THREE GREAT NOVELS

THREE GREAT NOVELS

A NEW LEASE OF DEATH
VANITY DIES HARD
THE SECRET HOUSE OF DEATH

Ruth Rendell

CRESSET PRESS

This Omnibus edition first published in 1992 by
CRESSET PRESS

Incorporating

A New Lease of Death
First published by Hutchinson and Co (Publishers) Ltd 1969
© Ruth Rendell 1969

Vanity Dies Hard
First published by Hutchinson and Co (Publishers) Ltd 1966
© Ruth Rendell 1966

The Secret House of Death
First published by Hutchinson and Co (Publishers) Ltd 1968
© Ruth Rendell 1968

Printed and bound in Great Britain by
Mackays of Chatham PLC, Chatham, Kent

A NEW LEASE OF DEATH

For
MY FATHER AND SIMON

All the chapter heading quotations are extracts from
The Book of Common Prayer

1

> The laws of the Realm may punish Christian men with death for heinous and grievous offences.
>
> *The Thirty-nine Articles.*

It was five in the morning. Inspector Burden had seen more dawns than most men, but he had never quite become jaundiced by them, especially summer dawns. He liked the stillness, the sight of the little country town in a depopulated state, the hard blue light that was of the same shade and intensity as the light at dusk but without dusk's melancholy.

The two men they had been questioning about last night's fight in one of Kingsmarkham's cafés had confessed separately and almost simultaneously just a quarter of an hour before. Now they were locked into two stark white cells on the ground floor of this incongruously modern police station. Burden stood by the window in Wexford's office, looking at the sky which had the peculiar greenish tint of aquamarine. A flock of birds flying in dense formation crossed it. They reminded Burden of his childhood when, as at dawn, everything had seemed bigger, clearer and of more significance than it did today. Tired and a little sickened, he opened the window to get rid of cigarette smoke and the sweaty smell of youths who wore leather jackets in the height of summer.

Outside in the corridor he could hear Wexford saying good night—or good morning—to Colonel Griswold, the Chief Constable. Burden wondered if Griswold had guessed when he arrived just before ten with a long spiel about stamping out hooliganism that he was in for an all-night session. That, he thought unfairly, was where meddling got you.

The heavy front door clanged and Griswold's car started.

Burden watched it move off the forecourt, past the great stone urns filled with pink geraniums and into Kingsmarkham High Street. The Chief Constable was driving himself. Burden saw with approval and grudging amusement that Griswold drove at just about twenty-eight miles per hour until he reached the black and white derestriction sign. Then the car gathered speed and flashed away out of sight along the empty country road that led to Pomfret.

He turned round when he heard Wexford come in. The Chief Inspector's heavy grey face was a little greyer than usual, but he showed no other sign of tiredness and his eyes, dark and hard as basalt, showed a gleam of triumph. He was a big man with big features and a big intimidating voice. His grey suit—one of a series of low fastening, double-breasted affairs—appeared more shabby and wrinkled than ever today. But it suited Wexford, being not unlike an extension of his furrowed pachydermatous skin.

'Another job jobbed,' he said, 'as the old woman said when she jobbed the old man's eye out.'

Burden bore with such vulgarisms stoically. He knew that they were meant to horrify him; they always succeeded. He made his thin lips crease into a tight smile. Wexford handed him a blue envelope and he was glad of the diversion to hide his slight embarrassment.

'Griswold's just given me this,' Wexford said. 'At five in the morning. No sense of timing.'

Burden glanced at the Essex postmark.

'Is that the man he was on about earlier, sir?'

'Well, I don't have fanmail from beautiful olde worlde Thringford as a general rule, do I, Mike? This is the Rev. Mr Archery all right, taking advantage of the Old Pals' Act.' He lowered himself into one of the rather flimsy chairs and it gave the usual protesting creak. Wexford had what his junior called a love-hate relationship with those chairs and indeed with all the aggressively modern furnishings of his office. The glossy block floor, the square of nylon carpet, the chairs with their sleek chrome legs, the primrose venetian blinds—all these in Wexford's estimation were not 'serviceable', they were dust-traps and they were 'chichi'. At the same time he took in them an enormous half-secret pride. They had their effect. They served to impress visiting strangers such as the writer of this letter Wexford was now taking from its envelope.

It too was written on rather thick blue paper. In a painfully authentic upper-class accent, the Chief Inspector said affectedly, 'May as well get on to the Chief Constable of Mid-Sussex, my dear. We were up at Oxford together, don't you know?' He squeezed his face into a kind of snarling grin. 'All among the bloody dreaming spires,' he said. 'I hate that sort of thing.'

'Were they?'

'Were they what?'

'At Oxford together?'

'I don't know. Something like that. It may have been the playing fields of Eton. All Griswold said was, "Now we've got those villains wrapped up, I'd like you to have a look at a letter from a very good friend of mine called Archery. Excellent fellow, one of the best. This enclosure's for you. I'd like you to give him all the help you can. I've a notion it's got something to do with that scoundrel Painter." '

'Who's Painter?'

'Villain who got the chop about fifteen or sixteen years ago,' said Wexford laconically. 'Let's see what the parson has to say, shall we?'

Burden looked over his shoulder. The letter was headed St Columba's Vicarage, Thringford, Essex. The greek e's awakened in him a small hostility. Wexford read it aloud.

' "Dear sir, I hope you will forgive me for taking up your valuable time . . ." Don't have much choice, do I? ". . . but I regard this matter as being of some urgency. Col. Griswold, the Chief Constable of blah blah blah and so on, has very kindly told me you are the gentleman who may be able to assist me in this problem so I am taking the liberty, having first consulted him, of writing to you." ' He cleared his throat and loosened his crumpled grey tie. 'Takes a hell of a time coming to the point, I must say. Ah, here we go. "You will remember the case of Herbert Arthur Painter . . ." I *will*. "I understand you were in charge of it. I therefore supposed I should come to you before pursuing certain enquiries which, much against my will, I am compelled to make." '

'Compelled?'

'That's what the man says. Doesn't say why. The rest's a load of compliments and can he come and see me tomorrow—no, today. He's going to phone this morning, but he "anticipates my willingness to meet him." ' He glanced at the window to where the sun was coming up over York Street and with one of his distorted quotations, said, 'I suppose he's sleeping in Elysium at this moment, crammed with distressful cold mutton or whatever parsons go to bed on.'

'What's it all about?'

'O God, Mike, it's obvious, isn't it? You don't want to take any notice of this "being compelled" and "against his will" stuff. I don't suppose his stipend amounts to much. He probably writes true crime stories in between early Communion and the Mothers' Meeting. He must be getting desperate if he reckons on titillating the mass appetite by resurrecting Painter.'

Burden said thoughtfully, 'I seem to remember the case. I'd just left school . . .'

'And it inspired your choice of a career, did it?' Wexford mocked. ' "What are you going to be, son?" "I'm going to be a detective, Dad." '

In his five years as Wexford's right hand man, Burden had grown immune to his teasing. He knew he was a kind of safety valve, the stooge perhaps on whom Wexford could vent his violent and sometimes shocking sense of humour. The people of this little town, indiscriminately referred to by Wexford as 'our customers' had, unless suspected of felony, to be spared. Burden was there to take the overflow of his chief's rage, ridicule and satire. Now he was cast as the sponge to soak up the scorn that was rightly the due of Griswold and Griswold's friend.

He looked shrewdly at Wexford. After a trying, frustrating day and night, this letter was the last straw. Wexford was suddenly tense with irritation, his skin more deeply wrinkled than usual, his whole body flexed with the anger that would not suffer fools gladly. That tension must find release.

'This Painter thing,' Burden said slyly, slipping into his role of therapist, 'a bit run of the mill, wasn't it? I followed it in the papers because it was the big local sensation. I don't remember it was remarkable in any other way.'

Wexford slipped the letter back into its envelope and put it in a drawer. His movements were precise and under a tight control. One wrong word, Burden thought, and he'd have torn it up, chucked the pieces on the floor and left them to the mercy of the cleaner. His words had apparently been as right as possible under the circumstances for Wexford said in a sharp cool voice, 'It was remarkable to me.'

'Because you handled it?'

'Because it was the first murder case I ever handled on my own. It was remarkable to Painter because it hanged him and to his widow, I daresay. I suppose it shook her a bit as far as anything could shake that girl.'

Rather nervously Burden watched him observe the cigarette burn one of the men they had been interviewing had made in the lemon-coloured leather of a chair seat. He waited for the explosion. Instead Wexford said indifferently:

'Haven't you got a home to got to?'

'Too late now,' said Burden, stifling a yawn that threatened. 'Besides, my wife's away at the seaside.'

A strongly uxorious man, he found his bungalow like a morgue when Jean and the children were absent. This was a side of his character that afforded Wexford many opportunities for quips and snide remarks, this coupled with his comparative youth, his stolid stick-in-the-mud nature and a certain primness of outlook. But all Wexford said was, 'I forgot.'

He was good at his job. The big ugly man respected him for that. Although he might deride, Wexford appreciated the advantage of having a deputy whose grave good looks were attractive to women. Seated opposite that ascetic face, warmed by a compassion Wexford called 'softness', they were more inclined to open their hearts than to a majestic fifty-five-year-old heavyweight. His personality, however, was not strong and his superior effaced him. Now, in order to channel off that sharp-edged vitality, he was going to have to risk a rebuke for stupidity.

He risked it. 'If you're going to have to argue the toss with this Archery, wouldn't it be a good idea if we had a re-cap of the facts?'

'We?'

'Well, you then, sir. You must be a bit rusty yourself on the case after so long.'

The outburst came with an undercurrent of laughter. 'God Almighty! D'you think I can't see your brain working? When

I want a psychiatrist I'll hire a professional.' He paused and the laughter became a wry grin. 'O.K. it might help me . . .' But Burden had made the mistake of relaxing too soon. 'To get the facts straight for Mr Bloody Archery, I mean,' Wexford snapped. 'But there's no mystery, you know, no cunning little red herrings. Painter did it all right.' He pointed eastwards out of the window. The broad Sussex sky was becoming suffused with rose and gold, bands of soft creamy pink like strokes from a water-colour brush. 'That's as sure as the sun's rising now,' he said. 'There never was any doubt. Herbert Arthur Painter killed his ninety-year-old employer by hitting her over the head with an axe and he did it for two hundred pounds. He was a brutal savage moron. I read in the paper the other day that the Russians call anti-social people "unpersons" and that just about describes him. Funny sort of character for a parson to champion.'

'If he's championing him.'

'We shall see,' said Wexford.

They stood in front of the map that was attached to the yellow 'cracked ice' wallpaper.

'She was killed in her own home, wasn't she?' Burden asked. 'One of those big houses off the Stowerton road?'

The map showed the whole of this rather sleepy country district. Kingsmarkham, a market town of some twelve thousand inhabitants, lay in the centre, its streets coloured in brown and white, its pastoral environs green with the blotches of dark veridian that denoted woodland. Roads ran from it as from the meshy heart of a spider's web, one leading to Pomfret in the South, another to Sewingbury in the North-east. The scattered villages, Flagford, Clusterwell and Forby, were tiny flies on this web.

'The house is called Victor's Piece,' said Wexford. 'Funny sort of name. Some general built it for himself after the Ashanti Wars.'

'And it's just about here.' Burden put his finger on a vertical strand of the web that led from Kingsmarkham to Stowerton, lying due north. He pondered and light dawned. 'I think I know it,' he said. 'Hideous dump with a lot of green woodwork all over it. It was an old people's home up until last year. I suppose they'll pull it down.'

'I daresay. There are a couple of acres of land to it. If you've got the picture we may as well sit down.'

Burden had moved his chair to the window. There was something consoling and at the same time rejuvenating in watching the unfolding of what was going to be a lovely day. On the fields tree shadows lay long and densely blue and bright new light glinted on the slate roofs of ancient houses. Pity he hadn't been able to get away with Jean. The sunlight and the fresh heady air turned his thoughts towards holidays and prevented him from recalling details of this case that had long ago shocked Kingsmarkham. He searched his memory and found to his shame that he could not even remember the murdered woman's name.

'What was she called?' he asked Wexford. 'A foreign name, wasn't it? Porto or Primo something?'

'Primero. Rose Isabel Primero. That was her married name. Far from being foreign, she'd been brought up at Forby Hall. Her people were by way of being squires of Forby.'

Burden knew Forby well. What tourists there were in this agricultural country with neither seaside nor downs, castles nor cathedrals, made a point of going to Forby. The guide books listed it absurdly as the fifth prettiest village in England. Every local newsagent's contained postcards of its church. Burden himself regarded it with a certain affection because its inhabitants had shown themselves almost totally devoid of criminal tendencies.

'This Archery could be a relative,' he suggested. 'Maybe he wants some gen for his family archives.'

'I doubt it,' Wexford said, basking in the sun like a huge grey cat. 'The only relatives she had were her three grandchildren. Roger Primero, the grandson, lives at Forby Hall now. Didn't inherit it, had to buy it. I don't know the details.'

'There used to be a family called Kynaston at Forby Hall, or so Jean's mother says. Mind you, that was years and years ago.'

'That's right,' Wexford said with a hint of impatience in his rumbling bass voice. 'Mrs Primero was born a Kynaston and she was going on for forty when she married Dr Ralph Primero. I imagine her people looked on it a bit askance—this was at the turn of the century, remember.'

'What was he, a G.P.?'

'Some sort of specialist, I think. It was when he retired that they came to live at Victor's Piece. They weren't all that well-off, you know. When the doctor died in the thirties Mrs Primero was left with about ten thousand pounds to live on. There was one child of the marriage, a son, but he'd died soon after his father.'

'D'you mean she was living alone in that great place? At her age?'

Wexford pursed his lips, reminiscing. Burden knew his chief's almost supernatural memory. When he was sufficiently interested he had the nearest thing to total recall. 'She had one maid,' Wexford said. 'Her name was—is, she's still alive—her name was Alice Flower. She was a good bit younger than her employer, seventy odd, and she'd been with Mrs Primero for about fifty years. A real ancient retainer of the old school. Living like that, you might think they'd have become friends rather than mistress and servant, but Alice kept to her place and they were "Madam" and "Alice" to each other till the day Mrs Primero died. I knew Alice by sight. She was quite a local character when she came into town to do their shopping, particularly when Painter started bringing her in in Mrs Primero's Daimler. D'you remember how nursemaids used to look? No, you wouldn't. You're too young. Well, Alice always wore a long navy coat and what's called a "decent" navy felt hat. She and Painter were both servants, but Alice put herself miles above him. She'd pull her rank on him and give him his orders just like Mrs Primero herself. He was Bert to his wife and his cronies but Alice called him "Beast". Not to his face, mind. She wouldn't have quite dared that.'

'You mean she was frightened of him?'

'In a way. She hated him and resented his being there. I I wonder if I've still got that cutting.' Wexford opened the bottom drawer of his desk, the one where he kept personal, semi-official things, grotesqueries that had interested him. He hadn't much hope of finding what he sought. At the time of Mrs Primero's murder Kingsmarkham police had been housed in an old yellow brick building in the centre of the town. That had been pulled down four or five years ago and replaced by this block of startling modernity on the outskirts. The cutting had very probably got lost in the move from the high pitch pine desk to this one of lacquered rosewood. He leafed through notes, letters, odd little souvenirs, finally surfacing with a grin of triumph.

'There you are, the "unperson" himself. Good-looking if you like the type. Herbert Arthur Painter, late of the Fourteenth Army in Burma. Twenty-five years old, engaged by Mrs Primero as chauffeur, gardener and odd-job man.'

The cutting was from the *Sunday Planet*, several columns of type surrounding a double-column block. It was a clear photograph and Painter's eyes were staring straight at the camera.

'Funny, that,' said Wexford. 'He always looked you straight in the eye. Supposed to denote honesty, if you've ever heard such a load of rubbish.'

Burden must have seen the picture before, but he had entirely forgotten it. It was a large well-made face with a straight though fleshy nose, spread at the nostrils. Painter had the thick curved lips that on a man are a coarse parody of a woman's mouth, a flat high brow and short tightly waving hair. The waves were so tightly crimped that they looked as if they must have pulled the skin and pained the scalp.

'He was tall and well-built,' Wexford went on. 'Face like a handsome overgrown pug, don't you think? He'd been in the Far East during the war, but if the heat and the privation had taken it out of him it didn't show by then. He had a sort of glistening good health about him like a shire horse. Sorry to use all these animal metaphors, but Painter was like an animal.'

'How did Mrs Primero come to take him on?'

Wexford took the cutting from him, looked at it for a moment and folded it up.

'From the time the doctor died,' he said, 'until 1947 Mrs Primero and Alice Flower struggled to keep the place going, pulling up a few weeds here and there, getting a man in when they wanted a shelf fixed. You can imagine the kind of thing. They had a succession of women up from Kingsmarkham to help with the housework but sooner or later they all left to go into the factories. The place started going to rack and ruin. Not surprising when you think that by the end of the war Mrs Primero was in her middle eighties and Alice nearly seventy. Besides, leaving her age out of it, Mrs Primero never touched the place as far as housework went. She hadn't been brought up to it and she wouldn't have known a duster from an antimacassar.'

'Bit of a tartar, was she?'

'She was what God and her background had made her,' Wexford said gravely but with the faintest suspicion of irony in his voice. 'I never saw her till she was dead. She was stubborn, a bit mean, what nowadays is called "reactionary", inclined to be an autocrat and very much monarch of all she surveyed. I'll give you a couple of examples. When her son died he left his wife and kids very badly off. I don't know the ins and outs of it, but Mrs Primero was quite willing to help financially provided it was on her terms. The family was to come and live with her and so on. Still, I daresay she couldn't afford to keep up two establishments. The other thing was that she'd been a very keen churchwoman. When she got too old to go she insisted on Alice going in her place. Like a sort of whipping boy. But she had her affections. She adored the grandson, Roger, and she had one close friend. We'll come to that later.

'As you know, there was an acute housing shortage after the war and a hell of a servant problem too. Mrs Primero was an intelligent old woman and she got to thinking how she could use one to solve the other. In the grounds of Victor's Piece was a coach house with a sort of loft over the top of it. The place for the coach was used to house the aforesaid Daimler. No one had driven it since the doctor died—Mrs Primero couldn't drive and, needless to say, Alice couldn't either. There was precious little petrol about but you could get your ration, enough to do the shopping and take a couple of old dears for a weekly jaunt around the lanes.'

'So Alice was that much of a friend?' Burden put in.

Wexford said solemnly, 'A lady can be accompanied by her maid when she goes driving. Anyway, Mrs Primero put an advert in the Kingsmarkham *Chronicle* for a young able-bodied man, willing to do the garden, perform odd jobs, maintain and drive the car in exchange for a flat and three pounds a week.'

'*Three pounds*?' Burden was a non-smoker and no lover of extravagant living, but he knew from doing his wife's weekend shopping what a little way three pounds went.

'Well, it was worth a good bit more in those days, Mike,' Wexford said almost apologetically. 'Mrs Primero had the loft painted up, divided into three rooms and piped for water. It wasn't Dolphin Square but, God, people were glad of one room back in 1947! She got a lot of answers but for some reason—

God knows *what* reason—she picked Painter. At the trial Alice said she thought the fact that he had a wife and a baby daughter would keep him steady. Depends what you mean by steady, doesn't it?'

Burden shifted his chair out of the sun. 'Was the wife employed by Mrs Primero too?'

'No, just Painter. She'd got this little kid, you see. She was only about two when they came. If she'd worked up at the house she'd have had to bring the child with her. Mrs Primero would never have stood for that. As far as she was concerned between her and the Painters there was a great gulf fixed. I gathered she'd hardly exchanged more than a couple of words with Mrs Painter all the time Painter was there and as for the little girl—her name was Theresa, I think—she barely knew of her existence.'

'She doesn't sound a very nice sort of woman,' Burden said doubtfully.

'She was typical of her age and class,' Wexford said tolerantly. 'Don't forget she was a daughter of the lord of the manor when lords of the manor still counted for something. To her Mrs Painter was comparable to a tenant's wife. I've no doubt that if Mrs Painter had been ill she'd have sent old Alice over with a bowl of soup and some blankets. Besides, Mrs Painter kept herself to herself. She was very pretty, very quiet and with a sort of deadly respectability about her. She was a bit scared of Painter which wasn't hard to understand, she being so small and Painter such a great hulking brute. When I talked to her after the murder I noticed she'd got bruises on her arm, too many bruises for her just to have got them through the usual kitchen accidents, and I wouldn't mind betting her husband used to knock her about.'

'So, in fact,' Burden said, 'they were two completely separate units. Mrs Primero and her maid living alone at Victor's Piece, the Painter family in their own home at the bottom of the garden.'

'I don't know about "bottom of the garden". The coach house was about a hundred feet from the back door of the big house. Painter only went up there to carry in the coal and receive his instructions.'

'Ah,' said Burden, 'there was some complicated business about coal, I seem to remember. Wasn't it more or less the crux of the whole thing?'

'Painter was supposed to chop wood and carry coal,' Wexford continued. 'Alice was past carrying coal and Painter was supposed to bring a scuttleful at mid-day—they never lit a fire before that—and another one at six-thirty. Now, he never objected to the gardening or the car maintenance, but for some reason he drew the line at the coal. He did it—apart from frequent lapses—but he was always grumbling about it. The midday duty cut across his dinner time, he said, and he didn't like turning out on winter evenings. Couldn't he bring two scuttles at eleven? But Mrs Primero wouldn't have that. She said she wasn't going to have her drawing room turned into a railway yard.'

Burden smiled. His tiredness had almost worn off. Given breakfast, a shave and a shower down, he would be a new man. He glanced at his watch, then across the High Street to where the blinds were going up on the Carousel Café.

'I could do with a cup of coffee,' he said.

'Two minds with but a single thought. Root someone out and send them over.'

Wexford stood up and stretched, tightened his tie and smoothed back the hair that was too sparse to become untidy. The coffee arrived in wax cups with plastic spoons and little cubes of wrapped sugar.

'That's better,' said Wexford. 'D'you want me to go on?' Burden nodded.

'By September 1950 Painter had been working for Mrs Primero for three years. The arrangement appeared to work pretty well apart from the difficulties Painter made about the coal. He never brought it in without complaining and he was always asking for a rise.'

'I suppose he thought she was rolling in money?'

'Of course, he couldn't have known what she'd got in the bank or in shares or whatever it was. On the other hand it was an open secret she kept money in the house.'

'In a safe, d'you mean?'

'Not on your life. You know these old girls. Some of it was in drawers stuffed into paper bags, some of it in old handbags.'

With a feat of memory Burden said suddenly, 'And one of those handbags contained *the* two hundred pounds?'

'It did,' Wexford said grimly. 'Whatever she might have been able to afford, Mrs Primero refused to raise Painter's wages. If he didn't like the set-up he could go, but that would mean giving up the flat.

'Being a very old woman, Mrs Primero felt the cold and she liked to start fires in September. Painter thought this unnecessary and he made the usual fuss about it. . . .'

He stopped as the telephone rang and he took the receiver himself. Burden had no idea from Wexford's reiterated, 'Yes, yes . . . all right,' who it could be. He finished his coffee with some distaste. The rim of the wax cup had become soggy. Wexford dropped the phone.

'My wife,' he said. 'Am I dead? Have I forgotten I've got a home of my own? She's run out of housekeeping and she can't find the cheque book.' He chuckled, felt in his pocket and produced it. 'No wonder. I'll have to nip back.' He added with sudden kindness, 'Go home and have a bit of shut-eye, why don't you?'

'I don't like being left in the air,' Burden grumbled. 'Now I know how my kids feel when I break off in the middle of a bedtime story.'

Wexford began bundling things into his briefcase.

'Leaving out all the circumstantial stuff,' he said, 'there isn't much more. I told you it was straightforward. It was the evening of September 24th it happened, a cold wet Sunday. Mrs Primero had sent Alice off to church. She went at about a quarter past six, Painter being due to bring the coal at half past. He brought it all right and departed two hundred pounds to the good.'

'I'd like to hear the circumstantial stuff,' Burden said.

Wexford was at the door now.

'To be continued in our next,' he grinned, 'You can't say I'm leaving you in suspense.' The grin faded and his face hardened. 'Mrs Primero was found at seven. She was in the drawing room lying on the floor by the fireplace in a great pool of blood. There was blood on the walls and on her armchair, and in the hearth was a blood-stained wood chopper.'

2

When sentence is given upon him let him be condemned
. . . let his children be fatherless and his wife a widow.

Psalm 109, appointed for the 22nd Day.

The nap Wexford had prescribed for him would have been attractive on a dull day, but not this morning when the sky was blue and cloudless and the sun promised tropical heat by midday. Moreover, Burden remembered that he had not made his bed for three days. Better have that shower and that shave instead.

After a canteen breakfast of two eggs and a couple of rashers of the greenback he liked, he had made up his mind what he was going to do. An hour could easily be spared. He drove northwards along the High Street with all the car windows down, past the shops, over the Kingsbrook Bridge, past the Olive and Dove and out on to the Stowerton road. Apart from a new house here and there, a supermarket on the site of the old police station, and aggressive road signs all over the place, things had not changed much in sixteen years. The meadows, the tall trees burdened with the heavy foliage of July, the little weatherboard cottages were much the same as when Alice Flower had seen them on her shopping trips in the Daimler. There would have been less traffic, then, he thought. He braked, pulled in and raised his eyebrows at the youth on a motor-bike who, overtaking the oncoming stream, had missed him by inches.

The lane where Victor's Piece was must be somewhere about here. Those circumstantial details Wexford had been so tantalising about were coming back to him from his own memory. Surely he had read about a bus stop and a telephone box at the end of the lane? Would these be the meadows he remembered reading that Painter had crossed, desperate to conceal a bundle of blood-stained clothing?

Here was the phone box now. He indicated left and turned slowly into the lane. For a short way its surface was metalled, then it petered out into a track ending in a gate. There were only three houses: a white-plastered semi-detached pair and opposite them the late Victorian pile he had described as 'a hideous dump'.

He had never been as near to it as this before, but he saw nothing to make him change his opinion. The roof of grey slates had been constructed—tortured almost—into a number of steep gables. Two of these dominated the front of the house, but there was a third on the right hand side and out of it grew another smaller one that apparently overlooked the back. Each gable was criss-crossed with timbering, some of it inexpertly carved into chevrons and all painted a dull bottle green. In places the plaster between the wood had fallen away, exposing rough pinkish brick-work. Ivy, of the same shade of green, spread its flat leaves and its rope-like grey tendrils from the foot of the downstairs windows to the highest gable where a lattice flapped open. There it had crept and burrowed into the mealy wall, prising the window frame away from the bricks.

Burden observed the garden with a countryman's eye. Never had he seen such a fine selection of weeds. The fertile black soil, cultivated and tended for many years, now nourished docks with leaves as thick and glossy as rubber plants, puce-headed thistles, nettles four feet tall. The gravel paths were choked with grass and mildewed groundsel. Only the clarity of the air and the soft brilliance of sunlight prevented the place from being actually sinister.

The front door was locked. No doubt this window beside it belonged to the drawing room. Burden could not help wondering with a certain wry humour what insensitive administrator had decreed that this scene of an old woman's murder should be for years the home—indeed the last refuge—of other old women. But they were gone now. The place looked as if it had been empty for years.

Through the window he could see a large shadowy room. In the grate of the amber-coloured marble fireplace someone had prudently placed crumpled newspaper to catch the drifts of soot.

Wexford had said there had been blood all over that fireplace. There, just in front of the copper kerb, was where the body must have lain.

He made his way round the side, pushing through a shrubbery where elders and strong little birches were threatening to oust the lilac. The panes in the kitchen casement were blurred with dirt and there was no kitchen door, only a back door that apparently opened off the end of the central passage. The Victorians, he reflected, were not too hot on design. Two doors with a straight passage between them! The draught would be appalling.

By now he was in the back garden but he literally could not see the wood for the trees. Nature had gone berserk at Victor's Piece and the coach house itself was almost totally obscured by creeper. He strolled across the shady flagged yard, made cool by the jutting walls of the house, and found himself skirting a conservatory, attached apparently to a kind of morning or breakfast room. It housed a vine, long dead and quite leafless.

So that was Victor's Piece. Pity he couldn't get inside, but he would, in any case, have to get back. Out of long habit—and partly to set a good example—he had closed all the windows of his car and locked the doors. Inside it was like an oven. He drove out of the broken gateway, into the lane and joined the traffic stream on the Stowerton road.

A greater contrast between the building he had left and the building he entered could hardly have been found. Fine weather suited Kingsmarkham Police Station. Wexford sometimes said that the architect of this new building must have designed it while holidaying in the South of France. It was white, boxy, unnecessarily vast and ornamented here and there with frescoes that owed something to the Elgin marbles.

On this July morning its whiteness glared and glistened. But if its façade seemed to welcome and bask in the sun its occupants did not. There was far too much glass. All right, said Wexford, for hothouse plants or tropical fish, but a mixed blessing for an elderly Anglo-Saxon policeman with high blood pressure and a low resistance to heat. The telephone receiver slid about in his large hand and when he had finished talking to Henry Archery he pulled down the venetian blinds.

'Heat wave's coming,' he said to Burden. 'I reckon your wife's picked a good week.'

Burden looked up from the statement he had begun to read. Lean as a greyhound, his face thin and acute, he often had the hound's instinct for scenting the unusual, coupled with a man's eager imagination.

'Things always seem to happen in a heat-wave,' he said. 'Our sort of things. I mean.'

'Get away,' said Wexford. 'Things are always happening around here.' He raised his spiky toothbrush brows. 'What's happening today,' he said, 'is Archery. He's coming at two.'

'Did he say what it's all about?'

'He's leaving that for this afternoon. Very la-di-da manner he's got with him. All part of the mystique of how to be a gentleman on nothing a year. One thing, he's got a transcript of the trial so I shan't have to go through the whole thing again.'

'That'll have cost him something. He must be keen.'

Wexford looked at his watch and rose. 'Got to get over to the court,' he said. 'Polish off those villains who lost me my night's sleep. Look, Mike, I reckon we deserve a bit of gracious living and I don't fancy the Carousel's steak pie for my lunch. What about popping into the Olive and booking a table for one sharp?'

Burden smiled. It suited him well enough. Once in a blue moon Wexford would insist on their lunching or even dining in comparative style.

'It shall be done,' he said.

The Olive and Dove is the best hostelry in Kingsmarkham that can properly be called an hotel. By a stretch of the imagination the Queen's Head might be described as an inn, but the Dragon and the Crusader cannot claim to be more than pubs. The Olive, as locals invariably call it, is situated in the High Street at the Stowerton end of Kingsmarkham, facing the exquisite Georgian residence of Mr Missal, the Stowerton car dealer. It is partly Georgian itself, but it is a hybrid structure with lingering relics of Tudor and a wing that claims to be pre-Tudor. In every respect it conforms to what nice middle-class people mean when they talk about a 'nice' hotel. There are always three waiters, the chambermaids are staid and often elderly, the bath water is hot, the food as well as can be expected and the A.A. Guide has given it two stars.

Burden had booked his table by phone. When he walked into the dining room just before one he saw to his satisfaction that he had been placed by the High Street window. Here it was just out of the sun and the geraniums in the window box looked fresh and even dewy. Girls waiting on the other side of the street for the Pomfret bus wore cotton frocks and sandals.

Wexford marched in at five past. 'I don't know why he can't get up at half twelve like they do in Sewingbury,' he grumbled. 'He' Burden knew, meant the chairman of the Kingsmarkham bench. 'God, it was hot in court. What are we going to eat?'

'Roast duck,' said Burden firmly.

'All right, if you twist my arm. As long as they don't mix a lot of rubbish up with it. You know what I mean, sweet corn and bananas.' He took the menu, scowling. 'Look at that, Polynesian chicken. What do they think we are, aborigines?'

'I went and had a look at Victor's Piece this morning,' said Burden while they waited for the duck to come.

'Did you now? I see it's up for sale. There's a card in the agent's window with a highly misleading photograph. They're asking six thousand. Bit steep when you think Roger Primero got less than two for it in 1951.'

'I suppose it's changed hands several times since then?'

'Once or twice before the old folks moved in. Thanks,' he said to the waiter. 'No we don't want any wine. Two halves of bitter.' He spread his napkin over his capacious lap and to Burden's controlled distaste sprinkled wing and orange sauce liberally with pepper.

'Was Roger Primero the heir?'

'One of the heirs. Mrs Primero died intestate. Remember I told you she'd only got ten thousand to leave and that was divided equally between Roger and his two younger sisters. He's a rich man now, but however he got his money it wasn't from his grandmother. All kinds of pies he's got his finger in—oil, property development, shipping—he's a real tycoon.'

'I've seen him around, I think.'

'You must have. He's very conscious of his status as a landowner since he bought Forby Hall. Goes out with the Pomfret hounds and all that.'

'How old is he?' Burden asked.

'Well, he was twenty-two when his grandmother was killed. That makes him about thirty-eight now. The sisters were much younger. Angela was ten and Isabel nine.'

'I seem to remember he gave evidence at the trial.'

Wexford pushed his plate away, signalled rather imperiously to the waiter and ordered two portions of apple pie. Burden knew that his chief's notion of gracious living was somewhat limited.

'Roger Primero had been visiting his grandmother that Sunday,' Wexford said. 'He was working in a solicitor's office in Sewingbury at the time and he used to make quite a habit of having Sunday tea at Victor's Piece. Maybe he had his eye on a share of the loot when Mrs Primero went—God knows he hadn't a bean in those days—but he seemed genuinely fond of her. It's certainly a fact that after we'd seen the body and sent for him from Sewingbury as next of kin, we had to restrain him forcibly from going over to the coach house and laying violent hands on Painter. I daresay his grandmother and Alice made a lot of him, you know, buttered him up and waited on him. I told you Mrs Primero had her affections. There'd been a family quarrel but apparently it didn't extend to the grandchildren. Once or twice Roger had taken his little sisters down to Victor's Piece and they'd all got on very well together.'

'Old people usually do get on well with kids,' said Burden.

'They had to be the right kind of children, Mike. Angela and Isabel, yes, and she had a very soft spot for young Liz Crilling.'

Burden put down his spoon and stared at the Chief Inspector.

'I thought you said you'd read all this up at the time?' Wexford said suspiciously. 'Don't say it was a long time ago. My customers are always saying that to me and it makes me see red. If you read the account of that trial you must remember that Elizabeth Crilling, aged precisely five at the time, found Mrs Primero's body.'

'I assure you I can't remember, sir.' That must have been the day he'd missed, the day he hadn't bothered with the papers because he'd been nervous about an interview. 'She didn't appear at the trial, surely?'

'Not at that age—there are limits. Besides, although she was actually the first to go into the drawing room and come upon the body, her mother was with her.'

'Digressing a little,' Burden said, 'I don't quite get this stuff about the right kind of children. Mrs Crilling lives over there in Glebe Road.' He turned to the window and waved his hand in the direction of the least attractive part of Kingsmarkham where long streets of small terraced brown houses had sprung up between the wars. 'She and the girl live in half a house, they haven't a penny to bless themselves with . . .'

'They've come down a lot,' said Wexford. 'In September 1950 Crilling himself was still alive—he died of T.B. soon after—and they lived opposite Victor's Piece.'

'In one of those white semi-detached places?'

'That's right. A Mrs White and her son lived next door. Mrs Crilling was about thirty at the time, little bit over thirty.'

'You're joking,' said Burden derisively. 'That makes her only in her late forties now.'

'Look, Mike, people can say what they like about hard work and childbearing and all that. I tell you there's nothing like mental illness to make a woman look old before her time. And you know as well as I do Mrs Crilling's been in and out of mental hospitals for years.' He paused as their coffee came and pursed his lips censoriously at the anaemic brown liquid.

'You did say black, sir?' the waiter asked.

Wexford gave a sort of grunt. The church clock struck the last quarter. As the reverberation died away, he said to Burden:

'Shall I keep the parson waiting ten minutes?'

Burden said neutrally, 'That's up to you, sir. You were going to tell me how Mrs Primero and the Crilling woman became friends. I suppose they were friends?'

'Not a doubt of it. Mrs Crilling was ladylike enough in those days and she had a way with her, sycophantic, sucking up, *you* know. Besides, Crilling had been an accountant or something, just enough of a professional man, anyway, in Mrs Primero's eyes to make his wife a lady. Mrs Crilling was always popping over to Victor's Piece and she always took the child with her. God knows, they must have been pretty close. Elizabeth called Mrs Primero "Granny Rose" just as Roger and his sisters did.'

'So she "popped over" that Sunday night and found Granny Rose dead?' Burden hazarded.

'It wasn't as simple as that. Mrs Crilling had been making the kid a party frock. She finished it by about six, dressed Elizabeth up and wanted to take her over and show her off to Mrs Primero. Mind you, she and Alice Flower were always at loggerheads. There was a good bit of jealousy there, spheres of influence and so on. So Mrs. Crilling waited until Alice had gone off to church and went over alone, intending to go back and fetch the child if Mrs. Primero was awake. She dozed a good bit, you see, being so old.

'That first time—it was about twenty past six—Mrs Primero *was* asleep and Mrs Crilling didn't go in. She just tapped on the drawing room window. When the old woman didn't stir she went back and returned again later. By the way, she saw the empty scuttle through the window so she knew Painter hadn't yet been in with the coal.'

'You mean that Painter came in and did the deed between Mrs Crilling's visits?' Burden asked.

'She didn't go back again till seven. The back door had to be left unlocked for Painter, so she and the child went in, called out "yoo-hoo" or some damn' thing, and marched into the drawing room when they didn't get an answer. Elizabeth went first—more's the pity—and Bob's your uncle!'

'Blimey,' said Burden, 'that poor kid!'

'Yes,' Wexford murmured, 'yes . . . Well, much as I should like to while away the rest of the afternoon, reminiscing over the coffee cups, I do have to see this clerical bloke.'

They both got up. Wexford paid the bill, leaving a rather obviously exact ten per cent for a tip.

'I can't see where the parson comes into it at all,' Burden said when they were in the car.

'He can't be an abolitionist because they've done away with the death penalty. As I say, he's writing a book, expects to make a big thing out of it and that's why he's laid out good money on a transcript.'

'Or he's a prospective buyer of Victor's Piece. He's a haunted house merchant and he thinks he's got another Borley Rectory.'

An unfamiliar car stood on the forecourt of the police station. The numberplate was not local and beside it was a little metal label that bore the name Essex with the country coat of arms of three scimitars on a red field.

'We shall soon know,' said Wexford.

3

There are false witnesses risen up against me and such as speak wrong.

Psalm 27, appointed for the 5th Day.

In general Wexford disliked the clergy. To him the dog collar was like a slipped halo, indicating a false saintliness, probable hypocrisy and massive self-regard. As he saw it vicars were not vicarious enough. Most of them expected you to worship God in them.

He did not associate them with good looks and charm. Henry Archery, therefore, caused him slight surprise. He was possibly not much younger than Wexford himself, but he was still slim and exceedingly good-looking, and he was wearing an ordinary rather light-coloured suit and an ordinary collar and tie. His hair was thick enough and fair enough for the grey not to show much, his skin was tanned and his features had a pure evenly cut regularity.

During the first preliminary small-talk remarks Wexford had noticed the beauty of his voice. You felt it would be a pleasure to hear him read aloud. As he showed him to a chair and sat down opposite him, Wexford chuckled to himself. He was picturing a group of tired ageing female parishioners working their fingers to the bone for the pitiful reward of this man's smile. Archery was not smiling now and he looked anything but relaxed.

'I'm familiar with the case, Chief Inspector,' he began. 'I've read the official transcript of the trial and I've discussed the whole thing with Colonel Griswold.'

'What exactly do you want to know, then?' Wexford asked in his blunt way.

Archery took a deep breath and said rather too quickly:

'I want you to tell me that somewhere in your mind there is just the faintest doubt, the shadow of a doubt, of Painter's guilt.'

So that was it, or part of it. Burden with his theories that the parson was a Primero relative or seeking to buy the Primero house couldn't have been more wrong. This man, whatever axe he might be grinding, was bent on whitewashing Painter.

Wexford frowned and after a moment said, 'Can't be done. Painter did it all right.' He set his jaw stubbornly, 'If you want to quote me in your book you're quite welcome. You can say that after sixteen years Wexford still maintains that Painter was guilty beyond the shadow of a doubt.'

'What book is this?' Archery inclined his handsome head courteously. His eyes were brown and now they looked bewildered. Then he laughed. It was a nice laugh and it was the first time Wexford had heard it. 'I don't write books,' he said. 'Well, I did once contribute a chapter to a work on Abyssinian cats but that hardly . . .'

Abyssinian cats. Bloody great red cats, thought Wexford. Whatever next? 'Why are you interested in Painter, Mr Archery?'

Archery hesitated. The sun showed up lines on his face that Wexford had not realised were there. Funny, he thought ruefully, how dark women age slower than fair ones but the reverse was true of men.

'My reasons are very personal, Chief Inspector. I can't suppose that they would interest you. But I can assure you that there's no possibility of my publishing anything you tell me.'

Well, he had promised Griswold—as to that, he didn't have much choice. Hadn't he, in any case, already resigned himself to giving up most of the afternoon to this clergyman? Weariness was at last beginning to gain a hold on him. He might be equal to reminiscing, going over past familiar words and scenes; on this hot afternoon he was quite unequal to anything more exacting. Probably the personal reasons—and he confessed mentally to an almost childish curiosity about them—would emerge in due course. There was something frank and boyish in his visitor's face which made Wexford think he would not be particularly discreet.

'What d'you want me to tell you?' he asked.

'Why you are so determined Painter was guilty. Of course I don't know any more about this sort of thing than the average layman, but it seems to me there were a good many gaps in the evidence. There were other people involved, people who had quite definite interests in Mrs Primero's death.'

Wexford said coldly, 'I'm fully prepared to go over any points with you, sir.'

'Now?'

'Certainly now. Have you got that transcript with you?'

Archery produced it from a very battered leather briefcase. His hands were long and thin but not womanish. They reminded Wexford of saints' hands in what he called 'churchy' paintings. For five minutes or so he scanned the papers in silence, refreshing his memory on tiny points. Then he put them down and raised his eyes to Archery's face.

'We have to go back to Saturday, September 23rd,' he said, 'the day before the murder. Painter didn't appear with the coal at all that evening. The two old women waited until nearly eight o'clock when the fire was almost out, and Mrs Primero said she would go to bed. Alice Flower was incensed at this and went out to get what she called "a few lumps".'

'That was when she hurt her leg,' Archery said eagerly.

'It wasn't a serious injury but it made Mrs Primero angry and she blamed Painter. At about ten on the following morning she sent Alice down to the coach house to tell Painter she wanted to see him at eleven thirty sharp. He came up ten minutes late, Alice showed him into the drawing room and afterwards she heard him and Mrs Primero quarrelling.'

'This brings me to the first point I want to raise,' Archery said. He flipped through the transcript and, putting his finger at the beginning of a paragraph, passed it to Wexford. 'This, as you know, is part of Painter's own evidence. He doesn't deny the quarrel. He admits that Mrs Primero threatened him with dismissal. He also says here that Mrs Primero finally came round to see his point of view. She refused to give him a rise because she said that would put ideas into his head and he would only ask for another increase in a few months' time. Instead she'd give him what she understood was called a bonus.'

'I remember all that well,' Wexford said impatiently. 'He said she told him to go upstairs and into her bedroom where he'd find a handbag in her wardrobe. He was to bring that handbag down to her and this, he said, he did. There was about two hundred pounds in the handbag and this he could have, take it away in the handbag and look upon it as a bonus on condition he was absolutely circumspect about bringing the coal at the required times.' He coughed. 'I never believed a word of it and neither did the jury.'

'Why not?' Archery asked quietly.

God, thought Wexford, this was going to be a long session. 'Firstly, because the stairs at Victor's Piece run up between the drawing room and the kitchen. Alice Flower was in the kitchen cooking the lunch. She had remarkably good hearing for her age, but she never heard Painter go up those stairs. And, believe me, he was a big heavy lout if ever there was one.' Archery winced faintly at this but Wexford went on, 'Secondly, Mrs Primero would never have sent the gardener upstairs to poke about in her bedroom. Not unless I'm very mistaken in her character. She would have got Alice to have fetched the money on some pretext or other.'

'She might not have wanted Alice to know about it.'

'That's for sure,' Wexford retorted sharply. 'She wouldn't have. I said on some pretext or other.' That made the parson draw in his horns. Wexford said very confidently, 'In the third place Mrs Primero had a reputation for being rather mean. Alice had been with her for half a century but she'd never given Alice anything bar her wages and an extra pound at Christmas.' He jabbed at the page. 'Look, she says so here in black and white. We know Painter wanted money. The night before when he hadn't brought the coal he'd been drinking up at the Dragon with a pal of his from Stowerton. The pal had a motor-bike to sell and he'd offered it to Painter for a bit less than two hundred pounds. Apparently Painter hadn't a hope of getting the money but he asked his friend to hold on to the bike for a couple of days and he'd contact him the minute anything came up. You're saying he got the money before noon on Sunday. I say he stole it after he brutally murdered his employer in the evening. If you're right, why didn't he get in touch with his friend on Sunday afternoon? There's a phone box at the bottom of the lane. We checked with the pal, he didn't move out of his house all day and the phone never rang.'

It was a very tempest of fact and Archery yielded, or appeared to yield, before it. He said only:

'You're saying, I think, that Painter went to the wardrobe after he'd killed Mrs Primero in the evening. There was no blood on the inside of the wardrobe.'

'For one thing he wore rubber gloves to do the deed. Anyway, the prosecution's case was that he stunned her with the flat side of the axe blade, took the money, and when he came downstairs, finished her off in a panic.'

Archery gave a slight shiver. 'Doesn't it strike you as odd,' he then said, 'that if Painter did it he should have been so transparent about it?'

'Some are. They're stupid, you see.' Wexford said it derisively, his mouth curling. He still had no notion what Archery's interest in Painter might be, but that he was pro-Painter was apparent. 'Stupid,' he said again, intent on flicking the clergyman on the raw. Another wince from Archery rewarded him. 'They think you'll believe them. All they've got to say is it must have been a tramp or a burglar and you'll go away satisfied. Painter was one of those. That old tramp thing,' he said. 'When did you last *see* a tramp? More than sixteen years ago, I'll bet.'

'Let's come to the murder itself,' Archery said quietly.

'By all means.' Again Wexford took the transcript, gathering with a quick glance the information he needed. 'Now, then,' he began, 'Painter said he went over to fetch the coal at half six. He remembered the time—twenty-five past six when he left the coach house—because his wife said five minutes to go before the child's bedtime. The time's not all that important, anyway. We know it was between twenty past six and seven o'clock that she was killed. Painter went over, chopped some wood and cut his finger. Or so he said. He certainly did cut his finger—cut it deliberately.'

Archery ignored this last. 'He and Mrs Primero belonged to the same blood group,' he said.

'They were both Group O. They weren't quite so accurate about the minute grouping of blood sixteen years ago as they are now. It was handy for Painter, that. But it didn't do him any real good.'

The clergyman crossed his legs and leaned back. Wexford could see he was trying to appear relaxed and making a poor job of it. 'I believe you personally went to interview Painter after the crime was discovered?'

'We were round at the coach house by a quarter to eight. Painter was out. I asked Mrs Painter where he was and she said he'd come back from the big house some time after six-thirty, washed his hands and gone straight out again. He'd told her he was going to Stowerton to see his friend. We'd only been there about ten minutes when he came in. His story didn't stand up, there was far too much blood around to have come from a cut finger and—well, you know the rest. It's all down there. I charged him on the spot.'

The transcript fluttered a little in Archery's hand. He could not keep his fingers quite steady. 'In evidence,' he said, speaking slowly and evenly, 'Painter said he hadn't been to Stowerton. "I waited at the bus stop at the end of the lane, but the bus never came. I saw the police cars turn into the lane and I wondered what was up. Presently I felt a bit faint on account of my finger bleeding a lot. I came back to my flat. I thought my wife might know what it was all about." ' After a pause, he added with a kind of pleading eagerness, 'That doesn't sound like the evidence of the complete moron you make him out to be.'

Wexford answered him patiently as if he were talking to a precocious teenager. 'They edit these things, Mr Archery. They condense them, make them sound coherent. Believe me. You weren't in court and I was. As to the truth of that statement, I was in one of those police cars and I was keeping my eyes open. We overtook the Stowerton bus and turned left into the lane. There wasn't anyone waiting at that bus stop.'

'I imagine you mean that while he said he was at the bus stop he was in fact hiding some clothes.'

'Of course he was hiding the clothes! When he was working he habitually wore a raincoat. You'll see that in Mrs Crilling's evidence and in Alice's. Sometimes it hung in the coach house and sometimes on a hook behind the back door of Victor's Piece. Painter said he had worn it that evening and had left it hanging on the back door. That raincoat couldn't be found. Both Alice and Roger Primero said they remembered having seen it on the back door that afternoon, but Mrs Crilling was certain it wasn't there when she brought Elizabeth in at seven.'

'You finally found the raincoat rolled up in a ball under a

hedge two fields away from the bus stop.'

'The raincoat plus a pullover,' Wexford retorted, 'and a pair of rubber gloves. The lot was sodden with blood.'

'But anyone could have worn the raincoat and you couldn't identify the pullover.'

'Alice Flower went so far as to say it looked like one Painter sometimes wore.'

Archery gave a deep sigh. For a time he had been firing questions and statements briskly at Wexford, but suddenly he had fallen silent. Little more than indecision showed on his face. Wexford waited. At last, he thought, Archery had reached a point where it was going to become necessary to reveal those 'personal reasons'. A struggle was going on within him and he said in an artificial tone:

'What about Painter's wife?'

'A wife cannot be compelled to give evidence against her husband. As you know, she didn't appear at the trial. She and the child went off somewhere and a couple of years later I heard she'd married again.'

He stared at Archery, raising his eyebrows. Something he had said had made the clergyman's mind up for him. A slight flush coloured Archery's even tan. The brown eyes were very bright as he leaned forward, tense again.

'That child . . .'

'What of her? She was asleep in her cot when we searched Painter's bedroom and that's the only time I saw her. She was four or five.'

Archery said jerkily, 'She's twenty-one now and she's a very beautiful young woman.'

'I'm not surprised. Painter was a nice enough looking fellow if you like the type, and Mrs Painter was pretty.' Wexford stopped. Archery was a clergyman. Had Painter's daughter taken after her father and somehow come into his care as a result of her transgressions? Archery could be a prison visitor. It was right up his street, Wexford thought nastily. Anger rose in his throat as he wondered if all this sparring discussion had been engineered merely because Archery wanted his help in getting the right psychological approach to a convicted thief or confidence woman. 'What about her?' he snapped. Griswold could go to hell! 'Now come on, sir, you'd better tell me and have done.'

'I have a son, Chief Inspector, an only child. He also is twenty-one . . .'

'Well?'

Obviously the clergyman had difficulty in framing the words. He hesitated and pressed his long hands together. At last he said diffidently and in a low voice, 'He wishes to marry Miss Painter.' When Wexford started and stared at him, he added, 'or Miss Kershaw, as her legal name now is.'

Wexford was all at sea. He was astonished, a rare thing for him, and he felt a sharp-edged excitement. But he had shown all the surprise he thought consistent with policy and now he spoke soberly.

'You must excuse me, Mr Archery, but I can't see how your son, the son of an Anglican clergyman, came to meet a girl in Miss Painter's—er, Miss Kershaw's—position.'

'They met at Oxford,' Archery said easily.

'At the *university*?'

'That is so. Miss Kershaw is quite an intelligent young woman.' Archery gave a slight smile. 'She's reading Modern Greats. Tipped for a First, I'm told.'

4

> If any of you know cause or just impediment why these two persons should not be joined together in holy matrimony, ye are to declare it.
>
> *The Banns of Marriage.*

If he had been asked to predict the future of such a one as Theresa Painter, what would he have foreseen for her? Children like her, Wexford reflected as he recovered from his second shock, children like Painter's little girl started life with a liability and a stain. The surviving parent, well-meaning relatives and cruel schoolfellows often made matters worse. He had hardly thought about the fate of the child until today. Now, thinking quickly, he supposed he would have counted her lucky to have become an anonymous manual worker with perhaps already a couple of petty convictions.

Instead to Theresa Painter had apparently come the greatest blessings of civilised life: brains, advanced education, beauty, friendship with people like this vicar, an engagement to this vicar's son.

Wexford cast his mind back to the first of only three encounters with Mrs Painter. A quarter to eight it had been on that Sunday in September. He and the sergeant with him had knocked on the door at the foot of the coach house stairs and Mrs Painter had come down to let them in. Whatever might have been fashionable in London at that time, the young women of Kingsmarkham were still doing their hair in a big pile on the forehead with tight curls falling to the shoulders. Mrs Painter was no exception. Hers was naturally fair, her face was powdered and her mouth painted diffidently red. Respectable provincial matrons did not go in for eye make-up in 1950 and Mrs Painter was of all things respectable. There seemed to be very little else to her. On her dry fine skin lines had already begun to form, little indentations which marked a regular prudish pursing of the lips, a setting of the chin that accompanied an outraged flounce.

She had the same attitude to the police as others might have to bugs or mice. When they came upstairs she alternated her replies to their questions with reiterated remarks that it was a disgrace to have them in the house. She had the blankest, most obtuse blue eyes he had ever seen on anyone. At no time, even when they were about to take Painter away, did she show the least pity or the least horror, only this fixated dread of what people would think if they found the police had been questioning her husband.

Perhaps she had not been so stupid as he had thought. Somewhere in that pretty respectable mouse and that great hunk of sub-humanity, her husband, must have been the spring from which their daughter drew her intelligence. 'Quite an intelligent girl,' Archery had said casually. Good God, thought Wexford, remembering how he had boasted when his own daughter got eight O Level passes. Good God! What were Modern Greats, anyway? Were they the same as Mods and did that mean Modern Languages? He had a vague idea that this might be the esoteric and deliberately deceptive name given to Philosophy and Political Economy. He wouldn't show his ignorance to Archery. Philosophy! He almost whistled. Painter's daughter reading—yes, that was the term, reading—philosophy! It made you think all right. Why, it made you doubt . . .

'Mr Archery,' he said, 'you're quite sure this *is* Herbert Arthur Painter's girl?'

'Of course I'm sure, Chief Inspector. She told me.' He looked almost defiantly at Wexford. Perhaps he thought the policeman would laugh at his next words. 'She is as good as she is beautiful,' he said. Wexford's expression remained unaltered. 'She came to stay with us at Whitsun. It was the first time we'd seen her, though naturally our son had written to us and told us about her. We took to her at once.

'Chief Inspector, times have changed since I was at college. I had to face the possibility that my son would meet some girl at Oxford, perhaps want to marry her at an age when I'd thought of myself as still a boy and when Orders were a lifetime away.

I'd see my friends' children marry at twenty-one and I was prepared to try and manage something for him, give him something to start life on. All I hoped was that the girl would be someone we could like and understand.

'Miss Kershaw—I'll use that name if you don't mind—is just what I would have chosen for him myself, beautiful, graceful, well-mannered, easy to talk to. Oh, she does her best to hide her looks in the uniform they all wear nowadays, long shaggy hair, trousers, great black duffel coat—you know the kind of thing. But they all dress like that. The point is she can't hide them.

'My wife is a little impulsive. She was hinting about the wedding before Theresa had been with us for twenty-four hours. I found it hard to understand why the young people were so diffident about it. Charles's letters had been paeans of praise and I could see they were deeply in love. Then she told us. She came out with it quite baldly. She said—I remember the very words—"I think you ought to know something about me, Mrs Archery. My father's name was Painter and he was hanged for killing an old woman."

'At first my wife didn't believe it. She thought it was some sort of a game. Charles said, "It's true. It doesn't matter. People are what they are, not what their parents did." Then Theresa—we call her Tess—said, "It would matter if he had done it, only he didn't. I told you *why* he was hanged. I didn't mean he'd done it." Then she began to cry.'

'Why does she call herself Kershaw?'

'It's her stepfather's name. He must be a very remarkable man, Chief Inspector. He's an electrical engineer, but . . .' You needn't come that rude mechanicals stuff with me, thought Wexford crossly. '. . . but he must be a most intelligent, perceptive and kind person. The Kershaws have two children of their own, but as far as I can gather, Mr Kershaw has treated Tess with no less affection than his own son and daughter. She says it was his love that helped her to bear—well, what I can only call the stigma of her father's crime when she learnt about it at the age of twelve. He followed her progress at school, encouraged her in every way and fostered her wish to get a County Major Scholarship.'

'You mentioned "the stigma of her father's crime". I thought you said she thinks he didn't do it?'

'My dear Chief Inspector, she *knows he didn't do it.*'

'Wexford said slowly, 'Mr Archery, I'm sure I don't have to tell a man like yourself that when we talk of somebody *knowing* something we mean that what they know is a fact, something that's true beyond a reasonable doubt. We mean that the majority of other people *know* it too. In other words, it's history, it's written down in books, it's common knowledge.' He paused. 'Now I and the Law Lords and the official records and what your son means when he talks about the Establishment, know beyond any reasonable doubt, that Painter did kill Mrs Rose Primero.'

'Her mother told her so, ' said Archery. 'She told her that she had absolute irrefutable personal knowledge that Tess's father did not kill Mrs Primero.'

Wexford shrugged and smiled. 'People believe what they want to believe. The mother thought it was the best thing for her daughter. If I'd been in her shoes I daresay I'd have said the same.'

'I don't think it was like that,' Archery said stubbornly. 'Tess says her mother is a very unemotional woman. She never talks about Painter, never discusses him at all. She just says quite calmly, "Your father never killed anybody" and beyond that she won't say any more.'

'Because she can't say any more. Look, sir, I think you're taking a rather romantic view of this. You're visualising the Painters as a devoted couple, kind of merry peasants, love in a cottage and all that. It wasn't like that. Believe me, Painter was no loss to her. I'm certain in my own mind he was in the habit of striking her just when the fancy took him. As far as he was concerned, she was just his woman, someone to cook his meals, wash his clothes and—well,' he added brutally, 'someone to go to bed with.'

Archery said stiffly, 'I don't see that any of that's material.'

'Don't you? You're picturing some sort of declaration of innocence plus incontrovertible proof made to the one person he loved and whom he knew would believe in him. Forgive me, but that's a load of rubbish. Apart from the few minutes when he came back to the coach house to wash his hands—and incidentally hide the money—he was never alone with her. And he couldn't have told her then. He wasn't supposed to know about it. D'you understand me? He could have told her he had done it, he couldn't have told her he had *not*.

'Then we came. We found blood flecks in the sink and faint blood marks on the kitchen wall where he'd stripped off that pullover. As soon as he came back he took the bandage off his hand to show us the cut and he handed the bandage to his wife. But he didn't speak to her, didn't even appeal to her for support. He made just one reference to her . . .'

'Yes?'

'We found the handbag with the money in it under the mattress in their double bed. Why hadn't Painter told his wife if he'd been given that money in the morning? Here it is, find it in your transcript. "I knew the wife would want to get her hooks on it. She was always nagging me to buy things for the flat." That's all he said and he didn't even look at her. We charged him and he said, "O.K., but you're making a big mistake. It was a tramp done it." He came straight down the stairs with us. He didn't kiss his wife and he didn't ask to go in and see his child.'

'She must have seen him in prison?'

'With a prison officer present. Look, sir, you appear to be satisfied and so do all the parties concerned. Surely that's the main thing. You must forgive me if I can't agree with you.'

Silently Archery took a snapshot from his wallet and laid it on the desk. Wexford picked it up. Presumably it had been taken in the vicarage garden. There was a great magnolia tree in the background, a tree as tall as the house it partly concealed. It was covered with waxen cup flowers. Under its branches stood a boy and a girl, their arms round each other. The boy was tall and fair. He was smiling and he was plainly Archery's son. Wexford wasn't particularly interested in him.

The girl's face was in sad repose. She was looking into the camera with large steady eyes. Light-coloured hair fell over her forehead in a fringe and down to the shoulders of a typical undergraduate's shirtwaister, faded, tightly belted and with a crumpled skirt. Her waist was tiny, her bust full. Wexford saw the mother again, only this girl was holding a boy's hand instead of a bloody rag.

'Very charming,' he said dryly. 'I hope she'll make your son happy.' He handed the photograph back. 'No reason why she shouldn't.'

A mixture of emotions, anger, pain, resentment, flared in the clergyman's eyes. Interestedly, Wexford watched him.

'I do not know what or whom to believe,' Archery said unhappily, 'and while I'm in this state of uncertainty, Chief Inspector, I'm not in favour of the marriage. No, that's putting it too coolly.' He shook his head vehemently. 'I'm bitterly, bitterly against it,' he said.

'And the girl, Painter's daughter?'

'She believed—perhaps accepts is the better word—in her father's innocence, but she realises others may not. When it come to it, I don't think she would marry my son while his mother and I feel as we do.'

'What are you afraid of, Mr Archery?'

'Heredity.'

'A very chancy thing, heredity.'

'Have you children, Chief Inspector?'

'I've got two girls.'

'Are they married?'

'One is.'

'And who is her father-in-law?'

For the first time Wexford felt superior to this clergyman. A kind of *schadenfreude* possessed him. 'He's an architect, as a matter of fact, Tory councillor for the North Ward here.'

'I see.' Archery bowed his head. 'And do your grandchildren already build palaces with wooden bricks, Mr Wexford?' Wexford said nothing. The only sign of his first grandchild's existence was so far envinced in its mother's morning sickness. 'I shall watch mine from their cradle, waiting to see them drawn towards objects with sharp edges.'

'You said if you objected she wouldn't marry him.'

'They're in love with each other. I can't . . .'

'Who's going to know? Palm Kershaw off as her father.'

'I shall know,' said Archery. 'Already I can see Painter when I look at her. Instead of her mouth and her eyes I can see his thick lips and his bloodlust. It's the same blood, Chief Inspector, the blood that mingled with Mrs Primero's, on the floor, on the clothes, down the water pipes. That blood will be in my grandchild.' He seemed to realise that he had allowed himself to be carried away, for he stopped suddenly, blushed, and shut his eyes briefly as if wincing at the sight he had described.

Wexford said gently, 'I wish I could help you, Mr Archery, but the case is close, over, finished. There is nothing more I can do.'

Archery shrugged and quoted softly, almost as if he could not stop himself, ' "He took water and washed his hands before the multitude, saying, I am innocent of the blood of this just person . . ." ' Then he jumped up, his expression suddenly contrite. 'Forgive me, Chief Inspector. That was an appalling thing to say. May I tell you what I intend to do?'

'Pontius Pilate, that's me,' said Wexford. 'So see you show more respect in future.'

Burden grinned. 'What exactly did he want, sir?'

'Firstly to tell him Painter may have been unjustly executed, which I can't. Damn it all, it would be tantamount to saying I didn't know my job. It was my first murder case, Mike, and it was fortunate for me it was so straightforward. Archery's going to do a spot of enquiry on his own. Hopeless after sixteen years but it's useless telling him. Secondly, he wanted my permission to go around hunting up all the witnesses. Wanted my support if they come round here, complaining and foaming at the mouth.'

'And all he's got to go on,' said Burden thoughtfully, 'is Mrs Painter's sentimental belief in her husband's innocence?'

'Aah, that's nothing! That's a load of hooey. If you got the chop, wouldn't Jean tell John and Pat you were innocent? Wouldn't my wife tell the girls? It's natural. Painter didn't make any last-minute confessions—you know what the prison authorities are like for watching out for things like that. No, she dreamed it up and convinced herself.'

'Has Archery ever met her?'

'Not yet, but he's making a day of it. She and her second husband live in Purley and he's got himself an invite for tea.'

'You say the girl told him at Whitsun. Why has he waited so long? It must be a couple of months.'

'I asked him that. He said that for the first couple of weeks he and his wife just let it ride. They thought the son might see reason. But he wouldn't. He got his father to get hold of a transcript of the trial, nagged him into working on Griswold. Of course he's an only child and as spoilt as they come. The upshot was that Archery promised to start poking his nose into it as soon as he got his fortnight's holiday.'

'So he'll be back?'

'That will depend on Mrs Painter,' said Wexford.

5

. . . That they may see their children christianly and virtuously brought up.

The Solemnisation of Matrimony.

The Kershaws' house was about a mile from the town centre, separated from shops, station, cinema and churches by thousands of other large suburban villas. For number 20 Craig Hill was large, half-heartedly Georgian and built of raspberry red brick. The garden was planted with annuals, the lawn was clover-free and the dead heads had been nipped off the standard rose bushes. On the concrete drive a boy of about twelve was washing down a large white Ford.

Archery parked his car at the kerb. Unlike Wexford he had not yet seen the coach house at Victor's Piece, but he had read about it and it seemed to him that Mrs Kershaw had climbed high. Sweat started on his forehead and his upper lip as he got out of the car. He told himself that it was unusually hot and that he had always been prone to feel the heat.

'This is Mr Kershaw's house, isn't it?' he asked the boy.

'That's right.' He was very like Tess, but his hair was fairer and his nose was freckled. 'The front door's open. Shall I give him a shout?'

'My name is Archery,' said the clergyman and he held out his hand.

The boy wiped his hands on his jeans. 'Hallo,' he said.

By now a little wrinkled man had come down the porch steps. The bright hot air seemed to hang between them. Archery tried not to feel disappointment. What had he expected? Certainly not someone so small, so unfinished looking and so wizened as this scrawny creature in old flannels and tieless knitted shirt. Then Kershaw smiled and the years fell from him. His eyes were a bright sparkling blue and his uneven teeth white and clean.

'How do you do?'

'Good afternoon, Mr Archery. I'm very happy to meet you. As a matter of fact I've been sitting in the window, looking out for you.'

In this man's presence it was impossible not to feel hope, cheerfulness almost. Archery detected at once a rare quality in him, a quality he had come upon perhaps only half a dozen times in his life. This was a man who was interested in all things. Energy and enthusiasm radiated from him. On a winter's day he would warm the air. Today, in this heat, his vitality was overwhelming.

'Come inside and meet my wife.' His voice was a hot breeze, a cockney voice that suggested fish and chips, eels and mash and East end pubs. Following him into the square panelled hall, Archery wondered how old he was. Perhaps no more than forty-five. Drive, the fire of life, lack of sleep because sleep wasted time, could prematurely have burnt away his youth. 'We're in the lounge,' he said, pushing open a reeded glass door. 'That's what I like about a day like this. When I get home from work I like to sit by the french windows for ten minutes and look at the garden. Makes you feel all that slogging in the winter was worthwhile.'

'To sit in the shade and look upon verdure?' After the words were out Archery was sorry he had spoken. He didn't want to put this suburban engineer in a false position.

Kershaw gave him a quick glance. Then he smiled and said easily, 'Miss Austen certainly knew what she was talking about, didn't she?' Archery was overcome. He went into the room and held out his hand to the woman who had got up from an armchair.

'My wife. This is Mr Archery, Rene.'

'How do you do?'

Irene Kershaw said nothing, but holding out her hand, smiled a tight bright smile. Her face was Tess's face as it would be when time had hardened it and finished it. In her youth she had been blonde. Now her hair, evidently set that day and perhaps in his honour, was dyed a dull leaf-brown and arranged in unreal feathery wisps about her forehead and ears.

'Sit down, Mr Archery,' said Kershaw. 'We won't keep you a minute for your tea. Kettle's on, isn't it, Renee?'

Archery sat in an armchair by the window. Kershaw's garden was full of experimental rose pergolas, eruptions of rockery and stone sporting generaniums. He gave the room a quick glance, noting at once its cleanliness and the enormous mass of things which had to be kept clean. Books abounded, Readers' Digests, encyclopaedias, dictionaries, works on astronomy, deep sea fishing, European history. There was a tank of tropical fish on a corner table, several model aircraft on the mantelpiece; stacks of sheet music covered the grand piano, and on an easel was a half-finished, rather charming, portrait in oils of a young girl. It was a large room, conventionally furnished with Wilton carpet and chintz covers, but it expressed the personality of the master of the house.

'We've had the pleasure of meeting your Charlie,' said Kershaw. 'A nice unassuming boy. I liked him.' Charlie! Archery sat very still, trying not to feel affronted. Charles's eligibility, after all, was not in question.

Quite suddenly Renee Kershaw spoke. 'We all like him,' she said. Her accent was just the same as Wexford's. 'But I'm sure I don't know how they plan to manage, what with everything being such an awful price—the cost of living, you know—and Charles not having a job in line . . .' Archery felt amazement. Was she really concerned with this trivia? He began to wonder how he would broach the subject that had brought him to Purley. 'I mean where will they live?' Mrs Kershaw asked primly. 'They're just babies really. I mean, you've got to have a home of your own, haven't you? You've got to get a mortgage and . . .'

'I think I can hear the kettle, Renee,' said her husband.

She got up, holding her skirt modestly down to cover her knees. It was a very suburban skirt of some permanently pleated material banded in muted blue and heather pink and of dead sexless respectability. With it she wore a short-sleeved pink jumper and around her neck a single string of cultured pearls. If cultured meant tended and nurtured, Archery thought he had never seen such obviously cultured pearls. Each night, he was sure, they were wrapped in tissue and put away in the dark.

Mrs Kershaw smelt of talcum powder, some of which lingered in the lines of her neck.

'I don't think we've got to the mortgage stage yet,' said Kershaw when she had gone. Archery gave a wry smile. 'Believe me, Mr Archery, I know you haven't come here just for an in-laws' get-together over the tea cups.'

'I'm finding it more awkward than I thought possible.'

Kershaw chuckled. 'I daresay. I can't tell you anything about Tess's father that isn't common knowledge, that wasn't in the papers at the time. You know that?'

'But her mother?'

'You can try. At times like this women see things through a cloud of orange blossom. She's never been very keen on Tess being an educated woman. She wants to see her married and she'll do her best to see nothing stands in her way.'

'And you, what do you want?'

'Me? Oh, I want to see her happy. Happiness doesn't necessarily begin at the altar.' Suddenly he was brisk and forthright. 'Frankly, Mr Archery, I'm not sure if she can be happy with a man who suspects her of homicidal tendencies before she's even engaged to him.'

'It isn't like that!' Archery hadn't expected the other man to put him on the defensive. 'Your stepdaughter is perfect in my son's eyes. I'm making the inquiries, Mr Kershaw. My son knows that, he wants it for Tess's sake, but he doesn't even know I'm here. Put yourself in my position . . .'

'But I *was* in your position. Tess was only six when I married her mother.' He looked quickly at the door, then leaned closer to Archery. 'D'you think I didn't watch her, look out for the disturbance to show itself? When my own daughter was born Tess was very jealous. She resented the baby and one day I found her leaning over Jill's pram striking her on the head with a celluloid toy. Luckily, it *was* a celluloid toy.'

'But, good heavens . . . !' Archery felt the pallor drawing at his face muscles.

'What could I do? I had to go to work and leave the children. I had to trust my wife. Then we had a son—I think you bumped into him outside cleaning the car—and Jill resented him in just the same way and with just the same violence. All children behave like this, that's the point.'

'You never saw any more—any more of these tendencies?'

'Tendencies? A personality isn't made by heredity, Mr Archery, but by environment. I wanted Tess to have the best sort of environment and I think I can say, with all due modesty, that she has.'

The garden shimmered in the heat haze. Archery saw things he hadn't noticed at first, chalk lines on the lawn, where, regardless of herbaceous borders, the grass had been marked out for a tennis court; a shambles of rabbit hutches attached to the garage wall; an ancient swing. Behind him on the mantelpiece he saw propped against ornaments two party invitations. A framed photograph above it showed three children in shirts and jeans sprawled on a haystack. Yes, this had been the best of all possible environments for the murderer's orphan.

The door was pushed open and the girl in the portrait came in pushing a tea trolley. Archery who was too hot and troubled to feel hungry, saw with dismay that it was laden with home-baked pastries, strawberries in glass dishes, fairy cakes in paper cases. The girl looked about fourteen. She was not so beautiful as Tess and she wore a bunchy school tunic, but her father's vitality illumined her face.

'This is my daughter Jill.'

Jill sprawled in a chair, showing a lot of long leg.

'Now, sit nicely, dear,' said Mrs Kershaw sharply. She gave the girl a repressive look and began to pour tea, holding the pot with curled fingers. 'They don't realise they're young women at thirteen these days, Mr Archery.' Archery was embarrassed but the girl didn't seem to care. 'You must have one of these cakes. Jill made them.' Unwillingly he took a pastry. 'That's right. I've always said to both my girls, schooling is all very well in its way, but algebra won't cook the Sunday dinner. Tess and Jill are both good plain cooks . . .'

'Mummy! I'm not plain and Tess certainly isn't.'

'You know what I mean. Now don't take me up on everything. When they get married their husbands won't be ashamed to have anybody for a meal.'

'This is my managing director, darling,' said Jill pertly. 'Just cut a slice off him and put it under the grill, will you?'

Kershaw roared with laughter. Then he took his wife's hand 'You leave Mummy alone.' All this jollity and family intimacy was making Archery nervous. He forced a smile and knew it looked forced.

'What I really mean is, Mr Archery,' said Mrs Kershaw earnestly, 'is that even if your Charlie and my Tessie have their ups and downs at first, Tess hasn't been brought up to be an idle wife. She'll put a happy home before luxuries.'

'I'm sure she will.' Archery looked helplessly at the lounging girl, firmly entrenched in her chair and devouring strawberries and cream. It was now or never. 'Mrs Kershaw, I don't doubt Theresa's suitability as a wife . . .' No, that wasn't right. That was just what he did doubt. He floundered. 'I wanted to talk to you about . . .' Surely Kershaw would help him? Jill's brows drew together in a small frown and her grey eyes stared steadily at him. Desperately he said, 'I wanted to speak to you alone.'

Irene Kershaw seemed to shrink. She put down her cup, laid her knife delicately across her plate and, folding her hands in her lap, looked down at them. They were poor hands, stubby and worn, and she wore just one ring, her second wedding ring.

'Haven't you got any homework to do, Jill?' she asked in a whisper. Kershaw got up, wiping his mouth.

'I can do it in the train,' said Jill.

Archery had begun to dislike Kershaw, but he could not help admiring him. 'Jill, you know all about Tess,' Kershaw said, 'what happened when she was little. Mummy has to discuss it with Mr Archery. Just by themselves. We have to go because, although we're involved, it's not quite our business. Not like it is theirs. O.K.?'

'O.K.' said Jill. Her father put his arm round her and took her into the garden.

He had to begin, but he was hot and stiff with awkwardness. Outside the window Jill had found a tennis racquet and was practising shots against the garage wall. Mrs Kershaw picked up a napkin and dabbed at the corners of her mouth. She looked at him, their eyes met, and she looked away. Archery felt suddenly that they were not alone, that their thoughts concentrated on the past, had summoned from its prison grave a presence of brute strength that stood behind their chairs, laying a bloody hand on their shoulders and listening for judgment.

'Tess says you have something to tell me,' he said quietly.

'About your first husband.' She was rolling the napkin now, squashing it, until it was like a golf-ball. 'Mrs Kershaw, I think you ought to tell me.'

The paper ball was tipped soundlessly on to an empty plate. She put her hand up to her pearls.

'I never speak of him, Mr Archery. I prefer to let the past be the past.'

'I know it's painful—it must be. But if we could discuss it just once and get it over, I promise I'll never raise the subject again.' He realised that he was speaking as if they would meet again and often, as if they were already connected by marriage. He was also speaking as if he had confidence in her word. 'I've been to Kingsmarkham today and . . .'

She clutched at the straw. 'I suppose they've built it all up and spoiled it.'

'Not really,' he said. Please God, don't let her digress!

'I was born near there,' she said. He tried to stifle a sigh. 'A funny little sleepy place it was, my village. I reckon I thought I'd live and die there. You can't tell what life will bring forth, can you?'

'Tell me about Tess's father.'

She dropped her hands from fidgeting with the pearls and rested them in her respectable blue lap. When she turned to him her face was dignified, almost ridiculously prim and shuttered. She might have been a mayoress, taking the chair at some parochial function, clearing her throat preparatory to addressing the Townswomen's Guild. 'Madam chairman, ladies . . .' she should have begun. Instead she said:

'The past is the past, Mr Archery.' He knew then that it was hopeless. 'I appreciate your difficulty, but I really can't speak of it. He was no murderer, you'll have to take my word. He was a good kind man who wouldn't have harmed a fly.' It was curious, he thought, how she jumbled together old village phrases with platform jargon. He waited, then burst out:

'But how do you know? How *can* you know? Mrs Kershaw, did you see something or hear something . . . ?'

The pearls had gone up to her mouth and her teeth closed over the string. As it snapped pearls sprayed off in all directions, into her lap, across the tea things, on to the carpet. She gave a small refined laugh, petulant and apologetic. 'Look what I've done now!' In an instant she was on her knees, retrieving the scattered beads and dropping them into a saucer.

'I'm very keen on a white wedding.' Her face bounced up from behind the tea trolley. Politeness demanded that he too should get on his knees and help in the hunt. 'Get your wife to back me up, will you? Oh, thanks so much. Look, there's another one, just by your left foot.' He scrambled round after her on all fours. Her eyes met his under the overhanging cloth. 'My Tess is quite capable of getting married in jeans if the fancy takes her. And would you mind if we had the reception here? It's such a nice big room.'

Archery got up and handed her three more pearls. When the tennis ball struck the window he jumped. The sound had been like a pistol shot.

'Now, that's quite enough, Jill,' said Mrs Kershaw sharply. Still holding the saucer full of pearls, she opened the window. 'If I've told you once, I've told you fifty times, I don't want any more breakages.'

Archery looked at her. She was annoyed, affronted, even slightly outraged. He wondered suddenly if this was how she had looked on that Sunday night long ago when the police had invaded her domain at the coach house. Was she capable of any emotion greater than this, of mere irritation at disturbance of her personal peace?

'You just can't settle to a quiet discussion with children about, can you?' she said.

Within an instant, as if at a cue, the whole family was upon them, Jill truculent and protesting, the boy he had encountered on the drive now demanding tea, and Kershaw himself, vibrant as ever, his little lined face showing a certain dry acuteness.

'Now, you're to come straight out and give me a hand with these dishes, Jill.' The saucer was transferred to the mantelpiece and stuck between an Oxfam collecting box and a card inviting Mrs Kershaw to a coffee morning in aid of Cancer Relief. 'I'll say good-bye now, Mr Archery.' She held out her hand. 'You've such a long way to go, I know you'll want to be on your way.' It was almost rude, yet it was queenly. 'If we don't meet again before the great day—well, I'll see you in church.'

The door closed. Archery remained standing.

'What am I to do?' he said simply.

'What did you expect?' Kershaw countered. 'Some sort of inconvertible evidence, an alibi that only she can prove?'

'Do *you* believe her?' Archery cared.

'Ah, that's another matter. I don't care, you see. I don't care one way or the other. It's so easy *not* to ask, Mr Archery, just to do nothing and accept.'

'But I care,' said Archery. 'If Charles goes ahead and marries your stepdaughter, I shall have to leave the church. I don't think you realise the sort of place I live in, the sort of people . . .'

'Aah!' Kershaw wrinkled up his mouth and spread his hands angrily fanwise. 'I've no patience with that sort of out-dated rubbish. Who's to know? Everybody round here thinks she's my kid.'

'I shall know.'

'Why the hell did she have to tell you? Why couldn't she keep her mouth shut?'

'Are you condemning her for her honesty, Kershaw?'

'Yes, by God I am!' Archery winced at the oath and shut his eyes against the light. He saw a red haze. It was only eyelid membrane, but to him it seemed like a lake of blood. 'It's discretion, not honesty, that's the best policy. What are you worrying about, anyway? You know damn' well she won't marry him if you don't want it.'

Archery snapped back, 'And what sort of a relationship should I have with my son after that?' He controlled himself, softened his voice and his expression. 'I shall have to try to find a way. Your wife is so sure?'

'She's never weakened.'

'Then I shall go back to Kingsmarkham. It's rather a forlorn hope, isn't it?' He added with an absurdity he realised after the words had come, 'Thanks for trying to help and—and for an excellent tea.'

6

Yet, forasmuch as in all appearance the time of his dissolution draweth near, so fit and prepare him . . . against the hour of death.

The Visitation of the Sick.

The man lay on his back in the middle of the zebra crossing. Inspector Burden, getting out of the police car, had no need to ask where he was or to be taken to the scene of the accident. It was all there before his eyes like a horrible still from a Ministry of Transport warning film, the kind of thing that makes women shudder and turn quickly to the other channel.

An ambulance was waiting, but nobody was making any attempt to move the man. Inexorably and with a kind of indifference the twin yellow beacons went on winking rhythmically. Up-ended, with its blunt nose poking into the crushed head of a bollard, was a white Mini.

'Can't you get him away?' asked Burden.

The doctor was laconic. 'He's had it.' He knelt down, felt the left wrist and got up again, wiping blood from his fingers. 'I'd hazard a guess the spine's gone and he's ruptured his liver. The thing is he's still more or less conscious and it'd be hell's own agony to try to shift him.'

'Poor devil. What happened? Did anybody see it?'

His eye roved across the knot of middle-aged women in cotton dresses, late homegoing commuters and courting couples on their evening stroll. The last of the sun smiled gently on their faces and on the blood that gilded the black and white crossing. Burden knew that Mini. He knew the stupid sign in the rear window that showed a skull and the words: *You have been Mini-ed*. It had never been funny and now it was outrageous, cruel in the way it mocked the man in the road.

A girl lay sprawled over the steering wheel. Her hair was short, black and spiky, and she had thrust her fingers through it in despair or remorse. The long red nails stuck out like bright feathers.

'Don't worry about her,' said the doctor contemptuously. 'She's not hurt.'

'You, madam . . .' Burden picked out the calmest and least excited looking of the bystanders. 'Did you happen to see the accident?'

'Ooh, it was awful! Like a beast she was, the little bitch. Must have been doing a hundred miles an hour.'

Picked a right one there, thought Burden. He turned to a white-faced man holding a sealyham on a lead.

'Perhaps you can help me, sir?'

The lead was jerked and the sealyham sat down at the kerb. 'That gentleman . . .' Blanching afresh, he pointed towards the crumpled thing lying on the stripes. 'He looked right and left like you're supposed to. But there was nothing coming. You can't see all that well on account of the bridge.'

'Yes, yes. I get the picture.'

'Well, he started to cross to the island like, when that white car came up out of nowhere. Going like a mad thing she was. Well, not a hundred, but sixty, I reckon. Those Minis can go at a terrible lick when they've had their engines hotted up. He sort of hesitated and then he tried to go back. You know, it was all in a flash. I can't rightly go into details.'

'You're doing very well.'

'Then the car got him. Oh, the driver slammed on her brakes for all she was worth. I'll never forget the noise to my dying day, what with the brakes screaming and him screaming too, and sort of throwing up his arms and going down like a ninepin.'

Burden set a constable to take names and addresses, turned away and took a step in the direction of the white car. A woman touched his arm.

'Here,' she said, 'he wants a priest or something. He kept on asking before you came. Get me Father Chiverton, he says, like he knew he was going.'

'That right?' said Burden sharply to Dr Crocker.

Crocker nodded. The dying man was covered now, a folded mac under his head, two policemen's jackets across his body. 'Father Chiverton is what he said. Frankly, I was more concerned for his physical than his spiritual welfare.'

'R.C. then, is he?'

'God, no. Bunch of atheists, you cops are. Chiverton's the new vicar here. Don't you ever read the local rag?'

'*Father?*'

'He's very high. Genuflecting and Sung Eucharist and all that jazz.' The doctor coughed. 'I'm a Congregationalist myself.'

Burden walked over to the crossing. The man's face was blanched a yellowish ivory, but his eyes were open and they stared back. With a little shock Burden realised he was young, perhaps no more than twenty.

'Anything you want, old chap?' He knew the doctor had given him a pain-killing injection. With his own bent body he shielded him from the watchers. 'We'll get you away from here in a minute,' he lied. 'Anything we can get you?'

'Father Chiverton . . .' it was a toneless whisper, as detached and inhuman as a puff of wind. 'Father Chiverton . . .' A spasm crossed the waning face. 'Confess . . . atone . . . spare Thou them which are penitent.'

'Bloody religion,' said the doctor. 'Can't even let a man die in peace.'

'You must be an asset to the Congregationalists,' Burden snapped. He got up, sighing. 'He obviously wants to confess. I suppose they do have confession in the Church of England?'

'You can have it if you want it but you needn't if you don't fancy it. That's the beauty of the C of E.' When Burden looked murderous, he added. 'Don't get in a tiz with me. We've been on to Chiverton, but he and his curate are off at some conference.'

'Constable Gates!' Burden beckoned impatiently to the man noting down addresses. 'Nip into Stowerton and fetch me a—a vicar.'

'We've tried Stowerton, sir.'

'O God,' said Burden quietly.

'Excuse me, sir, but there's a clergyman got an appointment with the Chief Inspector now. I could get on to the station and . . .'

Burden raised his eyebrows. Kingsmarkham police station had

apparently become the battleground of the Church Militant.

'You do that, and quick . . .'

He murmured something useless to the boy, and moved towards the girl who had begun to sob.

She was not crying because of what she had done, but because of what she had seen two hours before. It was two or three years now since she had what she called a waking nightmare—though at one time they were more real than reality—and she was crying because the nightmares were going to begin again and the remedy she had tried had not erased the picture from her mind.

She had seen it in the estate agent's window when she was coming home from work. It was a photograph of a house, but not as it was now, dirty and weathered, set in a tangled wilderness. The estate agents deceived you, they meant you to think it was like it had once been long ago . . .You? As soon as she found she was addressing herself as 'You' she knew it was beginning again, the re-telling of the nightmare. So she had got into the Mini and driven to Flagford, away from associations and memories and the hateful You voice, to drink and drink and try to send it away.

But it would not go away and you were back in the big house, listening to the voices that went on coaxing, cajoling, arguing until you were bored, so bored until you went out into the garden and met the little girl.

You went up to her and you said, 'Do you like my dress?'

'It's pretty,' she said, and she didn't seem to mind that it was much nicer than her own.

She was playing with a heap of sand, making pies in an old cup without a handle. You stayed and played and after that you came to the sand every day, down there out of sight of the big windows. The sand was warm and nice and you could understand it. You could understand the little girl too, even though she was the only little girl you had ever known. You knew a lot of grown ups, but you could not understand them, nor the ugly words and the funny wheedling way the talk was always about money, so that you seemed to see coins dropping out of wriggling lips and sliding dirtily through twitching fingers.

The little girl had some magic about her, for she lived in a tree. Of course it was not really a tree but a house inside a kind of bush all shivering with leaves.

The sand was not dry like the desert you lived in now, but warm and moist, like beach sand washed by a tepid sea. It was dirty too and you were afraid of what would happen if you got it on your dress . . .

You cried and stamped your foot, but you never cried as you were crying now as the good-looking inspector came up to the car, his eyes full of anger.

Did he seriously imagine he was going to find anything new after so long? Archery considered Wexford's question. It was, he decided, more a matter of faith than of any real belief in Painter's innocence. But faith in what? Not, surely, in Mrs Kershaw. Perhaps it was just a childlike certainty that such things could not happen to anyone connected with him, Archery. The child of a murderer could not be as Tess was, Kershaw would not have loved her, Charles would not want to marry her.

'It can't do any harm to see Alice Flower,' he said. He felt he was pleading, and pleading weakly. 'I'd like to talk to the Primero grandchildren, particularly the grandson.'

For a moment Wexford said nothing. He had heard of faith moving mountains, but this was simply absurd. To him it was almost as ridiculous as if some crank had come to him with the suggestion that Dr Crippen was the innocent victim of circumstances. From bitter experience he knew how difficult it was to hunt a killer when only a week had elapsed between a murder and the beginning of an investigation. Archery was proposing to open an enquiry a decade and a half too late and Archery had no experience at all.

'I ought to put you off,' he said at last. 'You don't know what you're attempting.' It's pathetic, he thought, it's laughable. Aloud he said, 'Alice Flower's in the geriatric ward at Stowerton Infirmary. She's paralysed. I don't even know if she could make herself understood.'

It occurred to him that Archery must be totally ignorant of the geography of the place. He got up and lumbered over to the wall map.

'Stowerton's there,' he said, pointing with the sheathed tip of a ballpoint pen, 'and Victor's Piece is about here, between Stowerton and Kingsmarkham.'

'Where can I find Mrs Crilling?'

Wexford made a wry face. 'In Glebe Road. I can't recall the number off-hand, but I'll get it looked up or you could find it on the electoral register.' He turned round ponderously and fixed Archery with a grey glare. 'You're wasting your time, of course. I'm sure I don't have to tell you to be very careful when it comes to throwing out a lot of unfounded accusations.'

Under those cold eyes it was difficult for Archery not to drop his own. 'Chief Inspector, I don't want to find someone else guilty, just prove that Painter was innocent.'

Wexford said briskly, 'I'm afraid you may find the former consequent upon the latter. It would be a wrong conclusion, of course—I don't want trouble.' At a knock on the door he spun round testily. 'Yes, what is it?'

Sergeant Martin's bland face appeared. 'That fatal on the zebra in the High Street, sir?'

'What of it? It's hardly my province.'

'Gates has just been on, sir. A white Mini, LMB 12M, that we've had our eye on—it was in collision with a pedestrian. It appears they want a clergyman and Gates recalled that Mr Archery was . . .'

Wexford's lips witched. Archery was in for a surprise. In the courtly manner he sometimes assumed, he said to the vicar of Thringford, 'It looks as if the secular arm needs some spiritual assistance, sir. Would you be so good . . .?'

'Of course I will.' Archery looked at the sergeant. 'Someone has been knocked down and is—is *dying*?'

'Unfortunately, yes, sir,' said Martin grimly.

'I think I'll come with you,' said Wexford.

As a priest of the Anglican Church Archery was obliged to hear confession if a confessor was needed. Until now, however, his only experience of this mystery concerned a Miss Baylis, an elderly female parishioner of his who, having been (according to Mrs Archery) for many years in love with him, demanded that he should listen to a small spate of domestic sins mumbled out each Friday morning. Hers was a masochistic, self-abasing need, very different from the yearning of the boy who lay in the road.

Wexford shepherded him across the black and white lines to the island. Diversion notices had been placed in the road, directing the traffic around Queen Street, and the crowd had been induced to go home. There were several policemen buzzing and pacing. For the first time in his life Archery realised the aptness of the term 'bluebottles'. He glanced at the Mini and averted his eyes hastily from the bright bumper with its ribbon of blood.

The boy looked at him doubtfully. He had perhaps five minutes to live. Archery dropped to his knees and put his ear to the white lips. At first he felt only fluttering breath, then out of the soft sighing vibration came something that sounded like 'Holy orders . . .', with the second word rising on a high note of enquiry. He bent closer as the confession began to flow out, jerky, toneless, spasmodic, like the gulping of a sluggish stream. It was something about a girl, but it was utterly incoherent. He could make nothing of it. We fly unto Thee for succour, he thought, in behalf of this Thy servant, here lying under Thy hand in great weakness of body . . .

The Anglican Church provides no order quite comparable to that of Extreme Unction. Archery found himself saying urgently over and over again, 'It will be all right, it will be all right.' The boy's throat rattled and a stream of blood welled out of his mouth, splashing Archery's folded hands. 'We humbly commend the soul of this Thy servant, our dear brother, into Thy hands . . .' He was tired and his voice broke with compassion and with horror. 'Most humbly beseeching Thee that it may be precious in Thy sight . . .'

It was the doctor's hand that appeared, mopping with a handkerchief at Archery's fingers, then feeling a still heart and an inert pulse. Wexford looked at the doctor, gave an infinitesimal shrug. Nobody spoke. Across the silence came the sound of brakes, a horn braying and an oath as a car, taking the diversion too late, veered into Queen Street. Wexford pulled the coat up over the dead face.

Archery was shattered and cold in the evening heat. He got up stiffly, feeling an utter loneliness and a terrible desire to weep. The only thing to lean on now the bollard was gone was the rear of that lethal white car. He leaned on it, feeling sick.

Presently he opened his eyes and moved slowly along the body of the car to where Wexford stood contemplating a girl's shaggy black head. This was no business of his, Archery's. He wanted no hand in it, only to ask Wexford where he could find an hotel for the night.

Something in the other man's expression made him hesitate. The big Chief Inspector's face was a study in irony. He watched Wexford tap on the glass. The window was slid back and the girl inside lifted to them a face drowned in tears.

'This is a bad business,' he heard Wexford say, 'a very bad business, Miss Crilling.'

'God moves in a mysterious way,' said Wexford as he and Archery walked over the bridge, 'His wonders to perform.' He hummed the old hymn tune, apparently liking the sound of his rather rusty baritone.

'That's true,' said Archery very seriously. He stopped, rested his hand on the granite parapet and looked down into the brown water. A swan sailed out from under the bridge, dipping its long neck into the drifting weed. 'And that is really the girl who found Mrs Primero's body?'

'That's Elizabeth Crilling, yes. One of the wild young things of Kingsmarkham. A boy friend—a very *close* friend, I may add—gave her the Mini for her twenty-first and she's been a menace in it ever since.'

Archery was silent. Tess Kershaw and Elizabeth Crilling were the same age. Their lives had begun together, almost side by side. Each must have walked with her mother along the grass verges of the Stowerton Road, played in the fields behind Victor's Piece. The Crillings had been comfortably off, middle-class people; the Painters miserably poor. In his mind's eye he saw again that tear-wrecked face down which grease and mascara ran in rivulets, and he heard again the ugly words she had used to Wexford. Another face superimposed itself on Elizabeth Crilling's, a fair aquiline face with steady intelligent eyes under a page-boy's blonde fringe. Wexford interrupted his thoughts.

'She's been spoilt, of course, made too much of. Your Mrs Primero had her over with her every day, stuffing her with sweets and what-have-you, by all accounts. After the murder Mrs Crilling was always taking her to psychiatrists, wouldn't let her go to school till they had the kid-catcher down on her. God knows how many schools she *has* been to. She was what you might call the female lead in the juvenile court here.'

But it was Tess whose father had been a murderer, Tess who might have been expected to grow up like that. 'God knows how many schools she's been to . . .' Tess had been to one school and to one ancient, distinguished university. Yet the daughter of the innocent friend had become a delinquent; the killer's child a paragon. Certainly God moved in a mysterious way.

'Chief Inspector, I want very much to talk to Mrs Crilling.'

'If you care to attend the special court in the morning, sir, she'll in all likelihood be there. Knowing Mrs Crilling, I'd say you might again be called upon in your professional capacity and then, who knows?'

Archery frowned as they walked on. 'I'd rather it was all above-board. I don't want to do anything underhand.'

'Look, sir,' said Wexford in a burst of impatience, 'if you're coming in on this lark you'll have to be underhand. You've no real authority to ask questions of innocent people and if they complain I can't protect you.'

'I'll explain everything frankly to her. May I talk to her?'

Wexford cleared his throat. 'Are you familiar with *Henry the Fourth,* Part One, sir?'

Slightly puzzled, Archery nodded. Wexford stopped under the arch that led to the coaching yard of The Olive and Dove. 'The quotation I had in mind is Hotspur's reply to Mortimer when he says he can call spirits from the vasty deep.' Startled by Wexford's deep voice, a little cloud of pigeons flew out from the beams, fluttering rusty grey wings. 'I've found that reply very useful to me in my work when I've been a bit too optimistic.' He cleared his throat and quoted, ' "And so can I and so can any man. But will they come when you do call to them?" Good night, sir. I hope you find the Olive comfortable.'

7

Into how high a dignity . . . ye are called, that is to say to be Messengers, Watchmen and Stewards . . .

The Ordering of Priests.

Two people sat in the public gallery of Kingsmarkham court, Archery and a woman with sharp, wasted features. Her long grey hair, oddly fashionable through carelessness rather than intent, and the cape she wore gave her a medieval look. Presumably she was the mother of this girl who had just been charged with manslaughter, the girl whom the clerk had named as Elizabeth Anthea Crilling, of 24A Glebe Road, Kingsmarkham in the County of Sussex. She had a look of her mother and they kept glancing at each other, Mrs Crilling's eyes flicking over her daughter's string-thin body or coming to rest with maudlin watery affection on the girl's face. It was a well-made face, though gaunt but for the full mouth. Sometimes it seemed to become all staring dark eyes as a word or a telling phrase awakened emotion, sometimes blank and shuttered like that of a retarded child with an inner life of goblins and things that reach out in the dark. An invisible thread held mother and daughter together but whether it was composed of love or hatred Archery could not tell. Both were ill-dressed, dirty-looking, a prey, he felt, to cheap emotion, but there was some quality each had—passion? Imagination? Seething memory?—that set them apart and dwarfed the other occupants of the court.

He had just enough knowledge of the law to know that this court could do no more than commit the girl to the Assizes for trial. The evidence that was being laboriously taken down on a typewriter was all against her. Elizabeth Crilling, according to the licensee of The Swan at Flagford, had been drinking in his saloon bar since six-thirty. He had served her with seven double whiskies and when he had refused to let her have another, she had abused him until he had threatened to call the police.

'No alternative but to commit you for trial at the Assizes at Lewes,' the chairman was saying. '. . . Nothing to hope for from any promise of favour, and nothing to fear from any threat which may be . . .'

A shriek came from the public gallery. 'What are you going to do to her?' Mrs Crilling had sprung up, the tent-like cape she wore billowing out and making a breeze run through the court. 'You're not going to put her in prison?'

Hardly knowing why he did so, Archery moved swiftly along the form until he was at her side. At the same time Sergeant Martin took half a dozen rapid strides towards her, glaring at the clergyman.

'Now, madam, you'd far better come outside.'

She flung herself away from him, pulling the cape around her as if it were cold instead of suffocatingly hot.

'You're not going to put my baby in gaol!' She pushed at the sergeant who stood between her and her view of the bench. 'Get away from me, you dirty sadist!'

'Take that woman outside,' said the magistrate with icy calm. Mrs Crilling spun round to face Archery and seized his hands. 'You've got a kind face. Are you my friend?'

Archery was horribly embarrassed. 'You can ask for bail, I think,' he muttered.

The policewoman who stood by the dock came over to them. 'Come along now, Mrs Crilling . . .'

'Bail, I want bail! This gentleman is an old friend of mine and he says I can have bail. I want my rights for my baby!'

'We really can't have this sort of thing.' The magistrate cast an icy scornful look upon Archery who sat down, wrenching his hands from Mrs Crilling's. 'Do I understand you wish to ask for bail?' He turned his eyes on Elizabeth who nodded defiantly.

'A nice cup of tea, Mrs Crilling,' said the policewoman. 'Come along now.' She shepherded the demented woman out, her arm supporting her waist. The magistrate went into conference with the clerk and bail was granted to Elizabeth Crilling in her own recognisance of five hundred pounds and that of her mother for a similar sum.

'Rise, please!' said the warrant officer. It was over.

On the other side of the court Wexford shovelled his papers into his briefcase.

'A friend in need, that one,' he said to Burden, glancing in Archery's direction. 'You mark my words, he'll have a job getting out of old Mother Crilling's clutches. Remember when we had to cart her off to the mental unit at Stowerton that time? You were her friend then. Tried to kiss you, didn't she?'

'Don't remind me,' said Burden.

'Funny affair altogether last night, wasn't it? Him being on hand, I mean, to show that poor kid his way to heaven.'

'It was lucky.'

'I only remember that happening once before, except in the case of R.C.s, of course.' He turned as Archery slipped between the wooden forms and came up to them. 'Good morning, sir. I hope you slept well. I was just saying to the inspector, there was a fellow killed out Forby way soon after I came here. Must be all of twenty years. I've never forgotten it. He was just a kid too and got it in the neck from an army lorry. But he wasn't quiet, he was screaming. All about a girl and a kid it was.' He paused. 'Did you speak, sir? Sorry, I thought you did. He wanted a clergyman, too.'

'I hope and trust he got what he wanted.'

'Well, no he didn't as a matter of fact. He died—unshriven is the word, I think. The vicar's car broke down on the way. Funny, I've never forgotten it. Grace was his name, John Grace. Shall we go?'

The Crillings had departed. As they came out into the sunshine, the policewoman came up to Wexford.

'Mrs Crilling left a note with me, sir. She asked me to give it to a Mr Archery.'

'Take my advice,' said Wexford. 'Tear it up. She's as mad as a hatter.' But Archery had already slit open the envelope.

Dear Sir, he read.

They tell me that you are a man of God. Blessed is he that sitteth not in the seat of the scornful. God has sent you to me and my baby. I will be at home this afternoon, waiting to thank you in person.

Your affectionate friend, Josephine Crilling

Archery's bedroom combined charmingly the best of old and new. The ceiling was beamed, the walls painted pink and decorated with a tooled design of chevrons, but there was also a fitted carpet, an abundance of lights on walls and bedhead and a telephone. He rinsed his hands at the pink washbasin (a private bathroom he felt to be an unwarranted extravagance), lifted the receiver and asked for a call to Thringford in Essex.

'Darling?'

'Henry! Thank heaven you've phoned. I've been trying over and over again to get you at that Olive Branch place or whatever it's called.'

'Why, what's the matter?'

'I've had a dreadful letter from Charles. Apparently poor darling Tess phoned her people late yesterday afternoon and now she's told Charles the engagement's definitely off. She says it wouldn't be fair on him or us.'

'And . . . ?'

'And Charles says if Tess won't marry him he's going to come down from Oxford and go out to Africa to fight for Zimbabwe.'

'How utterly ridiculous!'

'He says if you try and stop him he'll do something dreadful and get sent down.'

'Is that all?'

'Oh, no. There's lots and lots of it. Let me see. I've got the letter here. ". . . What's the use of Father always ballsing on"—sorry, darling, does that mean something awful?—"on about faith and taking things on trust if he won't take Tess's word and her mother's? I've been into the whole fiasco of the case myself and it's full of holes. I think Father could get the Home Secretary to have the case re-opened if he would only make some sort of effort. For one thing there was an inheritance involved but it never came up at the trial. Three people inherited vast sums and at least one of them was buzzing around the place the day Mrs Primero died . . ." '

'All right,' said Archery wearily. 'If you remember, Mary, I have a transcript of the trial myself and it cost me two hundred pounds. How are things apart from that?'

'Mr Sims is behaving rather oddly.' Mr Sims was Archery's curate. 'Miss Bayliss says he keeps the communion bread in his pocket, and this morning she got a long blonde hair in her mouth.'

Archery smiled. This parish chit-chat was more in his wife's line than solving murders. It brought her to him visually, a handsome strong woman who minded the lines on her face that he never noticed. He was beginning to miss her mentally and physically.

'Now, listen, darling. Write back to Charles—be diplomatic. Tell him how well Tess is behaving and say I'm having some very interesting talks with the police. If there's the slightest chance of getting the case re-opened I'll write to the Home Secretary.'

'That's wonderful, Henry. Oh, there go your second lot of pips. I'll ring off. By the way, Rusty caught a mouse this morning and left it in the bath. He and Tawny are missing you.'

'Give them my love,' said Archery to please her.

He went downstairs into the dark cool dining room, ordered something called a *Navarin d'agneau*, and in a burst of recklessness, a half-bottle of Anjou. All the windows were open but on some of them the green shutters had been closed. A table in one of these embrasures reminded him with its white cloth, its tilted cane chairs and its vaseful of sweet peas of a Dufy that hung on the walls of his study at home. Filtered sunlight lay in primrose-pale bars across the cloth and the two places laid with silver.

But for himself and half a dozen elderly residents, the dining room was deserted, but presently the door from the bar opened and the head waiter ushered in a man and a woman. Archery wondered if the management would object to the apricot poodle the woman fondled in her arms. But the head waiter was smiling deferentially and Archery saw him pat the tiny woolly head.

The man was small and dark and would have been good-looking but for his glassy, red-rimmed eyes. Archery thought he might be wearing contact lenses. He sat down at the Dufy table, ripped open a packet of Peter Stuyvesant and poured the contents into a gold cigarette case. In spite of the man's obvious polish—his sleek hair, svelt suit, taut bone-smooth skin—there was something savage in the way his white fingers tore the paper. A wedding ring and a big bold signet gleamed in the soft light as he tossed the mutilated packet on to the cloth. Archery was amused to see how much jewellery he wore, a sapphire tie pin and a watch as well as the rings.

By contrast the woman wore none. She was plainly dressed in a cream silk suit that matched her hair, and everything about her from the gauzy hat and hair to her crossed ankles was the colour of faint sunlight, so that she seemed to glow with a pale radiance. Outside the cinema and the pictures in Mary's magazines, she was the most beautiful woman he had seen for years. Compared to her Tess Painter was just a pretty girl. Archery was reminded of an ivory orchid or a tea rose which, when lifted from the florist's cube of cellophane, still retains its patina of dew.

He gave himself a little shake and applied himself determindely to his *Navarin*. It had turned out to be two lamb chops in a brown sauce.

Between Kingsmarkham High Street and the Kingsbrook Road lies an estate of ugly terraced houses covered with that mixture of mortar and grit builders call pebble dashing. On a hot day when the roads are dusty and flickering with heat mirage these rows of dun-coloured houses look as if they have been fashioned out of sand. A giant's child might have built them, using his crude tools unimaginatively.

Archery found Glebe Road by the simple and traditional expedient of asking a policeman. He was getting into the habit of asking policemen and this one was low in the hierarchy, a young constable directing traffic at the crossroads.

Glebe Road might have been designed by the Romans, it was so straight, so long and so uncompromising. The sand houses had no woodwork about them. Their window frames were of metal and their porch canopies excrescences of pebbly plaster. After every fourth house an arch in the façade led into the back and through these arches sheds, coal bunkers and dustbins could be seen.

The street was numbered from the Kingsbrook Road end and Archery walked nearly half a mile before he found twenty-four. The hot pavements running with melted tar made his feet burn. He pushed open the gate and saw that the canopy covered not one front door but two. The house had been converted into two surely tiny flatlets. He tapped the chromium knocker on the door marked 24A and waited.

When nothing happened he tapped again. There was a grinding trundling sound and a boy on roller skates came out from under the arch. He took no notice at all of the clergyman. Could Mrs Crilling be asleep? It was hot enough for a siesta and Archery felt languid himself.

He stepped back and looked through the arch. Then he heard the door open and slam shut. So somebody was at home. He rounded the sandy wall and came face to face with Elizabeth Crilling.

At once he sensed that she had not answered, nor probably even heard, his knock. Evidently she was going out. The black dress had been changed for a short blue cotton shift that showed the outlines of her prominent hip bones. She wore backless white mules and carried a huge white and gilt handbag.

'What d'you want?' It was obvious she had no idea who he was. He thought she looked old, finished, as if somehow she had been used and wrecked. 'If you're selling something,' she said, 'you've come to the wrong shop.'

'I saw your mother in court this morning,' Archery said. 'She asked me to come and see her.'

He thought she had rather a charming smile, for her mouth was well-shaped and her teeth good. But the smile was too brief.

'That,' she said, 'was this morning.'

'Is she at home?' He looked helplessly at the doors. 'I—er—which one is it, which flat?'

'Are you kidding? It's bad enough sharing a house with her. Only a stone-deaf paralytic could stick living *underneath* her.'

'I'll go in, shall I?'

'Suit yourself. She's not likely to come out here.' The bag strap was hoisted on to the right shoulder, pulling the blue stuff tight across her breasts. Without knowing why, Archery remembered the exquisite woman in the dining room of the Olive and Dove, her petal skin and her easy grace.

Elizabeth Crilling's face was greasy. In the bright afternoon light the skin had the texture of lemon peel. 'Well, go on in,' she said sharply, unlocking the door. She pushed it open and turned away, her mules flapping and clacking down the path. 'She won't bite you,' she said over her shoulder. 'At least, I shouldn't think so. She bit me once, but there were—well, extenuating circumstances.'

Archery went into the hall. Three doors led off it but they were all closed. He coughed and said tentatively, 'Mrs Crilling?'

The place was stuffy and silent. He hesitated for a moment, then opened the first of the doors. Inside was a bedroom divided into two by a hardboard partition. He had been wondering how the two women managed. Now he knew. The middle room must be where they lived. He tapped on the door and opened it.

Although the french windows were ajar the air was thick with smoke and the two ashtrays on a gateleg table were filled with stubs. Every surface was covered with papers and debris and the debris with dust. As he entered a blue budgerigar in a tiny cage broke into a stream of high brittle chatter. The cage swung furiously.

Mrs Crilling wore a pink nylon dressing gown that looked as if it had once been designed for a bride. The honeymoon, Archery thought, was long over, for the dressing gown was stained and torn and hideous. She was sitting in an armchair looking through the window at a fenced-in piece of land at the back. It could hardly be called a garden for nothing grew in it but nettles, three feet high, rose-pink fireweed, and brambles that covered everything with fly-infested tendrils.

'You hadn't forgotten I was coming, Mrs Crilling?'

The face that appeared round the wing of the chair was enough to intimidate anyone. The whites of the eyes showed all the way round the black pupils. Every muscle looked tense, taut and corrugated as if from some inner agony. Her white hair, fringed and styled like a teenager's, curtained the sharp cheekbones.

'Who are you?' She dragged herself up, clinging to the chair arm and came slowly round to face him. The vee at the dressing gown front showed a ridged and withered valley like the bed of a long-dried stream.

'We met in court this morning. You wrote to me . . .'

He stopped. She had thrust her face within inches of his and seemed to be scrutinising it. Then she stepped back and gave a long chattering laugh which the budgerigar echoed.

'Mrs Crilling, are you all right? Is there anything I can do?'

She clutched her throat and the laugh died away in a rising wheeze. 'Tablets . . . asthma . . . ,' she gasped. He was puzzled and shocked, but he reached behind him for the bottle of tablets on the littered mantelpiece. 'Give me my tablets and then you can . . . you can get out!'

'I'm sorry if I've done anything to distress you.'

She made no attempt to take a tablet but held the bottle up against her quaking chest. The movement made the tablets rattle and the bird, fluttering its wings and beating against the bars, began a frenzied crescendo, half song and half pain.

'Where's my baby?' Did she mean Elizabeth? She must mean Elizabeth.

'She's gone out. I met her in the porch. Mrs Crilling, can I get you a glass of water? Can I make you a cup of tea?'

'Tea? What do I want with tea? That's what she said this morning, that police girl. Come and have a cup of tea, Mrs Crilling.' A terrible spasm shook her and she fell back against the chair, fighting for breath. 'You . . . my baby . . . I thought you were my friend . . . Aaah!'

Archery was really frightened now. He plunged from the room into the dirty kitchen and filled a cup with water. The window ledge was stacked with empty chemist's bottles and there was a filthy hypodermic beside an equally dirty eye dropper. When he came back she was still wheezing and jerking. Should he make her take the tablets, dare he? On the bottle label were the words: *Mrs J. Crilling. Take two when needed.* He rattled two into his hand and, supporting her with his other arm, forced them into her mouth. It was all he could do to suppress the shudder of distaste when she dribbled and choked over the water.

'Filthy . . . nasty,' she mumbled. He half-eased, half-rolled her into the chair and pulled together the gaping edges of the dressing gown. Moved with pity and with horror, he knelt down beside her.

'I will be your friend if you want me to be,' he said soothingly.

The words had the opposite effect. She made a tremendous effort to draw breath. Her lips split open and he could see her tongue rising and quivering against the roof of her mouth.

'Not my friend . . . enemy . . . police friend! Take my baby away . . . I saw you with them . . . I watched you come out with them.' He drew back from her, rising. Never would he have believed her capable of screaming after that spasm and when the scream came, as clear and ear-splitting as a child's, he felt his hands go up to his face. '. . . Not let them get her in there! Not in the prison! They'll find it out in there. She'll tell them . . . my baby . . . She'll have to tell them!' With a sudden galvanic jerk she reared up, her mouth open and her arms flailing. 'They'll find it all out. I'll kill her first, kill her . . . D'you hear?'

The french windows stood open. Archery staggered back into the sun against a stinging prickling wall of weeds. Mrs Crilling's incoherent gasps had swollen into a stream of obscenity. There was a gate in the wire netting fence. He unlatched it, wiping the sweat from his forehead, and stepped into the cool dark cave of the sand-walled arch.

'Good afternoon, sir. You don't look very well. Heat affecting you?'

Archery had been leaning over the bridge parapet, breathing deeply, when the detective inspector's face appeared beside him.

'Inspector Burden, isn't it?' He shook himself, blinking his eyes. There was comfort in this man's steady gaze and in the shoppers who flowed languidly across the bridge. 'I've just come from Mrs Crilling's and . . .'

'Say no more, sir. I quite understand.'

'I left her in the throes of an asthma attack. Perhaps I should have got a doctor or an ambulance. Frankly, I hardly knew what to do.'

There was a crumb of stony bread on the wall. Burden flicked it into the water and a swan dived for it.

'It's mostly in the mind with her, Mr Archery. I should have warned you what to expect. Threw one of her scenes on you, did she?' Archery nodded. 'Next time you see her I daresay she'll be as nice as pie. That's the way it takes her, up one minute, down the next. Manic-depressive is the term. I was just going into Carousel for a cup of tea. Why don't you join me?'

They walked up the High Street together. Some of the shops sported faded striped sunblinds. The shadows were as black as night, the light cruelly bright under a Mediterranean blue sky. Inside the Carousel it was darkish and stuffy and it smelt of aerosol fly spray.

'Two teas, please,' said Burden.

'Tell me about the Crillings.'

'There's plenty to tell, Mr Archery. Mrs Crilling's husband died and left her without a penny, so she moved into town and got a job. The kid, Elizabeth, was always difficult and Mrs Crilling made her worse. She took her to psychiatrists—don't ask me where the money came from—and then when they made her send her to school it was one school after another. She was in St Catherine's, Sewingbury for a bit but she got expelled. When she was about fourteen she came up before the juvenile court here as being in need of care and protection and she was taken away from her mother. But she went back eventually. They usually do.'

'Do you think all this came about because she found Mrs Primero's body?'

'Could be.' Burden looked up and smiled as the waitress brought the tea. 'Thanks very much, miss. Sugar, Mr Archery? No, I don't either.' He cleared his throat and went on, 'I reckon it would have made a difference if she'd had a decent home background, but Mrs Crilling was always unstable. In and out of jobs, by all accounts, until she ended up working in a shop. I think some relative used to give them financial assistance. Mrs Crilling used to take days off from work ostensibly on account of the asthma but really it was because she was crazy.'

'Isn't she certifiable?'

'You'd be surprised how difficult it is to get anyone certified, sir. The doctor did say that if ever he saw her in one of her tantrums he could get an urgency order, but they're cunning, you see, By the time the doctor gets there she's as normal as you or me. She's been into Stowerton once or twice as a voluntary patient. About four years ago she got herself a man friend. The whole place was buzzing with it. Elizabeth was training to be a physiotherapist at the time. Anyway, the upshot of it all was that the boy-friend preferred young Liz.'

'*Mater pulchra, filia pulchrior,*' Archery murmured.

'Just as you say, sir. She gave up her training and went to live with him. Mrs Crilling went off her rocker again and spent six months in Stowerton. When she came out she wouldn't leave the happy couple alone, letters, phone calls, personal appearances, the lot. Liz couldn't stand it so eventually she went back to mother. The boy friend was in the car trade and he gave her that Mini.'

Archery sighed. 'I don't know if I ought to tell you this, but you've been very kind to me, you and Mr Wexford . . .' Burden felt the stirring of guilt. It wasn't what he would call kind. 'Mrs Crilling said that if Elizabeth—she calls her her baby—went to prison . . . it might mean prison, mightn't it?'

'It might well.'

'Then she'd tell you something, you or the prison authorities. I got the impression she'd feel compelled to give you some information Mrs Crilling wanted kept secret.'

'Thank you very much, sir. We shall have to wait and see what time brings forth.'

Archery finished his tea. Suddenly he felt like a traitor. Had he betrayed Mrs Crilling because he wanted to keep in with the police?

'I wondered,' he said, justifying himself, 'if it could have anything to do with Mrs Primero's murder. I don't see why Mrs Crilling couldn't have worn the raincoat and hidden it. You admit yourself she's unbalanced. She was there, she had just as much opportunity as Painter.'

Burden shook his head. 'What was the motive?'

'Mad people have motives which seem very thin to normal men.'

'But she dotes on her daughter in her funny way. She wouldn't have taken the kid with her.'

Archery said slowly, 'At the trial she said she went over the first time at twenty-five past six. But we've only her word for it. Suppose instead she went at twenty to seven when *Painter had already been and gone*. Then she took the child back later because no-one would believe a killer would wittingly let a child discover a body she knew was there.'

'You've missed your vocation, sir,' said Burden, getting up. 'You should have come in on our lark. You'd have been a superintendent by now.'

'I'm letting my fancy run away with me,' Archery said. To avoid a repetition of the gentle teasing, he added quickly, changing the subject, 'Do you happen to know the visiting times at Stowerton Infirmary?'

'Alice Flower's next on your list, is she? I'd give the matron a ring first, if I were you. Visiting's seven till seven-thirty.'

8

> The days of our age are threescore years and ten; and though men be so strong that they come to fourscore years, yet is their strength then but labour and sorrow.
>
> Psalm 90. *The Burial of the Dead.*

Alice Flower was eighty-seven, almost as old as her employer had been at the time of her death. A series of strokes had battered her old frame as tempests batter an ancient house, but the house was strong and sturdily built. No gimcrack refinements of decoration or delicacy had ever belonged to it. It had been made to endure wind and weather.

She lay in a narrow high bed in a ward called Honeysuckle. The ward was full of similar old women in similar beds. They had clean pink faces and white hair through which patches of rose-pink scalp showed. Every bed trolley held at least two vases of flowers, the sops to conscience, Archery supposed, of visiting relatives who only had to sit and chat instead of handing bed-pans and tending bed-sores.

'A visitor for you, Alice,' said the sister. 'It's no use trying to shake hands with her. She can't move her hands but her hearing's perfectly good and she'll talk the hind leg off a donkey.'

A most un-Christian hatred flared in Archery's eyes. If she saw it the sister took no notice.

'Like a good gossip, don't you, Alice? This is the Reverend Archery.' He winced at that, approached the bed.

'Good evening, sir.'

Her face was square with deeply ridged rough skin. One corner of her mouth had been drawn down by the paralysis of the motor nerves, causing her lower jaw to protrude and reveal large false teeth. The sister bustled about the bed, pulling the old servant's nightgown higher about her neck and arranging on the coverlet her two useless hands. It was terrible to Archery to have to look at those hands. Work had distorted them beyond hope of beauty, but disease and oedema had smoothed and whitened the skin so that they were like the hands of a misshapen baby. The emotion and the feel for the language of 1611 that was with him always welled in a fount of pity. Well done, thou good and faithful servant, he thought. Thou hast been faithful over a few things, I will make thee ruler over many things . . .

'Would it upset you to talk to me about Mrs Primero, Miss Flower?' he asked gently, easing himself into a bentwood chair.

'Of course it wouldn't,' said the sister, 'she loves it.'

Archery could bear no more. 'This is rather a private matter, if you don't mind.'

'Private! It's the whole ward's bedtime story, believe me.' She flounced away, a crackling navy and white robot.

Alice Flower's voice was cracked and harsh. The strokes had affected her throat muscles or her vocal cords. But her accent was pleasant and correct, learnt, Archery supposed, in the kitchens and nurseries of educated people.

'What was it you wanted to know, sir?'

'First tell me about the Primero family.'

'Oh, I can do that. I always took an interest.' She gave a small rattling cough and turned her head to hide the twisted side of her mouth. 'I went to Mrs Primero when the boy was born . . .'

'The boy?'

'Mr Edward, her only child he was.'

Ah, thought Archery, the father of rich Roger and his sisters.

'He was a lovely boy and we always got on a treat, him and me. I reckon it really aged me and his poor mother when he died, sir. But he'd got a family of his own by then, thanks be to God, and Mr Roger was the living spit of his father.'

'I suppose Mr Edward left him pretty well off, did he?'

'Oh, no, sir, that was the pity of it. You see, old Dr Primero left his money to madam, being as Mr Edward was doing so well at the time. But he lost everything on something in the city and when he was taken Mrs Edward and the three kiddies were quite badly off.' She coughed again, making Archery wince. He fancied he could see a terrible vain effort to raise those hands and cover the rattling lips. 'Madam offered to help—not that she had more than she needed—but Mrs Edward was that proud, she wouldn't take a penny from her mother-in-law. I never shall know how she managed. There was the three of them, you see. Mr Roger he was the eldest, and then there was the two little mites, ever so much younger than their brother, but close together if you take my meaning. No more than eighteen months between them.'

She rested her head back on the pillows and bit at her lip as if trying to pull it back into place. 'Angela was the oldest. Time flies so I reckon she'd be twenty-six now. Then there was Isabel, named after madam. They was just babies when their Daddy died and it was years before we saw them.

'It was a bitter blow to madam, I can tell you, not knowing what had become of Mr Roger. Then one day just out of the blue he turned up at Victor's Piece. Fancy, he was living in digs just over at Sewingbury, studying to be a solicitor with a very good firm. Somebody Mrs Edward knew had got him in. He hadn't no idea his granny was still alive, let alone in Kingsmarkham, but he was looking up somebody in the phone book, in the line of business, sir, and there it was: Mrs Rose Primero, Victor's Piece. Once he'd come over there was no stopping him. Not that we wanted to stop him, sir. Pretty nearly every Sunday he came and once or twice he fetched his little sisters all the way from London and brought them with him. Good as gold they were.

'Mr Roger and madam, they used to have some laughs together. All the old photographs they'd have out and the tales she used to tell him!' She stopped suddenly and Archery watched the old face swell and grow purple. 'It was a change for us to have a nice gentlemanlike young fellow about the place after that Painter.' Her voice changed to a shrill whistling shriek. 'That dirty murdering beast!'

Across the ward another old woman in a bed like Alice Flower's smiled a toothless smile as of one hearing a familiar tale retold. The ward's bedtime story, the sister had said.

Archery leant towards her. 'That was a dreadful day, Miss Flower,' he said, 'the day Mrs Primero died.' The fierce eyes flickered, red and spongey blue. 'I expect you feel you'll never forget it . . .'

'Not to my dying day,' said Alice Flower. Perhaps she thought of the now useless body that had once been so fine an instrument and was already three-quarters dead.

'Will you tell me about it?'

As soon as she began he realised how often she must have told it before. It was likely that some of these other old women were not absolutely bedridden, that sometimes in the evenings they got up and gathered round Alice Flower's bed. A tale, he thought, paraphrasing, to draw children from play and old women from the chimney corner.

'He was a devil,' she said, 'a terror. I was scared of him but I never let him know it. Take all and give nothing, that was his motto. Six pounds a year, that was all I got when I first went out into service. Him, he had his home and his wages, a lovely motor to drive. There's some folks want the moon. You'd think a big strong young fellow like that'd be only too glad to fetch the coal in for an old lady, but not Mr Bert Painter. Beast Painter was what I called him.

'That Saturday night when he never come and he never come madam had to sit all by herself in the icy cold. Let me go over and speak to him, madam, I said, but she wouldn't have it. The morning's time enough, Alice, she said. I've said to myself over and over again, if he'd come that night I'd have been in there with them. He wouldn't have been able to tell no lies then.'

'But he did come the next morning, Miss Flower . . .'

'She told him off good and proper. I could hear her giving him a dressing down.'

'What were you doing?'

'Me? When he come in first I was doing the vegetables for madam's lunch, then I popped on the oven and put in the meat tin. They asked me all that at the court in London, the Old Bailey it was.' She paused and there was suspicion in the look she gave him. 'You writing a book about it all, are you, sir?'

'Something like that,' said Archery.

'They wanted to know if I was sure I could hear all right. My hearing's better than that judge's, I can tell you. Just as well it is. If I'd been hard of hearing we might have all gone up in smoke that morning.'

'How was that?'

'Beast Painter was in the drawing room with madam and I'd gone into the larder to get the vinegar for the mint sauce, when all of a sudden I heard a kind of a plop and sizzle. That's that funny old oven, I said, and sure enough it was. I popped back quick and opened the oven door. One of the potatoes had kind of spat out, sir, and fallen on the gas. All in flames it was and sizzling and roaring like a steam engine. I turned it off quick and then I did a silly thing. Poured water on it. Ought to have known better at my age. Ooh, the racket and the smoke! You couldn't hear yourself think.'

There had been nothing about that in the trial transcript. Archery caught his breath in the excitement. 'You couldn't hear yourself think . . .' While you were choked with smoke and deafened by hissing you might not hear a man go upstairs, search a bedroom and come down again. Alice's evidence in this matter had been one of the most important features of the case. For if Painter had been offered and had taken the two hundred pounds in Mrs Primero's presence in the morning, what motive could he have had for killing her in the evening?

'Well, we had our lunch and Mr Roger came. My poor old leg was aching from where I'd bruised it the night before getting a few lumps in on account of Beast Painter being out on the tiles. Mr Roger was ever so nice about it, kept asking me if there was anything he could do, wash up or anything. But that isn't man's work and I always say it's better to keep going while you can.

'It must have been half past five when Mr Roger said he'd have to go. I was up to my neck what with the dishes and worrying if Beast would turn up like he'd promised. "I'll let myself out, Alice", Mr Roger said, and he come down to the kitchen to say good-bye to me. Madam was having a little snooze in the drawing room, God rest her. It was the last she had before her long sleep.' Aghast, Archery watched two tears well into her eyes and flow unchecked down the ridged sunken cheeks. 'I called out, "Cheeri-by, Mr Roger dear, see you next Sunday", and then I heard him shut the front door. Madam was sleeping like a child, not knowing that ravening wolf was lying in wait for her.'

'Try not to upset yourself, Miss Flower.' Doubtful as to what he should do—the right thing is the kind thing, he thought—he pulled out his own clean white handkerchief and gently wiped the wet cheeks.

'Thank you, sir. I'll be all right now. You do feel a proper fool not being able to dry your own tears.' The ghastly cracked smile was almost more painful to witness than the weeping. 'Where was I? Oh, yes. Off I went to church and as soon as I was out of the way along comes Madam Crilling, poking her nose in . . .'

'I know what happened next, Miss Flower,' Archery said very kindly and quietly. 'Tell me about Mrs Crilling. Does she ever come to see you in here?'

Alice Flower gave a kind of snort that would have been comical in a fit person. 'Not she. She's kept out of my way ever since the trial, sir. I know too much about her for her liking. Madam's best friend, my foot! She'd got one interest in madam and one only. She wormed that child of hers into madam's good books on account of she thought madam might leave her something when she went.'

Archery moved closer, praying that the bell for the end of visiting would not ring yet.

'But Mrs Primero didn't make a will.'

'Oh, no, sir, that's what worried Mrs Clever Crilling. She'd come out into my kitchen when madam was sleeping. "Alice," she'd say, "we ought to get dear Mrs Primero to make her last will and testament. It's our duty, Alice, it says so in the Prayer Book." '

'Does it?'

Alice looked both shocked and smug. 'Yes, it does, sir. It says, "But men should often be put in remembrance to take order for the settling of their temporal estates whilst they are in health." Still I don't hold with everything that's in the Prayer Book not when it comes to downright interference—saving your presence, sir. "It's in your interest too, Alice," she says. "You'll be turned out into the streets when she goes."

'But madam wouldn't have it, anyway. Everything was to go to her natural heirs, she said, them being Mr Roger and the little girls. It'd be theirs automatically, you see, without any nonsense about wills and lawyers.'

'Mr Roger didn't try to get her to make a will?'

'He's a lovely person is Mr Roger. When Beast Painter had done his murdering work and poor madam was dead Mr Roger got his bit of money—three thousand it was and a bit more. "I'll take care of you, Alice," he said, and so he did. He got me a nice room in Kingsmarkham and gave me two pounds a week on top of my pension. He was in business on his own then and he said he wouldn't give me a lump sum. An allowance, he called it, bless his heart, out of his profits.'

'Business? I thought he was a solicitor.'

'He always wanted to go into business on his own, sir. I don't know the ins and outs of it, but he came to madam one day—must have been two or three weeks before she died—and he said a pal of his would take him in with him if he could put up ten thousand pounds. "I know I haven't got a hope," he said, speaking ever so nice. "It's just a castle in the air, Granny Rose." "Well, it's no good looking at me," says madam. "Ten thousand is all I've got for me and Alice to live on and that's tucked away in Woolworth's shares. You'll get your share when I'm gone." I don't mind telling you, sir, I thought then, if Mr Roger liked to do his little sisters down he could try getting round madam to make that will and leave him the lot. But he never did, never mentioned it again, and he'd always made a point of bringing the two mites just whenever he could. Then Beast Painter killed madam and the money went like she said it would, to the three of them.

'Mr Roger's doing very well now, sir, very well indeed, and he comes to see me regular. I reckon he got the ten thousand from somewhere or maybe another pal came up with something else. It wasn't for me to ask, you see.'

A nice man, Archery thought, a man who had needed money perhaps desperately, but would do nothing underhand to get it; a man who provided for his dead grandmother's domestic while he was struggling to get a business going, who still visited her and who doubtless listened patiently over and over again to the tale Archery had just heard. A very nice man. If love, praise and devotion could reward such a man, he had his reward.

'If you should see Mr Roger, sir, if you want to see him about the story you're writing, would you give him my best respects?'

'I won't forget, Miss Flower.' He put his hand over her dead one and pressed it. 'Good-bye and thank you.' Well done, thou good and faithful servant.

It was gone eight when he got back to the Olive and Dove. The head waiter glared at him when he walked into the dining room at a quarter past. Archery stared about him at the empty room, the chairs arranged against the walls.

'Dance on tonight, sir. We did make a point of asking residents to take their dinner at seven sharp, but I expect we can find you you something. In here, if you please.'

Archery followed him into the smaller of the two lounges that led off the dining room. The tables had been crammed in and people were hastily gobbling their meal. He ordered, and through the glass doors, watched the band take its place on the dais.

How was he to spend this long hot summer evening? The dancing would probably go on until half-past twelve or one and the hotel would be unbearable. A quiet stroll was the obvious thing. Or he could take the car and go and look at Victor's Piece. The waiter came back with the braised beef he had ordered, and Archery, resolutely economical, asked for a glass of water.

He was quite alone in his alcove, at least two yards from the next table, and he jumped when he felt something soft and fluffy brush against his leg. Drawing back, he put his hand down, lifted the cloth and met a pair of bright eyes set in a golden woolly skull.

'Hallo, dog,' he said.

'Oh I'm so sorry. Is he being a nuisance?'

He looked up and saw her standing beside him. They had evidently just come in, she, the man with the glassy eyes and another couple.

'Not a bit.' Archery's poise deserted him and he found himself almost stammering. 'I don't mind, really. I'm fond of animals.'

'You were here at lunch, weren't you? I expect he recognised you. Come out, Dog. He doesn't have a name. We just call him Dog because he is one and it's just as good a name as Jock or Gyp or something. When you said, "Hallo, dog," he thought you were a personal friend. He's very intelligent.'

'I'm sure he is.'

She gathered the poodle up in her arms and held him against the creamy lace of her dress. Now that she wore no hat he could see the perfect shape of her head and the high unshadowed brow. The head waiter minced over, no longer harassed.

'Back again, Louis, like the proverbial bad pennies,' said the glassy-eyed man heartily. 'My wife took a fancy to come to your hop, but we must have a spot of dinner first.' So they were married, these two. Why hadn't it occurred to him before, what business was it of his and, above all, why should it cause him this faint distress? 'Our friends here have a train to catch, so if you can go all out with the old speed we'll be eternally grateful.'

They all sat down. The poodle mooched between diners' legs, scavenging for crumbs. Archery was faintly amused to see how quickly their dinner was brought to them. They had all ordered different dishes, but there was little delay and at the same time little hustle. Archery lingered over his coffee and his bit of cheese. Surely he was no bother to anyone in his small corner. People were coming in to dance now, passing his table and leaving in their wake the faint scent of cigars and floral perfume. In the dining room, a ballroom, now, the garden doors had been opened and couples stood on the terrace listening to the music in the tranquillity of the summer night.

The poodle sat on the threshold, bored, watching the dancers.

'Come here, Dog,' said his owner. Her husband got up.

'I'll take you to the station, George,' he said. 'We've only got ten minutes, so get a wiggle on, will you?' He seemed to have a variety of expressions to imply the making of haste. 'You don't have to come, darling. Finish your coffee.'

The table was veiled in smoke. They had smoked throughout the courses. He would be gone perhaps only half an hour but he bent over and kissed his wife. She smiled at him, lit another cigarette. When they had gone, she and Archery were alone. She moved into her husband's chair from where she could watch the dancers, many of whom she seemed to know, for she waved occasionally and nodded as if promising she would soon join them.

Archery suddenly felt lonely. He knew no one in this place except two rather hostile policemen. His stay might be for the whole fortnight. Why hadn't he asked Mary to join him? It would be a holiday for her, a change, and—heaven knew—she needed a change. In a minute, when he had finished his second cup, he would go upstairs and telephone her.

The girl's voice startled him. 'Do you mind if I have your ash-tray? Ours are all full.'

'Of course not, take it.' He lifted the heavy glass plate and as he handed it to her the tips of her cool dry fingers touched his own. The hand was small, childlike, with short unpainted nails. 'I don't smoke,' he added rather foolishly.

'Are you staying here long?' Her voice was light and soft, yet mature.

'Just a few days.'

'I asked,' she said, 'because we come here so often and I hadn't seen you before today. Most of the people are regulars.' She put out the cigarette carefully, stubbing it until the last red spark was dead. 'They have these dances once a month and we always come. I love dancing.'

Afterwards Archery wondered what on earth had induced him, a country vicar neary fifty years old, to say what he did. Perhaps it was the mingled scents, the descending twilight or just that he was alone and out of his environment, out of his identity almost.

'Would you like to dance?'

It was a waltz they were playing. He was sure he could waltz. They waltzed at church socials. You simply had to make your feet go one, two, three in a sort of triangle. And yet, for all that, he felt himself blush. What would she think of him at his age? She might suppose he was doing what Charles called 'picking her up.'

'I'd love to,' she said.

Apart from Mary and Mary's sister, she was the only woman he had danced with in twenty years. He was so shy and so overcome by the enormity of what he was doing, that for a moment he was deaf to the music and blind to the hundred or so other people who circled the floor. Then she was in his arms, a light creature of scent and lace whose body so incongruously touching his had the fluidity and the tenuousness of a summer mist. He felt that he was dreaming and because of this, this utter unreality, he forgot about his feet and what he must make them do, and simply moved with her as if he and she and the music were one.

'I'm not very good at this sort of thing,' he said when he found his voice. 'You'll have to overlook my mistakes.' He was so much taller than she that she had to lift her face up to him.

She smiled. 'Hard to make conversation when you're dancing, isn't it? I never know what to say but one must say something.'

'Like "Don't you think this is a good floor?"' Strange, he remembered that one from undergraduate days.

'Or "Do you reverse?" It's absurd really. Here we are dancing together and I don't even know your name.' She gave a little deprecating laugh. 'It's almost immoral.'

'My name's Archery. Henry Archery.'

'How do you do, Henry Archery?' she said gravely. Then as they moved into a pool of sunset light, she looked steadily at him, the glowing colour falling on her face. 'You really don't recognise me, do you?' He shook his head, wondering if he had made some terrible *faux pas*. She gave a mock sigh. 'Such is fame! Imogen Ide. Doesn't it ring a bell?'

'I'm awfully sorry.'

'Frankly, you don't look as if you spend your leisure perusing the glossy magazines. Before I married I was what they call a top model. The most photographed face in Britain.'

He hardly knew what to say. The things that came to mind all had some reference to her extraordinary beauty and to speak them aloud would have been impertinent. Sensing his predicament, she burst out laughing, but it was a companionable laugh, warm and kind.

He smiled down at her. Then over her shoulder he caught sight of a familiar face. Chief Inspector Wexford had come on to the floor with a stout pleasant-looking woman and a young couple. His wife, his daughter and the architect's son, Archery supposed, feeling a sudden pang. He watched them sit down and just as he he was about to avert his eyes, Wexford's met his. The smiles they exchanged were slightly antagonistic and Archery felt hot with awkwardness. Wexford's expression held a mocking quality as if to say that dancing was a frivolity quite out of keeping with Archery's quest. Abruptly he looked away and back to his partner.

'I'm afraid I only read *The Times*,' he said, feeling the snobbishness of the remark as soon as the words were out.

'I was in *The Times* once,' she said. 'Oh, not my picture. I was in the High Court bit. Somebody mentioned my name in a case and the judge said, "Who is Imogen Ide?"'

'That really is fame.'

'I've kept the cutting to this day.'

The music that had been so liquid and lullaby-like suddenly jerked into a frightening tempo with a stormy undertone of drums.

'I haven't a hope of doing this one,' Archery said helplessly.

He released her quickly, there in the middle of the floor.

'Never mind. Thank you very much, anyway. I've enjoyed it.'

'So have I, very much indeed.'

They began to thread their way between couples who were shuddering and bounding about like savages. She was holding his hand and he could hardly withdraw it without rudeness.

'Here's my husband back,' she said. 'Won't you join us for the evening if you've nothing better to do?'

The man called Ide was coming up to them, smiling. His evenly olive face, dead black hair and almost feminine standard of grooming gave him the look of a waxwork. Archery had the absurd notion that if you came upon him at Madame Tussaud's the old joke of the naive spectator mistaking a model for a flesh and blood attendant would be reversed. In this case you would pass the real man by, thinking him a figure in wax.

'This is Mr Archery, darling. I've been telling him he ought to stay. It's such a beautiful night.'

'Good idea. Perhaps I can get you a drink, Mr Archery?'

'Thank you, no.' Archery found himself shaking hands, astonished because of his fantasy at the warmth of Ide's hand. 'I must go. I have to phone my wife.'

'I hope we shall see you again,' said Imogen Ide. 'I enjoyed our dance.' She took her husband's hand and they moved away into the centre of the floor, their bodies meeting, their steps following the intricate rhythm. Archery went upstairs to his bedroom. Earlier he had supposed that the music would annoy him but here in the violet-coloured dusk it was enchanting, disturbing, awakening in him forgotten, undefined longings. He stood at the window, looking at the sky with its long feathery scarves of cloud, rose pink as cyclamen petals but less substantial. The strains of the music had softened to match this tranquil sky and now they seemed to him like the opening bars of an overture to some pastoral opera.

Presently he sat down on the bed and put his hand to the telephone. It rested there immobile for some minutes. What was the point of ringing Mary when he had nothing to tell her, no plans even for what he would do in the morning? He felt a sudden distaste for Thringford and its small parochial doings. He had lived there so long, so narrowly, and outside all the time there had been a world of which he knew little.

From where he sat he could see nothing but sky, broken continents and islands on a sea of azure. 'Here will we sit and let the sound of music creep in our ears . . .' He took his hand from the telephone and lay back, thinking of nothing.

9

> The words of his mouth were softer than butter, having war in his heart: his words were smoother than oil, and yet be they very swords.
>
> Psalm 55, appointed for the Tenth Day.

'I suppose there isn't anything in it?'

'In what, Mike? Liz Crilling having some dark secret her mother doesn't want extorted from her under the third degree?'

Burden lowered the blinds against the brazen morning sky. 'Those Crillings always make me uneasy,' he said.

'They're no more kinky than half our customers,' Wexford said breezily. 'Liz'll turn up at the Assizes all right. If not for any other reason simply because Mrs Crilling doubts her ability to get a thousand quid out of her brother-in-law, or whoever it is supports them. And then if she's got something to tell us, she'll tell us.'

Burden's expression, though apologetic, was obstinate.

'I can't help feeling it's got some connection with Painter,' he said.

Wexford had been leafing through a thick orange-coloured trade directory. Now he dropped it on the desk with a deliberate bang.

'By God, I won't have any more of this! What is it, anyhow, some sort of conspiracy to prove I can't do my job?'

'I'm sorry, sir, you know I didn't mean that.'

'I don't know a damn' thing, Mike. I only know the Painter case was an open and shut affair, and nobody's got a hope in hell of showing he didn't do it.' He began to calm down slowly, and he spread his hands in two large implacable fans on the directory cover. 'Go and question Liz by all means. Or tell Archery to do it for you. He's a fast worker that one.'

'Is he? What makes you say so?'

'Never mind. I've got work to do if you haven't and . . .' said Wexford, splendidly co-ordinating his metaphors, 'I'm fed up to my back teeth with having Painter rammed down my throat morning, noon and night.'

Archery had slept deeply and dreamlessly. It occurred to him that he had done all his dreaming while he was awake and there was none left for sleep. The telephone roused him. It was his wife.

'Sorry it's so early, darling, but I've had another letter from Charles.'

There was a cup of cold tea by the bed. Archery wondered how long it had been there. He found his watch and saw that it was nine.

'That's all right. How are you?'

'Not so bad. You sound as if you're still in bed.'

Archery grunted something.

'Now, listen. Charles is coming down tomorrow and he says he's coming straight over to Kingsmarkham.'

'Coming *down*?'

'Oh, it's all right, Henry. He's going to cut the last three days of term. Surely it can't matter much.'

'As long as it isn't the thin end of the wedge. Is he coming to The Olive?'

'Well, naturally. He's got to stay somewhere. I know it's expensive, darling, but he's got himself a job for August and September—something in a brewery. It sounds awful but he's going to get sixteen pounds a week and he says he'll pay you back.'

'I hadn't realised I made such an avaricious impression on my son.'

'You know he doesn't mean that. You *are* touchy this morning . . .'

After she had rung off he still held the receiver for some moments in his hand. He wondered why he hadn't asked her to join him as well. He had meant to last night and then . . . Of course, he had been so drowsy while she was speaking that he hardly knew what he was saying. The operator's voice broke in.

'Have you finished or did you want to make a call?'

'No thank you. I've finished.'

The little sandy houses in Glebe Road seemed to have been bleached and dried up by the sun. This morning they looked even more like desert dwelling, each surrounded by its own scanty oasis.

Burden went first to number a hundred and two. An old acquaintance of his lived there, a man with a long record and a nasty sense of humour called by some 'Monkey' Matthews. Burden thought it more than likely that he was responsible for the home-made bomb, a bizarre affair of sugar and weed killer stuffed into a whisky bottle that a blonde woman of easy virtue had received that morning through her letter box. The bomb had done no more than wreck the hall of her flat, she and her current lover being still in bed, but Burden thought it might amount to attempted murder just the same.

He knocked and rang but he was sure the bell didn't work. Then he went round the back and found himself ankle-deep in garbage, pram wheels, old clothes, newspapers and empty bottles. He looked through the kitchen window. There was a packet of weed killer—sodium chlorate crystals—on the window sill and the top had been torn off. How confident could you get, or how stupid? He went back up the street to a call box and told Bryant and Gates to pick up the occupant of a hundred and two Glebe Road.

Twenty-four was on the same side. Now he was so near there would be no harm in having a chat with Liz Crilling. The front door was closed but the latch was down. He coughed and walked in.

In the back room a plastic transistor was playing pop music. Elizabeth Crilling sat at the table reading the Situations Vacant in last week's local paper and she was wearing nothing but a slip, its broken shoulder strap held together with a safety pin.

'I don't remember inviting you in.'

Burden looked at her distastefully. 'D'you mind putting something on?' She made no move but kept her eyes on the paper. He glanced around the dismal, untidy room, and from the various miscellaneous heaps of clothes, selected something that might have been a dressing gown, a pink floppy thing whose flounces recalled withered petals. 'Here,' he said, and he wondered if she were not quite well, for she shuddered as she put the dressing gown round her. It was far too big, obviously not her own.

'Where's your mother?'

'I don't know. Gone out somewhere. I'm not her keeper.' She grinned suddenly, showing her beautiful teeth. 'Am I my mother's keeper? That's good, don't you think? Which reminds me . . .' The smile died and she exclaimed sharply, 'What's that clergyman doing here?'

Burden never answered a question if he could help it.

'Looking for a new post, are you?'

She gave a sulky pout. 'I phoned my firm yesterday when I got back from that bloody court and they gave me the push. I've got you lot to thank for that.' Burden inclined his head politely. 'Well, I've got to have a job, haven't I? They want girls at the raincoat factory and they say you can pick up twenty quid a week with overtime.'

Burden remembered her education, the expensive schools the Crilling relatives had paid for. She stared at him boldly.

'I may as well go and see them,' she said. 'What's the harm? Life's hell anyway.' She gave a strident laugh, walked to the mantelpiece and leaned against it, looking down at him. The open dressing gown, the tatty underclothes were provocative in a raw, basic way, that seemed to go with the hot weather and the dishevelled room. 'To what do I owe the honour of this visit? Are you lonely, Inspector? I hear your wife's away.' She took a cigarette and put it between her lips. Her forefinger was rusty with nicotine, the nail yellow, the cuticle bitten. 'Where the hell are the matches?'

There was something in the quick wary look she gave over her shoulder that impelled him to follow her to the kitchen. Once there, she turned to face him, grabbed a box of matches and stood as if barring his way. He felt a thrill of alarm. She thrust the matches into his hand.

'Light it for me, will you?'

He struck the match steadily. She came very close to him and as the flame shrivelled the tobacco, closed her fingers over his hand. For a split second he felt what his rather prudish nature told him was vile, then that nature, his duty and a swift suspicion took over. She was breathing hard, but not, he was certain, because of his nearness to her. From long practice he sidestepped neatly, freeing the long bare leg from between his own, and found himself confronting what she perhaps had hoped to hide from him.

The sink was crammed with dirty crocks, potato peelings, tea leaves, wet paper, but the Crillings were long past middle-class concealment of squalor.

'You could do with a few days off, I should think,' he said loudly. 'Get this place in some sort of order.'

She had begun to laugh. 'You know, you're not so bad-looking on the other side of a smoke-screen.'

'Been ill, have you?' He was looking at the empty pill bottles, the one that was half full and the syringe. 'Nerves, I daresay.'

She stopped laughing. 'They're hers.'

Burden read labels, saying nothing.

'She has them for her asthma. They're all the same.' As he put out his hand to find the hypodermic she seized his wrist. 'You've no business to turn things over. That amounts to searching and for searching you need a warrant.'

'True,' said Burden placidly. He followed her back to the living room and jumped when she shouted at him:

'You never answered my question about the clergyman.'

'He's come here because he knows Painter's daughter,' said Burden guardedly.

She went white and he thought she looked like her mother. 'Painter that killed the old woman?'

Burden nodded.

'That's funny,' she said. 'I'd like to see her again.' He had a queer feeling she was changing the subject, and yet her remark was not inconsequential. She turned her eyes towards the garden. But it wasn't, he thought, the nettles, the brambles and the mean wire fence she could see. 'I used to go over to the coach house and play with her,' she said. 'Mother never knew. She said Tess wasn't my class. I couldn't understand that. I thought, how can she have a class if she doesn't go to school?' She reached up and gave the birdcage a vicious push. 'Mother was always with the old woman—talk, talk, talk, I'll never forget it—and she used to send me into the garden to play. There wasn't anything to play with and one day I saw Tessie, mucking about with a heap of sand . . . Why are you looking at me like that?'

'Am I?'

'Does she know about her father?' Burden nodded. 'Poor kid. What does she do for a living?'

'She's some kind of a student.'

'*Student?* My God, I was a student once.' She had begun to tremble. The long worm of ash broke from her cigarette and scattered down the pink flounces. Looking down at it, she flicked uselessly at old stains and burn marks. The movement suggested the uncontrollable jerking of chorea. She swung round on him, her hate and despair striking him like a flame. 'What are you trying to do to me?' she shouted. 'Get out! Get out!'

When he had gone she grabbed a torn sheet from a stack of unironed linen and flung it over the birdcage. The sudden movement and the gust of breeze it had caused fluttered the thing her mother called a negligee but that she had never feared until it touched her own skin. Why the hell did he have to come here and rake it all up again. Perhaps a drink would help. True, it hadn't done so the other day . . . There never was a drink in this house, anyway.

Newspapers, old letters and unpaid bills, empty cigarette packets and a couple of old laddered stockings tumbled out when she opened the cupboard door. She rummaged in the back among dusty vases, Christmas wrapping paper, playing cards with dog-eared corners. One vase had an encouraging shape. She pulled it out and found it was the cherry brandy Uncle had given her mother for her birthday. Filthy, sweet cherry brandy . . . She squatted on the floor among the debris and poured some of it into a grimy glass. In a minute she felt a lot better, almost well enough to get dressed and do something about the bloody job. Now she had begun she might as well finish the bottle—it was wonderful how little it took to do the trick provided you started on an empty stomach.

The neck of the bottle rattled against the glass. She was concentrating on keeping her hand steady, not watching the liquid level rise and rise until it overbrimmed, spilt and streamed over the spread pink flounces.

Red everywhere. Good thing we're not houseproud, she thought, and then she looked down at herself, at red on pale pink

. . . Her fingers tore at the nylon until they were red and sticky too. O God, God! She trampled on it, shuddering as if it were slimy, alive, and threw herself on the sofa.

. . . You had nothing pretty on now, nothing to show to Tessie. She used to worry in case you got yourself dirty and one day when Mummy was indoors with Granny Rose and the man they called Roger she took you upstairs to see Auntie Rene and Uncle Bert, and Auntie Rene made you put an old apron on over your frock.

Uncle Bert and Roger. They were the only men you knew apart from Daddy who was always ill—'ailing' Mummy called it. Uncle Bert was rough and big and once when you came upstairs quietly you heard him shouting at Auntie Rene and then you saw him hit her. But he was kind to you and he called you Lizzie. Roger never called you anything. How could he when he never spoke to you, but looked at you as if he hated you?

It was in the Autumn that Mummy said you ought to have a party frock. Funny really, because there weren't any parties to go to, but Mummy said you could wear it on Christmas day. Pink it was, three layers of pale pink net over a pink petticoat, and it was the most beautiful dress you had ever seen in your life . . .

Elizabeth Crilling knew that once it had begun it would go on and on. Only one thing could stop it now. Keeping her eyes from the pink thing, all spattered with red, she stumbled out into the kitchen to find her temporary salvation.

Irene Kershaw's voice on the telephone sounded cold and distant. 'Your Charlie seems to have had a bit of a tiff with Tessie, Mr Archery. I don't know what it's all about, but I'm sure it can't be her fault. She worships the ground he treads on.'

'They're old enough to know what they're doing,' said Archery insincerely.

'She's coming home tomorrow and she must be upset if she's cutting the last days of term. All the people round here keep asking when the wedding is and I just don't know what to say. It puts me in a very awkward position.'

Respectability, always respectability.

'Did you ring me up about something special, Mr Archery, or was it just for a chat?'

'I wondered if you'd mind giving me your husband's business number?'

'If you two think you can get together,' she said more warmly, 'and have a go at patching things up, that would suit me down to the ground. I really can't contemplate the idea of my Tess being—well, thrown over.' Archery did not answer. 'The numbber's Uplands 62234,' she said.

Kershaw had an extension of his own and a bright cockney secretary.

'I want to write to Painter's commanding officer,' Archery said when the civilities had been exchanged.

Kershaw seemed to hesitate, then said in his usual eager, vital voice, 'Don't know the bloke's name, but it was the Duke of Babraham's Light Infantry he was in. Third Battalion. The War Office'll tell you.'

'The defence didn't call him at the trial, but it might help me if he could give Painter a good character.'

'If. I wonder why the defence didn't call him, Mr Archery?'

The War Office was helpful. The Third Battalion had been commanded by a Colonel Cosmo Plashet. He was an old man now and living in retirement in Westmorland. Archery made several attempts to write to Colonel Plashet. The final letter was not what he would have wished, but it would have to do. After lunch he went out to post it.

He strolled up towards the Post Office. Time hung heavy on his hands and he had no notion what to do next. Tomorrow Charles would come, full of ideas and extravagant plans, but comforting, an assistant. Or, knowing Charles, a director. He badly needed someone to direct him. Police work is for policemen, he thought, experts who are trained and have all the means for detection at their disposal.

Then he saw her. She was coming out of the florist's next door to the Post Office and her arms were full of white roses. They matched and mingled with the white pattern on her black dress so that you could not tell which were real and which a mere design on silk.

'Good afternoon, Mr Archery,' said Imogen Ide.

Until now he had hardly noticed the beauty of the day, the intense blue of the sky, the glory of perfect holiday weather. She smiled.

'Would you be very kind and open the car door for me?'

He jumped to do her bidding like a boy. The poodle, Dog, was sitting on the passenger seat and when Archery touched the door, he growled and showed his teeth.

'Don't be such a fool,' she said to the dog and dumped him on the back seat. 'I'm taking these up to Forby cemetery. My husband's ancestors have a sort of vault there. Very feudal. He's in town so I said I'd do it. It's an interesting old church. Have you seen much of the country round here yet?'

'Very little, I'm afraid.'

'Perhaps you don't care for clerestories and fonts and that sort of thing.'

'Quite the contrary, I assure you. I'll get the car and go over to Forby tonight if you think it's worth seeing.'

'Why not come now?'

He had meant her to ask him. He knew it and he was ashamed. Yet what was there to be ashamed about? In a way he was on holiday and holiday acquaintances were quickly made. He had met her husband and it was only by chance her husband was not with her now. In that case he would have accepted without a qualm. Besides, in these days there was no harm in a man going on a little excursion with a woman. How many times had he picked up Miss Baylis in Thringford village and driven her into Colchester to do her shopping? Imogen Ide was much farther removed from him in age than Miss Baylis. She couldn't be more than thirty. He was old enough to be her father. Suddenly he wished he hadn't thought of that, for it put things in an unpleasant perspective.

'It's very good of you,' he said. 'I'd like to.'

She was a good driver. For once he didn't mind being driven, didn't wish he was at the wheel. It was a beautiful car, a silver Lancia Flavia, and it purred along the winding roads. All was still and they passed only two other cars. The meadows were rich green or pale yellow where they had been shorn of hay, and between them and a dark ridge of woodland ran a glittering brown stream.

'That's the Kingsbrook,' she said, 'the same one that passes under the High Street. Isn't it strange? Man can do almost anything, move mountains, create seas, irrigate deserts, but he can't prevent the flow of water. He can dam it, channel it, pass it through pipes, make bridges over it . . .' He watched her, remembering with wonder that she had been a photographic model. Her lips were parted and the breeze blew her hair. 'But still it springs from the earth and finds its way to the sea.'

He said nothing and hoped she could sense if not see his nod. They were coming into a village. A dozen or so cottages and a couple of big houses surrounded a sprawling green; there was a little inn and through a mass of dark green foliage Archery could see the outlines of the church.

The entrance to the churchyard was by way of a kissing gate. He followed Imogen Ide and he carried the roses. The place was shady and cool but not well-tended and some of the older gravestones had tumbled over on their backs into the tangle of nettles and briars.

'This way,' she said, taking the left hand path. 'You mustn't go widdershins around a church. It's supposed to be unlucky.'

Yews and ilexes bordered the path. Underfoot it was sandy, yet green with moss and the delicate tufts of arenaria. The church was very old and built of rough-hewn oaken logs. Its beauty lay in its antiquity.

'It's one of the oldest wooden churches in the country.'

'There's one like it in my county,' said Archery. 'At Greensted. I believe it's ninth century.'

'This one's Nine something. Would you like to see the leper squint?'

They knelt down side by side and, bending forward, he peered through the small triangular gap at the base of the log wall. Although it was not the first of its kind he had seen, it pained him to think of the outcast, the unclean, who came to this tiny grille and listening to the Mass, received on his tongue the bread that some believe is the body of God. It made him think of Tess, herself an outcast, condemned like the leper to an undeserved disease. Within he could see a little stone aisle, wooden pews and a pulpit carved with saints' faces. He shivered and he felt her shiver beside him.

They were very close together under the yew boughs. He had a strange feeling that they were quite alone in the world and that they had been brought here for the working out of some destiny. He lifted his eyes, and turning to her, met hers. He expected her to smile but instead her face was grave, yet full of wonder and a kind of fear. He felt in himself, without analysing it, the emotion he saw in her eyes. The scent of the roses was intoxicating, fresh and unbearably sweet.

Then he got to his feet quickly, a little quelled by the stiffness of his knees. For a moment he had felt like a boy; his body betrayed him as bodies always do.

She said rather brightly, 'Have a look inside while I put these flowers on the grave. I won't be long.'

He went softly up the aisle and stood before the altar. Anyone watching him might have taken him for an atheist, so cool and appraising was his glance. Back again to look at the unassuming little font, the inscriptions on wall plaques. He put two half-crowns in the box and signed his name in the visitors' book. His hand was shaking so badly that the signature looked like that of an old man.

When he came out once more into the churchyard she was nowhere to be seen. The lettering on the older stones had been obliterated by time and weather. He walked into the new part, reading the last messages of relatives to their dead.

As he came to the end of the path where the hedge was and on the other side of the hedge a meadow, a name that seemed familiar caught his eye. Grace, John Grace. He reflected, searching his mind. It was not a common name and until quite recently he had associated it only with the great cricketer. Of course—a boy had lain dying in the road and that death and that boy's request had reminded Wexford of another, similar tragedy. Wexford had told him about it in the court. 'Must be all of twenty years . . .'

Archery looked to the engraved words for confirmation.

Sacred to the Memory of
John Grace
Who departed This Life
February 16th, 1945
In the Twenty-First Year
of His Age

Go, Shepherd, to your rest;
Your tale is told.
The Lamb of God takes
Shepherds to his fold.

A pleasant, if not brilliant, conceit, Archery thought. It was apparently a quotation, but he didn't recognise it. He looked round as Imogen Ide approached. The leaf shadows played on her face and made a pattern on her hair so that it looked as if it was covered by a veil of lace.

'Are you reminding yourself of your mortality?' she asked him gravely.

'I suppose so. It's an interesting place.'

'I'm glad to have had the opportunity of showing it to you. I'm very patriotic—if that's the word—about my county though it hasn't been mine for long.'

He was certain she was going to offer herself as his guide on some future occasion and he said quickly: 'My son is coming tomorrow. Well have to explore together.' She smiled politely. 'He's twenty-one,' he added rather fatuously.

Simultaneously their eyes turned to the inscription on the stone.

'I'm ready to go if you are,' she said.

She dropped him outside the Olive and Dove. They said good-bye briskly and he noticed she said nothing about hoping to see him again. He didn't feel like tea and he went straight upstairs. Without knowing why he took out the photograph he had of Painter's daughter. Looking at the picture, he wondered why he had thought her so lovely. She was just a pretty girl with the prettiness of youth. Yet while he looked he seemed to realise for the first time why Charles longed so passionately to possess her. It was a strange feeling and it had little to do with Tess, with Tess's appearance or with Charles. In a way it was a universal diffused empathy, but it was selfish too and it came from his heart rather than from his mind.

10

> And if he hath not before disposed of his goods, let him be admonished to make his will . . . for the better discharging of his conscience and the quietness of his executors.
>
> *The Visitation of the Sick.*

'You don't seem to have got very far,' said Charles. He sat down in an armchair and surveyed the pleasant lounge. The maid who was operating a floor polisher thought him very handsome with his rather long fair hair and his scornful expression. She decided to give the lounge a more than usually thorough do. 'The great thing is to be businesslike about it. We haven't got all that long. I start at the brewery on Monday week.' Archery was rather nettled. His own parochial duties were being overlooked. 'I'm sure there's something fishy about that fellow Primero, Roger Primero. I rang him up before I got here last night and I've got a date to see him this morning at half eleven.'

Archery looked at his watch. It was almost ten.

'You'd better get a move on, then. Where does he live?'

'You see? Now if I'd been in your shoes that's the first thing I'd have found out. He lives at Forby Hall. I suppose he fancies himself as the lord of the manor.' He glanced at his father and said quickly, 'Be all right if I have the car?'

'I suppose so. What are you going to tell him, Charles? He might have you thrown out.'

'I don't think he will,' Charles said thoughtfully. 'I've found out a bit about him and it seems he's mad keen on publicity. Always trying to create an image.' He hesitated, then added boldly, 'I told him I was the top features man on the *Sunday Planet* and we were doing a series on tycoons. Rather good, don't you think?'

'It doesn't happen to be true,' said Archery.

Charles said rapidly, 'The end justifies the means. I thought I could put across a line about his early life being dogged by misfortune, father dying, grandmother murdered, no prospects—that sort of thing. And look at him now. You never know what will come out. He's supposed to be very forthcoming to the Press.'

'We'd better go and get the car out.'

It was as hot as ever, but more sultry. A thin mist covered the sun. Charles wore an open necked white shirt and rather tapering trousers. Archery thought he looked like a Regency duellist.

'You won't want to start yet,' he said. 'Forby's only about four miles away. Would you like to look round the place?'

They walked up the High Street and over the Kingsbrook bridge. Archery was proud to have his son beside him. He knew they were very much alike but he didn't for a moment deceive himself they might be taken for brothers. The heavy muggy weather had brought on a twinge of lumbago and today he had utterly forgotten what it felt like to be twenty-one.

'You're reading English,' he said to Charles. 'Tell me where this comes from.' His memory hadn't begun to fail, at any rate. He was word perfect in the little verse.

' "Go, Shepherd, to your rest;
Your tale is told.
The lamb of God takes
Shepherds to his fold." '

Charles shrugged. 'Sounds vaguely familiar, but I can't place it. Where did you see it?'

'On a gravestone in Forby churchyard.'

'You really are the end, Father. I thought you wanted to help me and Tess and all you've been doing is messing about in cemeteries.'

Archery controlled himself with difficulty. If Charles was going to take everything into his own hands there seemed no reason why he shouldn't just go back to Thringford. There was nothing to keep him in Kingsmarkham. He wondered why the prospect of returning to the vicarage seemed ineffably dull. Suddenly he stopped and nudged his son's arm.

'What's the matter?'

'That woman outside the butcher's, the one in the cape—it's that Mrs Crilling I told you about. I'd rather not come face to face with her.'

But it was too late. She had evidently seen them already, for with her cape flying, she came bearing down upon them like a galleon.

'Mr Archery! My dear friend!' She took both his hands in hers and swung them as if she were about to partner him in an eightsome reel. 'What a lovely surprise! I was only saying to my daughter this morning, I do hope I shall see that dear man again so that I can thank him for ministering to me in my wretched affliction.'

This was a new mood. She was like a dowager at a successful garden party. The cape was familiar but the dress she wore under it was an ordinary cotton frock, simple and dowdy, somewhat splashed with gravy stains on its front. She gave a broad, calm and gracious smile.

'This is my son, Charles,' Archery muttered. 'Charles, this is Mrs Crilling.'

To his surprise Charles took the outstretched, none-too-clean hand and half-bowed over it.

'How do you do?' Over her head he gave his father an angry glance. 'I've heard so much about you.'

'Nice things, I hope.' If it occurred to her that Archery had seen nothing nice about her to relate she gave no sign of it. She was quite sane, gay, even frivolous. 'Now, don't refuse to gratify my little whim. I want you both to come into the Carousel and take a wee cup of coffee with me. My treat, of course,' she added archly.

'Our time,' said Charles grandiloquently—absurdly, Archery thought, 'is quite at your disposal. Until eleven fifteen, that is. Don't let us discuss anything so absurd as treats in the company of a lady.'

Evidently it was the right line to take with her. 'Isn't he *sweet?*' she gurgled. They went into the cafe. 'Children are such a blessing, don't you think? The crown of the tree of life. You must be proud of him, even though he quite puts you in the shade.'

Charles pulled out a chair for her. They were the only customers and for a while no one came to take their order. Mrs Crilling leant confidingly towards Archery.

'My baby has got herself a situation and she starts tomorrow. An operative in a ladies' wear establishment. I understand the prospects are excellent. With her intelligence there's no knowing how far she can go. The trouble is she's never had a real chance.' She had been speaking in a low genteel voice. Suddenly she turned her back on him, banged the sugar basin on the table and screamed loudly in the direction of the kitchen:

'Service!'

Charles jumped. Archery shot him a glance of triumph.

'Always having her hopes raised and then it comes to nothing,' she went on just as if the scream had never happened. 'Her father was just the same—struck down with T.B. in the flower of his age and dead within six months.' Archery flinched as she jerked away from him once more. 'Where the flaming hell are those bloody girls?' she shouted.

A woman in a green uniform with Manageress embroidered on the bodice came out from the kitchen. The look she gave Mrs Crilling was bored and withering.

'I asked you not to come in here again, Mrs Crilling, if you can't behave yourself.' She smiled frostily at Archery, 'What can I get you, sir?'

'Three coffees, please.'

'I'll have mine black,' said Charles.

'What was I talking about?'

'Your daughter,' said Archery hopefully.

'Oh, yes, my baby. It's funny really she should have had such a bad break because when she was a little tot it looked as if everything in the garden was lovely. I had a dear old friend, you see, who simply doted on my baby. And she was rolling in money, kept servants and all that kind of thing . . .'

The coffee came. It was the espresso kind with foam on the top.

'You can bring me some white sugar,' said Mrs Crilling sulkily. 'I can't stomach that demerara muck.' The waitress flounced away, returned with another sugar bowl and banged it down on the table. Mrs Crilling gave a shrill little shriek as soon as she was out of earshot. 'Silly bitch!'

Then she returned to her theme. 'Very old my friend was and beyond being responsible for her actions. Senile, they call it.

Over and over again she told me she wanted to do something for my baby. I passed it off, of course, having an absolute revulsion about stepping into dead men's shoes.' She stopped suddenly and dropped four heaped teaspoonfuls of sugar into her coffee.

'Naturally,' said Charles. 'The last thing anyone would call you is mercenary, Mrs Crilling.'

She smiled complacently and to Archery's intense amusement, leant across the table and patted Charles's cheek.

'You dear,' she said. 'You lovely, understanding dear.' After a deep breath she went on more practically, 'Still, you have to look after your own. I didn't press it, not till the doctor told me Mr Crilling had only got six months to live. No insurance, I thought in my despair, no pension. I pictured myself reduced to leaving my baby on the steps of an orphanage.'

For his part. Archery was unable to picture it. Elizabeth had been a sturdy youngster of five at the time.

'Do go on,' said Charles. 'It's most interesting.'

'You ought to make a will, I said to my friend. I'll pop down the road and get you a will form. A thousand or two would make all the difference to my baby. You know how she's gladdened your last years, and what have those grandchildren of yours ever done for you? Damn all, I thought.'

'But she didn't make a will?' Archery said.

'What do you know about it? You let me tell it in my own way. It was about a week before she died. I'd had the will form for weeks and weeks and all the time poor Mr Crilling was wasting away to a shadow. But would she fill it in? Not her, the old cow. I had to use all my most winning powers of persuasion. Every time I said a word that crazy old maid of hers would put her spoke in. Then that old maid—Flower, her name was—she got a bad cold and had to keep to her bed. "Have you thought any more about disposing of your temporal estates?" I said to my friend in a light-hearted, casual manner. "Maybe I should do something for Lizzie," she said and I knew my opportunity was at hand.

'Back across the road I flew. I didn't like to witness it myself, you know, on account of my baby being a beneficiary. Mrs White, my neighbour, came over and the lady who helped with her housework. They were only too delighted. You might say it brought a ray of sunshine into their humdrum lives.'

Archery wanted to say, 'But Mrs Primero died intestate.' He didn't dare. Any hint that he knew whom she was talking about and the whole narrative might be brought to a halt.

'Well, we got it all written out. I'm a great reader, Mr Archery, so I was able to put it in the right language. "Blood is thicker than water", said my old friend—she was wandering in her mind—but she only put the grandchildren down for five hundred apiece. There was eight thousand for my baby and I was to have charge of it till she was twenty-one, and a bit left over for the Flower woman. My friend was crying bitterly. I reckon she realised how wicked she'd been in not doing it before.

'And that was that. I saw Mrs White and the other lady safely off the premises—more fool I, though I didn't know it at the time. I said I'd keep the will safe and I did. She wasn't to mention it to anybody. And—would you believe it?—a week later she met with her death.'

Charles said innocently, 'That was a good start for your daughter, Mrs Crilling, whatever misfortunes came afterwards.'

He started as she got up abruptly. Her face had blanched to the whiteness it had worn in court and her eyes blazed.

'Any benefits she got,' she said in a choking voice, 'came from her dead father's people. Charity it was, cold charity. "Send me the school bills, Josie," her uncle'd say to me. "I'll pay them direct, and her auntie can go with her to get her uniform. If you think she needs treatment for her nerves her auntie can go with her to Harley Street, too." '

'But what about the will?'

'That bloody will!' Mrs Crilling shouted. 'It wasn't legal. I only found out after she was dead. I took it straight round to Quadrants, the solicitors that were in the High Street. Old Mr. Quadrant was alive then. "What about these alterations?" he said. Well, I looked and, lo and behold, the old cow had scribbled in a lot of extra bits while I was at the front door with Mrs White. Scribbled in bits and scratched out bits too. "These invalidate the whole thing," said Mr Quadrant. "You have to get the witnesses to sign them, or have a codicil. You could fight it," he said, looking me up and down in a nasty way, knowing I hadn't got a bean. "But I wouldn't say much for your chances." '

To Archery's horror she broke into a stream of obscenities,

many of which he had never heard before. The manageress came out and took her by the arm.

'Out you go. We can't have this in here.'

'My God,' said Charles, after she had been hustled away. 'I see what you mean.'

'I must confess her language shook me a bit.'

Charles chuckled. 'Not fit for your ears at all.'

'It was most enlightening, though. Are you going to bother with Primero now?'

'It can't do any harm.'

Archery had to wait a long time in the corridor outside Wexford's office. Just as he was beginning to think he would have to give up and try again later, the main entrance doors opened and a little bright-eyed man in working clothes came in between two uniformed policemen. He was plainly some sort of criminal, but everyone seemed to know him and find him a source of ironic amusement.

'I can't stand these contemporary-type nicks,' he said impudently to the station sergeant. Wexford came out of his office, ignoring Archery, and crossed to the desk. 'Give me the old-fashioned kind every time. I've got a slummy mind, that's my trouble.'

'I'm not interested in your views on interior decoration, Monkey,' said Wexford.

The little man turned to him and grinned.

'You've got a nasty tongue, you have. Your sense of humour's sunk as you've gone up. Pity, really.'

'Shut up!'

Archery listened in admiration. He wished that he had the power and the authority to talk like that to Mrs Crilling, or that such authority could be vested in Charles, enabling him to question Primero without the inhibitions of subterfuge. Wexford, talking silkily about bombs and attempted murder, ushered the little man into his office and the door closed on them. Such things did go on, Archery thought. Perhaps his own new-forming theories were not so far-fetched after all.

'If I could just see Inspector Burden for a moment,' he said more confidently to the station sergeant.

'I'll see if he's free, sir.'

Eventually Burden came out to him himself.

'Good morning, sir. Doesn't get any cooler, does it?'

'I've got something rather important to tell you. Can you spare me five minutes?'

'Surely.'

But he made no move to take him into a more private place. The station sergeant occupied himself with perusing a large book. Sitting on a ridiculous spoon-shaped chair outside Wexford's office, Archery felt like a school boy, who having waited a long time to see the headmaster, is compelled to confide in and perhaps take his punishment from an underling. Rather chastened, he told Burden briefly about Mrs Crilling.

'Most interesting. You mean that when Mrs Primero was murdered the Crilling woman thought the will was valid?'

'It amounts to that. She didn't mention the murder.'

'We can't do anything. You realise that?'

'I want you to tell me if I have sufficient grounds to write to the Home Secretary.'

A constable appeared from somewhere, tapped on Wexford's door and was admitted.

'You haven't any circumstantial evidence,' Burden said. 'I'm sure the Chief Inspector wouldn't encourage it.'

A roar of sardonic laughter sounded through the thin dividing wall. Archery felt unreasonably piqued.

'I think I shall write just the same.'

'You must do as you please, sir.' Burden got up. 'Been seeing much of the country round here?'

Archery swallowed his anger. If Burden intended to terminate the interview with small talk, small talk he should have. Hadn't he promised his old friend Griswold and, for that matter, the Chief Inspector, not to make trouble?

'I went to Forby yesterday,' he said. 'I was in the churchyard and I happened to notice the grave of that boy Mr Wexford was talking about in court the other day. His name was Grace. Do you remember?'

Burden's face was a polite blank but the station sergeant glanced up.

'I'm a Forby man myself, sir,' he said. 'We make a bit of a song and dance about John Grace at home. They'll tell you all about him in Forby for all it was twenty years ago.'

'All about him?'

'He fancied himself as a poet, poor kid, wrote plays too. Sort of religious mystic he was. In his day he used to try and sell his verses from door to door.'

'Like W.H.Davis,' said Archery.

'I daresay.'

'Was he a shepherd?'

'Not as far as I know. Baker's roundsman or something.'

Wexford's door swung open, the constable came out and said to Burden, 'Chief Inspector wants you, sir.'

Wexford's voice roared after him, 'You can come back in here, Gates, and take a statement from Guy Fawkes. And give him a cigarette. He won't blow up.'

'It seems I'm wanted, sir, so if you'll excuse me . . .'

Burden went with Archery to the entrance doors.

'You had your chat with Alice Flower just in time,' he said. 'If you had it, that is.'

'Yes, I talked to her. Why?'

'She died yesterday,' said Burden. 'It's all in the local rag.'

Archery found a newsagent. The *Kingsmarkham Chronicle* had come out that morning and fresh stacks of papers lay on the counter. He bought a copy and found the announcement at the bottom of the back page.

'Death of Miss A. Flower.'

He scanned it and took it back with him to the terrace of the hotel to read it properly.

'The death occurred today . . .' That meant yesterday, Archery thought, looking at the dateline. He read on. 'The death occurred today of Miss Alice Flower at Stowerton Infirmary. She was eighty-seven. Miss Flower, who had lived in the district for twenty-five years, will be best remembered for the part she played in the notorious Victor's Piece murder trial. She was for many years maid and trusted friend of Mrs Primero . . .'

There followed a brief account of the murder and the trial.

'The funeral will take place at Forby parish church on Monday. Mr Roger Primero has expressed a wish that the last rites may be celebrated quietly and that there will be no sightseers.'

Roger Primero, faithful to the end, Archery thought. He found himself hoping that Charles had done nothing to distress this kindly and dutiful man. So Alice Flower was dead at last, death had waited just long enough to let her tell him, Archery, all she knew. Again he seemed to feel the working of destiny. Well done, thou good and faithful servant. Enter thou into the joy of thy Lord!

He went in to lunch, feeling jaded and depressed. Where on earth was Charles? He had been gone more than two hours. By now Primero had probably seen through that absurd cover story and . . .

His imagination showing him his son being interrogated by Wexford at his nastiest, he was just picking at his fruit salad and warm ice-cream when Charles burst into the dining room, swinging the car keys.

'I was wondering where you'd got to.'

'I've had a most instructive morning. Anything happened here?'

'Nothing much. Alice Flower is dead.'

'You can't tell me anything about that. Primero was full of it. Apparently he was at her bedside for hours yesterday.' He threw himself into a chair next to his father's. 'God, it was hot in that car! As a matter of fact, her dying like that was a help if anything. Made it easier to get him on to the murder.'

'I didn't think you could be so callous,' said Archery distastefully.

'Oh, come off it, Father. She'd had her allotted span plus seventeen. She can't have wanted to live. Don't you want to hear what I got out of him?'

'Of course.'

'You don't want any coffee, do you? Let's go outside.'

There was no one on the terrace. A yellow climbing rose had shed its petals all over the ground and the battered cane chairs. What residents there were had left possessions out here as if to reserve permanent perches, magazines, library books, a roll of blue knitting, a pair of glasses. Ruthlessly Charles cleared two chairs and blew away the rose petals. For the first time Archery noticed that he looked extremely happy.

'Well,' he said when they had sat down, 'the house first. It's quite a place, about ten times the size of Thringford Manor, and it's all built of grey stone with a kind of pediment thing over the front door. Mrs Primero lived there when she was a girl and Roger bought it when it came up for sale this spring. There's a park with deer in it and a vast drive coming up from a pillared entrance. You can't see the house from the road, only the cedars in the park.

'They've got an Italian butler—not so classy as an English one, d'you think? But I suppose they're a dying race. Anyway, this butler character let me in and kept me hanging about for about ten minutes in a hall the size of the ground floor of our house. I was a bit nervous because I kept thinking, suppose he's rung up the *Sunday Planet* and they've said they've never heard of me? But he hadn't and it was all right. He was in the library. Superb collection of books he's got and some of them looked quite worn, so I suppose someone reads them, though I shouldn't think he does.

'It was all furnished in leather, black leather. You know that rather sexy modern stuff. He asked me to sit down and have a drink . . .'

'A bit early, wasn't it?'

'People like that, they slosh it down all day. If they were working class they'd be alcoholics, but you can get away with anything when you've got a butler and about fifty thousand a year. Then his wife came in. Rather a nice-looking woman—a bit past it, of course—but magnificent clothes. Not that I'd want Tess to dress like that . . .' His face fell and Archery's heart moved with pity. 'If I ever get a say in what Tess wears,' he added dolefully.

'Go on.'

'We had our drinks. Mrs Primero wasn't very talkative, but her husband was most expansive. I didn't have to ask him much, so you needn't get all steamed up about your conscience, and he got on to the murder, quite naturally. He kept saying he wished he hadn't left Victor's Piece so early that Sunday evening. He could easily have stayed.

' "I was only going to meet a couple of chaps I knew at a pub in Sewingbury," he said. "And, as it happened, it was a dead loss because they never turned up. Or, at least, they did turn up but I got the wrong pub. So I waited about for an hour or so and then I went back to my lodgings. I wonder," he said, "how many times I've cursed myself for not staying at Victor's Piece."

'What d'you think of that? I thought it was fishy.'

'He didn't have to tell you,' Archery said. 'In any case the police must have questioned him.'

'Maybe they did and maybe they didn't. He didn't say.' Charles lounged back in his chair, and swinging his feet up poked them through the trellis. 'Then we got on to money,' he said. 'Money, I may add, is the mainspring of his existence.'

Inexplicably, Archery felt himself marked out as Primero's defender. Alice Flower had painted him in such glowing colours. 'I had the impression he was rather a nice sort of man,' he said.

'He's all right,' Charles said indifferently. 'He's very modest about his success and about his money.' He grinned. 'The kind of character who cries all the way to the bank. Anyway, now we come to the crux of the whole thing.

'Just before Mrs Primero was killed some mate of his asked him if he'd like to go into business with him. Importing or exporting. I don't quite know what it was but it doesn't matter. The friend was to put up ten thousand and so was Primero. Well, Primero hadn't got it, hadn't got a smell of it. As far as he was concerned it was hopeless. Then Mrs Primero died.'

'We know all this,' Archery objected. 'Alice Flower told me as much . . .'

'All right, wait for it. Alice Flower didn't know this bit. "That was the making of me," he said very breezily. "Not that I wasn't devastated by my grandmother's death," he added as a sort of hasty afterthought. His wife was sitting there all the time with a blank look on her face. He kept looking at her uneasily.

' "I put up the money and we were away," he said, talking rather fast. "And since then I've never looked back."

'I was in a bit of a dilemma. Everything was going so smoothly and I didn't want to mess things up. I thought he was looking defiant and suddenly I realised why. *He didn't know how much I knew about Mrs Primero's money*. She'd died intestate, it was sixteen years ago, I was a newspaper reporter and for all he knew I was interested in him, not his grandmother.'

'A lot to read into a defiant look,' said Archery.

'Perhaps there was a bit of hindsight in that. But just wait a minute. Then I asked a question. It was a shot in the dark but it came off.

' "So you got your ten thousand just when you needed it?" I said casually. Primero didn't say anything, but his wife looked at me and said, "Just the exact sum after death duties. You should really be asking me. Roger's told me about it so often I know it better than he does."

'Well, I couldn't leave it there. I persisted. "I understand you've got two sisters, Mr Primero," I said. "I suppose they inherited similar amounts?" He began to look terribly suspicious. After all, it wasn't my business and it had nothing to do with the story I was supposed to be writing. "Are they successful in business too?" I asked, trying to justify myself. It was a stroke of genius. Sorry to be big-headed but it was. I could actually see him relax.

'"I really don't see much of them," he said. "Oh, Roger," said his wife, "you know we *never* see them." Primero gave her an icy look. "One's married," he said, "and the other has a job in London. They're much younger than I am." "It must be nice to inherit ten thousand pounds when you're still a child," I said. "I imagine it's always nice," he said, "but I've never had the pleasure of inheriting any more. Shall we leave the subject and get on with the story of my life?"

'I pretended to take notes. I was doodling really but he thought it was shorthand. When we'd finished he got up and shook hands and said he'd keep his eye open for the *Sunday Planet*. I felt a bit awkward at that and I didn't quite know what to say but his wife saved me by asking me to lunch. So I accepted and we had a splendid lunch, smoked salmon and enormous steaks, great sides of oxen they were, and raspberries in framboise liqueur.'

'You've got a nerve,' said Archery in grudging admiration. He pulled himself up. 'It was very wrong of you. Most unethical.'

'All in a good cause. You do see the point, don't you?'

Why do one's children always think one senile yet childish, dully practical yet irrational, capable of supporting them but unintelligent to the point of imbecility?

'Of course I do,' Archery said irritably. 'Alice Flower and Mrs Crilling both said Mrs Primero had only ten thousand to to leave, but apparently Roger Primero didn't get only a third of that, he got the whole ten thousand.'

Charles jerked round to face him, scattering more rose petals from the trellis. 'Now, why? There definitely wasn't a will. I've checked on that. And there were just the three heirs, Roger, Angela and Isabel. Mrs Primero hadn't another relative in the world and according to the law it should have been divided between the three grandchildren. But Roger got the lot.'

'I can't understand it.'

'Neither can I—yet. Maybe I shall when I've seen the sisters. I couldn't ask Roger where they lived, but Primero isn't a common name and the single one may be in the London phone directory. I haven't quite made up my mind about the line I'll take with them, but I've got the glimmerings of an idea I might say I've come from the Inland Revenue . . .'

'*Facilis descensus Averni.*'

'In matters of this kind,' Charles said crisply, 'you have to be bloody, bold and resolute. Can I have the car again tomorrow?'

'If you must.'

'I thought you might like to go out to Victor's Piece,' Charles said in a hopeful tone, 'and just have a look round. See if you can see if Primero could have hidden himself anywhere, sneaked upstairs or something, instead of letting himself out of the front door that Sunday night.'

'Aren't you letting your imagination run away with you?'

'It's a family failing.' His eyes clouded suddenly and to Archery's dismay he put his head in his hands. Archery didn't know what to do. 'Tess hasn't spoken to me for two days,' the boy said. 'I can't lose her, I can't.' If he had been ten years younger his father would have taken him in his arms. But if he had been ten years younger the whole thing would never have happened.

'I don't give a damn,' Charles said, controlling himself, 'what her father was or what he did. I don't care if every one of her ancestors was hanged. But you do and she does and . . . Oh, what's the use?' He got up. 'Sorry to make an exhibition of myself.' Still looking down, he scuffed his feet against the eddies of petals. 'You're doing all you can,' he said with a dreadful prim gravity, 'but you can't be expected to understand at your age.' Without looking at his father, he turned and went into the hotel.

11

From fornication, and all other deadly sin; and from all the deceits of the world, the flesh and the devil,
Good Lord, deliver us.

The Litany.

Angela Primero lived in a flat at Oswestry Mansions, Baron's Court. She was twenty-six years old and the elder of Mrs Primero's granddaughters. That was all Charles Archery knew about her—that and her telephone number which he had easily found. He rang her up and asked if he could see her on the following morning. Thinking better of his original plan, he said he represented the *Sunday Planet,* and the death of Alice Flower having brought once more into prominence Mrs Primero's murder, his newspaper were running a feature on the fate of the other people concerned in the case. He was rather pleased with that. It had the ring of verisimilitude.

Miss Primero had a grim voice for so young a woman. It was gravelly, abrupt, almost masculine. She would be glad to see him, but he did realise, didn't he, that her recollection of her grandmother was slight? Just a few childhood memories were what he wanted, Miss Primero, little touches to add colour to his story.

She opened the door to him so quickly that he wondered if she had been waiting behind it. Her appearance surprised him for he had kept a picture of her brother in his mind and he had therefore expected someone small and dark with regular features. He had seen a photograph of the grandmother too, and though the old face was both wizened and blurred by age, there were still to be seen vestiges of an aquiline beauty and a strong resemblance to Roger.

The girl whose flat this was had a strong plain face with bad skin and a big prognathous jaw. Her hair was a dull flat brown. She wore a neat dark blue frock bought at a chain store and her figure, though over-large, was good.

'Mr Bowman?'

Charles was pleased with the name he had invented for himself. He gave her a pleasant smile.

'How do you do, Miss Primero?'

She showed him into a small very sparsely furnished sitting room. He could not help adding to the mystery by contrasting this with the library at Forby Hall. Here there were no books, no flowers, and the only ornaments were framed photographs, half a dozen perhaps, of a young blonde girl and a baby.

She followed his gaze towards the studio portrait of the same girl that hung above the fireplace. 'My sister,' she said. Her ugly face softened and she smiled. As she spoke there came from the next room a thin wail and the murmur of a voice. 'She's in my bedroom now, changing the baby's napkin. She always comes over on Saturday mornings.'

Charles wondered what Angela Primero did for a living. A typist perhaps, or a clerk? The whole set-up seemed too scanty and poor. The furniture was brightly coloured but it looked cheap and flimsy. In front of the hearth was a rug woven out of woollen rags. Needy nothing trimmed in jollity . . .

'Please sit down,' said Angela Primero.

The little orange chair creaked as it took his weight. A far cry, he thought, from the brother's voluptuous black leather. From the floor above he could hear music playing and someone pushing a vacuum cleaner.

'What do you want me to tell you?'

There was a packet of Weights on the mantelpiece. She took one and handed them to him. He shook his head.

'First, what you remember of your grandmother.'

'Not much. I told you.' Her speech was brusque and rough. 'We went there to tea a few times. It was a big dark house and I remember I was afraid to go to the bathroom alone. The maid used to have to take me.' She gave a staccato, humourless laugh and it was an effort to remember she was only twenty-six. 'I never even saw Painter if that's what you mean. There was a child across the road we used to play with sometimes and I believe Painter had a daughter. I asked about her once but my grandmother said she was common, we weren't to have anything to do with her.'

Charles clenched his hands. He felt a sudden desperate longing for Tess, both for himself, and also to set her beside this girl who had been taught to despise her.

The door opened and the girl in the photographs came in. Angela Primero jumped up at once and took the baby from her arms. Charles's knowledge of babies was vague. He thought this one might be about six months old. It looked small and uninteresting.

'This is Mr Bowman, darling. My sister, Isabel Fairest.'

Mrs Fairest was only a year younger than her sister, but she looked no more than eighteen. She was very small and thin with a pinkish-white face and enormous pale blue eyes. Charles thought she looked like a pretty rabbit. Her hair was a bright gingery gold.

Roger's hair and eyes were black, Angela's hair brown and her eyes hazel. None of them was in the least like either of the others. There was more to genetics than met the eye, Charles thought.

Mrs Fairest sat down. She didn't cross her legs but sat with her hands in her lap like a little girl. It was difficult to imagine her married, impossible to think of her as having given birth to a child.

Her sister scarcely took her eyes off her. When she did it was to coo at the baby. Mrs Fairest had a small soft voice, tinged with cockney.

'Don't let him tire you, darling. Put him down in his cot.'

'You know I love holding him, darling. Isn't he gorgeous? Have you got a smile for your auntie? You know your auntie, don't you, even if you haven't seen her for a whole week?'

Mrs Fairest got up and stood behind her sister's chair. They both gurgled over the baby, stroking its cheeks and curling its fingers round their own. It was obvious that they were devoted to each other, but whereas Angela's love was maternal to both sister and nephew, Isabel showed a clinging dependence on the older girl. Charles felt that they had forgotten he was there and he wondered how Mr Fairest fitted into the picture. He coughed.

'About your early life, Miss Primero . . . ?'

'Oh, yes. (Mustn't cry, sweetie. He's got wind, darling.) I really can't remember any more about my grandmother. My mother married again when I was sixteen. This is the sort of thing you want, is it?'

'Oh, yes.'

'Well, as I say, my mother married again and she and my stepfather wanted us to go out to Australia with them. (Up it comes! There, that's better.) But I didn't want to go. Isabel and I were still at school. My mother hung it out for a couple of years and then they went without us. Well, it was their life, wasn't it? I wanted to go to training college but I gave that up. Isabel and I had the house, didn't we, darling? And we both went out to work. (Is he going to have a little sleep, then?)'

It was an ordinary enough tale, fragmentary and very clipped. Charles felt that there was far more to it. The hardship and the privation had been left out. Money might have changed it all but she had never mentioned money. She had never mentioned her brother either.

'Isabel got married two years ago. Her husband's in the Post Office. I'm a secretary in a newspaper office.' She raised her eyebrows, unsmiling. 'I'll have to ask them if they've ever heard of you.'

'Yes, do,' said Charles with a suavity he didn't feel. He must get on to the subject of the money but he didn't know how to. Mrs Fairest brought a carry-cot in from the other room, they placed the baby in it, bending tenderly over him and cooing. Although it was nearly noon neither of them had mentioned a drink or even coffee. Charles belonged to a generation that has accustomed itself to almost hourly snacks, cups of this, glasses of that, bits and pieces from the refrigerator. So, surely, did they. He thought wistfully of Roger's hospitality. Mrs Fairest glanced up and said softly.

'I do like coming here. It's so quiet.' Above them the vacuum cleaner continued to whirr. 'My husband and me, we've only got one room. It's nice and big but it's awfully noisy at weekends.'

Charles knew it was impertinent but he had to say it.

'I'm surprised your grandmother didn't leave you anything.'

Angelo Primero shrugged. She tucked the blanket round the baby and stood up. 'That's life,' she said in a hard voice.

'Shall I tell him, darling?' Isabel Fairest touched her arm

and looked timidly into her face, waiting for guidance.

'What's the point? It's of no interest to him.' She stared at Charles and then said intelligently, 'You can't put that sort of thing in newspapers. It's libel.'

Damn, damn, damn! Why hadn't he said he was from the Inland Revenue? Then they could have got on to money at once.

'But I think people ought to know,' said Mrs Fairest, showing more spirit than he had thought her capable of. 'I do, darling. I always have, ever since I understood about it. I think people ought to know how he's treated us.'

Charles put his notebook away ostentatiously.

'This is off the record, Mrs Fairest.'

'You see, darling? He won't say anything. I don't care if he does. People ought to know about Roger.'

The name was out. They were all breathing rather heavily. Charles was the first to get himself under control. He managed a calm smile.

'Well, I *will* tell you. If you put it in the paper and I have to go to prison for it, I don't care! Granny Rose left ten thousand pounds and we should all have had a share, but we didn't. Roger—that's our brother—he got it all. I don't quite know why but Angela knows the ins and outs of it. My mother had a friend who was a solicitor where Roger worked and he said we could try and fight it, but Mother wouldn't on account of it being awful to have a court case against your own son. We were just little kids, you see, and we didn't know anything about it. Mother said Roger would help us—it was his moral duty, even if it wasn't legally—but he never did. He kept putting it off and then Mother quarrelled with him. We've never seen him since I was ten and Angela was eleven. I wouldn't know him now if I saw him in the street.'

It was a puzzling story. They were all Mrs Primero's grandchildren, all equally entitled to inherit in the event of there being no will. And there had been no will.

'I don't want to see all this in your paper, you know,' Angela Primero said suddenly. She would have made a good teacher, he thought, reflecting on waste, for she was tender with little children, but stern when she had to be.

'I won't publish any of it,' Charles said with perfect truth.

'You'd better not, that's all. The fact is, we couldn't fight it. We wouldn't have stood a chance. In law Roger was perfectly entitled to it all. Mind you, it would have been another story if my grandmother had died a month later.'

'I don't quite follow you,' said Charles, by now unbearably excited.

'Have you ever seen my brother?'

Charles nodded, then changed it to a shake of the head. She looked at him suspiciously. Then she made a dramatic gesture. She took her sister by the shoulders and pushed her forward for his inspection.

'He's little and dark,' she said. 'Look at Isabel, look at me. We don't look alike, do we? We don't look like sisters because we aren't sisters and Roger isn't our brother. Oh, Roger is my parents' child all right and Mrs Primero was his grandmother. My mother couldn't have any more children. They waited eleven years and when they knew it was no good they adopted me. A year later they took Isabel as well.'

'But . . . I . . .' Charles stammered. 'You were legally adopted, weren't you?'

Angela Primero had recovered her composure. She put her arm round her sister who had begun to cry.

'We were legally adopted all right. That didn't make any difference. Adopted children can't inherit when the dead person has died without making a will—or they couldn't in September 1950. They can now. They were making this Act at the time and it became law on October 1st, 1950. Just our luck, wasn't it?'

The photograph in the estate agent's window made Victor's Piece look deceptively attractive. Perhaps the agent had long given up hope of its being sold for anything but its site value, for Archery, enquiring tentatively, was greeted with almost fawning exuberance. He emerged with an order to view, a bunch of keys and permission to go over the house whenever he chose.

No bus was in sight. He walked back to the stop by the Olive and Dove and waited in the shade. Presently he pulled the order to view out of his pocket and scanned it. 'Splendid property of character,' he read, 'that only needs an imaginative owner to give it a new lease of life . . .' There was no mention of the old tragedy, no hint that violent death had once been its tenant.

Two Sewingbury buses came and one marked Kingsmarkham Station. He was still reading, contrasting the agent's euphemisms with the description in his transcript, when the silver car pulled into the kerb.

'Mr Archery!'

He turned. The sun blazed back from the arched wings and the glittering screen. Imogen Ide's hair made an even brighter silver-gold flash against the dazzling metal.

'I'm on my way to Stowerton. Would you like a lift?'

He was suddenly ridiculously happy. Everything went, his pity for Charles, his grief for Alice Flower, his sense of helplessness against the juggernaut machinery of the law. An absurd dangerous joy possessed him and without stopping to analyse it, he went up to the car. Its bodywork was as hot as fire, a shivering silver blaze against his hand.

'My son took my car,' he said. 'I'm not going to Stowerton, just to a place this side of it, a house called Victor's Piece.'

She raised her eyebrows very slightly at this and he supposed she knew the story just as everyone else did, for she was looking at him strangely. He got in beside her, his heart beating. The continual rhythmic thudding in his left side was so intense as to be physically painful and he wished it would stop before it made him wince or press his hand to his breast.

'You haven't got Dog with you today,' he said.

She moved back into the traffic. 'Too hot for him,' she said. 'Surely you're not thinking of buying Victor's Piece?'

His heart had quietened. 'Why, do you know it?'

'It used to belong to a relative of my husband's.'

Ide, he thought, Ide. He couldn't remember hearing what had become of the house after Mrs Primero's death. Perhaps it had been owned by some Ides before it became an old people's home.

'I have a key and an order to view, but I'm certainly not going to buy. It's just—well . . .'

'Curiosity?' She could not look at him while she was driving but he felt her thoughts directed on him more powerfully than any eyes. 'Are you an amateur of crime?' It would have been natural to have used his name, to end the question with it. But she didn't. It seemed to him that she had omitted it because 'Mr Archery' had suddenly become too formal, his Christian name still too intimate. 'You know, I think I'll come over it with you,' she said. 'I don't have to be in Stowerton until half-past twelve. Let me be your guide, may I?'

Imogen Ide will be my guide . . . It was a stupid jingle and it tinkled in his ears on a minor key like an old, half-forgotten madrigal. He said nothing but she must have taken his silence for assent, for instead of dropping him at the entry she slowed and turned into the lane where dark gables showed between the trees.

Even on this bright morning the house looked dark and forbidding. Its yellow-brown bricks were crossed with fretted half-timbering and two of its windows were broken. The resemblance between it and the agent's photograph was as slight as that of a holiday postcard to the actual resort. The photographer had cunningly avoided or else subsequently removed the weeds, the brambles, the damp stains, the swinging rotted casements and the general air of decay. He had also succeeded in somehow minimising its rambling size. The gates were broken down and she drove straight through the gap, up the drive and stopped directly before the front door.

This moment should have been important to him, his first sight of the house where Tess's father had committed—or had not committed—his crime. His senses should have been alert to absorb atmosphere, to note details of place and distance that the police in their jaded knowledge had overlooked. Instead he was conscious of himself not as an observer, a note-taker, but only as a man living in the present, dwelling in the moment and discarding the past. He felt more alive than he had done for years and because of this he became almost unaware of his surroundings. Things could not affect him, not recorded fact. His emotions were all. He saw and experienced the house only as a deserted place into which he and this woman would soon go and would be alone.

As soon as he had thought this in so many words he knew that he should not go in. He could easily say that he only wanted to look at the grounds. She was getting out of the car now, looking up at the windows and wrinkling her eyelids against the light.

'Shall we go in?' she said.

He put the key in the lock and she was standing close beside him. He had expected a musty smell from the hall but he was hardly aware of it. Shafts of light crossed the place from various dusty windows and motes danced in the beams. There was an old runner on the tiled floor and catching her heel in it, she stumbled. Instinctively he put out his hand to steady her and as he did so he felt her right breast brush his arm.

'Mind how you go,' he said, not looking at her. Her shoe had sent up a little cloud of dust and she gave a nervous laugh. Perhaps it was just a normal laugh. He was beyond that kind of analysis, for he could still feel the soft weight against his arm as if she had not stepped quickly away.

'Terribly stuffy in here,' she said. 'It makes me cough. That's the room where the murder was committed—in there.' She pushed open a door and he saw a deal board floor, marble fireplace, great bleached patches on the walls where pictures had hung. 'The stairs are behind here and on the other side is the kitchen where poor old Alice was cooking the Sunday dinner.'

'I don't want to go upstairs,' he said quickly. 'It's too hot and dusty. You'll get your dress dirty.' He drew a deep breath and, moving far from her, stood against the mantelpiece. Here, just on this spot, Mrs Primero had felt the first blow of the axe; there the scuttle had stood, here, there, everywhere, the old blood had flowed. 'The scene of the crime,' he said fatuously.

Her eyes narrowed and she crossed to the window. The silence was terrible and he wanted to fill it with chatter. There was so much to say, so many remarks even mere acquaintances could make to each other on such a spot. The noonday sun cast her shadow in perfect proportion, neither too tall nor grossly dwarfed. It was like a cut-out in black tissue and he wanted to fall to his knees and touch it, knowing it was all he would get.

It was she who spoke first. He hardly knew what he had expected her to say, but not this—certainly not this.

'You are very like your son—or he's like you.'

The tension slackened. He felt cheated and peeved.

'I didn't know you'd met,' he said.

To this she made no reply. In her eyes was a tiny gleam of fun. 'You didn't tell me he worked for a newspaper.'

Archery's stomach turned. She must have been there, at the Primeros'. Was he expected to sustain Charles's lie?

'He's so very like you,' she said. 'It didn't really click, though, until after he'd gone. Then, taking his appearance and his name together—I suppose Bowman's his pseudonym on the *Planet*, is it?—I guessed. Roger hasn't realised.'

'I don't quite understand,' Archery began. He would have to explain: 'Mrs Ide . . .'

She started to laugh, stopped when she saw the dismay in his face. 'I think we've both been leading each other up the garden,' she said gently. 'Ide was my maiden name, the name I used for modelling.'

He turned away, pressing the hot palm of his hand against the marble. She took a step towards him and he smelt her scent. 'Mrs Primero was the relative who owned this house, the relative who's buried at Forby?' There was no need to wait for her answer. He sensed her nod. 'I don't understand how I can have been such a fool,' he said. Worse than a fool. What would she think tomorrow when the *Planet* came out? He offered up a stupid ashamed prayer that Charles had found out nothing from the woman who was her sister-in-law. 'Will you forgive me?'

'There's nothing to forgive, is there?' She sounded truly puzzled, as well she might. He had been asking pardon for future outrages. 'I'm just as much to blame as you. I don't know why I didn't tell you I was Imogen Primero.' She paused. 'There was no deceit in it,' she said. 'Just one of those things. We were dancing—something else came up . . . I don't know.'

He raised his head, gave himself a little shake. Then he walked away from her into the hall. 'You have to go to Stowerton, I think you said. It was kind of you to bring me.'

She was behind him now, her hand on his arm. 'Don't look like that. What are you supposed to have done? Nothing, nothing. It was just a—a social mistake.'

It was a little fragile hand but insistent. Not knowing why, perhaps because she too seemed in need of comfort, he covered it with his own. Instead of withdrawing it, she left her hand under his and as she sighed it trembled faintly. He turned to look at her, feeling shame that was as paralysing as a disease. Her face was a foot from his, then only inches, then no distance, no face but only a soft mouth.

The shame went in a wave of desire made the more terrible and the more exquisite because he had felt nothing like it for twenty years, perhaps not ever. Since coming down from

Oxford he had never kissed any woman but Mary, scarcely been alone with any but the old, the sick or the dying. He did not know how to end the kiss, nor did he know whether this in itself was inexperience or the yearning to prolong something that was so much more, but not enough more, than touching a shadow.

She took herself out of his arms quite suddenly, but without pushing or struggling. There was nothing to struggle against. 'Oh, dear,' she said, but she didn't smile. Her face was very white.

There were words to explain that kind of thing away. 'I don't know what made me do that' or 'I was carried away, the impulse of the moment . . .' He was sick of even the suggestion of lying. Truth itself seemed even more compelling and urgent than his desire and he thought he would speak it even though tomorrow and in the days to come it too would appear to her as a lie.

'I love you. I think I must have loved you from the first moment I saw you. I think that's how it was.' He put his hands up to his forehead and his fingertips, though icy cold, seemed to burn just as snow can burn the skin. 'I'm married,' he said. 'You know that—I mean my wife is living—and I'm a clergyman. I've no right to love you and I promise I'll never be alone with you again.'

She was very surprised and her eyes widened, but which of his confessions had surprised her he had no idea. It even occurred to him that she might be amazed at hearing from him lucid speech, for up to now he had been almost incoherent. 'I mustn't suppose,' he said, for his last sentence seemed like vanity, 'that there's been any temptation for you.' She started to speak, but he went on in a hurry, 'Will you not say anything but just drive away?'

She nodded. In spite of his prohibition, he longed for her to approach him again, just touch him. It was an impossible hunger that made him breathless. She made a little helpless gesture as if she too were in the grip of an overpowering emotion. Then she turned, her face held awkwardly away from him, ran down the hall and let herself out of the front door.

After she had gone it occurred to him that she had asked no questions as to his reasons for coming to the house. She had said little and he everything that mattered. He thought that he must be going mad, for he could not understand that twenty years of discipline could fall away like a lesson imparted to a bored child.

The house was as it had been described in the transcript of the trial. He noticed its layout without emotion or empathy, the long passage that ran from the front door to the door at the back where Painter's coat had hung, the kitchen, the narrow, wall-confined stairs. A kind of cerebral paralysis descended on him and he moved towards that back door, withdrawing the bolts numbly.

The garden was very still, overgrown, basking under a brazen sky. The light and the heat made him dizzy. At first he could not see the coach house at all. Then he realised he had been looking at it ever since he stepped into the garden, but what he had taken for a great quivering bush was in fact solid bricks and mortar hidden under a blanket of virginia creeper. He walked towards it, not interested, not in the least curious. He walked because it was something to do and because this house of a million faintly trembling leaves was at least a kind of goal.

The doors were fastened with a padlock. Archery was relieved. It deprived him of the need for any action. He leant against the wall and the leaves were cold and damp against his face. Presently he went down the drive and through the gateless entrance. Of course, the silver car would not be there. It wasn't. A bus came almost immediately. He had quite forgotten that he had omitted to lock the back door of Victor's Piece.

Archery returned the keys to the estate agent and lingered for a while looking at the photograph of the house he had just come from. It was like looking at the portrait of a girl you had known only as an old woman, and he wondered if it had perhaps been taken thirty years before when Mrs Primero had bought the house. Then he turned and walked slowly back to the hotel.

Half-past four was usually a dead time at the Olive and Dove. But this was a Saturday and a glorious Saturday at that. The dining room was full of trippers, the lounge decorously crowded with old residents and new arrivals, taking their tea from silver trays. Archery's heart began to beat fast as he saw his son in conversation with a man and a woman. Their backs were towards him and he saw only that the woman had long fair hair and that the man's head was dark.

He made his way between the armchairs, growing hot with

trepidation and weaving among beringed fingers holding teapots, little asthmatic dogs, pots of cress and pyramids of sandwiches. When the woman turned he should have felt relief. Instead bitter disappointment ran through him like a long thin knife. He put out his hand and clasped the warm fingers of Tess Kershaw.

Now he saw how stupid his first wild assumption had been. Kershaw was shaking hands with him now and the man's lively face, seamed all over with the wrinkles of animation, bore no resemblance at all to Roger Primero's waxen pallor. His hair was not really dark but thin and sprinkled with grey.

'Charles called in on us on his way back from town,' Tess said. She was perhaps the worst dressed woman in the room in her white cotton blouse and navy serge skirt. As if explaining this, she said quickly, 'When we heard his news we dropped everything and came back with him.' She got up, threaded her way to the window and looked out into the bright hot afternoon. When she came back she said, 'It feels so strange. I must have walked past here lots of times when I was little, but I can't remember it at all.'

Hand in hand with Painter perhaps. And while they walked, the murderer and his child, had Painter watched the traffic go by and thought of the way he could become part of that traffic? Archery tried not to see in the fine pointed face opposite his own, the coarse crude features of the man Alice Flower had called Beast. But then they were here to prove it had not been that way at all.

'News?' he said to Charles and he heard the note of distaste creep into his voice.

Charles told him. 'And then we all went to Victor's Piece,' he said. 'We didn't think we'd be able to get in, but someone had left the back door unlocked. We went all over the house and we saw that Primero could easily have hidden himself.'

Archery turned away slightly. The name was now invested with many associations, mostly agonising.

'He said good-bye to Alice, opened and closed the front door without actually going out of it, then he slipped into the dining room—nobody used the dining room and it was dark. Alice went out and . . .' Charles hesitated, searching for a form of words to spare Tess. 'And, after the coal was brought in, he came out, put on the raincoat that was left hanging on the back door and—well, did the deed.'

'It's only a theory, Charlie,' said Kershaw, 'but it fits the facts.'

'I don't know . . .' Archery began.

'Look, Father, don't you want Tess's father cleared?'

Not, thought Archery, if it means incriminating *her* husband. Not that. I may already have done her an injury, but I can't do her that injury.

'This motive you mentioned,' he said dully.

Tess broke in excitedly, 'It's a marvellous motive, a *real* motive.' He knew exactly what she meant. Ten thousand pounds was real, solid, a true temptation, while two hundred pounds . . . Her eyes shone, then saddened. Was she thinking that to hang a man wrongfully was as bad as killing an old woman for a bag of notes? And would that too remain with her all her life? No matter which way things fell out, could she ever escape?

'Primero was working in a solicitor's office,' Charles was saying excitedly. 'He would have known the law, he had all the facilities for checking. Mrs Primero might not have known about it, not if she didn't read the papers. Who knows about all the various Acts of Parliament that are going to be passed anyway? Primero's boss probably had a query about it from a client, sent him to look it up, and there you are. Primero would have known that if his grandmother died intestate before October 1950 all the money would come to him. But if she died after the Act his sisters would get two-thirds of it. I've been looking it all up. This is known as the Great Adoption Act, the law that gave adopted children almost equal rights with natural ones. *Of course* Primero knew.'

'What are you going to do?'

'I've been on to the police but Wexford can't see me before two on Monday. He's away for the weekend. I'll bet the police never checked Primero's movements. Knowing them, I'd say it's likely that as soon as they got hold of Painter they didn't trouble with anyone else.' He looked at Tess and took her hand. 'You can say what you like about this being a free country,' he said hotly, 'but you know as well as I do that everyone has a subconscious feeling that "working class" and "criminal class" are more or less synonymous. Why bother with the respectable, well-connected solicitor's clerk when you've already got your hands on the chauffeur?'

Archery shrugged. From long experience he knew it was useless to argue with Charles when he was airing his quasi-communist ideals.

'Thank you for your enthusiastic reception,' Charles said sarcastically. 'What is there to look so miserable about?'

Archery could not tell him. A load of sorrow seemed to have descended on him and in order to answer his son, he sorted out from conflicting pain something he could express to them all.

'I was thinking of the children,' he said, 'the four little girls who have all suffered from this crime.' He smiled at Tess. 'Tess, of course,' he went on, 'those two sisters you saw—and Elizabeth Crilling.'

He did not add the name of the grown woman who would suffer more than any of them if Charles was right.

12

Is it not lawful for me to do what I will with mine own?

The Gospel for Septuagesima Sunday.

The man who was shown into Wexford's office at nine on Monday morning was small and slender. The bones of his hands were particularly fine and with narrow delicate joints like a woman's. The dark grey suit he wore, very expensive looking and very sleek, made him look smaller than he actually was. He seemed to be surrounded, even so early in the morning and away from his own home, with a great many adjuncts of elegance. Wexford, who knew him well, was amused by the sapphire tie-pin, the two rings, the key chain with its heavy drop of chased—amber, was it?—the briefcase of some kind of reptile skin. How many years, he asked himself, was Roger Primero going to need to get used to wealth?

'Lovely morning,' said Wexford. 'I've just had a couple of days at Worthing and the sea was like a millpond. What can I do for you?'

'Catch a con man,' said Primero, 'a lousy little squirt posing as a journalist.' He unclipped the briefcase and flicked a Sunday newspaper across Wexford's desk. It slipped on the polished surface and fell to the floor. Raising his eyebrows, Wexford let it lie.

'Hell,' said Primero. 'There's nothing for you to see, anyway.' His glazed eyes had a sore look in the handsome expressionless face. The man's vanity had made him rebel against glasses at last, Wexford thought, blinking slightly behind his own heavy tortoiseshell frames. 'Look here, Chief Inspector, I don't mind telling you, I'm hopping mad. This is how it was. Mind if I smoke?'

'Not at all.'

A gold cigarette case spilled out from his pocket, followed by a holder and a lighter in peculiar black and gold mosaic. Wexford watched this production of props, wondering when it was going to end. The man is furnished like a room, he thought.

'This is how it was,' he said again. 'Character rang me up on Thursday, said he was on the *Planet* and wanted to do an article about me. My early life. You get the picture? I said he could come along on Friday and he did. I gave him a hell of a long interview, all the dope and the upshot of it was my wife asked him to lunch.' He screwed up his mouth and nose like a man smelling something offensive. 'Hell,' he said, 'I don't suppose he's ever seen a lunch like that in all his life . . .'

'But no article appeared and when you rang the *Planet* this morning they'd never heard of him.'

'How did you know?'

'It happens,' said Wexford dryly. 'I'm surprised at you, sir, a man of your experience. The time to ring the *Planet* was *Friday* morning.'

'It makes me feel such a frightful ass.'

Wexford said airily, 'No money passed, I daresay?'

'Hell, no!'

'Just the lunch, then, and you told him a lot of things you'd rather have left unsaid.'

'That's the thing.' His expression had been sulky, but suddenly he smiled and it was a likeable smile. Wexford had always rather liked him. 'Oh, hell's bells, Chief Inspector . . .'

'Hell's bells, as you say. Still, you were wise to come to us, though I don't know that we can do anything unless he makes a move . . .'

'A move? What d'you mean, a move?'

'Well, let me give you an example. Nothing personal, you understand. Just supposing a wealthy man, a man who is somewhat in the public eye, says something a shade indiscreet to a reputable journalist. Ten to one he can't use it because he's laying his paper open to libel action.' Wexford paused and gave the other man a penetrating look. 'But if he says those same indiscreet things to an impostor, a confidence trickster . . .' Primero had grown very pale. 'What's to stop the impostor following a few leads and ferreting out something really damaging. Most people,

Mr Primero, even decent law-abiding people, have something in their pasts they'd rather not have known. You have to ask yourself, if he's not on the level, what's he up to? The answer is either he's after your money or else he's crazy.' He added more kindly, 'In my experience nine out of ten of them are just crazy. Still, if it'll help to set your mind at rest perhaps you could give us a description. I suppose he gave you his name?'

'It wouldn't be his real name.'

'Naturally not.'

Primero leant confidingly towards him. During the course of his long career Wexford had found it valuable to make himself *au fait* with perfumes and he noticed that Primero smelt of Lentheric's Onyx.

'He seemed nice enough,' Primero began. 'My wife was quite taken with him.' His eyes had begun to water and he put his fingers very cautiously up to them. Wexford was reminded of a weeping woman who dare not rub her eyes for fear of smudging mascara. 'I haven't told her about this, by the way. I passed it off. Wouldn't want to upset her. He was well-spoken, Oxford accent and all that. A tall fair fellow, said his name was Bowman, Charles Bowman.'

'A-ha!' said Wexford but not aloud.

'Chief Inspector?'

'Mr Primero?'

'I've just remembered something. He was—well, he was extraordinarily interested in my grandmother.'

Wexford almost laughed.

'From what you've told me I think I can assure you there won't be any serious repercussions.'

'You think he's a nut?'

'Harmless, anyway.'

'You've taken a load off my mind.' Primero got up, retrieved his briefcase and picked up the newspaper. He did it rather awkwardly as if he was unused to performing even so simple a service for himself. 'I'll be more careful in future.'

'An ounce of prevention, you know.'

'Well, I won't take up any more of your time.' He pulled a long, but possibly sincerely sad face. The watering eyes added to his look of melancholy. 'Off to a funeral, as a matter of fact. Poor old Alice.'

Wexford had noticed the black tie on which the sapphire glowed darkly. He showed Primero to the door. Throughout the interview he had kept a solemn face. Now he permitted himself the indulgence of gargantuan, though almost silent, laughter.

There was nothing to do until two o'clock except sight-seeing. Charles had been out early and bought a guide book. They sat in the lounge studying it.

'It says here,' said Tess, 'that Forby is the fifth prettiest village in England.'

'Poor Forby,' said Charles. 'Damned with faint praise.'

Kershaw began organising them.

'How about all piling into my car . . .' He stuck his finger on the map '. . . and going down the Kingsbrook Road to Forby—keep clear of Forby Hall, eh, Charlie?—have a quick look at the church, and then on to Pomfret. Pomfret Grange is open every weekday in the summer—we might have a look over it—and back into Kingsmarkham along the main road.'

'Lovely,' said Tess.

Kershaw drove and Archery sat beside him. They followed the same route he had taken with Imogen Ide when she had come to put flowers on old Mrs Primero's grave. As they came within sight of the Kingsbrook he remembered what she had said about the implacability of water and how, notwithstanding the efforts of man, it continues to spring from the earth and seek the sea.

Kershaw parked the car by the green with the duckpond. The village looked peaceful and serene. Summer was not as yet so far advanced as to dull the fresh green of the beech trees or hang the wild clematis with its frowsty greyish beard. Knots of cottages surrounded the green and on the church side was a row of Georgian houses with bow windows whose dark panes glistened, showing chintz and silver within. There were just three shops, a post office, a butcher's with a canopy and white colonnade, and a place selling souvenirs for tourists. The cottagers' Monday morning wash hung drying in the windless warm air.

They sat on the seat on the green and Tess fed the ducks from a packet of biscuits she had found on the shelf under the dashboard. Kershaw produced a camera and began taking photographs.

Suddenly Archery knew he did not want to go any further with them. He almost shivered with distaste at the thought of trailing round the galleries of Pomfret Grange, gasping with false pleasure at the china and pretending to admire family portraits.

'Would you mind if I stayed here? I'd like to have another look at the church.'

Charles glared. 'We'll all go and look at the church.'

'I can't, darling,' said Tess. 'I can't go into a church in jeans.'

'Not in these trousers,' Kershaw quipped. He put away his camera. 'We'd better get moving if we're going to see the stately home.'

'I can easily go back on the bus,' said Archery.

'Well, for God's sake, don't be late, Father.'

If it was going to be any more than a sentimental journey, he too would need a guide. When the car had gone he made his way into the souvenir shop. A bell rang sweetly as he opened the door and a woman came out from a room at the back.

'We don't keep a guide to St Mary's, but you'll find them on sale inside the church door.'

Now he was here he ought to buy something. A postcard? A little brooch for Mary? That, he thought, would be the worst kind of infidelity, to commit adultery in your heart every time you saw your wife wearing a keepsake. He looked drearily at the horse brasses, the painted jugs, the trays of costume jewellery.

A small counter was devoted entirely to calendars, wooden plaques with words on them in pokerwork, framed verses. One of these, a little picture on a card, showing a haloed shepherd with a lamb, caught his eye because the words beneath the drawing were familiar.

'Go, Shepherd, to your rest . . .'

The woman was standing behind him.

'I see you're admiring the efforts of our local bard,' she said brightly. 'He was just a boy when he died and he's buried here.'

'I've seen his grave,' said Archery.

'Of course a lot of people who come here are under the impression he was a shepherd, you know. I always have to explain that at one time shepherd and poet meant the same thing.'

'Lycidas,' said Archery.

She ignored the interruption. 'Actually he was very well-educated. He'd been to High School and everyone said he should have gone to college. He was killed in a road accident. Would you like to see his photograph?'

She produced a stack of cheap framed photographs from a drawer beneath the counter. They were all identical and each bore the legend: John Grace, Bard of Forby. Those whom God loves, die young.

It was a fine ascetic face, sharp-featured and ultra-sensitive. It also, Archery considered, gave the impression that its owner suffered from pernicious anaemia. He had a curious feeling that he had seen it somewhere before.

'Was any of his work published?'

'One or two bits in magazines, that's all. I don't know the ins and outs of it because I've only been here ten years, but there was a publisher who had a week-end cottage here and he was very keen on making his poetry into a book when the poor boy died. Mrs Grace—his mother, you know— was all for it, but the thing was most of the stuff he'd written had disappeared. There were just these bits you see here. His mother said he'd written whole plays—they didn't rhyme, if you know what I mean, but they were kind of like Shakespeare. Anyway, they couldn't be found. Maybe he'd burnt them or given them away. It does seem a shame, though, doesn't it?'

Archery glanced out of the window towards the little wooden church. 'Some mute inglorious Milton here may rest . . .' he murmured.

'That's right,' said the woman. 'You never know, they may turn up, like the Dead Sea Scrolls.'

Archery paid five and sixpence for the picture of the shepherd and the lamb and strolled up towards the church. He opened the kissing gate and, walking in a clockwise direction, made for the door. What was it she had said? 'You must never go widdershins around a church. It's unlucky.' He needed luck for Charles and for himself. The irony was that however things fell out, one of them would lose.

There was no music coming from the church, but as the door opened he saw that some sort of service was in progress. For a moment he stood, looking at the people and listening to the words.

'If after the manner of men I have fought with beasts at Ephesus, what advantageth it me, if the dead rise not?'

It was a funeral. They were almost exactly half way through the service for the burial of the dead.

'Let us eat and drink for tomorrow we die . . .'

The door gave a slight whine as he closed it. Now, as he turned, he could see the funeral cars, three of them, outside the other gate. He went to look again at Grace's grave, passed the newly dug trench where this latest coffin was to be laid, and finally sat down on a wooden seat in a shady corner. It was a quarter to twelve. Give it half an hour, he thought, and then he would have to go for his bus. Presently he dozed.

The sound of gentle footfalls awakened him. He opened his eyes and saw that they were carrying the coffin out of the church. It was supported by four bearers, but it was a small coffin, a child's perhaps or a short woman's. On it were a few bunches of flowers and a huge wreath of madonna lilies.

The bearers were followed by a dozen people, the procession being headed by a man and a woman walking side by side. Their backs were towards Archery and besides that the woman, dressed in a black coat, wore a large black hat whose brim curved about her face. But he would have known her anywhere. He would have known her if he were blind and deaf, by her presence and her essence. They could not see him, had no idea they were watched, these mourners who had come to bury Alice Flower.

The other followers were mostly old, friends of Alice's perhaps, and one woman looked as if she must be the matron of the Infirmary. They gathered at the graveside and the vicar began to speak the words that would finally commit the old servant to the ground. Primero bent down and, taking rather fastidiously a handful of black earth, cast it on to the coffin. His shoulders shook and a little hand in a black glove reached out and rested on his arm. Archery felt a savage stab of jealousy that took away his breath.

The vicar spoke the Collect and blessed them. Then Primero went a little way apart with him, they spoke together and shook hands. He took his wife's arm and they walked slowly towards the gate where the cars were. It was all over.

When they were out of sight Archery got up and approached the gradually filling grave. He could smell the lilies five yards off. A card was attached to them and on it someone had written simply: 'From Mr and Mrs Roger, with love.'

'Good day,' he said to the sexton.

'Good day, sir. Lovely day.'

It was gone a quarter past twelve. Archery hurried towards the kissing gate, wondering how often the buses ran. As he came out from under the arch of trees, he stopped suddenly. Charles was striding towards him up the sandy lane.

'Good thing you didn't come,' Charles called. 'The place was shut for redecorating. Can you beat it? We thought we might as well drift back and pick you up.'

'Where's the car?'

'Round the other side of the church.'

They would be gone by now. Just the same Archery wished he were safely back at the Olive and Dove eating cold beef and salad. As they rounded the yew hedge a black car passed them. He forced himself to look towards the gate. The Primeros were still there, talking to the matron. His throat grew suddenly dry.

'Let's cut across the green,' he said urgently.

'Mr Kershaw happens to be waiting on this side.'

They were now only a few yards from the Primeros. The matron shook hands and stepped into a hired limousine. Primero turned and his eyes met those of Charles.

He grew first white, then a curious vinegary purple. Charles went on walking towards him and then Primero too began to move. They were approaching each other menacingly, ridiculously, like two gunmen in a Western.

'Mr Bowman, of the *Sunday Planet*, I believe?'

Charles stopped and said coolly. 'You can believe what you like.'

She had been talking to the women in the car. Now she withdrew her head and the car began to move off. They were alone, the four of them, in the centre of the fifth prettiest village in England. She looked at Archery first with embarrassment, then with a warmth that conquered her awkwardness.

'Why, hallo, I . . .'

Primero snatched at her arm. 'Recognise him? I shall need you for a witness, Imogen.'

Charles glared. 'You what?'

'Charles!' said Archery sharply.

'Do you deny that you made your way into my home under false pretences?'

'Roger, Roger . . .' She was still smiling, but her smile had grown stiff. 'Don't you remember we met Mr Archery at the dance? This is his son. He's a journalist, but he uses a pseudonym, that's all. They're here on holiday.'

Charles said rigidly, 'I'm afraid that isn't quite true, Mrs Primero.' She blinked, her lashes fluttering like wings, and her gaze came to rest softly on Archery's face. 'My father and I came here with the express purpose of collecting certain information. That we have done. In order to do it we had to make our way into your confidence. Perhaps we have been unscrupulous, but we thought the end justified the means.'

'I'm afraid I don't understand.' Her eyes were still on Archery and he was unable to draw his own away. He knew that his face registered a tremendous plea for forgiveness, a disclaimer of Charles's statement, and also registered the agony of love. There was, however, no reason why she should read there anything but guilt. 'I don't understand at all. What information?'

'I'll tell you . . .' Charles began, but Primero interrupted him.

'Since you're so frank, you won't have any objection to coming down to the police station right now and laying your "information" before Chief Inspector Wexford.'

'None at all,' Charles drawled, 'except that it happens to be my lunchtime and in any case I have an appointment with the Chief Inspector already. At two sharp. I intend to tell him, Mr Primero, just how opportunely for you your grandmother died, how—oh, perfectly legally, I admit—you managed to cheat your sisters out of their inheritance, and how you concealed yourself in Victor's Piece on a certain evening in December sixteen years ago.'

'You're out of your mind!' Primero shouted.

Archery found his voice. 'That's enough, Charles.' He heard her speak, a tiny disembodied sound.

'It isn't true!' And then, terribly afraid. 'It isn't true, is it?'

'I'm damned if I'll argue it out in the street with this crook!'

'Of course it's true.'

'It was all above board.' Primero suddenly broke. They were all hot, standing there in the noon sun, but only Primero's face showed actual sweat, water drops on the cheesy sallow skin. 'Hell, it was a matter of law,' he blustered. 'What's it got to do with you, anyway? Who *are* you?'

Without taking her gaze from Archery, she took her husband's arm. All the gaiety had left her face and she looked almost old, a faded blonde who was effaced by her black clothes. Because she had become ugly she suddenly seemed for the first time within Archery's reach, yet she had never been farther from it. 'Let's go home, Roger.' Her mouth trembled and cobweb lines had appeared at its corners. 'In the course of your enquiries, Mr Archery,' she said, 'I hope you managed to combine pleasure with business.'

Then they were gone. Charles gave a great gasp.

'I must say I rather enjoyed that. I suppose by pleasure she meant the lunch they gave me. You can rely on these tycoons' wives to tot up every egg in the caviare. Still it was hard on her. You needn't look so shattered, Father. It's awfully middle-class to have a phobia about scenes.'

13

I deal with the thing that is lawful and right . . . and all false ways I utterly abhor.

Psalm 119, appointed for the 26th Day.

'Public General Acts and Measures, 1950.' Wexford took the book—was it a White Paper? Archery was ashamed to confess that he did not know—and read the title aloud. 'There's something here you want me to look at?'

Charles found the page for him. 'Here.' Wexford began to read. The silence was tense, almost agonised. Archery looked surreptitiously at the others, Charles who was flushed with eagerness, Kershaw trying to sit casually, but whose bright darting eyes betrayed his anxiety, Tess who looked confident, serene. Was it her mother in whom she trusted so completely or was it Charles? A good deal of Charles's poise had deserted him when, on entering the office five minutes before, he had had to introduce Tess to the Chief Inspector.

'Miss Kershaw,' he had said, 'my . . . the girl I'm going to marry. I . . .'

'Ah, yes.' Wexford had been very urbane. 'Good afternoon, Miss Kershaw, Mr Kershaw. Won't you sit down? Heatwave's coming to an end at last, I'm afraid.'

And indeed a change had come over the bright blue un-English sky. It had begun just after lunch with the appearance of a cloud that was truly no bigger than a man's hand, and this cloud had been followed by more, driven by a sudden wind. Now, as Wexford, frowning a little, read steadily, Archery contemplated the window from which the yellow blind had been fully raised, and through it the lumpy blotchy mass of cumulus, hollowed and pock-marked with grey.

'Very interesting,' said Wexford, 'and new to me. I didn't know the Primero sisters were adopted. Convenient for Primero.'

'Convenient?' said Charles. Archery sighed within himself. He could always tell when his son was going to be rude or what Charles himself called forthright. 'Is that all you've got to say?'

'No,' said Wexford. Few people have the confidence and the restraint to say 'yes' or 'no' without qualification. Wexford was big and heavy and ugly; his suit had seen better days, too many wet ones and too many hot dusty ones, but he radiated strength. 'Before we go any further on this tack, Mr Archery,' he said to Charles, 'I'd like to say that I've had a complaint about you from Mr Primero.'

'Oh, that.'

'Yes, that. I've been aware for some days that your father had made the acquaintance of the Primeros. Perhaps it wasn't a bad idea and I'm sure it wasn't an unpleasant one to do so through Mrs Primero.' Archery knew his face had become white. He felt sick. 'And let me say in all fairness,' Wexford went on, 'that I told him it was all right as far as I was concerned to make contact with the people concerned in the Primero case.' He glanced briefly at Tess who didn't move. 'Make contact, I said, not make trouble. Your little escapade on Friday is what I call making trouble and that I won't have!'

Charles said sulkily, 'All right, I'm sorry.' Archery saw that he had to justify himself before Tess. 'You're not going to tell me that your people don't occasionally invent a cover story to get what they want.'

'My people,' Wexford snapped, 'happen to have the law on their side.' He added grandiloquently, 'They *are* the law.' The frown thawed. 'Now we've got the lecture over you'd better tell me just what you and your father have found out.'

Charles told him. Wexford listened patiently, but as the evidence against Primero mounted, instead of surprise, his face registered a strange blankness. The heavy features had become brutish, like those of an old bull.

'Of course, you'll say he had an alibi,' said Charles. 'I realise your people would have checked his alibi and after all these years it's going to be difficult to crack, but . . .'

'His alibi was not checked,' said Wexford.

'What did you say?'

'His alibi was not checked.'

'I don't understand.'

'Mr Archery . . .' Wexford got up and rested his massive hands on the desk, but he didn't move away from behind it. 'I am quite happy to discuss this whole matter with you, answer any questions you may like to ask.' He paused. 'But not in the presence of Miss Kershaw. If I may say so, I think you were unwise to bring her with you.'

Now it was Charles's turn to get to his feet.

'Miss Kershaw is going to be my wife,' he said hotly. 'Anything you say to me you can say to her. I won't have any secrets from her in this.'

Casually Wexford sat down again. He drew a bunch of papers from a desk drawer and began to study them. Then he lifted his eyes slowly and said: 'I'm sorry this has been a fruitless interview for you. With a little co-operation I think I could have saved you a lot of useless enquiry. But, if you'll forgive me, I'm a very busy man so I'll say good afternoon.'

'No,' said Tess suddenly. 'I'll go. I'll wait in the car.'

'Tess!'

'Of course I'm going, darling. Don't you see? He can't talk about my father in front of me. Oh, darling, be your age!'

He is being his age, thought Archery miserably. Wexford knew something—something that was going to be horrible. But why was he playing this pouncing cat and mouse game with them all, why had he played it with Archery all along? Confidence and strength—but did it cover a fierce inverted snobbism, a fear that the Archeries might shake his authority and trouble the still waters of his district? And yet the man held such sway and was, beyond a doubt, a good, just man. He would never lie or even shift truth to cover a lapse. 'His alibi was not checked . . .' If only they would stop fencing!

Then, suddenly, Wexford stopped it.

'No need to leave the building, Miss Kershaw,' he said. 'If your—your father would care to take you upstairs—straight along the corridor and turn left when you come to the double doors—you'll find we've got quite a reasonable canteen, even for a lady. I suggest a cup of strong tea and an eccles cake.'

'Thanks.' Tess turned and just touched Kershaw's shoulder. He rose at once. Wexford closed the door after them.

Charles took a deep breath, and making a brave attempt to lounge casually in his chair, said, 'All right, then. What about this alibi that for some mysterious reason was never investigated?'

'The reason,' said Wexford, 'was not mysterious. Mrs Primero was killed between six-twenty-five and seven o'clock on the evening of Sunday, September 24th, 1950.' He paused to allow Charles's inevitable interruption of 'Yes, yes', uttered with fierce impatience. 'She was killed in Kingsmarkham and at six-thirty Roger Primero was seen in Sewingbury five miles away.'

'Oh, he was seen, was he?' Charles scoffed, crossing his legs. 'What do you think, Father? Doesn't it seem remotely possible to you that he could have fixed it beforehand that he'd be "seen"? There's always some shifty mate who'll perjure himself and say he's seen you for twenty quid.'

'Some shifty mate, eh?' Wexford was now hardly bothering to conceal his amusement.

'Somebody saw him. All right. Who saw him?'

Wexford sighed and the smile was erased.

'I saw him,' he said.

It was a blow in the face. Archery's love for his son, dormant over the past days, rose within his breast in a hot tide. Charles said nothing, and Archery who had been doing this sort of thing rather a lot lately, tried hard not to hate Wexford. He had taken an unconscionable time coming to the point, but this, of course, was his revenge.

The big elbows rested on the desk, the fingers meeting and pressing together in an implacable pyramid of flesh. The law incarnate. If Wexford had seen Primero that night, there was no gainsaying it, for here was incorruptibility. It was almost as if God had seen him. Horrified, Archery pulled himself up in his chair and gave a dry painful cough.

'You?' said Charles at last.

'I,' said Wexford, 'with my little eye.'

'You might have told us before!'

'I would have,' said Wexford mildly and, oddly enough,

believably, 'if I'd had the remotest idea you suspected him. Chatting up Primero about his grandmother was one thing, pinning murder on him quite another.'

Polite now, stiff and very formal, Charles asked, 'Would you mind telling us the details?'

Wexford's courtesy matched his. 'Not at all. I intend to. Before I do, however, I'd better say that there was no question of hindsight. I knew Primero. I'd seen him in court with his chief on a good many occasions. He used to go along with him to learn the ropes.' Charles nodded, his face set. Archery thought he knew what was going on in his mind. Loss was something he knew about, too.

'I was in Sewingbury on a job,' Wexford continued, 'and I'd got a date to meet a man who sometimes gave us a bit of information. What you might call a shifty mate, but we never got twenty quidsworth out of him. The appointment was for six at a pub called the Black Swan. Well, I had a word with my—my friend, and I was due back in Kingsmarkham at seven. I walked out of the public bar at just on half past six and ran slap bang into Primero.

'"Good evening, Inspector," he said, and I thought he looked a bit lost. As well he might. I found out afterwards that he'd been going to meet some pals, but he'd got the wrong pub. They were waiting for him at The Black Bull. "Are you on duty?" he said. "Or can I buy you a short snort?"'

Archery nearly smiled. Wexford had given a very fair imitation of the absurd slang Primero still affected after sixteen years of affluence.

'"Thanks all the same," I said, "but I'm late as it is." "Good night to you, then," he said and he went up to the bar. I'd only been in Kingsmarkham ten minutes when I got called out to Victor's Piece.'

Charles got up slowly and extended a stiff, mechanical hand.

'Thank you very much, Chief Inspector. I think that's all anyone can say on the subject, don't you?' Wexford leaned across the desk and took his hand. A faint flash of compassion softened his features, weakened them, and was gone. 'I'm sorry I wasn't very polite just now,' Charles said.

'That's all right,' said Wexford. 'This is a police station, not a clerical garden party.' He hesitated and added, 'I'm sorry, too.' And Archery knew that the apology had nothing to do with Charles's ill manners.

Tess and Charles began to argue even before they had all got into the car. Certain that they had said it all or something very like it before, Archery listened to them indifferently. He had kept silent for half an hour and still there was nothing he could say.

'We have to be realistic about it,' Charles was saying. 'If I don't mind and Mother and Father don't mind, why can't we just get married and forget you ever had a father?'

'Who says they don't mind? That's not being realistic, anyway. I'm being realistic. One way and another I've had a lot of luck . . .' Tess flashed a quick watery smile at Kershaw. 'I've had more than anyone would have thought possible, but this is one bit I have to dip out on.'

'And what does that mean exactly?'

'Just that—well, it was ridiculous ever to imagine we could be married, you and I.'

'You and I? What about all the others who'll come along and fancy you? Are you going to go through the same melodrama with them or d'you think you'll weaken when the thirties rear their ugly heads?'

She winced at that. Archery thought Charles had almost forgotten they were not alone. He pushed her into the back seat of the car and banged the door.

'I'm curious, you see,' Charles went on, bitterly sarcastic. 'I'd just like to know if you've taken a vow of perpetual chastity. O God, it's like a feature in the *Sunday Planet*—Condemned to lonely spinsterhood for father's crime! Just for the record, since I'm supposed to be so far above you morally, I'd like to know the qualifications the lucky man has to have. Give me a specification, will you?'

Her mother had built up her faith, but the Archery family with their doubts had knocked it down; still it had lived until Wexford had killed it. Her eyes were fixed on Kershaw who had given her reality. Archery was not surprised when she said hysterically:

'I suppose he'd have to have a murderer for a father.' She

gasped, for she was admitting it to herself for the first time. 'Like me!'

Charles tapped Archery's back. 'Just nip out and knock someone off,' he said outrageously.

'Oh, shut up,' said Kershaw. 'Give it a rest, Charlie, will you?'

Archery touched his arm. 'I think I'll get out, if you don't mind. I need some air.'

'Me too,' said Tess. 'I can't stand being boxed up in here any longer and I've got a ghastly head. I want some aspirins.'

'Can't park here.'

'We'll walk back to the hotel, Daddy. If I don't get out I'll pass out.'

Then they were all three on the pavement, Charles's face as black as thunder. Tess swayed a little and Archery caught her arm to steady her. Several passers-by gave them curious looks.

'You said you wanted aspirins,' said Charles.

It was only a few yards to the nearest chemist's, but Tess was shivering in her thin clothes. The air was heavy and cloying. Archery noticed that all the shopkeepers had furled their sun-blinds.

Charles seemed about to begin again but she gave him a pleading look, 'Don't let's talk about it any more. We've said it all. I needn't see you again till October, not then if we're careful . . .'

He frowned silently, made a little gesture of repudiation. Archery held the shop door open for Tess to pass through.

There was no one inside but the assistant and Elizabeth Crilling.

She did not appear to be buying anything, just waiting and gossiping with the shopgirl. It was the middle of a weekday afternoon and here she was shopping. What had become of the job in the 'ladies' wear establishment'? Archery wondered if she would recognise him and how he could avoid this happening, for he did not want to have to introduce her to Tess. It gave him a little thrill of awe when he realised what was happening in this small town shop, a meeting after sixteen years of the child who was Painter's daughter and the child who had discovered Painter's crime.

While he hovered near the door. Tess went up to the counter. They were so close together that they were almost touching.

Then Tess reached across in front of Liz Crilling to select one of the aspirin bottles, and in doing so brushed her sleeve.

'I beg your pardon.'

'That's O.K.'

Archery could see Tess had nothing smaller than a ten shilling note. His trepidation, his fears for the effect of illumination on Tess at this moment were so great, that he almost cried aloud, 'Never mind. Leave it! Only, please God, let us all get away and hide ourselves!'

'Haven't you anything smaller?'

'I'm sorry.'

'I'll just go and see if we've got any change.'

The two young women stood side by side in silence. Tess stared straight in front of her, but Liz Crilling was playing nervously with two little scent bottles displayed on a glass shelf, moving them about as if they were chessmen.

Then the pharmacist in his white coat came out from the back.

'Is there a Miss Crilling waiting for a prescription?'

Tess turned, her face flooded with colour.

'This is a repeat prescription, but I'm afraid it's no longer valid...'

'What d'you mean, no longer valid?'

'I mean that it can only be used six times. I can't let you have any more of these tablets without a fresh prescription. If your mother...'

'The old cow,' said Liz Crilling slowly.

The swift animation on Tess's face died as if she had been struck. Without opening her purse she tumbled the change loose into her handbag and hurried out of the shop.

The old cow. It was her fault, everything bad that had ever happened to you was her fault—beginning with the beautiful pink dress.

She was making it for you and she worked at the sewing machine all day that cold wet Sunday. When it was finished you put it on and Mummy brushed your hair and put a ribbon in it.

'I'll just pop over and show you off to Granny Rose,' Mummy said and she popped over, but when she came back she was cross because Granny Rose was asleep and hadn't heard when she'd tapped on the window.

'Give it half an hour,' Daddy said, 'and maybe she'll be awake then.' He was half asleep himself, lying in bed, white and thin on the pillows. So Mummy had stayed upstairs with him, giving him his medicine and reading to him because he was too weak to hold a book.

'You stay in the sitting room, Baby, and mind you don't get that frock dirty.'

You had done as you were told but it made you cry just the same. Of course you didn't care about not seeing Granny Rose, but you knew that while she was talking to Mummy you could have slipped out into the passage and down the garden to show it to Tessie, now, while it was brand-new.

Well, why not? Why not put on a coat and run across the road? Mummy wouldn't come down for half an hour. But you would have to hurry, for Tessie always went to bed at half-past six. Auntie Rene was strict about that. 'Respectable working class,' Mummy said, whatever that meant, and although she might let you into Tessie's bedroom she wouldn't let you wake her up.

But why, why, why had you gone?

Elizabeth Crilling came out of the shop and walked blindly towards the Glebe Road turning, bumping into shoppers as she went. Such a long way to go, past the hateful little sand houses that were like desert tombs in this spectral form light, such a long long way . . . And there was only one thing left to do when you got to the end of the road.

14

> It is lawful for Christian men . . . to wear weapons and serve in the wars.
>
> *The Thirty-nine Articles.*

The letter with the Kendal postmark was awaiting Archery on the hall table when they got back to the Olive and Dove. He glanced at it uncomprehendingly, then remembered. Colonel Cosmo Plashet, Painter's commanding officer.

'What now?' he said to Charles when Tess had gone upstairs to lie down.

'I don't know. They're going back to Purley tonight.'

'Do we go back to Thringford tonight?'

'I don't know, Father. I tell you I don't know.' He paused, irritable, pink in the face, a lost child. 'I'll have to go and apologise to Primero,' he said, the child remembering its manners. 'It was a bloody awful way to behave to him.'

Archery said it instinctively, without thinking. 'I'll do that, if you like. I'll ring them.'

'Thanks. If he insists on seeing me I'll go. You've talked to her before, haven't you? I gathered from something Wexford said.'

'Yes, I've talked to her, but I didn't know who she was.'

'That,' said Charles, severe again, 'is you all over.'

Was he really going to ring her up and apologise? And why should he have the vanity to suppose that she would even come to the phone? 'In the course of your enquiries, Mr Archery, I hope you managed to combine pleasure with business.' She was bound to have told her husband what she had meant by that. How the middle-aged clergyman had suddenly gone sentimental on her. He could hear Primero's reply, his colloquialism, 'Didn't actually make the old pass, did he?' and her light dismissive laughter. His soul cringed. He went into the empty lounge and ripped open Colonel Plashet's letter.

It was handwritten on rough white vellum almost as thick as cartridge paper. By the occasional fading of the ink from deep black to pale grey Archery could tell that the writer had not used a fountain pen. An old man's hand, he thought, a military man's address, 'Srinagar', Church Street, Kendal . . .

Dear Mr Archery, he read,

I was interested to receive your letter and will do my best to provide you with what information I can on Private Herbert Arthur Painter. You may be aware that I was not called to give evidence as to character at Painter's trial, though I held myself in readiness to do so should it have been necessary. Fortunately I have retained in my possession certain notes I then made. I say fortunately, for you will appreciate that Private Painter's war service covered a period of from twenty-three to twenty years ago, and my memory is no longer what I should like it to be. Lest you should be under the impression, however, that I am the possessor of information sympathetic to Painter's relatives, I must reluctantly disabuse your mind. In deciding not to call me, Painter's defending counsel must have been aware that any statements I could truthfully have made would, instead of assisting their cause, have merely made the task of prosecution easier.

That was it, then. There would follow only another loathsome catalogue to Painter's propensities. Colonel Plashet's very idiosyncratic style and writing brought home to him more forcibly than the cold print of the transcript had done, the kind of man Charles was prepared to accept as a father-in-law. Curiosity, not hope, made him read on.

Painter had been serving with His Majesty's Forces for one year when he entered my regiment. This was shortly prior to our embarkation for Burma as part of the Fourteenth Army. He was a most unsatisfactory soldier. We saw no action until we had been in Burma for three months, during which time Painter was twice put on a charge for being drunk and disorderly and sentenced to seven days' detention for gross insolence on an officer.

In action his manner and bearing improved considerably. He was a naturally pugnacious man, brave and aggressive. Soon after this, however, an incident occurred in the village in which we had our camp and a young Burmese woman was killed. A Court Martial was held before which Painter was charged with her manslaughter. He was found not guilty. I think I had better say no more on this matter.

In February 1945, six months before the cessation of hostilities in the Far East, Painter succumbed to a certain tropical affliction which manifests itself in severe ulceration of the legs, accelerated, I am told by his complete disregard of certain elementary hygienic precautions and his refusal to take a proper diet. He became seriously ill and responded badly to treatment. There was at this time a troopship lying off Calcutta, and as soon as Painter's condition allowed, he and certain other sick men were transported there by air. This troopship reached a United Kingdom port during the latter part of March, 1945.

I have no further information as to Painter's fate except that I believe he was shortly afterwards demobilised on health grounds.

If you have any other questions whatsoever to put to me regarding Painter's war service, you may be assured of my willingness to answer them to the best of my ability and discretion. You have my full permission to publish this letter. May I, however, ask your indulgence to an old man's whim, and request a copy of your book when it comes out?

Yours sincerely,

Cosmo Plashet

They all assumed he was writing a book. Archery smiled a little at the colonel's grandiose style, but there was nothing to smile at in the brief lines about the Burmese woman's death. The colonel's guarded, 'I think I had better say no more on this matter . . .' told him more than a page of explanations.

Nothing new, nothing vital. Why, then, did he have this urgent sensation of having missed something of importance? But no, he couldn't see it . . . He looked again, not knowing what he was looking for. Then, as he stared at the spidery loops and whorls, he was engulfed by a hot wave of trepidation and longing. He was afraid to speak to her, yet he longed to hear her voice.

He looked up, surprised to find how dark it had become. The summer afternoon sky simulated dusk with its covering of slate-coloured cloud. Over the housetops away to the east it was leaden tinged with angry purple and as Archery began to fold the letter, a vivid flash of lightning shocked across the room, flashing the words on the paper into relief and bleaching his hands livid white. The thunder followed it as he reached the stairs, and echoes were still curling and growling round the old building when he entered his bedroom.

She could only refuse to speak to him. She wouldn't even have to do that herself, for she could send the Italian butler. There was no question of her berating or reproaching him personally —she could do it with far more crushing effect by proxy.

'Forby Hall. Mr Primero's residence.'

It *was* the butler. The Italian accent distorted every word except the name to which it gave true Latin emphasis.

'I should like to speak to Mrs Primero.'

'What name shall I say, sir?'

'Henry Archery.'

Perhaps she would not be with her husband when the message came. People situated as they were in an enormous house of many rooms tended to live individual lives, he in the library, she in the drawing room. She would send the butler back with a message. As a foreigner the butler would be without that intimate feel for the nuances of English and that would give her scope. She could tell him to say something subtle and apparently polite and he would not appreciate the cutting sting that underlay the words. He heard footsteps, echoing footsteps across the big hall Charles had described. The phone crackled, perhaps because of the storm.

'Hallo?'

Out of a bone-dry throat he tried to speak. Why hadn't he rehearsed something? Because he had been so sure she wouldn't come?

'Hallo, are you still there?'

'Mrs Primero . . .'

'I thought you might have got fed-up with waiting. Mario took so long about it.'

'Of course I waited.' Rain burst against his window, smacking and sobbing at the glass. 'I want to apologise to you for this morning. It was unforgivable.'

'Oh, no,' she said. 'I've forgiven you—for this morning. You didn't really take any part in it, did you? It was the other times that seem so—well, not unforgivable, just incomprehensible.'

He could imagine her little helpless gesture, the white hands spreading out.

'One doesn't like to feel one's been used, you see. It's not that I'm hurt. I'm not likely to be hurt because I'm really very tough, much tougher than Roger. But I am a bit spoilt and I feel as if I've been kicked off my pedestal. Good for me, I expect.'

Archery said slowly, 'There's so much to explain. I thought I could explain on the phone, but now I find I can't.' And yet the violence of the storm made it easier for him. He could hardly hear his own words. 'I want to *see* you,' he said, forgetting his promise.

Apparently she had forgotten it too. 'You can't come here,' she said practically, 'because Roger's somewhere about and he might not look on your apology in the same light as I do. And I can't come to you because the Olive and Dove, being a respectable hostelry, doesn't allow visitors in residents' bedrooms.' He made an inarticulate murmur. 'That's the second cheap thing I've said to you today,' she said. 'Oh, my dear, you wouldn't want to talk in the lounge among all the fuddy-duddies, would you? I know, what about Victor's Piece?'

'It's locked,' he said, adding stupidly, 'and it's raining.'

'I've got a key. Roger's always kept one. Shall we say eight? The Olive will be only too happy if you have an early dinner.'

He dropped the receiver almost guiltily as Charles put his head round the door. And yet the telephone call had not been clandestine but made at Charles's instigation.

'I think I've made it all right with the Primeros,' he said, and he reflected on words from an unremembered source. God gave men tongues that they might conceal their thoughts.

But Charles, with the quixotry of youth, had lost interest. 'Tess and her father are just off,' he said.

'I'll come down.'

They were standing in the hall, waiting. For what? Archery wondered. The storm to cease? A miracle? Or just to say good-bye?

'I wish we hadn't seen Elizabeth Crilling,' Tess said. 'And yet now I wish I'd talked to her.'

'Just as well you didn't,' said Archery. 'You're worlds apart.

The only thing you'd have in common is your age. You're both twenty-one.'

'Don't wish away my life,' Tess said oddly and he saw there were tears in her eyes. 'I'm not twenty-one till October.' She picked up the duffel bag that served her as a weekend case and held out her hand to Archery.

'We must love you and leave you,' said Kershaw. 'Doesn't seem anything more to be said, does there, Mr Archery? I know you hoped things would work out, but it wasn't to be.'

Charles was gazing at Tess. She kept her eyes averted.

'For God's sake say I can write to you.'

'What's the use?'

'It would give me pleasure,' he said tightly.

'I shan't be at home. I'm going to Torquay to stay with my aunt the day after tomorrow.'

'You won't be camping on the beach, will you? This aunt, doesn't she have an address?'

'I haven't got a piece of paper,' said Tess and Archery saw that she was near to tears. He felt in his pocket, pulled out first Colonel Plashet's letter—not that, not for Tess to see—then the illuminated card with the verse and the picture of the shepherd. Her eyes were misted and she scrawled the address quickly, handing it to Charles without a word.

'Come on, lovey,' said Kershaw. 'Home, and don't spare the horses.' He fished out his car keys. 'All fifteen of them,' he said, but no one smiled.

15

> If he hath offended any other . . . ask them forgiveness; and where he hath done injury or wrong to any man . . . make amends to the uttermost of his power.
>
> *The Visitation of the Sick.*

It was raining so heavily that he had to dash from the car into the dilapidated porch and even there the rain caught him, blown by the gusty wind and tossed in icy droplets off the evergreens. He leant against the door and staggered because it gave with his weight and swung noisily open.

She must have arrived already. The Flavia was nowhere to be seen and he felt a shiver of self-disgust and trepidation when it occurred to him that she was being purposely discreet. She was well known in the district, she was married and she was having a secret meeting with a married man. So she had hidden her conspicuous car. Yes, it was cheap, cheap and sordid, and he, a priest of God, had engineered it.

Victor's Piece, dry and rotten in drought, smelt wet and rotten now the rain had come. It smelt of fungus and dead things. There were probably rats under these knotted flaking floorboards. He closed the door and walked a little way down the passage, wondering where she was and why she had not come out to him when she heard the door. Then he stopped, for he was facing the back door where Painter's raincoat had hung, and there was a raincoat hanging there now.

Certainly nothing had hung there on his previous visit to the house. He moved up to the raincoat, fascinated and rather horrified.

Of course, it was obvious what had happened. Someone had bought the place at last, the workmen had been in and one of them had left his raincoat. Nothing to be alarmed about. His nerves must be very bad.

'Mrs Primero,' he said, and then, because you do not call women with whom you have secret assignations by their surnames, 'Imogen! Imogen!'

There was no answer. And yet he was sure he was not alone in the house. What about knowing her if you were deaf and blind, jeered a voice within him, what about knowing her by her essence? He opened the dining room door, then the drawing room. A damp cold smell came to meet him. Water had leaked under the window sill and formed a spreading pool, dark in colour, hideously evocative. This and the rusty veining on the marble of the fireplace recalled to him splashed blood. Who would buy this place? Who could bear it? But someone had bought it for there was a workman's coat hanging behind the door . . .

Here she had sat, the old woman, and bade Alice go to church. Here she had sat, her eyes closing easily into sleep, when Mrs Crilling had come tapping at the window. Then he had come, whoever he was, with his axe and perhaps she had still been sleeping, on and on over the threats and the demands, over the blows of the axe, on and on into endless sleep. Endless sleep? *Mors janua vitae*. If only the gateway to life had not been through an unspeakable passage of pain. He found himself praying for what he knew was impossible, that God should change history.

Then Mrs Crilling tapped on the window.

Archery gave a start so violent and galvanic that he seemed to feel a hand squeeze his heart with slippery fingers. He gasped and forced himself to look.

'Sorry I'm late,' said Imogen Ide. 'What a ghastly night.'

She should have been on the inside, he thought, pulling himself together. But she had been outside, tapping, tapping, because she had seen him standing there like a lost soul. This way it altered the aspect of things, for she had not hidden the car. It stood on the gravel beside his own, wet, silver, glittering, like something alive and beautiful from the depths of the sea.

'How did you get in?' she said in the hall.

'The door was open.'

'Some workman.'

'I suppose so.'

She wore a tweed suit and her pale hair was wet. He had been silly enough—bad enough, he thought—to imagine that when they met she would run to him and embrace him. Instead she stood looking at him gravely, almost coldly, two little frown lines between her brows.

'The morning room, I think,' she said. 'There's furniture in there and besides it doesn't have—associations.'

The furniture consisted of two kitchen stools and a cane-back chair. From the window, heavily encrusted with grime, he could see the conservatory to whose walls of cracked glass the tendrils of a dead vine still clung. He gave her the chair and sat down on one of the stools. He had a strange feeling—but a feeling not without a charm of its own—that they had come here to buy the house, he and she, had come early and were reduced to wait thus uncomfortably until the arrival of the agent who would show them round.

'This could be a study,' he would say. 'It must be lovely on a fine day.'

'Or we could eat in here. Nice and near the kitchen.'

'Will you be able to bear getting up in the morning to cook my breakfast?' (My love, my love . . .)

'You were going to explain,' she said, and of course, there would never be a shared bed or a shared breakfast or any future at all. This was their future, this interview in a damp morning room, looking at a dead vine.

He began to tell her about Charles and Tess, about Mrs Kershaw's belief. Her face grew even harder and colder when he came to the bit about the inheritance and before he had finished, she said:

'You really meant to pin the murder on Roger?'

'What could I do? I was torn between Charles,' he said, 'and you.' She shook her head quickly, the blood running into her face. 'I beg you to believe I didn't try to know you because you were his wife.'

'I believe you.'

'The money . . . his sisters . . . you didn't know about that?'

'I knew nothing. Only that they existed and that he never saw them. Oh God!' She screwed up her face, pushed her hands over her cheeks, across her eyes and up to the temples. 'We've been talking about it all day. He can't see that he was morally obliged to help them. Only one thing matters to him, that Wexford won't take it seriously as a motive for murder.'

'Wexford saw him himself that night at the crucial time in Sewingbury.'

'He doesn't know or he's forgotten. He's going to go through hell until he can pluck up courage to ring Wexford. Some people might say that's his punishment.' She sighed. 'Are his sisters very badly off?'

'One of them is. She lives in a single room with her husband and her baby.'

'I've got Roger to agree to let them have what they should have had in the first place, three thousand, three hundred odd each. I think I'd better go to see them myself. He won't even notice it's gone. It's funny, you know, I knew he was unscrupulous. You can't make that amount of money without being, but I didn't know he'd stoop to that.'

'It hasn't made you . . . ?' He hesitated, wondering what he had destroyed.

'Never feel the same about him again? Oh, my dear, you are funny. Listen, I'll tell you something. Seven years ago it was and the month of June. My face was on the cover of six separate magazines that month. The most photographed girl in Britain.'

He nodded, puzzled and out of his depth.

'If you reach a peak there's nothing left but to go downhill. In June of the next year I had my face on one magazine. So I married Roger.'

'You didn't love him?'

'I liked him, you know. He saved me in a way and all the time I'm saving him.' Archery knew what she meant, recalling her soft tranquillity in the Olive dining room, her hand touching a mourner's trembling arm. He expected always from her calm serenity and he was shocked when she raged suddenly: 'How was I to know there was a middle-aged clergyman waiting for me—a clergyman with a wife and a son and a guilt complex as big as a mountain?'

'Imogen!'

'No, you're not to touch me! It was stupid to come here and I should never have done it. Oh God, How I hate these sentimental scenes!'

He got up and walked as far from her as the little room

allowed. It had stopped raining but the sky was sludge-coloured and the vine was as dead as a doornail.

'What will they do now,' she said, 'your son and this girl?'

'I don't think they know themselves.'

'And you, what will you do?'

' "Go to the wife of my bosom," ' he quoted, ' "the same as I ought to go." '

'Kipling!' She gave a hysterical laugh, and he was pained by the depths he was discovering too late. 'Kipling! That's all I need.'

'Good-bye,' he said.

'Good-bye, dear Henry Archery. I've never known what to call you. Do you know that?' She lifted his hand, kissed the palm.

'Perhaps it's not a name for dalliance,' he said ruefully.

'But it sounds well with Rev. in front of it.'

She went out, closing the door soundlessly behind her.

'Jenny kissed me,' he said to the vine. Jenny could just be short for Imogen. 'So what?'

Presently he came out into the hall and he wondered why the place seemed emptier and more lifeless than before. Perhaps it was his own fresh sense of loss. He turned towards the back door and then he saw. It was not an imagined but an actual diminishing. The raincoat had gone.

Had it ever been there or was his fancy, morbid and hypersensitive, creating hallucinations? It was a vision that might naturally come to someone involved as he was in Painter's story. But if the raincoat had never been there what would account for those penny-sized puddles on the floor, made surely by rain rivulets running from a sleeve?

He had no belief in the vulgar supernatural. But now as he stood looking at the hook where the raincoat had hung, he remembered how he had jumped at the tap on the window and had likened the marble veining to blood. It was not impossible that some evil hung over places such as this, fermenting the imagination and re-creating on the mind's retina images from a past tragedy.

The door was glazed in square panes. All were dirty yet all glinted faintly in the evening light—all but one. He peered, then smiled wryly at his absurd fancies. The glass had been completely removed from the frame nearest to the lock. An arm could have passed through it to turn the key and slide back the bolts.

It was unbolted now. He stepped out on to the flagged yard. Beyond, the garden lay enveloped in thin wet mist. The trees, the bushes, the lush blanket of weed sagged under their weight of water. Once he would have felt the responsible citizen's anxiety as to the whereabouts of whoever had broken that window, might even have considered going to the police. Now he was simply apathetic, indifferent.

Imogen filled his mind, but even on this subject, his thoughts were no longer passionate or ashamed. He would give her five more minutes to get away and then he would return to the Olive. Mechanically he stooped down and for something to do began carefully picking up the shards of broken glass, stacking them against the wall where no one, not even the burglar, might tread on them.

His nerves were bad, he knew that, but surely that was a footfall, the sound of indrawn breath.

She was coming back! But she must not—it was more than he could stand. The sight of her would be joy, but anything she said could only mean a fresh parting. He set his teeth, tightened the muscles of his hands and before he could stop himself his fingers had closed on a sliver of glass.

The blood came before the pain. He stood up, looking stupidly and aloud in that empty place, and he turned to meet the tap-tap of high heels.

Her scream burst in his face.

'Uncle Bert! Uncle Bert! Oh, my God!'

His hand was all bloody but he put it out, the hurt hand and the other, to catch Elizabeth Crilling as she fell.

'You ought to have it stitched,' she said. 'You'll get tetanus. You'll have an awful scar.'

He wrapped the handkerchief more tightly about the wound and sat grimly on the step, watching her. She had come round in seconds but her face was still white. A little gust of wind flicked through the tangled mass of green and showered them with water drops. Archery shivered.

'What are you doing here?' he asked.

She lay back in the chair he had fetched her from the morning room, her legs stretched out and limp. He noticed how thin they were, thin as the legs of an Oriental, the stockings wrinkled at the ankles.

'I've had a row with my mother,' she said.

He said nothing, waiting. For a moment she remained inert, then her body seemed to snap forwards, a trap with a steel spring. Instinctively, he shifted a little away from her, for she had brought her face towards his, her hands clutching each other between knees and breast. Her mouth moved before the words found sound.

'Oh Christ!' He kept still, controlling his inevitable reaction to the oath. 'I saw you with blood on you,' she said, 'and then you said it, what he said. "I've cut myself." ' A great shudder rocked her as if she had been grasped and shaken by an invisible force. Amazed, he watched her slacken again and heard her say in cold contrast, 'Give me a cigarette.' She tossed her bag to him. 'Light it!' The flame guttered in the damp air and the tugging wind. She cupped her thin hands with their big knuckles around it. 'Always snooping, aren't you?' she said, drawing back. 'I don't know what you thought you'd find, but this is it.'

Bewildered, he found himself staring at the garden, up at the overhanging gables, down at the wet broken paving.

'Me, I mean,' she said with savage impatience. 'You've been telling tales to the police about me and you don't even know what it's all about.' Again she snapped forward and shamelessly—he was horrified—pulled up her skirt and exposed her thigh above her stocking top. The white skin was covered all over with needle punctures. 'Asthma, that's what it's about. Asthma tablets. You dissolve them in water—and that's a hell of a job on its own—and then you fill up a hypodermic.'

Archery did not think himself easily shocked. But he was shocked now. He felt the blood run into his face. Embarrassment silenced him, then gave place to pity for her and a kind of diffused indignation with humanity.

'Does it have any effect?' he asked as coolly as he could.

'It gives you a lift, if you follow me. Much the same as you get from singing psalms, I expect,' she jeered. 'There was this man I lived with, he put me on to it. I was in the right place for getting supplies, you see. Until you sent that bastard Burden down and he put the fear of God into my mother. She's got to get a new prescription every time she wants them now and she's got to collect them herself.'

'I see,' he said, and hope went. So that was what Mrs Crilling had meant. In prison there would be no tablets, no syringe, and because she had become addicted to them she would have to reveal her addiction or . . .

'I don't think the police can do anything to you,' he said, not knowing whether they could or not.

'What would you know about it? I've got twenty left in a bottle so I came here. I've made myself a bed upstairs and . . .'

He interrupted her. 'It's your raincoat?'

The question surprised her, but only for a moment, then scorn returned to make her look twice her age.

'Sure it is,' she said scathingly. 'Whose did you think it was, Painter's? I went out for a bit to get something from my car, left the door on the latch and when I came back you were here with that tarty piece.' He kept his eyes on her, controlling himself. For the only time in his life he felt an urge to strike another person's face. 'I didn't dare come back for a bit,' she said, returning to the only other mood she had, a self-pitying childishness. 'But I had to get my raincoat—the tablets were in the pocket.'

She inhaled deeply and flung the cigarette away from her into the wet bushes.

'What the hell were you doing, returning to the scene of the crime? Trying to get under his skin?'

'Whose skin?' he whispered urgently.

'Painter's of course. Bert Painter's. My Uncle Bert.' She was defiant again, but her hand shook and her eyes glazed. It was coming now. He was like a man awaiting bad news, knowing it was inevitable, knowing even exactly what it was going to be, but still hoping that there would be some detail, some facet to mitigate it. 'That night,' she said, 'he stood there just like you. Only he was holding a piece of wood and there was blood on it and all over him. "I've cut myself," he said. "Don't look, Lizzie, I've cut myself." '

16

> When the unclean spirit is gone out of a man, he walketh through dry places seeking rest and finding none. He saith, I will return unto my house whence I came out.
>
> *The Gospel for the Fourth Sunday in Lent.*

She told it in the second person, 'You did this,' 'You did that.' Archery realised he was hearing what no parent and no psychiatrist had ever heard, and he marvelled. The peculiar use of the pronoun seemed to draw his own mind into the child's body so that he could see with her eyes and feel with her overweening terror.

She sat in the damp dusk on the spot where it had all begun for her, utterly still now. Only her eyelids moved. Sometimes, at agonising moments in the narrative, she would close her eyes, then open them again with a slow exhalation of breath. Archery had never been to a seance—would indeed have disapproved of such a thing as being theologically untenable—but he had read of them. Elizabeth Crilling's steady outpouring of terrible events told in a flat monotone was reminiscent, he thought, of mediumistic revelation. She was coming to the end now and a weary relief crossed her face as of one shedding a load.

. . .You put your coat on, your best coat because it was your best frock, and you ran across the road, down the sideway and past the greenhouse. Nobody saw you because there was no one about. Or was there? Surely that was the back door closing softly.

You came very quietly around the side of the house and then you saw it was only Uncle Bert who had come out of the house into the garden.

'Uncle Bert, Uncle Bert! I've got my best frock on. Can I go and show it to Tessie?'

Suddenly you were very frightened, more frightened than you had ever been in all your life, because Uncle Bert was breathing in such a funny way, gasping and coughing like Daddy did when he had one of his attacks. Then he turned round and there was red stuff all over him, on his hands and all down the front of his coat.

'I've cut myself,' he said. 'Don't look, Lizzie. I've just cut myself.'

'I want Tessie! I want Tessie!'

'Don't you go up there!'

'You're not to touch me. I've got my new dress on. I'll tell my mummy.'

He just stood there with the red stuff on him and his face was like the face of a lion, big thick mouth, thick nose, curly tawny hair. Yes, it was like the lion in that picture book Mummy said you must not look at . . .

The red stuff had splashed on to his face and trickled to the corner of his mouth. He brought that dreadful face down close to yours and shouted right at you:

'You tell her, Lizzie Crilling, you stuck-up little snob, and d'you know what I'll do? Wherever I am—wherever, d'you hear me?—I'll find you and I'll give you what I gave the old girl.'

It was over. He could tell that by the way she came out of her trance, sat up and gave a kind of moan.

'But you went back,' Archery murmured. 'You went back with your mother?'

'My mother!' Weeping would not have surprised him. This violent bitter laughter did. On a high discordant peal, she stopped suddenly and rushed into her answer. 'I was only five, only a kid. I didn't know what he meant, not then. I was much more frightened of letting her know I'd been over there.' He noted that 'her' and knew intuitively she would not mention her mother by name again. 'You see, I didn't even know it was blood and I reckon I must have thought it was paint.'

'Then we went back. I wasn't afraid of the house and I didn't know what he meant by the old girl. I think when he said about giving me what he'd given the old girl I thought he meant his wife, Mrs Painter. He knew I'd seen him hit her. I found the body. You knew that? God, it was terrible. I didn't understand, you see. D'you know what I thought at first? I thought she'd sort of burst.'

'Don't,' said Archery.

'If you can't take it now, what d'you think it was like for me? I was *five*. Five, my Christ! They put me to bed and I was ill for weeks. Of course, they'd arrested Painter, but I didn't know that. You don't tell children that sort of thing. I didn't know what had happened at all, only that Granny Rose had burst open and he had made it happen and if I said I'd seen him he'd do the same to me.'

'But afterwards. Didn't you tell anyone then?'

She had talked about finding the body and said it was terrible, but then there had been affectation in her voice. A child finding a murdered woman, he thought. Yes, all the world would recoil in shock from that. Yet for her that had not been the worst. Now as he asked her about afterwards he saw the trance begin once more to mist her face as the spectre of Painter—Painter on this very spot—rose before it.

'He'd find you,' she mumbled. 'He'd find you wherever you were, wherever he was. You wanted to tell *her*, but she wouldn't listen to you. "Don't think about it, Baby, put it out of your mind." But it wouldn't go *out* . . .' Her features worked and the blank eyes flickered.

'Miss Crilling, let me take you home.'

She was standing up now, moving mechanically towards the house wall, a robot whose programming has failed. When her hands touched the bricks she stopped and spoke again, talking to him but into the house itself.

'It wouldn't go out. It went in and in, till it was just a little black wheel spinning and playing the same thing over and over again.'

Had she realised she was speaking in metaphor? He had thought of a medium's utterances, but now he knew it had been more like a discordant record, playing the same horror each time it was pricked by the stylus of association. He touched her arm and was surprised when she followed him meekly and limply back to the chair. They sat in silence for some minutes. She was the first to speak and she was almost her normal self.

'You know Tessie, don't you? She's going to marry your son?' He shrugged. 'I think she was the only real friend I ever had,' she said quietly. 'It was her birthday the next week. She was going to be five, and I thought I'd give her one of my old dresses. Sneak it round when *she* was with the old girl. Generous little beast, wasn't I? I never saw her again.'

Archery said gently, 'You saw her this afternoon in the chemist's.'

Her new tranquillity was very finely balanced. Had he pushed it too far?

'In the white blouse?' she said in a dead even voice, so low that he had to lean forward and strain to catch it. He nodded. 'That girl who hadn't got any change?'

'Yes.'

'She was standing beside me and I never knew.' There was a long silence. The only sound was the faint rustling of wet bushes, water-loaded gleaming leaves on the coach-house walls. Then she tossed her head. 'I reckon I don't notice women much,' she said. 'I saw you all right and the boy that was with you. I remember I thought the talent's looking up in this dump.'

'The talent,' Archery said, 'is my son.'

'Her boy-friend? I never would have told you!' She gave a low cry of exasperation. 'And, my God, I never would have told her—not if you hadn't caught me out like that.'

'It was chance, coincidence. Perhaps it's better that I do know.'

'You!' she said. 'That's all you think about, you and your precious son. What about me?' She stood up, looked at him and moved towards the door with the broken pane. It was true he thought, ashamed. He had been prepared to sacrifice all these other people to save Charles, the Crillings, Primero, even Imogen—but his quest had been doomed from the beginning because history could not be changed.

'What will they do to me?' Her face was turned away from him and she spoke softly. But there was such urgency and such fear in those six short words that their impact was as if she had shouted.

'Do to you?' He could do no more than get to his feet and stand helplessly behind her. 'Why should they do anything to you?' He remembered the dead man on the crossing and he remembered the needle punctures, but he said only, 'You've been more sinned against than sinning.'

'Oh, the Bible!' she cried. 'Don't quote the Bible to me.' He said nothing for he had not done so. 'I'm going upstairs now,' she said strangely. 'When you see Tess would you give her my love? I wish,' she said, 'I wish I could have given her something for her birthday.'

By the time he had found a doctor's house he felt all hand, nothing but hand, a throbbing thing that beat like a second heart. He recognised Dr Crocker at once and saw that he, too, was remembered.

'You must be enjoying your holiday,' Crocker said. He stitched the finger, filled a syringe with anti-tetanus serum. 'First that dead boy and now this. Sorry, but this may hurt. You've got thick skin.'

'Really?' Archery could not help smiling as he bared his upper arm. 'I want to ask you something.' Without stopping to explain he put the question that had been troubling him all the way from Victor's Piece. 'Is it possible?'

'Beginning of October?' Crocker looked closely and not unsympathetically at him. 'Look, how personal is this?'

Archery read his thoughts and managed a laugh. 'Not that personal,' he said. 'I am, as they say, enquiring for a friend.'

'Well, it's extremely unlikely.' Croker grinned. 'There have been cases, very few and far between. They make minor medical history.'

Nodding, Archery got up to go.

'I shall want to see that finger again,' the doctor said. 'Or your local G.P. will. You'll need another couple of injections. See to it when you get home, will you?'

Home . . . yes, he would be home tomorrow. His stay in Kingsmarkham had not been a holiday, anything but that, yet he had that curious end-of-a-holiday feeling when the resort one has stayed in becomes more familiar than home.

He had walked along this High Street every day, more frequently even than he trod the main village street at Thringford. The order of the shops, chemist, grocer, draper, were as well known to him as to the housewives of Kingsmarkham. And the place was certainly pretty. Suddenly it seemed sad that he should hardly have noticed its prettiness—more than that really, for prettiness does not go with grace and dignity—but would associate it for ever with a lost love and a failed search.

Street lamps, some of them of ancient design and with wrought iron casings, showed him alleys winding between stone walls, coaching yards, flowers in a few cottage gardens. The weak yellow light bleached these flowers to a luminous pallor. Half an hour ago it had been just light enough to read print by; now the darkness had come down and lamps appeared in windows fronting the street. The sky had a rainy look and stars showed only in the crevices between bulbous bloated cloud. There was no moon.

The Olive and Dove was brightly lit and the car park full. Glass doors separated the hall from the cocktail bar and he saw that it was crowded. There were groups and pairs of young people, sitting on high stools, gathered round the small black oak tables. Archery thought he would give everything he possessed to see Charles among them, throwing back his head in laughter, his hand resting on the shoulder of a pretty girl. Not a beautiful, intellectual, tainted girl—just someone pretty and dull and uncomplicated. But Charles was not there. He found him alone in the lounge writing letters. Only a few hours had elapsed since his parting from Tess, but already he was writing . . .

'What on earth have you done to your hand and where have you been?'

'Hacking away at the past.'

'Don't be cryptic, Father. It doesn't suit you.' His tone was bitter and sullen. Archery wondered why people say that suffering improves the character, why indeed he had sometimes thoughtlessly said it to his own parishioners. He listened to his son's voice, carping, querulous and selfish. 'I've been wanting to address this envelope for the past two hours, but I couldn't because I don't know where Tess's aunt lives.' Charles gave him a sour accusing look. 'You wrote it down. Don't say you've lost it.'

'Here.' Archery took the card from his pocket and dropped it on the table. 'I'm going to phone your mother, tell her we'll be home in the morning.'

'I'll come up with you. This place goes dead at night.'

Dead? And the bar crowded with people, some of whom were

surely as exacting as Charles. If Tess had been with them it would not have been dead. Quite suddenly Archery made up his mind that Charles must be made happy, and if happiness meant Tess, he should have Tess. Therefore the theory he was formulating would have to be made to work.

He paused on the threshold of his bedroom, put his hand to the light switch but did not press it. There in the darkness with Charles behind him there flashed across his brain a picture of himself and Wexford that first day at the police station. He had been firm then. 'Bitterly, bitterly against this marriage,' he had told the Chief Inspector. How utterly he had come round! But then he had not known what it was to crave for a voice and a smile. To understand all was not merely to forgive all, it was utter identification of the spirit and the flesh.

Over his shoulder Charles said, 'Can't you find the switch?' His hand came up and met his father's on the dry cold wall. The room flooded with light. 'Are you all right? You look worn-out.'

Perhaps it was the unaccustomed gentleness in his voice that did it. Archery knew how easy it is to be kind when one is happy, how nearly impossible to feel solicitude in the midst of one's own misery. He was suddenly filled with love, an overflowing diffused love that for the first time in days had no specific object but included his son—and his wife. Hoping unreasonably that her voice would be soft and kind, he moved towards the telephone.

'Well, you are a stranger,' were the first words he heard and they were sharp with resentment. 'I was beginning to wonder what had happened to you. Thought you must have eloped.'

'I wouldn't do that, darling,' he said, sick at heart. And then, because he had to set his foot back on the path of constancy, he took a grotesque echo, 'Kingsmarkham isn't conspicuous for its talent. I've missed you.' It was untrue and what he was going to say next would also be a lie. 'It'll be good to be home with you again.' That lie would have to be changed into truth. He clenched his hand till the hurt finger burned with pain, but as he did so he thought that he and time could make it true . . .

'You do use some extraordinary expressions,' Charles said when he had rung off. 'Talent, indeed. Very vulgar.' He was still holding the card, staring at it with utter absorption. A week ago Archery would have marvelled that a woman's address and a woman's handwriting could provide such fascination.

'You asked me on Saturday if I'd ever seen this before. You asked me if I'd heard it. Well, now I've *seen* it, it's rung a bell. It's part of a long religious verse play. Part of it's in prose but there are songs in it—hymns really—and this is the last verse of one of them.'

'Where did you see it? In Oxford? In a library?'

But Charles was not listening to him. He said as if he had been meaning to say it for the past half-hour, 'Where did you go tonight? Had it any connection with me and—and Tess?'

Must he tell him? Was he obliged to root out those last vestiges of hope before he had anything real and proven to put in their place?

'Just to have a last look at Victor's Piece.' Charles nodded. He appeared to accept this quite naturally. 'Elizabeth Crilling was there, hiding.' He told him about the drugs, the wretched attempts to secure more tablets, but he did not tell him everything.

Charles's reaction was unexpected. 'Hiding from what?'

'The police, I suppose, or her mother.'

'You didn't just leave her there?' Charles asked indignantly. 'A crazy kid like that? God knows what she might do. You don't know how many of those tablets would poison her. She might take them deliberately to that end. Have you thought of that?'

She had accused him of not considering her but even that taunt had not prompted him. It had simply not crossed his mind that he was doing something irresponsible in leaving a young girl alone in an empty house.

'I think we ought to go to Victor's Piece and try to get her to come home,' Charles said. Observing the sudden animation on his son's face, Archery wondered how sincere he was and how much of this spurt of energy was due to a desire to do something, anything, because he knew that if he went to bed he would not sleep. Charles put the card away in his pocket. 'You won't like this,' he said, 'but I think we ought to take the mother with us.'

'She's quarrelled with her mother. She behaves as if she hates her.'

'That's nothing. Have you ever seen them together?'

Only a glance across a courtroom, a glance of indecipherable passion. He had never seen them together. He knew only that if Charles were alone somewhere and miserable, on the verge perhaps of taking his own life, he, Archery, would not want strangers to go to his succour.

'You can drive,' he said and he tossed the keys to his son.

The church clock was striking eleven. Archery wondered if Mrs Crilling would be in bed. Then it occurred to him for the first time that she might be worrying about her daughter. He had never attributed to the Crillings ordinary emotions. They were different from other people, the mother deranged, the girl delinquent. Was that why, instead of being merciful, he had merely used them? As they turned into Glebe Road he felt a new warmth stir within him. It was not too late—especially now she had found some release—to bring Elizabeth back, to heal that old wound, to retrieve something out of chaos.

Outwardly he was cold. He was coatless and the night was chilly. You expect a winter's night to be cold, he thought. There was something depressing and wrong about a cold summer night. November with flowers, a November wind that ruffled the ripe leaves of summer. He must not find omens in nature.

'What d'you call it,' he said to Charles, 'when you ascribe emotions to nature? What's the expression?'

'The Pathetic Fallacy,' Charles said. Archery shivered.

'This is the house,' he said. They got out. Number twenty-four was in darkness upstairs and down.

'She's probably in bed.'

'Then she'll have to get up,' said Charles and rang the bell. He rang again and again. 'Pointless,' he said. 'Can we get round the back?'

Archery said, 'Through here,' and led Charles through the sandy arch. It was like a cavern, he thought, touching the walls. He expected them to be clammy but they were dry and prickly to the touch. They emerged into a dark pool among patches of light which came from french windows all along the backs of houses. A yellow square segmented by black bars lay on each shadowed garden but none came from Mrs Crilling's window.

'She must be out,' said Archery as they opened the little gate in the wire fence. 'We know so little about them. We don't know where she'd go or who her friends are.'

Through the first window the kitchen and the hall showed dark and empty. To reach the french windows they had to push through a tangle of wet nettles which stung their hands.

'Pity we didn't bring a torch.'

'We haven't *got* a torch,' Archery objected. He peered in. 'I've got matches.' The first he struck showed him the room as he had seen it before, a muddle of flung-down clothes and stacked newspapers. The match died and he dropped it on wet concrete. By the light of a second he saw that on the table were the remains of a meal, cut bread still in its paper wrapping, a cup and saucer, a jam jar, a single plate coated with something yellow and congealed.

'We might as well go,' he said. 'She isn't here.'

'The door's not locked,' said Charles. He lifted the latch and opened it quietly. There came to them at once a peculiar and unidentifiable odour of fruit and of alcohol.

'You can't go in. There isn't the slightest justification for breaking in.'

'I haven't broken anything.' Charles's foot was over the threshold, but he stopped and said over his shoulder to his father, 'Don't you think there's something odd here? Don't you feel it?'

Archery shrugged. They were both in the room now. The smell was very strong but they could see nothing but the dim outlines of cluttered furniture.

'The light switch is on the left by the door,' he said. 'I'll find it.' He had forgotten that his son was a man, that his son's adult sense of responsibility had brought them there. In that dark, evilly scented place, they were just a parent and his child. He must not do as Mrs Crilling had done and let the child go first. 'Wait there,' he said. He felt his way along the side of the table, pushed a small armchair out of his path, squeezed behind the sofa and felt for the switch. 'Wait there!' he cried again, much more sharply and in a spasm of real fear. Previously in his passage across the room his feet had come into contact with debris on the floor, a shoe, he thought, a book dropped face-downwards. Now the obstruction was larger and more solid. His scalp crept. Clothes, yes, and within those clothes something heavy and inert. He dropped to his knees, thrusting forward hands to palpate and fumble. 'Dear God . . . !'

'What is it? What the hell *is* it? Can't you find the light?'

Archery could not speak. He had withdrawn his hands and they were wet and sticky. Charles had crossed the room. Light pouring into and banishing that darkness was a physical pain. Archery closed his eyes. Above him he heard Charles make an inarticulate sound.

He opened his eyes and the first thing he saw was that his hands were red. Charles said, 'Don't look!' and he knew that his own lips had been trying to frame those words. They were not policemen, not used to sights such as this, and each had tried to save the other from seeing.

Each had to look. Mrs Crilling lay spread on the floor between the sofa and the wall and she was quite dead. The chill of her body came up to Archery's hands through the pink flounces that covered it from neck to ankles. He had seen that neck and at once had looked away from the stocking that made a ligature around it.

'But she's all over blood,' said Charles, 'It's as if—God!—as if someone had sprinkled her with it.'

17

I held my tongue and spake nothing; I kept silence, yea, even from good words; but it was pain and grief to me.

Psalm 39. *The Burial of the Dead.*

'It isn't blood,' said Wexford. 'Don't you know what it is? Couldn't you smell it?' He lifted the bottle someone had found under the sideboard and held it aloft. Archery sat on the sofa in Mrs Crilling's living room, worn, tired, utterly spent. Doors banged and footsteps sounded as Wexford's two men searched the other room. The people upstairs had come in at midnight, Saturday night happy, the man a little drunk. The woman had had hysterics during Wexford's questioning.

They had taken the body away and Charles moved his chair round so that he could not see the crimson splashes of cherry brandy.

'But why? Why did it happen?' he whispered.

'Your father knows why.' Wexford stared at Archery, his grey gimlet eyes deep and opaque. He squatted opposite them on a low chair with wooden arms. 'As for me, I don't know but I can guess. I can't help feeling I've seen something like this before, a long, long time ago. Sixteen years to be exact. A pink frilly dress that a little girl could never wear again because it was spoilt with blood.'

Outside the rain had begun again and water lashed against the windows making them rattle. It would be cold now inside Victor's Piece, cold and eerie like a deserted castle in a wood of wet trees. The Chief Inspector had an extra uncanny sense that almost amounted to telepathy. Archery willed his thoughts to alter course lest Wexford should divine them, but the question came before he could rid his mind of its pictures.

'Come on, Mr Archery, where is she?'

'Where is who?'

'The daughter.'

'What makes you think I know?'

'Listen to me,' said Wexford. 'The last person we've talked to who saw her was a chemist in Kingsmarkham. Oh, yes, we went to all the chemists first naturally. This one remembers that when she was in the shop there were two men and a girl there too, a young man and an elder one, tall, fair, obviously father and son.'

'I didn't speak to her then,' Archery said truthfully. The smell sickened him. He wanted nothing but sleep and peace and to get out of this room where Wexford had kept them since they had telephoned him.

'Mrs Crilling's been dead six or seven hours. It's ten to three now and you left the Olive at a quarter to eight. The barman saw you come in at ten. Where did you go, Mr Archery?'

He sat silent. Years and years ago—Oh, centuries ago!—it had been like this in school. You own up, you betray someone, or everyone suffers. Funny, once before he had thought of Wexford as a kind of headmaster.

'You know where she is,' Wexford said. His voice was loud, threatening, ominous. 'D'you want to be an accessary? Is that what you want?'

Archery closed his eyes. Quite suddenly he knew why he was prevaricating. He wanted the very thing that Charles had warned him might happen and although it was contrary to his religion, wicked even, he wanted it with all his heart.

Charles said, 'Father . . .' and when he got no reply shrugged, turned his dull shocked eyes to Wexford. 'Oh, what the hell? She's at Victor's Piece.'

Archery realised that he had been holding his breath. He let it out in a deep sigh. 'In one of the bedrooms,' he said, 'looking at the coach house and dreaming of a heap of sand. She asked what they would do to her and I didn't understand. What will they do to her?'

Wexford got up. 'Well, sir . . .' Archery noted that 'sir' as one might notice the re-assuming of a velvet glove. 'You know as well as I do that it's no longer lawful to punish with death for certain . . .' His eyes flickered over the place where Mrs Crilling had lain. '. . . certain heinous and grievous offences.'

'Will you let us go now?' Charles asked.

'Until tomorrow,' said Wexford.

The rain met them at the front door like a wave or a wall of spray. For the past half hour it had been drumming on the roof of the car and seeping in through the half-open quarter light. There was water laying in a small pool at Archery's feet but he was too tired to notice or care.

Charles came with him into his bedroom.

'I shouldn't ask you now,' he said. 'It's almost morning and God knows what we'll have to go through tomorrow, but I have to know. I'd rather know. But what else did she tell you, that girl at Victor's Piece?'

Archery had heard of people pacing a room like caged beasts. He had never imagined himself so strung with tension that in spite of utter exhaustion he would have to find release by crossing and re-crossing a floor, picking up objects, replacing them, his hands shaking. Charles waited, too wretched even for impatience. His letter to Tess lay in its envelope on the dressing table and beside it the card from the gift shop. Archery picked it up and kneaded it in his hands, crumpling the deckle edging. Then he went up to his son, put his hands gently on his shoulders and looked into the eyes that were young replicas of his own.

'What she told me,' he said, 'needn't matter to you. It would be like—well, someone else's nightmare.' Charles did not move. 'If you will only tell me where you saw the verse that is printed on this card.'

The morning was grey and cool, such a morning as occurs perhaps three hundred times a year out of the three hundred and sixty-five, when there is neither rain nor sun, frost nor fog. It was a limbo of a morning. The policeman on the crossing had covered his shirt sleeves with his dark jacket, the striped shop blinds were rolled up and sluggish steps had grown brisk.

Inspector Burden escorted Archery along the drying pavements to the police station. Archery was ashamed to answer Burden's kindly question as to how he had slept. He had slept heavily and soundly. Perhaps he would also have slept dreamlessly had he known what the inspector now told him, that Elizabeth Crilling was alive.

'She came with us quite willingly,' Burden said and added

rather indiscreetly, 'To tell you the truth, sir, I've never seen her so calm and sane and—well, at peace, really.'

'You want to go home, I suppose,' Wexford said when Burden had left them alone in the blue and yellow office. 'You'll have to come back for the inquest and the magistrates' court hearing. You found the body.'

Archery sighed. 'Elizabeth found a body sixteen years ago. If it hadn't been for her mother's self-seeking-vanity, greed for something she had no claim to—that would never have happened. You might say that that greed reached out and destroyed long after its original purpose had been frustrated. Or you might say that Elizabeth bore her mother a grudge because Mrs Crilling would never let her talk about Painter and bring her terrors to the light of day.'

'You might,' said Wexford. 'It could be all those things. And it could be that when Liz left the chemist's she went back to Glebe Road, Mrs Crilling was afraid to ask for another prescription, so Liz, in the addict's frenzy, strangled her.'

'May I see her?'

'I'm afraid not. I'm beginning to guess just what she saw sixteen years ago and what she told you last night.'

'After I'd talked to her I went to see Dr Crocker. I want you to look at this.' Archery gave Wexford Colonel Plashet's letter, silently indicating the relevant passage with his bandaged finger. 'Poor Elizabeth,' he murmured. 'She wanted to give Tess a dress for her fifth birthday. Unless Tess has changed a lot it wouldn't have meant much to her.'

Wexford read, closed his eyes briefly and then gave a slight smile. 'I see,' he said slowly and restored the letter to its envelope.

'I am right, aren't I? I'm not juggling things, imagining things? You see, I can't trust my own judgment any more. I have to have an opinion from an expert in deduction. I've been to Forby, I've seen a photograph, I've got a letter and I've talked to a doctor. If you had the same clues would you have come to the same conclusions?'

'I'm sure you're very kind, Mr Archery.' Wexford gave a broad ironic grin. 'I get more complaints than compliments. Now, as to clues and conclusions, I would, but I'd have been on to it a whole lot sooner.

'You see, it all depends on what you're looking for and the fact is, sir, you didn't know what you *were* looking for. All the time you were trying to disprove something in the face of—well, you said it—expert deduction. What you've found now achieves the same result as the other thing would have. For you and your son, that is. But it hasn't changed what for justice is the *status quo*. We would have made sure we knew precisely what we were looking for at the start, the basic thing. When you come down to that, it doesn't matter a damn to you who committed the crime. But you were looking through a pair of spectacles that were too big for you.'

'A glass darkly,' said Archery.

'I can't say I envy you the coming interview.'

'Strange,' said Archery thoughtfully as he got up to go, 'that although we both held such opposing opinions in the end we were both right.'

Wexford had said he must come back. He would make his visits short, though, short and blind, his eyes opening only in the court he could see out of this window, his words mere evidence. He had read stories of people transported to strange places, blindfolded and in shuttered cars, so that they should not see the country through which they passed. In his case he would be prevented from seeing visions and associations with those visions, by the presence of those he was legitimately allowed to love. Mary should come with him and Charles and Tess to be his shutters and his hood. Certainly he would never see this room again. He turned to give it a last glance, but if he hoped to have the last word he was disappointed.

'Both right,' said Wexford, giving Archery's hand a gentle clasp. 'I by reason and you by faith. Which, taken all in all,' he added, 'is only what one might expect.'

She opened the door to them carefully, grudgingly, as if she expected to see gypsies or a brush salesman from a disreputable firm.

'I hope you'll forgive us, Mrs Kershaw,' Archery said with too loud heartiness. 'Charles wanted to see Tess and as we were coming this way . . .'

It is difficult to greet callers, even unwelcome callers, without some kind of a smile. Irene Kershaw did not smile, but she made muttering noises in which he caught the occasional word: 'very welcome, I'm sure,' 'unexpected . . .' and 'not really prepared . . .' They got into the hall, but it was an awkward manœuvre and it almost involved pushing past her. She had grown rather red and she said to Charles, now quite coherently:

'Tess has popped down to the shops to get a few last-minute things for her holiday.' Archery could see that she was angry and that she did not know how to vent her anger on people who were at the same time adults and from a different background from her own. 'You've quarrelled, haven't you?' she said. 'What are you trying to do, break her heart?' Apparently she was capable of emotion, but once she had shown it, not capable of control. Tears welled into her eyes. 'Oh dear . . . I didn't mean to say that.'

Archery had explained everything to Charles in the car. He was to find Tess, get her alone and tell her. Now he said, 'You might go down the hill, Charles, and see if you can meet her coming up. She'll be glad of a hand with her basket.'

Charles hesitated, possibly because he was at a loss to answer Mrs Kershaw's accusation and could not bring himself to echo so exaggerated an expression as 'a broken heart'. Then he said, 'I'm going to marry Tess. That's what I've always wanted.'

The colour died out of her face and now that there was no occasion for them the tears trickled down her cheeks. Archery would, under other circumstances, have been embarrassed. Now he realised that this mood of hers, tears, a lukewarm resentment that might be her nearest approach to passion, would make her receptive to what he had to say. A tired tigress apparently lurked under that dull suburban exterior, a mother beast capable of being roused only when its young was threatened.

Charles let himself out of the front door. Archery, left alone with her, wondered where the other children were and how soon Kershaw himself would return. Again he was finding himself, when in the sole company of this woman, at a loss for words. She made no effort to help him, but stood stiff and expressionless, dabbing at the tearmarks with the tips of her fingers.

'Perhaps we could sit down?' He made a vague gesture towards the glass door. 'I should like to have a talk, settle things, I . . .'

She was recovering fast, tunnelling back into the sanctuary of her respectability. 'You'd like some tea?'

The mood must not be allowed to peter out into small-talk over the cups. 'No,' he said, 'no, really . . .'

She went before him into the living room. There were the books, the Reader's Digests, the dictionaries and the works on deep sea fishing. The portrait of Jill on the easel was finished and Kershaw had made the amateur's mistake of not knowing when to stop, so that the likeness had been lost in last-minute touches. In the garden which was spread before him with the unreality and the garish colours of a cushion cover in gros point, the Paul Crampel geraniums burned so brightly that they hurt his eyes.

Mrs Kershaw sat down genteelly and crimped her skirt over her knees. Today, now that it was cold again, she wore a cotton dress. She was that kind of woman, Archery thought, who would wear her winter clothes on and on cautiously until she was sure a heatwave was fully established. Then, just as the hot weather was ending and the storm about to break, then at last the carefully laundered thin dress would be brought out.

The pearls had been restrung. She put her hand up to them and drew it away quickly, curbing temptation. Their eyes met and she gave a tiny nervous giggle, perhaps aware that he had noticed her tiny vice. He gave a small inner sigh, for all her emotion had gone and her face showed only the natural bewilderment of a hostess who does not know the purpose of a call and is too discreet to question the caller.

He must—he *must*—awaken something from behind that pale lined brow. All his carefully prepared openings died. In a moment she would begin on the weather or the desirability of white weddings. But she did not quite do that. He had forgotten the other stock remark that is so handy a conversation starter between strangers.

'And how did you enjoy your holiday?' said Irene Kershaw.

Very well. That would do as well as anything.

'Forby is your native village, I believe,' he said. 'I went to see a grave while I was there.'

She touched the pearls with the flat of her hand. 'A grave?' For an instant her voice was as raw as when she had talked of a broken heart, then all passionless Purley again as she added, 'Oh, yes, Mrs Primero is buried there, isn't she?'

'It wasn't her grave I saw.' Softly he quoted, ' "Go, shepherd to your rest . . ." Tell me, why did you keep all the works he left behind him?'

That there would be reaction and that that reaction might be anger he had expected. He was prepared for a flouncing hauteur or even that damning, dulling response so dear to the heart of the Mrs Kershaws of this world: 'We needn't discuss that.' He had not thought she would be frightened and at the same time stricken with a kind of awe. She cowered a little in the armchair—if cowering is compatible with perfect stillness—and her eyes wide and glistening now, had the utter immobility of the dead.

Her fear had the effect of frightening him. It was as communicable as a yawn. Suppose she were to have a fit of hysterics? He went on very gently:

'Why did you keep them hidden away in the dark? They might have been published, they might have been acted. He could have had posthumous fame.'

She made no answer at all, but now he knew what to do, the answer came to him like a gift of God. He only had to go on talking, gently, mesmerically. The words tumbled out, platitudes and clichés, praise of work he had never seen and had no reason to suppose he would admire, assurances and unfounded promises he might never be able to honour. All the time, like a hypnotist, he kept his eyes on her, nodding when she nodded, breaking into a wide fatuous smile when for the first time a tiny vague one trembled on her lips.

'May I see them?' he dared. 'Will you show me the works of John Grace?'

He held his breath while with torturing slowness she mounted a stool and reached for the top of the book case. They were in a box, a large cardboard grocer's box that had apparently once contained a gross of tinned peaches. She handled it with a peculiar reverence, her care all concentrated on it, so that she let the magazines which had been stacked on it cascade to the floor.

There must have been a dozen of them but only one cover picture splashed at Archery like acid on the eyes. He blinked away from the beautiful photographed face, the pale hair under a hat of June roses. He had waited for Mrs Kershaw to speak now and her words pulled him out of shock and misery.

'I suppose Tess told you,' she whispered. 'It was supposed to be our secret.' She lifted the lid of the box so that he was able to read the writing on the topmost sheet of manuscript. '*The Fold. A Prayer in Dramatic Form* by John Grace.' 'If you'd told me before I would have shown them to you. Tess said I should show them to anyone who would be interested and would—would understand.'

Again their eyes met and Irene Kershaw's tremulous stare was caught and steadied in his strong one. He knew his face was mobile and expressive of his thoughts. She must have read them for she said, thrusting the box towards him, 'Here, have them. You can have them.' He drew away his hands and his body, horrified and ashamed. At once he had realised what she was doing, that she was trying to pay him off with her most precious material possession. 'Only don't ask me.' She gave a little thin cry. 'Don't ask me about him!'

Impulsively, because he could not bear those eyes, he covered his own with his hands. 'I've no right to be your inquisitor,' he murmured.

'Yes, yes . . . It's all right.' Her fingers touching his shoulder were firm with a new strength. 'But don't ask me about him. Mr Kershaw said you wanted to know about Painter—Bert Painter, my husband. I'll tell you everything I can remember, anything you want to know.'

Her inquisitor and her tormentor . . . Better a swift knife thrust than this interminable twisting on the rack. He clenched his hands till the only pain he could feel came from the wound where the glass had gone in and he faced her across the yellowing sheets of verse.

'I don't want to know about Painter any more,' he said. 'I'm not interested in him. I'm interested in Tess's father . . .' The moan she gave and the feel of those fingers scrabbling at his arm could not stop him now. 'And I've known since last night,' he whispered, 'that Painter *couldn't* have been her father.'

18

. . . As ye will answer at the dreadful day of judgment when the secrets of all hearts shall be disclosed . . .

The Solemnisation of Matrimony.

She lay on the floor and wept. To Archery, standing by helpless, it was some measure of her total breakdown that she had come so far wide of her conventional limits as to lie there prone and shake with sobs. Archery had never in his life reached such a nadir of despair. He pitied with an anxiety that had something of panic in it this woman who cried as if the power to weep had long fallen into disuse, as if she were experimenting with some new and shattering exercise.

He did not know how long this abandonment to grief had lasted or would last. This room with all its apparatus for living what some call a 'full life' contained no clock and he had removed his watch to make room for the wrist anchorage of the bandage. Just as he was beginning to feel that she would never stop, she made a curious humping movement so that she rested like a flogged overburdened beast.

'Mrs Kershaw . . .' he said. 'Mrs Kershaw, forgive me.'

She got up slowly, her breast still heaving. The cotton dress was creased into a faded rag. She said something but he could not hear her at all and he realised what had happened. She had utterly exhausted her voice.

'Can I get you a glass of water, some brandy?'

Her head shook as if it were not part of her body but a separate thing quivering on a pivot. Her voice came in a hoarse croak. 'I don't drink.' Then he knew that nothing could fully pierce the layers of respectability. She fell into the chair from which his questions had prised her and let her arms hang limply over its sides. When he came back from the kitchen and gave her the glass of water she had recovered sufficiently to sip it and to rub with the old refinement at the corners of her lips. He was afraid to speak.

'Does she have to know?' The words had a hollow sound to them but the roughness had gone. 'My Tessie, does she have to know?'

He did not dare to tell her that Charles would have told her already. 'It's nothing these days,' he said, and shed with a word two thousand years' teaching of his faith. 'Nobody thinks anything of it any more.'

'Tell me what you know.' He knelt at her feet, praying that all his guesses would approximate to the truth and that there would be few gaps for her to fill. If only he could deal well with this last task and save her the shame of confession.

'You and John Grace,' he said, 'you lived close together in Forby. You were in love with each other, but he was killed . . .'

On an impulse he took the manuscript in his hands and laid it gently in her lap. She took it as a religious takes a talisman or a relic and she said softly:

'He was so clever. I couldn't understand the things he wrote, but they were beautiful. His teacher wanted him to go to college but his mother wouldn't let him. You see, his father had a bakery business and he had to go into that.' Let her go on, he prayed, edging away to squat on the edge of his chair. 'He still wrote his poems and his plays,' she said, 'and in the evenings he used to study for some exam. He wasn't strong enough to go into the forces, anaemia or something he had.' Her fingers tightened on the manuscript but her eyes were dry and drained. Archery had a quick vision of the pale pointed face in the souvenir shop picture, only now it was blending into and becoming one with Tess's.

He let his eyes linger on Irene Kershaw for a brief moment with painful compassion. They had reached a point in this telling where she must, unless he could save her, touch on that which would humiliate her most.

'You were going to be married,' he said.

Perhaps she was afraid to hear the words he might choose. 'We never did anything wrong but the once,' she cried. 'Afterwards—well, he wasn't nasty like other boys, and he was just as ashamed as me.' Justifying herself, her head turned from him, she whispered, 'I've had two husbands and then there was John, but I've never been much for that side of things.' Her head swung back and her face was aflame. 'We were engaged, we were going to be married . . .'

Archery knew he must rush on with his conjectures. 'After he was killed you knew you were going to have a child?' She nodded, silent now with the enormity of her embarrassment. 'You had nowhere to go, you were afraid so you married Painter. Let me see, John Grace was killed in February 1945 and Painter got home from Burma at the end of March. You must have known him before,' he said, guessing, improvising. 'Perhaps he was stationed at Forby before he went to the Far East?' A tiny nod rewarded him and he was prepared to go on, drawing someone else's story out of an inspired imagination, out of a letter from Kendal, a photographed face, the bruises on a woman's arm. He lifted his eyes from her and clasped his hands tightly to stop the sound that might have been no more than a sigh. Even a sigh would tell her. At the open french window, against the blaze of red petals, Kershaw was standing, silent, still and powerfully alert. How long had he been there? How much had he heard? Archery, transfixed, sought momentarily in his expression for suffering or anger and saw a sweetness that brought a sudden strength to his heart.

Perhaps he was betraying this woman, perhaps he was doing the unforgivable. It was too late for such recriminations.

'Let me try to finish,' he said, and he had no idea whether he kept his voice on the same level he had used before. 'You were married and you let him think he was Tess's father. But he suspected and that was why he never loved her as a father loves his child? Why didn't you tell Mr Kershaw?'

She leant forward and he could tell she had not heard the man behind her move almost soundlessly into the room. 'He never asked me about my life with Bert,' she said. 'But I was so ashamed of it, of being married to a man like that. Mr Kershaw's so good—you don't know him—he never asked me, but I had to tell him some of it, didn't I?' She was suddenly eloquent. 'Think what I had to tell him, think what I had to bring him—nothing! People used to point to me out in the street like I was a freak. He had to take that on his shoulders—Mr Kershaw who'd never touched dirt in all his life. He said he'd take me away and give me a new life where no one'd know, he said I wasn't to blame, I was innocent. D'you think I was going to give up the one chance I'd ever had by telling him Tess was—was illegitimate?'

Archery gasped and staggered to his feet. By the power of his eyes and his will he had been trying to force the man behind her chair to retreat the way he had come. But Kershaw remained where he was, still, a man apparently without breath or heart-beats. His wife had been rapt, her own story dulling all outer stimuli, but now she seemed to sense the atmosphere in the room, the soundless passion of two other people whose sole desire was to help her. She twisted in her chair, sketched a strange little gesture of pleading and rose to confront her husband.

The scream Archery expected never came. She lurched a little, but whatever she was trying to gasp out was lost and muffled by Kershaw's strong embrace. He heard her say only, 'Oh, Tom, Oh, Tom!' but his energy was so drained that his brain was filled with just one foolish thought. It was the first time he had ever heard Kershaw's christian name.

She did not come downstairs again for that time. Archery supposed that he would not see her again until they all met among flowers and bridesmaids and wedding cake. Tess sat pale-faced and almost shy, her hand clasped in that of Charles, the manuscript on her knees.

'I feel so strange,' she said. 'I feel I have a new identity. It's as if I had three fathers and the most remote of them was really my father . . .'

Charles said tactlessly, 'Well, wouldn't you choose to have had this one, a man who could write like this?' But Tess lifted her eyes momentarily to the man Archery would have to learn to call Tom and he knew she had made her choice.

Then she thrust the heavy stack of paper towards Archery. 'What can we do with them?'

'I could show them to a publisher I know. I once wrote part of a book myself . . .' He smiled. 'On Abyssinian cats. I do know someone who might be interested. Something I can do to make amends,' he said.

'You? You've got nothing to reproach yourself with.' Kershaw moved to stand between him and the lovers. Only marred one marriage to make another, Archery thought. 'Listen,' said Kershaw, his face scored with the lines of effort to make himself understood. 'You did nothing but what I should have done years ago, talked to her. I couldn't, you see. I wanted to get off on the right foot. Now I can see you can be too tactful, too damned diplomatic. Oh, there were a thousand little things, how she'd never cared for Painter but he'd been pestering her to marry him. I never asked her what made her change her mind when he came home from Burma. God help me, I thought it wasn't my business! She didn't want me to tell Tess about Painter and I went through agony trying to put that across to a kid of twelve.' Here, unafraid of sentimentality, he caught his stepdaughter's free hand and held it briefly. 'I remember I even got mad at Rene because she seemed to be contradicting every blessed word I said.'

Tess quoted softly, '"Never mind what Daddy says. Your father was no murderer."'

'And she was right but I turned a deaf ear. She'll talk to me now as she's never talked in all these years. She'll talk to you, Tess, if you'll go up to her now.'

Like a child she hesitated and her lips trembled into a nervous smile of indecision. But obedience—happy, reasonable obedience—was natural in that house. Archery had seen an instance of it before.

'I don't know what to say, how to begin,' she said, getting slowly to her feet. 'I'm so desperately afraid of hurting her.'

'Begin with your wedding, then,' Kershaw said robustly. Archery watched him stoop to the floor where the magazines had fallen. 'Show her this and let her dream of seeing you in something like it.'

Tess was in jeans and a white shirt, an Olivia or a Rosalind finding her lost birthright and with it a new womanhood. She took the magazine from Kershaw and glanced at the cover picture, the hat that was a pyramid of flowers crowning the most photographed face in Britain.

'That's not for me,' she said, but she took it with her and Archery watched them depart together, Charles's flesh and blood love and his own, a paper fantasy. Not for me, not for me . . .

'We must go soon,' he said to his son. 'It's time we shared all this with your mother.'

VANITY DIES HARD

For the Savilles:
Patricia and Derek, Mark and Caroline

Vanity dies hard; in some obstinate cases it outlives the man.
Robert Louis Stevenson: *Prince Otto*

1

The rain stopped as they came into the town, but puddles lay everywhere, whipped and wrinkled by the wind. Wet leaves smacked against the windscreen and lay on the pavement like torn rags.

'This do you all right?' Hugo asked. He pulled the car on to a parking area marked with criss-crossed white lines as if for some intricate game. 'We're a bit tight for time, so if you think you can . . .'

'You might take her all the way,' said his wife. 'I call it mean, dumping people as if you were a bus. Besides, it's going to pour.'

'I said we were late,' Hugo snapped. He turned to his sister. 'O.K., Alice? Now the programme is, Jackie and I make a quick tour round Amalgamated Lacquers—there's some kind of a reception at four—but we should be through before five. Pick you up here again at five?'

'Lovely,' said Alice. She gathered up her umbrella and her handbag and opened the car door.

'Don't take any notice of him,' Jackie said quickly. 'Of course we'll call for you at Nesta's. Tell me the address again, will you?'

'Saulsby—S, a, u, l, s, b, y—Chelmsford Road, but I can easily——'

'Rubbish.' She glared at her husband and her black

saucer-sized curls vibrated like antennae. 'If he had an ounce of—of chivalry . . . Oh, what's the use?' For Hugo had already started the car, was putting it in gear. In silent rage he held his left wrist extended, displaying the face of his watch. Alice stood on the pavement and gave a little wave.

'Love to Nesta and all that,' Jackie shouted. 'I hope she won't be in one of her moods. Mind you cheer her up before we come.'

In one of her moods. . . . It was not improbable; it would account for her long silence, her apparent refusal to answer most of Alice's letters. Perhaps she shouldn't have come. Certainly it would have been better to come in her own car, instead of impulsively begging a lift from her brother. Chelmsford Road might be anywhere, might be a mile away on the other side of the town.

So this was Orphingham, a narrow high street rather consciously unspoilt, houses that were called 'period' because they had mostly been built before the nineteenth century, a few new shops, plane trees from whose trunks the bark peeled like flakes of olive-coloured paint. Above her on a bright green mound Alice could see the castle; between gaps in the buildings the Orph could be seen winding between water-meadows. Alice thought it had changed little since the days when Constable painted it, a brown looped river walled with willows. A pretty place for a woman of taste, or a sanctuary for a weary spirit.

Outside the town hall there was a street plan, framed and glazed. Alice found Chelmsford Road at once. She smiled at her own trepidation when she realised that Nesta's street was one of the arms leading from the junction where she now was. As soon as she entered it she saw that it was literally what it called itself, the road to Chelmsford. Wider than the street by which she had entered, it was affluent rather than beautiful and suggestive at first of a wealthy suburb. Many of the houses lay back, half concealed by high walls with gates let into them under arched openings.

It was not quite what she had pictured for Nesta. She had imagined a cottage with espalier apple trees and a porch of cockle-shells. 'A little house,' in Herrick's words, 'whose humble roof is weatherproof.' There was nothing like that here, only huge gabled and turreted villas. Nesta probably had a flat in one of them.

A light drizzle had begun to fall. Alice put on her grey uncompromising 'Pakamac' and opened her umbrella. As she did so she couldn't help remembering how perfect Nesta always looked, how svelte. Her umbrella had been a pagoda-shaped affair, black with a slender handle that looked as if it was made of onyx. Alice sighed. Even without a mirror she knew exactly what she must look like, a pleasant, blue-eyed Englishwoman, no longer very young and never worth a second glance. She put up her left hand to smooth back a trailing strand of fair hair and as she did so a raindrop splashed her new wedding ring. The sigh changed to a smile. What did anything matter, age, indifferent looks, competition, when she had Andrew?

She began to walk briskly down Chelmsford Road. As she had supposed from Nesta's address, none of the houses had numbers. Orphingham Lodge—the abode surely of a successful dentist—El Kantara, The Elms. . . . On the opposite side she noted a succession of similarly obvious names. The last big house had a bungalow next to it, its barren garden planted with Japanese cherries whose stark branches stuck upwards like the spokes of umbrellas turned inside out.

Beyond it there remained only a single terrace. Alice's

eyebrows went up in surprise. The block of coke-dark late-Victorian houses was so out of character in this prosperous street that she could hardly believe her eyes. They were small and cramped, incongruous against the background of swelling green hills, and they reminded Alice of miners' dwellings, blackened by smoke from pit chimneys.

Each bore a stucco plate under its eaves with its name and the date, 1872. Dirt and time had obscured the lettering. To read the plate on the first house she had to come right up to the iron gate, lean over it and peer.

Alice felt a bitter let-down, a cold stab of disappointment. The house was called Kirkby. Nesta's house was going to be one of these, of course it was. But Nesta *couldn't* live here. To come to this after Salstead? Helicon Lane and The Bridal Wreath had been so exquisite. Scotch pines sheltered the little shop with its steep steps and its iron railings; out of the pavement by its forecourt grew the historic Salstead Oak through whose split trunk it was said a man could ride on horseback and from whose branches mistletoe hung in a loose green ball.

She told herself not to jump to conclusions. That dark side of her character, that pessimistic side that had always been liable to fear the worst, had never manifested itself since her marriage. Andrew had taught her to be gay, frivolous almost. Stoically she looked up again. Kirkby, Garrowby, Sewerby and—yes, Revesby. So it wasn't one of these, after all. She heaved a sigh of relief.

And yet . . . Wasn't it rather odd to come upon four houses whose names all ended in the same way as Saulsby and Saulsby not be one of them? Perhaps there were more—prettier than these or smartened up in some way—right at the end of the road. But the houses petered out after the next fifty yards and the pavements changed to grass verges blackened with mud and diesel. In this direction the only building was Orphingham Castle, standing out grey and gaunt against a background of fast-flowing cloud. She had come to the end of the town.

'Excuse me . . .'

A woman in a tweed suit and mackintosh was approaching the road from a field path. She clambered heavily over a stile and came diffidently up to Alice with the suspicious look people wear when accosted by strangers.

'Can you tell me where there's a house called Saulsby?'

'In Chelmsford Road?'

'Yes, Saulsby. I can't find it anywhere.'

The woman pointed in the direction of the terrace. Under the pall of cloud the squat houses seemed to frown back. Alice frowned too.

'That's Sewerby.'

'Canvassing, are you? They do make these mistakes over names. It'll be Sewerby you want, all right.'

'I'm not canvassing. I'm going to see a friend of mine.' Alice got out her address book. 'Look, Saulsby.' Interested, the woman peered over her shoulder. 'She wrote to me and told me her address.'

'Somebody's made a mistake somewhere, if you ask me. You take my advice and ask at Sewerby.'

You take my advice . . . Well, she had asked for advice and she might as well take it. There was no bell on the shabby front door of Sewerby, only a knocker in the shape of a Lincoln Imp. Alice tapped and waited. For a while—half a minute perhaps—she heard nothing. Then from within there came a shambling shuffling sound. The door was bolted and the bolt squeaked as it was drawn back. It opened and she saw a very old man, as pale and purblind as if he had been shut up for years in the dark. From the dim hole of a hall came a stench of boiled cabbage, unwashed clothes and camphor.

'Good afternoon. Is Mrs Drage at home?'

'Who?'

'Mrs Drage. Mrs Nesta Drage.'

'There's only me here, lady.' He wore an ancient over-large suit and his collarless shirt was fastened at the neck by a bone stud. His face was rough and wrinkled, the skin had the texture of rind on old cheese. 'Been all on my own since the wife went,' he said. 'All on my own since fifty-four.'

'But Mrs Drage used to live here,' Alice persisted. 'A young woman, a girl really. She's very pretty with fair hair. She came here about three months ago from Salstead. I thought she had a . . .' She paused, realising that the standards she had set for Nesta were falling all the time. '. . . a room or something,' she said.

'I never let no rooms. It'll be Mrs Currie at Kirkby you want, her what's got a girl nursing at the hospital, but she only takes young fellers.'

So it wasn't Sewerby. She *had* been right. From the page in the address book she read it again: Saulsby. Nesta had written to her—written to her twice—and although she had thrown away the letters, she had copied the address down at once. It was incomprehensible, absurd.

Slowly she walked back the way she had come. The Elms, El Kantara, Beechwood, St Andrew's, Orphingham Lodge and twenty more. But no Saulsby, no Saulsby in the whole street.

Suppose you knew the name of a house and the name of the street it was in, but you couldn't find the house, how did you go about finding it? 'Canvassing, are you?' That was it. The electoral register, the voters' list!

The police station was in the centre of the town between

a public house called The Lion and Lamb and the cottage hospital. Alice went in. The station sergeant had naturally never heard of Saulsby but he provided a copy of the electoral register.

'She won't be on it,' he said, 'not if she's new here.'

But Saulsby would be. Here it was, Chelmsford Road.

'Kirkby, Garrowby, Sewerby, Revesby,' she read aloud and her voice faltered.

'She's written to you from that address, madam?'

'Of course she has, twice.'

'Well, now, I don't rightly know what to suggest.' He hesitated and then, suddenly inspired, added: 'What does she do for a living?'

'She's a florist. She used to have a flower shop in Salstead. You mean I could enquire at all the florists?'

'All two of them,' he said. 'Wouldn't do any harm, would it?'

At the first she drew a blank. The second was larger and busier. Inside the air was humid yet fresh with scent. That particular perfume, a mixture of roses, acrid chrysanthemums and the heavy languor of carnations, brought Nesta back to her as perhaps nothing else could. It seemed to go naturally with the plump pretty face, the golden hair and the commonplace prattle.

The woman ahead of her was ordering wedding flowers. Back in May, when Alice and Andrew had been married, Nesta had given them all the flowers for a wedding present, sewing with her own hands the white orchid to a length of satin ribbon Alice had carried in a prayer book; early in the morning she had come to Vair Place and banked the walls of Uncle Justin's drawing-room with Whitsun Lilies.

'Do you have a Mrs Drage working for you?'

She smiled and opened her eyes in wide delight when the

manageressy girl replied: 'Yes, dear. She's just gone out the back to see to an order. She won't be a minute.'

The search was over. As she waited she felt a quick little twinge of shame and of—envy? Only a woman who had never had to work for her living would come looking for a friend who did work, come on a weekday and expect to find her at home. Of course Nesta would have to work and perhaps she wouldn't be able to leave the shop for long. But then, she comforted herself, something could surely be done to persuade the manageress to let her leave early, or at least get away for a few minutes. She, Alice, could buy something —she slipped her hand into her bag and felt the thick roll of notes she always carried—something extravagant to give to Nesta. Those orchids, possibly, or a dozen long-stemmed red roses.

'I'll give her a call, shall I? I'm sure I don't know what's keeping her.'

Alice wandered about the shop, making plans. It was going to be so good to see Nesta again. I do hope she's got over that depression, she thought. Surely the change of air and environment would have cured it by now. In a moment she would come through that door, ducking her head to avoid an ivy in a hanging basket. She would be wearing a black nylon overall and her hands would be damp, with leaf shreds adhering to them. A sleepy smile would cross her face, for she had always looked lately as if she had just been awakened from a disturbing dream, and she would come out with one of her characteristic, endearing catch-phrases.

'Well, this is a surprise. Long time no see!'

A surprise? No, she wouldn't say that, for Alice had written to her to tell her she was coming, and in five minutes the mystery of the house that wasn't there would be cleared up.

From the back of the shop came the sound of paper being

crumpled, then footsteps. Alice smiled eagerly and took a step forward.

'Nesta . . .'

She blinked and put her hand up to her lips.

'This lady here is Mrs Drake. Sorry to have kept you.'

The disappointment was so sharp that she felt her face muscles fall into an almost comical dismay. Her eyeballs prickled. Mrs Drake was thin, red-armed and middle-aged.

'I said Mrs *Drage*.'

'I'm sorry, I'm sure, but I could have sworn . . .'

She shook her head and turned her back on them. So much frustration was past bearing. She stood on the pavement in the rain, the umbrella dangling from her wrist like a wet deflated pod, staring drearily at the shoppers. Nesta might be among them. Surely . . . ? She started, looked again, and began to run after the little figure in the black shiny raincoat whose bright hair was escaping under a scarf. But as she put out her hand to touch the sleeve the woman turned and showed a pig's face with rosy corrugated skin and scarlet lips.

A sob rose in her throat and with it the beginning of panic. It was an old familiar feeling, this sudden fear, this dread of something terrible about to happen. Familiar but old, half forgotten in the happiness of the past year. Calm, practical, matter-of-fact. That, she knew, was how everyone thought of her.

Suddenly she felt very young, almost childish. She wanted to cry and she wanted Andrew. Strange, because the two impulses were incompatible. In his eyes she was strong, calm and maternal. With a little catch of her breath she turned and caught sight of herself in the rain-dashed glass of a shop window, a tall substantial woman with broad shoulders made to cry on, not to shake with sobs.

Nesta had often cried on them. When you are young and pretty you can cry and nobody minds, nobody reprimands you. Why think of that now? Pull yourself together, she told herself in another of Nesta's clichés. She lifted her sleeve and glanced at the little platinum and diamond watch. Almost four. In an hour's time Hugo and Jackie would come looking for Nesta's house, driving up and down the street, growing angrier and more impatient. She could hardly sit on the wall outside Sewerby, waiting for them in the pouring rain. It was almost funny when you thought of it like that, not a crying matter at all.

In all her thirty-eight years Alice had hardly ever used a public telephone box. For communication with its outlying villages Orphingham had a complicated dialling system, a series of codes. What was the name of the firm whose factory Hugo was visiting? He had only mentioned it once. Amalgamated something-paints, varnishes, sprays. . . . She opened the directory and found it quickly. Amalgamated Lacquers, Orph Bridge. Away from Salstead and the people she had known all her life, Alice was always a little ill-at-ease, uncertain, shy. Never having had to make her own way in the world, she was daunted by the unfamiliar. Tentatively she studied the code and worked the dial slowly. Outside it was beginning to grow dark. Water drummed on the roof and washed down the glass walls.

'May I speak to Mrs Whittaker, please?'

She found she had to explain more fully than that. There followed clicks and trills as someone worked a switchboard, then Jackie's puzzled, slightly apprehensive voice.

'Hallo? Is that you, Mummy?'

'It's Alice.'

'Oh God! I thought there was something wrong with the kids. What's the matter?'

Alice told her. In the background she could hear voices, restrained laughter.

'You've obviously made a mistake,' Jackie said rather sharply. 'Got the address wrong. Have you got her letters with you?'

'I haven't got them at all. I threw them away.'

'Well, there you are, then. You got the address mixed up.'

'That's not possible, Jackie. Nesta left a ring at Cropper's to have it enlarged. I sent it to her at Saulsby and I sent letters too. She got the ring, she wrote to me and thanked me for it. She even sent two pounds to cover the cost of the enlargement.'

'You mean you sent letters and a parcel to a place that doesn't exist and you got answers?' Jackie's tone was gentler now, yet high-pitched with a sort of excitement. 'Listen, I'll come over and fetch you and then we'll come back for Hugo.'

2

'Now, let's see. She moved away from Salstead at the beginning of August and she was very vague about where she was going. She said she hadn't got anything fixed but she'd write and let you know when she was settled. Right?'

Alice nodded. 'I didn't like to bother her with a lot of questions, Jackie. She'd been so depressed lately. She'd been in Salstead three years at that shop and she said that was enough. It can't be much fun being a widow and having to earn your own living. She's so young.'

'Young!' Jackie stretched her trousered legs. 'She's older than I am. Twenty-eight if she's a day.' She added thoughtfully: 'A cross between a Jersey cow and a china doll, that's how she struck me.'

That was not at all how Nesta had struck Alice. Looking back to a couple of years before she was married, she remembered how she had gone into The Bridal Wreath when it had first come under Nesta's management. The wreaths of variegated laurel and the pots of solanum sprouting little orange balls had all been taken away and replaced by specie fuchsias and orchids in green metal trays. In her slow dreamy way Nesta had loved orchids. Their gleaming opaque flesh seemed to have an affinity with her own, their petals curved and pearly like her nails. Alice recaptured that first sight of her now, in one of the black dresses she always wore, the only brightness about her pale vivid hair, stacked and interwoven into a filagree cone.

'It was about a month after she moved that I went into Cropper's to get that watch for Andrew. Nesta had taken her engagement ring in to have it enlarged——'

'I'm not surprised,' Jackie interrupted. 'She was putting on weight like mad. I noticed the way her ankles absolutely bulged when she tottered about in those crazy high heels.'

'Anyway, she must have forgotten to collect the ring before she left. I told Mr Cropper I'd send it to her, but I didn't know her address.'

'Was that when you were going to put an advertisement in *The Times*?'

'I knew Nesta wouldn't read *The Times*, but I thought she might have a friend or a relative who would. I was still thinking about it when I had a letter from her. It was just a couple of lines, but I sent the ring and she wrote back and thanked me for it. But that's weeks and weeks ago now.'

From the scuffed handbag of tooled leather she always carried Jackie took a packet of Sobranie Cocktail cigarettes, selected a pale green one and lit it reflectively. The smoke curled up to the car roof like a feather or a branching flower. 'How could she have got the ring if you sent it to a place that isn't there?'

'I don't know,' said Alice.

Above them the rain pattered rhythmically. The sound it made was like the regular tap-tap of little scurrying heels or long-nailed fingers drumming nervously on metal.

'You'd better tidy yourself up a bit,' Jackie said as she started the car. 'You look as if you've got caught in a storm on a cross-country run.'

A year before Alice would have resented the remark. Now she only smiled. 'I'll never be a glamour queen.'

'A *glamour* queen? Where do you get these expressions, out of the ark?'

'I don't need to—to attract people. I've got a husband.'

'Your Andrew,' said Jackie slyly, 'is a very attractive man.'

'I know.'

'I always think dark men are much more sexy than fair men, don't you?'

'Oh, Jackie, I've never thought about it.'

'Well, you can take it from me, they are. Frankly, lovey—I known you won't mind my saying this, you're too sensible, aren't you?—frankly I've often wondered how you managed to catch Andrew in the first place. Picked him up at some tin-pot school sports, didn't you?'

'It wasn't a school sports, it was Founder's Day. And I didn't pick him up. I went with a friend whose little boy was at school there. We were talking to the English master. . . .'

'And the English master was Andrew.'

'Jackie, dear, I thought every Whittaker in the place knew the story by now. We wrote to each other and had dinner together. Isn't that how most women meet their husbands?'

'I met Hugo in a pub.'

'Yes, I remember, but for goodness' sake don't let Uncle Justin know.'

Jackie giggled. When they were about a mile out of Orphingham she took a left-hand turn down a recently concreted lane. The factory where Hugo was resembled a great fungoid growth, plaster white and rubbery looking among the fields. Presently he came out to the car. His manner was ebullient if slightly nervous and he launched at once into an account of the contract he assured them was 'in the bag'.

'Who cares, anyway?' said Jackie truculently.

'It's your bread and butter, isn't it? And Alice's, come to that. Shove over, you'd better let me drive. All you lot, you batten on Whittaker's like a bunch of parasites.' He gave an irascible grunt. Jackie lit a blue cigarette, elaborately calm. Hugo sniffed. 'Give me one, will you? Not one of those, a real cigarette. Couldn't care less about the works, could you?' All the Whittakers referred to their factory as 'the works'. 'Never think about it, do you? Grasshoppers living it up while the ants do all the work, the ants being Justin and me.' He grunted again. 'Oh, and Andrew of course,' he added as an afterthought and as a sop to Alice.

She was used to his quick gusts of temper, spurts of rage that evaporated quickly and usually meant nothing. 'I'm sorry Jackie had to come back,' she said peaceably, 'but I suppose you've gathered that I couldn't find Nesta. The house just wasn't there.'

'What d'you mean, wasn't there? Oh, damn and blast him!' He braked sharply, stuck his head out in the rain and shouted at the driver of a molasses tanker. The traffic was dense, a glittering sluggish caterpillar.

'It's useless trying to talk to you,' said Jackie. She gasped and exclaimed suddenly, 'Why didn't we think of it? We should have gone to the Post Office.' The car jerked almost into the tanker's tail lights and the big sign attached to its rear, *Caution, Air Brakes*, seemed to leap against the windscreen. 'Hugo!' she screamed. 'What the hell are you doing? Will you still love me when I've had plastic surgery?'

'Oh, Jackie,' said Alice miserably, 'I wish I'd thought of the Post Office. It was the obvious place. I went to the police, but I never thought. . . .'

'You went to the *police*?' Hugo sounded aghast.

'Only for the voters' list. Could we go back, Hugo? It's worrying me rather.'

'Go back? It'd worry me rather if I had to go back through this hell's delight in the middle of the rush. Besides, they'll be closed.'

'I suppose so. I didn't think.'

In fact it was difficult to see how anyone could turn and go back. The crawling queue remained unbroken and serpentine all the way to the Brentwood fork. Then one in three trickled away.

'Thank God this'll be a thing of the past when the by-pass opens next week.'

The whole stream came to a shivering stop as the first cars edged into the bottleneck of Salstead High Street. To her right Alice could see the white mouth of the twin-track road and across it a row of oil drums set about with red warning lights. The new lamps were in place but unlighted. It was a ghost road, a virgin stretch of concrete over which no tyre had yet passed. Still and silent, it dwindled away between dark embankments of piled-up clay. Alice could just make out the big flat direction sign in the distance and the acute-angled branch where the slip road forked away to meet the High Street in the centre of the town. On the other side of that slip road lay Helicon Lane. It was a stump now, its lower end lopped off to allow the passage of the by-pass, but The Bridal Wreath was still there, the oak and the swinging mistletoe. . . .

At the cross roads they left the High Street and turned down Station Road. The lights were on in the doctor's surgery and Mr Cropper was veiling his window display in the metal night guard that looked like a curtain of chain mail. At any rate, Nesta had got her ring. Somewhere in the elusive Saulsby she might even now be slipping it on above her wedding ring, twisting it and smiling as the light caught the facets of the diamond chips.

People were going into The Boadicea. It must be gone six. The car sped smoothly between new developments of semi-detached houses, under the railway bridge, past 'the works' —Whittaker-Hinton, est. 1856. The last of the workers were leaving, in cars, on bicycles, some on foot. Hugo slowed, raising his hand in a salute, and Alice recognised his secretary coming down the steps. Uncle Justin's Bentley and Andrew's Sprite were missing from the executives' car park. The car moved on quickly into the peace of the wet sequestered countryside.

Vair House was much smaller than Vair Place, but built at the same period and of the same tulip-red bricks, and it clung close to its side without being joined to it. It was rather as if the parent building had actually given birth to Vair House, had delivered a child unmistakably its own, though not its replica.

The larger house topped the other by perhaps a dozen feet and this extra space consisted of an overhanging roof from which four dormers protruded. From these windows, and indeed from all the upper windows of both houses, an unscarred view was to be had of Salstead's outlying meadows. Justin Whittaker, who lived at Vair Place, said that just as there was nothing ugly or incongruous about what he called the demesne, so nothing unsightly was visible from it.

Even the new service station on the Pollington Road was concealed by a fine wall of limes, whitebeams and larches. Only St Jude's spire could be seen, a tenuous needle of stone above a web of branches. By building their factory just outside the station the Whittakers had for ever ruined the visitor's first prospect of Salstead; their own dwelling they had taken care to guard from depredations.

Alice and Hugo, orphaned as children, had been brought

up by their father's brother, the present head of the firm. But when Hugo married he had chosen to build himself a new bungalow a quarter of a mile away. Vair House fell vacant when the last Hinton aunt died and had remained so until Uncle Justin gave it to Alice on her marriage to Andrew.

Andrew . . . It was just the place for him, she thought as Hugo dropped her at the entrance to the drive and she began to walk towards the house. She could hardly remember anything that had given her greater pleasure than that first day she had shown him Vair House and had told him it was to be their home instead of one of the stucco-fronted bungalows reserved for married masters at Pudsey School. Unless—unless it was giving him the little red Sprite for a wedding present or the gold watch on his birthday or the William and Mary bookcase for his Trollope first editions.

The Sprite was on the drive now, dwarfed by Uncle Justin's Bentley on the other side of the hedge. Of course, he would be home by now. Alice looked at her watch. Almost half past six. She rounded the only bend in the path and then she saw him waiting for her to come.

She knew he was waiting for her although he was not looking into the garden. The curtains had not yet been drawn and through the small square panes she could see the pink light from one of the lamps falling on his face and on the book he was reading. As she came up the steps, tiptoeing because she loved to come upon him unawares, she could see every detail of the cameo in the embrasure of the window: Andrew's long hands that always reminded her of the hands in Titian's *L'homme au Gant*, the signet ring on his finger, even the cover of one of his favourite Palliser novels, brown and duck-egg blue with the Huskinson drawing.

She let herself in quietly. In front of the hall glass she

paused and looked at herself. When she had married and brought Andrew to Salstead she had made a firm resolution. Nothing about her appearance should be changed. Let them laugh and gossip because dowdy Alice Whittaker had found herself a husband at last—and what a husband! They would have laughed and talked more, she thought, if she had taken to wearing high heels and short skirts and had had her hair cut.

In the great hall at Pudsey she had looked the way she always did, a woman with a splendid figure—a fine woman, Andrew said—in a Macclesfield silk dress and sensible low-heeled sandals, her hair done in the way it had been since she had first put up the plaits when she was seventeen. Andrew had spoken to her, sat with her, fallen in love with her just the way she was. Why should she change?

Still . . . She remembered Jackie's reproaches and felt a tiny stab of doubt. The scarf might look better draped against the neck of her sweater with the brooch pinned to it, or knotted perhaps. She fumbled unsuccessfully; then, smiling at her small vanities, discarded the scarf and fastened the brooch again. Behind her the door swung and she knew he was standing there. His face appeared in the glass over her shoulder.

' "She well knew",' he quoted, laughing, ' "the great architectural secret of decorating a construction and never descended to construct a decoration." '

'Darling Andrew!'

'I was beginning to get worried about you.'

He put out his arms and she went into them, just as if they had been parted for a month.

'You weren't really worried?'

'I would have been if you hadn't come soon. Hungry?' She nodded. 'I sent Pernille off to the pictures. Apparently some early gem of Bergman has found its way to the Pollington Plaza. She'll be back in time to get dinner.'

He followed her into the drawing-room. The tea things were arranged on a low table with thin bread and butter and pastries from the cake shop in York Street.

'I waited tea for you.'

'Waited? Oh, Andrew, you got all this ready specially, didn't you?'

'*Madame est servie.*'

The fire was just beginning to come up. She imagined him letting it die down, not noticing. Then, when it was six o'clock and still she hadn't come, rushing to pile logs on the ashes. She warmed her hands at the thin yellow flames, remembering the first time he had ever handed her a cup of tea in the hall at Pudsey on Founder's Day.

He too had felt it or read her thoughts, for he said gravely, 'Do you take milk, Miss Whittaker?'

She laughed, lifting her face to his and meeting there a shared tenderness, an awareness of the miracle that had happened to them both. It was still impossible for her to believe that he loved her as much as she loved him, yet impossible to doubt when she saw in his eyes that glow of wonder and delight. Love had come to her late and unlooked for. 'It's so romantic,' Nesta had sighed, 'it makes me want to cry,' and her pale blue eyes had filled with tears. Nesta might be crying somewhere now because she had waited for Alice and Alice had failed to come. She drew away from Andrew, keeping hold of his hand. If Nesta had really been waiting for her, surely she would have telephoned.

'Tell me what you've been doing,' she said. 'Anything happened, anyone phoned?'

'Harry Blunden came in, ostensibly to lend me something and to return a book he'd borrowed. You see, he's torn the cover.' He shrugged, indicating a long rent in the jacket of the novel he had been reading. 'He's a ham-handed character for a doctor. I hope he never has to give me an injection.'

So Nesta, wherever she was, had kept silence and was content to do so. 'I haven't seen Harry for weeks and weeks,' she said. Harry might know, he had been Nesta's doctor. 'What did you mean, ostensibly?'

'Of course, he really came to see you, Bell.' He always called her Bell, for it was the Victorian diminutive of her second Christian name. 'I shall call you Bell,' he had said when she had told him she was called Alice Christabel. 'Alice is too hard for you. Alice is for old spinsters, not young wives. . . .'

'What did Harry want?'

He laughed. 'Just to see you, I imagine. He hung about flapping his great hands for half an hour, more or less tongue-tied, and then he had to take his evening surgery.'

'You don't like Harry, do you?'

'Naturally I don't like men who are in love with my wife,' he said lightly. 'I don't like men who treat her house as if it were a shrine and I don't like men who make a point of sitting in her favourite chair because they know she sat there last. He carries his torch aloft over the ground you tread on.' Smiling a little, he sat down on the floor at her feet. 'Which age-old platitudes,' he said, 'bring me to your friend Nesta. How was she? Tell me all about it.'

'There's nothing to tell. I didn't see her. It's awfully odd, darling, but I couldn't find her.'

'What d'you mean, Bell?' He listened in silence, relaxed and perfectly still, as she told him about it.

'What did you say the house was called?'

She took a pastry basket full of marzipan fruit and bit into it.

'Saulsby. I know Jackie thinks I've got it wrong, but I haven't. It's in my book. Wait a minute and I'll get it.'

'Don't get up now. I know you don't make mistakes like that.' He shifted comfortably, looking up at her. 'You really have the most delightful cushiony lap I ever rested my head in.'

'Have you rested it in many?'

'Hundreds.'

She smiled at that, pitying the other women that had been rejected when she was chosen. 'What ought I to do about Nesta?'

'Do? Why should you do anything?'

'It seems so strange.'

'There's probably some quite simple explanation.'

'I hope so. I can't help feeling she may be in some kind of trouble. Do you remember how depressed and strange she was when she left?'

'I remember she went around saying good-bye to everyone, metaphorically rattling her collecting box.'

'Oh, darling!'

'She foisted herself on us because she said everything was packed up for the move and she couldn't cook herself a meal.'

'Pernille was ill so I had to cook it, but the cheese soufflé went flat and it was ghastly.'

'It wasn't particularly ghastly,' he said, and added teasingly: 'You should have invited Harry as well. I'm sure he'd guzzle . . .' He paused, selecting the worst thing he could think of. '. . . chocolate-coated ants if he thought you'd cooked them.'

'Horrible!' Alice shuddered. 'And then she had one of her little weeps,' she went on, 'and you drove her back to The

Bridal Wreath. Goodness knows why because she was going to spend the night with the Feasts. That was the first night they began moving the old graves to make room for the slip road. Nesta had a thing about it.'

'The uncontrolled imagination of the ill-educated,' Andrew said pompously. He grinned at her.

'Don't be so unkind. Even you wouldn't have been awfully keen on sleeping a hundred yards from where a lot of people were unearthing corpses. I know I wouldn't. They even had a policeman and the vicar there, and I think that made it worse. But she wasn't there, anyway. I do wish I knew where she is now, Andrew.'

'Bell?' He sat up suddenly. 'Could we give Nesta Drage a rest?'

She looked at him questioningly.

'I was glad when she went away,' he said. 'I never have been able to see what you saw in her, Bell. When you said she'd borrowed money off you—I didn't like that.' When she began to protest he went on soothingly: 'All right, she paid it back. Today when you went to Orphingham I confess I thought you'd come back several hundred pounds poorer and a partner in another hopeless bit of private enterprise like the last one. But you didn't see her. Darling, I'm not much of a one for signs and portents, but I can't help seeing this mix-up over addresses as the interposition of a kindly Providence.'

'I was going to go back to Orphingham tomorrow.'

'I wouldn't if I were you.' She had never been clever at concealing her thoughts. Now she felt disappointment must show in every feature, for he said impulsively, 'You're really worried about this, aren't you?'

She nodded.

He sat back on his heels and, taking both her hands,

smiled at her tenderly. 'I'm so afraid you'll be hurt. Why not wait till Saturday and then I can come with you?'

'Oh, Andrew, I don't need a bodyguard!'

He was still looking at her with that strange mixture of solicitude and amusement. 'Not a bodyguard,' he said, and his voice held a kind of sad intensity. 'There are other kinds of vulnerability.'

'Sticks and stones,' she said lightly. 'You know how it goes on.'

'Perhaps the most insensitive proverb of them all, certainly the most obtuse.'

Alice went upstairs to dress. It was absurd of Andrew to be so protective. If any of her relatives had heard him they would hardly have been able to keep from laughing, knowing how strong and self-sufficient she was. Maternal was the word they used to describe her, a fit adjective for a woman who had married a man nine years younger than herself.

3

'And where,' asked Uncle Justin as he got out of the Bentley, 'do you think you're going? Why aren't you having your luncheon?'

He came towards the hedge and looked her up and down. What he saw must have displeased him, for he gave no hint of a smile.

Alice recalled that some wit had once said of the family that all the Whittakers looked like the descendants of a monstrous union between a golden cocker and an Arab mare, but that only the males favoured the distaff side. Certainly Justin Whittaker looked very like a horse. His forehead was low but saved from ignobility by its width. The distance between his eyes and his mouth was great and made illusorily greater by the deep parallel lines which his constantly compressed lips had cut from his nose to his chin. His large teeth were all his own but he seldom showed them, keeping his underlip in a position of what he called determination, others pugnacity.

'I'm going to the starvation lunch, Uncle Justin, the bread and cheese lunch for Oxfam,' said Alice bravely, remembering that she was a married woman now. 'They have one every Friday.'

'Roman Catholic rubbish.'

It was useless to argue with him. Better for him to think

she was toying with the Church of Rome than for him to fling at her his most opprobrious taunt, 'Socialist!'

'You don't have to pay for it, do you?'

'Of course we pay for it. That's the point.' She drew a deep breath. 'The proceeds go to Oxfam. I told you. At the moment we're trying to raise enough to buy agricultural machinery for an Indian village.'

He frowned, shaking his head. His silver tie was always so tightly knotted that he had to hold his chin up.

'I wonder what you think we're going to do with all these people you're feeding on the fat of the land. You aren't going to like it, Alice, when they come over here and live in prefabs all over Vair.'

'I can't argue now, Uncle Justin, I'll be late.'

'A lot of old tabbies, I suppose.' His look indicated that he included her among them, not a real woman, a pretty woman. Women in his view should be seen, and should be worth seeing, but should seldom be heard. 'You don't get any men there, I'm sure.'

'Yes, we do.' Alice owned to herself that he was almost right, and then named the only four men who ever attended. 'Mr Feast from the dairy—he's the treasurer—and Harry Blunden often comes. The vicar's almost always there and Father Mulligan from Our Lady of Fatima.'

'There you are, what did I say? You'd much better come and eat your luncheon with me.'

She was almost tempted. Lunch at Vair Place was delightful. She pictured her uncle eating the meal that seldom varied. A small glass of Manzanilla always preceded it, then came a steak and an apple pie cooked by Mrs Johnson and served by Kathleen. His version of bread and cheese was Thin Wine biscuits and a triangle of Camembert.

'I must go,' she said. 'Don't forget you're having dinner with us tonight.'

It was now much too late to walk. By the time she had battled through the lunchtime traffic and found a place to park she saw that it was a quarter past one. But the pitch pine door of St Jude's Hall was still hopefully open.

The hall floor was covered with light brown lino that, because it was never polished, looked like milk chocolate that has been left too long exposed to the air. At a trestle table just inside the door, a table laden with collecting boxes and hung with posters, sat a very thin man. He was even more emaciated than the starved children who, with distended bellies and feverish eyes, stared hopelessly from the flapping photographs.

'I'm sorry I'm late, Mr Feast.' Alice had known him too long to be amused by or even to notice the incongruity of his name.

'Better late than never.' In his throat a huge bulge, like an Adam's Apple swollen to monstrous proportions, stuck out above his collar. It was the only prominent thing about him. If only, Andrew had once proposed, he could be induced to stand at the hall entrance in a loincloth even Uncle Justin's hostility to the cause would melt. The most reactionary would join the bread and cheese eaters, perhaps unaware of the true objects of their fast.

She passed on quickly.

'Good morning, Miss Whit—Mrs Fielding, I should say,' said the vicar. He had married her but it would take him more than six months to get over the habit of twenty years. 'We haven't seen as much of you lately as we should like.' It was the very phrase he used to church backsliders.

I have married a husband and therefore I cannot come, Alice nearly said. Instead she smiled. 'Well, I'm here now.'

'Yes, indeed, and most welcome.'

He led her to one of the long deal tables and hesitated between the many empty chairs. Her eyes travelled from the oil painting of James Whittaker, builder of this hall, splendid in frock coat, watch and chain, to the different pictures beneath. Under each piously Gothic window hung a poster of a hungry child with an empty bowl, so that from where she stood it seemed as if a queue of malnourished infants stretched the length of the hall, watching and waiting.

'Alice! Come and have a place in the sun.' Harry Blunden pushed back his bentwood chair and stood up. 'Here you are, the warmest place in the room.'

She smiled up into his lean ugly face, trying not to show the embarrassment she felt when she saw in his blue eyes so much naked love.

'Thank you, Harry.'

His extreme height had always been a nuisance to him—she imagined him ducking beneath hospital bed curtains, bending almost double over the sick—that he now had a permanent stoop. 'There, what's it going to be?' He eased her coat from her shoulders. 'Mousetrap or best-quality kitchen soap?' It was the no longer funny remark he always made when they met at the Friday lunch.

'Oh, mousetrap. But please not that bit with the evil-looking hole in it.'

The table was covered with a cloth of white plastic. There were bread rolls and rough-hewn chunks of French stick all tumbled together in Pyrex bowls, cheese in bricks as dry and unappetising as the wood of the table, and, in a jam-jar, a small bunch of attenuated watercress. Everyone had a plate, a knife and a Woolworth glass tumbler.

'Hallo, Mrs Fielding.'

Alice looked across the table and met the eyes of a thin

girl with long shaggy hair that reached to her shoulder blades.

'Hallo, Daphne. You're the very person I wanted to see.'

Daphne Feast parted the strands of hair and peered at her.

'I know. I've been talking to your sister-in-law.'

'*Jackie*? Is Jackie *here*?'

Reaching a long arm rudely across the plate of a plump woman sitting two places from her, Daphne pointed to the far end of the table where Jackie sat between her two small children.

'She said you'd been looking for Nesta Drage. She'd given you a false address or something.'

'Well, it wasn't quite——' Alice stopped as Harry interrupted her. She wished he wouldn't always try to monopolise her.

'Gave you a false address?' he said. 'But you went to see her, didn't you?'

'Yes, I did, but . . .'

She lifted up her glass as the vicar approached their section of the table with a jug of water.

'How much do we have to pay for this?' asked the plump woman suspiciously.

The vicar beamed. 'Just whatever you would have paid for your normal lunch at home.'

'But I don't have any lunch at home! My mother-in-law won't let me. She says if I put on any more weight I'll get a coronary. I won't get a coronary, will I, Dr Blunden?'

Harry turned towards her reluctantly. 'Just as well to be on the safe side,' he said.

'I wish you'd come and sit by me, Doctor, and tell me what I ought to do so that I can tell my mother-in-law.'

Alice could see he didn't want to move. For a moment he

hesitated. Then he got up and, smiling abstractedly, walked round the table carrying his plate.

'I thought you might know where Nesta really is,' she said to Daphne. 'You were such close friends.'

'Oh, I don't know. We used to have a bit of a giggle together. That's all.'

'Didn't she tell you where she was going either? She must have given you an address to write to.'

'She knew I'd never write, Mrs Fielding. We were—what-d'you-call-it?—ships that pass in the night. She never even said a proper good-bye, but I'm not breaking my heart over it.'

Alice was bewildered. 'But she stayed with you and your father on her last night. August the seventh, that Friday night. She had supper with us and then she went to stay with you.'

'She never turned up.'

'I though it was a definite arrangement.'

'Not what you'd call an arrangement. She did *say* she'd come and Pop and me waited for her, but there was a play on the telly and what with her having the phone cut off I couldn't get in touch with her. You know how it is.'

No, she didn't know. She wrote down all her engagements in a twin to the big address book and she had never failed to keep a coffee-morning date, let alone break a promise to spend the night in a friend's house.

'Didn't you go round to The Bridal Wreath to find out?'

The suggestion almost seemed to shock Daphne. She nibbled at her last fragment of cheese. 'I told you, there was this play on. Pop just went up to The Boadicea for a beer and I said, 'Keep your eyes open for Nesta,' but he never had sight nor sound of her. When it got to ten I gave her up.' She leaned confidingly across the table. 'Quite frankly, Mrs Fielding, I didn't go much on going down Helicon Lane in the dark, not with all those graves being turned up.'

Heavens! Alice gave herself a little shake. There was something ghoulish about Daphne's pallid face in which only the eyes were made up, the streaming hair that trailed across the bread bowl.

'Well,' she said, 'it's a mystery, isn't it? Before I sent the ring off to Nesta—when I didn't know anything of her whereabouts—I asked everyone in Salstead who knew her and no one had her address.'

'You asked me then,' said Daphne mournfully, 'and I asked Pop and all the shop people.'

On the other side of the table Harry looked as if his patience was being exhausted. The plump woman's voice rang out, 'I suppose there's nothing to stop me going into The Boadicca when I've finished this and having a proper lunch, is there?'

'On your own head be it,' said Harry. He came round behind Alice's chair, stopped and patted her shoulder. 'I wouldn't do too much of this, if I were you, Alice.' His voice had dropped and she swivelled round quickly because his words were plainly intended only for her ears. 'You need proper meals. You've been looking tired lately.'

'But I feel fine.'

The words were almost a whisper and she had to strain to catch them. 'If there's ever anything troubling you—*anything*, Alice, you'll come to me, won't you?'

'You know I'm never ill, Harry.'

He shook his head, increased the pressure of his hand and then withdrew it. Puzzled, she watched him cross to the table where Mr Feast sat taking the money. Harry was a doctor, *her* doctor. Why then had she received such a strong impression that the trouble he feared for her wasn't physical at all?

'You said it was a mystery,' said Daphne Feast. 'Well, I'll tell you something. There were a lot of mysteries about Nesta.'

At the hint of gossip Alice felt herself shrink. All she wanted was to find out where Nesta was and why she was hiding herself.

'For one thing she was involved with some man.'

'Oh, come!' Nesta had been devoted to the memory of her dead husband, even to the extent of still wearing mourning three years after his death. One day certainly she would get married again. Anyone as pretty as she was was bound to. But, involved with a man? Nesta had been lonely and forlorn. It was because of this and in an effort to save her from the company of people like the Feasts that Alice had made a point of cultivating her.

'She wouldn't tell me who he was,' Daphne said firmly, 'only that he was a big man in Salstead and that some people would have a bit of a shock when it came out.' She lit a cigarette and dropped the match among the crusts and cheese rinds on her plate. 'I reckon he was married. There was some reason he didn't want it known. Nesta said he'd have to marry her one of these fine days. We had a bit of a giggle about it.'

'That sounds like day-dreaming to me,' said Alice severely.

'There was another funny thing. Nothing to do with her love life, but a funny thing.' Daphne flicked her ash across the table.

I'm not surprised Nesta didn't want to stay with the Feasts, Alice thought.

'Did you ever notice her eyebrows?'

'Her *eyebrows*?'

'You think I'm daft, don't you? No, you wouldn't have noticed, not with her being so neurotic about the way she looked. Well, when she first came here she had thick sort of fair eyebrows and very long lashes. Right?'

Yes, Nesta had beautiful eyebrows and long soft lashes. Her blonde hair had been abundant too.

'Well, naturally she used to pluck her eyebrows, but one day she was a bit heavy-handed and she pulled too much out. She said she'd have to let them grow . . .'

'Well?'

'Well, they never did. That's all. They never did and she used to have to sort of pencil them in. I popped into her flat once—she didn't know I was coming and, God, she jumped out of her skin—she'd taken her make-up off and she hadn't got any eyebrows at all. I can tell you, Mrs Fielding, it gave me the creeps. Just eyes she had and then nothing till her hair started.'

Daphne, Alice thought, had missed her vocation. She would have made a startling impact on filmgoers as a kind of female Boris Karloff. First the graves and now this.

'Her eyelashes were—well, they were quite luxuriant.'

'False,' said Daphne Feast. 'I'm not kidding.'

So poor Nesta had had alopecia. Horrible, when you remembered how proud she had been of her appearance.

'Thanks, Daphne. I expect she'll turn up.'

She began to put on her gloves.

'When you do root her out you might tell her to come and collect her stuff.'

'Her stuff?'

'She got Snows to fetch round some stuff of hers the day before she left. I reckon it was a load of junk or some of those kids' jigsaw puzzles she was so crazy on doing. Anyway, you can tell her I'm fed-up with it cluttering the place up.'

'I'll tell her.'

The trouble with being a Whittaker was that everybody expected you to dispense largesse wherever you went. Glad that Uncle Justin would never know the extent of her generosity, Alice took two pound notes from her wallet and laid them on the table in front of Mr Feast.

'Quite a good——' She had nearly said 'audience', '—attendance here today, Mr Feast.'

He began mournfully on a long diatribe. 'Always the upper crust and the working class, though, you'll notice, Mrs Fielding. The bourgeoisie keep their feet under their own fat tables. That's why I've always said and always shall say, the Popular Front's an impossibility. The upper crust and the working class——'

'Do tell me, Mr Feast, which do I come in?' At Jackie's voice, Alice turned. 'I didn't know what to do with the brats so I brought them along to see how the other half lived.'

Alice bent down and swung the three-year-old up into her arms. 'He's getting heavy, Jackie! What did you think of your funny old dinner, darling?'

Her nephew flung his arms around her neck. 'I'm partial to cheese, aren't I, Mum?'

'Partial?'

'It's his latest word. Put him down, Alice. You'll strain yourself.'

'I've just made up my mind,' Alice said. 'I'm going back to Orphingham. Now. This afternoon.'

'And we're coming with you,' said Mark and Christopher together.

Smiling, Alice squatted in front of them.

'Would you like to? You can. I'd love some nice jolly company.'

'Well, you've had that for a start,' said Jackie. 'You're coming to the dentist with me.'

As the double wail went up she put her hands over her ears.

'It's a pity you haven't got any of your own, Alice. If you'd got married ten years ago you'd have had kids and all the jolly company you wanted.'

Ten years ago Andrew had been nineteen, in his second year at Cambridge. Alice wondered if Jackie knew what she had said, but although she felt the blood mounting in her own cheeks there was no sign of embarrassment on her sister-in-law's face. Jackie and Hugo, Uncle Justin, all of them, only thought of Andrew's luck, the sudden rapid step he had taken into affluence. They never considered what he had lost by marrying a woman on the verge of middle age.

She took a hand of each of the boys. 'If you're very grown-up about going to the dentist, I promise I'll have something lovely for you at Vair. You get Mummy to bring you at—let me see—half past five.'

'That's a vicious circle,' said Jackie. 'Fill their beastly little fangs and then rot them all over again.'

Alice walked out into the cold sunlight. If she made haste and started at once she would be in Orphingham by three.

4

The post office was crowded. Alice had to push her way in past prams and tethered dogs. Behind the rail on the counter top, three people were serving, a thin young man with a face so pale as to be almost green, a plump woman and another man, older and dignified, with a heavy grey moustache. Alice glanced ruefully at a legend on a poster: 'Someone, somewhere, wants a letter from you.' She joined the shortest of the queues. It was moving very slowly. Pension books were brought out and presented with dogged patience, secreted once more in bags and wallets.

'Next, please.'

'I've been sending letters to a house in Chelmsford Road,' Alice began. 'To a friend of mine. But when I went to Chelmsford Road yesterday I couldn't find the house.' Behind her an old woman pushed forward to listen. 'The name of the house is Saulsby, but there isn't a Saulsby in the whole street.'

'You mean your letters have gone astray?' The young man's voice was rough with impatience. He kept his head bent while he rummaged in a drawer. 'If they've been wrongly addressed they'll be returned to sender in due course. It's a wise precaution to put your own address. . . .'

'I don't think they can have gone astray. I've been getting replies.'

At last he looked at her. 'You don't want us at all, do you? What you want is the council offices. They'll let you have a street plan. Next, please?'

Standing her ground, Alice said desperately: 'I know the name of the street. I told you, it's Chelmsford Road. I'm sorry if you're busy . . .'

'Always busy on a Friday afternoon on account of everybody coming in then because it gets so crowded on Saturday.'

His lack of logic almost defeated her. She stepped back and immediately an arm in moth-eaten ocelot thrust across her and laid a pension book on the counter.

'Isn't there anyone I could talk to about this? Surely there must be someone who would know?'

'If you'd like to line up over there you could have a word with Mr Robson. He's the postmaster.'

To join Mr Robson's queue she had to go right back to the door. She counted fifteen people waiting while the postmaster served a woman in an orange sari. Five minutes passed and nobody moved. The Indian woman was buying half a dozen stamps of each denomination to send home to a philatelic relative in Calcutta. The queue began to mutter and shuffle.

Suppose I were to go back there just once more, Alice thought, and make another check on those house names now it isn't raining. Ignoring the queue, she walked straight up to the pale man's counter. 'Will it be less crowded if I come back later?'

'Pardon?'

'If I come back later?'

'You can come back later if you like.' Counting notes, he hardly bothered to look at her. 'It gets a bit slacker around half-five.'

'Do you mind not going out of your turn?' asked a tired young woman carrying a child.

Alice went back to her car and drove up the High Street to the Chelmsford Road turning. Even under the wintry sky the place had the higgledy-piggledy, typically English prettiness of a calendar or a Christmas card. The townspeople evidently took pride in their rainbow variety of painted front doors, lime-washed walls and sanded steps. This place, she thought, but without malice or contempt, would have made a particular appeal to Nesta's snobbishness and her love of beauty kept within orderly bounds. Its residents could turn up their noses at certain utilitarian workaday aspects of Salstead.

Chelmsford Road was deserted. Dead chestnut leaves like ancient wrinkled hands, brown and crepitating, rustled in the gutters. None of the houses had numbers and none was called Saulsby. She walked up one side examining name plates and down the other.

The only sound to disturb the cathedral-like hush came from the front path of El Kantara where a woman was sweeping leaves. The round-topped gate in the wall was open and just inside was a sign which read:

Orphingham Hospital Management Committee, Nurses' Home.

'I'm looking for a house called Saulsby,' Alice said.

'Saulsby? I don't think . . .' It was almost sinister the way she whispered and looked furtively over her shoulder. She held the broom a foot from the ground and the leaves began to eddy back, covering the swept path once more. 'You don't mean one of the eyesores?' she said in a voice so low that Alice had to strain to catch it.

'The eyesores?'

'Four nasty little slums. If you've been up the road you

must have passed them. They've been due for demolition goodness knows how long.'

Why whisper about it? Why keep glancing up at those blind closed windows? In the heavy shadowed silence of the tree-grown drive Alice suddenly felt a little thrill of fear. If only she had waited until tomorrow when Andrew could have come with her.

'No, it isn't one of those,' she said softly. She glanced behind her quickly into the thick bushes and jumped as the woman hissed suddenly:

'Sorry I had to keep my voice down.' She smiled, breaking the tension, and pointed the broom handle aloft. 'You see, the night-duty girls are all asleep.'

Alice almost laughed as she went once more into the street. She must be letting this business get her down. Of course that was the obvious explanation. Why read ridiculous nuances into it?

While she had been inside the gate someone had parked a bicycle beside her car, a red bicycle. A postman would have a red bicycle, she thought. But where was he? As she stood looking at the blank wall, the long row of gates all overhung with chestnut branches, holly and yellow-spotted laurel, a sudden gust of wind caught the bicycle and knocked it over into the gutter. Its wheels spun. She bent to pick it up. He must have heard the crash and the whirr of wheels, for he came running, slamming the gate of The Laurels.

'Thanks very much.' He was very young with yellow hair and a characterless face in which the colour was oddly distributed, for his chin, nose and forehead were chapped and reddish while his lips and cheeks had a sickly pallor. 'You shouldn't have got yourself dirty.' He hoisted his canvas bag on to the handlebars and stood waiting for her to go.

'Tell me,' she said, 'do you deliver letters down here in the mornings, all the letters? Are you the regular postman?'

'Been on here a couple of months. What were you wanting?'

'Have you ever delivered any letters to a Mrs Nesta Drage at a house called Saulsby?'

'Not what you'd call delivered. There's a redirection notice on Saulsby.'

She stared at him. Her heart had begun to beat very fast. At last the name made sense to somebody besides herself.

'What's a redirection notice?'

'It's like when you change your address, see? You fill in a form at the post office and all the post—well, it doesn't go to your old address. It goes to the new one. We do our own sorting and when we get mail for this said person, the one that's filled in the form, we write the new address on the envelope and it goes back in the post. Saves your letters getting lost like.'

'Would you be very kind and tell me where Mrs Drage's letters are going?'

He shook his head. 'Can't do that. That'd be an invasion of privacy.'

The wind had grown suddenly cold. Twilight was coming and with it a light, needle-sharp frost. She shivered. She was seldom angry but now she could feel herself growing edgy with frustration.

'I suppose it didn't occur to you that there isn't a Saulsby in Chelmsford Road, that it doesn't exist?'

'Now, look,' he said, truculent and defensive, 'it's on the notice. I've seen it on her letters, plain as a pikestaff.'

'Where is it, then? Show me.'

'Up there. 'He pushed the bicycle up to the grey terrace and Alice followed.

'Sewerby, you see,' she said quietly, and she was glad she

had made no more of this small triumph, for he stared aghast at the name plaque and the flush spread across his whole face, dark as a naevus.

'But I've never had no letters for Sewerby.'

'I'm not surprised. He's a very old man and he's all on his own. I don't suppose anyone ever writes to him, and if you've only been on here two months——'

He interrupted her raggedly. 'I don't know what come over me.' His voice was pleading and he turned towards her as if he would clutch at her clothes. She moved away, lifting her hand. 'I reckon I must have misread that name and what with them always coming and going at Kirkby and them houses not having numbers like . . . Mr Robson did say I was to check, but—I don't know—things kind of got on top of me.' His hands tightened on the handlebars. 'He'll have the hide off me,' he said.

'I don't want to make trouble for you. I only want to know where my letters are going.'

'That's easy,' he said eagerly. 'There was a letter come for her Wednesday.' Alice nodded. She had posted it herself on Tuesday night. 'One hundred and ninety-three, Dorcas Street, Paddington. I've got it by heart on account of my mother's name being Dorcas.'

Alice wrote it down. 'I won't say a word to Mr Robson,' she joked feebly. 'He's not an easy man to see.'

One hundred and ninety-three, Dorcas Street, Paddington. Of Paddington Alice knew only the station and that small pretty corner known as Little Venice. Those streets she had seen from Western Region trains taking her on holiday to Cornwall had been far from prepossessing. Could Dorcas Street be one of them? It sounded charming but its very euphony made her uneasy. In present-day civilisation the pretty names belonged to sordid venues while a street that was called The Boltons or Smith Square was all that was respectable and affluent.

This, then, was the most likely explanation: Nesta had gone to an ugly slummy part of London but she had been unable to bring herself to admit it. Snobbery, a desire to seem grand to her friends, had made her give Alice a fine-sounding address.

Her heart contracted with pity as she gave Chelmsford Road a last look. Nesta must have been to Orphingham and seen in its peace the sanctuary she longed for. Chelmsford Road was the very place she might have chosen for her home if circumstances had been different. Perhaps that too was the explanation of her languor and her depression. A day-dreamer continually baulked could have conceived such a plan. Only a woman with a deranged mind would have carried it out. Or—or a woman who lived puzzles, jigsaws, problems on television quiz programmes, the easier crosswords in the evening papers?

Suddenly Alice felt quite excited. Then doubt and disquiet returned. There could be nothing amusing in the motives which had prompted Nesta. She must be rescued. Friendship was pointless if it stopped short at material aid. Alice felt in her handbag the shiny blue book whose cheques never bounced. Why, oh why, instead of this constant effort to keep up appearances, hadn't Nesta told her?

'I'd rather you didn't go.'

'Why on earth shouldn't I, darling?' She was at the dressing-table, combing her hair, when Andrew had come in, already dressed, slightly impatient. As soon as he had heard she meant to go to Paddington he had said he would go with her, but she had protested. Nesta was proud. She might tolerate Alice enquiring into her affairs, never Andrew.

'Do as you like, but it'll upset you, Bell, if you find she's living with a man.'

'*Nesta?*'

He came towards her and in the mirror she watched him approach and put his hands on her shoulders. 'You're such a child in some ways. I don't mean you're immature and God knows you're always exaggerating your age, but you're innocent. I wonder what you'd do if you found her in some horrible back room with a man—say, Nesta trailing about in a black négligé and the lover not bothering to hide himself, but bellowing things from the bedroom?'

'That's not funny, Andrew.'

'Darling, forgive me, but wouldn't you just whip out the little cheque-book—money, the universal healer?'

She was hurt and she showed it.

'You mean I'm mercenary? I make a god of money?'

'Not a god—a key to open all doors. Bell, I have to tell you this, but that's the way a child feels. Jackie brought Mark and Christopher in tonight—' Diverted, she held the comb poised. She was suddenly appalled because she had forgotten all about them. 'It's all right. I gave them some sweets I found in a drawer. Mark didn't want to go home. D'you know what he said? Let's stay, Mummy. I'll give you sixpence if you'll let me stay.'

'And I'm like that?'

'You're—you're an angel.' He dropped a kiss on to the top of her head. Still troubled, she looked up and in the glass he met her eyes.

Now, as she lifted the heavy mass of hair in both hands and, seeking some way of doing it more flatteringly, held it loosely above her head, he drew back, not touching her any more.

'What's the matter?'

'Don't do your hair like that. I don't like it.' He sounded ridiculously annoyed.

'I thought it made me look younger.'

'For heaven's sake, Bell, don't keep harping on your age as if you were a candidate for a geriatric ward!'

'Sorry.' Still twisting her hair into a soft loose coil, she averted her head from the glass and turned to face him. To her surprise he let out his breath in a sigh.

'It's not so bad, I suppose. I imagine I could get used to it.'

'You won't have to. The old way's easiest. 'Rapidly she began weaving the two plaits. 'Look, darling, will you feel better if I promise you that when I find Nesta I'll try to help her without actually giving her money?'

'What other help could you give her?' He was still shaken and she wondered why.

'If she was in need I could bring her here.'

'Bring her *here*? I'd rather you gave her money to stay away than adopted her!'

'Andrew! Adopt—why did you use that word? What did you mean?'

He shook his head. 'Nothing. Forget it.'

Her hands travelled down over her useless, ageing body. Jackie had been there, Jackie with her two sons. It was not hard to unravel the workings of his subconscious.

'I'm ready now,' she said in a carefully neutral voice. 'Let's go down.'

'Good heavens,' said Uncle Justin, 'it makes you wonder what the Post Office is coming to! If you had any idea of your duty as a citizen, Alice, you'd report the whole thing to that fellow-what's-his-name?—Robson.' Suspiciously he ran his tongue round the rim of his glass. 'Where did you get this sherry, Andrew? I may be wrong but to me it has a distinct flavour of the Southern Hemisphere.'

'Well, it can't have,' said Alice firmly. She had recovered her poise, 'since it came from Jerez. What do *you* think I ought to do about Nesta?'

'Ah, yes, Mrs Drage.' Alice remembered with exasperation that he had to know someone for at least twenty years before venturing on the Christian name. 'A comely woman, very easy to look at. Not at all the sort of person one would expect to see keeping a shop. I daresay she found it difficult to make ends meet.'

'She borrowed some money off Alice once,' said Andrew. Why had she ever told him that? 'Before we were married. I'm afraid there might be a repetition and that's one reason why I think it's better for Alice not to see her.'

'She paid it back,' Alice said pleadingly, 'besides it wasn't much.'

'A couple of hundred pounds and you call it not much!'

'Not enough to make a song and dance about,' said Uncle Justin unexpectedly. 'I'm happy to say I was able to give her a little help myself occasionally in that direction.'

Dumbfounded, Alice looked at him. He was sitting stiffly, not resting his head against the soft back of the chair. His thinness and the straight set of his shoulders took ten years from his age. His hair was grey but abundant. The bone formation of his face and the sparse flesh had suffered few of the effects of time. There were lines and cavities, deep pouches under the eyes, but there were no wrinkles.

Of all the big men in Salstead he was the biggest. Just as she was wondering if she dare ask him the obvious question Andrew asked it for her. 'And may one ask if you ever got it back?'

His answer would make all the difference. As she waited,

half terrified, half curious, for the outburst, the door opened and Pernille appeared on the threshold, beaming at them.

'Ah, dinner!' said Uncle Justin. 'I hope you're going to give us some of your Scandinavian delicacies. I'm particularly fond of those little cup things with asparagus.'

'*Krustader*, Mr Whittaker.'

'That's it. Crustarther. You'll have to give Mrs Johnson the receipt for those.'

Too far away from him to warn him off further indiscreet questioning with a touch, Alice gave Andrew a glance of loving anger.

But he said no more and now her uncle was beaming in happy anticipation of the meal. She felt a sudden impatience, a wish to get the evening over quickly, the night that must pass before she could go to a hundred and ninety-three, Dorcas Street, Paddington.

5

A kaleidoscope of green, grey and rose-pink whirled and rocked; then it began to spin round an intensely bright, burning vortex. But just as she thought it must engulf her and destroy the last remaining steadiness of balance the colours split and settled back into the bathroom décor. Just grey tiles, a rectangle of green soap and three pink towels hanging on a wickedly bright rail. The window was like a square of gingham, white bars crossing the black sky of early morning. It was still now, no longer bouncing or swimming in a mist. But the sickness remained. Alice sat down on the edge of the bath. She could not remember ever having felt so ill.

It must be very early. The cold she felt could have nothing to do with the true temperature, for she had turned on the heater when she had first staggered here from the bedroom. Shivers fluttered along her arms and legs and seemed only to increase when she put her hands on the hot rail. In Andrew's shaving glass her face looked white and aged by the bile that was moving again, rising horribly into her mouth. She twisted over to the basin and retched.

Presently, when the spasm had passed, leaving her drained and trembling, she made her way back to the bedroom. Andrew was asleep. The dark blue light that precedes a winter dawn showed her a boy's cheek and a hand curled like a child's round the pillow edge. She moved in beside him warily, afraid to let him see her in the ignominy of a repulsive illness.

But she was *never* ill. Something in Pernille's dinner must have disagreed with her, the pink *silde salat* perhaps, or the *krustader*. Andrew had opened a bottle of wine, *Entre Deux Mers*, a dry white Bordeaux, but she had taken less than a glassful. And afterwards they had eaten chocolates that Uncle Justin had brought. She shifted away from Andrew, keeping her head up. The very thought of food was bringing the sickness back and the shivers that made her teeth chatter.

She pressed her hands against her diaphragm, willing the nausea to go. Perhaps it had been the yoghurt she had grown so fond of lately and took every night for her supper. As she remembered the gelatinous curd, white, decomposing into whey as the spoon broke it, she threw back the bedclothes and rushed across the room. Let me make it to the bathroom, she prayed.

Of course it had awakened him. She clung to the basin rim, knowing that he was standing behind her.

'Go back to bed,' she said harshly, 'I don't want you to see——'

'Don't be silly.' She knew she would have been sick again if anyone had touched her and yet because he did not touch her she felt, in the midst of her misery, the deprivation.

'I'll be all right in a minute.'

'Why didn't you wake me, Bell? How long have you been like this?'

She ran cold water into the basin, splashing her hands and face. 'Hours,' she said. 'I don't know.'

'Come on.' He put his arm around her and she turned her face away. 'I'll get Pernille to bring you some tea.'

'Leave me alone, please, Andrew.' She fell on to the bed

and buried her head in the warm hollow where his had been. 'You mustn't see me like this.'

'Darling, don't be absurd. Aren't you supposed to be the flesh of my flesh and the bone of my bone?' It was a phrase from one of his favourite Victorian novels, half joke, half sincere. 'I'll get Pernille.'

She couldn't drink the tea. It grew cold and bitterly yellow on the bedside table beside the dregs of hot milk Andrew had brought her the night before.

'Pernille,' she said feebly, 'that yoghurt, where did it come from?'

The Danish girl shook out the pillows and pummelled them. 'I took it home from Mr Feast's, Mrs Fielding.'

Alice felt too ill to do her duty and correct the usage. She would never appreciate the difference between 'to bring' and 'to take'.

'Did you have any of it?'

'I? No, thank you. Nobody takes yoghurt but you.'

Andrew came back softly, bringing the morning papers. She wished he would leave her to the dimness and not snap on the overhead light.

'Any better, darling?'

'I feel terribly ill, Andrew. Do you think we could get Harry?'

'Just because you feel a bit sick?' He sat on the edge of the bed and lifted the long fair hair from her cheeks. 'You'll be better in a little while.'

'And I was going to London today,' she wailed.

'In that case you'd better have Harry. I'm sure he won't let you go out, darling. It's bitterly cold.' To emphasise his words he drew back the curtain and showed the cruel windy morning, clouds white as piled snow, lurching across purplish-black cumulus. The wind was tossing scotch pine branches against the glass, fist-shaped bunches of needles tapping and jerking away again.

'He needn't come till he's finished his other calls.'

His quick jealousy was a better tonic than any medicine Harry could prescribe. 'Don't worry,' he said sharply. 'He'll come.' Catching her eye, he laughed at himself and added ruefully: 'You know very well, darling, if the whole of Salstead was down with bubonic he'd still be here first thing.'

'Andrew!' He must love her, looking not with the eyes but with the mind. 'Go and have your breakfast.' He kissed her, picked up the book he had been reading the night before, and went downstairs.

Harry came as soon as his morning surgery was over. She blushed a little when he came in. Andrew's prophecy had been fulfilled. Bubonic was an exaggeration, but surely Harry had countless patients awaiting him. Andrew must be sitting in the dining-room now, smiling a little, the man in possession. It gave her a little warm thrill to think that, though apart, they shared the same thoughts.

'How do you feel, Alice?'

'Not quite so bad now.' She gave him her hand and he put his fingers to the pulse. 'I was terribly sick earlier. Did Andrew tell you about it?'

His face was expressionless. 'He said something about it on the phone. I didn't disturb him when I came in.' Taking his hand away, he said in a repressed tone, 'He was reading.'

You make him sound like Nero, she thought resentfully, fiddling while Rome burns. Andrew's jealousy was reasonable, the natural corollary to a husband's love, Harry's pathetic.

'I just kept being sick, on and on. I suppose Pernille's dinner was too rich.'

He smiled in disbelief and put the thermometer in her mouth.

'It's more likely to be one of these viruses.'

When she was beginning to think she would vomit again if the glass tube remained any longer between her lips, he took it from her and went to the window.

'It isn't anything serious, is it, Harry? I wanted to go to London today, to Paddington.'

He shook the thermometer down with a swift jerky movement.

'Paddington? You're not going away, are you?'

Strange how to everyone Paddington meant only the station. She shook her head.

'You mustn't think of going out,' he said. 'You'd far better stay where you are. I'll look in again tomorrow.'

Illness was unfamiliar. It made her at once into a hypochondriac. 'You'd tell me if it was anything serious?' But she knew he wouldn't. Doctors never did.

'I told you, Alice. You've probably got a virus infection. I thought you were looking pale yesterday.'

'Is that why you said I was to come to you if anything was troubling me?'

He blushed as hotly as the young postman in the twilit street. 'Of course,' he said abruptly. At the best of times he had no poise, only a vulnerable boyish gaucheness. Now as, all thumbs, he bundled his instruments back into the case, she thought briefly back over the ten years since he had come to Salstead. She had lost count of how many times he had asked her to marry him. And yet for all that, their relationship had never advanced beyond friendship, he had never kissed her or even put his arm round her shoulders. They were doctor and patient. She almost smiled as she thought that in spite of the love and the proposals the question of ending *that* relationship had never arisen. Her physical health had been so splendid she had never had to call him in.

'I hope I'm not going to be ill long,' she said fretfully. It was going to be awkward and embarrassing if he had to come here daily to attend her.

'Here's someone to cheer you up,' he said.

It was Hugo. Muffled in a rugger scarf, he tiptoed up to the bed and dumped a squashy parcel on his sister's stomach. 'Grapes,' he said. 'Hallo, Harry.'

'How did you know I was ill?'

'News travels fast in this neck of the woods. Jackie bumped into Pernille Madsen at the shops.' He rubbed his hands and sat down heavily on the bed. 'You're in the best place. It's enough to freeze the——'

'All right, Hugo!' Alice laughed weakly. 'Good-bye, Harry. It was nice of you to come.' He hesitated, waiting—for what? What did he expect her to say to him, what could she say that was kind, generous and meaningless all at the same time? 'You mustn't think that because I'm a friend . . .' As the smile on his face gradually chilled, she blundered on, 'I mean, you mustn't neglect your other patients for me. . . .'

His hand was resting on the glass fingerplate of the door. Then she saw that it was no longer resting, but pressing, pressing, until the nails showed white.

'What makes you think you're different from anyone else, Alice?' he snapped. Hugo coughed and, making a great display of loosening his scarf, flung it on the bed. 'Are you criticising my professional conduct?'

She was horrified, almost at a loss for words. 'I didn't . . . I wouldn't . . . You know what I meant!'

'I'm sorry. Forget it.' He cleared his throat and managed

a smile. 'I'll leave a prescription with Miss Madsen,' he said abruptly. 'Take care of yourself.' Then he was gone.

'What was all that about?' Hugo asked.

'I don't know.'

'He's very fond of you, you can see that. It's written all over him.'

'Never mind that,' said his sister impatiently. 'Oh, Hugo, I did so want to go up to London today. D'you think . . .?'

'No, I don't. You'll get pneumonia.'

'You wouldn't go for me, would you?'

'Not on your life. We've got people coming to lunch. Why d'you want to go there, anyway?'

She told him about the postman and the redirection notice, and he laughed in grudging admiration of Nesta's cunning.

'Good psychology, that. Women always read such a hell of a lot into an address. I know Jackie always wants to pick our holiday hotels by their names, and when you get there the Miramar turns out to be a slum on top of the marshalling yards.'

'But Saulsby wasn't there at all.'

'I can't see why she bothered to write. Why not just vanish?'

Yes, why not? The second letter was explained by the receipt of the parcel. But why had Nesta written the first letter suddenly, out of the blue? She couldn't have known Alice had the ring, for she hadn't mentioned it then. It was uncanny that she should have been silent for a month and then have written just as Alice was going to advertise for her. It was, at any rate, a remarkable coincidence.

'I didn't keep either of the letters, but I remember what they said. The first one said something like this: *Dear Alice, just a line to let you know I'm settled in temporarily, but I shan't be staying for very long. I don't suppose we shall meet again, but thanks for the meal and everything. Best wishes to Andrew and your uncle.*'

'Just an ordinary sort of letter,' said Hugo. Alice sighed, knowing from experience that his own were very much like that. 'It told you the basic essentials.'

'It told me nothing,' said Alice unhappily. 'The second one was even worse. *Thanks for the ring. I enclose two pounds to cover cost.* . . . And, Hugo, that was another odd thing. I've only just thought of it. I'd paid Cropper's but I didn't say what it had cost and I didn't ask for the money. But the bill was for two pounds and Nesta sent me exactly two pounds.'

'Coincidence?'

'Well, it *must* have been. Then she wrote: *Don't put yourself out to answer this as I've never been much of a correspondent*, and then something about being too preoccupied to bother. Not as rude as I've made it sound of course. She ended up with the usual regards to Andrew and Uncle Justin.'

'Keen on him, wasn't she?'

Something seemed to grip her chest, something which released a cold bubble of nausea.

'What *do* you mean?'

'Justin.'

'Oh.' She was able to smile again. 'What makes you think so?'

'She used to make him up a buttonhole every morning.'

'You're romancing, Hugo. Those flowers came from the garden.'

'Did they hell! Not for the last two years they didn't. Your little Nesta had an eye for the men.' He smiled and in the smile was a kind of wry vanity. 'She made a pass at me once,' he said thoughtfully.

'She did what?'

'Come off it, Alice. You know what a pass is as well as I do.' He glanced at her doubtfully. 'Almost as well, anyway. She'd been baby-sitting for us and I drove her home. She said would I see her into the shop because she was nervous in the dark. You know how slow and languid she was. There wasn't much in it but she sort of swayed against me in the dark. I put out my arm to stop her falling and she—well, she took hold of me and said she was so miserable, I mustn't leave her alone. I yanked her upstairs, put all the lights on and got out double-quick.'

As Alice stared at him he went on hurriedly: 'The funny thing was after that, whenever we were alone together—you know, if we met in the street just for a moment—she'd talk to me—Oh, damn it! It's so hard to explain. She'd talk to me as if we'd had a full-blown affair and had to kind of—well, keep it secret. She kept saying Jackie mustn't ever know. But there wasn't anything *to* know. I don't mind telling you, just between ourselves, I used to wonder what she would say if she ever got to be alone with Jackie and she was manic as against depressive.'

Alice was rather shocked. 'Manic-depressive? You mean she was really ill in her mind? Oh, Hugo, I think it was just loneliness and perhaps envy.' He shrugged, disbelieving. 'I don't think we any of us realised how lonely she was.' She looked up at him, wondering how he would take sentimentality. 'She told me once losing her husband had been like losing a leg or an arm. Part of her was in the grave with him.'

'She was a mistress of the cliché.' The door had swung open and Andrew was on the threshold, holding the coffee tray. Alice sat up, startled by his silent, almost supernatural arrival.

'Oh, darling! I remember she said——'

'And I remember,' he interrupted her, 'how she used to call a sheaf a sheath and a corsage a cortège.' As Hugo chuckled he moved towards the bed and took her face gently in his hands. 'You're better, Bell. You've got some colour in your cheeks.'

With a word, a smile, he could make her feel like a beauty. Feeling warmth coming back to flush her face, she put up her hands to the things she was proud of, the white, still unlined neck and the long loose hair.

'I think I could drink some coffee,' she said.

'I've brought you another visitor.'

He brushed his lips against her forehead in a fluttering kiss. Embarrassed, Hugo shifted uneasily.

'What's supposed to be the matter with you?' asked Uncle Justin from the doorway. He was frowning. Alice noticed the chrysanthemum bud in his buttonhole and remembered the roses, wound and wired in silver foil, he had worn in the summer.

'I'm supposed to have a virus.'

'A virus! I don't know what we're all doing in here, then. That's a fine thing to spread about the works.' With extreme ostentation, he shook out a large white handkerchief and held it yashmak-wise across his nose and mouth. 'I suppose a virus is a new-fangled name for the flu?'

'I'll get up when I've had my coffee,' she said meekly, knowing he would discourage malingering.

His reply surprised her. 'I wouldn't.' He sat on the dressing-table stool as far away from the bed as possible. 'You've got Andrew here and what's-her-name to wait on you.' Pausing, he added characteristically: 'It isn't as if you've got anything to do.'

Perhaps it would be better to stay where she was. Certainly everyone was very anxious that she should stay in bed. The coffee tasted strong and bitter. Over the rim of the cup she watched them all in silence.

Harry hadn't actually said it was a virus, just that it probably was. He hadn't said that she had a raised temperature either. It was true what Uncle Justin said about a virus just being the flu, but she had never had flu before. Surely there would be more to it than these waves of sickness that came so chillingly and overmasteringly, but when they had gone, left her feeling well and even cheerful?

As she sipped the coffee a strange thought visited her. That was how Nesta had been, alternating between illness and health, only Nesta's had been not of the body but of the mind. Nesta had been manic-depressive, Hugo said. Why had she, Alice, she who was never ill, suddenly developed this strange illness, when she was on the point of finding Nesta?

The malaise returned sharply, washing over her, and drawing the blood from her face. She felt the pallor and the chill which came with it and her whole body jerked in a big convulsive shudder.

Hugo and her uncle were discussing some change at the works. Only Andrew noticed. He took her hand and held it until the spasm had passed. She leant back against the pillows, spent, and inexplicably afraid.

6

On Monday morning, as soon as Andrew had gone, she got up. After two days in bed she still felt tired, but in her weariness there was no desire for sleep, only a weakness that seemed to come from some inner core of her body. The sickness had passed, leaving her languid and strangely prone to tears. She had no appetite except for liquids, but even tea and the yoghurt she had lately grown so fond of tasted odd, bitter yet otherwise flavourless. The fluid seemed to burn her throat.

But there was nothing really wrong with her. Harry had come again on Sunday and shrugged off her fears. It was just a mild virus, he thought, not absolutely committing himself. His words were reassuring, but she hadn't liked the look in his eyes. There was bewilderment in them, doubt and concern.

The fresh air would do her good. It was a pity the wind was so strong, stirring the bare black branches of the Vair shrubs so that their tops looked like a dark and stormy sea, but it couldn't be helped. She would wrap up warm and wear a scarf on her head. Besides it was always warmer and more sheltered in London than in the country.

The thought that in less than two hours' time she would see Nesta again provided her with a little spurt of energy. The house in Dorcas Street might be a bit of a shock. Of course Nesta didn't own it, nor even have a flat in it, but a single poor little back room. She, Alice, would make a stoical effort not to show her dismay. If Nesta were out at work—as she probably would be, a very minor assistant in a huge West End shop—she would just ask the landlady where the shop was and make her way there. She would take Nesta out to lunch. Dizzily she thought of taxis, of the Savoy, of wine brought by a deferential waiter.

'When I've gone,' she said to Pernille, 'you can ring up Dr Blunden and tell him I'm so much better he needn't bother to call.'

'I am not good with the telephone, Mrs Fielding.' The Danish girl had brown skin, darker than her hair, and eyes as blue and pleading as a Siamese kitten's.

'Then you obviously need practice,' said Alice firmly. 'I'll tell you what, when I'm out I'll get you a five-shilling stamp and a half-crown one for your brother. Is he still collecting?'

Pernille's willing-to-please smile quirked up even further at the corners and she broke into a giggle. 'Oh, yes, Knud is a famous . . .' The word came out on a bubble of proud laughter, '. . . philatelist!'

'I won't forget.'

Nesta ought to have a present, too. Alice wondered why she hadn't thought of it before. It was unlike her to go and visit someone empty-handed. She felt ashamed of herself, almost thankful that she hadn't found Nesta in Orphingham. To arrive without a gift when Nesta was probably in need.... She was appalled and puzzled at her own thoughtlessness.

Alice sincerely believed that she knew London. You must know a city if all your life you had lived only twenty-five miles from it. In fact she knew it less well than certain holiday resorts. The City itself she had seen only from car windows, its buildings like a series of photographs in a guide book that has been quickly flipped through. She was well acquainted with a few square yards of pavement outside most of the theatres and could easily visualise the river between the Tower and Westminster Bridge. At the age of ten she had been able to name all the bridges in their correct sequence just as she could count up to twenty in French. In fact she knew her capital as well as most Englishwomen know it; all her knowledge was of the two or three streets in which she had bought clothes.

From Liverpool Street she took the Tube and she remembered how often she had made just this same journey with Nesta. They had always got out at Marble Arch and walked back, window-gazing. Nesta's tastes had been expensive—the black she always wore had to cost a lot if it was to look nice—and sometimes Alice had slipped her a couple of pounds when the salesgirl wasn't looking. It seemed cruel not to be able to have the sombre dresses you only wore out of respect for your dead husband's memory. Alice had bought nothing for herself, but only followed where Nesta led.

Today she had no guide. Still, it was easy to buy presents for someone as pretty and vain as Nesta, floral scent, a scarf of white silk scribbled all over with black. Alice came out of the shop and hailed a taxi. It was only the second time in her life she had ever done such a thing in London. The driver accepted her directions, questioned nothing. She felt brave and rather sophisticated. London was just a place like any other, Salstead or Orphingham magnified.

Once past Marble Arch again, she was lost. They might be anywhere, in any great city. She leaned back and closed her eyes. The tiredness was coming back and with it a physical unease that was too faint to amount to sickness or even the warning of sickness to come. It was just discomfort and nervous anticipation. She sat up and looked out of the window.

They were nearly there. As they turned out of a big busy thoroughfare she caught sight of a name on a house wall, Dorcas Street. This, at last, was where Nesta lived.

It was neither sordid nor romantic and it was not a slum. The houses were very tall and ranged in long plaster-covered terraces, each with a pillared portico and little iron-railed balconies. They had a shabby, neglected look. The roadway, treeless and uniformly grey, seemed like a reflection of the wind-stirred grey sky, itself an avenue between long architraves.

She couldn't see much of a hundred and ninety-three. Stopping directly outside it, the taxi's bulk hid everything but its two fat pillars and its flight of steps. At home Alice would hardly have thought twice about how much to tip Mr Snow. Now she was a little flustered. A ten-shilling note? It seemed all right, enough, at any rate, to evoke a large pleased smile. It was only after he had turned that it occurred to her she might have asked him to wait. Her new-found courage was unequal to calling after him.

She sighed and went to the steps. Where the number should have been on the column that supported the canopy was only a blank rectangle, a paler patch on the plaster. Slowly she lifted her head and let her gaze travel upwards. There on the pediment, scrawled in neon tubing with a frail attempt at smartness, were the words *Endymion Hotel.*

It was happening all over again. For a brief wild moment her brain registered a mad picture of another redirection notice, indeed a whole series of them, directing her from one house to another, back and forth the length and breadth of the country. No, that was impossible, just stupid panicky guesswork.

She stood under the canopy, looking up at the name, at the plaster patch where the number should have been, and suddenly as she waited, half afraid to take that first look through the glass, a violent spasm of nausea washed over her so that she swayed against the wall. It passed with slow cruelty, leaving her legs cramped and stiff.

She took a deep breath of not very fresh air and pushed the door open.

Because she had expected squalor her first sight of the foyer came as a pleasant surprise. It had been recently modernised. The Victorian panelled doors had been faced with hardboard, the moulded ceiling boxed in with polystyrene tiles and a new floor laid of black and white blocks. At ceiling level she could see a curly plaster leaf, part perhaps of a Corinthian capital, peeping between strips of plastic. Gladioli and roses, made out of wafer-thin wax, stuck out like a sunburst from a simulated marble urn. Behind the acid-yellow counter sat a young man on a high stool writing something in a book.

The doors had made no noise and for a moment he didn't see her. She stood by the flowers—seen close-to, they were grimed with dust which had settled into and become part of their petals and calyxes—and as she hesitated somebody opened a door at the back of the hall.

It swung back as if of its own accord and through it she caught a disillusioning glimpse of what the rest of the place must be like. She saw a passage, its walls faced with ochre-coloured lincrista, its floor covered by threadbare haircord torn on the threshold into a frayed hole. Then someone pushed the door suddenly, a woman who heaved her back against it and whose hair was a bright gauzy blonde.

Sickness and shyness were dispelled by excitement. Alice went up to the counter.

'Can you tell me if Mrs Drage is in?'

'Not what you'd call *in.* She's not a resident.' His complexion had the thick bloodlessness of skin on wet white fish. He wetted his fleshy lips and stared at her with blank boredom, swinging his legs as if to the tempo of some silent but remembered pop tune.

'But you do know her? She has been here?'

He just glanced at her handbag and her expensive gloves, then at the delicate wrappings on Nesta's presents. 'I haven't seen Mrs Drage for, let's see—three months. Oh, it'd be all of that. It's funny you asking. I wouldn't remember her on account of all . . .' He grinned ironically and she felt the grin was aimed at her, '. . . all the thousands we get passing through our doors.' Alice shifted impatiently. 'I say I wouldn't remember her only Mr Drage come in himself about half an hour ago.'

'*Mr Drage?*' Alice clasped the edge of the counter, longing for a chair. Before she could stop herself she burst out, 'But she's a widow, there isn't a Mr Drage!'

He didn't wink. He yawned very slightly and gave a faint shrug. His background was perhaps as different from hers as possible, his outlook as unlike hers as was consistent with their both being human beings and of British nationality. 'Is that so? Yeah, well, live and let live. Maybe she got married again. I'd say it was her business, wouldn't you?'

The telephone rang. He gabbled into it, using a good many yeahs. Alice stood looking at him helplessly. Nesta hadn't been at the Endymion for three months, but her letters had been sent on to her from Orphingham to the Endymion.

While he talked she got out her diary and turned back to August. Nesta had left Salstead on August the eighth. She put on her reading glasses and walked away from the counter to stand under the rather dim centre light. *August seventh, Friday, Pernille not well. Harry says mostly mental, probably homesickness. Must do what I can to cheer her up. Perhaps a really nice present? Nesta to supper. Still very hot.*

August eighth, Saturday. Nesta leaving today. Raining hard.

'Did Mrs Drage come here on August eighth?'

He put the receiver down. 'You the police?'

'Do I look like the police?'

Perhaps policewomen dressed like she did when they were in plain clothes. As soon as she had asked the question she wished instead that she had had the courage to sustain the bluff. On the other hand—how much did you tip or bribe people like him?

'If it's her address you want,' he said suddenly, 'I haven't a clue. Mr Drage only come in to collect her mail.'

'Her mail?' Alice's voice sounded hollow and echoing as if someone else had spoken the words.

'Yeah. Well, if that's all I've got things to do.'

The sickness was coming back. Fighting it off, she said rather wildly, 'Please tell me . . .' It wouldn't do to give him too little. She opened her handbag, and, firmly shutting away thoughts of Andrew's and Uncle Justin's horror, laid a five-pound note on the counter top.

For a moment his face hardly changed. Then the wet red lips melted into a knowing smile.

'What's she done, then?'

'Nothing. I can't find her. I only want to find her.'

'Yeah, well . . .' The plump little hand had long nails. It closed over the note and thrust it into the pocket of his jacket through which gold thread ran, appearing occasionally like a recurrent vein of ore. He opened the book he had been writing in when Alice arrived.

'August eighth, you said? Mrs Drage booked up for that night but she never come. Mr Drage called up and cancelled it. She never come at all but we got mail for her. Three or four letters it was and a little parcel.'

'And you gave them to this man who came in this morning?'

'I gave them to Mr Drage, yeah. Why not?'

A big man in Salstead. . . . If he could only give her some clue to the appearance of 'Mr Drage'. He wriggled a little on his stool and began to buff his nails on his jacket lapel.

'You knew him well?' she said tentatively.

'Sure I did. Him and his wife been coming here on week-ends God knows how long. From the country it was—some dump in Essex.'

Her heart leapt. This man might well be someone she knew.

'Then you must often have had a close look at him,' she said, forcing a smile and trying to make her voice persuasive. A description, she prayed, make him give me a description. 'You were alone with him this morning. I'm sure you . . .' She stopped. Suddenly his face had become hideously aggressive and he got slowly and deliberately off his stool. What had she said? Was there some limit to how much the bribe would buy? He leant across the counter and thrust his face into hers.

'What are you getting at?' he said. He was no more than five feet four, small-boned and sinuous as a girl. 'You insinuating something, are you?'

Alice had no idea what he meant, but she sensed something foul and alien. With a little gasp she backed away from him, slipping on the waxed floor. Her hands found the door as if by instinct and she stumbled out into the windy street.

A taxi, she must find a taxi. Clutching Nesta's presents she ran along Dorcas Street until she came to the main road. It was full of office workers hurrying to lunch places. After her encounter with the Endymion receptionist it was a comfort just to be with ordinary people, but how strange, how frightening, to notice how many of them looked like Nesta! Little heels tapped, short skirts lifted by the wind showed plump knees; pretty dolls' faces, their pink mouths snapping as they chattered, were topped by twists and bunches and doughnuts of yellow hair. She realised, but not newly, rather as if subconsciously she had always known it, that this was supposed to be the ideal type of womanhood. The fairness, the silliness, the porcelain skin—these were what attracted the majority of men, what they made jokes about, yet coveted.

She came up to the wider pavement and mingled with the crowd of little blonde ghosts. Ghosts, why had she thought of that? It made her shiver.

The first taxi was taken, the second pulled in beside her as she gave a feeble wave. It had been a disastrous morning and suddenly she knew she couldn't face the Tube.

'Will you take me all the way to Liverpool Street?'

The notes she could feel in her wallet were as comforting as a drug.

'My poor Bell,' said Andrew, smiling, 'I wish I'd been there. I'd love to have seen you taken for a policewoman.'

'It was horrible.' She began to pull the curtains, shutting

out the garden, the windy night and the dark orange moon that was rising above Vair Place. 'I suppose I shall have to give up looking for her now.'

Andrew pulled the sofa up to the fire and tucked a cushion behind her head. 'You suppose? I thought the mystery was solved.'

'It isn't really. Not all of it. How could she write and thank me for the ring when she hadn't even got it? And why did that man go to the Endymion only this morning to get the letters? It's—well, it's such a fantastic coincidence.'

'It would be, but for one thing.' She looked up at him enquiringly, hoping wistfully for reassurance. He dropped a quick kiss on her cheek. 'You don't know the letters and the parcel were yours at all, do you?'

'But I—Andrew, I didn't actually ask him where they came from. I just assumed——'

'You just assumed. If the place is used as an accommodation address they might have dozens of letters for her. The boy friend could have been coming in once a week to fetch them.'

'That wasn't the impression I got, darling. I'm sure he meant that that was his first visit and that he took *all* the letters.'

A flicker of impatience crossed his face and pulled at the mouth muscles. Then he controlled it and, smiling, looked at her searchingly.

'How can you talk about impressions when you say yourself you weren't feeling well?'

Firelight like candlelight is flattering. She could feel it playing on her face, then realised with a little pang that she had not powdered her nose or painted her lips since the morning. Was that why he was staring at her so closely?

'You were ill and nervous and uneasy,' he said. 'Don't underrate your imagination, Bell.'

'No, you're right. You're always right.' She curled her legs under her and rested her head on his shoulder. The book he had been reading lay face-downwards on the cushions, a book with a chocolate-brown jacket, its title and illustration enclosed in rectangles of greenish blue. She watched his hand creep across to it. There was something loving and hungry and at the same time surreptitious in the way he slid it on to his lap.

'Go on,' she laughed, 'you can read if you like. I won't disturb you.'

Compulsive reading was just escapism. Why should he want to escape, and what was he escaping from? He was tired, she thought, it was only natural.

The fireplace wall was lined with bookshelves. The Trollope clericals and politicals had pride of place at eye level on the third shelf from the top. All the politicals had that same blue and brown cover. She smiled to herself as she realised that she had never yet seen the complete set there on the shelves. At least one was always out, actually in Andrew's hands, on the table or by their bed.

She looked at him covertly but he was already too preoccupied to notice the movement of her eyes. Wasn't it rather odd for a man to keep reading the same novels over and over again? He must know them by heart. She wondered vaguely how important to him was the world they presented. By now it must be very real to him, part of his daily consciousness, a source of metaphor, a guide to speech. Amid these reflections came a sudden conviction that to be a true companion to him she ought also to be acquainted with that world. It was what people meant when they talked about 'having things in common'. You needed as much of that as you could get when you had disadvantages that couldn't be overcome—the difference in age, for instance, the threat of childlessness. . . .

She got up. He turned a page and smiled at some favourite expression that had caught his eye. Smiling like that, uninhibitedly, indifferent to observation as a child is, he looked terribly young, younger even than he was. She was suddenly very much aware of her thirty-eight years.

The dining-room door was ajar. As she crossed the hall she peered through the dark room towards the uncurtained french windows that showed the shrubbery and the side of Vair Place. It was unpleasant to think that she had sat on that lawn, under those trees, a big strong child nearly five feet tall and already reading quite grown-up books, when Andrew had not even been born.

She went upstairs into her bedroom and switched on the light over the dressing-table glass. Then she felt in the drawer for the only lipstick she possessed.

Slowly she lifted her head and her eyes met her own reflection. There was not much light in the room and the furniture behind her lay in shadow. Apart from her own face the mirror showed only vague shapes and the pale shimmer of flowers in a vase.

Her hair was very untidy, coming loose in front from its braids and irradiated into translucent gold by the overhead light. Puzzled, very slightly alarmed, she drew back and closed her eyes. After an interval she opened them again. The impression was still there. Her own face looked unfamiliar and at the same time familiar. It seemed fuller, blanker, drained of intelligence. In some ways it looked younger for the skin was clear and glowing and the eyes bright.

'Pull yourself together,' she said aloud, but the brisk, hackneyed phrase which she could see as well as hear herself speak only enhanced the—the what? Hallucination?

Quickly she combed back her hair. As she painted two lines of strawberry red on her mouth the illusion vanished. With a sigh of relief she straightened up. She was herself again.

7

A wicked wind from the north-east whistled down the twin-track road and howled away under the concrete bridge. At the entrance to the by-pass the oil-drums had been taken away and in their place someone had stretched a long white ribbon of the kind seen on wedding cars.

In spite of the cold a crowd had gathered to watch the official opening: children from the primary school, shepherded by a harassed teacher; shop assistants out for their lunchtime break; housewives with baskets. Behind the ribbon stood the Parliamentary Secretary to the Ministry of Transport, surprisingly feminine as if it were not surprise enough that she was female; Justin Whittaker who was chairman of the highways committee; the chairman of the council; and a host of hangers-on who had nothing to do but watch, applaud and ultimately eat smoked salmon and roast chicken with the great ones at The Boadicea.

'There can scarcely be an inhabitant of Salstead,' Justin Whittaker was saying, 'who will not regard the opening of this by-pass as an unmixed blessing. I think I speak for all of us when I say that it is with disquiet and apprehension that we have watched the daily shaking—nay, undermining—of our historic buildings by the constant passage . . .'

Andrew squeezed Alice's arm. 'Oh, adjourn, adjourn!' he yawned.

'Sssh!'

'Nor will it deprive us of the trade necessary to our continued prosperity, for the slip road which leaves it and meets the town centre will allow access to those vehicles whose entry is a commercial necessity. This slip road is a triumph of contemporary engineering. Not only is it a most modern highway of its kind, but its designers have seen to it that Helicon Lane, to which it runs parallel, remains untouched to continue as a beauty spot of which we may all be justly proud.'

An icy drizzle had begun to fall. He raised the collar of his barathea overcoat and stepping back, handed a pair of shears to the Parliamentary Secretary. She drew her furs more closely around her and, still clasping the violets presented to her by one of the schoolchildren, cut the ribbon.

'I declare the Salstead By-pass well and truly open.' She had a voice like the Queen's, high-pitched, poised, remote.

Andrew nudged Alice. 'And may God save her and all who drive on her,' he said. She laughed and held his arm more tightly, flinching from the bitter, rain-bearing wind.

The Parliamentary Secretary scuttled back to her car in thin court shoes. Her driver stood holding the door open. Presently the car moved off along the virgin track, followed by Justin Whittaker's Bentley, the chairman's Rolls and so on down to the Mini that belonged to the assistant sanitary inspector. The Parliamentary Secretary waved graciously, again like a royal lady in a state procession.

'Come along, children,' said the schoolmistress. 'I'd like the first dinner people in the vanguard, please.'

'Are you going to the luncheon?' Alice asked Harry Blunden.

'I'm not a local dignitary. G.P.s are hoi-polloi these days.'

'We've got a double ticket,' Alice said. 'Nepotism, really, because I'm a Whittaker, but Andrew's got to get back to the works.' She realised suddenly what she had said and what he might expect. There was no reason why he shouldn't come with her in Andrew's place. Walking between the two men, she glanced quickly from the smooth handsome head to the tousled one. Then Andrew's hand holding hers pressed very gently, relaxing again at once. It was an indication that he wouldn't care for the substitution. 'Of course I shan't go,' she said too emphatically.

'And you're better now, Alice?' Again that odd, solicitous look. 'Miss Madsen rang me yesterday and said you were better.'

'Nearly back to normal.'

'I'll look in again in a day or two, shall I?'

Andrew was holding the Sprite door open for her. 'Really, I don't think that's necessary,' he said smoothly. Harry blushed, screwing up his face against the squally wind. 'We can always contact you if . . .' He paused and said emphatically, '. . . if my wife needs another prescription.' The speed with which he hustled her into the car was almost rough. 'We may as well take advantage of the triumph of contemporary engineering,' he said.

The slip road left the by-pass smoothly and gradually at a narrow acute angle. Inside this angle the end of Helicon Lane could be seen, cut off by the great embankments of still grassless earth. They were like the raw edges of a wound made in the fields.

Reflecting that she had not been down Helicon Lane since Nesta's departure, Alice leaned over and looked down. The branches of the Salstead Oak seemed to sweep the sky like the bristles of a huge brush. She could just see The Bridal Wreath, its twin bow windows now filled with skeins of wool and canvases printed for gros point. The sign had been replaced by another, The Workbasket. She sighed, losing sight of it in the mist her breath had made on the glass.

The road passed between stretches of barren earth. A fence had been put up almost against the nave of St Jude's Church and nothing remained of the old churchyard. It was rather awe-inspiring to think that the new concrete over which they were driving covered what had once been consecrated ground. Here had been green mounds, moss-grown slabs and between them long yew-shaded avenues. Mourners had walked there, country people in smocks and print gowns, bringing stocks and nasturtiums from cottage gardens. Alice shook herself and said prosaically:

'I can't very well go to the luncheon now.'

'For heaven's sake, darling!'

'How can I, after what I said to Harry?' And after what you said, she thought.

'You can change your mind at the last moment,' he said jesuitically. 'Pernille won't have anything for you at home.' He glanced into the wing mirror. 'I'd better speed up if we don't want to get involved with the motorcade, or whatever it's called.'

Still doubtful, she let him drop her in the High Street. It was full of people, mostly people she knew. What did it matter if they saw him take her in his arms and kiss her full on the mouth? They were still on their honeymoon and it would go on being like this until they were both old, so old that the nine years between them was nothing. She was still radiant from the kiss as she crossed the road and went into The Boadicea.

The lounge was already crowded. A waiter approached her with a tray of glasses and she took one containing something pale yellow with a crescent of lemon peel slotted on to its rim. Through the glass door that led by way of a beamed tunnelly passage to the dining-room she could see tables laid with white cloths, silver, late dahlias in long narrow vases. The door swung and stuck open as a waitress came through. With her drifted a pungent garlicky smell of soup.

Alice put down her glass abruptly, suddenly and sharply sickened. The dry martini trickled coldly down her throat meeting a fierce surge of something that made her gasp. It was exactly as if her chest and stomach were being scalded from within. She sagged against the table, avoiding the solicitous eyes of Mrs Graham whose husband kept the hotel.

How could she dream of eating in company, feeling as she did? Before she was half-way through that soup she would be jerking back her chair, flying for the door with a napkin pressed against her mouth. Far better to go now before people came with their questions and their steadying arms.

She staggered towards the door, burrowing between knots and guests. Their laughter and their bright brittle talk stabbed at her with little points of pain. The wind that met her was cruel too, assailing her with mischievous teasing gusts. Just as she gained the shelter of Mr Cropper's shop porch Uncle Justin and the Parliamentary Secretary left their cars. He hadn't seen her. She kept her back turned for a moment, gazing at the swimming mass of rings and brooches, until they had crossed the pavement.

Then she began to walk up the High Street. The cutting wind seemed to beat at her with little slaps. No wonder the ancients had personalised winds, she thought, seeing them as gods or puff-cheeked cherubs, blowing with capricious malice.

It was half a mile to Vair House and Andrew had taken

the car with him to the works. The hourly bus service to Pollington which had formerly passed Vair had been diverted from this moment to the by-pass. The obvious person to help her was Harry, but she couldn't go to Harry now. I shall *have* to walk, she told herself fiercely.

She managed another twenty yards or so until her legs threatened to buckle and yield. Her whole body felt unutterably weak and beaten, empty of everything but urgent fear. She had never been ill in all her life and now when illness had come it was like some huge venomous snake that wrapped her in coils of pain and panic. Gasping, she tottered up to the seat on the war memorial green and sank on to the thick oak board.

There was only one thing to do. She would have to hire a car. When she had had five minutes' rest she could probably just make it to Snow's.

Presently the drumming in her ears stopped and the coils relaxed. It was, she imagined, just like having a bandaged limb unbound, only in this case it wasn't a limb but her entire body. She raised herself gingerly and set off again along the pavement.

'Salstead Cars. Self-drive or chauffeur-driven cars for every occasion.' They had hired her wedding cars from here. From the windows of one of these black limousines she had waved to Mrs Johnson as she and Uncle Justin drove off down the drive of Vair Place.

The office was a creosoted wooden hut around which the great glossy cars clustered like seals. Perched on a high stool, his hat pushed to the back of his head, the proprietor sat eating sandwiches off a copy of the *Daily Mirror*. He got off the stool when she came in.

'Oh, Mr Snow, I'm afraid I'm not very well. I suddenly felt so awfully faint and I wondered . . .' She tried to smile, averting her face from the slabs of bread and corned beef.

'Here, have a chair, Mrs Fielding.' She dropped heavily into a bentwood chair with a broken cane seat. 'You're as white as a ghost. Now, if you were to ask me, what I would advise is a little drop of brandy.'

'Brandy? Oh, no, I couldn't . . .'

'It's wonderful for settling the stomach.' Ignoring her objections, he fetched a quarter-bottle from the shelf and with it a surprisingly clean glass. 'Warm the cockles of your heart, that will.'

'Thank you. It's very kind of you.'

The effect of the brandy was immediate. Unexpectedly it didn't burn, but flooded her with soft civilising warmth like the newly inhaled scent of fresh flowers. Fountains and sprays, healing and gentle, grew and cascaded all over her body.

Mr Snow wrapped up his sandwiches and stood by the small grimy window, whistling softly through his teeth.

'Don't happen to have heard from Mrs Drage, do you?' he asked suddenly.

'Well . . .'

'I only wondered, you and her being so friendly like. Feeling better now, are you?'

'Much better. Mr Snow, why did you ask about Mrs Drage?'

'Well, it was in the way of business, Mrs Fielding. But I won't worry you now, you being under the weather.'

'Oh, no, really, I'd like to hear.'

'You understand there's no offence meant, Mrs Fielding?' He took the glass, rubbed it with a bit of newspaper and inverted it on the shelf. Firmly she suppressed a shudder. 'Only it's like this, we did a couple of jobs for Mrs D. and seeing as she didn't leave no address . . .'

'You mean she owes you money?'

He opened the booking ledger on top of the desk. 'August seventh it was. Seventh and eighth.' Alice bit her lip, once more uneasy. 'She booked one of my vehicles to take some stuff up to Feasts' for her. Three p.m.' Those were the words Daphne had used—'some stuff', 'she left some stuff at our place!' We did the job and she says to come to The Bridal Wreath the next morning, August eighth, eight sharp, she said, and pick her up and take her to the station. She was staying the night at Feasts' but coming back the next morning to see to the removals. We was to take her to the station and stop at Feasts' for the stuff on route. Eight o'clock sharp, she said. I don't mind telling you I was a bit narked. I took the car round myself but she'd gone. Not a word from her. She'd flitted on her own.'

'Are you sure?'

'They were taking out the furniture, Mrs Fielding. Cox's from York Street it was. The doors were all open and I went up. Len Cox was there taking out her bits and pieces. Where is she then? I said, not wanting to hang about on account of Saturday always being busy. Gone, he said. We was here at seven and the key was in the door so we come up. The place was as neat as a pin, Len said, all packed up and ready to go. You can't just take it, I said, not without her here, but Len's very hasty. It was going into store, he said, and she'd paid up when he give her the estimate. I can't have some bloody woman messing me about, he said—— Pardon me, Mrs Fielding, but that's what he said.

'Well, I wasn't laughing, I can tell you. I'd turned down two jobs for eight o'clock and one of them would have brought in five nicker. Not only that. There was what she owed me for going to Feasts' with the van in the afternoon.'

Alice said quickly, 'Of course I'll make that good, Mr Snow.' She found her cheque-book and began to write, surprised at the firmness of her hand. 'I suppose Mrs Drage changed her mind and forgot she booked your car.'

'That's what happened. It stands to reason. I'm not saying she did it deliberate.'

Alice folded the cheque.

'You wouldn't think folks could be that forgetful, would you? Being as she booked the vehicle and when she saw me in the afternoon she reminded me about the next morning. The funny thing was she rang up again about five and said I wouldn't forget, would I? I was a bit narked, Mrs Fielding, I can tell you.'

'I expect you were,' said Alice faintly.

The incident of the car was a wholly unexpected development. Of course, it was possible that Nesta had forgotten. Her nervous depression had made her forgetful. But still Alice didn't like it. Perhaps she was growing forgetful too, for it was not until she was back in the High Street that she remembered her original purpose in calling on Mr Snow.

She paused under a shop awning and took her diary from her handbag. *August eighth, Saturday, Nesta leaving today. Raining hard.* Raining hard. She thought back to that summer morning. Friday, August the seventh, had been the last day of a long heatwave. She had got up quite early. The rain had awakened her and, pulling back the curtains, she had said to Andrew over her shoulder, 'It's pouring with rain. The drive's almost flooded. It must have been coming down for hours.'

How could she be sure it was that Saturday morning? Because Andrew had answered, 'Nesta's furniture will get wet.'

If the drive was flooded at eight it must have been raining for hours. Helicon Lane was a long way from the station. Nesta wouldn't have walked. And yet she hadn't been there when Cox's came at seven.

Alice began to walk slowly back along the High Street. She was building in her mind a picture and a timetable of Nesta's last evening. In the middle of the afternoon Mr Snow had taken the stuff, whatever it was, round to Feasts', and at five Nesta had telephoned him to remind him of the morning call. She must have used the afternoon for tidying the flat and preparing the furniture for Cox's. Then, soon after that telephone call she had gone out to make her round of farewell visits. Mr and Mrs Graham at The Boadicea, Harry probably—he had been her doctor—Hugo and Jackie, then Uncle Justin, last of all to Vair House where she had had supper.

Very weary she had seemed, more depressed than ever. It had been a warm evening and she had worn no coat over her thin dress of black pleated lawn. Her ankles, Alice remembered, had been swollen, bulging over the vamps of flimsy black patent shoes. She had gone up to say good-bye to Pernille and then she had come down and shared the flat cheese soufflé with them. It was soon after eight when Andrew had driven her back to The Bridal Wreath.

'Why not stay the night here?' Alice had said, for Nesta, clasping her hand tightly, had looked so tired and there had been tears in her eyes.

'Too late to change my plans now. I've fixed up I'm stopping at the Feasts'.'

That night they had begun shifting the graves. The very discretion with which it had been done must have heightened the atmosphere of ghostliness. From Nesta's bedroom window you would have been able to see the tarpaulin screens and hear the sound of earth being moved. That in itself would have been bad enough, but worse, far worse, the aftermath, when just before the first of the light, the coffins had been shrouded, abandoned, to await the coming of the vans. Of course she hadn't gone to Feasts'. Was it possible that she had forgotten that arrangement too? She had forgotten about the car, even though she must have gone to all the trouble of telephoning Mr Snow from a call box. Her own phone, Daphne said, had been disconnected.

'I'm stopping at the Feasts',' she had said, and her face close to Alice's smelt of a summer garden. Then she had meandered down the drive in front of Andrew, moving languidly in the hot dusty air.

Mr Feast was stacking cream cartons against a wall tiled like Covent Garden Tube station in khaki and white. He looked thinner than ever in his grocer's coat. She noticed for the first time a certain resemblance in that bulbous brow and hollow cheeks to Abraham Lincoln; the same crusading fire burnt in his eyes.

'I wonder if I might have a word with Daphne, Mr Feast?'

'If it's about the Freedom from Hunger, Mrs Fielding . . .' He glanced almost apologetically about his land of plenty. 'That's more my province, if you know what I mean.'

'No, it's something personal.'

'I hope the yoghurt's been to your taste. We've had to switch to a different brand, but it's very good.'

'Oh, yes, delicious.' It was strange that in the past few days sometimes the only food she could face had been the thin sourish whey in the green and white cartons. 'If I could just . . .'

'Through there, then.' He opened the door behind him and shouted, unnecessarily loudly, she thought: 'Daph! Mrs

Fielding to see you. Go right up, Mrs Fielding. You'll make allowances, I know, for a certain amount of disarray.' She smiled, murmuring something. 'Did you want to take any yoghurt today? That's right. I'll pop it in a bag for you when you come down. Eat wisely and you'll live long, that's what I always say.' His voice, harsh and bird-like with a mechanical chattering note, pursued her up the staircase. 'The tragedy is that so many who would eat wisely if they only had the chance are deprived by man's inhumanity of the bare. . . .'

Daphne came out on to the landing. 'You've got Pop started.'

'He makes me feel virtuous because I didn't go to the official luncheon.'

'Have a bit of something with me, will you?'

Alice shook her head. The half-eaten pork pie on the tray without a cloth might be what Mr Feast called 'the bare' but the sight of it brought back a wriggle of nausea.

'You said you were keeping some things for Nesta. I wondered . . . Daphne, would you show them to me? Could I see them?'

'Them? It's not them, it's it. It's a sort of box. As a matter of fact Pop's got it in his room. He's using it as a bedside table.'

Mr Feast's bedroom was a long narrow cell that overlooked the High Street. Alice crossed to the window and looked down. The street was quiet, almost empty of traffic. Of course! The by-pass was in use, the plan was working.

'This is it,' said Daphne.

Alice turned. She could see only a single divan with beside it what appeared to be a table covered by a cloth and laden with magazines—*Peace News*, *China Today*, the journal of The United Nations Association—medicine bottles, an alarm clock, a green Anglepoise lamp.

She took a step towards it, then jumped violently. From somewhere behind her a bell began to ring, insistent, shrill, growing louder and clearer. Daphne glanced up and shrugged.

'It's only an ambulance. Some mad-brain's come a cropper on the new road.'

Only an ambulance . . . Why had the bell seemed like a warning, Go away, don't look? She watched the big white van turn out of the slip road, its blue light revolving. Her hands had gone up to cover her ears. She drew them down and gave herself a little shake, turning her attention once more to the table.

'But that's a trunk!' she exclaimed. 'A huge trunk.'

'I told you she left a lot of stuff.'

It was a wooden trunk, old-fashioned and long ago painted vandyke brown. Where a corner of the cloth hung was a hasp secured by a padlock.

'Is it locked?'

'I don't know.' Daphne wrenched at the padlock. 'Yep. I can't shift it.'

'I wonder whether we should. I can't make up my mind if we're justified. . . .' She hesitated and all the things that had alarmed her came back to her mind: letters which had never been received yet had been answered; the Endymion Hotel; the man who called himself Mr Drage; a car expressly, doubly ordered, that had called in vain.

'I reckon she can't want it all that much,' Daphne said eagerly, 'otherwise she wouldn't have dumped it here.' Her eyes shone. 'Here, I wonder what's inside.' She pushed up the sleeves of her brown mohair sweater. It was less like a garment than an extension of her own shaggy hair. 'My

God, it's heavy!' She had lifted the trunk by its leather handles and dropped it again, gasping. It made a dull thud on the square of matting by Mr Feast's bed.

'We could get a locksmith, I suppose, or perhaps your father.'

'Pop can't leave the shop unless I take over.' This Daphne was plainly unwilling to do. 'I don't mind having a go.'

'*You?*'

At Vair when they wanted anything done they sent for the gardener or Uncle Justin's chauffeur. If it was too big a job for amateurs a man with the appropriate skill was summoned from Salstead. Nobody, least of all a woman, would attempt anything as violent as breaking a lock.

'All you want,' said Daphne, 'is a screwdriver.'

Alice sat down on the bed and watched her dubiously as she came back with a toolbox. Daphne's eyes troubled her. They moved like a ferret's, darting between beaded lashes.

'What's happened to her, anyway?' The first of the three screws was coming unloose now. Alice shrugged. 'She's sort of disappeared, hasn't she?' The screwdriver twisted smoothly. 'Here . . .' Daphne stopped and glared. 'You don't think she's in here, do you? In bits, I mean. You know, like you read about in horror books.'

'Of course I don't,' Alice said sternly. 'Don't be silly.'

A wave of colic washed over her. The Feasts' flat smelt of sour milk.

'Here she goes,' said Daphne. The hasp had come away and hung against the brown wood. 'If it's anything nasty I warn you I shall be sick.' Her suet-coloured face showed two red spots on the low cheekbones. 'You look a bit queer yourself.'

Alice was breathing quickly now, clenching her cold

hands. Why did Daphne have such horrible ideas? There couldn't be anything 'nasty' in the trunk. Nesta had been alive and well after it had been sent to Feasts'.

Daphne gave a snorting giggle and threw back the lid in a rush.

8

Alice sighed with relief and shuddered at the foul taste in her mouth. She gave a quick deprecating laugh. The trunk was full of clothes.

There was a black nightgown on top and underneath it a layer of underclothes. Daphne pulled them out and threw an armful on the bed. Beneath were dresses, skirts, trews, a black and white check suit and four topcoats.

'All her clothes,' said Alice in wonder. 'Oh, but it can't be!'

Daphne was burrowing in the trunk. 'There are ever so many pairs of shoes under the coats.' She emerged, her arms full of shoes, packed heel to toe and wrapped in tissue. 'Look, Mrs Fielding, every pair of shoes she had. No, I tell a lie. She had some old black patent things. They aren't here.'

'She was wearing black patent that night she came to us. I noticed them because the heels were so high and her ankles were swollen.'

Daphne dived again and came out clutching a flat case perhaps twelve inches by eight. It was covered in black leatherette and initialled N.D. Before Alice could stop her she had opened that lid as well and a sweet powdery scent tickled Alice's nostrils, dissipating for a moment the dairy smell. Together they looked at the array of bottles and jars, lotions, creams, green eye shadow and blue eye shadow, lacquer for the hair and lacquer for the nails, brushes for the lips and brushes for the lashes.

'It's what used to be called a vanity case,' said Alice.

'Fancy her leaving that! And all her best shoes and all her coats. Wouldn't you have thought she'd have gone away in her summer coat? Look, this white orlon thing.'

'Then which coat did she wear that Saturday morning?'

'She can't have worn a coat. She only had the four, Mrs Fielding. I know Nesta's wardrobe like I know my own. I'd been through it often enough. We used to swap clothes.'

'Then, what . . . Daphne, what did she take with her?'

'If you're asking me, I'd say nothing except what she stood up in. There's a black lawn dress missing. I reckon she was wearing that on the Friday night.' Alice nodded. 'What I don't understand is how she came to leave all her best things. She'd saved up for that check suit and it cost her twenty quid.'

'Why send them all here anyway? I can understand she might want a suit or a coat for the morning but she was only staying with you for one night.'

'That's easy. I told you we used to swap clothes. I reckon she meant us to have a good go through her things. You know how keen she was on black?'

'It was her mourning, Daphne.'

'Mourning my foot! She said she looked so smashing in the suit she had for her husband's funeral that she stuck to black ever after. If you don't mind me saying so, you are a bit naive, Mrs Fielding. Well, as I was saying, she meant us to go through her things. I've got a little black lurex number she'd had her eye on for ages, but when she didn't turn up I thought she'd changed her mind.'

'But what is she wearing now? She can't have lived for

nearly three months in a cotton dress and a pair of court shoes.'

Lived? You needed clothes for living and if you were Nesta above all you needed the precious little case that smelt of musk and lilies and vanity itself. She closed the lid abruptly and as she did so the thought came to her that for dying you needed only a shroud, a thin, black shroud.

'Unless,' said Daphne doubtfully, 'she got herself a rich boy friend who bought her a whole new wardrobe.'

In that case, Alice reflected wretchedly, she would surely have given the lot to Daphne. Certainly she wouldn't have tried to drive a hard bargain to get possession of the dress esoterically described as a 'lurex number'.

'Mucky lot of stuff she wore next to herself, didn't she?' Daphne was shovelling through the underwear. Alice had already noticed how tattered it was, some of the garments hastily cobbled, most left in holes, shoulder straps coming away, elastic stretched and puckered. 'She was always one for top show was Nesta. I can't say I'm sorry I didn't get her for my step-mum, though it seemed a bit of a giggle at the time.'

'Your stepmother?' Alice was aghast. Mr Feast had seemed to belong to a different generation until she realised unpleasantly that he was perhaps no more than ten years older than herself. 'I had no idea . . .'

'Well, no. I reckon nobody had. We got to know Nesta at first at the Chamber of Commerce. Pop got into the way of seeing her home from the meetings. He was very keen on her but it sort of petered out. I don't know as I believe in marriages where there's a big age difference.'

Alice looked down, feeling the flimsy back stuff and hoping Daphne had not seen her blush.

'There were no hard feelings, you know. Not between me

and Nesta, that is. If you ask me she'd got her sights set on someone a cut above Pop. Mind you, he felt it. Funny, you wouldn't think anybody'd be jealous at his age, would you? What d'you think I ought to do with the things, Mrs Fielding?' There was a flicker of desire in her eyes as they lingered over the suit and the knitted coat.

'Hold on to them. What else can you do?'

Daphne must have misunderstood her. She pulled the coat round her and thrust her arms into the sleeves.

Horrified, Alice said, 'I didn't mean . . .' She broke off and stood up suddenly. A lapful of brassières and petticoats fell on to the floor.

Mr Feast was standing in the doorway looking at them, his face twisted with anger.

'D'you fancy me in it?' said Daphne. She pirouetted clumsily and jumped when she saw her father.

'Where did you get all them things?' It must be a very strong emotion, Alice thought, to make him lapse into cockney. 'What you doing with my bed table?'

'It's not your bed table, Pop. It belongs to Nesta Drage. We got it open and it's full of clothes.'

He fell on his knees among the piles of garments and began scooping them back into the trunk. 'Haven't you any respect for other people's property?' he shouted. 'That box was in our care. We're responsible for it. That's why the world's in the state it is, big people riding roughshod over the feelings of little people.' Stiff with horror, Alice backed away from him. 'Hitler and—and all that lot,' he said wildly. His face had become a dark red, the blood pumping through raised veins. 'Smarming their dirty hands over the—the household gods of the people!'

With a little pettish gesture Daphne shrugged the coat

from her shoulders. Her father grabbed it and clutched it against his hollow chest.

'Haven't you got no ethics? You're no better than a dirty little Fascist.' He crammed the clothes back, flung the cloth over the trunk and began replacing the copies of *Peace News*. 'Stealing her clothes, tarting yourself up . . . Now if you was in a Free People's Democracy——'

'Calm down, for God's sake,' said Daphne mildly. 'I'm sure I don't know what Mrs Fielding's going to think of you.'

'Mrs Fielding . . .' He seemed to see her for the first time.

'Come on. You're due at the Orphingham Branch at half-three.'

The name struck Alice like a burning point of fire in the midst of her swimming brain. Blindly she put out her hand, but it caught only at the empty air. She might have been standing on ice or in a quagmire for all the support the floor gave her. Her legs yielded at the knees and a great curtain of blackness, muffling and utterly silent, slid down over her eyes and her consciousness.

Daphne's voice, cheerful and excited, was the last thing she heard. 'Here, she's going to pass out!'

The children were sitting in the corner of the big untidy room helping themselves to Smarties out of a coloured canister. On the fireplace wall the huge green abstract painting seemed to be hanging crookedly. Perhaps it was only her eyes. The brightness of this familiar room hurt them, the red and citron chairs, the waxen snake-like house plants, the toys flung all over the carpet into which someone's heel had ground a strip of plasticene.

'Jackie . . .?'

'It's all right. Mr Feast phoned me and I brought you here because it was nearer.'

'Where's Andrew?'

'At work, of course. Where else? I phoned him, but you moaned something at me about not fetching him.'

'Yes, yes, I know. I remember now. I just thought he might . . .' Her voice trailed away. She tried to smile at Christopher and he stared back shyly. The crumpled dress felt hot and constricting. Suddenly she longed desperately for Andrew and the tears welled into her eyes. 'That awful man, Feast. He got into a rage, a violent rage, Jackie, because we opened a trunk full of Nesta's clothes. I can't get his face out of my mind, those burning eyes and that lump in his neck.'

'It's only thyroid,' said Jackie placidly. Mark rattled the Smartie box listlessly. 'An over-active thyroid. That's why he's so thin and always brimming over with vim and vigour. I know I was only a nurse for about a year but that's one thing I do remember. Too much thyroid and you get like Mr Feast, too little—that's called myxoedema—and you get fat and sluggish.'

'He was going to Orphingham,' Alice said. 'Did you know they'd got a branch there? I didn't. That means he knows Orphingham well. Oh, Jackie . . .' She stopped, looking at the children.

'Go and get Aunt Alice a glass of water, will you?' said Jackie promptly to her elder son.

'Jackie, I think Nesta's dead. No, I don't *think* so. I know she is. I'm certain of it. A woman doesn't leave her home late in the evening or very early in the morning in a thin cotton dress without a coat. It was an old dress, Jackie, and Nesta was vain. No matter how miserable she felt she wouldn't go off to make a new start somewhere dressed like that when she'd got a new suit to wear. Besides, it was pouring with rain. I don't think she ever left The Bridal Wreath.'

'But the letters, Alice.'

'She didn't write those letters. For one thing they were typed. I never thought of it before but I don't think Nesta could type. All right, she signed them, but anyone could forge a five-letter name like that, particularly someone who'd had letters from her before.'

'But that means . . .' Jackie hesitated and forced a bright absurd smile as Mark came back slopping water from a nursery rhyme mug. 'Thank you, darling. Now you can go over to the playroom and—and *play*.' Alice felt too weak and preoccupied to laugh.

'Here.' She felt in her bag. The disgruntled faces brightened at the sight of sixpences. 'Go and buy something nice.'

'And for God's sake, mind the road!'

The two women looked at each other after they had gone, at each other and away again in the embarrassment that comes from an awful incredible realisation. It was impossible. Such things couldn't happen in a world that also contained nursery rhyme mugs and green abstract pictures and empty boxes of Smarties.

'Suicide?' said Jackie.

'They would have found her, Jackie. Cox's or Mr Snow would have found her in the morning. Besides, if she killed herself, why the letters?'

'You mean *someone* killed her?'

Alice drank some of the water and looked at the design of Jack and Jill on the side of the mug. 'Daphne said her father had been in love with Nesta. He was jealous of her. If he was jealous there must have been other men. I've got a feeling now that she liked to get a hold on them.' With a kind of outrage she shivered violently. 'It's loathsome, I know. I hate women like that but that's what Nesta was. I've found out so many horrible things about her.'

'What sort of things?' Jackie asked in a small voice. She kept glancing about the room, looking fearfully over her shoulder towards the door.

'She had all those clothes, but dreadful scruffy underwear. She had alopecia too, but I couldn't quite understand it when you remember her lovely hair. You used to nag me to do my hair like Nesta's.'

'You mean you don't know? That topknot thing of Nesta's wasn't her own. It was nylon. Haven't you seen those switches hanging up in Boot's?'

Alice didn't answer her. She was wondering why she had always thought Nesta beautiful. Beauty couldn't consist of false hair, plucked and painted eyebrows, skin that showed dry and mealy when the light fell on it. Was it perhaps only Nesta's own desperate seeking after beauty, her confidence in her own good looks—a confidence that sometimes seemed shaky, feverish—that made Alice believe in it too? Nesta had been taken at her own valuation.

'Alice . . .' Jackie found one of her coloured cigarettes among a mêlée of plastic soldiers and tea cards on the bookcase. 'What do you think has happened to her?'

Alice said slowly: 'She wouldn't tell anyone where she was going. It didn't seem so odd to me at the time, but it does now. It must have been because she was going away with a man. I can't help feeling she was killed by someone who was jealous.' Her eyes, roving across the room as she sought for words, fell on the framed photograph of Hugo on the sideboard. *She made a pass at me once.* Hugo had said that, but suppose it had been the other way about? Oh, absurd, stupid . . . Her own brother? People always tell lies about sex. She had read that somewhere and it had appalled her. Perhaps it had shocked because it was so true. 'Jackie,' she said firmly, 'tell me exactly what happened when she came here to say good-bye to you.'

'I don't remember all that well.' Jackie wrinkled her brows. 'You see, I was putting the brats to bed and she was in here most of the time with Hugo.' Alice sipped some water. Had they been planning to elope, those two? Hugo often seemed bored with his marriage, his children. From business associations he knew Orphingham well. She remembered how he had refused to go back to the post office. 'She was very upset when she said good-bye to me,' Jackie continued. 'She kissed me—funny, really, we didn't know each other all that well. Then she simply ran away.' Thin and boyish, her face white and intense, she presented, Alice thought, a complete contrast to Nesta. 'I can't think why she was so emotional about it all.'

'Perhaps because she thought we'd think ill of her when we found out what she'd done.'

Jackie shrugged. 'She went on to Uncle Justin after she'd left us, then to you.'

'She was very quiet,' said Alice. 'While I was getting the dinner Andrew took her up to see Pernille. She came down ahead of him and I noticed she had to hang on to the banisters. I asked her if she was all right and she said she'd taken a couple of aspirins. I knew she'd been going to Harry about her depression but she'd told me he wouldn't give her anything for it. It was all in the mind or something. She slipped a little brown bottle into her handbag but I didn't take much notice—I thought it must be aspirins.'

'I wonder . . .' Jackie was suddenly thoughtful and excited, as if she was on the verge of a discovery. 'I wonder if it wasn't aspirin at all, but tranquillisers?'

'Harry had given her tranquillisers, or so she said, but they didn't do her any good and she wouldn't take them.'

'Someone else could have given them to her. People are such fools, Alice. I know that from my nursing days. They won't rely on their doctor but they'll take stuff that's been prescribed for other people. They think all sorts of drugs with awful side effects are all right for anyone to take. For instance, Mummy was taking some tablets when she was staying here in the summer—she's been feeling low since Daddy died—and she left the bottle behind when she went. Well, you'd hardly believe it, but Hugo wanted to take a couple just because some business thing had gone wrong. I soon put a stop to that. For one thing, they were the things you mustn't eat with cheese. . . .'

'With *cheese*, Jackie? You don't mean it.'

'I know it sounds funny, but it's a fact. It's quite a fashionable drug, lots of people have it. I can't remember what it's called but it raises the blood pressure and the cheese raises it some more.'

'We had a cheese soufflé for supper that night,' Alice said. 'Nesta always had a good appetite but she didn't eat much of it. It didn't taste very nice and I felt awkward about it. After we'd finished she lay back in her chair and put her hand on her heart. She said her heart felt all fluttery as if it was beating too fast.'

'Tachycardia.'

'What?'

'Fluttery heart-beat. Go on.'

'Well, there isn't any more. I asked her again where she was going, but all she said was something about a holiday and then "fresh fields and pastures new". I remember that because afterwards Andrew said it ought to have been "fresh woods". Then he took her home. She was very unsteady going down the path.'

She hardly knew how to put it but she was too worried

for tact. 'What happened to your mother's tablets, Jackie?'

'Don't know,' said Jackie carelessly. 'I expect they got thrown away. They aren't there now, anyway. Hugo probably slung them out. You know what a mania your family have for tidying up. Look, Alice, I'm not saying she actually took that particular drug—I *wish* I could remember what it's called—it was just a suggestion.'

Smoothing things over quickly, Alice said, 'I suppose practically anyone in Salstead could have had them prescribed. So many people have neuroses these days.' She paused, pondering. 'Mr Feast's terribly nervous and jittery, don't you think?' If only I dared ask Harry, she thought, recalling how sensitive he was about his professional honour. 'But, no. It won't do, Jackie. Nobody would know Nesta was going to eat cheese at my house.'

Jackie took another cigarette from the packet. The table lighter she picked up was fashioned ridiculously like a Queen Anne teapot. In the light from the flame her face looked wary and ill at ease. Wasn't she smoking rather more than usual, almost chain-smoking?

'Most people eat cheese after an evening meal,' she said softly. 'You can more or less take it for granted. And, Alice—my God!—it was *Friday*. Nesta often went to the bread and cheese lunch. She told everyone she thought it would help her to lose weight. He might have given her the stuff in the morning, but she needn't have taken it until later.'

It was frighteningly true. And yet there was comfort in the thought that of all the three men Alice associated with Nesta only Mr Feast would have been likely to have encountered her that Friday morning. Mr Feast was jealous of Nesta—his own daughter had said so. He had a shop at Orphingham and would know the place as intimately as only a tradesman can. Besides, it was absurd to think of men as normal and matter-of-fact as Hugo and Uncle Justin stepping over the border of normalcy into homicide. But, if Jackie's hypothesis were true, Mr Feast was already disturbed, his violent nature intensified by disease.

'Then Nesta was poisoned,' she said. Poisoned? The word had come out quite naturally and impulsively. What she had meant to say, of course, was 'drugged'. It was she, not Nesta, who felt this dreadful burning in the stomach, this movement of bile as if her whole being was constantly longing to reject something alien.

Presently the children came back with bags of potato crisps.

'Cheese and onion flavour,' said Mark happily, thrusting the packet under her nose. 'You can have one if you like.'

The smell of grease and, above all, the smell of cheese, was so nauseating that she quivered with revulsion. The child stared at her. Then, at a repressive glance from his mother, he put down the crisps and stood on one leg. Alice could see he sensed the tension between the two adults. The room was quite silent, yet with a kind of vibration in the air.

Mark was so like Hugo and like his great-uncle as well. It was as if Jackie had contributed nothing to his looks but just been the vehicle through which another Whittaker had been bred. Because she was suddenly ashamed of her suspicions, and because she felt that soon if nobody moved she would scream aloud, she reached out and threw her arms round the child. It was a way of making amends, but Mark knew nothing of that. He struggled and pushed her away.

His rejection did more to hurt her and cow her than anything else. In it she sensed the scorn and dismissal of all her family.

'Why is Aunt Alice ill?' said Mark.

'I don't know,' said Jackie shortly. 'People do get ill sometimes. You know that.'

'Grandad got ill and he died.'

Alice wanted to cover Jackie's embarrassed giggle with reassuring, incredulous laughter. Her lips felt as rigid and as cold as pebbles.

'I'd better drive you home now,' said Jackie.

Andrew deposited the stack of novels carefully on the bedside table.

'Are you sure you want to read all this stuff? You'll probably find it as dry as dust.'

'You don't.'

'No . . .' He smiled distantly. Couldn't he see that she was trying to create a new bond between them?

'Are all the Trollope politicals here, Andrew?'

'Not quite all. There are a couple I want for myself downstairs.'

Downstairs. That meant he wasn't going to sit with her any longer. Still, she must try not to feel even a shred of bitterness. A compulsive reader like Andrew had to read like others had to have drugs. Drugs . . . She shivered. It was unjust to admit the thought that he preferred reading a book he had read over and over again to sitting with his wife.

'Which ones are missing?' she asked brightly.

'Two volumes of *Phineas Finn*. It'll take you days before you get to them.'

'Days, Andrew? I won't be here for days. I'm going to get up tomorrow and go to the police. No, don't say anything. I've decided. I've got to do something about Nesta.'

Exasperation crossed his face and tightened his mouth.

'Oh, Bell! What are you going to tell them? Don't you understand you can't prove anything without the letters and you haven't kept the letters. Nesta simply tried to deceive you into thinking she was in Orphingham when she was really in London. . . .' She shook her head violently and touched his arm, but he pushed her hand away gently. 'Of course she's in London. Try to be realistic. What you're feeling is hurt pride. At best your going to the police can only lead to your appearing in court as a witness when they find Nesta Drage and summons her for some paltry offence against the Post Office. And they can't even do that without the letters and without the redirection notice.'

It was all true. What one logical reasonable man believed other men would believe. Only she and Jackie were convinced, largely by evidence that appealed to the feminine instinct, that Nesta was dead.

Somewhere she was dead—and buried. The florist who had wound so many garlands had been buried without a wreath of her own. Where was she lying now? They had begun to move the graves that night and you could get into the old graveyard quite easily from the garden of The Bridal Wreath. The ancient coffins would contain nothing now but dust. Who of the midnight men moving silently among the yew clumps would notice that one was a little heavier?

If the coffins were too risky there were always the cavities left in the crumbly brown clay. A little could have been spaded away and later restored. A week afterwards tons of concrete had been poured over the rifled ground to make the slip road.

She hesitated fearfully, certain, but afraid to put her thoughts into words. Fancies such as these, spoken aloud in the still-warm room, would only serve to make her sound a neurotic. As she looked at him, straight and young with his smooth black hair, she was suddenly more than ever conscious of her age and that she was on the threshold of a woman's foolish years. She put her hand to her lips, then to the forehead that no longer had the satiny feel of youth.

He went coldly, slowly, without another word. She closed her eyes. When she opened them again Pernille was standing at the end of the bed with the yoghurt and some thin bread and butter on a tray.

'Mrs Fielding, I do not like to ask before because you are ill, but the stamps?'

She had forgotten all about them. A little half-hysterical laugh crept up and struggled in her throat. Stamps! Of all the trivial, prosaic things to have to remember when so many tumultuous things had happened!

'I forgot. I'm sorry. I'll get them as soon as I'm allowed out.'

'Knud will be so pleased. They are of more value when they are not postmarked, you see.'

Postmarks. . . . In the absence of the letters themselves, in the absence of the redirection notice, it might help if she could only say where those letters had come from and could show a sample of the typing.

'Pernille,' she said thoughtfully, 'd'you remember—Oh, way back in September—I had two letters from Mrs Drage?'

Pernille nodded, her clear dark skin growing increasingly pink. She stopped half-way to the door and looked back at Alice warily.

'You didn't happen to notice the postmarks, did you? I thought you might have seen by accident when you were taking the letters in.'

If she had been wearing an apron she would certainly have twisted it. Her face was a comical mask of shame, guilt and self-justification.

'The second letter,' she said at last. 'I kept the envelope, Mrs Fielding. You had finished with it and when I empty the wastepaper basket, there is the envelope with the beautiful new stamp. I look at the date on the postmark and I know at once . . . Oh, I do not know how to say it in English!'

Alice's mind went back thirty years to a rainy afternoon at Vair Place. She and Hugo had been sitting on the attic floor and between them was Hugo's new stamp album. Hugo had pulled her plaits and made her cry because, anxious to take part in this masculine pastime, she had wanted to soak a certain stamp off a certain envelope.

'A first-day cover!' she cried. 'You kept it for your brother because it was a first-day cover.'

Pernille nodded. 'It is the same in Danish,' she said simply. 'You do not mind?'

'Of course I don't mind. I'm glad, very glad. . . .' Her face fell in sudden disappointment. 'But you've sent it to Copenhagen?'

'No, I wait for Knud to come. Next week he comes for his holidays and then I will give him all the stamps I have saved. I long for him to come, Mrs Fielding.' Not bothering to hide her emotion, she said softly, 'I have been so—so homesad.'

'Homesick,' Alice corrected her gently. Suddenly her heart went out to the girl. She had been too happy with Andrew to notice this unhappiness on her own doorstep. Without hesitation she got out of bed and pulled on her dressing-gown.

'We'll go and find the envelope,' she said, 'and we'll have a look at your room. See if we can do something to cheer it up.'

Perhaps she hadn't devoted as much care as she should have done to furnishing it. It had a maid's room look about it, the floor uncovered but for the two stupidly bright goat-hair rugs. The curtains didn't match the bedspread and there were no ornaments, no books. Pernille's tiny transistor stood forlornly on the bedside table between a tiny brown glass bottle and a jar of hand cream. The envelope they had come for was retrieved pathetically from a writing case stowed under the Danish girl's pillow.

Alice took it eagerly and stared. It was clearly postmarked Orphingham.

But Nesta had never lived in Orphingham. Whoever had posted it there had done so to sustain the deception. The threepenny stamp was one of the new issue of Forth Road Bridge commemoratives, violet, blue and black. Its design of the great suspension arcs beside the Queen's head was almost obliterated by the name Orphingham in the twin circles of the postmark.

Tomorrow morning she would take it to the police. Surely they could deduce something from it, trace the typewriter, even find fingerprints? Delicately, as with tongs, she held the paper between her nail-tips. That greenish-pale assistant at Orphingham Post Office might even remember to whom he had sold stamps on that first day of issue.

'Pernille,' she said, 'I'm ashamed I let you sleep in this ghastly room.' Gratitude and hope were making her generous. 'I think we could run to a proper carpet, and would you like your own television?'

The pale blue kitten eyes met hers and looked away. Then Pernille smiled and nodded her thanks. Was it illness that made her see a kind of pity in those curling lips?

'You're eating properly, aren't you? Plenty of milk and meat and cheese?'

'I eat meat, yes,' Pernille justified herself. She shivered slightly, affecting disgust. 'But milk and that yoghurt you have—no, thank you!'

Smiling, Alice said a brisk 'Good night' and stepped out

on to the landing. It was almost funny a Dane disliking the dairy foods that were so closely associated with her native land. She was concentrating so hard on keeping back the hysterical laugh that had risen to her lips that she failed to catch Pernille's last words. Something about cheese and lucky she didn't like it.

Alice went back to bed and ate some of the yoghurt. Everything tasted strange these days. Wearily she pushed it away and opened the first of the Victorian novels, seeing only a blur of print and line drawings.

The house had been perfectly silent but as she turned the pages she heard from beneath her a faint tapping, chattering sound. She listened. No, it wasn't coming directly beneath but somewhere from the other side of the house where the morning room and the dining-room were with the kitchen behind them. It is always difficult, she knew, precisely to locate the invisible source of sound. Then a door closed and quiet returned. The noise must have come from some of Pernille's kitchen equipment, for whatever it sounded like, there was certainly no typewriter in the house.

9

The sun was as bright as on a spring day. The thick evergreen foliage on the bushes in the drive gave a look of spring too, but along the edges of the paths frost clung to the grass.

Alice turned away from the landing window and began to go downstairs. The sun made bright flame-coloured patches on the red turkey carpet in the hall. As she reached the half-landing where the stairs twisted before the final straight descent, she heard voices from the kitchen. The door was slightly ajar.

'Of course she's years and years older than him.' The voice was Mrs Johnson's, the subject of the conversation not difficult to guess at. Vexed, she bit her lip and stood still.

'I did not know.' That was Pernille. Dear Pernille! 'I do not think one would know that. She is so pretty, I think, and she has a lovely body.'

'We don't say that over here, dear. A lovely figure, or a nice bust if you want to go into details.' On the stairs Alice almost giggled. 'And she's got a beautiful head of hair, I grant you that. Always did have, even when she was a little tot.'

This was an instance of listeners hearing nothing but good of themselves. Alice took a step down, about to announce her presence with a cough when Mrs Johnson spoke again.

'Mind you I'm not saying anything against *him* . . .'

'Mr Fielding?'

'No names, dear, no pack drill. We know who we mean. Affection there may be, I don't doubt it. But as for taking him into the works that was a mistake. He's no more use to Mr Whittaker than the office boy.'

Alice froze again.

'Not that Mr Whittaker ever says anything, but you can tell from one or two things he's let slip. I'm a bit of a psychologist in my way, Miss Madsen, and I get to read between the lines. Every time there's anything in the paper about those schoolteachers wanting more money Mr Whittaker gets very hot under the collar. Scathing is the word. I said to Kathleen only yesterday, Blessed is he that sitteth not in the seat of the scornful.'

She could stand it no longer. Her grandmother would have burst in on them. Times had changed. Alice crept back to the landing and came down again, making an unnecessary amount of noise. Mrs Johnson's voice rang out loudly:

'I just popped over with an egg custard for Mrs Fielding, dear. Something light and sustaining. I'm not saying anything against continental cooking, but those made-up dishes are a bit highly seasoned when you've got gastric trouble.'

Alice opened the door. 'Good morning, Mrs Johnson.'

'Well, madam, this is a surprise.' Alice had known Mrs Johnson for thirty years. She had been a nanny to her, almost a mother. But when she came home from school at eighteen the Christian name had been replaced by 'miss' and from the moment she returned from St Jude's after her wedding, Mrs Johnson had begun to call her madam. 'We thought you were asleep and here you are dressed. Well, I always say it's better to keep going and not give way.'

'I feel much better this morning.'

'That's right, you keep going. When we had all that trouble over my cousin, I was that low, I can't tell you. Dr Blunden wanted to keep me under morphia day and night, but No, I said, I'll keep going with my usual. . . .'

'I'm going out, Pernille,' said Alice.

Now she was on the point of going to the police, something held her back; reluctance to put her fears into words, perhaps, or shyness. The overheard conversation had been upsetting and she felt a sudden bitter resentment against her uncle. What right had he to talk about Andrew like that, as if Andrew were mercenary? Even in the wind her cheeks felt hot with anger. They seemed to be muffled in warm, suffocating cloth.

Postponing her visit, she went first to the post office and bought the stamps, then into the carpet shop and took away a pattern book. Harry came out of his surgery on the other side of the street, waved at her, smiled his sweet smile and got into his car. Outside Mr Cropper's shop the jeweller was standing in the sunshine, talking to Mr Feast.

'Good morning, Mrs Fielding.' He looked at her as if he wanted to say more, apologise perhaps, but she passed on quickly. The sight of him, cadaverous, intense, febrile, a jealous, violent man, was the one spur she needed. She went up the steps into the police station.

The station was familiar but not this little room with C.I.D. on the door. The man on the opposite side of the table had a young handsome face creased with fatigue. She fancied strangely that so might Andrew have looked if his life had been different, without education and cloistered pedagogy. The face was like Andrew's and yet unlike. Fineness and grace were there but scarred, as it were, by the passing of a brutish hand in a rough glove. He had introduced himself and her heart sank a little when she heard he was only a detective constable.

She told him about the letters. His face was impassive. She told him about her illness and how it had inhibited her, preventing her from making all the enquiries she would have liked to make. Apparently listening, he asked her if she would smoke. Impatiently she shook her head.

'From what I've heard I think Mrs Drage may have been involved with several men. This is what I think happened: one of them wanted to kill her and he gave her some tablets he said were aspirins. But they weren't, you see. They were a drug that's potentiated by cheese. Everyone knew she went to the bread and cheese lunches because she wanted to slim. She didn't eat cheese that day until she came to my house.'

She stopped. Not until she was actually telling him had she realised that the meal which had contributed to Nesta's death had been eaten in her house, cooked by her. The realisation, appalling though it was, made her only the more anxious to find the truth.

His expression told her she had been talking in vain. Desperately she clenched her fists and brought them down hard on the desk. It was a mistake.

'So you've been unwell, Mrs Fielding?' he said.

'I'm not sick in my mind.'

'Nobody suggested such a thing. Don't you think being ill could have made you over-imaginative?'

'I haven't got a powerful imagination and I don't read sensational literature.' In her mind's eye she saw the Victorian novels she had left on her bedside table, but she couldn't smile.

'Well, if you could just show me the letters Mrs Drage sent you.'

'I've told you, I didn't keep them. I've shown you the envelope. The address is written down in my book. You see, it's like Sewerby and . . .'

'Yes,' he said. 'It's a very easy mistake to make. I know I've done it myself.'

'All right, suppose I made a mistake. Mrs Drage had never lived at Sewerby either. I spoke to the owner of the house and he'd never heard of her. Look, if you were to go—if you were to send someone to Dorcas Street, I'm sure that boy would tell you Mrs Drage hadn't collected the letters and the parcel.'

He corrected her gently, '*Some* letters and *a* parcel. Mrs Fielding, about the cheese and the drug. I'm interested in drugs and I keep a file. Would you like me to show you something?' It was a folder of newspaper cuttings. She glanced at them listlessly. 'The drug you're thinking of,' he said, placing his finger on the cutting he had been looking for, 'is a pep pill containing tranylcypromine.'

'Very possible, I . . .'

'It says here that if you take them with cheese they combine to produce a blood pressure rise which can be dangerous.'

She nodded eagerly. They were getting somewhere at last.

'Mrs Fielding, do you know how many deaths associated with this combination have been recorded in this country since 1960 out of an estimated million and a half patients?'

'Of course I don't.'

He closed the file. 'Fourteen,' he said.

'She could have been the fifteenth.'

He turned his graceful dark head from side to side in gentle incredulity. It might have been a younger, rougher Andrew sitting opposite her. He seemed to be growing more and more like Andrew every minute. There was the same black hair growing high on his forehead, the same narrow sceptical mouth. Suddenly she wondered if he thought she was mad. Mad women probably came in here and told him improbable stories. They would look like her with untidy hair and pale hectic faces.

'She wrote to me and told me her address.' No, that was wrong. Someone else had written. 'I had a letter from Orphingham but the address was false.'

'If she wrote to you, Mrs Fielding, I don't understand why you think she's missing.'

'Won't you do anything?' she pleaded. 'If you could just talk to that man Feast, if you could get some expert to go over the envelope . . .'

He got up and stood by the window. She could see she had made some sort of an impression on him and she leant across the desk, striving to make a last appeal. His eyes flickered. Suddenly she realised that he was silent not from dawning conviction but out of pity and a certain awe of her clothes, her manner and her name. It would not do to cry in front of him. She bent her head and began pulling on her gloves.

'Mrs Fielding . . .'

'It doesn't matter. You'd better forget I came in.' She put the envelope into the pocket of her fur coat.

'We keep a list of missing persons. I don't feel justified in putting Mrs Drage's name on it at present, but we'll keep our eyes open. In case of any unidentified . . .'

Bodies, he had been going to say. In the face of such disbelief how could she tell him that they should exhume the graves in the new cemetery?

'I should go back home, Mrs Fielding, if I were you. I think we could find a car to take you if . . .' He saw the ignition key in her fingers and stopped. 'The chances are,' he said, hearty and relieved because she was going, 'the chances are that you'll have a letter from your friend in a day or two.'

His solicitude was unbearable. When a spinster, Alice had never seen herself as an object of pity. Now she was a married woman, but she felt that to this young man she was exhibiting all the traditionally sad signs of ageing spinsterhood, frustration, loneliness, a longing to draw attention to herself, a desire to make and keep friends.

When she had gone he would talk about her to the station sergeant. 'Bit of a nut-case, that one.' He might even tap his head. And the station sergeant, from a longer experience, would add: 'They go that way when they're getting on and they haven't any kids.'

Who else was there for her to turn to? Not Andrew. His reaction was like the young detective constable's, a mixture of pity and scorn. Uncle Justin and Hugo were at the works. Who but Harry? He would listen to her and believe. The police would believe him.

She must find him, go to the surgery now and go over the whole thing with him in detail. As she came down the steps St Jude's clock struck one. Surely it wasn't as late as that? She looked up at the clock, half doubting, waiting for the other eleven strokes, and her gaze fell on the church hall, its doors wide open. Of course, it was Friday, the day of the weekly bread and cheese lunch. Harry would be there—Harry and Mr Feast. She must be brave and, if necessary, confront him with something like bravado.

But it was the vicar who sat at the deal table just inside the entrance, taking the money.

'Good morning, Miss Whit—Mrs Fielding. Such a pleasure to have you with us again.'

She could think of absolutely nothing to say to him. Instead she felt in her bag and dropped a pound note in front of him. I pay grossly, disproportionately, for everything, she thought as she passed down the hall. I pay my way into everything and out of everything.

Daphne Feast was sitting next to the wife of the council chairman. Alice nodded to them, unable to smile. Father Mulligan was bearing down on her, slopping water from an over-full jug. She paused, giving him a pointless, supplicating glance. Didn't the Catholic catechism cite murder as one of the four sins that cried aloud to heaven for vengeance? He smiled back at her, a pale holy smile from a face like a rack-stretched saint's.

Harry was sitting alone among the posters at the end table. He tried to take her coat from her, but she drew it more closely around her, suddenly realising how bitterly cold she was.

'Harry,' she said, bursting into the middle of things, 'you must tell me, have you ever prescribed tranylcypromine for anyone in Salstead?'

'Have I what? Alice, what is this?'

'Have you? That's all I want to know.'

'Yes, I have as a matter of fact . . .' He stopped, holding a wedge of bread six inches from his mouth. 'Alice, dear, I can't possibly confide in you about things like that. You must understand that as a doctor . . .'

'Have you ever given it to Mr Feast?'

'Certainly not. That would be the last thing. . . . Please, Alice, will you tell me what you're getting at?'

'It's Nesta,' she said quietly. 'If you won't believe me I don't know what I shall do.'

He had seemed annoyed, prickly and pompous, because of the questions she had no right to ask. While she had been the suppliant, a child with an empty bowl, he had been distant, unwilling to grant favours. Now she felt suddenly that they had changed places. Suddenly his face wore that look of hungry anxiety she had formerly felt on her own.

'Nesta?' he said, and then in a forced casual voice, 'What has she been telling you?'

'Telling me? Nothing. How could she tell me anything? Listen, Harry, nobody will believe me except Jackie. I've been nearly out of my mind with worry and Andrew won't listen to me. He won't talk about her.'

She was going to go on, pour out the details of her search, when he interrupted her with a remark so strange that for a moment she forgot all about drugs and letters and Mr Feast. His voice was practical and frighteningly kind.

'That's natural under the circumstances.'

At once she felt that she was on the threshold of a dreadful discovery, and at the same time that she was the last of all of them to make it. For a long time it had been there, a snake sleeping in a box, sometimes showing life but never venom. Now it was beginning to uncurl and to pulsate.

'What do you mean?'

'Alice, I can't discuss it with you. You must see that. When you married a man so much younger than yourself you surely realised there might be problems of this sort.'

The chatter in the hall rose and fell. A glass clinked. She pressed her hands together, suddenly very conscious of tiny sounds. By the vicar's table someone dropped a purseful of small change on to the floor. She heard the coins rolling and the scrabbling noise of someone groping for them. Her eyes compulsively fixed on pictured poverty, she said:

'I don't understand.'

'We'll come to Nesta in a minute,' he said, 'but, Alice, for your own sake you must stop connecting her with Andrew. It's essential for your own peace of mind.'

'Andrew with Nesta? I'm not, am I?' She could feel her

voice becoming shrill, slipping out of control. 'I didn't know I was, Harry.'

His understanding and his pity was more than she could bear. She pushed back her chair and its legs grated on the rough surface of the floor.

'I'm sorry,' he said. 'If I hadn't thought you knew already I wouldn't have said as much as I have. You must forget it, treat it like a bad dream.' He put his hand out to touch her arm but the fingers caught only at her fur sleeve. 'Oh God, Alice,' he whispered, 'I'd give anything to take back what I said.'

Nor all thy piety and wit . . . nor all thy tears wash out a word of it! 'Let me go,' she said. 'I want to go home.' She pulled away from him and walked blindly down the hall.

10

The car roared on to the Vair gravel. She was driving erratically, much too fast, and she saw that she had twice swerved on to the turf verges, breaking the edges and grinding down the grass. But she was home at last, home without giving way to the terrible temptation to burst in on him at the works, sobbing out violent reproaches.

'Are you all right, madam?' Mrs Johnson, aroused from silver cleaning by so much unaccustomed noise, reminiscent perhaps of rally driving and quite alien to the peace of Vair, was leaning out of a window. 'You're a bundle of nerves these days.'

'I'm just tired. And I'm cold.'

'You go straight in and get Miss Madsen to make you a nice cup of something hot. Nerves are very treacherous things, as I have cause to know.'

Alice leant against the bonnet of the car, almost spent with misery and the need to make stupid conventional conversation.

A cloud of plate powder flew out of the window as Mrs Johnson flapped her duster.

'It's a pity you can't bring yourself to have a nice confidential chat with Doctor about it. I know he brought me untold comfort.' The unconscious irony brought a hysterical sob into Alice's throat. 'Now, if you'll just hang on a minute, madam, I can let you have just the thing. . . .'

'No, no!' Alice cried wildly. If she looked any longer into that insensitive, nanny-ish face she felt she would scream. 'I'm going to lie down.' She fumbled with the lock, rushed upstairs and fell on to her bed.

Jealous. Whoever had killed Nesta had been jealous. A big man in Salstead, Daphne Feast had said. To someone with Nesta's background Andrew would have seemed like that with his academic past, his house, his Whittaker connections. But Andrew loved her, Alice. Of course he loved her.

Wretchedly she remembered the police station and the detective who, with his dark good looks and his patience that seemed occasionally to break into exasperation, had reminded her of her husband. He had shown her something she had refused to face before. Young men in their twenties *pitied* women like her, women who were approaching middle age and who had never been beautiful. If they were kind young men they pitied them, if they were not they laughed behind their hands. They didn't fall in love with them. Why had she never thought of it before?

But Andrew loves me, she thought fiercely, I know he loves me. 'For your own sake,' Harry had said, 'you must stop connecting Nesta with Andrew.' All those evenings when Andrew had driven her home, all those weekends before they were married when he had been too busy to come to Vair. . . . He had already met Nesta then.

Why had he married her, given up the job that was his life, changed his whole existence, unless he had loved her? Because you are a rich woman, said a small cold voice, because Nesta lived in Salstead too.

When they had first gone out together he hadn't known she was rich and the signs of love had shown themselves at once. You fool, snarled the canker that was growing inside her. Everything about you proclaimed it—your clothes, your rings, the photographs you showed him of Vair Place. On the second occasion they met she had spoken to him of Whittaker-Hinton. She could remember it all so clearly and now she thought she could remember that then, at that very moment, he had lifted his eyes from the picture, smiled, touched her hand, begun to show her the marked attentions of a lover.

It was on his first visit to Vair that she had introduced him to Nesta. Beforehand she had arranged the theatre foursome, Andrew and herself, Nesta for Harry. But Andrew and not Harry had taken Nesta home. He had been away so long, while she and Harry talked desultorily about nothing, and he had come back talking lightly of flowers he had been shown and carrying a rose-pink cyclamen in a pot. That had been a present for her from Nesta, he said. A present—or a peace offering, a payment for services rendered?

She turned into the pillows with a dry sob that seemed to tear her throat.

He came home earlier than usual, pale, tired, his hair blown by the wind into Byronic disorder. She was lying flat on her back, staring at the ceiling.

'Why did it have to happen, Andrew?' she said stupidly. Her mind was so full of haunting pictures of him and Nesta, excluding everything else, that she thought he must know at once what she meant.

Apparently he didn't. If he felt any guilt, had any inkling of her meaning, concern for her drove it away. He came to the bed and bent over her. 'Why did what happen? What's wrong, Bell?'

'You and . . .' It gave her a physical pain in the mouth

even to pronounce the name. 'You and—and Nesta!' She wetted her lips, shuddering. 'Harry told me.'

'Damn and blast him to everlasting hell!'

She had never heard him swear before. He had been pale when he came in but now he was white with rage.

'You were in love with her, weren't you?' she whispered.

He swung round, turning his back on her. He was a slight man, not broad or muscular, but now his shoulders seemed enormous, hostile, blocking out the light. She covered her eyes with her hands. With his soft careful tread he was walking away from her into the farthest corner of the room. She heard him close the door and the little metallic click, unnoticed a dozen times a day, was like a pistol shot. The mattress dipped as she felt him slump on to the other side of the bed with a heaviness that contained a world of despair.

'Andrew . . .' she moaned.

He would tell her now, confess, ask for her forgiveness, and at the same time admit what she could never forgive—a passion for the dead woman who had been her friend. Clasping her hands together tightly, she opened her eyes and waited.

'If I could only make you believe,' he said, 'how violently . . .' She let out her breath in a trembling sigh. 'How violently I loathed her! She was utterly repulsive to me. But you couldn't see it. I had to put up with that white slug of a woman with her false hair always around me because she was your friend. My God, Bell, I sometimes thought I'd strike her if I ever had to hear her call an anemone an *anenomee* again!' Hes hivered and she could see the tremor wasn't simulated. 'Those wrists of hers, so fat with a sort of dimple around them like a bracelet . . .!'

'Oh, my darling, why didn't you tell me? But, Andrew—

there was something—something between you you wanted hidden, wasn't there?'

'If there hadn't been,' he said dryly, 'I suppose I should hardly have felt the subsequent revulsion.'

'Tell me, then. You can tell *me*.'

'You remember that night we all went to see that play. *Rain*, it was. I remember afterwards thinking how apt of you it was to provide me with a Sadie Thompson.'

'But Nesta was invited for *Harry*.'

'You didn't make that clear, my love. You and Harry seemed to get on so well. I thought you were breaking it gently to me that here was the marriage of true minds. So, you see, when you asked me to take Nesta home I said I would. And when Nesta asked me in, all among the oxlips and the nodding violets, I went in. Oh, Bell dear, she made it very obvious she expected me to kiss her. I thought, why not? That is why I was asked to this particular party.'

'And then?'

'Nothing. I swear to you, nothing. The next time I saw her I was engaged to you.'

All the time he had been speaking he had been waiting, she could see, for a sign from her. Now she gave it. First her hands went out to him, then the smile which had begun in her eyes spread until it irradiated her whole face. He got up swiftly, came to her and took her in his arms.

'Oh, Bell, I've been so afraid for us,' he said, holding her close. 'I wanted to forget it all—what little there was—but Nesta wouldn't let me. When we were alone together she used to speak to me as if we'd been lovers, as if we had some secret we had to keep from you. Then she'd say it might be better if you knew. I watched her disintegrate into the manic-depressive she'd become and I wondered when it would come out, the confidences, the lies, the excuses.'

She nodded and her cheek rubbed warmly against his.

'She was like that with Hugo,' she said. 'Andrew, how many more were there? Why was she like that and how did Harry know?'

'I don't know,' he said thoughtfully. 'Overweening vanity, perhaps. As to how many more . . . Bell, I'll tell you something now. I felt I couldn't before.' He sat back, keeping his arm tightly around her shoulders. 'Back in the summer I was in your uncle's office at the works. You know how he always treats me rather like a minion?' She nodded, a tiny cloud passing across her new happiness. 'Well, that's fair enough—I'm not much good. He had to write a cheque for somebody. He just flung the cheque-book at me, asked me to see if there was one left in it, and went out of the room. As it happens there was just one left, Bell. I noticed some of the stubs—I couldn't help it. You know he uses a new cheque book about once a fortnight, but just the same two stubs were filled in for payments of ten pounds a time to N.D.'

The initials on the vanity case. . . . 'That's horrible, Andrew!'

He said quietly, 'He may have been as innocent as I was.' Tilting her face up to his, he gave her a gentle, passionless kiss. 'Don't worry about it,' he said. 'We'll never see her again.' He jumped up, springy and light, more carefree than she had ever seen him. 'I'll get you some tea.'

We'll never see her again. For more than a week all her energies had been devoted to an attempt to see Nesta again, then to an effort to find who had killed her. Nothing had been allowed to stand in her way but her illness. Now she was almost glad of that illness. The last thing she wanted was to see or hear anything more that could evoke a plump tripping figure, eyes brimming with foolish tears, a black and white check suit seductively tight.

Andrew came back rather noisily and hastily for him.

'Oh, darling, it's a bore but your uncle's downstairs with Hugo. Apparently Mrs Johnson's spun them some tale that you're ill again.'

'I'm coming,' she said. She would have to begin putting suspicions out of her mind and now was as good a time as any.

The tea was already poured out when she entered the drawing-room. Justin Whittaker, his silver tie stiff as a sword pointing at and threatening to pierce his lifted chin, gave a pettish glance at her swollen eyes.

'What's all this I hear about nerves?'

Hugo handed her a cup of tea, slopping it slightly and cursing. 'I've just driven Uncle back from Orphingham,' he said. 'I was dropping him at the gates when Mrs Johnson came flying out in a tear saying you'd nearly driven the car through the garage doors.'

Because she could think of nothing to say, she sat down beside Andrew and sipped the lukewarm tea. Uncle Justin contemplated the ceiling.

'Ten thousand years of civilisation shed in an instant when you put a woman behind the wheel of a car.' He put down his cup as if he had seen it and realised he was holding it for the first time. 'What do I want with tea at this time of night?' he said to no one in particular, then to Alice, shaking his head, 'I don't know where you pick up these proletarian customs.'

She was about to make some angry rejoinder—why were they here, what right had they to question her behaviour?—when the thought came to her that her uncle's bluster covered concern.

'I was worried about something,' she said calmly, 'and I was tired. It doesn't matter, does it? I didn't hit the doors.'

'What you need is a tonic,' he said, 'something to knock all this nonsense about being tired out of you.' Reluctant to betray any emotion, he added brusquely: 'I may as well tell you, Alice, I'm worried about you. You've got something serious the matter with you and if Andrew here doesn't look to it he's going to find himself tied to an invalid—or worse.'

Appalled she jumped up and took a step towards him. Andrew was breathing steadily, evenly, not moving.

'Uncle Justin!' The burning pain which caught at her diaphragm was the worst she had ever experienced. It had come suddenly from nowhere and it diffused at once, pouring into her limbs and flecking brilliant, flower-like colours across her vision. Her legs had become numb and immovable and as she put out her hands into intangible voids, a spasm of sickness flooded her so that she could hear with her physical ears a roaring like the waves of the sea.

'What's the matter, Bell? What on earth's the matter?'

It was going to happen again, just as it had in the Feasts' flat. This time his arms were there to save her, but she fell so heavily that they both crashed against the loaded table. The last things she heard were Hugo's oaths, the shattering of china and the dripping of milk and tea on to the carpet.

She had been conscious for a long time, but there seemed to be no reason for opening her eyes. Blackness and withdrawal were all she wanted. She had been aware of comings and goings and now she realised that Harry only was in the room with her and Andrew. The two men were arguing in harassed angry whispers.

'I fully realise I'm not here because you want me,' Harry was saying, 'but since Mr Whittaker telephoned me, and Alice is my patient, the least you might let me do is try and make a diagnosis.'

'Considering you've seen my wife almost every day since this trouble started, and so far all you've managed to come up with is some mythical virus, I should think "try" is the operative word.'

'Listen to me, Fielding, a virus is the last thing I'm considering at this moment, but something very different....'

'You make me tired!'

'Before I can be sure I shall have to make a very thorough examination and ask her some questions, so if you or Miss Madsen will help me get her upstairs . . .'

She felt his hand move under her arm. Then Andrew jerked it violently away. Still Harry didn't quite lose his temper.

'Come now. Alice won't mind talking to me. I think you forget she and I are old friends.'

'I've had about as much of this friend-patient stuff as I can stand. It's always been my impression that the less so-called friendship existing between a doctor and his woman patient the better.'

There was dead silence. When Harry spoke his voice was so quiet that she had to strain to catch it.

'If anyone—*anyone*—but Alice's husband had said that I'd have had him for slander.' She heard him take a deep breath. 'For heaven's sake let's leave personalities out of this. It's essential that Alice should see a doctor. She ought to have tests made, a special diet.' He stepped back clumsily and she heard his heel grind into broken china. 'What on earth has she been eating? Did she have any lunch?' His voice rose and suddenly she knew what he was trying to say and why his voice had that chilled, appalled edge to it. 'Fielding, can't you guess what's the matter with her, or are you too much of an escapist to face up to it?'

'I happen to be a layman,' said Andrew, 'not a provincial, back-street physician. Now, will you please go?'

She opened her eyes then and gave a faint moan. Harry was standing, looking down at her.

'Alice,' he said, hardly moving his lips.

'I understand,' she said. 'I should have realised before. Don't worry, I'll be careful now.'

'I have to go.' Harry's face was miserable and anxious; his blue eyes stared down at her, wide with shock. 'Promise me you'll call someone else in, get a second opinion.'

'Of course I will.'

'Get out!' said Andrew.

He went without looking back and she saw that for once instead of stooping he walked erect. As the door closed she leaned back, the tears streaming down her face.

Now that the worst of his rage had passed he stood beside her almost humbly, abject, with eyes cast down. Evidently he expected her to reproach him, but she could think of nothing but the awful momentousness of Harry's words. *What on earth has she been eating? We must have tests made. Fielding, can't you guess what's the matter with her?* Harry was a doctor and Harry had seen, had divined from her symptoms, what was the matter with her.

It should have been a surprise and yet it wasn't. Subconsciously she had suspected it all the time and that accounted for her fear, the dread which arose within her each time the nausea returned. Spasms of sickness had occurred at each fresh stage in her search for Nesta, or rather had occurred just before those stages were reached. Whoever had killed Nesta was frightened too, so frightened that he was prepared to make her ill, even to kill her, in his desperate effort to stop the truth coming out.

Harry would have helped her, but Harry had been sent away. Even if he had stayed there was nothing he could have done. Quite clearly there rose before her eyes a picture of them all as they had been before she had drunk that cup of tea, Hugo and her uncle watching her, waiting, talking to fill in time. The tea had been poured out before she had come into the room. One of them could have . . . Oh, it was horrible! But how could she allow Harry to make tests, discover whatever it was—arsenic, strychnine?—and then incriminate her uncle or her brother? It couldn't be possible. Yet Andrew had said Justin Whittaker was paying sums of money out to Nesta. An allowance perhaps, or blackmail? Hugo had confessed to his own small adventure with Nesta. Maybe it had been not a small but a big adventure, an escapade that he would do anything to prevent Jackie discovering.

'Bell, we'll get you another doctor,' Andrew said at last, 'someone who really knows, a specialist.'

'I don't know. I'm so afraid, Andrew.'

It might not be either of them. Other men had been involved with Nesta. Hadn't there been something almost sinister in the way Mr Feast had pressed her to take the yoghurt? He had known that no one else in the house would eat it. She mustn't stop to think about consequences, about police in the house, endless questions, a trial at which she must give evidence, when her own life was in danger.

Perhaps it was too late. Perhaps the poison had already taken a grip on her from which there was no escaping except into death. As if providing an affirmative answer, pain suddenly gripped her chest, diffusing out in flowing branches of agony, and as she moaned and hugged herself with numb cold arms, she seemed to sense death's grinning presence.

'If I should die, Andrew . . .' She shook her head against his expostulations. 'No, darling, listen. If I die it's all for you, this house and, oh, ever so many shares in the works. And everything that's in the bank. I made a will when we were married and it's all for you.'

'*Die?*' he said. 'People don't die, my darling, because they have food poisoning. You're so tired and overwrought you don't know what you're saying.'

If only she could get up and call them all back, shout to them that they were wrong, abysmally wrong, if they thought she wanted to find Nesta now. All she wanted was peace, a return to the normalcy of last week, a body that no longer need wage a battle against something too strong for it.

'Don't leave me,' she said. 'Stay with me.'

'Of course I'll stay. Try and get some sleep.'

Then he did a curious thing. With the tips of his fingers he touched her eyelids lightly and obediently she closed her eyes. It was only afterwards, just as she was slipping into exhausted, stunning sleep, that her brain associated his gesture with the closing of the eyelids of the dead.

11

Tomorrow the specialist would come. She had lain in bed for three days now and it seemed to her that hardly an hour had passed in which she had not rehearsed the coming interview, but still she hadn't made up her mind what she would say to him. Her association with crime, even though she was just a victim, seemed to have degraded her, smearing her with underworld dirt, and she pictured the distaste on the face of the great man as the truth began to become obvious to him.

The air in the bedroom was quite fresh—indeed she kept the windows open day and night in spite of the gale—but it seemed to her that the place was filled with a kind of miasma. Poison was in the air, in the mind of someone and in her own body. She had frightened Andrew by her refusal to eat anything that had not been prepared by himself or by Pernille, and frightened him more by her refusal to say why.

'I don't want to see them, I don't want them to bring me things,' was all she would say.

'But you could see Jackie, darling. She's made you a jelly and brought you some wonderful flowers.'

She reared up in the bed then and he flinched at her outburst of incoherent terror. And Jackie had gone away, hurt and indignant, leaving behind her a bunch of chrysanthemums with blossoms like curly golden wigs. Alice had always loved flowers and she had told Pernille to put these in a corner of the bedroom, out of scent but disturbingly within sight. They reminded her of the huge plumed flowers Nesta had woven into wreaths for winter funerals. Nesta had sat in her workroom with the chrysanthemums spread about her, her own golden head like an enlargement of one of the giant blooms.

Alice sat in bed, reading continuously, absorbing perhaps only one word in every ten, but turning the pages, keeping herself sane. Even so she couldn't keep her eyes from roving compulsively towards the vase in the corner. Then her body seemed to crystallise into a block of fear, a pillar of salt, while she stared rigid and terrified at twelve golden heads which the wind whipped and ruffled.

'When will he come?' she kept asking Andrew, for she longed for and feared the arrival of the specialist.

'Sir Omicron Pic?' Andrew always called him that, affecting to have forgotten his real name, and calling him instead after an eminent physician in one of his favourite novels. 'Tomorrow at three. You can't summon him at a moment's notice like some village quack.' And his mouth curled with a kind of scorn. 'How do you feel this morning?'

'I don't know,' she said. 'I wish I knew.'

The sickness which had been physical had undergone a subtle change. Now more than anything it resembled the dyspepsia that accompanies an anxiety neurosis. So many things could bring it on, the sound of her uncle's voice booming out enquiries in the hall below, the gleam of the golden flowers at twilight, her own thoughts that kept returning to the dead woman. But sometimes it came without provocation, mostly at evening or when she first awoke, and then it was so savage and unremitting that she knew no mental turmoil could have caused it.

'Pernille,' she said when the Danish girl came in with her lunch, 'would you take those flowers away?'

With only a hazy idea of what it had all been about, she closed the last page of the second volume in the series. Pernille rested the tray on her knees and she noticed the smart blue coat that was undoubtedly 'best', the white gloves, the black shiny pumps. For a moment the sight of those jetty pointed toes brought Nesta back to her so forcibly that she sank against the pillows, feeling a scented languid presence and hearing a voice whispering sad yet urgent words too far away to catch. Then, recovering, she said in a tone that sounded falsely bright:

'Are you going out?'

'It is my afternoon off, Mrs Fielding.' Pernille lifted the vase and held it in front of her.

'Are you going somewhere nice?' A pang of envy struck her. The girl looked so free, so happy, so radiant with animal good health.

'I think it is nice, yes. Today my brother comes for his holiday and I go to the airport to meet him.' Above the nodding blossoms her eyes sparkled. 'I am so excited to see him again.'

'Yes, you must be. Don't bother about getting back early.'

'Just think, I have not seen him during a whole year.' She hesitated and then burst out, 'Knud stays with a friend he has known at the university and . . .'

'Yes?'

'Mr Fielding said perhaps I need not come back till tomorrow, but you are ill so I . . .'

'Of course you mustn't come back!' A beautiful new idea was taking shape in her mind. 'Look, why don't you take two or three days off? Mr Fielding will look after me.'

'He will be home by five and all is ready for your tea and for your dinner.'

'You're an angel!' What could she do for this girl in gratitude for leaving her in solitude with Andrew? 'Pass me my bag, will you?' The notes snapped from their rubber band as flat and crisp as the pages of a book. Pernille's face flamed and her fingers crushed the green paper. She must be too overcome to thank me, Alice thought, watching her vanish in a flash of blue and gold.

It was only when she had gone that Alice remembered what she had meant to ask her. 'Go downstairs and see if you can find a book of Mr Fielding's called *Phineas Finn.*' It couldn't be helped; she would have to go herself.

Pernille's bedroom door was wide open, tidy but for signs of last-minute packing. A crumpled scarf lay on the bedside table. Beside it she saw what she had seen before but which her brain had not recorded as significant: a small brown glass bottle. Nesta had been holding a bottle like that the night she died. It means nothing, nothing, she told herself, as the bottle seemed to grow to huge dimensions, filling the room until it glowed like a great amber coloured tower of glass. Pernille had been ill with homesickness. . . .. Abruptly she turned her back on the room and closed the door.

Although it was still early afternoon the hall was already dark. The old sash windows rattled in their frames and the doors shook. Alice wasn't really cold but the sound of the wind, sighing and keening, made her shiver. The kitchen looked starkly clean and bare. Of course she had often been alone in it before, but seldom, she realised with a reassuring laugh, when there was no one else in the house. Her laughter echoed and she wondered why, all by herself as she was, she had made a noise at all.

Pernille had left the back door unlocked. Alice turned the key. She wanted to be alone, didn't she? The last thing she wanted was a visitor from the outside world, a malignant visitor bringing her some dainty prepared for an invalid.

Now to find the book. She walked softly into the drawing room and over to the shelves which lined the fireplace wall. Andrew had a complete set of Trollope and they were usually in the third shelf from the top. Yes, there were the clericals—from hearing him talk about them she knew their titles by heart—but where the politicals should have been was a long gap, just a stretch of blank polished wood with wallpaper behind it. Most of those volumes were in her bedroom—but where were the two parts of *Phineas Finn*?

Andrew was fanatically tidy about the arrangement of his books. It was unlikely that he could have stuffed these two precious volumes among the modern fiction and the poetry on the other shelves. Just the same, she looked, whispering the titles to herself as her fingers skimmed their spines. But the two books were missing. All the time really she had known they would be. The milk chocolate and blue design on their covers was too distinctive to miss even with only a cursory glance.

He wouldn't want her to take the first editions. She crossed to the antique bookcase she had given him to house them. Dull green and gilt, attractive only to a bibliophile, they looked forbidding behind the glass doors. The key was in the lock but it had been turned. The books seemed to say, touch us not.

Perhaps the missing copies were in the dining-room or the little dark morning room they seldom used because it gave on to the shrubbery. Andrew sometimes sat in there by himself, reading, always reading. As she approached the door a sound behind her made her stop dead. It was a kind of whirring crepitation, dull but quite clear.

But she was alone in the house. *She must be.* Her nerves, already on edge by the discovery of the bottle, the unlocked door and the blank space where the books should have been, now seemed to prickle and jump as if long feelers had been put out to snag her skin.

The whirring went on, piercing her ears as violently as a scream. She kicked open the kitchen door, holding her breath. Then she let it out in a sigh and shook her head impatiently.

'You fool!' she said aloud, for it was only the refrigerator, its pump working noisily as it did perhaps once an hour, reducing temperature. That must have been the sound she had heard the other night, she thought, contemptuous of herself. How could she have mistaken something heard so often and so familiarly for the tapping of a typewriter?

The morning room was empty, cupboardless, with neither desk nor chest that might conceal a book. She came to the dining room. Bleak winter light flooded it from the french windows. She felt a sudden settling, a new ease. After all, it was just an ordinary November day, and here she was alone in her own house, naturally anxious and on edge as any woman would be under the circumstances.

The books were nowhere to be seen. The only explanation must be that, incomprehensible as it was, Andrew had taken them to the works with him. She pulled open the sideboard drawers, but saw only silver slotted into velvet-covered mouldings, tablecloths, their two napkin rings both initialled A. A magazine or a newspaper would have to do instead. There was a pile of these on a stool. Impatiently she began to shift the topmost copies and as she did so two heavy volumes slid out on to the floor and with them a fluttering spray of white quarto sheets and carbon paper.

Brown and blue covers, a little line drawing of bearded men sitting round a club table . . . *Phineas Finn*, Volumes One and Two. Why on earth had careful meticulous Andrew hidden them like this? But, of course, it was absurd to suppose that he had. He must have left them on the table, meaning to bring them up to her, but he had forgotten and Pernille, hurrying to get away, had bundled them up with the papers.

She tucked them under her arm and went to the window. Vair Place seemed to frown at her, a tough old man of a house, gaunt and impregnable among the beating branches. As she stared at the red brickwork, the white facings against which shrub fronds tore vainly, she wondered afresh if it was possible that her uncle could have done this dreadful thing to her. Her uncle or her brother? Tomorrow when the specialist came it would be too late to stop the whole machinery of police procedure. They would have to be questioned, any man who had known Nesta would be questioned. . . .

Any man? Suddenly she felt a renewal of unease that had nothing to do with Hugo or Justin Whittaker. Then, as if with a healing balm flowing into and blocking all the dark frightened corners of her mind, the idea which had come to her when she was talking to Pernille returned. Why shouldn't they go away, she and Andrew? There was nothing to keep them in Salstead, every reason why they should leave a place that had become hateful to both of them. . . .

She went upstairs dreamily, pulled back the covers and got into bed. It was ridiculous to spend all that time hunting for a book and then to be too tired to read it. She would sleep for a little while and wake up refreshed for Andrew.

• • • • •

'Do you take milk, Miss Whittaker?'

She laughed, carefree, ecstatically happy to be alone with him. Looking back, it seemed to her that the whole hateful business had begun at tea-time and now at tea-time she was going to end it.

'Andrew, shall we leave here and go away? Permanently, I mean. Would you like that? We could go tomorrow. I've thought it all out.'

'Sir Omicron Pie is coming tomorrow.'

'We could put him off, couldn't we? I know I'll be all right if I can only get away from here.'

'But, Bell, what about Pernille?'

'I'll—Oh, I'll give her six months' money or something. She's longing to go home, anyway. She's terribly homesick. Darling, we could just pack up and go—go to an hotel somewhere. . . .'

He wasn't looking at her, but down at the silk bedcover, the thick soft carpet, the shell-thin china on the tray. The expression in his eyes was so strange that for a moment she couldn't tell whether it was delight or dismay. His hands were clenched so tightly that great white patches showed on the skin where the pressure of his fingers had driven away the blood.

'Andrew . . . ?'

'When we were engaged,' he said slowly, 'I came down here for the weekend.' Clearing his throat, he added carefully: 'My second weekend at Vair. I meant to tell you then that I'd have to take you away, Bell, that my work couldn't be here. But almost as soon as I arrived you brought me to this house. You showed it to me and said it was to be ours. Your face was like a little girl's, showing off a dolls' house, and I hadn't the heart then to say all the things I'd meant to say. We had lunch with your uncle. His face wasn't in the least like a little boy's. I know little boys, Bell, they were rather an important part of my life. . . .' She started to speak, but he stopped her, shaking his head. 'He gave me a glass of sherry. God, it was as dry as a bone and I happen to like sweet sherry. But he couldn't know that since he hadn't bothered to ask. Then he said to me—barked is the better word—"We'll have to find a niche for you at the works, I suppose. I daresay you're not picking up more than twenty-five a week, are you, at Dotheboys Hall or whatever it calls itself?" The next thing I knew I was sitting at that enormous table with Kathleen spooning asparagus over my left shoulder.'

'Oh, Andrew, I never knew—I never guessed it was as bad as that!'

'I'd often wondered what it feels like to be a commoner married to a royal princess. Oh, it's very nice going on the Civil List, of course, but I confess I feel a certain blow to my manhood when the works foreman makes a slip of the tongue and calls me Mr Whittaker.'

'Why did you stand it? Why didn't you tell me?'

He took her hands and said almost harshly, 'Don't you know?'

She nodded, too ashamed to speak.

'Did you mean what you said just now, that we could go away and not come back?'

'Of course. It's what I want.'

Expecting him to kiss her, she waited, holding up her face. Instead he gave her hand an absent pat, and getting up, stood apart from her. He seemed dazed, like a man who, hearing the first tidings of unbelievable joy, cannot yet face or grasp them.

He would put the car away, he had said. Then he would

see what Pernille had left them for dinner and bring something up to her on a tray. Or perhaps she felt well enough to come downstairs? He could put a match to the fire Pernille had laid.

After he had gone she remembered she hadn't touched the tea he had poured for her. It was almost cold and it had a stagnant look but she sipped it. She heard him lift the garage door and start the car. What was it Mrs Johnson used to say to her when she was a little girl? 'I always know I'm a bit off-colour, love, when the tea's got a funny taste.' She put the cup down and from the floor beside the bed where she had laid it, picked up the first volume of *Phineas Finn*.

All at once the house seemed very silent and stuffily still. A sound that had been part of her existence for a week now had ceased. Then she understood. While she had been asleep the wind had dropped.

For a moment or two, feeling a faint recurrence of malaise, she held the book unopened in her hands. The brown and blue cover was slightly torn. Andrew could bring her the Sellotape when he came up again and she would mend it for him.

If they were really to leave tomorrow she must make an effort, not just lie here listlessly. To see her reading would please him; he would understand that she was beginning to relax again, to take an interest in something apart from her own health.

Were Victorian women really attracted by husky men in Norfolk jackets, men with great bushy fair beards? She smiled at the delicate Huskinson drawings, lingering over them. Here was a winsome crinolined girl standing in front of a Gothic mansion and here a painfully real illustration of a hunting accident. The pictures were amusing but the text looked dreadfully political. How would she ever plough through all that stuff about the Ballot and the Irish Reform Bill? Besides the illustrations were few and the text vast, nearly three hundred and sixty pages in the first volume. She sighed. Like another Alice she wanted pictures and conversation.

Snuggling down in the warm bed, she turned back to the list of contents. The characters and the place names in the chapter headings were all new to her. 'Phineas Finn Takes His Seat', she read abstractedly, 'Lord Brentford's Dinner', 'The New Government', 'Autumnal Prospects'. Her eyes were beginning to close . . . Then, with a little gasp, suddenly wide awake, she struggled up, first rubbing her eyes, then bringing the print close to them.

No, it couldn't be! It must be a hallucination, a delusion. She shut her eyes tightly and frightened by the darkness and the drumming in her head, opened them again to stare and stare. Every number, every line on that page swam together into a greyish blur except two words in italics: *Saulsby Wood.*

12

With the drumming in her ears came a terrible swamping heat, a blaze comparable to that from an open furnace. Then the sweat broke from her rather as if an outer constricting skin was being shed.

Saulsby.

She looked at the page again and the print danced. There was no point in staring at it so compulsively. Did she think that by looking and willing she could work a miracle, change the name into something else?

Saulsby. She shut her eyes and slammed the pages together. Her body was wet, running with sweat, and her fingers left damp prints on the book jacket.

The names of the houses in the terrace in Chelmsford Road had been real places, but Saulsby wasn't a real place. An author had invented it for a country house. This wasn't a popular novel anyone might read; it was obscure, largely unknown. Only a connoisseur, an enthusiast would read it. She mustn't think along those lines, that way madness lay. . . . She pushed her fists into her eye sockets.

Others in Salstead could have read it besides—yes, she had to say it—besides Andrew. She began to feel dreadfully sick. Try to be detached, she urged herself, try to make a part of you stand aside and look at it as a stranger might. But who would know as well as he that she wanted to advertise for

Nesta? He had known first, seen it all happen, because he was on the spot, here in the house.

You haven't any proof, she thought, this is your husband that you love. She had come up the path the first time she had been to Orphingham, and seen him sitting in the window reading this same book. Hadn't he shown her the cover then and told her it had been torn? It had all begun at tea-time and at tea-time it would end. . . . He had asked her the name of Nesta's house and she had told him.

'Saulsby. I've got it written down in my book. I'll get it.'

'Don't get up now. I know you don't make mistakes like that.'

Ten minutes before he had been reading it, perhaps reading the very name.

But how had he done it, what had he done? In all her theories about Nesta's disappearance she had never yet been able to put a convincing face on the lover who called himself Mr Drage. It had been stupid to think of Uncle Justin or Hugo or Mr Feast. How could any of them have gone to London on all those weekends? Andrew could. Before they were married, separated as they had been by a hundred miles, whole weeks passed by when they saw nothing of each other. *Andrew*. Shock had delayed the action of pain. It struck her now as with a blow to the heart.

One part of her mind was wounded, agonised, the rest suddenly clear and analytical. It had been easy for him, a gift to an intelligent man. Pernille had been given tranquillisers—that was what the little brown bottle had contained. One white tablet looked very like another. When they had gone up to Pernille together, and Nesta had asked for aspirins, nothing could have been simpler than to have given her two tablets—or three?—from that bottle. And

Andrew knew they were all going to eat cheese. Only fourteen deaths, the young detective had said, out of one and a half million people. But he had also said that this particular combination *raised* the blood pressure. Suppose Nesta's blood pressure had been high already? Bitterly she thought of the many opportunities Nesta would have had for imparting this fact to Andrew. Oh, Andrew, Andrew . . . She stuffed the sheet into her mouth to stop herself crying aloud.

He had done it for her. To prevent her discovering his infidelity—had she threatened that very night to tell Alice everything as a parting shot?—he had killed Nesta. Could she live with him, knowing what he had done?

He must have loved her more than Nesta. What he had felt for Nesta wasn't love at all. Suppose it had been love but the lure of money and position was stronger? He had talked about being a consort, about going on the 'Civil List', but perhaps he had only married her to attain that. Rather than lose it he would do—had done—anything. If he loves me for my money, she thought desperately, it's because I *am* my money. I am what my money has made me, inseparable from it, part and parcel of it. A girl could love a man because he was rich and authoritative and assured. Surely the principle remained if the roles were reversed.

She would never let him know that she knew. Every day she would think of it, every hour. But not for always. Time would take it away. After years had passed she would probably be able to forget it for whole days at a time. The great thing would be to support herself now, tonight, just while he sat with her and they ate their dinner.

Their dinner. . . . The words brought another rush of heat and a fresh flow of sweat. The shudder which took her jerked the bed and set the tea cup rattling. He had brought her that tea and bent over her, smiling. A man may smile and murder while he smiles. He had done it because he loved her. She tore the sheets from her body and rushed trembling from the bed. Why hadn't she seen the flaw in that argument? Whoever had killed Nesta had tried to kill her. Nesta's killer had tried to kill or, at least, seriously to incapacitate the woman who sought him.

Chocolates, yoghurt, a jelly, an egg custard . . . What a fool she had been! No one outside the house would dare to poison food anyone inside it might eat. But Andrew had brought her food and drink with his own hands, knowing it would be touched by nobody but herself.

She fell against the door, pressing it with cold clammy hands. The foretaste of vomit was on her tongue and bent double with an excruciating shaft of pain, she remembered the foul taste of the tea. Suppose she died tonight? Harry had been sent away after an obviously staged quarrel. In her own innocence she had herself asked Andrew to cancel the specialist's visit.

Pernille was gone. Not she but Andrew had told her to stay away all night. Charitably he had sent her away so that he might be alone with his wife.

I must get away too, she said aloud. I must get out! With agonising slowness the sickness subsided. It seemed to draw away from her mouth and throat and travel into her limbs where it settled as a kind of paralysis. She stumbled to the window and wrenched back the curtains. Light from the drawing-room showed her the drive misted by a faint drizzle. The laurels and ilexes, still now after a week of turbulence, hung their immobile heads. Thank God Uncle Justin was next door!

She began to dress, clumsily and feebly because her hands were shaking. There was no time to plait her hair. She caught it up and twisted it into a coil on the back of her head, found the pins and stabbed them in haphazardly. A coat next. It would be cold out there tonight. She unhooked the fur from its hanger and seeking warmth, thrust her hands into the pockets. Something stiff and cool touched her right palm—Nesta's envelope, the first-day cover. The contact brought back humiliation. She had slipped that envelope into her pocket at the police station.

If he saw her on the stairs he would try to stop her.

'What are you doing, Bell?'

Nobody would ever call her that again. For ever now she would associate the diminutive with sweet insincerity, a subtle, smiling poisoner. Clutching at her body, she let out a little cry of pain.

But it was useless to think of that now. For that she had all the rest of her life. Now she must get out. Cautiously she opened the door. The house was full of light. Down the stairs next as swiftly as her weak legs would take her. The front door, could she make the front door without his hearing her?

There was a light in the dining-room and she thought at once of the french windows which faced the side of Vair Place. From the kitchen came the very faint clink as of plates being moved. She went into the room and reached for the curtains to draw them away from the lock.

The room was different, changed since she had visited it that afternoon. Something, some unfamiliar arrangement of objects, unnoticed at first, but registering by their very oddity on her subconscious, made her turn towards the table. She started and froze. On the table was a typewriter.

A pad of perhaps half a dozen quarto sheets were in the roller. She moved towards the machine fearfully as if it were alive, able to transmit her actions to its owner by some method of supernatural photography. Her breath made the sheets flutter. Where had she seen that perfect, print-like type-face before? Methodically, as if she really were an expert sent by detectives to furnish evidence, she slid the envelope from her pocket.

The lettering, the spacing, the little serifs were precisely identical.

Like a second degree burn the shock it gave her was mild in comparison with the searing her mind had suffered from the sight of the words in the book. This merely confirmed what had been almost a certainty. Had he still hoped, still thought to quiet her by other means than poison? Had he been going to forge another letter? She stood swaying, not shuddering at all, but hollow and sick with horror.

Even when she heard his steps behind her she didn't jump.

'Bell, darling!'

'I wanted to come down,' she said, and every word was an effort. It was as if she was speaking an unfamiliar language. 'To surprise you.' But why was she suddenly laughing, a merry trilling laugh that bubbled out gaily? 'Yes, I wanted to surprise you, Andrew.'

It must have been the high strained note in her voice that made him stare at her like that. Or perhaps it was the fact that she had seen the typewriter. The movement he made to pull out the sheets of paper was swift and furtive.

Her foolish laughter went on unchecked. She couldn't stop it, though the feeling it stemmed from and it in its turn caused, was more like grief than happiness.

'Stop it, Bell,' he said sharply. 'Come and sit down.' She stiffened her body to prevent the recoil. Then she began to laugh again, but the spasmodic giggling died suddenly as his outstretched hands rested on her shoulders, terribly near her neck, pulling her towards the armchair. 'Let me help you down.'

Her will was too weak to hinder the great shudder. She shook and the coat slid from her back.

He stooped down and gathered it up in his arms. 'You won't want it in here.' Some of her fear, although wordless, had communicated itself to him. First she saw in his eyes apprehension, then he made a quick recovery. His tone was velvety. 'You surely weren't thinking of going tonight?'

'No. Oh, no, no, no. . . .'

When his hand—a dry, calm hand—touched her forehead and rested there she gritted her teeth and tensed all her muscles. Another moment and she would have screamed aloud.

'We'll have dinner in here,' he said, 'and then I'm not going to let you out of my sight.' Her teeth had begun to chatter. 'What's the matter with you?' Stern, unsmiling now, he had moved away from her, but his eyes never left her face.

'I'm so cold.'

He wouldn't give her the fur. It looked feral, alive, hanging over his arm, a prey in the hunter's hands. She identified herself with this old valued possession and she held her cold hands pressed against her cheeks as he went towards the door.

'I'll get a rug for your knees,' he said.

It was only a dozen yards to the cloaks cupboard. As soon as he was out of the room she staggered from the chair to the french windows and, her knuckles knocking against the glass, undid the bolts. In the obliquely slanted light from the table lamps his long shadow came in before him, heralding him. She sat upright and stiff in the armchair, clutching the arms. He spread the rug across her knees.

'You're to stay there,' he said, no longer gentle. 'You're

not to move, d'you hear?' She nodded, terrified. Her head moved up and down, fast at first, then more and more slowly and automatically, like the head of a doll that has been wound up and is gradually running down. 'The sooner we get all this cleared up,' he said, 'the better.'

Only once before had she seen that hatred in his eyes, the day he had sent Harry away. Thoughtfully and deliberately he said, 'I'll light the fire.' He struck a match and the paper and logs caught at once.

Everything he did, she thought, shivering, he did well. The cold yellow blaze filled the corners of the room with flickering light.

'I may be a little while,' he said.

She heard him lift the telephone receiver in the hall and begin to dial. He pushed the door and it clicked closed but not before she had caught his first words. 'Is that Welbeck . . . ?' He was phoning the specialist, telling him not to come.

It would be bitterly cold out there in the garden. She wrapped herself in the rug and edged towards the windows. The turning of the key in the lock made no sound. A dry sob rose in her throat but she was too frightened to cry. The door gave soundlessly and cold moist air seeped in to meet her.

13

The evergreens in the shrubbery were wet with black reptilian leaves. She pushed her way through them, holding her hands in front of her face to prevent it being cut by holly. As she passed the greenhouse she saw in the blaze of light that streamed from her own house, a pile of yellow lying on the compost heap. It was Jackie's chrysanthemums. Pernille must have tipped them there before she went out. Checked for a moment and breathless, she stared at them briefly in fascinated horror. Each with its golden curled head was evocative of Nesta, dead, discarded, because its usefulness had ended and it was in the way.

Only one light showed in the windows of Vair Place and that was in the hall. She couldn't remember that she had ever rung the bell before, always letting herself in at the back or by one of the casement doors. Through the panes of glass she could see a glimmer of red carpet, polished oak and pale porcelain. As she waited the desire to giggle uncontrollably returned, to giggle madly at colours and shapes and bushes that poked spotted leaf-fingers into her face.

The door was opened by Mrs Johnson. Alice was stunned now and she felt nothing, only that it was funny and foolish of Mrs Johnson to be wearing her winter coat and a felt hat in the house.

'Where's my uncle?'

'Whatever's the matter, madam?'

It was surprisingly easy to smile, only difficult to stop bursting into laughter right in Mrs Johnson's face.

'Where's my uncle?'

'Mr Whittaker's dining with Mr and Mrs Hugo, being as it's their wedding anniversary.' It was a sudden sharp shock, as salutary as the prescribed slap in the face. Other people were doing other things, things apart from her; the world was going on. A wedding anniversary—how funny, something she would never have! But she clung to the newel post, not wanting to laugh any more.

Mrs Johnson's eyes flickered over the plaid rug.

'Whatever possessed you to come out without a coat, madam?'

'I'll wait for my uncle. What time is it?'

'Just gone seven.' Grudgingly the door was opened a little wider. 'As to waiting for him, madam, me and Kathleen was just on our way to Pollington to see my cousin Norman. But if you wanted to wait here we could always cancel our arrangements. . . .'

The heavy feet in their thick suède-collared boots edged back a few inches.

'No, no, not if you were going out to enjoy yourself. . . .'

'It's not a matter of enjoyment, madam,' Mrs Johnson bridled. 'Only with Norman being laid up all these months, and Mr Whittaker being so good to him, I always feel it's the least I can do. Goodness knows, the Dawsons are an idle lot in all conscience and Norman not the least, but when it's a case of genuine illness . . .'

'It doesn't matter!' She stopped, putting the names together. N.D., Norman Dawson. Uncle Justin had been paying an allowance to his housekeeper's sick cousin. Another door was slammed, another question mark erased.

'Of course you must go. I can wait by myself.'

'There, and just this minute Kathleen's raked out the boiler all ready for the sweep in the morning. Half an hour and them pipes get as cold as charity.'

'It doesn't matter! It doesn't matter!' Alice cried. She could go to Hugo. It wasn't far, less than a quarter of a mile. She turned, shaking her head feebly, exhausted with the effort of talking. The door was held open just long enough to light her way down the path between the laurels. She began to run along the street, stumbling and catching at the fences.

He would never dare to come after her. Or would he? If only her legs were less weak, the pavement dry instead of greasy with mud and water.

Your husband is trying to kill you. He has killed one woman and because you know too much about it, and because he wants your money, he is trying to kill you too. It was no good. They were just words, words that might have come back to her out of a book she had been reading. The facts were all there, clear in her head, but the magnitude of the horror provided an anaesthetic that blanked out all emotion. Your husband is trying to kill you. Her mouth twisted into a silly smile.

Hugo's bungalow was the first of an estate of large modern houses built behind the elms in what had been a country lane. Lights glimmered behind a web of tangled black branches. She was going to spoil their celebration, burst in on a group of happy people just as they raised their glasses in the first toast. It couldn't be helped.

As she put her hand to the gate the lights of a car loomed out of the black hole between the arched boughs. It seemed to roar as it emerged like a train coming out of a tunnel and she flattened herself against the hedge, all the breath driven from her body. But it was only a shooting brake with a retriever gazing placidly from the rear window. Drizzle speckled on to her lifted face and a cascade of liquid mud splashed against her legs. This is how the hare must feel, she thought, afraid by instinct, but not knowing what it fears, running with hysterical leporine laughter.

The path to the bungalow was long, a causeway of crazy paving, slightly raised above wet grass. This was the last lap and it gave her a spurt of energy. She flung herself into the porch and hammered on the door.

Jackie was coming. Thank God Jackie would be the first to see her! With the sound of human movement, the certainty of immediate human contact, there returned in piercing violence the awfulness of reality. Andrew has killed Nesta, Andrew is trying to kill you . . . For a little while Jackie would hide her from the men, take her to her bedroom and warm her until the worst of the panic was gone. What would come after the panic she didn't dare to think.

The door was tugged open abruptly.

'Oh, Jackie, I thought I'd never . . .'

She gasped. There on the doorstep with Christopher in her arms stood Daphne Feast.

Wedding anniversary cards propped on vases covered the mantelpiece. A big one with a slightly more pithy greeting than the others had been pinned to the frame of the lop-sided green picture. A peasant, a displaced person with a blotchy white face under a cowl of tartan, looked back at Alice from the mirror. Christopher had begun to cry.

'They've gone to The Boadicea,' said Daphne. 'Didn't you know? It stands to reason she wouldn't want to mess about with cooking on her anniversary.'

The mirrored face mouthed out, 'What are you doing here?'

'Baby-sitting. And it's not funny round here. He's been yelling his perishing head off ever since they went.' She held the child out to Alice and stared at her. 'Here, you take him for a bit. If you're not in too much of a state, that is.'

It was as well the chair happened to be there. Alice fell into it without looking behind her. She clutched the child tightly, taking comfort from him. Diverted by a new face, he stopped crying. She pulled the comb from her hair and gave it to him. He fingered his own wet cheeks and then touched hers down which weary tears had begun to trickle, laughing as if he had made a happy discovery.

'Is there anything to drink?' Her voice sounded harsh, more like that of a hard-bitten woman propping up a bar than her own.

'I don't know. It's not my house.'

'There ought to be some brandy in the sideboard.'

Round-eyed, Daphne slid back the doors and handed the bottle and a glass to Alice. She dumped Christopher on the floor. He began combing the long mohair strands of the hearthrug. Alice poured some brandy and drank it. The comfort it brought and the new warmth staggered her.

'I reckon you ought to phone Mr Fielding and get him to come and fetch you.'

'I will,' Alice lied.

Fortunately the telephone was in the hall. She shut the door on Daphne. It was nearly a year since she had dialled this number, but she knew it by heart. Taking a deep breath, she waited for him to answer.

Perhaps there had been something in what Jackie said. If she had done her hair like this years ago, taken trouble with her face, it might never have happened. Jackie's dressing-table afforded an array of things Alice had never thought of buying.

Busily she brushed her hair, but baulked at the thought of plaiting it. Instead she twisted it into a cone on the top of her head and with a strange excitement, stepped back to study the effect. She gasped, then in mimicry gave a tight little smile. So that was the explanation!

It was with a sense of indulging in a secret vice that she began to make up her face. The lips were a pale glossy pink now, the eyelids blue. As the final step in assuming another identity, she drew in dark arched brows over her own fair ones. The transformation was almost complete.

She couldn't go out into the road again draped in a travelling rug. Jackie's wardrobe was full of coats. Tiptoeing now, she slid one in black bouclé off a hanger and without looking back at the glass put it on.

The stage was set, the curtain about to go up. She opened her eyes and turned. Yes, it was just as she expected. Nesta Drage was walking forward to meet her.

She sat down heavily on the bed, euphoria displaced by shock. Had they all seen it, all of them but herself? Was that why Jackie had said, You ought to do your hair like Nesta's, because with a little juggling, a tiny change of make-up, she looked like Nesta? Her forehead was higher, her eyes larger than the florist's, but there was the same plumpness of figure, the same bud of a mouth. In spite of her illness, her face had filled out, heightening the resemblance.

Justin Whittaker had seen it. His affection for Nesta had been an uncle's, seeing in her the pretty womanly woman his own niece could never be. Andrew had seen it. He had married her because she reminded him of Nesta. Cold pain stabbed her and the face in the mirror responded with Nesta's look of melancholy.

Daphne's voice called her out of the nightmare.

'You all right, Mrs Fielding?'

She answered in a tone that was exclusively hers, cultivated and authoritative.

'I've borrowed one of Mrs Whittaker's coats. She won't mind.' Turning out the light, she stepped into the hall.

'Aren't you going to wait for Mr Fielding?'

'I expect I'll meet him on my way.'

'You do look nice. Quite with-it, if you know what I mean.' If Daphne had noticed the uncanny resemblance she said nothing about it. Her face was wistful, for whatever was going on she had played her small part in it and in a moment was to be excluded. 'Scared stiff you looked when you came in. Someone hanging about in the lane, was it? I thought to myself. She's seen some man and he's scared her. Was it a man, Mrs Fielding?'

'Yes, it was a man,' Alice said.

On the telephone to Harry she had explained nothing. It had seemed to her then under the pleasurably numbing influence of the brandy that once she was with him everything would ease and fall into place. He had always loved her and, seeing her husband with the eyes of an outsider, anticipating the inevitable, waited his own chance. He would take her away somewhere, and one day, when it was all over . . .

She walked along Station Road, under the bridge, past the works, no longer afraid. In a moment his car would appear, swing in to the kerb beside her. 'If anything is troubling you—anything, Alice—you'll come to me, won't you?' But he was her doctor as well as her friend; she couldn't compromise him. For the time being all she could expect was a sympathetic listener, a friend when all other friends had failed.

Things seldom happen just as and just when you expect them to. But at the point when her thoughts said, Now he will come, the car twisted out from the High Street and swung alongside her. It was a little like falling in love for the first time the way her heart leapt. This perfect achievement of timing did more than anything to dispel her doubts. How had she ever thought him clumsy or gauche?

She was in the car beside him before she looked at his face. Then, as at last she looked up at him, his gaunt tiredness brought her a quick twinge of physical displeasure, and she thought visually of Andrew's beauty. Andrew. . . . Would she ever see him again? At some distant future time, sitting like this perhaps with Harry, she might catch sight of him far away, a stranger in a crowd.

'I'm glad you phoned me,' Harry said quietly. 'I thought you might. We began a conversation, didn't we, in the church hall? Perhaps we ought to finish it now.' He suddenly seemed to realise that it was night, that it had been raining and that she had walked. 'What's Andrew thinking of to let you . . .?'

'I've left him,' she said flatly.

She knew he wouldn't be surprised. From the first he had expected it. He turned the car into the High Street without speaking. The orange lights on the slip road and the by-pass lit up the sky with a dull glare. It was as if some horizon town was on fire.

'Harry, I can't talk about it now. I thought I could right up until I met you, but it's too near, too recent. If you could just talk to me, be with me, till Hugo gets back . . . I don't want to be a nuisance, Harry. Perhaps it would be better if I went to an hotel. I just don't know any more.'

They passed The Boadicea. Hugo is in there, she thought, Hugo and my uncle. If she could not tell it to Harry, how could she ever tell it to them?

'I wish you could be with me,' Harry said under his breath. She began to cry. 'You'd feel better if you told me about it.' He gave her his arm and helped her out of the car across the pavement to the door with the brass plate beside it. In the waiting-room the chairs had been arranged against the wall and the magazines piled tidily. He didn't bother to switch on the light or lock the door behind him. 'You can lie down in here,' he said, 'and I'll give you something to calm you.'

Walking into the surgery in front of him, she saw her own reflection coming to meet her in the black rain-dashed window. At the sight of that gold and black blur she put her hand up to her eyes and sank into a chair. In silence he went to the medicine cupboard and handed her two tablets. The tumbler he gave her had about two inches of water in it. He had put on the light and the brightness hurt her eyes.

'Wouldn't you like to tell me about it now?' he asked gently.

She swallowed the tablets and took a deep breath. 'I wish I hadn't stopped you that day in the church hall,' she said. 'You were going to tell me, weren't you, Harry?' If only she had let him go on, not jumped up and run from him, she might have known it all before she had made those plans for herself and Andrew, plans that had been sweet and now seemed ludicrous. 'I could have borne it better, then.'

He was puzzled. 'I don't quite understand you, Alice.'

'Don't you remember? You said I mustn't connect Andrew with Nesta.'

'You haven't left him because of *that*?' He gave a little dry laugh. Surprised, she looked up at him.

'That—and other things.'

He sat beside her and a tremor of alarm crossed his features. 'Alice, I don't know what the other things were—

I'm not asking you—but I wasn't going to gossip to you about your husband.'

'What, then?'

Frowning, he said, 'I merely thought the time had come to tell you a few things about Nesta Drage. Oh God, I'd held out so long, but when you started to talk about her I—I braced myself for a confession, Alice.'

'Talk about her? Everybody knew I was nearly out of my mind with worry about her.'

There was no mistaking the shocked incredulity in his face. 'Why didn't you tell me?'

Like a jet of icy water the realisation hit her. He was right, she had never told him about it. Of all the people she might have consulted she had never consulted him, because she was afraid—with his swift warnings he had made her afraid—of discussing a patient with her doctor!

'But, Harry . . .' she stammered, 'Nesta hadn't been ill. Why should I ask you?'

Again the dry bitter laugh. 'Hadn't been ill! Did you think it was normal for a woman to get fat and lose her hair and be as depressed as she was?'

'No, but—Harry, I don't care about all that. I beg you to tell me where—where Andrew came into it all!'

She was calmer now. The tablets he had given her were taking quick effect. She bent towards him, gripping the table.

Suddenly he had the air of a man who, coming to the end of his world, may say anything, admit anything, because nothing matters any more. 'There were only two men in Nesta's life,' he said. 'Feast—and I don't think he was ever alone with her for more than five minutes at a time—and one other.'

'Andrew?' she whispered.

'Alice, I told you not to connect them. I meant it. Andrew,

Hugo, your uncle, they were just props for her ego. Believe me, you need props when you're a young pretty woman and suddenly, out of the blue, you get a loathsome disfiguring thing the matter with you. You need reassurance all the time—it's one of the signs. You want to be told all the time that you're still lovely and desirable.'

'What thing?' she cried. 'What thing? What was the matter with her?'

'You'll do anything to hide it,' he said slowly, 'but I think Feast sensed it. It might even explain the attraction, the drawing together of such physical opposites, one lacking what was such a burden to the other. I don't suppose you've ever heard the name. . . .'

A green picture, two children sent away out of earshot. . . . The difficult word Jackie had spoken came back to her and she faltered out the syllables.

'Myxoedema?'

'Clever of you.' He gave the ghost of a smile.

'But how do you know all this, about Feast, about Andrew and my uncle?'

'I made up my mind I'd tell you the lot once I'd started. You see, I was the other man.'

Mechanically her hand had gone to the telephone. She could only think, It's all right, I must phone Andrew. But he caught the fingers, stopping her. She was weak and his strength seemed suddenly great.

'Let me finish now. Don't desert me again, Alice. She reminded me a little of you, you see. There was an elusive something—like you in a distorting glass. I couldn't have you, but I had to live, didn't I?'

'I want Andrew, I must go to Andrew!'

Anger shook him. He grasped her wrists. 'Can't you

forget him for a single moment? Don't you owe it to me to give me one last half-hour of your time?'

'All right, but . . .'

'We used to go to a place she knew—a sordid dump in Paddington. I think I'm shocking you, Alice.' She shook her head wearily. 'It had to be like that, secret, sordid, underhand, because I was her doctor. Not very pretty, is it? Oh, I stopped needing her long ago, but she needed me. She used to say that if I left her she couldn't be responsible for what she might say. I knew she'd got myxoedema—how could I help knowing, a doctor and so—so close to her? I knew that if she wouldn't be treated for it eventually she'd become like an idiot, helpless, bloated, quite unable to look after herself. But she was so vain, and it didn't make any difference when I told her her vanity was just another symptom. She kept saying: "Leave me alone. I'll get all right in time. You're persecuting me because you want to get rid of me." '

To get rid of her. The words were like worms wriggling across Alice's brain. Suddenly she wanted to stop him, to get out into the clean cold air of the night outside.

'Please don't get up,' he said. She hated that near-hysterical tone in his voice and beads of sweat broke on her upper lip. 'Let me tell you everything.' He paused and went on in a rush: 'She said she couldn't work any more. She couldn't stand the pace. With what she got for the shop she was going to stay at this place in Paddington for a bit and think things out. I could go and—and see her there, she said. In a way it was a relief, but it was worse too. My God, I was frightened to death! Sooner or later, I knew, she'd have to get herself another doctor—she'd *have* to—and then, what would she tell him about me?'

'I don't want to hear! I don't want to know!'

'Sit down, Alice. Please!'

'I know what you're going to tell me, that you gave her a drug and she ate cheese and . . .'

'It wasn't like that,' he said in wonder. 'That wouldn't have harmed Nesta. It would only have raised her blood pressure and people with myxoedema have *low* blood pressure. Oh, Alice—poor Alice—is that what you've been thinking?'

'What was it, then?'

'I had a key to The Bridal Wreath,' he said. 'I was going to meet Nesta there the night before she went away. When she got back from saying good-bye to everyone I was going to make a final effort to get her to have treatment.' He hesitated. 'Look, Alice, I did try to get her to take thyroid. It's extract of thyroid, you know, that people like Nesta lack. I gave her tablets of thyroid and told her they were pep pills, but she wouldn't take them. By that time she wouldn't take anything I'd prescribed.'

The structure he was building up was growing to the proportions of a house in a nightmare, a house with many rooms through which you mounted until at last you came to the secret in the attic at the top. She wanted to get out of the house and run screaming down the stairs he was forcing her to climb.

'Harry, please . . .'

'I didn't get there till half past nine. I called to her but she didn't answer. Then I went upstairs and found her lying on the bed. All the bedding was packed and she was lying there on the bare mattress.' Again he paused as if afraid to go on. Alice made a little inarticulate sound. 'She was . . . she was unconscious. I didn't know what had happened, what she'd taken. . . . God, I wish I could make you understand what I felt at that moment. To be safe, to be free . . . One tiny push over the edge—not that even—just to do nothing and let her die. No one would ever know. Why let anyone see her, come to that? Acres of earth were all turned up outside. I looked at her lying there with that false hair coming adrift, and then I looked out of the window at a ready-made burial ground.'

A cry of sheer terror broke from her.

'What are you trying to tell me?' And her eye fell on the empty glass on the edge of his desk. 'No, no, Harry, no!'

She had come up all those stairs in the nightmare house with him behind her, prodding her on. The rooms had been laid open, one by one, and she had seen their contents, objects that grew uglier and more terrifying as each stage of the journey was passed. Now they had come to the summit of the top flight and there was just one door left.

Doors—the past weeks there had been doors everywhere, opening on hope, showing glimpses of black clothes and bright hair, and closing on despair. This was the last door and in a moment it would open too.

She backed away from him on the brink of a scream. He started towards her, murmuring something, very tall and bulky against the square window. Behind the door she could hear footsteps tapping, muffled at first, then coming nearer. It *mustn't* open. She had to get out, back to Andrew!

Was it the real door, or the one in her vision? There was a faint click as the latch began to move. It was an old door with a black finger-plate and a curly iron handle that crept slowly downwards like a snake, writhing and crawling across the wood.

Alice's stiff hands went up to cover her eyes. But they wouldn't close, instead growing wider, fixed and staring. The door opened an inch, stopped and moved again.

A little wind blew through the crack and with it came a cone of honey-coloured hair, a black pointed toe stepping over the threshold.

Her whole body had frozen into a taut knot of screwed-up muscles and nerves. Somewhere inside her was a scream that the back of her closed dry throat held imprisoned. Shock kept her fingers pressed against her forehead, but through them she could still see the bobbing blonde chignon and the black and white check suit. Between gloved fingers the initials on the vanity case gleamed out at her.

'Well, this is a surprise! Hallo, Alice. Long time no see.'

14

Bent double in the chair with her head touching her knees, she knew that she had never quite lost consciousness. The rim of the glass Harry was holding to her lips chattered against her teeth and water slopped down Jackie's coat.

There was deep silence in the room. She was aware of her own heart beating heavily. Then the silence was broken by the sound of Harry's lumbering tread as he crossed to the sink, the gush of water as he rinsed the glass, the nervous cough he gave.

The staring eyes were not Harry's. She lifted her own and met them. A Jersey cow, a china doll, a white slug of a woman—all those descriptions she was now remembering, but none fitted the girl who sat on the edge of the desk, looking back at her, swinging long slim legs. Nesta was beautiful. Her golden hair, framing her face in a cloud, blazed against the old walls, the green baize. Surely her skin had never had quite that translucency? She remembered it as strangely thick, always heavily *maquillée*. Nesta was no longer fat, but slender. Instead of being like a second skin the check suit fitted as a suit should.

Speechlessly they gazed at each other. Nesta's silence, her lips parted as if she longed to speak but could not, only heightened the impression that this was just a vision. It was Harry who brought reality in to shatter the long dream.

When he saw that Alice was recovering he went up to Nesta and said in a low angry whisper:

'It was inexcusable, creeping up on us like that. What are you doing, anyway? You're not due out till next week.'

Nesta blinked. Once she started to speak the words came tumbling out. 'I was as right as rain. They got fed-up with me so they gave me the push. I thought it was the least I could do to come and see my devoted physician.' Alice could hardly believe it. This was Nesta; every word, every phrase, was hers. But this was Nesta as she had been when she had first come to Salstead. She heard her foolish giggle, watched the fingers in their long black gloves tap the desk. 'I popped into Feasts' first, though, and dolled myself up. I wasn't going to be seen a minute longer than poss. in that ghastly red mac you bought me, Harry.' Turning again to Alice, she smiled conspiratorially, all girls together, and added: 'Red, I ask you!'

Without knowing why, unless it was from relief or as a prelude to forgiveness, Alice put out her hand and found Nesta's. The little hand squeezed hers. Nesta bent her head and sniffed the red rose in her buttonhole.

'I reckon I owe you an apology, Alice.' She looked so contrite that Alice shook her head vehemently. 'Oh, yes, I do. I've been awful to you and I've got a sort of feeling I've upset you a bit.'

'That,' said Harry, 'must be the understatement of the year.'

'But where have you been?' Alice found herself blushing. 'I thought you were dead,' she said.

'I very nearly was. Those last weeks in Salstead I was so ill I nearly went off my rocker.' She hesitated, then gave her hair a nervous pat. Glancing at Harry, she went on quickly: 'Something went wrong with . . . Oh, my metabolism or something. Nothing anyone could *see.* Mostly in the mind really.'

'Rubbish!' said Harry.

She gave him an indignant look. 'I was in quite a state that Friday. 'The too bright smile made her thin-drawn eyebrows go up. It didn't make me feel any better, I can tell you, seeing the Grahams all jolly and bouncing at The Boadicea, and then Hugo and Jackie with their kids. By the time I'd got to your uncle's I was at a pretty low ebb. Well, I went into the kitchen to say good-bye to Mrs Johnson....'

'And the silly old fool said she'd got just the thing for nerves and gave her a bottle with three Tofranil tablets in it,' Harry said. 'She *will* do it, hand out drugs I've prescribed for her to all and sundry.'

'She tried to give me some the other day,' said Alice, remembering.

'Nesta was a damned fool to take them.'

'When I'd been in to see Pernille,' said Nesta, 'I went into your bathroom and swallowed the lot with some water out of your tooth-mug.'

'Tofranil lower the blood pressure, the worst thing for someone with myxoedema.'

Nesta flinched at the word and Alice squeezed her hand.

'They have other side effects,' said Harry brutally, 'tremor, tachycardia, loss of appetite.'

'Well, I felt rotten when I got back and I thought I'd have a lay down. I must have passed out because I was nearly gone when Harry found me. I reckon I ought to be grateful to him and I am. They hadn't got a bed at Pollington so he whipped me off to hospital in Orphingham.'

'*Orphingham?* You mean you were there all the time?' It was unbelievable, yet truer than any of her conjectures. While she had gone to the police, to the post office, while she had pursued one shadow at the florist's and another down the pavement, the real Nesta had been lying a hundred yards away at the cottage hospital.

'Harry came down to see me two or three times a week. He didn't want anyone in Salstead to know about me and I went along with him in that. Then he told me I'd have to drop you a line. You were going to advertise for me in the paper, he said, and I'd have to let you know where I was. The nurses might see the advert or one of the patients. Well, I said, of course I'd write but—I don't know, Alice—I was a bit unbalanced and I thought it might upset you to see me so under the weather. . . .'

'That's nonsense and you know it,' said Harry testily. 'She was terrified to let you see her, Alice. They'd taken away that hair thing she wears and they wouldn't let her use make-up. They couldn't have the symptoms masked, could they? She didn't want you or Andrew to see the bloated flabby wreck she'd become because of her own vanity.'

'Don't,' said Alice. She got up and put a protecting arm around Nesta. 'Don't be so cruel!'

'I got used to the nurses,' Nesta whispered, 'but it was bad enough having them poke and prod me. All except one. I used to have a bit of a giggle with her.' She sighed and lifted her head. 'She was a nice girl. Harry wasn't very sympathetic, nag, nag, nag all the time through visiting. As soon as I got a bit better he brought me a load of stodgy novels to read and he said I ought to do some therapy, learn a useful job for when I got out. My nurse used to buy me all the women's weeklies.'

'The upshot of all this, Alice,' said Harry impatiently, 'is that I simply lent her my typewriter.' Nesta gave him a resentful glance. 'Flower selling had been a dead loss, anyway.'

'I feel ever so ashamed, Alice. I don't know how to explain. You see, I didn't want you to worry about me, but at the same time I didn't want you to see me. Well, here goes. That nurse I told you about—Nurse Currie—she said, wasn't it funny I didn't get any letters? Perhaps no one knew where I was. Why didn't I let her get me a redirection thing from the post office and have my stuff sent on to the hospital from Salstead? She said she didn't like to think of anyone not getting any letters. It reminded her of an old man who lived at a house called Sewerby in Chelmsford Road next door but one to her mum. He never got any letters, she said, and when he went into the post office for his pension he'd seen a notice that said *Someone, somewhere, wants a letter from you* and it had cut him to the heart. She laughed then and said it was a chance anyhow whether anyone in Chelmsford Road got their letters or not on account of the new postman being more or less half-witted.'

'Oh, Nesta!' Alice cried and she began to laugh weakly.

'You know me, Alice. I always was one for puzzles, crosswords, quizzes, something to occupy the mind.'

'Go on,' said Harry.

'All *right*. Only I want to tell it my way, d'you mind? I filled up the form, Alice, and put Sewerby as my last address.' Alice looked at her, but didn't interrupt. 'I thought I'd have the stuff sent on to the hospital—I did mean to, I swear I did—but then I thought, my God, Nurse Currie'll bring in my post and she'll see the Sewerby address, next door but one to her own mother, Alice, and then where'll I be? So I fixed on the Endymion. You see I knew they'd be safe there and I could pop up and fetch them when I got out. They were always saying, you'll be out in a week or two, Mrs Drage. How was I to know you'd keep writing and get all steamed up?'

'You did your best to stop me,' Alice said. 'Your letters weren't very encouraging.'

'That wasn't intentional, duckie. I never could get the hang of that machine. Just a few lines and that was about my limit. But, look, Alice, you're not to blame Harry. I never told him a thing.'

'I don't understand how you knew your plan was working, Nesta. I mean, the postman might have seen through it. I mightn't have sent off the ring . . .'

'That was where Harry came in. He hadn't seen you but he'd got wind of it by the old grapevine.'

Harry interrupted savagely, 'Let me tell her, will you? I met your sister-in-law, Alice. She said you'd been writing to Nesta. I didn't know the details and I didn't want to. I left it at that. You do see, don't you?'

Alice saw. He would have been too frightened, too apprehensive of the outcome to ask any questions.

'Nesta said she couldn't get on with the typing,' he went on, 'so I fetched the machine away. Andrew had told me he needed one and I took it in to him that day you came down to Orphingham. God knows I can't stand him—what's the use of pretending?—but I couldn't bear to think of him spending any more of your money. That car, that watch you gave him—I wasn't going to sit by and see him squander a hundred pounds on another expensive toy!'

She felt herself grow white with anger, but she set her teeth. When she spoke the rage vibrated through the mild words. 'You don't understand, Harry, you don't begin to understand . . .'

'I'm sorry. I shouldn't have said that. Never mind, skip it, forget it. Andrew told me you'd gone to Orphingham to look for Nesta. He said she was living there—living in a private house, I mean. God, I didn't know what was going on. I'd brought him back a book I'd borrowed—Nesta had been reading it—and I just dropped it on the table, muttered something about having to get down to the surgery and got out. Then, the next day I saw you at the bread and cheese lunch. You said you'd been looking for Nesta and you started asking Daphne Feast. I was going to tell you where Nesta was then, Alice, but there were all those people there—that damned woman wanted to talk to me about her diet . . . I said you were to come to me if anything was troubling you. It was a hint to come and see me by yourself, but you didn't come and . . .'

'And then I told him,' said Nesta, 'made a clean breast of the whole thing.' She giggled. 'They say open confession is good for the soul. My God, I thought he'd do me an injury, he was so mad. When I said all the stuff was going to the Endymion he nearly had a fit.'

'I went up and got the letters,' Harry muttered. 'I couldn't tell you about it after that, Alice. You'd have told Andrew and he'd have had me up before the Medical Council. I could just see it. Mr Drage, otherwise Dr Blunden, spending weekends with a patient in an hotel, and what an hotel!'

Nesta looked demurely down at her black gloves. 'Poor Harry would have been struck off,' she said. 'Can you picture him, Alice, all down at heel, peddling patent medicines from door to door? That's what happens to doctors who go off the rails. I've seen it on TV.'

'Oh, shut up!' said Harry. He turned to Alice. 'Once I'd got the letters, Alice, I thought it would all blow over. But when you started connecting Andrew with Nesta I knew I'd have to set things straight.'

'You don't have to go on,' said Alice. 'I can see it all, but for one thing. If you meant to give your address as Sewerby, Nesta, why didn't you?'

'I did. Of course I did.'

Her bewilderment was momentary. 'Did you enjoy *Phineas Finn*, Nesta?' she asked dryly.

'Did I what?'

'A Victorian novel with a blue and brown cover.'

'You mean Andrew's book? There are limits, Alice. I reckon Harry must have thought he was improving my mind. I flipped through it and had a look at the pictures and, believe me, that was enough.'

'Enough to make you have a mental aberration and write Saulsby when you meant Sewerby.' Recalling the young detective's words, she said softly, 'It's an easy mistake to make.'

Nesta put her hand up to her mouth. At last she said, 'No wonder I couldn't ever get those crosswords to come out.'

'I'll take you home, Alice,' said Harry wearily. He felt in his pocket and held out his hand to Nesta. Something in his palm winked and glittered as diamond chips caught the light. 'By the way, I've had this for a week. I forgot to give it to you.'

Slowly Nesta drew the black glove off her left hand. Then she waved her third finger showily.

'Somehow I don't think I'm going to need it.' The black diamond was large, square-cut and expensive-looking. 'My fiancé—oh, you don't know, do you?—he's quite a big man in his way. He broke his leg when his Jag ran into a lorry the first day the by-pass opened.' She laughed as they stared at her. Alice was remembering the ambulance she had heard that day at Feasts', and wondering strangely in the midst of that other greater wonder. That was the day she had first believed Nesta dead. Had the ambulance in fact been bringing her a new life? 'Of course he had a private room at Orphingham,' Nesta went on, 'but they've got a lovely lounge there—for first- and second-class passengers.' She giggled at her own joke. 'I've only known him a week. It's what they call a whirlwind romance. Don't look like that, Harry. I shan't tell him about you.' She drew on her glove and in a queer little gesture of hope, pressed both index fingers along the painted hairless lines of her brows. 'I've got something to lose now, too,' she said.

'I can't understand why I was so sure she was dead.'

'Perhaps you wished she was,' Harry said quietly.

'I wished Nesta was dead? But that's nonsense, that's horrible! I spent days and weeks looking for her. I was nearly out of my mind with worry. I spent pounds and pounds trying to find her.'

'Why did you try to make yourself look like her tonight?'

'I . . .' Why had she? She put her handkerchief up to her eyes and scrubbed at the blue on the lids.

He said impatiently: 'You're not really alike, you know. What you see in the mirror isn't the true image. It's lateral inversion. It's not what other people see, Alice. I believe you looked in the mirror and sometimes you saw her as if she were the other side of yourself.' She stared at him as he turned into Station Road and stopped the car. Then he turned to face her. 'You see, Nesta had succeeded where you had failed, Alice. You were a spinster at thirty-seven, rich but without a career. Nesta had married young, earned her own living, made herself attractive to men. It was only when she started to get ill that you really took her up.'

'I was *sorry* for her.'

'Perhaps you were. You weren't sorry for yourself any more because you were going to be married. Then Nesta moved away and disappeared. By then you'd changed places, but you didn't quite want to lose the other self that was lonely, just as you had been. Money would get her back just as money had got you everything.'

'No!' she cried, 'No, Harry, it isn't true.'

'Why not be detached about it? We all act this way. You began to find things out about her, the way she had attracted Andrew. Perhaps she'd been attractive to other people as well.' Alice put her hands up to her face. 'You were going to kill that other image with all the things it implied, particularly Andrew's infidelity.' With swift intuition, he added: 'Bury it deep in the coffins and make way for a new road. Maybe you had killed her. Where else did you get that mad idea about the cheese? Or if you hadn't Andrew had. Andrew had killed the young, the pretty, the desirable.'

'How you must hate me, Harry,' she said.

'Hatred, as Nesta might say, is akin to love.'

'Not your kind of hatred. Whatever Nesta was going to tell me about you it was enough to make you go to any lengths.' She sobbed and wrenched at the car door. 'Look, I can forgive you if you were only trying to make me ill, but... Why did you poison me? Why?'

She was breathing deeply, sobbing as she caught each breath. What he would do she hardly knew, but the orgy of fear she had experienced at Vair and afterwards at the surgery—a fear that had been none the less real because she now knew it was unnecessary—had left her indifferent to further terror.

As she was about to step out, he touched her arm. The question he asked her was totally unexpected, inconsequential, under the circumstances an insult.

'What d'you think? You talk to me about worry. How do you think it's been for me, ill, terrified to eat, suspecting everyone I loved of trying to kill me?'

'You aren't ill,' he said, 'and nobody's been trying to poison you. You're going to have a child.'

She said nothing, but she got out of the car. The air was cold and fresh. She leant against one of the wings and began to cry.

Presently he came out and stood beside her.

'I didn't know at first,' he said, 'but I guessed that day at the lunch when you got into such a state. When you fainted and I came up to Vair I wanted to examine you and make sure, but Andrew wouldn't let me.' He sighed heavily. 'I was glad in a way. You see, when you're in love with someone and she marries someone else the only way you can stop yourself going off your head is by self-deception. You can't face up to the facts and you tell yourself it's for companionship—what does the prayer book say?—the mutual society the one ought to have of the other. In your heart you know it isn't, it's a true marriage in every sense of the word, but you fool yourself, you get used to it and you achieve a kind of acquiescence.'

He looked at her as if he would have liked to take her hand. But she stood stunned, swaying a little, letting the wind play on her face.

'Then something else happens, what's happened to you. I couldn't fool myself any longer. I felt ten times worse than I did the day you told me you were engaged to him. It was as if the fact of the marriage had really been brought home to me at last. But I didn't want to have to tell you. The specialist could do that.' He gave a dry laugh. 'As if it needed a specialist! Any half-baked midwife could have seen it—the way you walked, the way your face had filled out and made you look ten years younger, that sickness. Why do you think you had all those fantastic ideas about Nesta? Didn't it ever occur to you—doesn't it now—that they were just the fancies of an imagination heightened by pregnancy?'

Still she was speechless. A thin rain had begun to fall, little more than a heavy mist. The cloying air was almost unbreathable. It dewed her face.

'Let someone else tell them, I thought. I knew I couldn't bear to see your happiness and his.' His voice broke and he cleared his throat. 'To see it,' he said, 'and to know it had nothing whatsoever to do with me.'

'I am happy,' she said.

She drew the black coat around her and pressed her hands to her waist. Happiness spiralled through her and seemed to burst into flower.

'Let's go,' he said.

'No.'

His eyelids fell and she looked into a face that was blank and blind.

'I'm going to telephone Andrew and get him to fetch me.'

'Andrew!' he said bitterly. 'Always Andrew. Funny, I always hoped, Alice. I thought it would only be a matter of time. He'd leave you and then—then you'd come to me.'

'Andrew will never leave me,' she said sternly.

She walked away from him quite fast, not looking back at all. The telephone box on the corner of the High Street and the slip road was empty. A gang of youth loitered outside The Boadicea and although her hair was coming down and she had bitten most of Jackie's lipstick from her mouth, one of them whistled. She slipped inside and closed the door, feeling her lips purse into that look of mock modesty and consciousness of beauty she had seen on the faces of other women but never felt on her own.

It was only when she lifted the receiver and touched the dial that she realised. She had no money. *She had no money.*

For years now she had bought her way into everything and out of everything; always about her person had been the shiny blue book and the wad of notes. But at this moment when she wanted to do something that even the poorest could afford she had no money, not even a few coppers.

It didn't matter. She could walk. Independence was like a tonic, invigorating and joyous, and it was coupled with a new dependence—on Andrew.

The lights of the car caught her in their beam as she stepped from the box. For a moment she thought it was Harry returning for her and pity fought with indignation. Dazzled, she blinked and moved into the light. This car was small, red, gay.

'Andrew,' she said as calmly as if they were meeting by a long-arranged appointment.

'Bell, darling!' He jumped out of the car and took her in his arms. The loiterers again broke into whistles. Andrew didn't seem to notice them. 'I've been looking for you everywhere. I thought you'd run away from me. I've even been into The Boadicea to see if you were with Justin. Where have you been?'

'Seeing ghosts,' she said. I'll tell you all about it, she had been about to add. The words died and she smiled instead. Tell him about it, tell him that she had suspected her own husband of murder, of adultery, of outrageous deception? No marriage, especially so young a one as theirs, could survive it. Dependence and trust, she thought, time and patience. Time would clear up all the mysteries that remained.

Suddenly exhausted, the last spark of energy used up, she got into the car. She moved her body carefully, treasuring it and longing for the first stir of life. But when they got home he would ask her again where she had been and she would have to tell him. The answer came to her. To whom does a woman go when she suspects pregnancy but to her own doctor? Leaving Andrew without a word, running down to the High Street in the rain, all that was compatible with her hopes and fears.

For the moment she didn't speak. He was looking at her tenderly. 'I've just seen someone we used to know.' Hesitating, he chose his words with care. 'She was outside the Feasts', getting into an enormous Jaguar with a dented wing.'

'I know.'

'You've seen her too? I didn't speak to her,' he said. 'I was looking for you.'

Epilogue

Alice tucked the baby up in his pram. He was already asleep, a placid olive-skinned child with his father's black hair. She wheeled the pram into the shade of the diminutive porch. Andrew liked to see him there when he came home from afternoon school.

Now she had a whole two hours before her in which to read the book. It had arrived from the publisher's by the late post and for the hundredth time she read the title: *Trollope and The House of Commons* by Andrew Fielding. Some people said that artistic creation was like giving birth to a child and theirs had been a simultaneous gestation.

Her eye caught the name Saulsby in the second chapter. She smiled, shamefacedly recalling a different reaction. She had kept her resolution never to tell him what she had suspected, but some questions had to be asked.

'Why didn't you recognise the name when I asked you? You remember, I'd come back from Orphingham and you'd got my tea ready.'

He had laughed at her then, holding her tightly in his arms to take away the sting of mockery. 'What does Saulsby sound like when you say it with your mouth full of marzipan cake?'

'I see. Oh, Andrew, you thought I said *Salisbury*.'

'There must be one in every English country town.'

Still smiling, she turned the page, marvelling that a seven-letter word, once the cause of so much anguish, was now just a tiny jigsaw piece in the general pattern of contentment.

THE SECRET HOUSE OF DEATH

For
Dagmar Blass

Then is it sin
To rush into the secret house of death
Ere death dare come to us?

Antony and Cleopatra

I

The man was heavily built and he drove a big car, a green Ford Zephyr. This was his third visit to the house called Braeside in Orchard Drive, Matchdown Park, and each time he parked his car on the grass patch in the pavement. He was in his early thirties, dark and not bad-looking. He carried a brief-case. He never stayed very long but Louise North who lived at Braeside with her husband Bob was always pleased to see him and admitted him with a smile.

These were facts and by now everyone who lived in the vicinity was aware of them. The Airedale who lived opposite and who belonged to some people called Winter obligingly kept them informed of the big man's visits. At day-long sentry-go behind his gate, the Airedale barked at strangers, kept silence for residents. He barked furiously now as the man strolled up Norths' path, knocked at the front door, and, thirty seconds later after a whispered word with Louise, disappeared inside. His duty done, the dog nosed out a brown earth-encrusted bone and began to gnaw it. One by one the women his outburst had alerted retreated from their windows and considered what they had seen.

The ground had been prepared, the seed sown. Now all that remained was for these enthusiastic gardeners to raise their crop of gossip and take it to market over the fences and over the tea-cups.

Of them all only Susan Townsend, who lived next door to Braeside, wanted to be left out of this exchange of merchandise. She sat typing each afternoon in her window and was no more proof than they were against raising her eyes when the dog barked. She wondered about the man's visits but, unlike her neighbours, she felt no lubricious curiosity. Her own husband had walked out on her just a year ago and the man's visits to Louise North touched chords of pain she hoped had begun to atrophy. Adultery, which excites and titillates the innocent, had brought her at twenty-six into a dismal abyss of loneliness. Let her neighbours speculate as to why the man came, what Louise wanted, what Bob thought, what would come of it all. From personal experience she knew the answers and all she wanted was to get on with her work, bring up her son and not get herself involved.

The man left forty minutes later and the Airedale barked again. He stopped abruptly as his owner approached and, standing on his hind legs—in which position he wriggled like a belly dancer—fawned on the two little boys she had fetched from school.

Susan Townsend went into her kitchen and put the kettle on. The side gate banged.

'Sorry we're so late, my dear,' said Doris Winter, stripping off her gloves and homing on the nearest radiator. 'But your Paul couldn't find his cap and we've been rooting through about fifty lockers.'

'Roger Gibbs had thrown it into the junior playground,' said Susan's son virtuously. 'Can I have a biscuit?'

'You may not. You'll spoil your tea.'

'Can Richard stay?'

It is impossible to refuse such a request when the putative guest's mother is at your elbow. 'Of course,' said Susan. 'Go and wash your hands.'

'I'm frozen,' Doris said. 'Winter by name and Winter by nature, that's me.' It was March and mild, but Doris was always cold, always huddled under layers of sweaters and cardigans and scarves. She divested herself gradually of her outer coverings, kicked off her shoes and pressed chilblained feet against the radiator. 'You don't know how I envy you your central heating. Which brings me to what I wanted to say. Did you see what I saw? Louise's boy-friend paying her yet another visit?'

'You don't know he's her boy-friend, Doris.'

'She says he's come to sell central heating. I asked her—

got the cheek of the devil, haven't I?—and that's what she said. But when I mentioned it to Bob you could see he didn't have the least idea what I meant. "We're not having central heating," he said. "I can't afford it." There now. What d'you think of that?'

'It's their business and they'll have to sort it out.'

'Oh, quite. I couldn't agree more. I'm sure I'm not interested in other people's sordid private lives. I do wonder what she sees in this man, though. It's not as if he was all that to write home about and Bob's a real dream. I've always thought him by far the most attractive man around here, all that cool fresh charm.'

'You make him sound like a deodorant,' said Susan, smiling in spite of herself. 'Shall we go in the other room?'

Reluctantly, Doris unpeeled herself from the radiator and, carrying shoes, shedding garments in her wake, followed Susan into the living-room. 'Still, I suppose good looks don't really count,' she went on persistently. 'Human nature's a funny thing. I know that from my nursing days . . .'

Sighing inwardly, Susan sat down. Once on to her nursing days and the multifarious facets of human idiosyncrasy to be observed in a hospital ward, Doris was liable to go on for hours. She listened with half an ear to the inevitable spate of anecdote.

'. . . And that was just one example. It's amazing the people who are married to absolutely marvellous-looking other people and who fall in love with absolute horrors. I suppose they just want a change.'

'I suppose they do,' Susan said evenly.

'But fancy trusting someone and having complete faith in them and then finding they've been deceiving you all along. Carrying on and making a fool of you. Oh, my dear, forgive me! What have I said? I didn't mean you, I was speaking generally, I was——'

'It doesn't matter,' Susan cut in. She was used to tactlessness and it wasn't the tactlessness she minded but the sudden belated awareness on the part of speakers that they had dropped bricks. They insisted on covering up, making excuses and embarking on long disquisitions aimed to show that Susan's was an exceptional case. Doris did this now, giggling nervously and rubbing her still cold hands.

'I mean, of course, Julian *did* carry on behind your back, meeting what's-her-name, Elizabeth, when he was supposed to be working. And you've got a trusting nature like poor Bob. But Julian never did it on his own doorstep, did he? He never brought Elizabeth here.' Doris added transparently, 'I know that for sure. I should have seen.'

'I'm sure you would,' said Susan.

The two little boys came downstairs, their arms full of miniature cars. Susan settled them at the table, hoping Doris would take the hint and go. Perhaps she was over-protective but Paul was, after all, the child of a broken marriage and on her rested the responsibility of seeing he didn't grow up with too jaundiced a view of matrimony. She glanced at Doris now and slightly shook her head.

'Just listen to my dog,' Doris said too brightly. 'It's a wonder the neighbours don't complain.' She trotted to the window, gathering up shed garments as she went, and shook her fist at the Airedale, a gesture which inflamed him to a frenzy. He stuck his big woolly head over the gate and began to howl. 'Be quiet, Pollux!' Susan often wondered why the Airedale had been named after one of the Gemini. Orchard Drive must be thankful the Winters had no Castor to keep him company. 'It's the new baker's roundsman that's set him off this time,' Doris said sagely. 'He never barks at us or you or the Gibbses or the Norths. Which just goes to show it's fear with him and not aggressiveness, whatever people may say.' She glared at her son and said, as if instead of placidly eating bread and butter, he had been urging her to stay, 'Well, I can't hang about here all night, you know. I've got Daddy's dinner to get.'

Susan sat down with the children and ate a sandwich. If you had no 'Daddy's dinner' to get, you certainly prepared none for yourself and tea was a must. Paul crammed a last chocolate biscuit into his mouth and began pushing a diminutive red fire engine across the cloth and over the plates.

'Not at the table, darling.'

Paul scowled at her and Richard, whose hands had been

itching to reach for a dumper truck, hid them under the table and gave him a virtuous glance. 'Please may I leave the table, Mrs Townsend?'

'I suppose so. Your hands aren't sticky, are they?'

But both little boys were on the floor by now, trundling their fleet of vehicles and making realistic if exaggerated engine sounds. They wriggled across the carpet on their stomachs, making for Susan's desk.

This was a Victorian mahogany affair full of niches and cubby-holes. Susan had sufficient empathy to understand its fascination for a five-year-old with a mania for Lilliputian vehicles and she tried to turn a blind eye when Paul used its shelves for garages, her writing paper boxes for ramps and her ribbon tins for turntables. She poured herself a second cup of tea and jumped, slopping it into her saucer, as the paper clip box fell to the floor and fasteners sprayed everywhere. While Richard, the ingratiating guest, scuttled to retrieve them, Paul stuck a jammy hand on Miss Willingale's manuscript and began to use it for a racing track.

'Now that's quite enough,' Susan said crisply. 'Outside both of you till bedtime.'

She washed the tea things and went upstairs. The children had crossed the road and were poking toys at Pollux through the curlicues of the wrought-iron gate. Susan opened the window.

'You're to stay on this side,' she called. 'All the cars will be along in a minute.'

The Airedale wagged his tail and made playful bites at a lorry bonnet Paul had thrust into his face. Susan, who hadn't been thinking about Julian nearly so much lately, suddenly remembered how he used to call Pollux an animated fun fur. This was the time Julian used to come home, the first of the commuting husbands to return. Pollux was still there and unchanged; as usual the children littered the front garden with their toys; the cherry trees were coming into bloom and the first lights of evening appearing in the houses. Only one thing had altered: Julian would never come again. He had always hated Matchdown Park, that detestable dormitory as he called it, and now he had a flat ten minutes from his office in New

Bridge Street. He would be walking home now to vent upon Elizabeth his brilliance, his scorn, his eternal fussing over food, his didactic opinions. Elizabeth would have the joy and the excitement—and the fever-pitch exasperation—until the day came when Julian found someone else. Stop it, Susan told herself sternly, stop it.

She began to brush her fair shiny hair—thinner and less glossy since the divorce. Sometimes she wondered why she bothered. There was no one to see her but a little boy and the chance of a friend dropping in was almost nil. Married couples wanted to see other married couples, not a divorcee who hadn't even the advantage of being the guilty and therefore interesting party.

She had hardly seen any of those smart childless friends since the divorce. Minta Philpot had phoned once and cooled when she heard Susan hadn't a man in tow, much less was planning on remarriage. What had become of Lucius and Mary, of lovely remote Dian and her husband Greg? Perhaps Julian saw them, but he was Julian Townsend, the editor of *Certainty,* eternally sought after, eternally a personage.

The children were safely occupied on the lawn by now and the first homing husband had arrived, Martin Gibbs with a bunch of flowers for Betty. That, at any rate, awoke no painful memories. Julian had never been what he called a 'hothouse hubby' and Susan had been lucky to get flowers on her birthday.

And here, exactly on time, was Bob North.

He was tall, dark and exceptionally good-looking. His clothes were unremarkable but he wore them with a grace that seemed unconscious and his masculinity just saved him from looking like a male model. The face was too classically perfect to suit modern cinematic requirements and yet it was not the face of a gigolo, not in the least Italianate. It was an English face, Celtic, clear-skinned and frank.

Susan had lived next door to him and his wife since they had moved to Braeside two years before. But Julian had despised his neighbours, calling them bourgeois, and of them all only Doris had been sufficiently pushing and thick-skinned to thrust her friendship on the Townsends. Susan knew Bob just well enough to justify the casual wave she now gave him from her window.

He waved back with the same degree of amiable indifference, took the ignition key from his car and strolled out on to the pavement. Here he stood for a few seconds gazing at the ruts the green Zephyr had made in the turf. His face had grown faintly troubled but when he turned and glanced upwards, Susan retreated, unwilling to meet his eyes. Herself the victim of a deceiver, she knew how quickly a fellow-feeling for Bob North could grow, but she didn't want to be involved in the Norths' problems. She went downstairs and called Paul in.

When he was in bed, she sat beside him and read the nightly instalment of Beatrix Potter. Strong-featured, flaxen-haired, he was his mother's son, as unlike Julian as could be.

'Now read it all again,' he said as she closed the book.

'You must be joking. It's ten to seven. *Ten to seven.*'

'I like that book, but I don't think a dog would ever go to tea with a cat or take it a bunch of flowers. It's stupid to give people flowers. They only die.' He threw himself about on the bed, laughing scornfully. Perhaps, Susan thought, as she tucked him up again, he wasn't so unlike Julian, after all.

'I tidied up all your papers,' he said, opening one eye. 'I can have my cars on your desk, if I tidy up, can't I?'

'I suppose so. I bet you didn't tidy up the garden.'

Immediately he simulated exhaustion, pulling the bedclothes over his head.

'One good turn deserves another,' Susan said and she went out into the garden to collect the scattered fleet of cars from lawn and flower-beds.

The street was deserted now and dusk was falling. The lamps, each a greenish translucent jewel, came on one by one and Winters' gate cast across the road a fantastic shadow like lace made by a giant's hand.

Susan was groping for toys in the damp grass when she heard a voice from behind the hedge. 'I think this is your son's property.' Feeling a little absurd—she had been on all-fours—she got up and took the two-inch long lorry from Bob North's hands.

'Thanks,' she said. 'It would never do to lose this.'

'What is it, anyway?'

'A kind of road sweeper. He had it in his stocking.'

'Good thing I spotted it.'

'Yes, indeed.' She moved away from the fence. This was the longest conversation she had ever had with Bob North and she felt it had been deliberately engineered, that he had come out on purpose to speak to her. Once again he was staring at the ruined turf. She felt for a truck under the lilac bush.

'Mrs Townsend—er, Susan?'

She sighed to herself. It wasn't that she minded his use of her christian name but that it implied an intimacy he might intend to grow between them. I'm as bad as Julian, she thought.

'Sorry,' she said. 'How rude of me.'

'Not at all. I just wondered . . .' He had dark blue eyes, a smoky marbled blue-like lapis, and now he turned them away to avoid hers. 'You do your typing at the window, don't you? Your writing or whatever it is?'

'I do typed copies of manuscripts, yes. But only for this one novelist.' Of course, he wasn't asking about this aspect of it at all. Anything to deflect him. 'I wouldn't consider . . .'

'I wanted to ask you,' he interrupted, 'if ever . . . Well, if today . . .' His voice tailed away. 'No, forget it.'

'I don't look out of the window much,' Susan lied. She was deeply embarrassed. For perhaps half a minute they confronted each other over the hedge, eyes downcast, not speaking. Susan fidgeted with the little car she was holding and then Bob North said suddenly:

'You're lucky to have your boy. If we, my wife and I . . .'

That doesn't work, Susan almost cried aloud. Children don't keep people together. Don't you read the newspapers? 'I must go in,' she stammered. 'Good night.' She gave him a quick awkward smile. 'Good night, Bob.'

'Good night, Susan.'

So Doris had been right, Susan thought distastefully. There was something and Bob was beginning to guess. He was on the threshold, just where she had been eighteen months ago when Julian, who had always kept strict office hours, started phoning with excuses at five about being late home.

'Elizabeth?' he had said when Susan took that indiscreet phone call. 'Oh, *that* Elizabeth. Just a girl who keeps nagging me to take her dreary cookery features.'

What did Louise say? 'Oh, *that* man. Just a fellow who keeps nagging me to buy central heating.'

Back to Miss Willingale. Paul hadn't exaggerated when he had said he had tidied her desk. It was as neat as a pin, all the paper stacked and the two ballpoint pens put on the left of the typewriter. He had even emptied her ashtray.

Carefully she put all the cars away in their boxes before sitting down. This was the twelfth manuscript she had prepared for Jane Willingale in eight years, each time transforming a huge unwieldy ugly duckling of blotted scribblings into a perfect swan, spotless, clear and neat. Swans they had been indeed. Of the twelve, four had been best sellers, the rest close runners-up. She had worked for Miss Willingale while still Julian's secretary, after her marriage and after Paul was born. There seemed no reason to leave her in the lurch just because she was now divorced. Besides, apart from the satisfaction of doing the job well, the novels afforded her a huge incredulous amusement. Or they had done until she had embarked on this current one and found herself in the same position as the protagonist. . . .

It was called *Foetid Flesh*, a ridiculous title for a start. If you spelt foetid with an O no one could pronounce it and if you left the O out no one would know what it meant. Adultery again, too. Infidelity had been the theme of *Blood Feud* and *Bright Hair about the Bone*, but in those days she hadn't felt the need to identify.

Tonight she was particularly sensitive and she found herself wincing as she reread the typed page. Three literal mistakes in twenty-five lines. . . . She lit a cigarette and wandered into the hall where she gazed at her own reflection in the long glass. Tactless Doris had hit the nail on the head when she said it didn't matter how good-looking a person's husband or wife was. It must be variety and excitement the Julians and the Louises of this world wanted.

She was thinner now but she still had a good figure and she knew she was pretty. Brown eyes and fair hair were an unusual combination and her hair was naturally fair, still the same shade it had been when she was Paul's age. Julian used to say she reminded him of the girl in some picture by Millais.

All that had made no difference. She had done her best to be a good wife but that had made no difference either. Probably Bob was a good husband, a handsome man with a pleasing personality any woman might be proud of. She turned away from the mirror, aware that she was beginning to bracket herself and her next-door neighbour. It made her uneasy and she tried to dismiss him from her mind.

2

Susan had just left Paul and Richard at the school gates when Bob North's car passed her. That was usual, a commonplace daily happening. This morning, however, instead of joining the High Street stream that queued to enter the North Circular, the car pulled into the kerb a dozen yards ahead of her and Bob, sticking his head out of the window, went through the unmistakable dumbshow of the driver offering someone a lift.

She went up to the car, feeling a slight trepidation at this sudden show of friendship. 'I was going shopping in Harrow,' she said, certain it would be out of his way. But he smiled easily.

'Fine,' he said. 'As it happens, I have to go into Harrow. I'm leaving the car for a big service. I'll have to go in by train tomorrow, so let's hope the weather cheers up.'

For once Susan was glad to embark upon this dreary and perennial topic. She got into the car beside him, remembering an editorial of Julian's in which he had remarked that the English, although partakers in the most variable and quixotic climate in the world, never become used to its vagaries, but comment upon them with shock and resentment as if all their lives had been spent in the predictable monsoon. And despite Julian's scornful admonitions, Susan now took up Bob's cue. Yesterday had been mild, today was damp with an icy wind. Spring was certainly going to be late in coming. He listened to it all, replying in kind, until she felt his embarrassment must be as great as her own. Was he already regretting having said a little too much the night before? Perhaps he had offered her the lift in recompense; perhaps he was anxious not to return to their old footing of casual indifference but attempting to create an easier neighbourly friendship. She must try to keep the conversation on this level. She mustn't mention Louise.

They entered the North Circular where the traffic was heavy and Susan racked her brains for something to say.

'I'm going to buy a present for Paul, one of those electrically operated motorways. It's his birthday on Thursday.'

'Thursday, is it?' he said, and she wondered why, taking his eyes briefly from the busy road, he gave her a quick indecipherable glance. Perhaps she had been as indiscreet in mentioning her son as in talking of Louise. Last night he had spoken of his sorrow at his childlessness. 'Thursday,' he said again, but not interrogatively this time. His hands tightened a little on the wheel and the bones showed white.

'He'll be six.'

She knew he was going to speak then, that the moment had come. His whole body seemed to grow tense beside her and she perceived in him that curious holding of the breath and almost superhuman effort to conquer inhibition that precedes the outpouring of confession or confidence.

The Harrow bus was moving towards its stop and she was on the point of telling him, of saying that she could easily get out here and bus the rest of the way, when he said with an abruptness that didn't fit his words, 'Have you been very lonely?'

That was unexpected, the last question she had been prepared for. 'I'm not sure what you mean,' she said hesitantly.

'I said, have you been lonely? I meant since your divorce.'

'Well, I . . .' Her cheeks burned and she looked down into her lap, at the black leather gloves that lay limply like empty useless hands. Her own hands clenched, but she relaxed them deliberately. 'I've got over it now,' she said shortly.

'But at the time, immediately afterwards,' he persisted.

The first night had been the worst. Not the first night she and Julian had slept apart but the night after the day when he had gone for good. She had stood at the window for hours, watching the people come and go. It had seemed to her then that no one but herself in the whole of her little world was alone. Everyone had an ally, a partner, a lover. Those married couples she could see had never seemed so affectionate, so bound together, before. Now she could remember quite distinctly how Bob and Louise had come home late from some dance or party, had laughed together in their front garden and gone into the house hand in hand.

She wasn't going to tell him any of that. 'Of course, I had a lot of adjusting to do,' she said, 'but lots of women get deserted by their husbands. I wasn't unique.'

Plainly he had no intention of wasting sympathy on her case. 'And husbands by their wives,' he said. Here we go, Susan thought. Surely it couldn't take more than ten minutes before they got into Harrow? 'We're in the same boat, Susan.'

'Are we?' She didn't raise her eyebrows; she gave him no cue.

'Louise is in love with someone else.' The words sounded cold, deliberate, matter-of-fact. But when Susan made no reply, he suddenly burst out raggedly, 'You're a discreet, cagey one, aren't you? Louise ought to thank you. Or maybe you're on her side. Yes, I suppose that's what it is. You've got a big anti-men thing because of what happened to you. It would be different, wouldn't it, if some girl came calling on me while Louise was out of the house?'

Susan said quietly, although her hands were shaking, 'It was kind of you to give me a lift. I didn't know I was expected to show my gratitude by telling you what your wife does while you're out.'

He caught his breath. 'Perhaps that's what I did expect.'

'I don't want to have any part in your private life, yours and Louise's. Now I'd like to get out, please.'

He reacted peculiarly to this. Susan had thought refusal impossible, but instead of slowing the car down, he swung with hardly any warning into the fast lane. A car immediately behind them braked and hooted. Bob cut into the roundabout, making the tyres screech, and moved on a skid into the straight stretch. His foot went down hard on the accelerator and Susan saw his mouth ease into the smile of triumph. Indignant as she was, for a moment she was also genuinely afraid. There was something wild and ungoverned in his face that some women might have found attractive, but to Susan he simply looked very young, a reckless child.

The needle on the speedometer climbed. There were men

who thought fast dangerous driving a sign of virility and this perhaps was what he wanted to demonstrate. His pride had been hurt and she mustn't hurt it further. So instead of protesting, she only said dryly, although her palms were wet, 'I should hardly have thought your car was in need of a service.'

He gave a low unhappy chuckle. 'You're a nice girl, Susan. Why didn't I have the sense to marry someone like you?' Then he put out the indicator, slowed and took the turn. 'Did I frighten you? I'm sorry.' He bit his lip. 'I'm so damned unhappy.' He sighed and put his left hand up to his forehead. The dark lock fell across it and once more Susan saw the bewildered boy. 'I suppose he's with her now, leaving his car outside for everyone to see. I can picture it all. That ghastly dog barks and they all go to their windows. Don't they? Don't they, Susan?'

'I suppose so.'

'For two pins I'd drop back to lunch one day and catch them.'

'That's the shop I want, Bob, so if you wouldn't mind . . .'

'And that's my garage.'

He got out and opened the door for her courteously. Julian had never bothered with small attentions of this kind. Julian's face had never shown what he was feeling. Bob was far better looking than Julian, franker, easier to know—and yet? It wasn't a kind face, she thought. There was sensitivity there, but of the most egocentric kind, the sensitivity that feels for itself, closes itself to the pains of others, demands, grasps, suffers only when its possessor is thwarted.

She stepped out of the car and stood on the pavement beside him in the cold wind. It whipped colour into the skin over his cheekbones so that suddenly he looked healthy and carefree. Two girls went past them and one of them looked back at Bob, appraisingly, calculatingly, in the way men look at pretty women. He too had caught the glance and it was something of a shock to Susan to watch him preen himself faintly and lean against the car with conscious elegance. She picked up her basket and said briskly, 'Thanks. I'll see you around.'

'We must do this more often,' he said with a shade of sarcasm.

The car was still at the pavement edge and he still sitting at the wheel when she came out of the toyshop. How hard the past year had made her! Once she would have felt deeply for anyone in his situation, her own situation of twelve months before. She couldn't escape the feeling he was acting a part, putting all the energy he could muster into presenting himself as an object of pity. He said he was unhappy, but he didn't look unhappy. He looked as if he wanted people to think he was. Where were the lines of strain, the silent miserable reserve? Their eyes met for a second and she could have sworn he made his mouth droop for her benefit. He raised his hand in a brief salute, started the engine and moved off along the concrete lane between the petrol pumps.

In another *Certainty* editorial, Julian Townsend had averred that almost the only green spaces remaining in north-west London were cemeteries. One of these, the overspill graveyard of some central borough, separated the back gardens of Orchard Drive from the North Circular Road. From a distance it still had a prettiness, an almost rural air, for the elms still raised their black skeletal arms against the sky and rooks still nested in them. But, taking the short cut home across the cemetery, you could only forget you were in a suburb, on the perimeter of a city, by the exercise of great imagination and by half closing your senses. Instead of scented grass and pine needles, you smelt the sourness of the chemical factory, and between the trees the traffic could always be seen as if on an eternal senseless conveyor belt, numberless cars, transporters carrying more cars, scarlet buses.

Susan got off one of these buses and took the cemetery path home. A funeral had taken place the day before and a dozen wreaths lay on the fresh mound, but a night of frost and half a day of bitter wind had curled and blackened their petals. It was still cold. The clouds were amorphous, dishcloth-coloured, with ragged edges where the wind tore them. A day, Susan thought, calculated to depress even the most cheerful. Struggling across the bleakest part of the expanse, she thought that to an observer she must appear as she held her coat collar up against her cheeks like Oliver Twist's mother on her last journey to the foundling hospital. Then she smiled derisively. At least she wasn't pregnant or poor or homeless.

Now as she came into the dip on the Matchdown Park side, she could see the backs of the Orchard Drive houses. Her own and the Norths' were precisely identical and this brought her a feeling of sadness and waste. It seemed too that their occupants' lives were destined to follow a similar pattern, distrust succeeding love, bitterness and rupture, distrust.

Two men were coming down the path from Louise's back door. They had cups of tea in their hands, the steam making faint plumes in the chill air, and Susan supposed they were labourers from the excavations on the road immediately below her. They had been digging up that bit of tarmac for weeks now, laying drains or cables—who knew what they ever did? —but it had never occurred to Susan to offer them tea. To her they had merely meant the nuisance of having clay brought in on Paul's shoes and the staccato screaming chatter of their pneumatic drills.

She let herself out of the cemetery gate and crossed the road. Inside the workmen's hut a red fire burned in a brazier made from a perforated bucket. As she approached the gate in her own fence the heat from this fire reached her, cheerful, heartening, a warm acrid breeze.

The men who had the tea cups moved up to the fire and squatted in front of it. Susan was about to say good morning to them when a third emerged from the trench that never seemed to grow deeper or shallower and gave a shrill wolf whistle. No woman ever really minds being whistled at. Does any woman ever respond? Susan fixed her face into the deadpan expression she reserved for such occasions and entered her own garden.

Out of the corner of her eye, she saw the whistling man march up Louise's path in quest of his tea. The fence was six feet high between the two back doors. Susan could see nothing, but she heard Louise laugh and the exchange of badinage that followed that laughter.

Susan went through the house and out of the front door to bring in the milk. Contrary to Bob's prediction, there was no green Zephyr on the grass patch, but wedged into the earth at the far side of the garden she caught sight of its counterpart in miniature. Inadvertently she had left one of Paul's cars out all night.

As she stooped to pick it up, shaking the earth from its wheels, Doris appeared from Betty Gibbs's house with Betty following her to prolong their conversation and their last good-byes as far as the gate.

'An endless stream of them,' Susan heard Betty say, 'always up and down the path. Why can't they make their own tea? They've got a fire. Oh, hallo.' Susan had been spotted. She moved towards them, wishing she felt less reluctant. 'Doris and I have been watching the way our neighbour runs her canteen.'

'No visit from lover-boy today,' said Doris. 'That's what it is.'

'Louise has been making tea for those men for weeks and weeks,' Susan protested, and as she did so she felt a violent self-disgust. Who decreed that she should always find herself in the role of Louise's defending counsel? The woman was nothing to her, less than nothing. How smug she must appear to these perfectly honest, ordinary neighbours! Smug and censorious and disapproving. There was earth on her hands and now she found herself brushing it off fastidiously as if it were a deeper defilement. 'Come,' she said and she managed an incredulous smile, 'you don't really think Louise is interested in any of those workmen?'

'I know *you* don't. You're too discreet to live.'

'I'm sorry, Doris. I don't mean to be a prig.' Susan took a deep breath. 'I just hope things will work out for the Norths, that's all, and that they won't be too unhappy.'

The other two women seemed for a moment taken aback. It was as if unhappiness as the outcome of the Norths' difficulties had never occurred to them. Excitement, perhaps, or huge scandal or further sensational food for speculation, but nothing as real as grief. Doris tossed her head and Susan waited for the sharp retort. Instead Doris said mildly and too loudly, 'I'll be in with Paul at the usual time.'

It was a sound characteristic of Louise North that had alerted her and caused the swift artificial change of subject. Behind them on the Braeside path came the sharp clatter of the metal-tipped high heels Louise always wore. Roped into this conspiracy of gossip, Susan didn't turn round. Her back was towards Louise but the other women faced her and it was both comic and distasteful to see the way they drew themselves up before Betty, the weaker of the two, managed a feeble smile and a twitch of the head.

Susan would have felt less weary of them and less sickened had they accorded the same treatment to Julian a year ago. But as soon as trouble between her husband and herself became evident these women had positively fawned on him. In Matchdown Park, surely the last bastion of Victorianism, the adulterer was still fascinating, the adulteress fallen. Deliberately she crossed back into her own garden and gave Louise a broad smile and a hearty untypical, 'Hallo, there!'

Her neighbour had come into the garden on the same mission as her own and in her hands she held two pint bottles of milk, their foil tops pecked to pieces by blue tits. 'Hallo,' said Louise in her little girl's voice that always had a whine in it.

'Bob gave me a lift into Harrow this morning.'

'Oh, yes?' Louise couldn't have sounded less interested, but just the same she approached the fence, picking her way across the soggy grass. Her heels sank in just as her lover's car tyres had sunk into the grass plot.

Louise always wore very high heels. Without them she would have been less than five feet tall, about the size of a girl of twelve, but like most tiny women she set herself perpetually on stilts and piled her hair into a stack on top of her head. Beneath it her little white face looked wizened and shrunken. Of course, it was particularly cold this morning and as usual Doris had begun to shout about the low temperature at the top of her voice, reiterating her urgent desire to get back to her fire as she made her slow way back across the road.

'Freezing! I've never known such weather. Goodness knows why we don't all pack up and go to Australia!'

'It isn't as cold as all that,' Louise whispered, and now she was leaning over the fence. It only reached to the average person's waist, but she rested her elbows on it and stared wistfully at Susan. 'There are worse things,' she said, 'than a bit of cold.'

'I must want my head tested, hanging about here,' Doris shouted, still on the pavement, still staring frankly at Louise. 'I'm a mass of chilblains as it is.'

'Well, I really am going in,' Susan said firmly and she closed the front door behind her. For a moment she had had the uneasy notion that Louise too wanted to confide in her, only it was impossible. She hardly knew the woman. The idea that an intimacy might be about to grow between her and the Norths really frightened her. Yesterday they had been the merest acquaintances, while now . . . It almost seemed that Julian had been right when he said you chose your friends but your neighbours were thrust upon you and the only protection was to hold yourself aloof. No doubt, she had been too forthcoming. It might even be that her reputation for discretion at which Doris had hinted had reached the North's ears, so that separately they had decided to make use of her as the repository of their secrets .

Susan shrugged, hardened her heart and settled herself at her desk. It was a bore, but there was nothing to be afraid of. And why did she suddenly feel this curious dichotomy, this desire both to be miles away and at the same time to go outside once more and look at Braeside, that strangely secret house where the windows were seldom opened and where no child ever played on the lawn? It was as if she wanted to reassure herself, to settle a doubt or allay a fear.

Presently she spread her hands across the keys and emptied her mind.

At half past three she went into the kitchen. A resolution had been forming subconsciously while she worked and now she brought it out into the open. In future she would have as little as possible to do with the Norths. No more accepting of lifts, no more garden talks. It might even be prudent to be on the alert for their comings and goings to avoid bumping into them.

The drills were screaming behind the back fence. Susan put the kettle on, watching the big elms sway in the wind with the pliability of grass blades. From here she could just see the workmen's fire glowing crimson in its punctured bucket and the workmen's faces, 'dark faces pale against that rosy flame' as they passed across the threshold of their hut. The sight of another's hearth which others share and enjoy always brings a sense of exclusion and of loneliness. The brazier, incandescent and vivid, its flames burning translucent blue against the red heart, brought to mind the improvised stoves of chestnut sellers and she remembered how she and Julian, on their way to a theatre, had sometimes stopped to buy and warm their hands.

The sky was blue now like arctic ice and the clouds which tumbled across it were pillowy glacial floes. Susan's kettle bumped, the drills shrilled and then, clearly and succinctly through the louder sounds, there came a gentle tap at the front door.

Pollux hadn't barked. It must be a neighbour or a familiar visitor to the street. Surely it was too early for Doris to be bringing Paul? Besides, Doris always came to the back door and Doris always shouted and banged.

The drills died away on a whine. Susan crossed the hall and the little tap was repeated. She opened the door and when she saw who her caller was she felt an actual dismal sinking of the heart.

What was the use of resolving to avoid people when those people intruded themselves upon you? Louise North wasn't wearing her little girl's size eight coat, but had wrapped it round her thin shoulders. She stepped inside, shivering, before Susan could hinder her and the little-hammer heels rattled on the wood-block floor. Louise was trembling, she was scarcely steady on her feet.

'Spare me five minutes, Susan? Five minutes to talk?' She lifted her eyes, bending her head back to look up into Susan's face. Those eyes, the pale insipid blue of glass beads, were watering from the cold. But she's only come from next door, Susan thought, unless she's crying. She *is* crying. 'You don't mind if I call you Susan, do you? You must call me Louise.'

You're at the end of your tether. Susan almost said it aloud. Two tears coursed down Louise's thin face. She brushed at them and scuttled towards the living-room. 'I know the way she muttered. 'It's just the same as my house.' Her heels left a twin trail of little pits, ineradicable permanent holes in the parquet.

Susan followed her helplessly. Louise's face was muddy with make-up applied over stale make-up and tear-stains. Now in the warm quiet living-room she dropped her head into her hands and tears trickled through her fingers on to the gooseflesh of her wrists.

3

Susan stood by the window and waited for Louise to stop crying. She was anxious not to prejudge her, but she felt impatient. Louise had no handkerchief. Now, in a feeble and embarrassed way, she was fumbling in the pockets of her coat and looking vaguely about her for the handbag she hadn't brought.

In the kitchen the kettle was bumping on the gas. Susan knew it was the sponge she had put inside it years and years ago to absorb the lime deposit the water made. The sponge had become petrified with time and the noise of this piece of rock lurching against the kettle lining made the only sound. Susan went into the kitchen, turned off the gas and fetched Louise a clean handkerchief.

'I'm ever so sorry,' Louise gulped. The tears had made her childish face pink and puffy. She put up a hand to her hair, retrieving wisps and poking them back into the piled lacquered structure that gave her an extra two inches. 'You must think me very uncontrolled, coming here and breaking down like this when we hardly know each other.' She bit her lip and went on miserably. 'But my friends are all Catholics, you see, and I don't like to talk to them about it. I mean, Father O'Hara and Eileen and people like that. I know what they'd say.'

Susan had forgotten Louise was a Catholic. Now she remembered seeing her go off to church sometimes with Eileen O'Donnell, black lace scarves in their hands to put over their heads at the mass. 'Of course, I can't get a divorce,' Louise said, 'but I thought—Oh, dear, I can't put it into words. I've taken up your time getting into a state and now I can't seem to say it.' She gave Susan a sidelong glance. 'I'm like you, you see, I'm rather reserved.'

Susan didn't altogether care for the comparison. Reserve

doesn't take itself into a neighbour's house and weep and borrow handkerchiefs. 'Well, suppose you sit there and calm down a bit while I make the tea?'

'You're awfully kind, Susan.'

The drills began their deafening clamour while Susan was cutting bread and butter. She began to think what she should say to Louise when she returned to the living-room, but she feared any advice she could give would differ hardly at all from that proffered by Eileen or the priest. As to what Louise was about to say to her, she had no difficulty at all in guessing. It would be a defiant recital of how love gave you the right to do as you chose; how it was better to spoil one life now than ruin two for ever; how you must take what you can get while you were still young. Julian had said it all already and had expressed it more articulately than Louise ever would. Should there be any hesitations or gaps in her narrative, Susan thought bitterly, she could always provide excuses from Julian's own logical and entirely heartless apologia. She went back with the teacloth and the plates. Louise was standing up now, watching the quivering elms and the cold rushing sky, her face stricken with woe.

'Feeling a bit better?' Susan asked, and she added rather repressively, 'Paul will be in in a moment.' She hoped her face made it plain to her visitor that she didn't want her son, the child of a broken marriage and already the witness of grown-up grief, to hear yet again an adult's marital problems and see an adult's tears.

But Louise, like her husband, had little interest or concern to spare for other people's anxieties. 'Oh, dear,' she said pathetically, 'and Doris Winter with him, I suppose. Susan, I've been screwing up my courage all afternoon to come to you. It took me hours and hours before I dared. But you were so nice and friendly to me in the garden and I . . . Look, Bob's going to be late tonight and I'll be all alone. Would you come in to me? Just for an hour?'

The side gate clicked and slammed. For a second the two women's eyes met and Susan thought how innocent Louise looked. As if she wouldn't hurt a fly. Why bother with flies when you can torture people?

'Hi, there!' Doris called from the back door. 'Late again. I'm dying for a cup of tea.'

'Will you stay and have one?'

Louise shook her head and picked up her coat from the chair. Her face was still blotched and tear-stained. She looked up when Doris came in and a small pathetic smile trembled on her lips.

'Oh, I didn't know you'd got company,' said Doris, 'or I wouldn't have come bursting in.' Her eyes were wide with excitement at the idea she might by chance have come upon adventure at the least likely time and in the least likely place. She drew her stiff red fingers out of the woollen gloves and, turning towards Susan, raised an interrogatory eyebrow. Susan didn't respond and it amused her to see Doris's greedy anticipation gradually give way to chagrin until, like a battery in need of recharging from some source of power, she attached herself to the radiator and said sulkily, 'All right for some. I've been frozen all day.'

Then Louise said it. Afterwards Susan often thought that if her neighbour had kept silent or merely made some harmless rejoinder, the whole ensuing tragedy would have taken a different course or perhaps have been altogether averted. In spite of her determination not to be involved, she would have accepted Louise's invitation for that night out of weakness and pity. She would have learned and understood and been in a position to defend.

But Louise, fumbling with her coat and hesitating whether to pocket Susan's handkerchief or leave it on the chair arm, turned those watery glass bead eyes on Doris and said, 'I'll have my central heating next winter. They're soon going to put it in.' A tiny spark of enthusiasm brought colour into her cheeks. 'I expect you've seen the man here.'

Doris's always active eyebrows jerked as if she had a tic and almost disappeared into her fringe.

'I'll just see you to the door,' Susan said coldly. Rage bit off the christian name she had meant to use and which would have softened the dismissal. That Louise should come here and cry about her love affair, then persist in employing the blind she had used to deceive everyone, filled her with choking anger. The dishonesty and the duplicity were past bearing.

Louise tripped as she crossed the hall and Susan didn't put out a hand to steady her. The metal heel left a pit and a long gash in the parquet Susan and her cleaner, Mrs Dring, kept so carefully polished. Illogically, this wanton damage was more maddening than Louise's slyness and her lack of control. At the front door she stopped and whispered:

'You'll come tonight?'

'I'm afraid I can't leave Paul.'

'Come tomorrow then, for coffee,' Louise pleaded. 'Come as soon as you've taken Paul to school.'

Susan sighed. It was on the tip of her tongue to say she would never come, that the Norths and their problems were nothing to her. Bob would be away for once, so like a child, Louise wanted Susan's shoulder to cry on. Didn't it occur to her that Susan was always alone, that Julian had gone away for good? It was all Julian's fault. If he had been here, he wouldn't have allowed her to be the Norths' mediator and counsellor, but then if he had been here none of this confiding would have begun. It was only because she had been deserted and divorced that the Norths thought her a suitable adviser. Her experiences qualified her; she might be supposed to understand the motives of wife and husband; her knowledge gave her the edge over the priest and the devout unworldly friends.

'Louise . . .' she said helplessly, opening the door and letting the chill damp air wash over her hot face.

'Please, Susan. I know it's ugly and beastly, but I can't help it. Please say you'll come.'

'I'll come at eleven,' Susan said. She could no longer resist that look of agonised supplication. Still exasperated but almost resigned, she followed Louise outside to call the boys in for their tea.

Louise's heels tap-tapped away into the side entrance. Her shoes had pointed toes, curled and wrinkled at the tips where her own toes were too short to reach. In her long floppy coat and those absurd over-large shoes, she reminded Susan of a little girl dressing up in her mother's clothes.

For a moment Susan let her gaze travel over the Braeside

façade. Of all the houses in the street it was the only one whose occupants had never troubled to improve its appearance. Susan was no admirer of rustic gnomes, of carriage lamps or birdbaths on Doric pediments, but she recognised a desire for individuality in the Gibbs's potted bay tree, a wistful need of beauty in the O'Donnells' window boxes.

Braeside was as stark now as it must have been when it was first built ten years before. Since that time it had never been painted and the perpetually closed windows looked as if they would never open. The house belonged to the Norths and yet it had an air of property rented on a short lease as if its owners regarded it as a place of temporary sojourn rather than a home.

No trees had been planted in the front garden. Almost every other house had a kanzan or cypresses or a prunus. The Braeside garden was just a big square of earth planted entirely with daffodils and with a few inches of turf bordering it. The daffodils looked as if they were grown by a market gardener to sell, they stood in such straight rows. But Louise never even cut them. Susan could remember how in springs gone by she had sometimes seen her neighbour walk carefully between the rows to touch the waxen green leaves or stoop to smell the fresh and faintly acrid scent of their blossoms.

They were as yet only in bud, each tightly folded yellow head as sealed as the house itself and, like it, seeming to hold secrets.

Susan called the children and hustled them in through the side gate. The Braeside windows looked black and opaque, effective shutters for a woman to hide behind and cry her eyes out.

Coping repressively with Doris's curiosity and trying to give Paul an adequate but necessarily untruthful answer to his question as to why Mrs North had been crying, left Susan exhausted and cross. She badly needed someone with whom she could discuss this crisis in the Norths' lives and she thought rather wistfully of how Doris must be now regaling John with its latest phase. A man would see the whole matter more straightforwardly—and less subtly—than she could; a man would advise how to avoid involvement with kindness and tact.

When the phone rang at seven-thirty she knew it must be Julian and for a moment she thought seriously of casting her troubles on his shoulders. If only Julian were more human, less the counterpart of an actor playing a brittle role in an eternal drawing-room comedy! And since his new marriage he had grown even more suave and witty and in a way unreal. Contemptuous he had always been, misanthropic and exclusive, besides having this odd conviction of his that dwellers in a suburb were quite alien to himself, sub-human creatures leading a vegetable or troglodyte existence. He was indifferent to their activities, although the doings of his own circle often aroused in him an almost feminine curiosity, and as soon as Susan heard his voice her hopes went. Consulting Julian would be only to invite a scathing rebuff.

'You said this was the most convenient time,' said the drawling pedantic voice, 'so, since I aim to please, I've dragged myself away in the middle of my prawn cocktail.'

'Hallo, Julian.'

His habit of plunging into the middle of things without greeting, preamble or announcing who he was, always irritated her. Of course an ex-wife might be expected to recognise her ex-husband's voice; that was fair enough. But Susan knew he did it to everyone, to the remotest acquaintance. In his own estimation he was unique, and it was unthinkable to him that even the deaf or the phone-shy could mistake him for anyone else.

'How are you?'

'I am well.' This strictly correct but unidiomatic reply was another Julianism. He was never 'fine' or even 'very well'. 'How are things in Matchdown Park?'

'Much the same,' said Susan, bracing herself for the sneer.

'I was afraid of that. Now, listen, my dear, I'm afraid Sunday's out as far as having Paul is concerned. Elizabeth's mamma wants us for the weekend and naturally I can't chicken out of that even if I want to, which I don't.'

'I suppose you could take him with you.'

'Lady Maskell isn't exactly mad about having tots around the place.'

It had always seemed odd to Susan that Julian, the editor of a left-wing review, should in the first place have married a baronet's daughter and secondly should set so much store by the landed gentry to which his in-laws belonged.

'This is the second time since Christmas you've put him off,' she said. 'It seems rather pointless the judge making an order for you to have him every fourth Sunday if you're always going to be too busy. He was looking forward to it.'

'Oh, you can take him out somewhere. Take him to the zoo.'

'It's his birthday the day after tomorrow. I thought I'd better remind you.'

'Flap not, my dear. Elizabeth's got it down on her shopping list to make sure we keep it in mind.'

'That's fine then, isn't it?' Susan's voice shook with annoyance. It had been an impossible day, thronged with impossible people. 'You'd better get back to your steak,' she said in the nagging tone he both provoked and hated, 'or whatever's next on the menu.' Elizabeth had got it on her shopping list! Susan could imagine that list: canned prawns, peppers, cocktail sticks, birthday present for 'tot', fillet steak, chocs for Mummy. . . . How maddening Julian was! Strange that whereas remembered words and phrases of his could sadden her and awaken pain, these weekly telephone conversations never did.

He was bound to send Paul something utterly ridiculous, an electric guitar or a skin-diving outfit, neither of which were outside the bounds of what Julian or Elizabeth would consider suitable for a middle-class suburban child on his sixth birthday. Susan went around the house bolting the doors for the night. Usually on this evening task she never bothered to glance up at the side of Braeside, but tonight she did and it disquieted her to see the place in darkness.

Could Louise already have gone to bed? It was scarcely eight o'clock. A simple curiosity, an inquisitiveness as indefensible as Doris's possessed her, drawing her into the front garden to stare frankly at the house next door. It was a blot of darkness amid its brightly lit neighbours. Perhaps Louise had gone out. Very likely she had gone out to meet her lover and was now sitting with him in some characterless North Circular Road pub or holding hands in a half-empty café. But Susan didn't think she had and it depressed her to imagine Louise lying sleepless in that house with her eyes open on the dark.

She listened, hardly knowing what she was listening for. She heard nothing and then, a little unnerved, she listened to the silence. Julian called Matchdown Park a dormitory and at night it was a dormitory indeed, its denizens enclosed like bees in their warm cells. And yet it was incredible that so many people should live and breathe around her, all in utter silence.

But if this was silence, it was nothing to the deep mute soundlessness of the back garden. Susan checked her back door lock, noticing that the wind had died. There was no movement in the black trees and, apart from the running river of traffic in the distance, no light but from the three red spots of the lamps the workmen had left on their pyramid of clay.

4

David Chadwick hadn't seen Bernard Heller for months and then, quite by chance, he bumped into him on a Tuesday evening in Berkeley Square. It was outside Stewart and Ardern's and Heller had his arms full of cardboard boxes. Some heating equipment, David thought, that he must going to dump at the offices in Hay Hill where *Equatair* had its headquarters.

Heller didn't look particularly pleased to see him, although he forced his features into an unsuccessful grin. David, on the other hand, was glad they had met. Last summer, on a generous impulse, he had lent Heller his slide projector and now he thought it was time he got it back.

'How are things?'

'Oh, so-so.' The boxes were stacked up under Heller's chin and perhaps it was this which gave to his face a set look.

'How about a drink if you're knocking off?'

'I've got some more stuff to unload.'

'I'll give you a hand,' David said firmly. He didn't want to lose him now.

'In the car, then.'

He still had the same green Zephyr Six, David noted as he lifted out the three remaining boxes from the boot which Heller had opened. The cardboard was torn on the top one and inside part of a gas burner could be seen.

'Thanks,' Heller said, and then, with an effort to be gracious, 'Thanks very much, David.'

Equatair's swing doors were still open. A couple of typists in white boots and fun furs passed them on the steps. Heller put his boxes on the floor of a small vestibule and David followed suit. Photographs of radiators and boilers and one of a lush living-room interior were pinned to the walls. It reminded David of his own designs for television film sets. That was how he had first met Heller, through work. *Equatair* made fireplaces too and David had borrowed one for the set of a series called, *Make Mine Crime*.

'How about that drink?'

'All right. I'm in no hurry to get home.' Heller didn't look at David when he said this and he mumbled something else with his head averted. It might have been, 'God knows, I'm not,' but David couldn't be sure of that.

He was a big heavy man, this heating engineer, with a round bullet head and hair that stuck up in short curly bristles. Usually he was almost irritatingly cheerful, inclined to slap people on the back while he told tedious jokes which, for all that, had about them an innocent slapstick quality. Tonight he had a hangdog look and David thought he had lost weight. His plump jowls sagged and they were greyish, perhaps not just because Heller, normally careful of his appearance, was in need of a shave.

'There's a nice little place in Berwick Street I sometimes go to,' David said. He hadn't got his car with him so they went in Heller's. For an engineer-cum-salesman, he was a lousy driver, David thought. Twice he was afraid they were going to go into the back of a taxi. It was his first experience of being driven by Heller as their encounters had usually been for a pre-lunch drink or a sandwich. Heller had been kindness itself over the fireplace and almost embarrassingly generous. It had been a job to stop him paying for all their drinks. Then, back in July, he had happened to say his twin brother had been staying with relatives in Switzerland—they were Swiss or half-Swiss or something—but couldn't show the slides he had taken because he hadn't a projector. For a long time David had wanted to show his gratitude, but it was difficult while Heller insisted on paying for everything. The loan of the projector had settled that question.

Paying off debts was one thing. He hadn't expected the man to hang on to it for eight months without a word.

'I wonder if I might have my projector back sometime?'

he said as they crossed Regent Street. 'The summer's coming and holidays . . .'

'Oh, sure,' Heller said without enthusiasm. 'I'll drop it off at the studios, shall I?'

'Please.' It wouldn't have hurt him to say thank you. Still, he evidently had something on his mind. 'That's the place, The Man in the Iron Mask. If you're quick you can nip in between that van and the Mercedes.'

Heller wasn't very quick. Twice he bungled the reversing manœuvre. The pub was tucked between an Indonesian restaurant and a strip club. Heller gave the pictures of nudes on leopard skin a sick look.

Over the entrance to The Man in the Iron Mask was a sign depicting this apocryphal character, his head encased in a cage. David went in first. Inside the place was cosy and overheated and with its black and white tiled floor and walls panelled in dark wood, suggested a Dutch interior. But the hunting prints could only be English and nowhere but in England would you see the facetious slogans and the pinned-up cartoons.

The area behind the bar was suffused with red light, making it look like the entrance to a furnace, and this same light stained the faces of the man and the girl who sat there. Her fingernails showed mauve when she moved her hands out of the red glow to caress her boy-friend's shoulders. The discerning would have recognised his grey tunic as the upper half of a Confederate uniform.

'What are you going to have?' David asked, anticipating the usual. 'No, let me.'

'Lime and lager,' Heller said only.

'Big stuff. What are we celebrating?'

'It's just that I have to drive.'

David went up to the bar. He was trying to remember where Heller lived. South London somewhere. If he was going to have to make conversation with this semi-conscious man, he would need something strong.

'Double scotch and a lime and lager, please,' he said to the barman.

'You mean lager and lime.'

'I don't suppose it would matter at that.'

Heller rubbed his big forehead as if it ached. 'D'you often come in here?'

'Off and on. It's quiet. You see some interesting characters.' And as he spoke, the Confederate kissed his girl on her oyster-coloured mouth. The door opened with an abrupt jerk and two bearded men came in.

They advanced to the bar and, because it was for an instant unattended, knocked sharply on the counter. The taller of the two, having given their order with a scowl, resumed an anecdote. The red glow turned his beard to ginger.

'So I said to this bank manager chappie, "It's all very well you moaning about my overdraft," I said. "Where would your lot be without overdrafts?" I said, "That's what I'd like to know. That's what keeps you banks going. You'd be out of a job, laddie," I said.'

'Quite,' said the other man.

Heller didn't even smile. His florid skin was puckered about his eyes and the corners of his mouth turned down.

'How's work?' David asked desperately.

'Just the same.'

'Still operating in the Wembley–Matchdown Park area?'

Heller nodded and mumbled into his glass, 'Not for long.'

David raised an eyebrow.

'I'm going abroad. Switzerland.'

'Then we are celebrating. I seem to remember your once saying that's what you wanted. Haven't *Equatair* got a footing out there?'

'Zürich.'

'When do you go?'

'May.'

The man's manner was only just short of rude. If he went on like that it was a wonder he ever sold anyone a thermostat replacement, let alone a whole central heating system. It struck David suddenly that May was only two months off. If he ever wanted to see his projector again he had better look sharp about it.

'You're fluent in German, aren't you? Bi-lingual?'

'I went to school in Switzerland.'

'You must be excited.' It was a stupid thing to say, like asking a shivering man if he was hot.

'Oh, I don't know,' Heller said. 'Might have been once.' He finished his drink and a spark of something fierce flashed momentarily in his dark eyes. 'People change, you get older.' He got up. 'There doesn't seem much point in anything, does there?' Without offering to buy David a drink, he said. 'Can I drop you anywhere? Northern Line for you, isn't it?'

David lived alone in a bachelor flat. He wasn't going anywhere that night and he intended to eat out. 'Look, I don't want to be a bore about this,' he said awkwardly, 'but if you're going straight home, would you mind if I came along with you and collected my projector?'

'Now, d'you mean?'

'Well, yes. You're going in May and I dare say you've got a lot on your mind.'

'All right,' Heller said ungraciously. They got into the car and David's spirits improved slightly when the other man said, with a ghost of his old grin, 'Bear with me, old man. I'm not very good company these days. It was decent of you to lend us the projector. I didn't intend to hold on to it.'

'I know that,' David said, feeling much better.

They went over one of the bridges and down past the Elephant and Castle. Heller drove by a twisty route through back streets and although he seemed to know his way, he was careless about traffic lights and once he went over a pedestrian crossing with people on it.

Silence had fallen between them and Heller broke it only to say, 'Nearly there.' The street was full of buses going to places David knew only by name, Kennington, Brixton, Stockwell. On the left-hand side a great blank wall with small windows in it ran for about two hundred yards. It might have been a barracks or a prison. There wasn't a tree or a patch of grass in sight. At a big brightly lit Odeon Heller turned right and David saw that they were at a typical South London crossroads, dominated by a collonaded church in the Wren style, only Wren had been dead a hundred and fifty years when it was put up. Opposite it was a tube station. David didn't know which one. All he could see was London

Transport's Saturn-shaped sign, glowing blue and red. People streamed out over the crossing, their faces a sickly green in the mercury vapour light.

Some of them took a short cut home through a treeless park with a cricket pavilion and public lavatories. Heller drove jumpily on the inside lane of the stream. The street was neither truly shopping centre nor residential. Most of the big old houses were in the process of being pulled down. Shops there were, but all of the same kind, thrust shabbily together in a seemingly endless rhythmic order: off-licence, café, pet foods, betting shop, off-licence, café . . . If he were Heller he wouldn't have been able to wait for May. The prospect of Zürich would be like heaven. What kind of a slum did the man live in, anyway?

Not a slum at all. A fairly decent, perhaps ten-year-old block of flats. They were arranged in four storeys around a grass and concrete court. Hengist House. David looked around for Horsa and saw it fifty yards ahead. Some builder with Anglo-Saxon attitudes, he thought, amused.

Heller put the car into a bay marked with white lines.

'We're on the ground floor,' he said. 'Number three.'

The entrance hall looked a bit knocked about. Someone had written, 'Get back to Kingston' on a wall between two green doors. David didn't think they had meant Kingston, Surrey. Heller put his key into the lock of number three. They had arrived.

A narrow passage ran through the flat to an open bathroom door. Heller didn't call out and when his wife appeared he didn't kiss her.

Seeing her gave David a jolt. Heller was only in his early thirties but he was already touched by the heavy hand of middle-age. This girl looked very young. He hadn't been thinking about her so he had no preconceived idea as to how she would look. Nevertheless, he was startled by what he saw and as he met her eyes he knew she expected him to be startled and was pleased.

She wore blue jeans and one of those skinny sweaters that there is no point in wearing if you really are skinny. Her figure was the kind that is photographed large and temptingly in the non-quality Sundays. Long black hair that a brush touch would set sparking fell to her shoulders.

'I don't think you've met,' Heller mumbled, and that was all the introduction David got. Mrs Heller peeled herself from the wall and now her glance was indifferent. 'Make yourself at home. I won't be a minute finding the projector.' He looked at his wife. 'That slide projector,' he said. 'Where did you put it when Carl brought it back?'

'In the bedroom cupboard, I suppose.'

Heller showed him into the living-room, if pushing open a door and muttering could be called showing anyone anywhere. Then he went away. The room had three white walls and one red one with a stringed instrument hanging above an *Equatair* radiator. A little bit of haircord clung to the centre of the floor space. Mrs Heller came in and rather ostentatiously placed cutlery for two persons on the table. It amused David to reflect on the domestic surroundings of real salesmen-executives. In the films and plays he did sets for they had open-plan apartments, forty feet long, split-level with wall-to-wall carpeting, room dividers festooned with ivy, leather furniture. He sat down in an armchair that was a woven plastic cone in a metal frame. Outside the buses moved in a white and yellow glare.

'Sorry to come bursting in on you like this,' he said. She put two glasses of water on the table. In his films they had bottles of Romani Conti served in straw baskets. 'I happened to run into Bernard and I remembered my projector.'

She swivelled, tilting her chin. 'Ran into him, did you?' Her voice had the remnants of a burr he couldn't place. 'D'you mind telling me where?'

'In Berkeley Square,' he said, surprised.

'Sure it wasn't Matchdown Park?'

'Quite sure.' What was all this? The man was legitimately employed in Matchdown Park, wasn't he? He watched her as she finished laying the table. An orchidaceous face, he thought. Horrible word, but it just described that lush velvety skin, the little nose and the full pink pearl lips. Her eyes were green with gold sparks. 'I hear you're going to Switzerland. Looking forward to it?'

She shrugged. 'Nothing's settled yet.'

'But surely Bernard said . . .'

'You don't want to listen to everything he says.'

David followed her into the kitchen because he couldn't hang about there any longer with the glasses of water and the mandoline or whatever it was. The blue jeans were provocative as she bent to light her cigarette from the gas. He wondered how old she was. Not more than twenty-four or twenty-five. In the next room he could hear Heller banging about, apparently shifting things from a high shelf.

A pan of water was heating on the cooker. Already cooked and lying dispiritedly on a plate were two small overdone chops. When the water in the pan boiled the girl took it from the gas and emptied into it the contents of a packet labelled, 'Countryman's Supper. Heavenly mashed potatoes in thirty seconds.' David wasn't sorry they weren't going to ask him to share it.

'Magdalene!'

Heller's voice sounded weary and fed-up. So that was her name, Magdalene. She looked up truculently as her husband lumbered in.

'I can't think where it's got to,' Heller said worriedly, glancing with embarrassment at his dusty hands.

'Leave it,' David said. 'I'm keeping you from your meal.'

'Maybe it's up there.' It was the girl who had spoken, indicating a closed cupboard on top of the dresser. David was a little surprised, for up till now, she had shown no interest in the recovery of his property and seemed indifferent as to whether he went or stayed.

Heller dragged out a stool from under the table and stuck it against the dresser on which was a pile of unironed linen. His wife watched him open the cupboard and fumble about inside.

'There was a phone call for you,' she said abruptly, her full mouth pouting. 'That North woman.' Heller mumbled something. 'I thought it was a bloody nerve, phoning here.' This time her husband made no reply. 'Damned cheek!' she said, as if trying to provoke from him a spark of anger.

'I hope you didn't forget your manners on the phone.'

David was rather shocked. Uncouth, graceless, Magdalene might be, jealous even. She had hardly deserved to be reproved with such paternal gruffness in front of a stranger. She was evidently drawing breath for an appropriate rejoinder, but David never found out what it would have been. Heller, whose arms and shoulders had been inside the cupboard, retreated and, as he emerged, something heavy and metallic fell out on to the linen.

It was a gun.

David knew next to nothing about firearms. A Biretta or a Mauser, they were all the same to him. He knew only that it was some sort of automatic. It lay there glistening, half on Heller's underpants and half on a pink pillow slip.

Neither of the Hellers said anything. To break the rather ghastly silence, David said facetiously, 'Your secret arsenal?'

Heller started gabbling very fast then. 'I know I shouldn't have it, it's illegal. As a matter of fact, I smuggled it in from the States. Went on a business trip. The Customs don't always look, you know. Magdalene had got scared, being here alone. You get some very funny people about out there, fights, brawls, that kind of thing. Only last week there was a bloke down in the alley shouting at some woman to give him his money. A ponce, I dare say. Hitting her and shouting he was. In Greek,' he added, as if this made things worse.

'It's no business of mine,' David said.

'I just thought you might think it funny.'

Suddenly Magdalene stamped her foot. 'Hurry up, for God's sake. We're going to the pictures at seven-thirty and it's ten past now. And there's the washing-up to do first.'

'I'll do that.'

'Aren't you coming, then?'

'No, thanks.'

She turned off the oven, lifted the plates and carried them into the living-room. David thought she would return, but she didn't. The door closed and faintly from behind it he heard the sound of spy thriller music.

'Here it is at last,' Heller said. 'It was right at the back behind the hair dryer.'

'I've put you to a lot of trouble.'

Heller passed the projector down to him. 'That's one thing I won't have to worry about, anyway,' he said. He didn't close the cupboard doors and he left the gun where it lay.

Perhaps it was the presence of the gun, grim, ugly, vaguely threatening, in this grim and ugly household that made David say on an impulse, 'Look, Bernard, if there's anything I can do . . .'

Heller said stonily, 'Nobody can do anything. Not a magician, are you? Not God? You can't put the clock back.'

'You'll be better when you get to Zürich.'

'If I get there.'

The whole thing had shaken David considerably. Once out of the courtyard, he found himself a pub, bigger and brassier and colder than the Man in the Iron Mask. He had another whisky and then he walked up to the tube station, discovering when he was a few yards from it that it was called East Mulvihill. As he walked under the stone canopy of the station entrance he caught sight of Magdalene Heller on the other side of the street, walking briskly, almost running, towards the big cinema he and Heller had passed. She looked jerkily to right and left before she went in. He watched her unzip her heavy shoulder bag, buy a ticket and go alone up the stairs to the balcony.

The cause of Heller's misery was no longer in doubt. His marriage had gone wrong. One of these ill-assorted, very obviously incompatible people, had transgressed, and from what Magdalene had hinted of a telephone call, David gathered the transgressor was Heller. It looked as if he had found himself another woman. Had he dwindled to this taciturn shadow of the cheerful buffoon he once had been because it was not she but Magdalene he must take with him to Switzerland?

5

On the way to school they passed the postman and Paul said, 'I don't have to go to school tomorrow until after he's been, do I?'

'We'll see,' Susan said.

'Well, I shan't,' he said mutinously for Richard's benefit. Richard ran ahead, jumping into the air at intervals to grab at the cherry branches. 'He'll be early anyway,' Paul said in a more conciliatory tone, taking his mother's hand. 'Daddy's going to send me a watch. He promised.'

'A watch! Oh, Paul . . .' Of all the vulnerable and ultimately—when Paul fell over in the playground as he did two or three times a week—tear-provoking presents for a six-year-old! 'You'll have to keep it for best.'

They reached the school gates and the two little boys were absorbed by the throng. Susan looked at the children with different eyes this morning, seeing them as potential adults, makers of misery. A cold melancholy stole over her. Determinedly she braced herself, waved to Paul and turned back towards Orchard Drive.

It was ten to nine, the time she usually saw Bob North. His car regularly passed the school gates about now. Susan didn't want to see him. She remembered their last encounter with distaste. He wouldn't offer her a lift today as he would be able to see she intended to go straight home, but she was certain he would stop. Probably he had found out about Louise's visit to her and their appointment for this morning and he would be anxious to put his own story across before Louise could blacken his character. People in Louise's situation always blamed their marriage partners. Julian had spent a long time pointing out her deficiencies as a wife, her nagging, her dislike of his more *avant-garde* friends, her old-fashioned morality, before embarking on the tale of his own infidelity.

She felt very exposed as she walked back under the cherry trees, nervously aware that any time now Bob's car would nose or back out of the Braeside drive. She thought wildly of bending down to retie her shoelace or, if this ploy failed, diving into the house of someone she slightly knew. The trouble was she hardly knew anyone well enough for that.

It was a still day, not quite foggy, but uniformly grey. Rain threatened in the clammy air. Susan quickened her pace as she approached Braeside and then she remembered. Bob's car was in for a service. He would go to work by train today, so therefore he had probably left much earlier, had certainly left by now. Her spirits lifted absurdly. Really, it was stupid to work herself up to such a nervous pitch because in a couple of hours time one of her neighbours was going to confide something rather unorthodox to her. That was all it amounted to.

Braeside had a dull dead look. The upstairs curtains were all drawn as if the Norths were away. Perhaps Louise was lying late in bed. Unhappiness made you want to do that. Jane Willingale would have attributed it to a desire to get back to the womb but Susan thought it was only because you felt there was nothing to get up for.

As usual there was not a single open window, not even a fanlight lifted an inch or two. It must be cold and stuffy in there, the air stale with angrily exhaled breath and tears and quarrels.

Mrs Dring would arrive at any moment. Susan let herself into her own warm house and began to grease tins and beat mixture for Paul's party cakes. Her hall clock chimed nine and as the last stroke died away, the pneumatic drills began.

Breaking across this shrill sound, the Airedale's bark sounded hollow. He was used to Mrs Dring by now and wouldn't bark at her arrival. Not for the first time Susan wondered why this canine summons was impossible to resist. Hardly anyone really interesting ever came to Orchard Drive and yet Pollux never barked in vain. She was as vulnerable to the alert as any of the women, although, unlike them, a change of delivery man or a new meter reader left her indifferent. She didn't want to speculate as to why Fortnum's van had called at Gibbs's or a couple of nuns at O'Donnells'. Sometimes she thought she rushed to the window when Pollux barked because, against all experience to the contrary, she always hoped the roar announced a newcomer into her own life, someone who would change it, who would bring hope and joy.

How pathetic and childish, she thought as, in spite of herself, she ran into the living-room and drew aside the curtain. Winters' gate clanged between its concrete posts and Pollux, who had half-mounted it in his rage, dropped back on to the path with a thump.

Susan stared. On the grass patch in the pavement, its tyres buried in the ruts they had made on Monday, stood the green Ford Zephyr.

Once again Louise North was entertaining her lover.

'Good morning, dear. Did you think I wasn't coming?'

Mrs Dring always bellowed this question on a triumphant note if she was more than a minute late. A large raw-boned redhead of forty-five, she put immense value on herself and the work she did, confident that her employers, in the event of her non-appearance, must be reduced to a helpless and desperate panic like abandoned infants.

'I'll do downstairs, shall I?' she said, putting her head round the door. 'Make it nice for the boy's party.' Cleaning a room before a children's party seemed pointless to Susan, but it was useless arguing with Mrs Dring. 'Want me to come and give you a hand tomorrow? There's nothing anyone can tell me about running kids' parties. Famous for them I am.'

Mrs Dring didn't explain how she came to know so much about the organisation of children's parties. She had no children of her own. But she was always making statements of this kind in a dark tone, as if implying that all her acquaintances were aware of her omnipotent versatility and took repeated advantage of it. She had a good word for no one except her husband, a man whose competence in the most unlikely fields rivalled her own and who possessed in equal measure to his manual and administrative skills a superhuman intelligence quotient.

'There's nothing that man doesn't know,' she would say.

Now she advanced into the room and went straight up to the window where she stood tying up her hair, almost scarlet this morning, in a scarf.

'I've been meaning to ask you,' she said, her eye on the green car, 'what's going on next door?'

'Going on?'

'You know what I mean. I got it from my friend who helps Mrs Gibbs. Mind you, my friend's a proper little liar and I reckon anyone who'd believe a word Mrs Gibbs says must want her head tested.' Drawing breath, Mrs Dring proceeded at once to place herself in this lunatic category. 'She says Mrs North is carrying on with the central heating fellow.'

'Do you know him?' Susan couldn't stop herself asking.

'I've seen him about. My husband could tell you his name. You know what a wonderful memory he's got. We was thinking about central heating ourselves and I said, You want to talk to that fellow—Heffer or Heller or something—who's always about in a green car. But my husband put the pipes in himself in the end. There's nothing he can't do it he puts his mind to it.'

'Why shouldn't he be calling on Mrs North just for business?'

'Yes, funny business. Well, it stands to reason he's in the right job for that kind of thing if he fancies it. It's her I'm disgusted with.' Seeing Susan wasn't to be drawn, Mrs Dring dropped the curtain and pulled two kiss-curls, as fluorescent red as Day-glo paint, out on to her forehead. 'What d'you think of my hair? It's called flamingo, this shade. My husband did it last night. I always tell him he ought to have gone into the trade. He'd have been in the West End by now.'

Susan began typing desultorily. Mrs Dring was never silent for long and these mornings she was on edge, constantly distracted from work by futile remarks. Her cleaner, engaged in the first place 'to do the rough' had soon made it clear that she preferred polishing and cleaning silver to heavy work and her favourite tasks were those which kept her at a vantage point near one of the windows.

Now, having observed all there was to see in Orchard Drive, she had stationed herself at the french windows with the plate powder and a trayful of Susan's silver ornaments. It was half past nine. Although it had begun to rain, the drills had scarcely ceased in the past half-hour. Susan could hardly believe there was anything of interest to see from that window, but Mrs Dring kept craning her neck and pressing her face against the streaming glass until at last she said, 'They won't get no tea this morning.'

'Mmm?' Susan looked up from her typewriter.

'Them men. Look, he's going down the path now.' The summons couldn't be refused without rudeness. Susan joined her at the window. A tall workman in a duffel coat, its hood pulled up over his head, was making his way down Norths' garden from the back door towards the gate at the far end. 'I heard him banging on the back door. Wants his tea, I said to myself. Canteen's closed this morning, mate. Madam's got other things on her mind. Funny that dog of Winters didn't bark, though. Have they got it shut up for once?'

'No, it's out.'

It was raining steadily. The workman opened the gate. His companions were deep in their trench where one of them was still plying his drill. The solitary man warmed his hands at the bucket fire for a moment. Then he turned, his shoulders hunched, and strolled off along the road that skirted the cemetery.

Nodding her head grimly, Mrs Dring watched him disappear. 'Gone to fetch himself a cup from the cafe,' she said and added because Susan had retreated, 'Is the car still there?'

'Yes, it's still there.' The rain streamed down its closed windows and over the pale green bodywork. Someone else was looking at it, too, Eileen O'Donnell, who was putting up her umbrella after scuttling out of Louise's garden.

'Mrs O'Donnell's coming round to the back door, Mrs Dring,' Susan said. 'Just see what she wants, will you?'

She was sure she would be called to the conference that

was about to ensue, but after a short conversation at the back door, Mrs Dring came back alone.

'Mrs North asked her to bring some fish fingers in for lunch in case her husband comes home. She says she's banged and banged at the front door but she can't make no one hear. She says the upstairs curtains are all drawn but that's on account of Mrs North not wanting the sun to fade the carpets. I reckon some folks go about with their eyes shut, don't know they're born. Sun, I said, what sun? A kid of five could tell you why she's drawn them curtains.'

Susan took the package, noting with amusement that it was wrapped in last week's edition of *Certainty*. How pained Julian would be! Its use as insulating material for frozen food was only one step up the scale from wrapping it round fish and chips.

'What am I supposed to do with them?'

'Mrs O'Donnell said you was going in there for coffee. And could you take them in with you just in case that poor wretch she's doing dirt to comes home for his lunch?'

But Susan had begun to doubt whether she was expected to keep that appointment. By the time Mrs Dring had finished the living-room and moved into what used to be Julian's study it was half past ten and the car was still outside. It looked as if Louise had forgotten. Love was generally supposed to conquer all and, although this was perhaps not what the adage meant, it certainly in Susan's experience, banished from the lover's mind firm promises and prior engagements. Curious, though. Louise had been so insistent.

But between ten-thirty and eleven the time went slowly. There was no need to watch the window. The Airedale, now sheltering in Winters' porch, would warn her of the man's departure. Eleven struck and on the last stroke Susan's oppression lifted. The rain was filling Monday's ruts with yellow clayey water, making pools round the wheels of the green car. Its driver was still inside Braeside and Susan sighed with relief. She wouldn't have to go now. There was no need for tact or kindness or firm advice because, by her own actions, Louise had cancelled the consultation.

Mrs Dring wrapped herself in a cocoon of blue polythene and trotted off into the rain, pausing to glower at the car and the curtained windows. Susan tried to remember how many times and for how long each time the car had been there before. Surely not more than three times and the man had never stayed as long as this. Didn't he have a job to go to? How could he afford to spend so much time—an entire morning—with Louise?

She opened the refrigerator door to make sandwiches for her lunch. The fish finger packet lay slightly askew on the metal slats. Did Bob ever come home to lunch? Eileen O'Donnell had seemed to think he might and now, as Susan considered, she remembered how Bob himself had told her he might come home one lunchtime.

Well, let him come home. Let him find them together. A show-down might be the best way out of this mess for all of them. But Susan took the packet from the refrigerator and went round to the front of the house from where she could see Braeside.

There was no one sitting in the through-room or in the little room at the other side of the front door. They must be still in the bedroom behind those closed curtains. Susan glanced at her watch and saw that it was gone half past twelve. How would she have felt if she had walked into that hotel, or wherever they had met, and found Julian in bed with Elizabeth? It would almost have killed her. Julian had been far more discreet than Louise—he was far cleverer—but still the process of discovery had been dreadfully painful to his wife. If Bob North came now it would be a far worse pain than that which would meet him.

That decided her. It was all very well deciding to have as little as possible to do with the Norths. Circumstances altered cases and this was a hard case with circumstances as different from those of everyday life as Susan's present existence was from that of a year ago. She went back into the house and slipped her arms into the sleeves of her raincoat. Then she banged hard on Norths' front door, banged and rang the bell, but no one came. They must be asleep.

Reluctantly she went round to the side. What she was about

to do would save Louise, at least for a time, from ignominy and possibly from violence, but Louise wouldn't be grateful. What woman would ever again be able to bear the sight of a neighbour who had found her in what the lawyers called *flagrante delicto*?

Better not to think about it. Get in, wake them up and go. Susan cared very little what Louise thought of her. She was going to give the Norths a very wide berth in future.

The back door was unlocked. If Louise was going to carry on with this sort of thing, Susan thought, she had a lot to learn. Julian would have made her a good adviser. The kitchen was untidy and freezing cold. Louise had stacked the breakfast things in the washing-up bowl but not washed them. There was a faint smell of cold fat from a water-filled frying-pan.

On the kitchen table stood the briefcase Susan had once or twice seen Louise's lover carrying up the path, and over the back of a chair was his raincoat. Susan put her package down and moved into the hall, calling Louise's name softly.

There was no answer, no sound from upstairs at all. In the little cloakroom a tap dripped. She came to the foot of the stairs and stood by the wall niche in which a plaster Madonna smiled down at her Child. It was grotesque.

No fires had been lighted in the house this morning and the ashes of yesterday's lay grey in the living-room hearth. All the windows streamed with water so that it was impossible to see out of them. Such heavy rain as this enclosed people like hibernating creatures, curled up dry, yet surrounded by walls of water. So it must have been for Louise and her lover, kissing, whispering, planning, while outside the rain fell and blotted out time.

Susan went upstairs. The bathroom door was open and the bathmat, a purple affair with a yellow scroll design in its centre, lay crookedly on the tiles. It looked as if none of the routine morning cleaning had been done. All the bedroom doors but one were open. She stood outside the closed door and listened.

Her reluctance to burst in on them had grown with every step and now she felt a strong revulsion. They might be naked.

She put her hand to her forehead and felt a faint dew of sweat. It must be at least ten to one and Bob could be turning the corner of Orchard Drive at this moment.

She grasped the handle and opened the door gradually.

They were both on the bed, but the man appeared to be fully clothed. Only Louise's stockinged feet could be seen, for her lover lay spreadeagled across her, his arms and legs flung wide in the attitude of someone crucified on a St Andrew's Cross. His face was slightly turned as if he had fallen asleep with his lips pressed to Louise's cheek. They were both utterly still.

No one slept like that.

Susan came round the side of the bed between it and the dressing table and as she did so she stumbled over something hard and metallic that lay on the carpet. She looked down on it, breathing fast, and at first she thought it was a child's toy. But the Norths had no little boys to run up and down the stairs, shouting, Bang, bang, you're dead!

Momentarily she covered her face with her hands. Then she approached the bed and bent over the couple. One of Louise's shoulders was exposed. Susan touched it and the man's head lolled. Where his ear should have been was a neat round hole from which something sticky had run and dried. The movement revealed a mat of blood, liquid and caked, grumming their faces together and smothering the front of Louise's nightdress and housecoat.

Susan heard herself cry out. She put her hand up to her mouth and backed away, stumbling, while the floor eddied and rocked beneath her and the furniture swayed.

6

The police asked her to wait there until they came. Susan's voice had shaken so much on the telephone that she was astonished she had made herself understood. She was almost numb with shock and long after the kind voice had stopped talking and told her to do nothing and to touch nothing, she sat staring at the Madonna while the receiver hung from her hand.

A rushing splash of water at the front of the house announced the arrival of the car. Susan was surprised she could stand. She made her way to the front door, clinging to the furniture and groping like a blind person.

The Airedale hadn't barked, but in her present state this didn't warn her. Then, in a kind of horror, she watched the latch turn from the inserted key.

Bob had come home to lunch.

He had dived through the rain from the newly serviced car to the door and he had stepped inside, shaking the drops from his hair, before he realised who waited for him in the cold shadowy hall.

'Susan?' She couldn't speak. Her lips parted, she drew a long breath. He looked at her, then past her at the dead ashes in the grate, the briefcase on the kitchen table. 'Where's Louise?'

Her voice came in a cracked whisper. 'Bob, I . . . She's upstairs. I . . . I phoned the police.'

'Tell me what's happened?'

'She's dead. They're both dead.'

'You came to coffee,' he said stupidly and then he plunged for the stairs.

'You mustn't go up there!' Susan cried. She caught his shoulders and they were stiff, without a tremor, under her hands. He gripped her wrists as if to free himself and then the dog Pollux began to bark, dully at first, then furiously as the police car splashed through the puddles in the street. Bob dropped limply on to the stairs and sat with his head in his hands.

There were three policemen, a little brown-faced inspector called Ulph, a sergeant and a constable. They spent a long time upstairs and questioning Bob in the kitchen before they came to her. The sergeant passed the open living-room door with a sheaf of papers that looked like letters in his hand. Susan heard Bob say:

'I don't know who he is. I don't even know his name. Ask the neighbours. They'll tell you he was my wife's lover.' Susan shivered. She couldn't remember ever having felt so cold before. They were searching through the briefcase now. She could see them through the serving hatch and see Bob, sitting pale and stiff, by the table. 'No, I didn't know he was married,' Bob said. 'Why would I? Bernard Heller, did you say his name was? Of course I never ordered central heating.' His voice rose and cracked. 'Don't you understand? That was just a blind.'

'What about your own movements this morning, Mr North?'

'My car was in for a service. I left for work on foot. About half past eight. My wife was all right then. She was in her dressing-gown, making the bed, when I left. I'm a quantity surveyor and I went to Barnet to look at a building site. Then I collected my car from Harrow where it was being serviced and drove back here. I thought . . . I thought my wife was expecting me home for lunch.'

Susan turned her head away. The sergeant closed the door and the hatch. The coat Louise had worn the day before lay slung over the back of one of the chairs. There was something very casual about that coat as if it had been put down only for a moment and any minute now Louise would come in and envelop her childish body in its comforting warmth. The tears came into Susan's eyes and she gave a little sob.

Upstairs the police were tramping heavily about. Then

she heard someone descending the stairs and the small brown-faced inspector came in. He closed the door behind him and said gently to Susan, 'Try not to upset yourself, Mrs Townsend. I know this has been a great shock to you.'

'I'm quite all right, really. Only it's so cold in here.' He might think her eyes were watering from the cold, but she didn't think he would. He had compassionate eyes. Not the sort of policeman, she thought, who would be briskly hearty in the face of death or make jokes about it with his companions.

'Did you know Mrs North was on intimate terms with this man, Heller?' Inspector Ulph asked presently.

'I . . . Well, it was common knowledge,' Susan began. 'I know she was very unhappy about it. She was a Catholic and couldn't be divorced.' Her voice shook. 'She was terribly distressed when she came to see me yesterday.'

'Distressed to the point of taking her own life, or to agreeing to a suicide pact?'

'I don't know.' This sudden taking of responsibility frightened Susan. Her hands were icy cold and trembling. 'A Catholic wouldn't commit suicide, would she? But she was in a bad state. I remember thinking she was at the end of her tether.'

He asked her quietly about the events of the morning and Susan, trying to keep her voice steady, told him how she had seen Heller's car outside soon after nine; how she had waited and waited for Heller to leave; how Mrs O'Donnell had called and how, at last, she had come here to Braeside to alert Louise and Heller, believing them to be asleep.

'No one else came to this house during the morning?' Susan shook her head. 'Did you see anyone leave?'

'Only Mrs O'Donnell.'

'Well, that's all for now, Mrs Townsend. I'm afraid you'll have to be present at the inquest. Now, if I were you, I should telephone your husband and see if he can come home early. You shouldn't be alone.'

'I'm not married,' Susan said awkwardly. 'Well, that is, I'm divorced.'

Inspector Ulph made no reply to this, but he came with

Susan to the door, lightly supporting her with one hand under her elbow.

As she came out into the garden, she blinked and started back. The crowd on the pavement affected her as bright sunlight shocks someone coming out of a dark room. Wrapped in coats, Doris and Betty and Eileen stood outside Doris's gate with the old woman who lived alone next to Betty, the bride from Shangri-La, the elderly couple from the corner house. Everyone who didn't go out to work was gathered there and everyone, their tongues stilled, was silent.

Even Pollux had been stunned into silence by those unprecedented comings and goings. He lay exhausted at his mistress's feet, his head between his paws.

The rain had ceased, leaving the roadway a glistening mirror of pools and wet tarmac. Raindrops dripped steadily from the cherry buds on to umbrellas and coat collars. Doris looked colder and more miserable than Susan had ever seen her, but for once she said nothing about the cold. She stepped forward, putting her arms around Susan's shoulders, and Inspector Ulph said:

'Will one of you ladies kindly look after Mrs Townsend?'

Susan let Doris lead her past the green Zephyr, the police car and the black mortuary van and into her own house. All the time she expected to hear her neighbours' chatter break out behind her, but there was only silence, a silence broken only by the steady drip-drip of water from the trees.

'I'll stay with you, Susan,' Doris said. 'I'll stay all night. I won't leave you.' She didn't cite her nursing experience as qualification for this duty and she didn't clutch at the radiators. Her face was grey and huge-eyed. 'Oh, Susan, Susan . . . ! That man, did he kill her and himself?'

'I don't know. I think he must have.'

And the two women, friends only from propinquity and mutual practical need, clung together for a moment, their heads bowed on each other's shoulders.

It was curious, Susan thought, how tragedy seemed to bring out in everyone the best qualities, tact, kindness, sympathy. Afterwards the only really tactless action she could remember was the arrival of Roger Gibbs at Paul's party with the present of a toy revolver.

'I reckon some women are downright daft,' said Mrs Dring. 'Fancy, a gun! You'd think Mrs Gibbs'd have had more thought. And she's sent that boy of hers with a streaming cold. What'll I get them on playing? Musical Parcel? Squeak, Piggy, Squeak?'

Murder was the favourite party game among the under-tens in Orchard Drive. When no one suggested playing it, Susan knew they must have been forewarned by their mothers. Had those mothers told their sons what she had told Paul, that Mrs North had had an accident and been taken away? What do you tell someone who is old enough to wonder and be frightened but too young, far too young by years and years, to understand?

'I hope to God,' said Mrs Dring, 'young Paul won't have an accident with that watch his dad sent him.' She was unusually subdued this afternoon, softer-voiced and gentler, for all the dazzling aggressiveness of her red hair and the lilac suit she declared her husband had knitted. 'Has Mr Townsend been in touch yet?'

The watch had arrived by the first post and with it a card bearing a reproduction of Van Gogh's *Mills at Dordrecht*, a gloomy landscape that Julian had evidently preferred to the more suitable teddy-bear mouthing, 'Hallo, six-year-old'. He approved of culture being rammed home during the formative years. But there was no note inside for Susan and he hadn't phoned.

'He must have read about it,' said Doris indignantly, passing with a tray of sausage rolls.

Mrs Dring frowned at her. 'Perhaps he'll put something about it in his own paper.'

'It isn't that sort of paper,' said Susan.

It was only because she had wanted to keep Paul's interest from the tragedy next door that she had decided to go ahead with the party as planned. But now, as the little boys shouted and romped to the loud music from the record player, she wondered how much of this noise was reaching Bob. Since Louise and Heller had been found, he had only left Braeside for two visits to the police station. All the curtains, not just those upstairs, remained drawn. Gossip had reached the workmen on the cemetery road and today none of them had come up to the back door for their tea. Susan didn't care to think of Bob alone in there, living, moving, sleeping in the house where his wife had been shot. If he heard the children, would he take their merriment as the outward sign of her own indifference to his sorrow?

She hoped he wouldn't. She hoped he would understand and understand, too, that she hadn't yet called on him because she felt as yet he was better alone. That was why she hadn't been among the stream of tip-toeing housewives who knocked almost hourly at the Braeside door, some of them with flowers, some with covered baskets, as if he was ill instead of sick at heart.

Doris met Susan after the inquest was over and took her back for lunch in the over-heated room the Winters called their 'through-lounge'. An immense fire was burning. Susan saw that Doris's gentle, sympathetic mood had passed now. Her curiosity, her avidity for gossip, had returned, and, wondering if she was being just, Susan recognised in the huge fire, the carefully laid tray and the gloss of the room, a bait to keep her there for the afternoon, a festive preparation in return for which she must supply the hostess with every juicy tit-bit the inquest had afforded.

'Tell me about the gun,' Doris said, helping Susan plentifully to fruit salad.

'Apparently this man Heller smuggled it in from America. His twin brother was in court and he identified the gun and said Heller had tried to commit suicide in September. Not with the gun. The brother found him trying to gas himself.' Doris made eager encouraging noises. 'He shot poor Louise twice, both times through the heart, and then he shot himself. The pathologist thought it rather strange that he'd dropped the gun, but he'd known that happen before in cases like this. They asked me if I'd heard the shots, but I hadn't.'

'You can't hear a thing when those drills are going.'

'I suppose that's why I didn't. The verdict was murder

and suicide by Heller, by the way. Apparently he was always threatening suicide. His brother and his wife both said so.'

Doris helped herself to more salad, picking out pieces of pineapple. 'What was the wife like?'

'Rather beautiful, I thought. Only twenty-five.' Susan recalled how Carl Heller and Magdalene Heller had both tried to speak to Bob while they all waited for the inquest to begin and how Bob had turned from them, brushing off their overtures as if stung. She thought she would never forget how that big, heavy man had approached Bob and attempted to talk to him in his strongly accented English, and Bob's near-snarl, his bitter contempt for the woman whose dead husband had killed Louise. She wasn't going to tell Doris any of that, nothing of Bob's frenzied outburst in court when Magdalene Heller had accused him of driving his wife, through his own neglect, into another man's arms; nothing of the girl's stony, stunned horror that had broken at last into vituperative ravings at Bob.

'She knew about Louise,' Susan said. 'Heller had promised to give her up and try to patch up his marriage but he didn't keep his promise. He was miserable and suicidal about it. He'd been like that for months.'

'Had they ever met before, she and Bob?'

'Bob didn't even know Heller was married. No one knows how Louise and Heller met. Heller worked for a firm called *Equatair* and the managing director was in court. He said Heller was going as their representative to Zürich in May—apparently he'd always wanted to go back to Switzerland. He was born and brought up there—but he didn't show any interest when he was offered the post. I suppose he thought it would take him away from Louise. The managing director said *Equatair* got their custom by sending out business reply cards to people, but they hadn't sent one to Louise and everyone seemed to think Heller must have given her one just so that she could fill it in and arrange for him to call. That would make his visits look innocent, you see.'

Doris digested all this with satisfaction. She poked the fire until it crackled and blazed. Then she said, 'I wonder why they didn't just go away together?'

'I gathered from the letters that Heller wanted to but Louise wouldn't. It seemed as if Louise had never even told Bob about it, not in so many words.'

'Letters?' Doris said excitedly, discarding the rest of this fresh information. 'What letters?'

The police had found them in a drawer of Louise's dressing table, two love-letters from Heller to Louise which had been written in November and December of the previous year. Carl Heller had identified his brother's handwriting which, in any case, had been confirmed by an examination of Heller's work notes. When they were read in court Bob's face had grown grey and Heller's widow, covering her face with her hands, had buried her head in her brother-in-law's massive shoulder.

'They were just love-letters,' Susan said, sickened by this inquisition. 'They only read out bits.' Strange and horrible that they had picked out those bits which most cruelly maligned Bob. 'I can't remember what he'd written,' she lied.

Her expression must have shown her unwillingness to talk about it any more, for Doris, realising that she had gone as far as she dared, dropped the subject with a, 'It'll all be in the paper, I expect,' and suddenly became solicitous for Susan's welfare. 'I'm a beast, aren't I?' she said. 'Pestering you after all you've been through. You don't look at all well, as if you're sickening for something.'

'I'm all right.' In fact, Susan had begun to feel dizzy and rather sick. Probably it was only nerves and the hothouse temperature in this room. She would be better at home.

'Now I hope your place is really warm,' Doris twittered in the icy hall. 'I know it usually is. The great thing with shock and all this upheaval is to keep in an even temperature.' She hunched her shoulders and wrapped her arms around her chest. 'An even temperature, that's one thing my sister tutor always impressed on me.'

For Susan's neighbours the inquest had been a kind of demarcation. It was over and with it most of the excitement, the terror and the scandal. Those involved and those looking on had reached a point at which they must again take up the strings of their lives. Susan had found two dead bodies, but Susan couldn't expect to be the centre of attraction, of sympathy and of comfort for ever.

But for all that, it gave her a slight shock to realise that Doris wasn't going to accompany her home. Mrs Dring had stayed with her last night, but she had said nothing about coming back. Quietly and as cheerfully as she could, Susan said good-bye to Doris and thanked her for lunch. Then she crossed the road, keeping her eyes averted from Braeside.

Work is generally recommended as the remedy for most ills and Susan went straight to her typewriter and Miss Willingale's manuscript. Her hands trembled and, although she flexed them and held them against the radiator, she found herself unable to type at all. Would she ever again be able to work in this house? It was so dreadfully like Braeside. With all her heart she wished she had minded her own business on Wednesday, even though that meant the discovery would have been Bob's and not hers.

Her first impression of it, her first sight of its interior, had left on her mind an image of a house of death and now her own, its facsimile, seemed contaminated. For the first time she wondered why she had ever stayed on here after her divorce. Like Braeside, it was a house where happy people had lived together and where that happiness had died away into misery. Now nothing remained of that happiness and there was nothing to replace it while these walls reflected back the sorrow they had seen.

Susan heard Bob's car come in but she couldn't look up. Now that it was all over, she might have been able to comfort him. He had needed a counsellor for loneliness and here she was, alone. She knew she had neither the physical strength nor the will-power to go out and knock on his door. It was a cold ugly place, this corner of suburbia, where a young man and a young woman could live next door to each other in identical houses, two walls only between them, yet be so bound by reticence and by convention that they could not reach out to each other in common humanity.

Many times she had cursed the daily arrival of Doris at teatime, but when Paul came in alone she missed her bitterly.

A craving for company, stronger than she had felt for months, made her want to lie down and weep. A child of six, no matter how much beloved, is no company for a woman who feels as troubled and insecure as a child and Susan wondered if in her eyes he saw the same bewilderment, masked by a determined effort to make a brave show, as she saw in his.

'Roger Gibbs says Mrs North got shot by a man.' Paul said it quite casually, stretching his white face into a broad manly smile. 'And she was all over blood,' he said, 'and they had a trial like on the TV.'

Susan smiled back at him and her smile was as matter-of-fact, as bravely reassuring as his. In a light even voice she embarked on a bowdlerised explanation.

'He says this man wanted to marry her and he couldn't, so he shot her. Why did he? He couldn't marry her when she was dead. Daddy didn't shoot Elizabeth and he wanted to marry her.'

'It wasn't quite the same. You'll understand when you're older.'

'That's what you always say.' The smile had gone, and with a quick glance at her, Paul went over to his toy box. The gun Roger Gibbs had given him lay on top of the little cars in their coloured boxes. He picked it up, looked at it for a moment and then dropped it listlessly. 'Can I wear my watch?' he said.

'Yes, darling, I suppose so.'

'Can I wear it right up until I go to bed?'

Susan heard Bob's car reverse out into the road. This time she went to the window and watched him. For a long time she stood there, staring at the empty street and remembering how she had told him of her loneliness on the night Julian had gone.

7

The inquest report was given a four-column spread on an inside page of the *Evening Standard*. David Chadwick bought a copy from a West End newsvendor and, reading it as he went, strolled along through the evening rush to where he had parked his car some ten minutes' walk away. Wednesday's evening paper had carried photographs of Magdalene Heller, of Robert North and of the young woman, a neighbour, who had found the bodies, but tonight there was only a shot of Mrs Heller leaving the court arm-in-arm with a man. The caption said he was Bernard's twin brother and from what David could see of him—his face and the girl's were shielded by a magazine he was holding up—the resemblance between the brothers was striking.

It must be he for whom the slide projector had been borrowed. David had unwrapped it on Tuesday night, a little amused by the care Heller had taken of it, swaddling it in newspapers under its outer covering of bown paper. And then he hadn't been quite so amused, but moved and saddened. For one of the newspapers, some South London weekly, yellowed now and crumpled, contained a tiny paragraph reporting Heller's wedding to a Miss Magdalene Chant. David only noticed it because the paragraph was ringed in ink and because Heller had written, just outside the ring, the date 7.6.62.

He had kept that paper as a souvenir, David thought, as simple people will. He had kept it until his marriage went wrong, until he had met Mrs North and wedding souvenirs were only a reminder of an encumbrance. So he had taken it, perhaps from a pile of other significant newspapers, and used it for wrapping someone else's property.

In the light of this notion and when he read of Heller's death, David had looked again at the sheets covering his projector and found, as he had suspected, newsprint commemorating Heller's success in some suburban swimming event and his inclusion among the guests at a darts club annual dinner. To Heller, evidently, these tiny claims to distinction, these printed chronicles, had once afforded the same pride as the record of his Order of Merit in *The Times* might give to a greater man. They had meant much and then suddenly, because his life had somersaulted and lost its meaning, they had meant nothing at all.

David thought of all this as he walked along Oxford Street and he thought also how strange it was that he, an acquaintance merely, should have been with Heller on the eve of his death, should indeed have spent more time with him on that occasion than at any time during the two or three years since their first meeting. He wondered if he should have attended the inquest, but he could have told them nothing that was not already known. Now he asked himself, as men do under such circumstances, whether he had failed Heller in his last hours, if he could have shown more sympathy and, worst of all, if there was any word he could have spoken of hope or encouragement that might have deflected the man from his purpose.

Who could tell? Who could have suspected what Heller had in mind? Nevertheless, David felt guilty and a sense of failure and inadequacy overcame him. He often thought of himself as a hesitant and indecisive person. Some men, hearty and brash perhaps but still the salt of the earth, would have sensed the depths of Heller's misery and, undeterred by his initial refusal to unburden his soul, have stayed and pumped his grief out of him. Others, the more sensitive of the dogooders would have taken warning from that gun and linked its presence with Heller's confessed *weltschmerz*. He had done nothing, worse than nothing, for he had made his escape from that flat with obvious relief.

And on the next day Heller had shot himself. David felt bleakly depressed. He was driving, but he needed a drink, and all the breathalysers in the world could go to hell for all he cared. Folding the newspaper and cramming it into his pocket, he made for Soho and The Man in the Iron Mask.

It was early and the pub was nearly empty. David had never been there on a Friday before. He usually went home early on a Friday. Often he had a date and, anyway, to him the weekend started at five on Friday afternoon.

He didn't want to be alone yet and he looked around him to see if there was anyone here he knew well enough to sit with and talk to. But although all the faces were familiar, none was that of a friend. A man and a woman in their fifties were walking about, looking in silence at some new cartoons the licensee had pinned to the panelling; an elderly man who looked like an out-of-work character actor sipped pernod at the bar; the men with beards sat at a table near the pub door. As he passed, David heard one of them say, ' "But that's share-pushing," I said in my naive way. "Call it what you like," he said, but he had a very uneasy look on his face.'

'Quite,' said the other.

' "Some people will do anything for money," I said. "Money's not everything." '

'That's a matter of opinion, Charles . . .'

The couple who had been looking at the cartoons sat down and David saw that behind them, in the most dimly lit corner, was a girl alone. Her back was turned to him and she had only a blank wall to stare at. He ordered a light ale.

'Buying on a margin like that,' said the man called Charles. 'Apart from the ethics of the thing, I personally like to sleep quiet in my bed. Shall we go?'

'I'm ready when you are.'

They went and while David was waiting for his change, he looked curiously at the solitary girl. He could only see her back, made shapeless by the vinyl jacket she wore, a head of glossy black hair, long legs in velvet trousers twined round the legs of her chair. She sat quite still, gazing at the brown panelling with the raptness of someone watching an exciting television programme.

He was surprised to see a girl in there alone. It used to be the practice, a kind of unwritten law among West End licensees, not to serve women on their own. Probably still was. However, this girl didn't seem to have a drink.

There was something familiar about the set of her shoulders and he was wondering whether he ought to know her when the door opened to admit four or five young men. The sudden cool draught caused her to turn her head swiftly and nervously. Instantly, but almost incredulously, David recognised her.

'Good evening, Mrs Heller.'

The expression on her face was hard to analyse. Fear? Caution? Dismay? Her curious green eyes, speckled with gold and iridescent like a fly's wing cases, flickered, then steadied. David wondered what on earth she could be up to, by herself in a West End pub on the very day of her dead husband's inquest.

'Is this your local or something?' she asked in a discouraging voice.

'I come here sometimes. Can I get you a drink?'

'No.' The negative exploded from her so loudly that several people turned to look. 'I mean, no, thanks. Don't bother. I'm just going.'

David had considered whether he ought to write her the conventional letter of condolence, but because offering sympathy to a woman released by death from an obviously unhappy marriage seemed misplaced, he had thought better of it. Now, however, he felt it incumbent on him to say something, if only to show he was aware of Heller's death, and he embarked on a little stilted speech of regret. But after murmuring, 'Yes, yes,' impatiently and nodding her head, she interrupted him inconsequentially.

'I was meeting someone, but she hasn't come.'

She? David thought of all the possible meeting places for two women in London in the evening. An office where the other girl worked? One of the shops that stayed open late? A café? A tube station? Never, surely, a pub in Soho. Magdalene Heller got up and began buttoning her coat.

'Can I take you to your station? My car's not far away.'

'Don't bother. It's not necessary.'

David drank up his beer. 'It's no bother,' he said. 'I'm sorry your friend didn't come.'

Politeness wasn't her strong suit, but in everyone except the savage, convention forbids actually running from an acquaintance and slamming the door in his face. That, he thought, was what she would have liked to have done.

They approached the door and she fumbled in her bag with fingers he thought none too steady. The cigarette was eventually found. David got out his lighter and held the flame up to her face.

Behind her the door opened. It opened perhaps a foot and then stuck. Magdalene Heller inhaled, turning her head. David didn't know why he kept his finger pressed on the light, the flame still flaring. The man who had opened the door stood on the step, staring in.

Again Magdalene Heller faced him. Her lips parted and she said with an unexpected effusiveness, 'Thank you so much, David. I'm glad we ran into each other.'

David was so taken aback by this sudden *volte-face* that he too stared into her beautiful, suddenly flushed face. Her cigarette had gone out. He lit it again. The man backed abruptly the way he had come, leaving the door swinging.

They were ready to go, on the point of leaving, but she opened her bag again, rummaging aimlessly in its contents.

'D'you know that fellow?' David asked and then, feeling that he had been rude, added truthfully, 'I'm sure I do. Might be someone I've come into contact with on television, of course. His face seemed awfully familiar.'

'I didn't notice.'

'Or I could have seen his picture in a newspaper. That's it, I think, in connection with some case or other.'

'More likely on TV,' she said casually.

'He seemed to know you.'

Or had it been that this girl was so outstandingly good-looking that even in the West End where beauty is common, men stared at her? She put her hand on his arm. 'David?' She was lovely, the face close to his as they came into the street, flawless with its orchid skin and gold-specked eyes.

Why then did her touch affect him strangely, almost as if a snake had flickered against his sleeve? 'David, if you haven't anything better to do, would you—would you drive me home?'

All the way to the car she chattered feverishly and she clung to David's arm. She had an accent, he noticed, that wasn't from London or from the North. He couldn't quite place it, although he tried while he pretended to listen to what she was saying, whether she would be able to keep her flat, her future, her lack of training for any sort of job.

She didn't look like a new widow. The clothes she was wearing were not those he had seen in the inquest report picture, although those had been indecorous enough. Now she was dressed shabbily, casually and—he observed this for the first time as she got into the car—provocatively. He disliked fly-fronted trousers on women and these were far too tight. She took off her shiny jacket and draped it over the seat. Her breasts, though undoubtedly real, had an inflated rubbery look and they were hoisted so high as to suggest discomfort, but as if the discomfort were worth suffering for the sake of the erotic appeal. All this was fair enough in a beautiful girl of twenty-five, all this sticky seductive make-up, long cheek-enveloping hair, and emphasis given to a bold figure. But she wasn't just a girl of twenty-five. She was a widow who that morning had attended the inquest on her husband and who was supposed to be, if not grief-stricken, stunned by shock and subdued by care.

They had been driving along for perhaps a quarter of an hour when she put her hand on his knee. He hadn't the courage to remove it and he began to sweat when the fingers caressed and kneaded his flesh. She smoked continuously, opening the window every couple of minutes to flick ash out into the street.

'Is it straight on,' he said, 'or left here?'

'You can take the back doubles. It's shorter.' She wound down the window and threw her cigarette-end on to the pavement, narrowly missing a little Chinese. 'Take the next exit. I'll navigate for you.'

David obeyed her, going left, right, left again, and plunging into a web of mean streets. It was still quite light. They came to a bridge with huge concrete pillars at either end, carved columns vaguely Egyptian, that might have come from the Valley of the Kings. Underneath was a kind of marshalling yard, overlooked by factories and tower blocks.

'Down here,' Magdalene Heller said. It was a narrow street of tiny slum houses. Ahead he could see a tall chimney, a gasometer. 'What's the hurry?'

'It's not exactly a beauty spot, is it? Not the sort of place one wants to hang about in.'

She sighed, then touched his hand lightly with one fingertip. 'Would you stop a moment, David? I have to get cigarettes.'

Why couldn't she have bought them in London? Anyway, the three or four she had smoked had come from a nearly full pack. He could see a shop on the corner and he could see that it was closed.

Reluctantly he pulled into the kerb. They were quite alone and unobserved. 'I'm so lonely, David,' she said. 'Be nice to me.' Her face was close to his and he could see every pore in that smooth fungoid skin, mushroom skin, rubbery as he could guess that too-perfect, pneumatic body to be. There was a highlight on her lips where she had licked them. 'Oh, David,' she whispered.

It was like a dream, a nightmare. It couldn't be happening. As if in a nightmare, for a moment he was stiff and powerless. She touched his cheek, stroking it, then curled her warm hands around his neck. He told himself that he had been wrong about her, that she was desperately lonely, devastated, longing for comfort, so he put his arms around her. The full wet lips he by-passed, pressing his cheek against hers.

He stayed like that for perhaps thirty seconds, but when her mouth closed on his neck with sea-anemone suction, he took his arms from her shoulders.

'Come on,' he said. 'People can see us.' There was no one to see. 'Let's get you home, shall we?' He had to prise her off him, a new and quelling experience. She was breathing heavily and her eyes were sullen. Her mouth drooped pathetically.

'Come and have a meal with me,' she said. Her voice had a dismayed whine in it. 'Please do. I can cook for you. I'm a good cook, really I am. You mustn't judge by what I was giving Bernard that night. He didn't care what he ate.'

'I can't, Magdalene.' He was too embarrassed to look at her.

'But you've come all this way. I want to talk to you.' Incredibly, the hand came back to his knee. 'Don't leave me all alone.'

He didn't know what to do. On the one hand, she was a widow, young, poor, her husband dead only days before. No decent man could abandon her. He had already abandoned the husband, and the husband had killed himself. But on the other hand, there was her outrageous behaviour, the clumsy seduction attempt. There was nothing cynical in concluding her offer of a meal was just eyewash. But was he justified in leaving her? He was a grown man, reasonably experienced; he could protect himself, and under the peculiar circumstances, do so with tact. Above all, he wondered why he need protect himself. Was she a nymphomaniac, or so unhinged by shock as to be on the edge of a mental breakdown? He wasn't so vain as to suppose against all previous evidence to the contrary, that women were spontaneously and violently attracted to him. The wild notion that he might suddenly have developed an irresistible sex appeal crossed his mind to be immediately dismissed as fantastic.

'I don't know, Magdalene,' he said doubtfully. They passed the prison or barrack wall and they passed the lighted cinema. There was a long bus queue at the stop by the park. David heard himself let out a small sound, a gasp, a stifled exclamation. His hands went damp and slithered on the wheel. Bernard Heller stood at the tail of the queue, reading his evening paper.

Of course, it wasn't Bernard. This man was even bigger and heavier, his face more ox-like, less intelligent than Bernard's. If David hadn't already been jumpy and bewildered he would have known at once it was the twin brother, Carl who had borrowed the slide pojector. But they were uncannily alike. The resemblance made David feel a bit sick.

He pulled the car in alongside the queue and Carl Heller lumbered into the back. Magdalene had gone rather pale. She introduced them snappily, her accent more pronounced.

'David's going to have dinner with me, Carl.' She added as if she had a part-share in the car and more than a part-share in David, 'We'll drop you off first.'

'I can't stay for dinner, Magdalene,' David said firmly. The presence of Bernard's twin both discomfited him and gave him strength. Here were capable hands in which he could safely leave the girl. 'I'm afraid I don't know where you live.'

Magdalene said something that sounded like Copenhagen Street and she had begun on a spate of directions when David felt a heavy hand, grotesquely like the comedy scene hand of the law, lower itself on to his shoulder and rest there.

'She's in no fit state for company tonight, Mr Chadwick.' The voice was more guttural than Bernard's. There was more in that sentence than a polite way of telling someone he wasn't wanted. David heard in it self-appointed ownership, pride, sorrow and—yes, perhaps jealousy. 'I'll look after her,' Carl said. 'That's what my poor brother would have wanted. She's had a bad day, but she's got me.'

David thought he had never heard anyone speak so ponderously, so slowly. The English was correct and idiomatic, yet it sounded like a still difficult foreign tongue. You would grow so bored, exasperated even, if you had to listen to this man talking for long.

Magdalene had given up. She said no more until they reached Hengist House. Whatever she had been trying on, she had given it up.

'Thanks for the lift.'

'I'm glad I saw you,' David said untruthfully. Carl's face was Bernard's, unbearably pathetic, dull with grief, and David heard himself say in a useless echo of his words to the dead man, 'Look, if there's anything I can do . . .'

'No one can do anything.' The same answer, the same tone. Then Carl said, 'Time will do it.'

Magdalene lagged back. 'Good night, then,' David said. He watched Carl take her arm, propelling her, while she tugged a little and looked back, like a child whose father has come to fetch it home from a dangerous game with the boy next door.

8

Julian and Susan had tried to be very civilised and enlightened. They had to meet for Julian to see his son. It had seemed wiser to try to maintain an unemotional friendship and Susan had known this would be difficult. How difficult, how nearly impossible, she hadn't envisaged. When life went smoothly, she preferred not to be reminded of Julian's existence and his telephone calls—incongruously more frequent at such times—were an uncomfortable disruption of peace. But when she was unhappy or nervous she expected him to know it and to a certain degree be a husband to her again, as if he were in fact a husband separated from his wife for perhaps business reasons, who had to live far away.

She knew this was an impossible hope, totally unreasonable. Nothing on earth would have made her disclose this feeling to anyone else. Julian had his own life to lead.

But was it so unreasonable to expect at this time some sign of concern from him? Louise's death had been in all the newspapers; tonight both evening papers featured the inquest. Julian was an avid reader of newspapers and the fact that the two Evenings had been delivered to her house, were now spread on the table before her, was a hangover from her marriage to Julian who expected his wife to be well-informed.

That he still hadn't phoned showed a careless disregard for her that changed her loneliness from a gathering depression to a panicky terror that no one in the world cared whether she lived or died. To spend the evening and night alone here suddenly seemed a worse ordeal to pass through than any she had encountered since her divorce. For the first time she resented Paul. But for him, she could have gone out tonight, gone to the pictures, rooted out a friend from the past. Here in this house there was nothing else to think about but Louise and the only conversation possible an interchange between herself and her *alter ego*. The sentences almost spoke themselves aloud, the answerless questions. Could she have helped? Could she have changed the course of things? How was she going to stand days, weeks, months of this house? Above all, how to cope with Paul?

He had gone on and on that evening about Louise and the man. Because someone had told him Louise had loved this man, he found curious childish parallels between her case and that of his parents. Susan too had found parallels and she couldn't answer him. She reproached herself for her inadequacy but she was glad when at last he fell silent and slid the beloved cars out of their boxes, playing with absorption until bedtime.

So it was unforgivable to feel this mounting anger when she went to her desk and saw how he had left it, a multistoried car park with miniscule bonnet and fender protruding from every slot and cranny. Black tyre marks were scored across each of the top three sheets of her typescript. Unforgivable to be angry, cruel perhaps not to control that anger.

But the words were out when she was halfway up the stairs, before she could stop herself and count to ten through set teeth.

'How many times have I told you to leave my things alone? You're never to do it again, never! If you do, I won't let you wear your watch for a whole week.'

Paul gave a heart-breaking wail. He made a grab for the watch, pulling it from its velvet-lined case, and cradling it against his face. Desperately near tears herself, Susan fell on her knees beside him and took him in her arms.

'Stop crying. You mustn't cry.'

'I'll never do it again, only you're not to take my watch.' How quickly a child's tears evaporated! They left no trace, no ugly swollen redness. Louise's weeping had left her face furrowed, old, distraught.

Paul watched her with a child's sharp intuition. 'I can't go to sleep, Mummy,' he said. 'I don't like this house any more.' His voice was small and muffled against her shoulder.

'Will they catch the man and put him in prison?'

'He's dead too, darling.'

'Are you sure? Roger's mother said he'd gone away, but she said Mrs North had gone away too. Suppose he isn't dead and he comes back here?'

Susan left the light on in his bedroom and the light on on the landing. When she got downstairs again she lit the twentieth cigarette of the day, but the smoke seemed to choke her, starting a long spasm of coughing. It left her shivering with cold. She ground out the cigarette, turned up the central heating and, going to the phone, dialled Julian's number.

Tonight, when nothing went right and all things seemed antagonistic, it would have to be Elizabeth who answered.

'Hallo, Elizabeth. Susan.'

'Susan . . .' The echoed name hung in the air. As always, Elizabeth's gruff schoolgirlish voice held a note of doubt. The impression was that she knew quite ten Susans, all of whom were likely to telephone her and announce themselves without surname or other qualification.

'Susan Townsend.' It was grotesque, almost past bearing. 'May I have a word with Julian?'

'Sure, if you want. He's just finishing his mousse.' How those two harped on food! They had plenty in common; one day, no doubt, they would share obesity. 'Good thing you rang now. We're just off for our weekend with Mummy.'

'Have a good time.'

'We always have a great time with Mummy. I do think all this killing in Matchdown Park is the end, and you up to your neck in it. But I expect you kept cool. You always do, don't you? I'll just fetch Julian.'

He sounded as if his mouth was full.

'How are you, Julian?'

'I am well.'

Susan wondered if her sigh of exasperation was audible at the other end. 'Julian, I expect you've read about all this business out here. What I want to ask you is, d'you mind if we sell this house? I want to move as soon as possible. I can't remember the way our joint property is tied up but I know it's complicated and we both have to agree.'

'You must do exactly as you like, my dear.' Had he brought the mousse with him? It sounded as if he was eating while he talked. 'You're absolutely free. I shan't interfere at all. Only don't think of taking less than ten thousand and wherever you choose to make your new home, see it's within distance of a decent school for my son and a good prep school when the time comes.' He swallowed and said breezily, 'Just put it in some agent's hands and let him do the lot. And if I meet anyone pining to vegetate in salubrious Matchdown Park I'll send him along. Tell me, were we ever on more than nodding terms with these Norths?'

'You weren't on more than nodding terms with anyone. Sneering terms might be more accurate.'

For a moment she thought he was offended. Then he said, 'You know, Susan, you've got a lot more waspish since we parted. It's rather becoming, almost makes me . . . well, no I won't say that. Rather a sexy-looking fellow, this North, as I recall, and a quasi-professional job, surely?'

'He's a quantity surveyor.'

'Whatever that may be. I suppose you and he are living in each other's pockets now, popping in and out of each other's houses. No wonder you want to move.'

'I don't imagine I shall ever speak to him again,' said Susan. Julian muttered something about finishing dinner, packing, setting off for Lady Maskell's. She said good-bye quickly because she knew she was going to cry. The tears rolled down her cheeks and she didn't bother to wipe them away. Every time Julian talked to her she hoped for kindness and consideration, forgetting for the moment that this was how he had always spoken to other people, waspishly, lightly, frivolously. She was the other people now and the tender kindness was Elizabeth's.

And yet she didn't love him any more. It was the habit of being a wife, of coming first in a man's scheme of things, that she missed. When you were married you couldn't ever be quite alone. You might be on your own which was different. And whoever she begged to come to her now would look on her necessarily as a nuisance, a bore that separated them from the person they would prefer to be with.

For all that, she considered phoning Doris or even Mrs Dring. Her pride prevented her as her fingers inched towards the receiver.

Paul had fallen asleep. She covered him up, washed and redid her face. There was no point in it, but she sensed that if she were to go to bed now, at seven-thirty, it might become a precedent. You went to bed early because there was nothing to stay up for. You lay in bed late because getting up meant facing life.

She was going to move. Cling on to that, she thought, cling on to that. Never again to see the cherry trees come into crêpe paper bloom, the elms swaying above the cemetery, the three dull red pinpoints burning by the roadworks trench. Never again to run to a window because a dog barked or watch Bob North's headlights swing across the ceiling and die in a wobble of shadow against the wall.

They were glazing through the room now. Susan pulled the curtains across. She opened a new packet of cigarettes and this time the smoke didn't make her cough. Her throat felt dry and rough. That must be the intense heat. Why did she keep feeling alternately cold and hot? She went outside to adjust the heating once more, but stopped, jumping absurdly with shock, when the front door bell rang.

Who would call on her at this hour? Not surely those friends of her marriage, Dian, Greg, Minta, their consciences alerted by the evening papers? The dog hadn't barked. It must be Betty or Doris.

The man on the doorstep cleared his throat as she put her hand to the latch. The sound, nervous, gruff, diffident, told her who it was before she opened the door. She felt an unpleasant thrill of trepidation that melted quickly into pure relief that anyone at all had come to call on her. Then, coughing again, as nervous as he, she let Bob North in.

At once he made it clear that this wasn't a mere doorstep call and Susan, who had told Julian she would probably never be on more than remote terms with her neighbour, was curiously glad when he walked straight into the living-room as if he were a friend and a regular visitor. Then she told herself with self-reproach, that Bob had far more cause to be lonely and unhappy than she.

His face now bore no sign of the misery and bitterness to which he had given vent in court and although he again apologised for Susan's involvement in his affairs, he said nothing of why he had come. Susan had already put her sympathy and her sorrow for him into awkward words and now she could find nothing to say. That he had come with definite purpose was made clear by his nervous manner and the narrow calculating look he gave her as they faced each other in the warm untidy room.

'Were you busy? Am I interrupting something?'

'Of course not.' His loss made him different from other men, a pariah, someone you had to treat warily, yet appear to be no different. She wanted to behave both as if the tragedy had never happened and at the same time as if he were deserving of the most solicitous consideration. An odd reflection came to her, that it was impossible to feel much pity for anyone as good-looking as Bob. His appearance called for envy from men and a peculiarly humiliating admiration from women. If the tragedy hadn't happened and he had called like this, she would have felt ill-at-ease alone with him.

'Won't you sit down?' she said stiffly. 'Can I get you a drink?'

'That's very sweet of you.' He took the bottle and the glasses from her. 'Let me.' She watched him pour gin into a glass and fill it high with bitter lemon. 'What can I get you? No, don't shake your head . . .' He gave a very faint crooked grin, the first smile she had seen on his face since Louise's death. 'This is going to be a long session, Susan, if you'll bear with me.'

'Of course,' she murmured. This, then, was the purpose of his visit, to talk to one near enough to listen, far enough to discard when the unburdening was complete. Louise had tried to do the same, Louise had died first. Somewhere in all this there was a curious irony. Bob's dark blue eyes were on her, fixed, cool, yet doubtful as if he had still a choice to make and wondered whether he was choosing wisely.

She moved away from him to sit down and the sofa suddenly seemed peculiarly soft and yielding. A moment ago she had been glad to see Bob; now she felt only deeply tired. Bob walked the length of the room, turned sharply and, taking a roll of paper from his pocket, dropped it on the coffee table between them. He had an actor's grace, an actor's way of moving because he had studied and learnt those movements. Susan thought this with slight surprise and then she wondered if his gestures looked calculated because he was keeping them under a painful control.

She reached for the papers, raising her eyebrows at him. He nodded sharply at her. Could these quarto sheets be connected with some legal business? Could they even possibly be Louise's will?

Susan unfolded the first page without much curiosity. Then she dropped it with a sharp exclamation as if it had been rolled round something red hot or something slimily disgusting.

'No, I can't possibly! I can't read these letters!'

'You recognise them, then?'

'Parts of them were read in court.' Susan's face burned. 'Why . . .' She cleared her throat which had begun to feel sore and swollen. 'Why do you want me to read them?' she asked fiercely.

'Don't be harsh with me, Susan.' His brow puckered like a little boy's. She thought suddenly of Paul. 'The police gave me these letters. They *belonged* to Louise, you see, and I've —well, I've inherited them. Heller sent them to her last year. *Last year*, Susan. Since I read them, I haven't been able to think of anything else. They haunt me.'

'Burn them.'

'I can't. I keep on reading them. They've poisoned every happy memory I have of her.' He put his face in his hands. 'She wanted to be rid of me. I was just an encumbrance. Am I so loathsome?'

She avoided the direct answer, for the question was absurd. It was as if a millionaire had asked for her opinion on the low state of his finances. 'You're overwrought, Bob. That's only natural. When people are having a love affair, they say things they don't mean, things that aren't true, anyway. I expect Julian's wife said a lot of exaggerated unpleasant things about me.' She had never considered this before. It cost her an effort to put it into words.

He nodded eagerly. 'That's why I came to you. I knew you'd understand.' Swiftly he got up. The letters were written on stiff quarto-size paper and they had once again sprung back into a roll. He flattened them with the heel of his hand and thrust them at Susan, holding them a few inches from her face.

She had spoken of the possibility of Elizabeth's having written defamotory things about her. If this had happened and such a letter come into her possession, nothing would have induced her to show it to a stranger. And yet the majority of strangers would jump at the chance. She must be exceptionally squeamish or perhaps just a coward, an ostrich. How avidly Doris, for instance, would scramble to devour Heller's words if, instead of coming here, Bob were baring his soul in the house across the street!

Susan reached for a cigarette. The thought came to her that she had never read a love-letter. During their courtship she and Julian had seldom been separated and when they were they phoned each other. Certainly she had never read anyone else's. Bob, who valued her for her experience, would be astonished at such innocence.

Perhaps it was this innocence that still held her back. Louise's love affair, a housewife and a salesman, a hole-in-the-corner ugliness, seemed to her merely sordid, unredeemed by real passion. The letters might be obscene. She glanced up at Bob and suddenly she was sure he would expose her to nothing disgusting. With a little sigh, she brought Heller's looped sloping writing into focus, the address: Three, Hengist House, East Mulvihill, S.E.29, the date, November 6th, '67, and then she began to read.

My darling,

You are in my thoughts night and day. Indeed, I do not know where dreaming ends and waking begins, for you fill my mind and I go about in a daze. I am a bit of a slow stupid fellow at the best of times, sweetheart—I can picture you smiling at this and maybe (I hope) denying it—but it is true and now I am half-blind and deaf as well. My love for you has made me blind, but I am not so blind that I cannot see into the future. It frightens me when I think we may have to go on like this for years, only seeing each other occasionally and then for a few snatched hours.

Why won't you make up your mind to tell him? It's no good saying something may happen to make everything come right for us. What can happen? He is not an old man and may live for years and years. I know you say you don't wish him dead but I can't believe it. Everything you say and the very look on your face shows me you feel he's just a burden to you. The rest is superstition and in your heart you know it. He has no rights, no hold over you that anyone would recognise these days.

What it boils down to, what you're really saying is that we just have to hang on and wait till he dies. No, I'm not trying to persuade you to put something in his tea. I'm telling you for the hundredth time to make him understand you have a right to your own life, to take it from him and give it to your loving but very miserable,

Bernard

No, it wasn't a disgusting letter—unless you happened to know the man Heller referred to as a tiresome encumbrance. And if you didn't know the man, you might even find the second letter poignant. If you didn't know the man and hadn't lived next door to the wife from whose betrayal Heller had drawn his insinuations.

The address was the same, the date nearly a month later. December 2nd, '67, Susan read, and then:

My sweet darling,

I can't go on living without you. I can't go on existing and working miles and miles away from you, thinking of you with him and wasting your life being a slave to him. You must tell him about me, that you have found someone who really loves you and will give you a proper home at last. You half promised you would when we met last week, but I know how weak you can be when actually with him.

Does he really need all this care and attention and wouldn't a housekeeper be able to do everything you do now? He has always been harsh and ungrateful, God knows, and you say sometimes violent. Tell him tonight, darling, while you are with him in what I can only call your prison.

Time goes on so quickly (it seems slow to me now but I know it really flies) and what will you be like in a few years time, growing older and still tied to him? He will never come to appreciate and love you now. All he wants is a servant. You will be bitter and soured, and do you really think our love can still last under those conditions? As for me, I sometimes think that without you I can only make an end to myself. I just can't envisage life dragging on like this much longer.

Write to me or, better still, come to me. You have never seen me happy yet, not happy as I will be when I know you have left him at last.

Bernard

Susan folded the letters and they stared at each other in a deep, sickened silence. To break it, she shied away from touching on the emotional content of the letters and, seizing on something mundane, said, 'Were there only these? Didn't he write any more?'

'Aren't they sufficient?'

'I didn't mean that. Only that I should have expected more, a whole series.'

'If there were more, she didn't keep them.'

'She may have been ashamed of them,' Susan said bitterly. 'They aren't exactly couched in deathless prose, not literary gems.'

'I hadn't noticed. I'm no judge of that sort of thing. Their meaning is clear enough. Louise hated me so much she was prepared to tell any lies about me.' He took the letters from her hand and kept hold of the hand, clutching it sexlessly, desperately, like a lifeline. 'Susan,' he said, 'you don't believe it, do you, that I was a violent, harsh, slave-driver?'

'Of course I don't. That's why I don't think there's any

point in keeping the wretched things. You'll only read and re-read them and torture yourself.'

For a dreadful moment she thought he was going to cry. His face twisted and it was almost ugly. 'I can't bring myself to destroy them,' he said. 'Susan, would you do it, would you—if I left them here?'

Slowly she took them from his lap, expecting her wrist to be seized again. She felt rather as she did when each night she surreptitiously slipped the watch from Paul's hands while he slept. Here was the same held-breath caution, the same fear of a cry of protest. But Paul loved his watch. Was a kind of love curiously combined with Bob's hatred of these letters?

He let her take them. 'I promise, Bob,' she said, and a trembling weariness washed over her. 'I promise, as soon as you've gone.'

She thought he would go then. It was still early, but she had forgotten about precedents, about giving in to depression and tiredness. Now she only wanted to sleep.

But, 'I ought not to bore you with all this,' he said in the tone of someone who has every intention of doing so. Evidently her tiredness didn't show. 'I've got to talk to someone. I can't bear to keep it all to myself.'

'Go ahead, Bob. I understand.'

So she listened while he talked of his marriage, his once great love for Louise, their disappointment at their childlessness. He speculated as to where Louise and Heller had met, what they could have had in common and how strange it was that Louise's faith had deserted her. He spoke with violence, with passion, with incredulity and once he got up to pace the room. But instead of exhausting him as they exhausted Susan, his outbursts seemed to invigorate him. Cleansed and renewed, he talked for half an hour, while Susan lay back, nodding sometimes and assuring him of her sympathy. The stubs in her ashtray piled up until they looked like the poster picture in the doctor's surgery. Her throat had become rasping, rubbing sandpaper.

'My God, I'm sorry, Susan,' he said at last. 'I've worn you out. I'll go.' She was beyond polite dissuasion. He took her hands impulsively and as he bent over her his dark vivid face went out of focus and swam above her. 'Promise I'll never see those foul things again,' he said. She nodded. 'I'll let myself out. I'll never forget what you've done for me.'

The front door closed and the sound of its closing reverberated in her head to settle into a steady throbbing. Long shivers were coursing through her now and her back had begun to ache. She closed her eyes and saw Bob's face suspended before them. Heller's spidery writing danced and the beating in a corner of her brain became the sharp clicking of Louise's heels.

When she awoke it was midnight. The air was foul with smoke. The heating had shut itself off and it was the cold which had awakened her, eating into her bones. Sometime before she slept she must have taken the glasses to the kitchen and emptied that spilling ashtray. She remembered nothing about it, but as she staggered to her feet she knew very well that her inertia and the sharp pain in her throat had little to do with the emotional vicissitudes of the day.

Symptoms like these had real physical cause. She had the flu.

9

Since Julian's departure Susan had slept in one of the two spare bedrooms at the back of the house. It was a small room with a north light but now she was glad she had chosen it. To be ill in a bedroom that was the twin of Louise's bedroom, to lie in a bed placed just where hers was, was the worst medicine Susan could think of.

She had passed a miserable night, getting sleep only in short snatches. By morning the bed was piled with every surplus blanket in the house, although Susan only dimly remembered fetching the extra ones. She took her temperature and found it was a hundred and three.

'Go over to Mrs Winter, darling,' she said when Paul pottered in at eight. 'Ask her to give you breakfast.'

'What's the matter with you?'

'I've just got a bad cold.'

'I expect you caught it off Roger Gibbs at the party,' said Paul, adding as if praising a friend for remarkable altruism, 'He gives his colds to everyone.'

The doctor came, arriving simultaneously with Doris who stood at the end of the bed, confirming his diagnosis and chipping in every few seconds with suggestions of her own.

'I don't want you to catch it, Doris,' Susan said feebly after he had gone.

'Oh, I shan't catch it. I never catch things.'

It was true. For all her vulnerability to low temperatures and her huddling into cardigans, Doris never even had a cold. 'I got immune to all that in my nursing days,' she said, punching pillows like a boxer. 'Just listen to my dog. He's kicking up a racket because all the funeral cars have come next door.' Cocking her head, she listened to the distant barking and what might have been an undertaker's subdued footfall. 'One thing, I've got an excuse for not going and it'd be suicide for you to get up.' She clapped her hand over her mouth. 'Oh dear, that's a dirty word round here, isn't it? I've heard the Catholics won't have Louise in their cemetery. Shame, really, when it was Heller who did it.' The dog barked hollowly, a door slammed. 'I've seen Bob and he sent his best wishes for a speedy recovery. Fancy, with all his troubles, he wanted to know if there was anything he could do. I said to John, Bob North's got a terrific admiration for Susan in his way, and John agreed with me. I've turned your heating full on, my dear. I hope you don't mind, but you know what a chilly mortal I am. I wonder if he'll get married again.'

'Who?'

'Bob, of course. Well, marriage is a habit, isn't it, and I should think it would be funny adapting yourself to the single life. Oh God, there I go again, both feet in it!' Doris blushed and hugged herself in her big double-knit jacket. 'Could you eat a cut off the joint? No, better not. By the way, I tidied up for you and dusted through. Not that it needed it, was was all as neat as a pin.'

'You're being awfully kind.'

'Just bossy and managing, lovey.' Doris's sudden unexpected self-analysis endeared her to Susan more than all her expert attention. She wished her painful throat and her huge weariness would allow her to speak her gratitude. She croaked out something about Paul, and Doris said, 'He's gone with Richard. You can leave him with us for the weekend. What are you going to do with yourself? Maybe we could have the telly fetched up here.'

'No, really, Doris. I might read a bit later on.'

'Well, if you get bored, you can always watch the workmen slogging themselves to death.' And, twitching the curtain, Doris laughed loudly. 'They're as bad as I am, must have their fire and their tea.'

Watching three workmen fill in a trench and dig another one six feet up the road would hardly have been Susan's idea of compelling entertainment when she was well. She had often thought, as most people do, that if she was ever confined to bed, mildly sick, she would use the time to read one of those classics that demand uninterrupted concentration. So when Doris returned at lunchtime she asked her to fetch *Remembrance of Things Past* from the collection of books Julian had left behind him.

But Proust defeated her. She was uninterrupted, but her powers of concentration were so diminished as to leave her mind a vague blur of half-remembered worries, disjointed fears and thoughts of her removal from Matchdown Park. She put the book down after ten minutes of peering at the dancing print and, impatient to find herself yielding to Doris's silly suggestion, turned her eyes to the window.

The sky was a pale cloudy blue across which the elm branches spread their black lace tracery. She could just see the sun, a yellow puddle in the clouds. It all looked dreadfully cold and she could understand the workmen's need of a fire. The three of them were standing round it now, stirring tea in mugs Susan could see were coarse and cracked. Louise had given them china cups with saucers.

She propped the pillows behind her so that she could see better. Oddly enough, there was something peculiarly diverting in watching three unknown people moving about and talking to each other. That she couldn't hear what they said only increased the piquancy. There was an oldish man, a younger man and a boy. The two older men seemed to be chaffing the boy, but he took their shoving and their laughter good-humouredly. It was his task to collect the three mugs and take them back into the shelter of the hut. Susan saw him shake the dregs on to the clay-plastered pavement and wipe the insides of the mugs out with newspaper.

Presently they clambered back into their trench and the old man bowed his body over the broad handle of the drill. The boy had got hold of a muddy tangle of cables and capered about with them, at which his companion started a mock fight. Only their heads and their flailing hands were visible over the ridge of the trench, but the boy's laughter was so shrill that, far away as she was, Susan could hear it above the reverberations of the drill.

Then a girl in a short red coat appeared around the corner of O'Donnells' fence and immediately, ceasing their sparring, the two younger men whistled her. She had to pass the road-works and she did so with her nose in the air. The boy ogled her and shouted something.

Susan relaxed against her pillows. She had forgotten Louise and Bob, Paul's terrors, Julian's flippant unconcern. A much older woman crossed the road this time, but she too earned a heartening whistle. Susan smiled to herself, a little ashamed of getting amusement from something so puerile. How old did a woman have to be, she wondered, to escape this salute, thirty-five, forty, *fifty*? Certainly there was an open-hearted generosity in this lack of discrimination. Perhaps you were never too old or perhaps the old man, silent and grim while the other two acknowledged passing femininity, reserved his personal whistles for his female contemporaries.

At three the boy fetched a black kettle from the hut and began to boil it on the fire. Did they know Louise was dead? Had the news reached them somehow on the winged winds of gossip? Or had one of them come innocently to the back door on Thursday to be met by Bob's bitter staring eyes and Bob's abrupt dismissal?

The tea was made, the mugs refilled. The amount of tea they drank, they obviously preferred brewing their own to fetching it from the café two hundred yards away. No doubt it had been a blow to them when their emissary had gone to bang on Louise's door on Wednesday and got no reply. They hadn't sent the boy that time, Susan thought, but the man in his twenties who was pulling a blue jersey over his head as he crouched by the brazier.

The trench cut halfway across the road now and, having collected the mugs, the boy stationed himself on a pile of earth, a flag in his hand, to direct what little traffic passed. He swaggered, fancying himself a policeman on crossing patrol, but presently, after only two cars had passed, the blue-jersey man beckoned him back into the hole with fierce gestures. Susan felt that she was watching a silent film that would launch soon into knockabout farce, or perhaps some modern epic from Italy or Sweden, fraught with symbolism, where movement and facial expression are of deep significance and the human voice a vulgar intrusion.

And it was thus that Doris found her when she brought Paul home to put him to bed at six. The workmen had gone home and Susan lay back, looking dreamily at the dull crimson lights they had left behind them. She was absurdly disappointed that it was Sunday tomorrow, resentful like an avid viewer who knows he must wait two days for the next instalment of the serial.

'I've brought you a visitor,' Doris said on Sunday afternoon. 'Guess who.'

It couldn't be Julian, for he was staying in the country with Lady Maskell, part, no doubt, of a jolly gathering that would include Minta Philpott, Greg and Dian, and heaven knew who else. Besides, Julian avoided sickrooms.

'It's Bob.' Doris glanced nervously over her shoulder as his tread sounded on the stairs. 'He *would* come. I told him that in his low state he was vulnerable to every germ that's going, but he *would* come.'

His arms were full of daffodils. Susan was sure they were the ones that grew in the Braeside front garden and now she pictured that big square bed covered with the stubble of broken stalks. Louise had loved her bulbs and Bob's action in picking these flowers reminded Susan of a story she had once heard of the gardeners at Lady Jane Grey's home lopping the heads off all the oaks on the estate when she was killed. She said nothing of this to Bob. At first the sight of him embarrassed her and she wondered if he regretted his lack of reserve on Friday evening. But he showed no awkwardness, although his manner, until Doris had left them, was somewhat guarded.

'I rather expected you'd have gone away,' Susan said. 'Not exactly for a holiday, but just for a change.'

'There's nowhere I fancy going. All the places I've ever wanted to go to, I went with her.' He fetched a vase and arranged the daffodils, but clumsily for so graceful a man, crowding the stalks together and snapping them off roughly when they were too long. 'I'm better here,' he said, and when

Doris thrust her head round the door with a bright smile. 'I've a lot of things to see to.'

'You're unlucky with your holidays, anyway,' Doris said. 'I remember last year Louise was ill and you were in that boat disaster.' Bob didn't say anything but his face darkened dangerously. 'Poor Louise had just what you've got now, Susan, and Bob had to amuse himself as best he could. Poor Louise said the holiday was just a dead loss as far as she was concerned. Oh dear, would you rather I didn't talk about her, Bob?'

'Please,' Bob said tightly. He sat down by Susan's bed, scarcely concealing his impatience as Doris twittered on about Paul's refusal to clean his teeth, his insistence on keeping the new watch under his pillow. 'Thank God she's gone,' he said when at last the door closed. 'Doesn't she drive you mad?'

'She's a good friend, Bob. Awfully kind.'

'She doesn't miss anything that goes on in this street. That dog of hers nearly sent me out of my mind when the funeral cars came.' He gave an unhappy sigh and suddenly Susan had for him what he had seemed to want all along, a fellow-feeling. Pity welled up in her so that, had she been well, she would have wanted to take him in her arms and hold him close to her as she might have held Paul. The thought startled her. Had it come to her because he looked so young, so pitiably vulnerable? He was older than she, four or five years older. For a moment she was embarrassed, almost dismayed.

He went to the door, opened it a fraction, then closed it softly. She thought he moved like a cat. No, like something less domestic. Like a panther. 'Got rid of those letters all right, did you?' His voice had the elaborate casual lightness of someone asking a question intensely but secretly important to him. 'That scum Heller's letters,' he said. 'You said you'd burn them.'

'Of course I did,' Susan said firmly. But the question jolted her, bringing the singing back to her head as if her temperature had swiftly taken a sharp rise. Until now she had forgotten all about the letters. They had been distasteful to her, she thought, and perhaps what had taken place in her mind was what Julian called a psychological block. Now, in spite of what she had said so reassuringly to Bob, she simply couldn't remember whether she had burnt the letters or not. Had she before, after or even during that dream-filled two-hour sleep that had almost been a coma, dropped the letters into the disused fireplace and set fire to them with her lighter? Or could they possibly be still on the table, exposed for Doris or Mrs Dring to read?

'I knew I could rely on you, Susan,' Bob said. 'Sorry if I was a bore the other night.' He picked up the book she had left face-downwards. 'Highbrow stuff you read! When I'm ill I only want to lie still and look out of the window.'

'That's what I did yesterday. I just watched the workmen most of the day.'

'Fascinating pastime,' he said rather coldly, and then, 'A rotten lonely life you lead, Susan. All these months you must have been lonely and I never gave it a thought.'

'Why should you?'

'I lived next door to you. I should have realised. Louise might have realised . . .' He paused and said, his voice charged with a dull anger, 'Only she was too busy with her own affairs. Or should I say affair? How old are you, Susan?'

'Twenty-six.'

'Twenty-six! And when you're under the weather you're stuck in a suburban bedroom with no one to look after you and nothing better to do than watch four or five labourers dig up the road.'

It would be useless to tell him that for a few hours that suburban bedroom had been like a theatre box and the men actors on a distant comedy stage. Bob was such a physical, down-to-earth person, a prey to strong emotions but hardly the sort of man to get pleasure from the quiet observation of human behaviour. With his looks and his extrovert attitude to life, he had probably seldom experienced the taking of a back seat. He was looking at her now with such concern that she wondered why she had ever thought him selfish. She tried to laugh but her throat was too sore.

'But I'm not alone all the time,' she said, her voice rapidly disintegrating into a croak. 'And Doris is looking after me beautifully.'

'Yes, you said she'd been a good friend. I wish you'd said it of me. I wish things had been different so you *could* have said it of me.'

There was no reply to that one. He got up abruptly and when he came back, Paul was with him, the watch still strapped round his wrist at the edge of his pyjama sleeve.

'I can't kiss you, darling. I'm all germs.'

'You haven't got a clock in here,' Paul said. 'Would you like my watch, just for tonight?'

'That's a kind thought, but I wouldn't dream of depriving you.'

His look of relief was unmistakable. 'Well, good night, then.'

'Here, let's see if I can lift you.' Bob put out his hands to clasp the boy's waist. 'You've got so tall. I bet you weigh a ton.' It gave Susan a faintly sad shock to see that hard bitter face so suddenly tender. He had no children of his own, but now . . . Of course he would marry again. Perhaps because it was too soon to have such hopes for him, the thought was vaguely displeasing.

Paul let Bob pick him up, but when the man's arms tried to swing him high as if he were a tiny child, he struggled and said babyishly, 'Put me down! Put me down!'

'Come on now, don't be silly.' Susan was tired now. She wished they would all go and leave her. Paul would take a long time getting off to sleep tonight. Let Bob think her son had protested because he didn't care to be babied; she knew that there was another, darker reason.

'Good night, Susan.' The rejection hadn't upset him at all and now he gave her the charming boyish smile that made her forget how sullenly that dark face could cloud. It was such a frank, untroubled smile, ingratiating almost. She felt strangely that he had made these overtures to her son to please her rather than from a fondness for children.

'Good night, Bob. Thank you for the flowers.'

'I'll come again soon,' he said. 'Don't think you've seen the last of me.' They were alone now. He went to the door and hesitated. 'You've been my lifeline, Susan. You've been a light in the darkness.'

Less than a week ago she had been prepared to go to any lengths to avoid him. Now it seemed a cowardly, impossibly exclusive way to have behaved. Far from being selfish, he was kind, thoughtful, impulsive, all those things that Julian had never been. But she didn't know why she should compare him with Julian at all—they were so utterly different, in looks, in temperament, in manner to her—unless it was because her former husband was the only other man she could truthfully say she knew.

When the repetitive sing-song, the 'Tick-tock, tick-tock', softly chanted from Paul's bedroom ceased, Susan put on her dressing-gown, checked that her son was asleep, and made her way downstairs. Her legs were weak and each step sent a throbbing through her body up into her head.

The living-room was neater than Mrs Dring ever left it. Susan's eyes went immediately to the coffee table where she last remembered having seen Heller's letters, but there was only a clean ashtray on the polished circular expanse. She moved slowly about the room, leafing absurdly through a pile of magazines, opening drawers. This, she thought, putting her hand to her forehead, was how an underwater swimmer must feel, struggling to make a free passage through a cumbersome, unfamiliar heaviness. The air in this room seemed thick, dragging her limbs.

Doris would have loved to read those letters.

It was an unforgivable thought to have about so kind a friend. Besides, Doris would never have taken them out of the house. Susan moved aside the firescreen and peered into the grate. There was no paper ash on the clean bars.

For all that, she must have burnt them herself. And now as she cast her mind back to those dazed fever-filled hours, she could almost convince herself that she remembered holding the letters in the fireplace and watching her lighter flame eat across the pages to devour Heller's words. She could see it clearly just as she could picture Doris tidying the grate, dustpan and brush in her hand.

Her relief nearly equalled total peace of mind and if she was again shivering uncontrollably it was only because she was still ill and had disobeyed the doctor's instructions to stay in bed.

10

The soft insinuating voice at the other end of the line was peculiarly persistent. 'Bernard thought such a lot of you, David. He often talked about you. It seems a pity to lose touch and I know Carl wants to meet you again. We were both disappointed when you couldn't stay and have a meal on Friday, so I wondered if you'd make it another time. Say tomorrow?'

'I'm afraid I couldn't make it tomorrow.'

'Tuesday, then?'

'I can't make it this week at all. I'll ring you, shall I?' David said good-bye firmly and hung up. Then he went back into the untidy, cluttered but interesting room he called a studio and thought about it.

She had a face like Goya's *Naked Maja*, full-lipped, sensuous. It didn't attract him. He was always finding resemblances between living people and people painted long ago. Portraits were pinned all over his walls, Ganymede reproductions, picture gallery postcards, pages cut out of Sunday paper colour supplements. Vigee Le Brun's *Marie Antoinette* was there, stuck up with Sellotape next to an El Greco *Pope*; Titian's *L'homme aux Gants* had a frame which was more than he had accorded to his Van Gogh peasants or the Naked Maja herself.

A peculiar inconsistent woman, he thought, and he wasn't thinking about the Goya. She had been surly to him on the night before her husband's death and actually dismayed to see him in The Man in the Iron Mask. And then, after five minutes stilted courtesy on his part and absent-minded rejoinders on hers, she had changed her entire personality, becoming sweet, seductive and effusive. Why?

They said that no man can resist a pretty woman who throws herself at him. His nature is such that he succumbs, unable to believe such good fortune. And if he has not himself made the slightest overture, he congratulates himself, while despising the woman, on his irresistible attractions. But it hardly ever happens that way, David thought. It had never happened to him before. There had been no difficulty at all in resisting. From the first he had been bewildered.

And yet he would have done nothing about it. The incident would have been dismissed to the back of his mind, along with various others of life's apparently insoluble mysteries. People were peculiar, human nature a perennial puzzle. You had to accept it.

But she had telephoned him, talking like an old friend who had every hope and every justification for that hope of becoming much more. From a vague uneasiness, his bewilderment grew until it crowded everything else from his mind. No matter how carefully he thought about it, going over and over the events of Friday night, he could only justify Magdalene Heller's conduct by assuming her to be not quite sane. But he knew that this conclusion is always the lazy and cowardly resort of a poor imagination. Mad she might be, but there would be method in her madness. Young widows do not go into West End pubs on the day of their husband's inquests; they do not dress in tight trousers and tight sweaters; above all they do not make inexplicable unprovoked passes at casual acquaintances.

She said she had been there to meet someone and he had never for a moment believed that someone was a woman. Then he remembered the man who had come in, who had stared at her, hesitating, before retreating in haste. From that precise moment her manner towards David had changed.

Suddenly David knew quite certainly that her appointment had been with this man. She had arranged to meet a man at the pub, but the meeting must be a secret one. Why else had she failed to make the necessary introductions, denied recognising that face which now, as David remembered it, had worn in that first instant a look of satisfaction, of pleasurable anticipation? She knew him. She guessed that David's curiosity had been aroused, so she had staged the scene in the car to blind him, to seduce him and, ultimately, to make him forget what he had seen.

It must be terribly important to her, he thought, and he recalled her nervous gabbling and the urgency of her caressing hand. She had detained him in the pub after the man had gone. Because, having speculated as to the man's identity, he might have looked for him in the street, and seeing his face in daylight, have made absolute recognition certain?

But he and the Hellers had, as far as he knew, no acquaintances in common. How could he have recognised a friend of Magdalene's? And, supposing he had, why did it matter so much to her?

Suddenly it had grown too warm for a fire, even outside. The roadmen had brought a spirit stove with them and the boy boiled their kettle on it inside the hut. For the first time, as if lured out by the fine weather, the man in the blue jersey was working above ground, and for the first time too, Susan saw him standing erect.

She was surprised to see that he was rather short, or, rather, short in the leg. Perhaps it was the length of his torso which had deceived her. She had a strong impression that she associated this man with height, but she didn't know why.

Then it came to her that on one previous occasion she had seen him walking along on level ground. She had seen him in Louise's garden on the day of Louise's death, and now, as she thought about it, the impression of a much taller man strengthened and grew vivid. Surely that man had been quite six feet tall and more slightly built than Blue Jersey who, swinging a pick, showed a thick waistline and a heavily muscled back.

The answer must be that at that time there had been more than three men working on the road. When he brought the daffodils, Bob had spoken of four or five men and no doubt he was better-informed on this matter than she who had scarcely spared the labourers a second glance until illness brought them into compelling perspective.

That illness was now receding and by the middle of the

week Susan had lost interest in the workmen. Their doings had lost their freshness or her own standard of entertainment, lowered by fever, had risen. She read her Proust, hardly distracted even by the spasmodic scream of the drill.

'Mr North popped in with some books.' Mrs Dring piled a stack of new magazines on the bed. 'I reckon it's been the best thing that could have happened for him, you being ill. It's taken him out of himself, stopped him brooding. He coming in here again tonight, is he? You want to mind your neighbours don't get talking. That Mrs Gibbs has got a tongue as long as your arm.'

'Oh, rubbish,' Susan said crossly. 'You said yourself he only comes for something to occupy his mind.'

'And he's the type that occupies his mind with women. You needn't look like that. I dare say there's no harm in it. Men are men when all's said and done. My husband's different, but then he's one in a million as I've always said. And talking of men, if you're going to start sitting up you want to watch that lot in the road don't see you all in your nothings.'

Mrs Dring's manner was more that of a nanny than a charwoman. Susan let her draw the curtains half across the window and accepted, with a meek shrug, the bedjacket that was tossed on to the pillow.

'How many men are there working on the road, Mrs Dring?'

'Just the three.'

'I thought there were four or five last week.'

'There was never more than three,' said Mrs Dring. 'That was your temperature making you see double. There's always been just the three.'

Magdalene Heller phoned David again on Wednesday evening. She was very lonely, she said, she hardly knew a soul but Carl.

'What about your friend you were meeting in the pub?'

'I don't know him that well.'

'Better than me, surely?' Did she know what she had said? He muttered a quick good-bye. Her voice after that fatal sentence had sounded stunned. This was no fear of being caught out in a clandestine adventure, no fear of scandal. David sensed that she was deathly afraid. He had guessed right and located the source of her fear, her sudden change of heart, her advances to himself, and briefly he was elated. She wouldn't bother with him again.

Of course she had set herself up as very pure, the essence of wronged womanhood in the coroner's court. It would look funny if it turned out she had a man friend of her own, and he remembered how he had thought she was going to meet a man when he had watched her visiting the cinema. It might be a thought to read that inquest report again and see just what she had said.

Presently he unearthed the old newspaper—he always kept newspapers for weeks and weeks, finally bundling them up and putting them on top of his tiny dustbin—but the report was brief and very little of what Magdalene had said was quoted. With a shrug, he folded the newspaper again and then his eye was caught by a front-page photograph on the previous Wednesday's copy of the *Evening News*. The caption beneath it said, 'Mr Robert North and his wife Louise, who was today found shot with Bernard Heller, a 33-year-old salesman. This picture was taken while the Norths were on holiday in Devon last year. Story on page 5.'

David's eyes narrowed and he looked searchingly into the photographed face. Then he turned quickly to page five. 'I had never even heard Heller's name,' North had told the coroner, 'until someone in the street where I live told me that *Equatair*'s rep. had repeatedly called at my house. I never saw him till he was dead and I certainly didn't know he was a married man.'

But six hours later he had walked into a Soho pub where he had arranged to meet that married man's widow.

A regular weekly feature of *Certainty* was a kind of diary written entirely by Julian Townsend and called 'Happenings'. In fact, as few things ever happened to Julian and he was incurably lazy, the diary consisted less of accounts of events attended by him than a *mélange* of his opinions. There was usually some local war going on for Julian to condemn and advise negotiation or arbitration; some bill being placed before Parliament which enraged him; some politician whose way of life annoyed him and offered him an occasion of mischief-making. When, as occasionally happened, a freak silly season occurred, Julian vented his vituperation on old-established customs and institutions, spitting venom at the Royal Family, the Church of England, horse racing, musical comedies and the licensing laws.

This week 'Happenings' was as usual headed by Julian's name writ large on a streamer beneath which the writer's face scowled from a single column block. The high bumpy forehead, glossy with the sweat of intellect, round metal-framed glasses and supercilious mouth were familiar to David as a constant reader of *Certainty* and now he scarcely noticed them. A girl-friend of his, a television actress called Pamela Pearce, claimed acquaintance with *Certainty*'s editor and occasionally threatened to introduce him to David. But up till now he had steered clear of the encounter, preferring to keep his illusions. Townsend could hardly be as pompous, as self-opinionated and as pedantic as his articles led the reader to believe. David felt he might lose his zest for 'Happenings' if its writer turned out to be unassuming.

There was always a discourse on food and today Julian had gone to town, devoting the whole of his first column to recipes for aphrodisiac meat dishes and puddings, with erudite references to Norman Douglas, and half his second to a violent condemnation of the lunch he had eaten in a country hotel while week-ending with his aristocratic in-laws.

Smiling, David passed on. Apparently the fellow was going to fill up the rest of his space with an attack on the suburbs of London. 'Happenings' was a misnomer for this spate of vitriol. Rural England castrated by the entrenching tool, the pneumatic drill,' David read, amused. From the ravaged countryside, Julian sped towards the metropolis. 'Matchdown Park, where never a month passes without the demolition of yet another Georgian jewel . . .'

Rather odd. Years went by without a mention of Matchdown Park and now it was constantly in the news. David was surprised to find Townsend actually lived there. But he evidently did. 'The present writer's knowledge,' the paragraph ended, 'is based on five years' sojourn in the place.'

David fetched the blue S to Z telephone directory and there it was: Julian M. Townsend, 16 Orchard Drive, Matchdown Park. He hesitated, pondering. But when he began to dial, it wasn't the number on the page in front of him.

'Julian Townsend?' said Pamela Pearce. 'You're in luck, as it happens, darling. I'm going to a party tomorrow night and he's bound to be there. Why not come along?'

'Will his wife be there?'

'His wife? I expect so. He never goes anywhere without her.'

A Mrs Susan Townsend had found Heller's body, and she lived next door to the Norths in Orchard Drive. It was all in the paper and it must be the same woman. What he would say when he met her David hardly knew, but it should be easy to bring the conversation round to the North tragedy. It would still be a hot topic with her. She had been a friend of Mrs North. Didn't the paper say she had been paying an ordinary morning call? She would know if North and Magdalene Heller had known each other before the inquest and, since she had been in court, could tell him if North's statements—'I didn't even know he was a married man' and so on—had been misreported or if, when heard in their full and proper context, were capable of a different, innocent interpretation. If she were co-operative, she could set his mind at rest.

For it was active and troubled enough now. North had come to meet Magdalene in The Man in the Iron Mask six hours after the inquest. That was just explicable. He could have done so and still not have lied to the coroner. But if something else which David suspected were true, he had lied blackly and irredeemably.

They had arranged to meet there. That he knew for certain. Had they ever met there before?

11

'It's a crying shame the mess them floors get in,' said Mrs Dring on all-fours. 'There's holes in this parquet you could put your finger in.' Louise's heels, Susan thought with a pang. Probably they would never be eradicated, but at least the new occupant need never know how they had been caused. Of this prospective buyer she now had high hopes, for, once well again, her first task had been to call at the estate agent's. She watched Mrs Dring obliterating small clayey footmarks, her interest caught when she said, 'Let's hope we've seen the last of all this mud. Did you know they've finished the road at last? The three of them filled up that hole of theirs last night and good riddance.'

She had seen the last act of their play, then. Settling at her typewriter, Susan wondered why they had ever dug that series of trenches and whether life in Matchdown Park would have been brought to a standstill without the monotonous rhythm of those drills and the renewing of those glimpsed cables. Her ability to concentrate and reason normally, rediscovered in the past two days, brought her intense pleasure. It seemed to her that her illness had marked the end of a black period in her life and during that illness she had found fresh resources, decided to break away from Matchdown Park and made a friend in Bob North.

But as she worked, congratulating herself on her recovery, a tiny thread of doubt crept across her mind. For some unexplored reason she was troubled by her recollections of the roadmen and although she should have shared Mrs Dring's relief at their departure, she began instead to feel a curious dismay.

There had never been more than three men, Mrs Dring insisted, and yet while Louise was lying dead with Heller she had seen a fourth man in Louise's garden. That man had knocked at Louise's back door—Mrs Dring had heard him do so—and then walked away, not to join the others, but off by himself down the road. Recapturing the scene, lifting her eyes from the type which had blurred, Susan remembered quite clearly that the three others, the old man, Blue Jersey and the boy, had been in their trench while he stood for a moment, hooded, anonymous, to warm his hands at their fire.

'Mrs Dring.' She got up, feeling a faint sickness, the aftermath of her flu. 'I've just remembered something, something rather worrying. I suppose I was getting this flu while I was at the inquest. Only—only they asked me if I'd seen anyone call next door during the morning and I said I hadn't. I said . . .' She stopped, appalled at the curiosity which almost amounted to hunger on Mrs Dring's uplifted face.

'Well, you didn't see no one, did you?'

'I'd forgotten. It can't matter now. We all knew what the verdict was going to be, but still . . .' And Susan bit her lip, not because of what she had said, but because she had said it to this woman, this bearer of malice, this arch troublemaker who had no kind word for anyone but her husband. Then she managed a strained smile and, convincing herself she was changing the subject, said, 'You'll have a chance to get the floors nice now Paul won't be bringing in any more clay on his shoes.'

Gin and the 'something fizzy' he always liked to drink with it, coffee cups on a tray, the last of the daffodils displayed in a vase. Susan had only made these preparations once before but already they were becoming a ritual. Bob would be late tonight—he couldn't be with her until ten, for he had a business call to make—but she had already given up going to bed early. There was something to stay up for.

'It's always so wonderfully warm in here, Susan,' he said as he entered the living-room. 'There's a lot to be said for central heating. I don't know why I didn't have it put in years ago.'

She turned her head away to hide the blush, but, although

she was aware of his solecism, she felt a rush of elation. In saying such a thing, he had showed her that while Louise's death was fresh in his mind, the circumstances which had led up to it were fading. Would it be right to trouble him now with the question she had been intending to put to him all day? In all their talks they had scarcely yet discussed any subject but that of Heller and Louise, and just the same she hesitated, waiting for him to begin as he always did, obsessively, minutely on the details of their love and death.

A lightness and a sense of relief came to her when instead he asked her casually if she knew of anyone who would do the Braeside housework for him.

'My Mrs Dring might. I'll ask her.'

'You've done so much for me, Susan, and here I am still asking favours.'

'A very small favour. She may not be able to.'

'Somehow I feel she will if you ask her. You're one of those people who make things come right. D'you know, in the past week I've often thought that if we'd really bothered to get to know you, if you and Louise had been friends, none of this would ever have happened.'

They were back to it again. Subject normal.

'If I'm really so powerful,' Susan said, an urgency entering her voice, 'if I can really make things come right, I'd like to begin by telling you to stop all that, Bob. Try to forget it, put it behind you.'

He reached out and took her hands, both her hands in a strong warm grasp. For a comforter, a safe refuge, she suddenly felt strangely weak and enervated.

Pamela Pearce was a pretty little blonde with a taste for glitter. Metallic threads ran through the materials of most of her clothes; she liked sequins and beads and studs, anything that sparkled. Tonight she wore lamé, and against the cobbles and the grey brick walls of the South Kensington mews she glittered like a goldfish in murky waters.

'Hadn't you better tell me who my host and hostess are?' David said as he locked his car. 'I don't want to feel like a complete gatecrasher.'

'Greg's one of those society photographers. You must have seen those lovely things he did of Princess Alexandra. His wife's called Dian and she's absolutely lovely. You'll fall madly in love with her. Believe me, just to see her is to adore her.'

The trouble was David was never quite sure whether he had seen her. He was hardly in a position to fall madly in love with her as nobody bothered to introduce him to anyone and, Pamela having been borne off up the narrow staircase, he found himself alone on an island of carpet, surrounded by indifferent backs. Presently he forced his way between barathea-jacketed backs and half-naked backs, moving his arms like a swimmer doing the breast stroke, and finally squeezing into a little lyre-backed chair. A screen behind him was perilously loaded with lighted candles which dripped wax on to an improvised bar.

For some minutes no one took any notice of him and Pamela didn't reappear. Then a voice behind him said incomprehensibly, 'Do you think you could get outside some cup?'

David looked over his shoulder, first at the young man with butter-coloured hair who had addressed him, then at the bar wherein a bowlful of pale golden liquid, cherries and pieces of cucumber were floating. Before he could say he would avoid this at any price, a ladleful had been scooped up and dribbled into a glass.

It tasted like fruit juice which someone had poured into a cough mixture bottle. David put his glass down behind a plate of smoked eel canapes, observing that everyone else seemed also to have shunned the cup.

The room was too small to accommodate so large a party, but even so the guests had succeeded in huddling themselves into distinctly isolated groups. The largest of these had for its nucleus a tall man with an enormous forehead and he stood beneath the central lamp which effectively spotlighted him. David had no difficulty in recognising Julian Townsend.

The editor's prim mouth was opening and shutting nineteen to the dozen while he gesticulated sweepingly with a large hand in which he held a sausage roll. Five women stood around him in a circle, hanging on his words.

One of them must be his wife, David thought, the innocent neighbour of Heller's mistress, she who had found the dead couple. There was a statuesque brunette with a cigar, two nearly identical blondes, a teen-ager in brown and an elderly lady who evidently intended to spend the rest of the weekend in the country, for she wore a tweed suit, mesh stockings and tall boots. Pamela was nowhere to be seen, although he could hear her shrill giggle occasionally from upstairs, and he felt a stab of annoyance. Short of introducing himself as a reader and a fan, he couldn't see how he was going to talk to Townsend without her.

Then the teen-ager detached herself from the sycophantic circle and made for the bar. Her movements had the rapid and entirely selfish directness of the very young and, to avoid her, David backed into the bamboo screen.

'Good gracious, you nearly set your hair on fire!' The butter-haired barman had seized his arm and David backed away from naked candle-flame.

'Thanks,' he said, his face inches from the girl's.

'You need someone to look after you, don't you?' said the barman. 'It quite upsets me to see you standing there all lost. Take him under your wing, Elizabeth, do.'

Having refused the cup and helped herself to brandy, the girl said baldly, 'I'm Elizabeth Townsend. What's your name?'

'David Chadwick.' He was very surprised and perhaps he showed it. In her very short shapeless dress of the colour and texture of brown bread and with her long untidy brown hair she looked about seventeen. No doubt accustomed to being in the company of a man never at a loss for words, she fixed him with an incredulous glare. 'I believe you live in Matchdown Park,' he heard himself say in exactly the tone of wistful awe someone might use when enquiring if an acquaintance had a grace and favour apartment at Hampton Court.

'My God, no. Whatever gave you that idea?'

'I read it in *Certainty*,' David said indignantly. 'You *are* Mrs Julian Townsend?'

'Of course I am.' She looked deeply affronted. Then her

brow, furrowed with impatience and some imagined slight, cleared. 'Oh, I see it all now. You've dropped a clang.' His discomfiture stirred a gurgle from the depths of the brown bread dress. 'That's his ex you're thinking of, my—well, what would you call her?—wife-in-law might fit, don't you think?' She giggled happily at her own joke. 'Wild horses wouldn't make me live in Matchdown Park.' She said this with violent defiance, but almost before the words were out something quick and sharp came into her expression to change it and make it assume a slight concupiscence. 'Why d'you ask, anyway? Have you got some sort of yen to live in the place?'

'I might,' David muttered, not knowing where all this was leading. Never in all his life had he met anyone so brutally direct and unselfconscious as this girl. He wondered on what her confidence was built, plain, dumpy and charmless as she was.

'Only my wife-in-law . . .' She grinned with delight at her invented expression. '. . . my wife-in-law wants to move, so Julian's got this house in Matchdown Park on his hands. It's a very good sort of house.' She seemed sublimely unconscious that two minutes before she had denounced its environs with a shudder. 'Julian would be absolutely ecstatic if I'd found a buyer for him.'

Next door to Norths, inhabited by the woman who knew the Norths, who had found Heller's body. The candles flared behind David's head and their reflections, tall, smoky, yellow-white, danced in Elizabeth Townsend's glass. 'How big is it?' he said cautiously.

'Come and meet Julian. He'll tell you all about it.' She grabbed his arm, her fingers, urgent and almost affectionate, digging into his elbow. 'Julian, do shut up a minute! Listen, I've found a bloke who actually wants to live in Matchdown Park!'

Susan hadn't warned Paul that Bob was coming in for the evening. She didn't want him to awaken and, troubled by fears and fantasies as he was, hear a man's voice downstairs. In his present world men who called on solitary women brought guns with them . . .

Murmuring an excuse to Bob, she went up to Paul's bedroom, tucked him in again, restored his watch to a more secure position on the bedside table and went out again, leaving the light burning. She was half-way down the stairs when the phone rang.

'I don't suppose you've sold the house yet?' Julian's voice sounded unnaturally enthusiastic against a background of music and hilarity.

'Hardly,' Susan said dryly.

'That's what I thought. However, not to worry. Now tell me, are you doing anything on Monday night?'

She no longer loved him but it was horrible to be asked such a question by the man who had once been her husband.

'Why?'

'I've told some fellow he can come and look over the house. Chadwell, Challis—something like that. He's here with me now as a matter of fact—well, not exactly with me but we're all at Dian's and Elizabeth picked him up.'

'I thought you must be. I can hardly hear you for the racket. How is Dian?'

'Absolutely lovely as usual.'

Susan cleared her throat. 'What time does this man want to come?'

'Eightish. By the by . . .' He lowered his voice to a barely audible mumble. 'I shouldn't mention that peculiar affair next door. It might put him off.'

'Julian, you must be more naive than I think you if you imagine anyone could go through all the fuss of buying this house without finding out about Louise's suicide.' She stopped, aghast. All the doors were open and Bob must have heard. Too late now. 'Oh, Julian!' she said, exasperated.

'He might not find out,' Julian said craftily, 'until he'd signed the contract. Don't tell me you're indifferent to the prospect of five thousand pounds. Now I must return to this do. I suppose you're all alone?'

'In point of fact,' Susan said, 'I'm not. A friend is with me, so if you'll excuse me, Julian, I'd better get back to him.'

Bob sat where she had left him, on his face the blank look of someone who has been unable to help overhearing a private conversation but who must pretend, from politeness, to a temporary total deafness.

'Sorry about that,' Susan said crisply. 'You must have heard.'

'I couldn't help it. I gather you're thinking of moving, Susan?'

'The atmosphere here isn't right for Paul, and besides that . . . I suppose I wasn't well, I was almost hysterical at the end of last week. I wanted to get away as soon as possible, but that was before . . .'

Before what? What had she been about to say? Confused, she turned her head away. She had waited for him to finish the sentence for her and instead his glance was cool, analytical, assessing.

'When d'you think you'll go?'

'As soon as I can,' she said evenly, and then she made herself smile, crushing down the absurd disappointment. Had she really supposed this widower, this lost soul almost, came to see her because he was growing fond of her? He wanted a shoulder to cry on merely, and hers was waiting.

'I can understand you want to shake the dust of this place off your feet,' he said, 'put all the misery behind you. You'll soon forget about Louise and me, won't you?' Then, obsessively, forgetting perhaps that he had said it all before a dozen times, he began step by step to go over every word, action and suspicion that had led him to suspect Louise's love affair, to search again into the circumstances of her death.

'Bob,' Susan said sharply, 'you'll have to stop this. You'll turn yourself into a neurotic. What do you hope to gain by it? They're both dead, it's all over.' He looked at her, shocked and silenced. For the first time she was asking herself why, when another man would put up an outward show of courage, he should be so obsessed by his wife's death. A little thrill of nervousness, not quite fear, at the enormity of what she was about to say, ran through her. 'It isn't because . . .' she began slowly, 'it isn't because you doubt that it *was* suicide, is it?'

He made no answer. His smoky blue eyes had a glazed look and his face went dead so that the lamplight seemed to fall on a copper mask.

Susan's own words had startled her and now that they were out she was sure they would have been better unsaid. She had no grounds at all for saying them, only a vague unease that during the day and the previous day had held her standing sometimes in a dream or sent her upstairs to stare meaninglessly out of the window.

'It's just that, while I was ill . . .' She blushed hotly. Was this how Doris felt when she made one of her gaffes? 'There were one or two things,' she said, 'one or two odd things that made me wonder.'

'You were delirious.'

'Come now, I wasn't that ill.'

'I shouldn't want,' he said, 'I couldn't bear . . . Susan, it was his gun, they found the powder marks on his hand. How could there be . . . ?'

'If you don't think so,' she said, 'of course there can't be any doubt.' And she felt cold and sick because he was on his feet now. She had been his comforter and now he must think her just like all the others, stirring up trouble for him, making use of him as a topic for speculation. Wordlessly, he had moved out into the hall to stand on the spot where Louise's heel had pierced the parquet.

'Bob,' she said, going to him.

'Susan?'

'I was delirious.'

He touched her shoulder, bent down and brushed her cheek with his lips. It seemed like ages since anyone but Paul had kissed her and as she felt the light touch of his mouth she fancied she could still hear quite clearly the laughter and the music from that party far away, as if the telephone was still open, still transmitting it. A loneliness that was abysmal and a desire to end that loneliness at all costs, made her put out her hand and take his, holding it tightly.

'Forgive me?'

He nodded, still too shaken to smile. She heard him walk swiftly into Braeside but although, after a sick empty interval, she too went out into the garden, she saw that no lights had come on in the house next door where the windows were always closed.

12

The trees which grew from rectangles in the pavement were the kind David most disliked, sterile ornamental cherries and prunuses which bear no fruit. They were in full blossom now and he guessed that he had picked for his visit the one day in the year on which Orchard Drive justified its name. The buds had all opened, not a petal had yet fallen, and the flowers reminded him of crêpe paper. Behind the pink cloudy masses street lamps glowed with the acid drop quality of milky quartz.

He drove along slowly, following the route Heller had taken to see his love. The houses would only appear large to those with small horizons. They were not all the same—he counted four different types—but each was detached, each had an integral garage and a biggish lawned or landscaped front garden. He passed doors painted lilac and doors painted lime; he noted here the pretentious bay tree and there the pair of mass-produced carriage lamps. No raised voice, no subdued strain of music, no footfall disturbed the silence. He was beginning to see why wild horses wouldn't have dragged Elizabeth Townsend to live here.

Rather like a wild horse herself or perhaps a shaggy Shetland pony, she had tugged him towards the group where the editor of *Certainty* was holding forth. With a shout of 'Do me a favour, Mintay', and 'Mind your backs!' she had shoved him unceremoniously under her husband's nose.

Julian Townsend raised his eyebrows and one deprecating hand in his wife's direction. '. . . And just that essential dash of cointreau,' he finished. 'It makes all the difference between common *potage* and *haute cuisine*. Now, what was it you wanted to say, my darling?'

The female sycophants edged away. David looked awkwardly into the face that each week launched a thousand outraged letters. A faint dew glistened on Townsend's bulbous forehead and it creased and smoothed again as his little brown wife introduced David inaccurately.

'A private transaction would be nice, of course,' the great man said at last. 'Not that I'd consider less than ten thousand.'

'Not exorbitant these days.'

This casual rejoinder threw Townsend slightly off balance. It was apparent that he was thinking quickly, perhaps dismayed that he had named so paltry a sum. But, the mobile supercilious face having worked for some seconds, he seemed to abandon that line to say almost meekly, 'It's a delightful area, *rus in urbe*, you know. The house itself is in excellent condition. Do you know the district well?'

David, who had occasionally passed through it on the tube and heard it twice mentioned by Bernard Heller, said that he did. Townsend beamed at him.

'I really do think this calls for a drink.' He made no move to fetch drinks himself, but a kind of telepathy seemed to pass between him and the woman called Minta. She trotted off and returned with a trayful of whiskies. Townsend raised his glass and shouted something which sounded like '*Terveydeksenne*!'

'A Finnish toast,' said Minta reverently.

So Townsend had gone off to find Dian and get her permission to use her phone. 'I do hope you buy it,' said his wife, tucking her arm into David's. 'We could do with our half-share in the ten thou. Give my love to poor old Susan.'

Well, he would see poor old Susan in a minute. This was the place next door to Braeside, innocent, respectable-looking Braeside where Heller had found something the green-eyed Magdalene could not give him and into which he had taken death.

Or had death come to him?

That, David thought, was presumably why he was here. To try to find out. To disturb this all-enveloping, blanket-like silence. The pale, dry papery flowers brushed his face as he got out of the car. He slammed the door and from behind him out of the dark stillness came an appalling frenzied roar. He jumped, wheeled round. But it was only a dog, a great ginger and black curly coated thing with a monstrous horror-film shadow that cavorted wildly in an opposite garden. David noted that a sturdy iron gate separated it from him. That was that. The noise put paid to all thoughts, very tempting natural thoughts, of giving up and returning the way he had come. Poor old Susan would have been alerted by now, was probably eyeing him from between those drawn curtains.

He marched up the drive, suddenly dreading the encounter. Would she be a facsimile of Elizabeth, strident and indiscreet, or a taboo-ridden housewife from whose genteellisms Townsend had thankfully escaped? The dog's fury pursued him embarrassingly. He rang the bell. The fact that it rang instead of evoking a carillon of Westminster chimes slightly cheered him. The hall light came on, the door opened and he stood face to face with the woman who had found Heller dead.

She was not what he had expected. Taking in the fair hair, the broad brow and the slender tilted nose, he knew at once where he had seen that face before. In the National Gallery, but not on a living woman. Effie Ruskin, he thought, Millais, *The Order of Release*. She smiled at him in a businesslike way.

'I'm sorry about the dog,' she said. 'Deafening, isn't it? He always barks like that at strangers.'

'Only at strangers?'

'Oh, yes. You needn't worry that he'll bark at you if you come to live here. Won't you come in? I'm afraid it's rather late for you to see the garden.'

A sudden dismay seized him. Pulling a fast one over Julian Townsend and his current wife was all very well. Shallow, unscrupulous, insincere, they had seemed to ask for it. This woman, who received him in good faith, impressed him at first sight as utterly honest. He sensed an old-fashioned integrity about her and it made him feel like a spy. For the past few days he had been living in a spy story world where the unconventional and the 'not done' thing was suspended.

She brought him up against the hard brick wall of reality with a jolt.

Following her inside and watching her meet her own reflection, tall, shapely stylish, in the long wall glass, he thought of her supplanter and his opinion of Julian Townsend sank still further. Very probably he would give up taking *Certainty*.

'This is the living-room,' she said, 'with a dining area, you see, and that door leads to the room my—Julian, that is —used to have for his study. I'll show you in a moment.'

There was something that looked like a manuscript—perhaps she wrote—on a desk, a full ashtray beside it—she smoked too much—and on the sofa arm a copy of *Within a Budding Grove*. She had a mind too. For a prospective buyer, he was looking at all the wrong things. It was not she that was for sale.

'I'm sure you won't mind if I ask you to keep fairly quiet when we go upstairs. My little boy is asleep.'

'I didn't know you had a child.'

'Why should you?' Her cool voice chilled. She began to instruct him in the controls of the central heating plant and he thought of Heller. On the sideboard he could see a tray with a gin bottle on it, a can of some fizzy mineral water, two glasses. She was expecting someone, a man probably. Two women alone together would drink coffee or tea or perhaps sherry.

Presently she led the way upstairs. The child slept in a lighted room and he liked the way she approached the bed, tenderly and gently, to rearrange the tumbled bedclothes, but he was less happy about her troubled frown and for the first time he noticed a gauntness in her face.

Nobody slept in the main bedroom now. Bachelor though he was, he could tell an unused bed and detect that nothing lay between mattress and counterpane. She must have moved out when Townsend left her. Damn Townsend! It gave him a very real pleasure to envisage the man's disappointment when the expected 'five thou' wasn't forthcoming. For two pins he'd keep him hanging on while he, David, ostensibly made up his mind. He could take weeks about it, months.

Only there was this girl. As she talked and pointed out the amenities of the place, he began to feel sick. He was practising on her a monstrous deceit, all the more reprehensible because she probably needed the sale.

She closed the bedroom door and said quietly, 'There's something I think you ought to know before we go any further. I don't know if you like the house, but I couldn't let you make an offer without telling you there was a double suicide next door. Only three weeks ago. It was in all the papers but perhaps you haven't connected it.'

Her honesty, in contrast to his deceit, brought the colour into his face. 'I did . . .'

'It wouldn't be fair not to tell you. Some people might feel superstitious about it. Mrs North and the man—a man called Heller—shot themselves in her bedroom. *This* bedroom. The houses are just the same inside.' She shrugged. 'Well, now you know,' she said.

He walked away from her and rested his hands on the banister rail. 'I did know,' he said, and in a rush, 'I knew Bernard Heller. I knew him quite well.'

The silence behind him was thick and almost frightening. Then he heard her say, 'I don't quite understand. You knew and yet you wanted . . .'

He began to go downstairs, all his natural diffidence depriving him of words. She came slowly after him. Without looking back, he felt a quite disproportionate sorrow that the tentative friendly harmony established between them had been destroyed.

At the foot of the stairs she stood a little distance from him. 'You want to buy a house next door to the one your friend died in? I really don't understand.'

'I know Mrs Heller too and I'll try to explain . . .'

She looked towards the front door, back at him. 'It's hardly my business, but it is my business to know if you want to buy this house or not. If you're a journalist or a private detective, you ought to be next door, not here.'

'Mrs Townsend . . .'

Her eyes opened wide—grey eyes, unbearably clear—and the Effie Ruskin mouth curled as it curled in the painting.

'What exactly *did* you think? That I'd gossip, give you revelations? I don't know anything about Mrs Heller, I only saw her once, but hasn't Mr North had enough?'

She glanced up upstairs, then trying to move casually, edged past him. She was frightened. It had never occurred to him that she might be frightened, for he had never before put himself into the shoes of a lonely woman who finds herself closeted with a strange man, an impostor. He felt his face go white with shame as he watched her eye the telephone, that lifeline, that communication with protection, and he moved away, his heart pounding.

In her eyes he was the salesman who wedges his foot in the door, the soft-spoken mechanic turned rapist, the insurance collector with warped desires, latent sadism. Her hand creeping towards the receiver, she said bravely, 'Mr North is a friend of *mine*. I don't understand what you're doing, only that he isn't going to be hurt any more. Tell Mrs Heller that.'

He opened the front door. The pink crêpe paper blossom covered the street light like a lampshade. He stepped out into the porch and once again the dog began to roar. She must know now that she was safe. 'Perhaps Mrs Heller has already told him,' he said loudly above the din.

'She has never spoken to him.' Abandoning the telephone, she lifted her head high. 'Now will you please go?'

'O God,' he said, stammering a little, cursing the dog, 'I won't hurt you. I'm going and you can phone the police if you like. I expect I've done something against the law, false pretences probably.' He couldn't meet her eyes, but he had to say it. 'Mrs Townsend, they do know each other. On the very day of the inquest they planned a meeting in a London pub. I saw them.'

The door slammed in his face, so near to his face that he had to jerk backwards quickly. The dog was so incensed by now that its antics made the gate rattle and clang. He got into his car, his hands actually shaking.

As he moved off another car passed him and swung smoothly into the Braeside drive. Only someone who did that manœuvre every day could perform it with such practised ease. David slowed. The man got out and David saw his head in his driving mirror, a dark head, neat, perfect, a gleaming, almost metallic coin relief in the pinkish-white lamp glow. Robert North. He had only seen that face in the flesh once before.

David braked and sat still. Without turning his head, he continued to observe North in the mirror. The other man was raising his garage door now, approaching his car, changing his mind. David wondered why the silence seemed wrong somehow and then he realised that the dog had ceased to bark. No one had taken it into the house. Its long monstrous shadow, magnified into a Hound of the Baskervilles, wriggled fawningly between the shadowed bars of the gate as North approached it and patted its head. The big black silhouettes quivered. North turned away and still the dog was silent. Susan Townsend had said it only barked at strangers. . . .

North's shadow moved across the road. It was much larger and more sinister than the man who cast it. David watched him go up to Mrs Townsend's front door and ring the bell.

They were on close terms those two, he thought as he drove away. The gin and the can of fizzy stuff were for him. No wonder the girl had reacted as she had! She was not merely a good discreet neighbour; she was emotionally involved with him. Why not use old-fashioned, more realistic terms? She was in love with him. On his looks alone, he was a man any woman might love. And he, David, had thought he could sound her about North's behaviour, North's attitude.

He must have been mad to suppose he could enter into a conspiracy with a strange woman, even if that woman had not been in love, enter with her into a plot to bring about North's downfall. This was not one of those serials for which he designed sets, but the real unromantic world. Had he really supposed that at a word from him she would break the barriers of convention and loyalty and confer with him an to her friend's actions and motives?

It seemed that he had. He had genuinely believed in the possibility of setting up with Mrs Townsend a kind of amateur detective bureau and, without prior contact, they were to have banded together in a scheme to overthrow two lives.

Bob put his arm gently around her shoulders and led her to a chair. 'What's happened, Susan? You look as if you've had a shock.'

'Someone was here,' she said, breathing quickly. 'A man . . . He said—insinuated, if you like—that you'd met Mrs Heller secretly on the day of the inquest.'

'So I did,' he said coolly. 'I met her in a London pub, but there was nothing secret about it.'

'You don't have to tell me.' Susan moved slightly to free herself from his encircling arm. 'It isn't my business, only I thought you didn't know her. I had the impression you'd never met till the inquest.'

'We hadn't. But afterwards I talked to her—she apologised to me, as a matter of fact, for the way she'd behaved in court. I was sorry for her. She's almost destitute, you know. That swine Heller hadn't left her a penny to live on. I felt I was bound to help and that's why we met. However, when we got there I found her with a man.'

'This Chadwick who came here?'

'Yes. Susan, the last thing I felt like was talking to strangers. I'm afraid I just bolted and then I came to see you. Of course, I've seen Mrs Heller since at her home. I've just come from there now.'

'How cruel people are,' she said wonderingly.

'Some are. And then you find someone who's sweet and good and lovely like you, Susan.'

She looked up at him incredulously.

'I meant that,' he said softly. 'Come here, Susan. You lived next door to me for years and years and I never saw you. And now, I suppose it's too late . . . I wonder . . . Would you kiss me, Susan?'

He would touch her forehead, brush her cheek, as he had done the other day at the door. She lifted her face passively and then, suddenly, it was not like the other day at all. She was in his arms, clinging to him, mouth to mouth and eyes closing at last on their loneliness and their shared rejection.

13

Detective Inspector Ulph knew that Robert North had killed his wife and his wife's lover. He knew it, not as he knew he was James Ulph, forty-eight years old, divorced, childless, but he knew it as a juror must, beyond a reasonable doubt.

There was nothing he could do about it. His superintendent laughed at him when he talked of North's motive and North's opportunity. Motive and opportunity cut no ice, unless it can be proved the man was there, the gun to which he had access, in his hand.

'Ever heard of a small point,' said the superintendent scathingly, 'of tracing the weapon from its source to the killer?'

Ulph had. It had perplexed him all along. Half-way through his interrogation of North he had met the man's eyes and read in them, under the simulated grief, a defiance which seemed to say, You know and I know it. It can never be proved. And as in a match there comes a point where one of the contestants knows the other will win—will win, at any rate, this hand or this game—Ulph knew that North held the good cards, that he had stacked them subtly long beforehand.

The gun was Heller's. Both Heller's widow and Heller's brother swore that it was in his possession the night before the killing. Except by unimaginable feats of burglary, by breaking into a flat of whose very existence North was certainly ignorant, he could not have gained possession of that gun. After the deaths Ulph had tested Heller's hand for powder burns and then, as if it were an embarrassing formality, North's hand also. Heller had fired shots, North none. Heller had been seen to enter Braeside at ten minutes past nine by a

Mrs Gibbs and a Mrs Winter and during the rest of the morning no one had left the house. North, carless as he was once every four weeks, had been in Barnet.

And yet Ulph knew that he had killed his wife. The picture, as in a peculiarly vivid and impressive film sequence, of how he had done it first came to him during the actual process of the inquest and since then it had returned often with the insistence of a recurring dream.

No one had seen North leave his house that morning, but this, this negative thing, this not seeing, not noticing, was pathetic, laughable, when it came to a question of proof and circumstantial evidence. 'I didn't see him leave,' Mrs Gibbs had said, 'but I often don't see him leave. Not seeing someone's no help really, is it? I saw Heller come.'

Because the dog had barked . . . North knew that, of course, that no one in Orchard Drive ever saw anything unless the dog barked. Ulph's dream picture unfolded at this point, or just before this point. North had shot his wife while she was making the bed and then, when the dog barked, he had gone downstairs to admit the lover.

Ulph had only seen the man dead, but again and again he saw how that heavy earnest face must have looked when the door was opened, not by his mistress but by her husband. North would have stood well behind the door so that his neighbours, watching, saw only the door itself sliding inwards. And who would have questioned this secretive and surreptitious method of admitting Heller, this action so typical of a woman conducting a clandestine adventure?

Then, after the first shock, the adrenalin rushing into Heller's bloodstream, came the quick gathering of his forces. The cover story, the subterfuge . . . But North would have forestalled him, saying mildly that he was becoming genuinely interested in this idea of a heating installation. He had stayed at home to discuss it. And Heller, concealing his dismay, had followed him upstairs, entering as best he could, into this unlooked-for, fantastic conversation about radiators.

Ulph saw the dead woman lying on the bed and heard North's cry of alarm. His wife must have fainted. What more natural than for Heller to join him at the bedside, bend over

—with a very real concern—the body of Louise North.

North had shot him then, shot him through the head. Had he been wearing rubber gloves? Had he perhaps come to the door with those gloves on and a tea-cloth in his hands? Ulph pictured those gloved hands closing the dead man's bare hand around the gun, aiming it at the dead woman's heart, pressing the trigger for the third time.

The picture stopped there, as if the projector had suddenly broken down.

North must have left the house. It was inconceivable that he could have done so and no one see him. All eyes had been on Braeside, regardless of the dog, waiting for Heller to come out. But North hadn't come out. He had come *in* at one-fifteen in his newly serviced car.

And the gun? Sometimes Ulph played fantastically with the idea that North might have taken it from him, out of his briefcase, while it stood on the kitchen table. But Heller never took that gun out of his flat. He would only have brought it with him to commit suicide....

That part of Ulph which was a policeman wanted North brought to justice; that part which was an ordinary man had for him a sneaking fellow-feeling. His own wife had left him for another man and he had divorced her, but there had been times when another fantasy had occupied his mind, a fantasy not unlike that in which he saw North playing the vital role. He knew what it was like to want to kill.

That North's actions showed a long and careful premeditation did not, in Ulph's estimation, make the killing any less of a crime of passion. North had been cool, he thought, with the coolness that is a thin veneer lying on humiliated burning rage, unbearable jealousy. And the grief he had at first believed simulated might in fact be real, the horror of an Othello, who unlike Othello, had real and undeniable grounds for his crime.

So Ulph felt no desire to act as the instrument of society's revenge on North. His interest was academic, detached. He simply wanted to know how the man had done it, to a lesser extent why, when in this case divorce was the easy and obvious solution, the man had done it.

But the whole matter was closed. The coroner and the superintendent between them had closed it.

Afterwards David wished he hadn't telephoned her to apologise. Her voice still stung in his ears.

'Mr North has arranged to lend her some money. It's a pity some of her friends of longer standing didn't think of that.'

She had crushed him with cool pointed sentences, calculated to wound. But as he listened to her meekly, he could only think of the first impression she had made on him, an impression of utter sincerity. He bore her no ill-will. Unable to forget her face, he went into the Tate Gallery after work, found *The Order of Release* and then bought a postcard copy. He had made no mistake in likening her to Effie Ruskin, but now as he made his way out on to the Embankment and hailed a taxi, he found that the card which he still held in his hand brought him no pleasure, nor any satisfaction at the accuracy of his visual memory. He had the feeling that to pin it on his wall with the others might curiously depress him.

When he got to The Man in the Iron Mask the two bearded men were the only customers and they sat at their usual table, drinking shorts.

'Covenanting's all very well, Sid,' David heard Charles say, 'for the other fellow, the one who benefits, but it's a mug's game for number one.'

'Quite,' said Sid.

'What's in it for you, I mean? Sweet Fanny Adams, unless you get a kick out of doing the Inland Revenue in the eye.'

The barman eyed David curiously as, with an anxious frown, he pretended to scan the empty room.

'You look as if you've lost something.'

'Someone,' David corrected him. 'A young lady.' The genteelism grated rather. 'I hoped to find her here.'

'Stood you up, has she?'

'Not exactly.' Sid and Charles weren't going to bite. Why should they? It wasn't going to be as easy as all that. He edged diffidently towards their table. 'Excuse me.' Charles gave him an indignant glare. David thought it a bad-tempered face. 'Excuse me, but have you been in here since they opened?'

'We have.' Charles seemed about to add So what? or did David want to make something of it?

'I wondered if you'd happen to see a girl come in, striking-looking dark girl. You saw me in here with her a couple of weeks back.'

'Rings a bell.' Charles's surly expression softened and he began to look less like Rasputin. 'Wait a minute. Dishy-looking piece in tight pants, would it be?'

'Come now, Charles,' said Sid.

'No offence meant, old man. Intended as a compliment actually.'

'That's all right.' David managed a quite easy, natural laugh. 'She used to be my secretary and now my present girl's leaving me, I thought . . . The fact is I believe she's often in here and as I don't know where she's living, I came in on the off-chance of catching her.' He marvelled at his own ability to lie glibly. 'You know how it is,' he said.

'She's not been in tonight,' said Charles. 'Sorry we can't help you. I wish I'd had the nous,' he said to Sid, 'to buy a hundred Amalgamated Asphalts last week. They touched thirty-eight-and-six this morning.'

'Quite.'

'Can I get you a drink?' David asked desperately.

'You could have knocked me down with a feather. Six months they've been stuck at twenty-five bob and . . . Did I hear someone say the magic word drink? That's very nice of you, old man.'

'Brandy,' said Sid, apparently for both of them.

David bought two brandies and a beer for himself. The barman tightened his lips. His expression was meaningful but David couldn't interpret that meaning.

'Her boy-friend would do,' he said as he put the glasses down. 'All I want is her address.'

'*Salud y pesetas*,' said Charles. 'Not that I'd say much for the peseta at this moment. You still worrying about that girl, old man?'

Casting aside caution, David said, 'Have you ever seen her in here with a man?'

Charles gave Sid a lugubrious wink. 'Time and time again. Tall, good-looking dark bloke. Always drank gin with something fizzy in it, didn't he, Sid?'

'Quite,' said Sid.

Excitement caught at David's throat, making him stammer. That Sid and Charles obviously thought him Magdalene Heller's cast-off lover, didn't bother him at all. 'Always?' he said. 'You mean they've been in here often?'

'About once a week for the past six months. No, I'm wrong there. More like eight months. You can put me right on that, Sid. When did we give up The Rose and start coming here?'

'August.'

'August it was. I remember it was August because the first day I got back from Majorca Sid and I went as usual to The Rose and, damn it, if they didn't short-change me. I've had about as much of this as I can stand, I said to Sid, and so we came here instead. Your girl and the dark bloke were here then.'

'I see. And they've been meeting regularly here ever since?'

'Not for the past fortnight.' Charles glanced in the barman's direction and then leant towards David confidingly. 'It's my belief they got fed up with this place. There's a lot of skulduggery goes on. Just before you came in that fellow tried to pull a fast one on me. Said I'd given him a pound when it was a fiver. Disgusting!' His brows drew together angrily and he rubbed his beard.

'It looks as if I'll have to advertise for a secretary after all.'

Sid glared at him derisively and, getting up suddenly, spoke the longest sentence David had ever heard him utter. 'Don't give me that, that secretary stuff, d'you mind? We're all men of the world, I hope, and personally I don't care to be talked down to like a school kid. You don't want another drink, do you, Charles?' He swung the door open. 'Secretary!' he said.

'Quite,' said Charles, reversing roles. They went.

David turned towards the bar and shrugged.

'Couple of comedians they are,' said the barman energetically. 'If you like your humour sick.'

Keyed up and tremendously elated by his discovery, David had felt he couldn't stand the pub a moment longer. He was filled with an urgent energy, and wasting it on chit-chat with the barman made him impatient. Nor did he want to drink any more, for drink might cloud his thought processes. He went out into the street and began to walk about aimlessly.

His excitement lasted about ten minutes. While it lasted he felt as he had done at other high spots in his life, when he had got his diploma, for instance, when he had landed his present job. There was no room for anything else in his mind but self-congratulation. Heller was temporarily forgotten in a pride and an elation that had nothing to do with morality or justice or indignation. He had found it out, done what he had set out to do and now he could only reflect with wonder on his achievement.

But he was not naturally vain and by the time he came, by a circuitous route, to Soho Square his swagger was less confident. It might have been someone he had passed that recalled her to his mind, a girl with straight fair hair like hers or one whose grey eyes met his for a moment. Her image entered his mind with startling clarity and suddenly he came down to earth with a bump. He sat down on one of the seats under the trees and as his hand touched the cold metal arm a shiver ran through him.

She ought to be told. She ought not to be left there alone with no one to protect her, a prey to North. It seemed absurd to equate her with the classic detective story victim who, knowing too much, must be silenced, but wasn't that in fact what she had become? Already she had alerted North, informing him of David's early suspicions. There was no knowing how much else she had seen, living next door to North as she did, what tiny discrepancies she had observed in his behaviour. David didn't for a moment believe North sought her company from honest motives of affection. She was in danger.

He knew he couldn't warn her off. He was the last man in the world she would listen to. For all that, he got up and made slowly for a phone box. There was someone inside and he waited impatiently, pacing up and down. At last he got in. He had found her number, begun to dial when his nerve failed him. There was something better he could do than this, something more responsible and adult. As soon as he thought of it, he wondered why he hadn't done it days ago. The green directory then this time. . . . He took a deep breath and, tapping his fingers nervously on the coin box, waited for Matchdown Park C.I.D. to answer.

Inspector Ulph was a small spare man with a prominent hooky nose and olive skin. David always tried to find counterparts in art for living human beings. He had likened Susan Townsend to Millais' portrait of Effie Ruskin, Magdalene Heller had about her something of a Lely or even a Goya, and this policeman reminded him of portraits he had seen of Mozart. Here was the same sensitive mouth, the look of suffering assuaged by an inner strength, the eyes that could invite and laugh at esoteric jokes. His hair was not as long as Mozart's but it was longer than is usual in a policeman, and when he was a boy it had no doubt been the silky pale brown of the lock David had seen preserved at Salzburg.

For his part, Ulph saw a tall lean young man, intelligent-looking, not particularly handsome, whose eager eyes for a moment took ten years off his age. He poured out an impulsive story and Ulph listened to it, not showing the excitement which the name of North had at first evoked. What had he expected to hear? Not this. Disappointment succeeded his small elation and he stalled, summing his visitor up. Only one sharp pinpoint of his original excitement remained, and he left it glimmering to say briskly:

'You're telling me that Mr North and Mrs Heller have been meeting, to your certain knowledge, at a London public house called The Man in the Iron Mask? Meeting there at regular intervals before her husband and his wife died?'

David nodded emphatically. He had hoped for a sharper reaction than this. 'Yes, I am. It may be far-fetched, but I think they met there to plot, conspire, if you like, to kill the others and make their deaths look like suicide.'

'Indeed?' Ulph's eyebrows had gone up. No one looking at him now would have supposed him to be a man obsessed by thoughts of a gun and a subtly contrived exit. He looked as if David's suspicions, the bare idea that North might be anything but totally innocent, were a revelation to him.

'I'm sure he did it,' David said impulsively, 'and if he did it she must have been in it too. Only she could have told him when Heller would arrive at Braeside and only she could have given him the gun. I visited Heller's flat the night before he died and I saw the gun. Later I saw her go into a cinema. I think North was inside that cinema, waiting for her to hand him the gun in the dark.'

The gun. This was the only way, Ulph thought, that North could have got it. Not by burglary, not by the unimaginable sleight of hand necessary to filching it from Heller himself, but through a conspiracy with Heller's wife. Immediately he saw pitfalls and he said, 'You say North and Mrs Heller first met at this pub in August?'

'Yes, I think it was this way. Bernard Heller had met Mrs North, fallen in love with her, started this affair of theirs, and North found out about it. So he got in touch with Magdalene Heller.' David paused and drew a deep breath. He was beginning to feel proud of himself again. His theory was forming as he spoke and it sounded good to him. 'They arranged to meet and discuss—well, the wrong that is being done them. For a while they don't do anything more. Bernard tried to commit suicide in September—I read that in the paper—and it must have shaken them. But when he took up with Louise again, they went on with their meetings and decided to kill the others.'

It was so full of holes, so remote from life as Ulph knew it, that he almost laughed. But then he remembered that, absurd as this theory was, a farrago of nonsense, he owed to it the one clue he had as to how North had come into possession of the gun, and he only sighed. The proper study of man is mankind, he thought, and he wondered how anyone as intelligent, as articulate and as alert as this man who confronted him, could have lived nearly thirty years on this earth yet be so blind to man's cautiousness and the pull convention exerts over his conduct.

He said gently, 'Listen to me, Mr Chadwick.' For this, he thought, is going to be quite a long speech. 'An ordinary middle-class quantity surveyor discovers that his wife is unfaithful to him. There are several things he can do. He can discuss it with her; he can discuss it with the man; he can divorce her.' Under the desk he felt his hands begin to clench and he relaxed them. Hadn't he done all these things himself? 'He can do violence to one or both of them, kill her, kill them both. Also he might just contact the wife of his wife's lover and reveal his discovery.

'This last is a possibility. You or I,' Ulph said, 'you or I might not do it, but it has been done. The innocent pair confront the guilty pair. More violence or more discussion follows. What the innocent pair do not do is meet in a pub and plot a murder. Strangers to each other? Knowing nothing of each other's emotions, propensities, characters? Can you hear it? Can you see it?'

Ulph began to speak in a tone quite unlike his natural voice, boyishly, impulsively. Was this North's manner of speech? David had no idea. He had never heard it. '"We both hate them, Mrs Heller, and want to be rid of them. Suppose we make a foolproof plan to kill them? Suppose we plan it together?"' But Magdalene's voice he did know and he flinched a little, so uncanny was Ulph's imitation of her long vowels and her sibilants. '"What a lovely idea, Mr North! Shall I help you work it all out?"'

David smiled in spite of himself. 'Not in those words, of course, but something like that.'

'Wouldn't she have run from him? Called the police? Are you saying that two people, brought together only because their marriage partners were lovers, found in each other a complementary homicidal urge? It says much for your virtue. You've evidently never tried to involve a stranger in a conspiracy.'

But he had. Only two days ago he had attempted just that with Susan Townsend. He had gone to a stranger in the absurd hope she would help him to hunt North down. Why hadn't he learned? Recent experience should have taught him that people don't behave like that.

'Suppose I go back to the pub,' he said diffidently. Was that amusement in Ulph's eyes? 'Suppose I get the names of those two men?'

'As long as you don't get yourself into trouble, Mr Chadwick.'

David walked slowly out of the police station. He felt humiliated, cut down to size by Ulph's expertise. And yet Ulph had only shown him that his reasoning had been at fault. He had done nothing to alter David's conviction of North's guilt or diminish the growing certainty that North was pursuing Susan Townsend to find out how much she knew.

14

It was just his luck that Sid and Charles weren't in The Man in the Iron Mask tonight. Perhaps they never came in on Thursdays. He couldn't remember whether he had ever been there on a Thursday himself before. Certainly he couldn't remember any occasion when he had been there and they hadn't. He hung about until eight and then he went home.

On the following night all the regulars were there, the middle-aged couple, the old actor, the girl with the mauve fingernails and her boy-friend, this time wearing a Battle of Waterloo tricorne hat, everyone but Sid and Charles. David waited, watching the clock, the door, and at last he asked the barman.

'Those two bearded characters, d'you mean?'

'That's right,' David said. 'You called them comedians. There's something I wanted to see them about.'

'I doubt if you'll see them in here.' The barman looked at him meaningfully, setting down the glass he had been polishing. 'Keep it under your hat, but I had a bit of a ding-dong with them yesterday lunchtime. Always money, money, money with them it was. Like a disease. The very first time they came in here they started on me about giving wrong change, over-charging, that sort of guff.' He lowered his voice. 'You wouldn't believe the insinuations. Well, yesterday I'd had about enough. Get the police if you're not satisfied, I said. We've nothing to hide. I'm within my rights to refuse to serve you, I said, and if you come back tomorrow I will.'

'The same sort of thing happened to them last August at The Rose,' David said hopelessly.

'I shouldn't be at all surprised. I'm right in thinking they're not friends of yours, aren't I?'

'I don't even know their names.'

'A pub crawl,' said Pamela Pearce. 'Well, I don't know, darling. It could be dreary.'

'There are two chaps I want to find. I've got to find them.'

'I suppose they owe you money.'

'No, they don't,' David said crossly. 'It's much more serious than that, but I'd rather not explain. Come on now, it might be fun having a drink in every pub in Soho.'

'Intoxicating. Still, I don't mind if it's Soho. But, darling, it's pouring with rain!'

'So what? You can wear your new raincoat.'

'That's a thought,' said Pamela, and when he came to pick her up she was glittering in silver crocodile skin.

At Tottenham Court Road tube station he said, 'They've both got beards and their conversation is almost exclusively concerned with money.'

'Is that all you've got to go on?'

He nodded and avoided meeting her eyes. It had occurred to him that Sid and Charles, when at last run to earth, would certainly make cracks about his concern to find a striking-looking dark girl, his ex-secretary. Pamela knew very well he had never had a secretary. Strange that this didn't worry him at all.

They would go first to The Man in the Iron Mask. There was just a chance some of the other regulars might remember North and Magdalene. But David doubted this. He had been a regular too, but he had no recollection of ever having seen the couple—the conspirators? The lovers?—until the inquest day. Did Sid and Charles only remember because like the majority of men they had been susceptible to Magdalene's beauty?

He must find them.

Pamela walked along beside him in silence while the rain fell softly and steadily through grey vapour.

It was Sunday and Julian Townsend was taking his son out for the day. Hand in hand they walked down the path towards the parked car. Susan watched them go, amused because the Airedale who only barked at unknown interlopers, had suddenly begun to roar at Julian. He had become a stranger.

She shrugged and went indoors. In the hall glass her reflection walked to meet her and she stopped to admire herself, the fair hair that had a new gloss on it, the grey eyes alight with happy anticipation, the new suit she had plundered her bank balance to buy. The fee from Miss Willingale could be used to make that good, for she had only four more chapters to complete.

Bob's footsteps sounded in the sideway. No more formal front door calling for him. Susan looked at the mirrored girl and saw in her face pleasure at the new intimacy, the beginning of taking things for granted.

She went to meet him a little shyly. He came in and took her in his arms without a word. His kiss was long, slow, expert, almost shocking in its effect on her. But they were only friends, she told herself, friends in need, each other's comforters. She broke away from him, shaken, unwilling to meet his eyes.

'Bob, I . . . Wait for me a moment. I have to get my gloves, my bag.'

Upstairs the gloves and the bag were ready where she had left them on the dressing table. She sat down heavily on the bed and stared at the sky, hard blue this morning, at the elms that swayed lazily, seeing nothing. Her hands were shaking and she flexed them, trying to control the muscles. Until now she had thought that the year passed without a man, a lover, had been nearly insupportable on account of the lack of companionship and the pain of rejection. Now she knew that as much as this she had missed sexual passion.

He was waiting for her at the foot of the stairs. She remembered how the girl in Harrow had turned to look at him, how Doris had spoken of his looks and his charm, and these opinions, the spoken and unspoken views of other women, seemed suddenly to enhance him even more in her eyes. All but his own wife were overpowered by that physical presence, that quintessence of all that a man should be and should look like. She thought of his wife fleetingly now as she came down towards him. Why had this one woman been impervious, indifferent?

He smiled at her, holding out his hands. There was something shameful in wanting a man because of his looks and because—ugly, shameful thought—you wanted a man. She came closer and this time it was she who put out her arms to him and held her face up to be kissed.

'We'll have lunch,' he said, 'in a little country pub I know. I've always liked little pubs.'

She held his hand, smiling up at him. 'Have you, Bob?'

He said nervously, 'Why did you say it like that? Why do you look like that?'

'I don't know. I didn't mean to.' She didn't know, nor did she know why Heller and Heller's widow had suddenly come into her mind. 'Let's make a pact,' she said quickly, 'not to talk about Heller or Louise while we're out today.'

'God,' he said, and she felt him sigh as briefly he held her against him, 'I don't want to talk about them.' He touched her hair and she trembled a little when she felt his fingers move lightly against her skin. Her relief should have matched his own, but she felt only a vague dismay. Had they anything else to talk about, anything at all in common? There was something painfully humiliating in the thought which had crept into her mind. That instead of going out with him she would have preferred to stay here like this, holding him, touching her cheek to his, in an eternal moment of warmth and of desire. Outside this room they would have, it seemed to her, no existence as a pair, as friends.

The sharp bright air shocked her as if out of a dream. She walked ahead of him to his car and she was appalled at herself, like someone who had committed an indiscretion at a party and now, in the light of day, is afraid to face both his neighbours and his partner in that fall from grace.

Doris looked out of her window and waved. Betty looked up from her gardening to smile at them. It was as if she and Bob were going off on their honeymoon, Susan thought, and the pink cherry petals fell on to her hair and her shoulders like confetti on a bride. She got into the car beside him and then she remembered how harsh he had been with her the day he had driven her to Harrow, violent almost as he drove deliberately fast to frighten her. It was the same man. He smiled at her, lifted her hand and kissed the fingers. But she didn't know him at all, she knew nothing about him.

Whatever she said it would come back to Heller. It always did. But she had promised not to mention him or Louise and now she realised that although Bob himself would do so and derive a strange comfort from the tragedy, he became uneasy if she took the initiative herself. It was as if the double suicide was his private possession that no one, not even she, might uncover and look at without his permission.

The idea was very disagreeable to her. He was thinking about it now. She could see it in his face. For the first time she put into silent words what she had known since that other drive in this car with him. He thought about it all the time, day and night without rest.

She must talk to him about something. 'How are you getting on with Mrs Dring?' she asked desperately.

'All right. It was good of you to persuade her, Susan, sweet of you.'

'She can only come on Saturdays?'

'Yes, when I'm there.' He took one hand from the wheel, touched her arm. Not from desire, she thought, not out of affection. Perhaps simply to assure himself that she was really there. Then he said, his voice very low, as if they were not alone in a car but walking in a crowded street were anyone could hear unless he whispered, 'She talks to me about it. I try to keep away from her, but every chance she can, she talks to me about it.'

'She's rather thoughtless,' Susan said gently.

He set his mouth, but not defiantly. He was controlling the trembling of his lips. 'She opens the windows,' he said.

And thereby let fresh air and sound into the secret thing he kept there? Susan suddenly felt cold in the stuffy car whose heater blew out a hot breeze. In a monotone, low yet rapid, he began to tell her about the questions Mrs Dring had asked him, of her maudlin tactless sympathy.

'I'll have a word with her.'

But he hardly seemed to hear her. Once more he had returned to that morning, to his arrival at Baeside, to the couple on the bed. And, pitying him, not wanting him to know she was also a little afraid, Susan put her hand on his arm and rested it there.

'I couldn't find them,' David said. Ulph's expression was that of an indulgent father listening to a child's tall stories. Perhaps he had never really believed in the existence of Sid and Charles. He made David feel like a crank, one of those people who go to the police with wild accusations because they want to make mischief or attract attention to themselves. And it was on account of this that he said no more of his quest with Pamela Pearce, of their visits to eighteen different pubs, of the perpetually repeated enquiries, all in vain. Nor, naturally, did he say anything of their subsequent quarrel when their tempers were frayed by frustration and the incessant rain.

'I should think they work in the City,' he said, feeling foolish. 'We could try the Stock Exchange or Lloyds, or something.'

'Certainly *you* could try, Mr Chadwick.'

'You mean you won't? You wouldn't put a man on it?'

'To what end? Do any of the other regulars at this pub remember seeing Mr North and Mrs Heller there?' David shook his head. 'From what you have told me of their conduct, your two bearded acquaintances aren't remarkable for their probity. Mr Chadwick, can you be sure they weren't—well, having you on?'

This time David nodded stubbornly. Ulph shrugged, tapping his fingers lightly on the desk. He too had much in his mind his professional discretion prevented him from revealing. There was no reason to tell this obstinate man how, since his last visit, North and Mrs Heller had again been separately questioned and had emphatically denied any knowledge of the other prior to the suicides. Ulph believed them. Mrs Heller's brother-in-law and Mrs Heller's neighbours all knew Robert North by now. They knew him as the kind benefactor who had first shown his face in East Mulvihill five days after the tragedy.

And, because of this, Ulph had lost his faith in David's theory as to the gun. He still believed in North's guilt, still had before his eyes that moving picture of North's actions on that Wednesday morning. But he had acquired the gun some other way. Ulph didn't know how, nor did he know how North had got out of the house. Answers to these questions would help him to get the case reopened, not unfounded theories as to a conspiracy.

'You see, Mr Chadwick,' he said patiently, 'not only do you have no real evidence of conspiracy existing, you have no theory to convince me such a conspiracy would be necessary. Mrs Heller offered her husband a divorce when she first discovered his infidelity and only failed to petition because for a time he wanted them to try to keep their marriage going. He couldn't have prevented her divorcing him as the guilty party. It wasn't even as if he tried to conceal the truth from her. He loved Mrs North, was committing adultery with her, and he told his wife so. As to North, he might have committed a crime of passion from jealousy or hurt pride. That's a very different matter from conspiring for months with a comparative stranger. His anger would cool in that time. Why take the enormous risk premeditated murder entails when with all the evidence he had, he too had only to seek a divorce?'

He said no more. Show me, he thought, how this man in the jealousy and the rage I can understand came into possession of a gun he could not have possessed and left a house unseen.

She had invited him often enough and yet, he thought, she would be dismayed to see him. By now North would have told her of his visit to Matchdown Park. He stood on the doorstep for a second or two, hesitating, before he pressed the bell. The red and yellow glare from the neon signs, the passing buses, rippled and flickered on the peeling wall and the chalk graffiti.

It was the brother-in-law who let him into the flat. In the half-dark it might have been Bernard Heller and not Carl on whose face the slow smile dawned, Bernard who stood aside to let him enter.

The flat smelt of greens and gravy. They had shared a meal and the dirty plates were still on the table. Magdalene Heller was standing against the wall underneath the mandoline, an unlighted cigarette in her fingers.

'I thought it was time I looked you up,' David said, and with a sense of rightness, of retribution, of destiny almost, he stepped forward with his lighter. The flame threw violet shadows on her face and her eyes widened. She said nothing for a moment but David felt that she too recalled the parallel forerunner of this scene and had, as he had, a sense of having been there before. He half-expected her to glance quickly over her shoulder, searching for North's face. She sat down, crossing her long beautiful legs.

'How are you getting on?'

'All right.' Her gruffness, her gracelessness almost, reminded him a little of Elizabeth Townsend. But whereas Mrs Townsend's sprang from the confidence born of background, upbringing, connections, Magdalene's was the attitude of a woman sure of her own beauty, of the lily that needs no gilding.

It was Carl who said, 'People have been very kind, Mr North most of all.' David fancied that the girl stiffened a little at the name. 'He's lent Magdalene money to tide her over.' Carl smiled bovinely as if to say, There, what do you think of that? 'More like an old friend,' he said, and when David slightly raised his eyebrows, 'The police even came here and asked Magdalene if she'd known him before.'

David's heart seemed to run a little, to trip. So Ulph *was* interested. . . . 'But of course she hadn't,' he said innocently.

Magdalene crushed out her cigarette. 'Why don't you put the coffee on, Carl?'

While Bernard's twin lumbered off to do her bidding, she fixed David with those green eyes in which the gold specks, particles of metal dust, moved sluggishly. 'Tell me something.' Her accent was strong tonight. 'Did Bernard ever tell you how he met that woman?'

'He told me nothing,' David said. 'How did they meet?'

'It was last August in Matchdown Park. She was in a friend's house and he came to fit a spare part to the heating. She'd been ill and she had a bad turn so he said he'd drive her home. That was how it started.'

Why are you telling me this? he wondered. The words had been bare, almost all monosyllabic.

'He told me it all,' she said. 'Bob North didn't know a thing. I had to tell him. It's not surprising, is it, we got together after the inquest? We had plenty to tell each other.'

'But the police somehow believe you and North had met before?'

Pure hatred flashed briefly in her eyes. She knew why the police had questioned her and who had alerted them, but she dared not say. 'I never set eyes on Bob till three weeks ago,' she said brusquely, tossing her head so that the black hair swept her shoulders. 'I'm not worried. Why should I be?'

'No coffee for me,' David said when Carl came in with the tray. He had a strong revulsion against eating or drinking anything in this flat and he rose. 'I suppose *Equatair* have given you something?' he said baldly, for there was no longer any question of impertinence or of tact between him and her. The memory of her full pink mouth pressed against his skin sickened him.

'Precious little,' she said.

'I don't suppose it was easy for them getting someone to go to Switzerland in Bernard's place.' David turned to look at Carl. 'Not in your line, I suppose?'

'I speak the language, Mr Chadwick, but, no, I am not clever like Bernard was. I shall go to Switzerland for my usual holiday. I was born there and my relatives are there.'

Magdalene poured her coffee very slowly as if she were afraid her hands would shake and betray her. Suddenly David felt sure he must keep in touch with her brother-in-law. Once before he had failed to secure an address. He nodded to the widow, keeping his hands behind his back, and he met her sullen eyes before following Carl into the hall.

'I may go to Switzerland myself,' he said when they were out of earshot, side by side, almost touching in the narrow passage. 'If I wanted a bit of advice . . . well, would you let me have your address?'

Carl's sad face lit with pleasure. He looked a man whose counsel is seldom sought. David gave him a pen and an old envelope on which he wrote in a long sloping hand his address and a landlady's phone number.

'Any time, Mr Chadwick.' He opened the door, peered out. 'I thought we might have the pleasure of seeing Mr North tonight,' he said. 'Once or twice I've been here when he has called to see Magdalene. But he is a busy man and his neighbours take up so much of his time. . . .'

His neighbours. One neighbour, David thought. He crossed the street and as he slipped the envelope into his pocket his hand touched the card he had bought in the National Gallery. Under a street lamp he stopped to look at it. Was North with her now? Was North making love to her, just as Magdalene Heller had tried to make love to him, David, and for the same reason?

She was very lovely, this girl that Millais had painted, had wrested from Ruskin and had finally married. Susan Townsend was exactly like her, as like as Carl was to Bernard. It might have been her photograph which, bent and a little soiled now, David carried with him in his pocket. He wondered how he would feel if, instead of buying it, he had received it from her as a gift.

At East Mulvihill station he bought his ticket and then, swiftly, before he had time to dwell too much on what he was about to do, he went into a phone box.

15

'Mrs Townsend, this is David Chadwick. Please don't ring off.' Did his voice sound as intense to her as it seemed to him? 'I wanted to talk to you. I couldn't just leave things.'

'Well?' It could be a warm word, a word denoting health or things excellently done, but she made it the coldest in the world. On her lips it was onomatopoeic, a well indeed, a place of deep, dark and icy waters.

'I haven't phoned to talk of—what I mentioned to you last week. I don't intend to discuss Mr North.'

'That's good, because I wouldn't discuss him.' She was neither scathing nor hectoring. It was hard to say what she was. Iron-firm, implacable, remote.

'It was appalling what I did last week and I apologise profoundly. Can you understand when I say I want to see you and explain that I'm not a lout or a practical joker? Mrs Townsend, would you have dinner with me?'

Unable to see her, he couldn't define the atmosphere of her silence. Then she said, but not scornfully, '*Of course not*,' and she laughed. In her laughter he detected neither mockery nor outrage. She wasn't even amused. She was incredulous.

'Lunch, then,' he persisted. 'In some big crowded restaurant where I couldn't—couldn't frighten you.'

'I was frightened.'

In that moment he fell in love with her. Until then it had been a silly dream. Why had he been such a fool as to telephone and create for himself in five minutes a load of sorrow?

'I was frightened,' she said again, 'because I was alone and it was dark.' Again the silence fell and the pips sounded, remote, careless of what they terminated. He had his coin ready, his breathless question.

'Are you still there?'

Her voice was brisk now. 'This is rather a ridiculous conversation, don't you think? I expect you acted in good faith and it doesn't matter now, anyway. But we don't really know each other at all and the only thing we could talk about—well, I wouldn't talk about it.'

'It isn't the only thing,' he said fiercely. 'I can think of a hundred things just offhand like that.'

'Good-bye, Mr Chadwick.'

He went down the escalator and when he was alone in the passage that led to the platform he dropped the picture card to be trampled underfoot in the morning rush.

She was almost sure Bob hadn't overheard that conversation, but when she returned to the living-room he lifted his eyes and they had a haunted look. Should she lie to him, tell him it was someone the agent had put on to her, a prospective buyer of the house?

'I heard,' he said. 'It was that fellow Chadwick.'

'Only to ask me out to dinner,' she said soothingly. 'I shan't go. Of course, I shan't.'

'What does he want, Susan? What's he getting at?'

'Nothing. Don't, Bob, you're hurting me.' His hands which were so soft when they stroked her cheek, seemed to crush the bones in her wrists. 'Sit down. You were saying, before he phoned . . . ?'

The hard fingers relaxed. 'About Louise,' he said. 'I was telling you how she and Heller met and how he drove her home. Magdalene Heller's told me the whole story. After that they used to meet when I had to work late.' His voice was feverish, desperate. 'In cafés, in pubs. He got in such a state he tried to kill himself. I wish to God he'd succeeded then. He started writing those horrible letters to her . . . Susan, you *did* burn those letters, didn't you?'

She was past caring now whether she told the truth to him or lied. What, anyway, was the truth? 'I burnt them, Bob.'

'Why can't I forget it all, put it behind me? You think I'm going mad. Yes, you do, Susan, I can see it in your face.'

She put her head in her hands, running her fingers through

her hair. 'Keep away from Mrs Heller, if she upsets you,' she said presently. 'You've done enough for her.'

'What d'you mean?'

'You've given her money, haven't you?'

He sighed and he sounded infinitely weary. 'I'd like to get away, go far away. Oh, Susan, if only I didn't have to go back to that house tonight! Or ever again to see Magdalene Heller.' He paused and said as if he were stating something profound, yet at the same time novel and appalling, 'I don't ever want to see Magdalene Heller again.'

'Nor me, Bob?' Susan asked gently.

'You? It would have been better if I'd never met you, never seen you . . .' He got up and his face was as white and strained as if he were ill or really demented. 'I love you, Susan.' His arms went round her and, his lips almost touching hers, he said, 'One day, when I'm—when I'm better and all this is past, will you marry me?'

'I don't know,' she said blankly, but she kissed him on a long sigh and it seemed to her that no kiss had ever been so pleasurable and so sweet. 'It isn't the time yet, is it?' she said as their mouths parted and she looked up into that strained haunted face.

'There's the boy, I know,' he said urgently, reading her thoughts. 'He's frightened of me. That'll pass. We could all go away, couldn't we? Away from Mrs Dring and this Chadwick and—and Mrs Heller.'

The play for which David had designed the sets ended and the credit titles came up. He thought he might as well watch the news. The first item was the result of some West Country by-election which interested him not at all and he had got up to turn it off when he stopped, intrigued by the voice of a speaker who had suddenly replaced the announcer. That lilting intonation, those stressed r's were familiar. He had heard them before that evening on the lips of Magdalene Heller. Her accent, far less strong than that of the commentator, had always puzzled him and now he located it at last. She came from Devon.

Immediately he remembered the newspaper picture of

Robert and Louise North. That had been taken in Devon while they were holidaying there last year. Did it mean anything or nothing?

Very carefully he repeated in his mind the conversation he had had with Magdalene two hours before and it seemed strange to him that she had taken such pains to tell him how her husband and Louise North had met. Because the circumstances of that meeting caused her real distress, or because in fact they had not met that way at all? Of course it was possible that Bernard had driven her home because she was unwell, had promised perhaps to enquire after her subsequently, and that from this beginning their love affair had grown. But wasn't it far more likely that they had all met on holiday?

Once more David felt excitement stir. Suppose they had met, the two couples, in an hotel or on a beach? Then, when Louise and Bernard returned respectively to Matchdown Park and East Mulvihill, intending to follow up the attraction which had already begun, the last thing they would have done was talk to friends or neighbours of this apparently brief holiday acquaintance. But North and Magdalene would have a knowledge of each other, a shared memory which, however casual, would make their later meetings natural.

In this case North might well have contacted Magdalene to disclose his wife's conduct, or Magdalene him to reveal Bernard's. Even Ulph, David thought, wouldn't find anything fantastic in such a supposition.

He hesitated for a moment and then he dialled Carl Heller's number. The landlady answered. Mr Heller had just come home from his sister-in-law's, he was taking off his coat at this moment. The telephone slightly distorted his voice, making it more guttural.

'There is nothing wrong, I hope, Mr Chadwick?'

'No, no,' David said. 'It was just that I thought of going to Switzerland for a few days at Easter and it occurred to me you might be able to recommend somewhere to stay.'

Carl began to reel off a list of names and places. He sounded almost animated, over-helpful, as Bernard had been when asked favours. And David recalled how this man's dead brother, when asked tentatively for the loan of a fireplace, had pressed on him not one but a dozen of the latest models. Thus Carl, instead of naming a couple of *pensions*, selected from his memory hotels and tourist centres in every Swiss canton, pausing only for David to make, or pretend to make, copious notes.

'That'll do fine,' David said when Carl drew breath. 'I suppose your brother and his wife often stayed at this one?' And he named a modest hotel at Meiringen.

'My brother never went back to Switzerland after he was married. He was trying, he told me, to become like an Englishman and he dropped all his continental ways. He and Magdalene had their holidays in England, in Devon where Magdalene comes from.'

'Really?'

'That is why I was so pleased for them, for the Zürich appointment. Wait till you see real mountains, I said to Magdalene. But then my brother does this wicked thing and . . .' Carl's heavy sigh vibrated through the earpiece. 'It is a funny thing, Mr Chadwick, it will amuse you, although in a way it is sad. Always in Devon they are staying in the same place at Bathcombe Ferrers, and the place they stay at it is a small *pension* called—what do you think?—the Swiss Chalet. Often my brother and I have laughed about this. But you are a great traveller, I know, and would not be content with such a place. No, you must go to Brunnen or maybe Lucerne. Mount Pilatus now—you have it on your list like I have told you? You have the name. . . .'

In his hand David had only the soiled envelope on which Carl had written his address and now, feeling a little ashamed of the deceit he had practised, he wrote beside it just five words.

16

A rustic sign with its name burnt on in pokerwork informed him that he had arrived. Nothing else gave a clue as to why this place had been named 'The Swiss Chalet'. It was an Edwardian house, three storeys high with scarcely any visible roof. A superabundance of drain-pipes, tangled like creeper, climbed all over its façade.

The entrance was through a conservatory full of pots of Busy Lizzie. David opened the inner glass door and found himself in a hall that in colour and decoration might have been the subject of a nineteenth-century sepia photograph. He approached a cubby-hole in the wall which reminded him of a ticket office window at an almost totally disused station. On its shelf stood a bell, a brass bell painted with edelweiss and the name Lucerne. Honour was satisfied. In the Swiss Chalet there was at least one genuinely Swiss object.

Its shrill-throated ring brought a little round woman from a door marked Private. David stuck his head through the aperture, wondering if this was how it had felt to be put in the stocks. The woman advanced aggressively upon him as if she might at any moment throw a rotten egg or a tomato.

'Chadwick,' he said hastily. 'From London. I booked a room.'

The threatening look faded but she didn't smile. He put her age at just over sixty. Her hair was dyed to the shade of coconut matting, which it also resembled in texture, and she wore a mauve knitted twinset, a miracle of cable stitch and bobbles and loops.

'Pleased to meet you,' she said. 'It's Mrs Spiller you talked to on the phone.' She wasn't a native. Retired here perhaps in the hope of making a fortune. He glanced at the pitch-pine woodwork in need of revarnishing, the lamp in its bakelite shade, the visitors' book she pushed towards him whose emptiness told of failure. 'Room number eight.' He put out his hand for the key. Outrage settled in a crease on her purplish forehead. 'We don't have no keys,' she said. 'You can bolt your door if you're particular. Breakfast's at eight sharp, dinner at one and I do a high tea at six.' David picked up his suitcase. 'Up two flights.' She bobbed out from under a hinged flap. 'The first door on your left. The lav's in the bathroom, so don't hang about washing too long. There's such a thing as consideration.'

Consideration for whom? he wondered. The season had scarcely begun and the place seemed dead. It was ten past eleven, but Mrs Spiller seemed to have forgotten her last exhortation, for as he mounted the stairs, she bellowed after him:

'You never said who recommended me.'

'A friend,' David said. 'A Mrs Heller.'

'Not little Mag?'

'Mrs Magdalene Heller. That's right.'

'Well, why didn't you say so before?'

Because he had thought he must come round to it subtly, with cunning and by degrees.

'You *are* a dark horse. I bet you'd never have said if I hadn't asked. I read all about her tragedy in the papers. It upset me properly, I can tell you. I've got the kettle on. Would you like a cuppa before you turn in? That's right. You leave them bags and I'll get my boy to take them up.'

Things were going well, far better than he had expected. There was one question he must ask. Her answer would make the difference between his staying the whole weekend or leaving in the morning. 'Of course, she was here only last year, wasn't she?'

'That's right, in July. End of July. Now you pop into the lounge and make yourself comfy.'

The room was small and shabby. It smelt of geranium leaves and fly spray. Mrs Spiller shut the door on him and went off to fetch the tea. Sitting down, he wondered how often Magdalene had sat in the same chair. Suppose the

Norths had stayed here too and the first encounter between Bernard and Louise had been in this very room? He contemplated the décor with his critical designer's eye, the potted plants, the wedding group on an upright piano, the snowstorm in a glass dome. Two pictures faced him, a water colour of Plymouth Hoe and a nasty little lithograph of some central European city. There was another picture in the corner, half hidden by a mahogany plant stand. He got up to look more closely and his heart gave a little jerk. What more suited to this mid-Victorian room than Millais' *Order of Delease*? Susan Townsend looked through him and beyond, her mouth tilted, her eyes cool, distant, indifferent.

Before driving down here, he had done a strange, perhaps a foolish, thing. He had sent her a dozen white roses. Would she look like that when she received them, her expression changing from cold politeness as she closed the door to disgust?

'Sugar?' said Mrs Spiller into his right ear.

He jumped, almost knocking the teacup out of her hand.

'Bit nervy, aren't you? A couple of days down here will set you up. Very bracing, Bathcombe is.'

'It always does Magdalene a world of good,' David said.

'Just as well. You need your health to face up to what she's been through. What a terrible thing, him doing himself in like that, wasn't it? I've often asked myself what was at the back of it all.' Not as often as he had, David thought, sipping the hot sweet tea. 'You being their friend, you must know what triggered it all off. You needn't mind telling me. I'm not exaggerating when I say I was more or less one of the family. Year after year Mr Chant used to bring little Mag here for their holidays and Mag always called me Auntie Vi.'

'Still does,' David said stoutly. 'She often talks about her Auntie Vi.' But who was Mr Chant? Her father, of course. In the newspaper bundling his slide projector had been the announcement of Heller's wedding, Bernard Heller to Miss Magdalene Chant.

'Yes,' said Mrs Spiller, reminiscing, 'she'd been coming here with her dad since she was so high and she knows all the locals. Ask anyone in the village if they remember little Mag Chant pushing her dad about in his wheelchair. Well, not his. They used to borrow one from old Mr Lilybeer and she'd take him down to the beach. Her and Bernard, they came here for their honeymoon and then most years after that.'

'I don't suppose that Mrs North ever stopped here?'

'North?' Mrs Spiller considered and her face reddened. 'Are you referring to that woman as was Bernard's fancy piece, by any chance?' David nodded. 'She certainly did not. Whatever gave you that idea?'

'Nothing really,' David began.

'I should think not indeed. He must have been out of his mind chasing a woman like that when he had a lovely girl of his own. All the local boys was after Mag when she was in her teens, or would have been if her father'd given them half a chance.'

'I can imagine,' David said soothingly, but he was aware that for the time being at least he had spoiled the hopeful *rapport* between himself and Mrs Spiller. She was staunchly Magdalene's ally, as if she were really her aunt, and she took his introduction of Louise North's name as criticism of this adopted niece, of her beauty, her desirability. 'I think Magdalene's exceptionally good-looking.'

But Mrs Spiller was not to be so easily mollified. 'I'm off up the wooden hill,' she said and she gave him an aggrieved frown. 'You can have the telly on if you want.'

'A bit cold for that.' The room was unheated and a vaseful of wax flowers had been placed in the grate.

'I never light no fires after April the first,' said Mrs Spiller sharply.

He had discovered one thing. The Norths had not only not stayed at the Swiss Chalet at the same time as Bernard and Magdalene. They had never stayed there at all. But they had been better off than the Hellers and perhaps they had stayed at one of the hotels in the village.

David breakfasted alone off cornflakes, eggs and bacon and very pale thick toast. He had finished and was leaving the dining-room when the only other residents appeared, a dour-looking man and a middle-aged woman in tight trousers. The woman eyed David silently while helping herself from the sideboard to four bottles of different kinds of sauce.

It was a cool cloudy morning, sunless and still. He found a path between pines which brought him within ten minutes to the top of a cliff. The sea was calm, grey and with a silver sheen. Between two headlands he saw a pointed heathy island rising out of the sea and he identified it from Turner's painting as the Mewstone. This association of nature with art again evoked Susan Townsend's face, and it was in a depressed frame of mind that he set off for the village.

At the Great Western Hotel he ordered morning coffee and was shown into a wintry lounge. The place was as yet barely prepared for visitors. Through a large curved bay window he could see a one-man manually punted ferry that plied between the Bathcombe shore and a tiny beach on the opposite side.

'A friend of mine, a Mr North,' he said to the waitress who came for the bill, 'stayed here at the end of July last year, and when he heard I was coming down he asked me if I'd enquire about a book he left in his room.'

'He's left it a long time,' said the girl pertly.

'He wouldn't have bothered only he knew I was coming down.'

'And what would this said book be called?'

'*Sesame and Lilies*,' said David because he kept thinking of Susan Townsend who was Ruskin's wife all over again. With what he thought must be a mad smile, he left all his change from a ten shilling note on his plate.

'I will enquire,' said the girl more pleasantly.

David watched the ferryman come to the Bathcombe shore. He unloaded a cargo of empty squash bottles in a crate. Possibly the single cottage on the other side was a guesthouse. Come to that, the Norths could have rented a cottage here or a flat or stayed with friends. They might not have come in July, they might not have come to this part of Devon at all.

The girl came back, looking sour. 'Your friend didn't leave that gardening book of his here,' she said. 'He didn't even stay here. I've checked with the register. You'd better try the Palace or the Rock.'

But the Norths hadn't stayed at either place. David crossed the inlet by the ferry to find that the solitary house was a youth hostel.

Shepherd's pie and queen of puddings was served at the Swiss Chalet for luncheon. 'Well, did you meet anyone who knows Mag?' asked Mrs Spiller when she came in to serve him instant coffee and pre-sliced processed cheese.

'I hardly saw a soul.'

The coconut matting curls bounced and all the bobbles on the lilac jumper quivered. 'If it's excitement you want, I don't know why you didn't settle for Plymouth. Folks come to Bathcombe to get a bit of peace.'

Suppose the Norths had 'settled for' Plymouth? They might have come to Bathcombe just once for a day's outing. But would a passionate love affair have arisen from one isolated encounter on a beach? David couldn't picture slow, stolid Bernard, his deck-chair moved alongside Louise's, exchanging addresses surreptitiously.

'I'm not complaining,' he lied. 'It's a charming place.'

Mrs Spiller sat down and put her fat mauve elbows on the table.

'That's what Mr Chant always used to say. "It's a charming place, Mrs Spiller. You get real peace and quiet here," he'd say, and him coming from Exeter where it's not what you'd call rowdy, is it? By the way, I've been meaning to ask you, how's Auntie Agnes?'

'Auntie Agnes?'

'I'd have thought Mag would mention *her*. Not that you could blame Mag, a bit of a kid like her, but I've always thought she had a lot to thank Auntie Agnes for. But for her she never would have gone to London and got married.'

His mind wandering, David remarked that perhaps this wouldn't have been a bad thing.

'You've got something there.' Mrs Spiller passed him Marie biscuits from a packet. 'But she didn't know how it was all going to turn out, did she? I remember back in 1960 thinking to myself, that poor kid, she'll never have a proper life tied to an old man like that.'

'Mr Chant, you mean?' David said absently.

'Well, maybe I shouldn't call him old. I dare say he wasn't above fifty-five. But you know how it is with invalids. You always think of them as old, especially when they're crippled like Mr Chant was.'

'Arthritis or something, was it?'

'No, you've got it wrong there. Multiple sclerosis, that Auntie Agnes told me. She came down with them in 1960 and he was real bad then. Too much for Mag on her own.'

'I suppose so.' David wanted to get on with the hunt. He wasn't interested in diseases of the central nervous system and he was awaiting his chance to escape from Mrs Spiller.

'They're very slow in developing, them illnesses,' she was saying. 'You can have sclerosis for twenty or thirty years. Mind you, he had his good days. Sometimes he was nearly as good as you or me. But other times . . . It went right to my heart, I can tell you, watching that lovely girl pushing him about in a chair and her only in her teens.'

'Her mother was dead by then, I suppose?' David said, bored.

'That's what they used to tell people.' Mrs Spiller put her face closer to his and lowered her voice. The middle-aged couple sat some fifteen feet from them, looking out of the window, but Mrs Spiller's extreme caution implied that they were spies whose sole mission in visiting her guesthouse was to satisfy themselves as to certain unsolved mysteries in the Chants' family history. 'I got it all out of that Auntie Agnes,' she whispered. 'Mrs Chant had run off with someone when Mag was a kid. They never knew where she ended up. Saw what her life would be, I reckon, and got out when the going was good.'

'Like Magdalene.'

'A wife's one thing,' Mrs Spiller bristled. 'A daughter's quite another. When Auntie Agnes wrote and said Mag was going up to London to find herself a job I thought, that's the best thing that could happen. Let her have a bit of life while she's young enough to enjoy it, I thought. Of course, Auntie Agnes wasn't young, her being Mr Chant's own auntie really, and it's no joke looking after an invalid when you're past seventy.'

'No doubt she managed.'

'I don't reckon she looked ahead when she took it on. She wasn't to know Mag'd meet Bernard and write home she was getting engaged. Mind you, I never knew any of this till Mag and Bernard came down for their honeymoon. That was two years later and Mr Chant had passed on by then. That's why I asked if you knew what had become of Auntie Agnes. Dead and gone too, I dare say. It happens to all of us in the fullness of time, doesn't it?'

'Depends what you mean by the fullness of time,' said David and he thought of Bernard with a bullet through his head because he had loved unwisely.

Susan had begun on the last chapter of *Foetid Flesh* when Bob opened the back door and came in softly. She stopped typing at once, a little dismayed at the look on Paul's face. He had been trundling his cars between the legs of her chair, but now he squatted still and stiff and his expression would have seemed a mere blank to anyone but his mother who could read it.

'Where did the flowers come from, Susan?'

It was Paul who answered him. 'A man called David Chadwick. Roses are the most expensive thing you can send anyone in April.'

'I see.' Bob stood with his back to them, staring out of the window at the elms on which not a bud, not a vestige of green, showed. 'Chadwick . . . And daffodils are the cheapest, aren't they?'

'You picked your daffodils out of the garden.'

'All right, Paul. That's enough,' Susan said. 'It's not so long ago you said it was silly to send people flowers.' She smiled at Bob's back. 'And you were quite right,' she said firmly. 'I can see Richard outside. I expect he's wondering where you are.'

'Then why doesn't he call for me?' But Paul went, dodging the hand which Bob suddenly and pathetically put out to him. Susan took it instead and, standing beside him, again felt the physical pull he exerted over her, the attraction that emptied her mind and left her weary.

'Have you thought about what I asked you?'

For a moment her only answer was to press more tightly the hand she held. And then it came to her in a swift unpleasant revelation that this was her reply. Physical contact and then renewed, stronger physical contact was the only way she could get through to him. The closer intimacy which awaited them if they married would be just this pressure of hands on a full and complete scale, the desperate soulless coupling of two creatures in a desert.

She looked up at him. 'It's too soon, Bob.' His face was grey and drawn, no longer even handsome, and it was tenderness rather than desire that made her want to kiss him. She moved away, for suddenly her delaying answer had made kissing wrong. 'Come and sit down,' she said. 'You don't mind about the roses, do you? I don't know why he sent them.'

'Because he wants to know you better, of course. Susan, the world is full of men who'll want to know you better. That's why I have to—you have to . . . Susan, if I'd seen you as I see you now, when Louise was still alive, would you have . . . ?'

'When Louise was alive?'

'If I'd fallen in love with you then, would you have come away with me?'

She was afraid without knowing the reason for her fear, 'Of course I wouldn't, Bob. Even if you'd wanted to marry me then, Louise couldn't have divorced you. She was a Catholic.'

'My God,' he shouted, 'I know that!'

'Then, don't torment yourself.' She hesitated and said, 'I suppose you could have divorced her.' And would it have been different, would there have been true companionship for them without the spectre of Louise's death and Heller's between them, their sole wearisome topic of conversation? 'Yes, you could have done that,' she said tiredly.

'But I couldn't have done that,' he said, and his eyes had darkened from blue to a frightening impenetrable black. 'It's because I couldn't have done that . . . Oh, Susan, what's the use? It's past, gone for ever. Heller loved my wife and killed her and I ought to be free . . . Susan, I'll never be free!' He quietened, shivered, and gradually his face assumed the look it wore when he explored his obsession. 'Everyone persecutes me,' he said. 'The police have been here again. Didn't you hear that dog? The whole street must have seen.'

'But why, Bob?'

'I suppose your friend Chadwick put them on to me.' There was a sneer on the fine-drawn mouth as he glanced at the white roses. 'They wanted to know if I'd known Magdalene Heller last August.' He turned to stare at her with those sombre eyes and she, meeting them, was for the first time afraid of him. 'She persecutes me, too,' he said in a dull, dead voice.

Susan said helplessly, 'I don't understand.'

'God knows, I hope you never will. Then there's your Mrs Dring.' He drew in his breath sharply. 'I gave her the sack this morning. It was bad enough having to listen to her going on about Louise, but I could have stuck that.'

'What happened, Bob?'

'I found her rooting through Louise's dressing table. I think she was looking for those letters. She must have read about them in the papers and thought she'd got the chance of a peepshow. There was a scene, I said things I shouldn't have and so did she. I'm sorry, Susan. Nothing goes right for me, does it?'

He put out his hand to her very slowly as if to pull her towards him, and she was on her feet, bewildered and uneasy, moving to clasp that outstretched hand, when the telephone rang urgently into their silence. He dropped his head into his hands with a gasp of despair.

Susan lifted the receiver and sat down heavily when she heard Julian's brittle chit-chat voice.

'I've found a buyer for the house, my dear. Our old friend Greg.'

Knowing him of old, Susan sensed that the pause had been made for her to fill with praise and congratulation. Like someone hazarding a half-learned foreign language, she felt she must speak just to prove she could. Anything she might say would do. 'Why does he want to live out here?'

'You may well ask,' Julian said, 'after that delicious little mews place of his. The fact is Dian has been playing up and he feels there are too many naughty temptations in London. So I'll send him along, shall I?'

'I hope I'll still recognise him.'

She was aware that Julian had made some sharp sarcastic reply to this, but the words were just words, meaningless, without power. At the sound of a movement from the living-room, she looked up and saw Bob framed in the doorway. His face and body were in shadow, a dark silhouette, and, poised there, his figure suggested a man on the brink of an abyss. She covered the mouthpiece with her hand.

'Bob . . .'

He made a queer little gesture with one of those shadowed hands as if staving something off. Then he moved out of her sight and she heard the door to the garden close.

'Are you still there, Susan?'

'Yes, I . . .' How different this conversation with Julian would have been if she could have used it as the opportunity to tell him she was going to be married! In that moment she knew quite certainly she could never marry Bob. 'I'll see Greg any time he likes to come,' she said calmly, and then, with the politeness of a distant business acquaintance, 'It was good of you to phone. Good-bye.'

She sat by the phone for a long time, thinking how she and Bob were separated now only by two thin walls and ten feet of air. But those barriers were as impenetrable to her as the enclosures of his mind. She shivered a little because when they kissed or sat in silence she was almost happy with a happiness quenched at once by glimpses into that hooded mind.

17

Using his story of the lost book, David spent Saturday afternoon calling at every hotel on the South Devon coast between Plymouth and Salcombe and at each he drew a blank. Plymouth itself defeated him. He counted twelve hotels and guesthouses in the A.A. guide alone and, having tried four of them, he gave up. The Norths must have rented a house or stayed inland.

Must have? The chances were that they had been to North Devon, that they had been there in May or June. And Magdalene might have been telling the truth. It was not on a beach or a seafront restaurant that Bernard had met Louise but in fact in a suburban kitchen, drinking tea.

'Had a good day?' asked Mrs Spiller, slapping a plateful of pork pie and lettuce in front of him. 'Pity it's too early in the year for you to do the boat trip to Plymouth. But they don't run till May. Mag always went on them boats. Still, I dare say you wouldn't fancy it, you being the nervy type.'

He had never thought of himself as a neurotic. Perhaps the urgency and at the same time the fruitlessness of his quest was telling on him. 'Is it a particularly perilous voyage?' he asked sarcastically.

'Safe as houses normally, only there was the *Ocean Maid*, after all, wasn't there?'

The name rang a faint bell and then he vaguely recalled distasteful headlines and remembered reading in the papers of a catastrophe, similar to the *Darlwyne* tragedy, but with a happier ending. A glance at Mrs Spiller told him she was avid for conversation and he had no one else to talk to, nothing to do. 'She was a pleasure boat,' he said. 'Didn't she go aground off the coast here?'

Mrs Spiller took a cup from a side table and filled it from David's teapot. 'She was taking folks on trips from Torquay and Plymouth, calling in here and at Newton. Due back at six she was. The next thing we knew it was on the wireless she was missing.' A few drops of tea fell on to her embossed lilac bosom. She took a paper napkin from a tumbler and scrubbed at the stain. 'Drat that tea! What was I saying? Oh, yes, well, Mag had been a bit bored and lonely, not knowing what to do with herself, so I said, Why not go on the boat trip? and she did. I got her a real nice packed lunch and I saw her off on the boat myself, never thinking they'd go and run out of fuel and get themselves stranded overnight.

'Just a pair of slacks and one of them thin tee shirts she had on. You've got a lovely figure, so why not show it off? I said. Mighty cold she must have got on that boat, though. Well, it got to six and it got to seven and still she hadn't come and then we heard about it on the news. I was in a proper state, on the point of sending a wire to Bernard. You don't know what to do in a case like that, do you? You don't know whether you're worrying them needlessly like. Especially as I'd egged Mag on to go, got her ticket and all. I blamed myself really.'

'Didn't he go on the trip, then?' David put his knife and fork down and looked up, suddenly chilled.

'Go on the trip? How could he? He was up in London.'

'But I thought you said . . .'

'You're miles away tonight, Mr Chadwick, you really are. This was *last* year, last July. Mag came down on her own. You're mixing it up in your mind with the other years when Bernard came with her. Anyway, as I said, I never wired him and it was all right and poor little Mag none the worse for what she'd been through. She didn't let it keep her in for the rest of the time she was here. Palled up with some folks she'd met on the boat, she told me, and she was off with them every day. I was glad I hadn't got Bernard down here all for nothing, I can tell you. You've gone quite white, Mr Chadwick. Not feeling queer, I hope?'

Magdalene hadn't lied. Bernard had met Louise just as she

had told him. Perhaps it was true also that she had never set eyes on North until the inquest, had never plotted with him to do a murder, never handed him a gun nor sat with him in The Man in the Iron Mask. Wasn't it possible too that Sid and Charles had never seen them there together, but had concocted an amusing story to while away half an hour while they drank the drinks he had paid for?

On Sunday morning he packed his case and left the Swiss Chalet. Five miles inland he stopped for petrol in a village called Jillerton.

'Clean your windscreen, sir?'

'Thanks, and would you check the tyre pressures while you're about it?'

'Can you hang on five minutes while I see to this gentleman?'

David nodded and strolled across the village street. One day, he thought, he might look back to this weekend and laugh at himself. It had taken him a two-hundred-mile drive and surely two hundred questions besides two wasted days to find out that Bernard Heller had never been here at all.

There was only one shop in the street and, although it was Sunday, the door was open. David went inside aimlessly, eyeing the coloured car stickers, the pixie statuettes and the carved wooden stags, replicas of which he had seen for sale in Vienna, in Lacock, in Edinburgh and on the pavement by Oxford Circus underground. On a shelf behind this array of mass-produced bric-à-brac stood mugs and jugs in Devon pottery, hand-painted in cream and brown and not unattractive. He could think of no one but Susan Townsend to whom he wanted to give a present and if he bought her a souvenir she would probably send it back. The white roses might be wilting on his doorstep at this moment.

Some of the pottery was lettered with obscure proverbs and this he disregarded, but the mugs, plain and prettily shaped had a christian name written on each of them, Peter, Jeremy, Anne, Susan . . . There would have to be one for Susan, of course. What was wrong with him, what sentimental madness had seized him, that everywhere he looked he had to see her name or her face?

There was a plain one at the end of the shelf that he could buy his mother for her nightly hot chocolate. He lifted it, turned it round and saw that it wasn't plain after all. In common with the rest it had a name written in elegant brown calligraphy.

Magdalene.

Could Bernard have ordered it for Magdalene on one of those previous visits of theirs, ordered it and neglected to collect it? He was setting it down again thoughtfully when a voice behind him said, 'A very uncommon name, isn't it, sir?' David turned in the direction from which the deep Devon burr had come and saw an assistant who was perhaps his own age. 'I've often said to my wife, we'll never sell that one, not with a name like Magdalene.' And, raising his voice, he called to someone in the room behind the shop, 'I'm saying to this gentleman, we'll never sell that mug Mr North ordered.'

'*Mr North?*'

'I remember because the circumstances were a bit—well, funny,' said the assistant. 'Last August it was, right in the height of the holiday season. Still, you won't want to be troubled with that, sir. The gentleman won't come back for it now, so if you're interested . . . But no, not with a name like Magdalene.'

'I'll have it,' David said in a bemused voice.

'I call that handsome of you, sir. Ten and sixpence, if you please.'

'You said there were funny circumstances.'

Wrapping paper in hand, the young man paused. 'If you're going to have it, I reckon you're entitled to know. The gentleman was staying at the King's Arms. That's the inn on far side of the green and my uncle keeps it. Mr North ordered the mug for his wife, he said, but when he didn't come for it and he didn't come I had a word with uncle. 'Tis a Mrs *Louise* North, he says, not Magdalene. Queer that, we thought. Looks as if 'twere for a lady friend and the gentleman not quite above board.'

'So you didn't want to embarrass him by taking the mug over to the hotel?'

'Proper embarrassing it would have been too, sir, seeing as the lady, his true wife that is, fell sick with one of these here old viruses the day after they came. 'Twould have set her back a bit to hear her husband was carrying on.'

'Is the King's Arms that smart-looking pub on the green, did you say?'

'That's it, sir.'

North had a fondness for smart little pubs. . . .

'Rather unfortunate for them, Mrs North being ill like that,' David said casually and, as he spoke, he remembered Magdalene Heller's words. When Bernard met her she had been ill. . . . So it was after this holiday, then, they had met? 'It must have spoilt their time here.'

'Mr North didn't let it get him down, sir.' The assistant shrugged, perhaps at the villainy of mankind in general or London people in particular. 'Went on that boat trip, he did, without his wife. The *Ocean Maid*, you'll have read of in the London papers. He told me the tale when he came in to order that little mug, how they'd been drifting for hours, never knowing how close they were to the rocks. 'Twould put you or me off our holiday properly, wouldn't it, sir? But that Mr North he didn't turn a hair. I said to my wife at the time, you can see it'd take a mighty big upheaval to get him down.'

Susan was almost sorry she was nearing the end of *Foetid Flesh*. In a way it had taken her mind off the tragedy next door and off Bob. Now her problems, only subconsciously present while she typed, would rush to fill the hours the finishing of the typescript must leave empty.

Page four hundred and two. The whole thing was going to run into four hundred and ten pages. Jane Willingale's handwriting had begun to deteriorate in the last fifty sheets and even to Susan, who was used to it, some words were nearly indecipherable. She was trying to interpret something that looked like an obscure shorthand outline when Doris hammered on the back door and walked in with Richard.

'You don't mind if I leave him with you for a bit, do you, my dear? Just while we go for drinks with the O'Donnells. Bob was asked but he won't go anywhere these days. If you ask me, he's got persecution mania. Still, you'll know more about what goes on in his mind than the rest of us, no doubt. The police were here for hours in the week. Did you see?'

'Bob told me.'

'And I heard him yelling at your Mrs Dring when I was passing yesterday. He's in a very nasty nervous state. Many a time I've seen them like that in the nerve wards. I expect you know best, but if I were you I shouldn't fancy being alone with him. White roses, I see. They'll soon wilt up in this temperature. Unlike me. I could stay here all day, but I can see you want to get on. Pity it's always so perishing at the O'Donnells'.'

The outline was 'murder'. Susan typed it with a faint feeling of inexplicable distress. She heard Richard go upstairs and the sound of little cars trundled out on to the landing. Seven more pages to go. To decipher the last, almost hysterical rush, of Miss Willingale's novel was going to demand all Susan's concentration.

The children had moved their toys to the stairs now. She must be tolerant, she must control the admonition until they became really unbearable. Bump, bump, crash, whirr. . . . That was the latest tank plummeting to make a fresh dent in the hall parquet.

'You're making an awful racket,' she called. 'Can't you go outside for a bit?'

'It's raining outside,' Paul's voice came indignantly.

'You know you're not to play on the stairs, anyway.'

She waded through a long sentence and turned the page. The writing had suddenly improved.

My darling,

You are in my thoughts night and day. Indeed, I do not know where dreaming ends and . . .

It didn't make sense. But this wasn't even Jane Willingale's writing. It sloped more, the capitals were larger, the ink different.

Susan frowned and, taking a cigarette, inhaled deeply. Then, holding the sheets up to the light, she contemplated Bernard Heller's love-letters.

18

'Can we take the motorway outside?' Paul asked, adding virtuously, 'It's stopped raining, but the grass is wet and I thought I ought to ask you.'

Susan hardly heard him. 'What, darling?'

'Can we take the motorway outside?'

'The electricity won't work outside and it's too cold to leave the door open.'

Paul stuck out his lower lip. 'It's not fair. We can't play on the stairs and we can't come in here because you're working. You've got your papers in an awful mess again and you've got ash all over them. If I mess them up you just get mad.'

So she had never burnt the letters. Perhaps in her heart she had always known she hadn't, but she also knew that she had certainly not tucked them between the main body of Miss Willingale's manuscript and the penultimate page. What reason would Doris have for doing such a thing, Doris or Mrs Dring?

'Paul, you haven't been playing with my papers again, have you?'

'No, I haven't!'

'Are you quite sure?'

'I haven't touched them,' the little boy flared. 'I *swear* I haven't. Cross my heart. I haven't been at your desk since the day before you were ill, the day you had to go to the trial about Mrs North.' Self-righteous indignation turned his face a bright tear-threatening red. 'You said if I touched them again you wouldn't let me wear my watch and I didn't touch them.'

'You needn't make a big thing out of it. I believe you.'

'Except for once,' he said defiantly, 'the day you were first ill. I wanted to *help*. Your papers were in an awful mess. You'd left some of them on the coffee table so I put them back with the others, all tidy. I thought you'd be pleased!'

David was jubilant. He had been right, he hadn't wasted his time. Beyond all doubt now, Robert North and Magdalene Heller had known each other since last summer.

He was jubilant, but there was much he didn't understand. All along he had assumed that their meeting, knowledge of each other, love perhaps for each other had grown from the love affair between their marriage partners. Now it seemed that these two, the widow and the widower, had met first. North had gone alone on a boat trip and when it seemed they would be stranded at sea all night had been drawn towards Magdalene who was very likely the only other solitary passenger on that holiday voyage. David could picture her, a little frightened perhaps, but still flaunting her body in her trousers and her thin tee shirt, and he could picture North comforting her, lending her his coat.

But Bernard had been in London and Louise ill in bed.

Was it credible that on returning home North or Magdalene had brought the four of them together? Hardly, David thought. North had ordered the piece of pottery for her, had surely met her every day for the rest of his holiday. Mrs Spiller had spoken to him of her having 'palled up' with someone she met on the boat. By the end of their holiday, David was sure, they were already in love. North would never have introduced Magdalene to his wife nor she North to her husband.

How, then, had they contrived that the others should meet?

David spent Monday morning in Knightsbridge among the antique shops, hunting for Chippendale furniture to dress the set of *Mansfield Park*. His search was fruitful and at half past twelve he crossed the street to the tube entrance on the corner of Hans Crescent.

A girl whose face seemed familiar came out of Harrods at that moment and bore down on him relentlessly. Recognition came with a sickening twist. It was ironical that he should encounter the second Mrs Townsend when more than anything in the world he wanted to see the first. The absurd coincidence made him smile and she took the smile as an enthusiastic greeting.

With a violent snort, she dumped an enormous coloured paper carrier on the pavement between them. 'So you didn't buy that place, then?' she said with the loud directness he found repellent. 'Did you know Greg was after it? Only he won't cough up more than eight thou and God knows we're on our beam ends. There's wads of it going out every month to that woman in Matchdown Park and what's left all goes on nosh.' She drew breath noisily. 'You wouldn't believe what I've just had to pay for a lobster.'

David eyed her warily. She looked younger than ever this morning and particularly uncouth. The one-piece garment she wore—a dress? a coat?—was made of thick oatmeal-coloured material, striped here and there with grey and fringed at hem and wrists. It made her look like a squaw, the juvenile delinquent of the tribe.

'My husband is bonkers about food,' she said. 'Here, you might as well carry that for me. It weighs a ton.'

In fact, it must have weighed close on half a hundredweight. As David lifted the bag, a protruding bundling of wrapping paper slipped and a large red claw sprang out. Elizabeth Townsend marched to the pavement edge.

'Can I get you a taxi?'

'You're joking. I'm going on the bus.' She glared at him. 'D'you know what I'm going to have for my lunch? Yoghourt. That's what I've come down to. And I love food, I just love it.' She sighed and said crossly, 'Oh, come on, before the lights change.'

He followed her, humping the bag.

'I thought I might go to lunch with Dian,' she said petulantly. He almost asked who Dian was and then he remembered the mews house and the flaming bamboo screen.

'Why don't you? It's only just down the road.'

'Well, I don't quite like to. I'm not usually funny about these things. Julian says I rush in where angels and all that jazz. No, the point is Dian's got a man giving her a whirl. Not really like Dian, is it?'

David said heartily that indeed it was not.

'I'd have said Dian was the complete prude. Frigid, I expect. But then Minta rang up this morning and when I said I'd drop in on Dian, she said, I wouldn't because her boyfriend's there again.' Thrusting back the red claw, David said he saw what she meant. 'I don't want to burst in on them, you see. For Christ's sake, don't say a word to Dian. I know she's a mate of yours. Live and let live, after all. Dian hasn't said anything to Minta—she wouldn't, would she?'

'I shouldn't think so.'

'But with Minta living opposite she couldn't expect to get away with it. Minta told me this bloke's car's been there half a dozen times in the past fortnight and she's seen him sneaking in after Greg's gone to the studio. Of course, she dropped a hint to Greg and that's why he wants to take Dian out of harm's way.'

Every step was taking him further and further from the tube station. As Elizabeth Townsend trailed relentlessly on past bus stops, he had been searching for an excuse to dump the shopping and make his getaway. And now he did dump it, but not because he wanted to escape.

'Is that all Minta has to go on?' he asked, trying to keep the breathlessness from his voice. 'Just seeing a man's car outside Dian's?'

'She saw him go in,' said Elizabeth Townsend sharply.

'But, Mrs Townsend . . .'

'Oh, call me Elizabeth. You make me feel about ninety-six.'

'But, Elizabeth . . .' It was a relief. The other name conjured up a very different face and voice. 'He could be a salesman, a surveyor, an interior decorator, anything.'

'Yeah? I tell you he's a sexy fellow of thirty and Dian's a real dish. You know damn' well Dian and Greg haven't been having it for two years now and Dian's always off on her own. You can take it from me, she's all mixed-up over this bloke. You're green, David, that's your problem. But Minta's not and I'm not and when we hear a fellow's been sneaking round to a girl when her old man's nicely out of the way, we know what to think.'

'Faithful Dian? Frigid Dian?'

'You are rooting for her, aren't you? So she's not faithful, she's not frigid. This proves it.'

At this point the bottom fell out of the bag. He looked at the aubergines, the lemons and the tins of *fois gras* which rolled into the gutter and said happily, 'Elizabeth, I'm awfully glad I met you. Tell me, if you could choose, what's the nicest place you can think of for lunch? The place you'd most like to go to?'

'The *Écu de France*,' she said promptly, stuffing two lemons into the pocket of her Red Indian garment and eyeing him optimistically.

'I can't bear to think of you eating yoghourt,' he said. 'I never liked it.' He hailed a taxi and, opening the door, bowled vegetables and fruit and cans on to the seat. 'Jermyn Street,' he said to the driver. 'The *Écu de France*.'

He heard a chair shift and scrape from inside the office as he approached the door and when he came in the woman who was waiting for him sat a yard or two from his desk, her expression grimly virtuous. Ulph was sure she had been examining the papers which lay face-upwards on his blotter. They were a draft of the programme for the police sports gala and Ulph smiled to himself.

'Good morning,' he said. 'You wanted to see me?'

'I don't care who I see,' the woman said, 'as long as it's someone high up, someone as knows the ropes.' She patted her fuzzy red hair with a hand in a Fair Isle glove and she looked at him in truculent disappointment as if she had expected to see someone big, aggressive, authoritative. 'You'll do,' she said. 'I reckon you'd be interested in a fellow called North.'

'May I have your name, madam?'

'As long as it doesn't go no further. Mrs Dring. Mrs Leonard Dring. My first name's Iris.' She took off her gloves and laid them on the desk beside her handbag. 'I work for this North, cleaning like, or I did till he give me the push Saturday. What I wanted to tell you was, I work next door too and I was working there the morning Mrs North was done in.'

Ulph nodded, his face reserved. This was not the first time he had encountered the spite of the discarded servant. 'Go on, please.'

'There was three fellows digging up the road at the bottom of them gardens. Mrs North used to give them their tea, regular like. Well, about nine-thirty it was, I was in Mrs Townsend's kitchenette and I heard this banging on the back door next door. Well, I didn't think no more about it and I was doing my windows, in the lounge that is, when I see this chap go down the garden path, tall chap in a duffel coat. Mrs Townsend and me, we thought it was one of them workmen. He lets himself out of the gate and goes off up the road.'

'Perhaps to get his tea at a café instead?'

'So we thought at the time. I reckon that's what he wanted us to think. The point is there wasn't never more than *three* men working on the road. I'll tell you how I know. I said to my husband, 'How many chaps was there working on the cemetery road?' And he says, 'Three.' Never more than three. And he's never wrong, my husband, there's nothing that man doesn't know. I said, 'You're pally with that old fellow, the foreman that was, you ask him.' And that's what he did. Three fellows there was, all the time, the old chap, the man and the young lad. And what's more, when I heard the banging at the door that dog never barked. It was out the front, laying in wait, and it could see the side door all right. Like my husband always says, them animals have got more sense than we have. They don't take no account of duffel coats and folks setting themselves up as workmen.'

'You delayed a long time before you came to me, Mrs Dring,' Ulph said quietly. 'Could it be that you've only come now because you have a grudge against Mr North?'

'If you don't believe me, you ask Mrs Townsend. She knows. It was her put the idea into my head.'

Probably she supposed that her departure would be the signal for him immediately to set the law in motion. Ulph sat quite still, reflecting. His own construction of the murder scene, almost totally visual, had shifted and changed. North had done it very simply, after all. Ulph saw that there had been scarcely any premeditation at all and North, who had acted on impulse, had merely covered his tracks afterwards.

He had stayed at home that morning not to contrive a false suicide but to have it all out with Heller. He would have told Louise and let her warn her lover if she liked. Ulph touched his forehead and felt the muscle that jumped above his eye when he was nervous. Hadn't he done just that thing, confronting his own wife and the man she loved? Hadn't he too tried to discuss matters with them rationally and calmly? His wife had shut herself in her bedroom, flinging herself on the bed in a storm of tears.

Very likely it had been that way with Louise North, and the two men had gone up to her together. But first Heller had slung his raincoat and his heavy briefcase on the kitchen table, keeping the gun in his jacket pocket. Ulph knew very well that if a man, even a peaceful, mild man, owns a gun he is liable to use it under stress. Louise had given Heller the idea, perhaps erroneous, perhaps true, that her husband was violent and tyrannical. Aware of the kind of scene which awaited him, Heller would have brought his gun. Just as a threat, of course, just as a tool of persuasion.

And North? Perhaps Heller had arrived later than expected and the husband, tired of waiting, was ready for work in coat and gloves. Thus they had entered the bedroom together. Had they struggled and the gun off? Ulph thought so. In the struggle Louise had been inadvertently shot by Heller and when, in his horror at what he had done, he had bent over her, fallen beside her on the bed, North had taken the gun and shot him as he lay. Taken it in a hand already, but perhaps not with murderous intent, protected by a strong driving glove. Then, later, the instinctive actions of self-preservation, Heller's hand to be closed for the second time round the gun —lest the glove had eradicated earlier prints—and, hideously, a third shot to be fired. It had been raining. A duffel coat with hood up, the moment's pause to knock at the back door as the workmen always knocked, and then the deliberately slow stroll, heart pounding, blood thundering, to the fence, the street, the wide unsuspecting world outside.

With a good counsel, Ulph thought, North might not get

very long. He had been intolerably provoked. The woman had turned his home into a house of assignation and written foul things of him to her lover. And suddenly Ulph remembered how North had spoken of his neighbour's kindness to him, as if he thought of her as more than just a doer of good deeds. She was divorced, he recalled. Was there a chance that she would wait for North?

Ulph got up and cursed himself for a sentimental fool. There had been no woman waiting for him when at last he had found himself a free man. He glanced at his watch. North would be still at work, home in three hours or so. As he prepared the things he must say and do, he thought with a faint amusement of David Chadwick and the theories borne of a fruitful imagination. What else could you expect of a scene designer? Still, for a day or two Ulph also had believed in the possibility of collusion, of conspiracy. He felt a little ashamed of himself.

19

He looked again at the photograph of the Norths that had been taken on their holiday and this time the background to their smiling faces was familiar. The inn sign was too blurred for its name to be readable, but he recognised the half-timbering on the gables of the King's Arms and the white fence that surrounded Jillerton's village green.

David had stacked this paper with other souvenirs, depressing, a little macabre, of Bernard Heller. Here were the records of his brief and humble intrusions into the public eye, and here the announcement of his marriage to the girl who had wheeled her sick father along the Bathcombe shore. The print was faded but Bernard's handwriting not at all, the figures of his wedding date sharp and blue with the little distinctive and very continental tick across the ascender of the seven.

He looked at them all musingly for a moment and then he went to the telephone. Inspector Ulph was out and no one could tell him when he expected to return. David hesitated, pushed away inhibition and the fear of a rebuff, and dialled again. It was the child who answered.

'May I speak to your mother?'

He sounded a nice sensible boy, older than the impression David had from a fair head once seen on a pillow. 'Who shall I say?'

'David Chadwick.'

'We've got your flowers in a vase.' He could never know how much pleasure he had caused with that simple statement. 'Wait a minute and I'll fetch her.'

David would have waited all night.

'Thank you for the flowers,' she said. 'I was going to write to you, only things—well, haven't been very easy.'

He had meant to be gentle, tactful, cunning in his approach. The sound of her voice stunned him into abruptness. 'I must see you this evening. Can I come now?'

'But, why?'

'I have to see you. Oh, I know you can't stand me and, I tell you frankly, it's North I want to talk about. Don't put the receiver down. I should still come.'

'You're an extraordinary man, aren't you?' There was no laughter in her voice. 'I wouldn't be frightened this time,' she said, and then, 'Perhaps it would clear the air.'

Paul fell asleep quickly that night and Susan wondered if it was because the house was almost certainly sold now. It was still daylight, the evening soft and spring-like, and she had no need of a coat to go next door.

The Braeside windows were all tightly closed. A secret shuttered house, she thought. Hadn't someone once likened death to a secret house? And she forced her eyes not to look upwards as she made her way to the back door.

Bob had taken upon himself the right to enter her house without knocking and, although until now she had never availed herself of it, she felt that with him she must have a similar privilege. This was the first time she had entered Braeside since that Wednesday morning. The door yielded to a push and the kitchen yawned emptily at her. Did it seem bare because Heller's coat and briefcase were missing from the table?

'Bob?'

She had called his dead wife's name like that and, getting no answer, had gone upstairs. Suppose history had repeated itself? The niche where the Madonna had stood was empty now, an open mouth in the wall.

'Bob?'

The living-room was stuffy, but clean and as tidy as if no one had lived in it for a long time. For a second she didn't see him, he was sitting so still in the chair where she too had sat and talked to the police inspector. A bar of sunlight made a wavering gold band down the length of his body, passing across his eyes, but he stared through it, undazzled, like a blind man.

She went over to him, knelt at his feet and took his hands. The touch of his skin was no more exciting to her now than Paul's, and she felt for him only as she sometimes felt for Paul, pity, tenderness and above all an inability to understand. But she loved Paul. Had she ever been close enough to Bob to love him?

'Susan, I've come to the end,' he said. 'The police came to me today at work, but never mind that. Never mind that now. I went mad, I was corrupted, I suppose. I don't want to blame anyone else. If I was led into things—well, I was a grown man and I don't want to blame anyone else.' He held her hands more tightly. 'I'm glad,' he said, 'that they can't get anyone else for all this. They can't find out. You don't know what I mean, do you?'

She shook her head.

'Just as well. I don't want you to know. Tell me, did you ever think I might, well, do you an injury?'

Speechless, she looked at him.

'The suggestion was made,' he said hoarsely, 'and I—for a while I . . . It was only for a day or two, Susan. I didn't know what you knew and what you'd seen. I really love you. I love you, Susan.'

'I know,' she said. 'I know.'

'And Louise loved Heller, didn't she? You know that Everyone knows that.' He gasped and, leaning forward so that the beam of light shivered and cut across his shoulder, said fiercely, 'What I did, it was from jealousy. I couldn't stand . . . I had provocation, didn't I, Susan? And maybe I won't have to go away for very long, I'll come back to you.' He took her face in his hands. 'Do you know what I'm trying to tell you?'

'I think so,' she faltered and she stayed where she was, kneeling, because she thought that if she got up she might fall. She had come here to tell him that she still had his wife's letters, that they had never been burnt. His hands palpatated her skin. She had thought of him as a blind man but now he was like someone who is deaf and who can only discern speech by feeling the subtle and tiny movements of the speaker's bones.

Perhaps he had really become deaf, for he gave no sign that he had heard the dog begin to bark, hollowly at first and then with fury as the car door slammed.

'You've been crying,' David said.

'Yes, I didn't know it showed.'

The traces of tears were not disfiguring, only the evidence of an unbearable vulnerability. The puffiness they gave to her eyes, like some beautician's exclusive treatment, served to make her look very young. 'I was boorish on the phone,' he said. 'I'm always boorish with you.'

'It doesn't matter,' she said indifferently. 'At the moment I can't feel that anything much matters. You came to talk to me about—about someone we both know. I think you're too late. I—I don't think he'll come back here.'

'Do you mean he's been arrested?'

'That's what you wanted, isn't it?' she said harshly. He couldn't tell if it was personal hatred in her eyes or despair at the world she lived in. She turned away her head and sat down as if she must, as if her legs would no longer support her. 'Oh, I don't condone it,' she said. 'It's too soon yet, I can't fully realise it.' She swept back the fair hair which had tumbled across her forehead. 'But, d'you know what jealousy is? Have you ever known it? Have you?'

David didn't answer that. 'Is that what he told you?' he asked. 'That he did it from jealousy?'

'Of course.' Her voice was hard and brittle. 'He went over the edge. It was an impulse, he wasn't sane.'

'You're so wrong, Susan.' She had let the christian name pass. From indifference, he thought bitterly. 'I want to tell you something. It might comfort you. I don't say it would make you feel differently towards North, although . . .' He sighed quickly. 'But it might make you think better of me. May I tell you?'

'If you like. I haven't anything else to do. It will pass the time.'

He had wanted very much to tell this story of his, and he would have told it to Ulph had the inspector not been otherwise occupied. It was a dreadful story and, as the truth of it had come to him by degrees during the day, he had shocked himself into a kind of horror. In a way it was as if he had invented it, as a writer of the macabre invents, and then is troubled by the sick fecundity of his own mind. But David knew that his story was true and therefore inescapable. Because it was true and it changed the whole aspect of North's conduct and North's motives, it had to be told. But this girl was the wrong audience, although to him she was right in every other respect. He already felt for her the tenderness that wants to save its object from cruel disillusionment, but it had come to him too that she might contemplate waiting for North and, during that long wait, arrive at what she now denied, condonation of an act that to her was the outcome of uncontrollable jealousy.

'North met Magdalene Heller on holiday in Devon last July,' he began. 'They fell in love. It might be better to call it a physical enslavement on North's part.' She wasn't looking at him and her face was impassive. 'When they came home,' he said, 'they began meeting, sometimes in a London pub and, no doubt, in other places as well. Magdalene wanted him because he's handsome and well-off by her standards. I've told you why he wanted her. Perhaps he also wanted children, but I don't know.' He watched her make a very faint movement of one hand. 'I think it was Magdalene who thought of the idea, who was perhaps, to put it dramatically, North's evil genius. Magdalene had a gun, you see, and in September Magdalene's husband had tried to gas himself because he knew she no longer loved him. A man who attempts suicide may attempt it again and may succeed.

'I don't know when they first began to plan it. Perhaps not until after Christmas. It would have been in January or February that Magdalene gave North one of Heller's business reply cards to hand to Louise and propose that they have central heating installed. No, it wasn't a coincidence that Heller happened to work in the Matchdown Park area. It was because he did that Magdalene formed their plan on these particular lines.'

'What lines?' she said in a low, scarcely audible voice.

'As soon as Louise had filled in the card and signed it,' he went on, 'she began to tell her neighbours about the central heating project. Heller came along in his car to discuss it with her and every time he came that dog barked so that everyone was aware of his visits. Louise North had been looking very unhappy because she too knew that her husband was being unfaithful to her. She talked to no one of it, but she couldn't help the misery that showed in her face. She had only one thing to distract her, the plan for improving the heating of her house, and of course she told her neighbours about it. But when North was asked by them for his opinion on the scheme, he simply denied all knowledge of it. For this was the one sure way of making certain that Heller's visits would be taken as illicit.'

Now, at last, she did turn her eyes to his. 'But that is quite absurd.' Indignation had replaced all the deadening effect of shock. 'Of course people asked Bob about his central heating and of course he denied it. He told a friend of mine quite decidedly that he couldn't afford central heating. This idea of yours—I don't know what you're leading up to—this idea is ridiculous. If Bob had been lying, what do you suppose would have happened if people had asked him and Louise about it when they were together? Very probably they did ask.'

'And if they did?' David asked quietly. 'Wouldn't it have made them believe all the more firmly in Louise's guilt to hear her insist while her husband turned away and looked embarrassed? Wouldn't they have felt sorry for him as the deceived husband doing everything he could to conceal his wife's treachery?'

'Louise North was in love with Heller,' she said stubbornly. 'He came here three or four times and Bob knew very well why he was coming. Look, I know you're obsessed with these ideas of yours, but you weren't living here. You don't know the people involved. The day before she died Louise came in here in tears to tell me all about it, to beg me to go in there the next day and hear the whole story.'

For a moment he was checked. Suppose his theory was all wrong, all hot imagination? Susan Townsend would never speak to him again. 'She actually told you,' he said urgently, 'that she was in love with Heller?'

A flicker of doubt creased the skin between her eyebrows. 'No, but I . . . Of course she came for that. Why else would she have come?'

'Perhaps to tell you that her husband was being unfaithful to her and to ask your advice.'

She looked at him blankly and then she blushed, deeply and painfully. 'You mean that I would have been a good adviser because my husband had been unfaithful to me?'

It was dreadful that he, of all people, should have to wound her in this way. His throat was dry and for a moment he couldn't speak. Then he said, 'Because of that, of what you said, she wouldn't have expected you to show much sympathy to the guilty partner of a marriage, would she? And yet that is what you believed she was.'

'I still believe it,' she said with sudden passion. 'I believe in Bob's unhappiness.'

'Yes, I expect he was unhappy. There can't be much happiness in being driven to do frightful acts by a woman like Magdalene Heller. They flared at each other at the inquest, didn't they? All acting, or perhaps the rage of Lady Macbeth?'

'What are you really trying to say?'

'That Bernard Heller and Louise North weren't lovers at all. That they were never more to each other than salesman and housewife.'

20

She took a cigarette and lit it before he could. Her hands were very steady. The puffiness under her eyes had almost gone, leaving blue shadows. He noticed how thin her hands were, so thin that the wedding ring slid to the first joint when she moved her fingers.

He stammered a little. 'You've taken it very calmly. I'm glad of that.'

'Only because I know it isn't true.'

He sighed, but not with exasperation. How could he expect her to understand inconstancy, disloyalty? 'I know it's hard to take at first,' he said quietly.

'Oh, no, it isn't that.' Her face was almost serene. 'When you began I was afraid it was all going to be true, and now I know it isn't I feel, well, easier. I don't bear you any malice,' she said seriously. 'I know you meant to do the right thing. I like that.' She gave him a stiff brisk smile. 'You're a kind considerate person, really. It's true that . . .' And now she lowered her eyes. 'It's true that I let myself get fond of Bob North. We needed comfort from each other very much because . . .' Her voice had grown very matter-of-fact, 'Because we'd reached a low ebb in our lives. I'm getting over the shock of it now. I'm used to shocks,' she said. 'He did a dreadful thing and we shall never see each other again. It wasn't as if we really ever had much in common. I'm going to move away quite soon and I've always got my little boy to think of. I shall never forget Bob, how frightened he was and how haunted.' She paused and cleared her throat. 'But you want to know why I'm so sure your idea's wrong.'

'Yes,' he said tiredly, 'yes.'

'Well, then. Heller and Louise were in love, I know they

were. You see, Heller was writing love-letters to Louise as far back as last November. I've got them here—Bob left them with me—and you can see them if you like.'

'Forged,' David said, as he turned them over in his hands, although he knew they couldn't be. He had remembered them now, letters which had been identified in court by Magdalene and by *Equatair*'s managing director and by Bernard's own brother. 'No, I know they can't be.' He read them while she, lighting a second cigarette from the first, watched him with gentle sadness.

'You see, they're both dated 1967, last year.'

He read them again, slowly and carefully, and he looked again at the dates, November 6th, '67, and December 2nd, '67. There was no doubt when they had been written, but there was something wrong with them just the same. 'He is not an old man and may live for years. He has no rights, no hold over you that anyone would recognise these days.'

'How old is North?' he asked.

'I don't know,' she said and she stopped, distress puckering her face. 'About thirty, in his early thirties.'

'Odd,' David said. 'Strange that Heller should have described him like that.'

'But it's true, he isn't an old man.'

'No, he's so young that it was absurd of anyone who knew his age to write of him like that. That's the way you talk of someone in late middle-age, someone of, say, fifty-five. It's as if Heller were arguing with someone very young, putting the maturer, more realistic viewpoint. And what about this? "We just have to hang on and wait till he dies." Why should North have died? He's strong and healthy, isn't he, as well as young? And that about his rights, about him having no rights that anyone would recognise these days. I should think ninety per cent of the population wouldn't deny that husbands and wives have legal and moral rights over each other, and the hold is pretty strong.'

'It takes a good deal of legal machinery to break it,' she said dryly. 'But you're forgetting that Heller was in an unstable state, he was writing hysterically.'

'And yet these letters aren't hysterical. Parts of them are calm and tender. May I ask why North gave them to you?'

'He wanted them burnt. He hadn't the strength of will to do it himself.'

David almost laughed. The man had wanted them burnt all right because although on first glance, on cursory examination, they seemed genuine, a closer perusal might have shown some oddity that revealed Louise could not have been their recipient. Why had he shown them to Susan Townsend? Because he wanted to be sure of her sympathy, her pity, her recognition of himself as injured. He had succeeded, David thought bitterly.

'Do you know what I think?' She didn't, she didn't seem to want to. She was listening to him out of politeness. He went on just the same. 'I believe the man referred to wasn't a husband at all. The woman who received these letters was tied to someone, certainly, but tied only by duty.' He looked up and saw that she was very tired. 'Forgive me,' he said. 'May I take these letters away with me?'

'I don't see why you shouldn't. No one else wants them.'

She gave him her hand, passed before him into the hall. It was as if he had called to see her on some practical business, as if he and not the society photographer had bought her house.

'You shouldn't be alone,' he said impulsively. 'I wouldn't leave you, only you must loathe the sight of me.'

'Of course I don't, but I'm quite used to being alone. I was in a bad state after the inquest, but I was ill then.' She opened the front door and as soon as he appeared, framed in light, the dog began to howl. No wonder North had stroked its head, patted it, that last night David had been here, for it had been his innocent henchman. 'I wish we could have met under different circumstances,' she said.

'But we have met.' He didn't wait for her answer, for it might have quenched hope.

Until she was married Magdalene Heller had lived with her father, a victim of multiple sclerosis, aged about fifty-five. She had been a devoted nurse to him until she went to London and met Bernard. But she couldn't get married and leave her father; she had to wait for him to die. Mr Chant must have needed a great deal of care and attention that could only be provided by the daughter who understood. The chronic invalid was harsh and ungrateful, resenting the health of the girl who nursed him and sometimes violent to her. But it was her duty to stay with him and see her fiancé only occasionally, when he could come and stay near her in Exeter or she manage a day in London.

David assembled these facts in his mind and when he came to East Mulvihill he had formed a theory, subsidiary to his first, like the tiny offshoot on the body of a hydra. Carl Heller opened the door of the flat to him. Did Magdalene retain him there like a porter to do her bidding? His dull lethargic face was abject tonight, the heavy jowls as pendulous as a bloodhound's.

'You have seen the morning papers?' he asked, pausing between each guttural word. 'They have arrested Mr North for killing my brother.' Never before had David seen anyone actually wring his hands. 'Oh, my brother and his wrongdoing . . .' He seized David's arm with a quick clumsy movement. 'I can't believe it. Magdalene is sick, lying down. Yesterday when he did not come and he did not phone I thought she would go mad.' He shook his head, threw up his hands. 'She is better now, calmer. And all this misery has come upon us through my brother's wrongdoing.'

'I don't believe he did anything wrong, Mr Heller. He wrote some letters once to Mrs North, didn't he?'

'Wicked letters. I shall never forget how in the court I had to say those letters were written by my brother to that woman.'

'But he did write them to her?' David followed him into the sitting-room. The table was bare and the place tidy, but every piece of furniture was filmed with two days' dust.

Carl sat down, but jumped up again immediately and began to lumber about the room like a carthorse in a stall made for a pony. 'I don't mean he did not write them,' he said, but that I was ashamed to say he had. My brother to write of poor Mr North that he was useless and better dead!'

'Mr Heller . . .' David knew that it would be pointless to try to explain anything to this man whose slow stupidity was intensified because he was distraught. 'Will you tell me something? It may be meaningless to you, not to the point at all, but tell me, how did Bernard make his sevens?'

Astonishment, anger even, at the apparent inconsequence of the question wrinkled Carl's brow while his face—did he think David was mocking righteous chagrin?—flushed a dull brick red. But he stopped pacing and, taking the pencil David handed to him, licking the tip of it, drew a seven with a tick across the ascender.

'I thought so. He was educated in Europe, in Switzerland. Now make a one the way Bernard did.'

For a moment it seemed as if Carl wouldn't comply. The frown deepening, he stared at David, and then, shrugging, drew on the paper an outline very like an English seven. David slid the paper from under the big hand and looked at it thoughtfully. Magdalene had married Bernard in 1962, had met him in 1961. It all fitted and yet . . . Why hadn't the police seen who had access to Bernard's current notebooks, why hadn't the managing director of *Equatair* who knew Bernard's writing and style of making figures, why hadn't Carl?

'You said to me once that for the sake of getting on in his job, Bernard wanted to appear as English as possible. Did he ever alter his way of making these continental ones and sevens?'

'I think he may have.' Carl nodded, not understanding, not wanting to understand. 'Five years ago he said to me he would make himself so English no one would know.'

David said softly, 'Five years ago, then, he began to write his sevens without the tick and his ones as an upright stroke . . .' He said it softly because he had heard a door open behind him and footsteps in the narrow passage.

She was in a dressing-gown. A negligée would have been wrong for her and the thing she wore was a long stiff bell of quilted stuff, black shot through with blood red. It caught the light like armour. Her face was white and stiff and quite old-looking. She was a queen on a court card, the queen of spades.

'Back again?' she said. She was trying to be defiant but she was too frightened to manage the strong voice necessary for defiance. 'I want a drink of water,' she said to Carl. He fetched it, nodding humbly. Her nails rattled against the glass and she spilled some of the water. It trickled down her chin and on to the black quilting. Now she had a voice again, a poor travesty of a voice, as if she had really aged. 'Bob North killed them, after all. Just as well we didn't have any more to do with him. He must have been a fool, letting himself get caught like that.'

'Murderers ought to be caught,' said Carl stupidly.

'They ought to be tough,' she said, 'and see they don't.'

'I wonder if you would be tough enough,' David said, and he added conversationally as he got up, 'It would be interesting to see.' It will be interesting, he thought, tonight, or tomorrow. The green eyes, iridescent, shallow, rested on him for a long moment, and then she went back into the bedroom, the glass in her hand, her long stiff skirts rustling on the floor. He listened as he passed the door but behind it there was only a silence so deep as to be stronger and more frightening than any sound.

'I wanted to know,' David said when she answered the phone, 'if you were all right.'

'But you phoned last night to know that,' she protested, 'and again this morning.' At least, he thought, she didn't say, 'Back again?' 'I'm quite all right. Really I am. Only the police are here all the time...'

'I want to see them myself, but afterwards, may I come and see you?'

'If you like.' she said. 'If you like, David.' She had called him by his name and his heart turned a little. 'But no stories, no theories. I couldn't stand any more.'

'I promise,' he said. She would have to attend the trial and by then she would know him well enough to let him go with her. She would hear it all there and she would need him beside her when she heard the evidence against the two people in the dock.

So David put the phone down and went to tell Ulph what

Magdalene Heller and Robert North had done. How they had invented a love affair between two mild and gentle people who had never harmed them except by existing; how they had spread upon their characters so much filth that her friends and neighbours and his twin brother had vilified them; how they had done it simply because Louise North could not divorce her husband and Heller was going to take his wife away to Switzerland.

But before he went into the station entrance, he paused for a moment and leaned against the railings of the treeless park. They had driven past this place, he and Bernard Heller, and yet it was not as he had been then that David suddenly saw him, nor as he had been when he lay dead in the arms of the dead woman he had never really known. He remembered instead the fat jovial clown and the tedious jokes and the unfailing generous kindness.

Perhaps he would tell Ulph of his last discovery first. He was not a vindictive man, but he wanted to see Ulph's face when he learned that Magdalene Heller had kept her own love-letters, the letters Bernard had sent her in 1961, and used them as the documentary evidence of an adultery that had never been. He wanted to see Ulph's expression and, ultimately that of a judge and a jury.